Also by Bret Easton Ellis

White
Imperial Bedrooms
Lunar Park
Glamorama
The Informers
American Psycho
The Rules of Attraction
Less Than Zero

The
SHARDS

The
SHARDS

MANY YEARS AGO I REALIZED THAT A BOOK, a novel, is a dream that asks itself to be written in the same way we fall in love with someone: the dream becomes impossible to resist, there's nothing you can do about it, you finally give in and succumb even if your instincts tell you to run the other way because this could be, in the end, a dangerous game—someone will get hurt. For a few of us the first ideas, images, the initial stirrings can prompt the writer to automatically immerse themselves in the novel's world, its romance and fantasy, its secrets. For others it can take longer to feel this connection more clearly, ages to realize how much you needed to write the novel, or love that person, to relive that dream, even decades later. The last time I thought about this book, this particular dream, and telling this version of the story—the one you're reading now, the one you just began—was almost twenty years ago, when I thought I could handle revealing what happened to me and a few of my friends at the beginning of our senior year at Buckley, in 1981. We were teenagers, superficially sophisticated children, who really knew nothing about how the world actually worked—we had the experience, I suppose, but we didn't have the meaning. At least not until something happened that moved us into a state of exalted understanding.

When I first sat down to write this novel, a year after the events had taken place, it turned out that I couldn't deal with revisiting this period, or any of those people I knew and the terrible things that befell us, including, most crucially, what had actually happened to me. In fact without even writing a word I shut the idea of the project down almost as soon as I began it—I was nineteen. Even without picking up a pen or sitting at my typewriter, only gently remembering what happened proved too unnerving in that moment and I was at a place in my life that didn't need the added stress and I forced myself to forget about that period, at least for a while, and it wasn't hard to erase the past in that moment. But the urge to write the book returned when I left New York after living there for over twenty years—the East Coast was where I escaped almost immediately upon graduation, fleeing the trauma of my last year at high school—and found myself living back in Los Angeles, where those events from 1981 had taken place, and where I felt stronger, more resolved about the past, and that I was capable of steeling myself from the pain of it all and entering the dream. But this turned out not to be the case then either, and after typing up a few pages of notes about the events that happened in the autumn of 1981, when I thought I had numbed myself with half a bottle of Ocho in order to keep proceeding, letting the tequila stabilize my trembling hands, I experienced an anxiety attack so severe that it sent me to the emergency room at Cedars-Sinai in the middle of that night. If we want to connect the act of writing with the metaphor of romance then I had wanted to love this novel and it seemed to be finally offering itself to me and I was so tempted, but when it came time to consummate the relationship I found myself unable to fall into the dream.

THIS HAPPENED WHEN I WAS WRITING specifically about the Trawler—a serial killer who had been haunting the San Fernando Valley starting in the late spring of 1980 and then announcing their presence more strongly in the summer of 1981 and who was frighteningly somehow connected to us—and a wave of stress so severe crashed over me that night I began making notes I actually moaned with fear from the memories and I collapsed, retching up the tequila I'd been gulping down. Xanax I kept in the nightstand by my bed was no help—I swallowed three and knew they weren't going to do anything quickly enough. In that moment: I was sure I was about to die. I dialed 911 and told the operator I was having a heart attack and then fainted. The landline I was calling from—this was in 2006, I was forty-two, I lived alone—alerted them as to where the location was and an alarmed doorman from the front desk of the high-rise

I lived in escorted the EMTs to the eleventh floor. My apartment was unlocked by the doorman and they found me on the floor in the bedroom. I regained consciousness in an ambulance as it sped along San Vicente Boulevard toward Cedars-Sinai, a short distance from the Doheny Plaza, where I lived, and after I was wheeled into the emergency room prone on a stretcher and had reoriented myself as to what had happened, I became embarrassed—the Xanax had kicked in and I was calm and I knew there was nothing physically wrong with me. I knew the panic attack was directly related to the memories I had of the Trawler and more specifically of Robert Mallory.

A doctor checked me out—I was basically fine but the hospital wanted me to stay the night so they could perform a battery of tests, including running an MRI, and my primary physician agreed, reminding me over the phone that my health insurance would cover almost all of the stay. But I needed to get home and opted out of whatever tests they wanted to administer because if I had stayed at Cedars that night I was sure I'd slip into madness, knowing that what happened to me had nothing to do with my body or any malady I may or may not have harbored. It was a reaction simply connected to memory, to the past and conjuring that awful year—to Robert Mallory, and the Trawler, and Matt Kellner and Susan Reynolds and Thom Wright and Deborah Schaffer, as well as the darkened tunnel I was traveling through at seventeen.

AFTER THAT NIGHT I abandoned the project and instead wrote two other books during the following thirteen years, and it wasn't until 2020 that I felt I could begin *The Shards*, or *The Shards* had decided that *Bret* was ready because the book was announcing itself to *me*—and not the other way around. I hadn't reached out to the book because I spent so many years pushing myself away from the dream, from Robert Mallory, from that senior year at Buckley; so many decades spent pushing away from the Trawler, and Susan and Thom and Deborah and Ryan, and what happened to Matt Kellner; I had relegated this story to the dark corner of the closet and for many years this avoidance worked—I didn't pay as much attention to the book and it stopped calling out to me. But sometime during 2019 it

The SHARDS

began climbing its way back, pulsing with a life of its own, wanting to merge with me, expanding into my consciousness in such a persuasive way that I couldn't ignore it any longer—trying to ignore it had become a distraction. This particular timing had coincided with the fact that I wasn't writing screenplays anymore, that I had decided at a certain point to stop chasing that game—a decade of being well compensated for TV pilots and scripts for movies that would mostly never be made—and I briefly wondered if there was a connection between the book beckoning to me and the new lack of interest in writing for Hollywood. It didn't matter: I had to write the book because I needed to resolve what happened—it was finally time.

THE SPARK FOR MY RENEWED INTEREST in the novel was initiated by a brief moment years after that anxiety attack landed me in Cedars. I'd seen a woman—I was going to say a girl, but she wasn't any longer; she was a woman in her mid-fifties, my age—on the corner of Holloway and La Cienega in West Hollywood. She was standing on the sidewalk outside the Palihouse Hotel, wearing sunglasses, a phone pressed against her ear, waiting for a car, and even though this was a much older version of the girl I used to know when we were in high school it was unmistakably her. I knew it even though I hadn't seen her in almost forty years: she was still effortlessly beautiful. I had just made a left turn onto Holloway and was stopped in traffic when I noticed the figure on the deserted sidewalk beneath the umbrella at the valet stand—she was maybe twenty feet away from me. Instead of the happy surprise at seeing an old friend I was frozen with a sheet of dread—it draped over me immediately and I went ice cold. That glimpse of this woman in the flesh caused the fear to return and it started swallowing everything—just like it had in 1981. She was a reminder that it had all been real, that the dream had actually happened, that even though four decades had passed since we last saw each other, we were still bound by the events of that fall.

I didn't suddenly pull over to the side of Holloway, near the mouth of the garage of the CVS across the street from the Palihouse, and present myself to the woman, exclaim surprise, get out of the car and offer her an embrace, marvel at how beautiful she still looked—I had successfully avoided contact with any of my classmates from our senior year on social media, with only a few having reached out to me over the years, usually in the weeks after I published a book. Instead I just stared through the windshield of the BMW I was driving as she stood on that deserted sidewalk, holding the phone to her ear, listening to whoever was talking to her, not saying anything, and even with the sunglasses on, there was something haunted in the way she held herself, or maybe I was imagining this was true—maybe she was fine, maybe she had completely adjusted and had processed what happened to her in the fall of 1981, the terrible injury she suffered, the awful revelation she experienced, the losses she endured. I was on my way to Palm Springs with Todd, someone I'd met in 2010 and who'd been living with me for the past nine years, to spend a week with a friend flying in from New York who had rented a house on the edges of the movie colony in Palm Springs before heading to San Diego to attend a series of conferences. I'd been having a conversation with Todd when I saw the woman in front of the Palihouse and was shut down mid-sentence. A car suddenly blared its horn behind me and when I glanced at the rearview mirror I realized the light on Holloway had turned green and I wasn't moving. "What's wrong?" Todd asked as I accelerated too quickly and lurched toward Santa Monica Boulevard. I swallowed, and numbly offered, trying to sound utterly neutral: "I knew that girl . . ."

OF COURSE SHE WASN'T a girl any longer—again, she was almost fifty-five, as I was—but that was how I'd known her: a girl. It didn't matter. Todd just asked, "What girl?" and I made a vague distracted motion with my hand—"Just someone outside Palihouse." Todd craned his neck but didn't see anyone—she was already gone. He shrugged and looked back at his phone. I realized that the satellite radio was tuned to the Totally 80s station and the chorus from "Vienna" by Ultravox was playing—*It means nothing to me*, the singer cried out, *this means nothing to me*—as the fear kept swirling forward, a variation on that same fear from the fall of 1981, when we played this song near the end of every party or made sure of its prominence on every mixtape we compiled. Letting the song take me back on that December day, I thought I'd acquired the tools to cope with

The SHARDS

the events that happened when I was seventeen and I even thought, naïvely, foolishly, that I had worked it out through the trauma in the fiction I published years later, in my twenties and thirties and into my forties, but *that* specific trauma rushed back to me, proving that whatever I thought I'd worked out on my own, without having to confess it in a novel, I obviously hadn't.

That week we were in the desert I couldn't sleep—perhaps a couple of hours each night at the most even with a steady intake of benzodiazepine. I might have knocked myself out with the Xanax I'd overdosed on but the black dreams kept me from sleeping for more than one or two hours, and I would lie awake exhausted in the master bedroom in the house on Azure Court combating the rising panic tied to the girl I had seen. The midlife crisis that began after that night in 2006 when I tried to write about what happened to us our senior year at Buckley, completed itself roughly seven years later—seven years spent in a fever dream where the free-floating anxiety alienated everyone I knew and the accompanying stress caused me to drop forty pounds—waned away with the help of a therapist, a kind of life coach whom I dutifully saw every week for a year in an office off Sawtelle Boulevard just a block past the 405 who was the only one out of half a dozen shrinks I'd seen not afraid of the things I was telling him. I had learned from the previous five therapists that I had to downplay the horror of what had happened—to me, to us—and that I had to rearrange the narrative so that it was more palatable in order not to disturb the sessions themselves.

I was finally in a long-term relationship and the minor problems that never actually threatened my life—addiction, depression—crept away. People who had been avoiding me those last seven years, when I was emaciated and furious, would run into the new Bret in a restaurant or at a screening and seemed confused when they saw I wasn't as freaked out and messed up as I used to be. And the prince-of-darkness literary persona readers thought I had always embodied was now vanishing, being replaced by something sunnier—the man who wrote *American Psycho* was actually, some people were surprised to find out, just an amiable mess, maybe even likable, and not nearly the careless nihilist so many people mistook me for, an image that I perhaps played along with anyway. But it had never been the intended pose.

—

SHE WAS STANDING across the street from a CVS pharmacy that used to be, decades ago, a New Wave roller-disco rink called Flipper's, and on the way out to Palm Springs the sight of the woman caused me to remember the last time I had been to Flipper's, in the spring of 1981, before Robert Mallory appeared that September and everything changed. I was with Thom Wright and two other guys from our class at Buckley, Jeff Taylor and Kyle Colson—we were four seventeen-year-old high-school students in the convertible Rolls-Royce of a mildly infamous but harmless gay con man in his early forties named Ron Levin who Jeff Taylor had introduced to the group, all of us a little wired from the cocaine we had done at Ron's condo in Beverly Hills earlier that evening. This was actually on a school night during the middle of our junior year and what this might suggest about our adolescence is, I suppose, open to interpretation. It also might suggest something about our world that Jeff, a handsome surfer who—after Thom Wright—was the second- or third-best-looking guy in our class, was supplying Ron Levin with mild sexual favors for cash even though Jeff was straight, most of it going to a new surfboard, stereo equipment and a weed supplier in Zuma.

It might also suggest something about our world that Ron Levin was murdered a few years later by two members of something called the Billionaire Boys Club—an investment and social group collective made up of many of the guys we vaguely knew from the private-school scene in Los Angeles, guys who went to the Harvard School for Boys, which, along with the Buckley School, was one of the two most prestigious private schools in Los Angeles, and students from both places often knew each other in the vaguely exclusive world of prep schools then. Later, I would meet the founder of the Billionaire Boys Club, a guy my age named Joe Hunt, during winter break from Bennington at a casual dinner with a few friends at La Scala Boutique in Beverly Hills in the months preceding Ron Levin's murder at the hands of BBC's security director that Joe ordered, and nothing about Joe Hunt, tall and handsome and quiet, ever suggested he would be capable of the crimes he was later imprisoned for.

I'm digressing because what happened to us that fall in 1981 had nothing to do with the Billionaire Boys Club or Ron Levin or Joe Hunt. This was just a segment of where the world we were a part of was heading toward during that deep span of empire, and by the time the Billionaire Boys Club "happened" in 1983, what "happened" to us had already occurred, and it was perhaps the casually hedonistic world of adults we were eagerly entering that opened a door that allowed Robert Mallory and the Trawler and the events of that fall to greet us—it later seemed, at least to me, an invitation we thoughtlessly sent out completely unaware of the price we would end up paying.

FLIPPER'S LOOMED CLOSER on that spring night in Ron Levin's convertible Rolls-Royce as we headed up La Cienega into West Hollywood from Beverly Hills, Donna Summer singing "Dim All the Lights" from the car's stereo, off the eight-track of *Bad Girls*. Ron was driving and Jeff was in the passenger seat, Kyle and Thom and myself in the back, but I could see from where I was squeezed between Thom and Kyle that Ron's hand was on Jeff's thigh and then Jeff gently pushed Ron's hand away without looking at him. Thom had leaned over and saw this after I nudged him and glanced at me with a shrug, rolling his eyes, whatever. Did the shrug imply that this was simply where we all were and we were okay with it? I wondered hopefully as I glanced back at Thom Wright. But we really didn't care: we were high and young and it was a warm spring night and entering into the world of adults—nothing else mattered. This night in 1981 took place before a placid and beautiful summer in L.A.—the summer before the horror began, though we found out it had actually started *before* that summer, had already been unfolding in ways we weren't aware—and that night, which I remember few specific details of, seems in retrospect like one of the last innocent nights of my life despite the fact that we should have never been there, underage and slightly high on cocaine and with a much older gay man who would be murdered three years later by one of our private-school peers.

I don't remember roller-skating but I remember sitting in a booth drinking champagne, the *Xanadu* soundtrack blasting, and I remember that we went back to Ron's apartment in Beverly Hills and Ron casually disappeared into the bedroom with Jeff—he wanted to show

Jeff a new Rolex he'd just bought. Kyle drove back to his parents' in Brentwood while Thom and I did some more coke and played records (and I remember those records that night: Duran Duran, Billy Idol, Squeeze), before I eventually left, while Thom waited for Jeff, and after Ron passed out the two of them headed to Jeff's father's place in Malibu, where they stayed up the rest of the night and finished the half-gram Ron gave Jeff and hit the beach in their wet suits at dawn to surf the waves cresting along the misty morning shores before they put on their school uniforms and made the long drive to Buckley, taking Sunset all the way to Beverly Glen and then over the hill into Sherman Oaks. Hours earlier I had already driven through the canyons back to my parents' place on Mulholland, where I took a Valium I found in a Gucci pillbox—the pillbox a Christmas gift from Susan Reynolds when I was fifteen and maybe another clue about where we all were—before falling into an easy and dreamless sleep.

WE WERE SO autonomous at sixteen but it never seemed like it was to our youthful detriment, because the week you got your driver's license in L.A. was when you became an adult. I remember when Jeff Taylor first got his car before any of us and on a school night picked up Thom Wright in Beverly Hills and then dropped by the house on Mulholland to get me and then drove into Hollywood with the eight-track of Billy Joel's *Glass Houses* blasting "You May Be Right" and we went to see a late show of *Saturn 3* in a deserted Cinerama Dome—this was in February of 1980. I don't remember the movie—R-rated sci-fi starring Farrah Fawcett—only the freedom of being out on our own and without any parents involved. This was the first time we had driven by ourselves to see a ten o'clock movie and I remember hanging out in the vast parking lot of the Cinerama Dome as midnight neared, a deserted Hollywood surrounding us, sharing a joint, the future wide open.

It was not unusual after I got my driver's license to decide at seven o'clock on a Wednesday after browsing my homework that I would drive down the hill from the house on Mulholland and into West Hollywood to see the first set of the Psychedelic Furs at the Whisky without asking my mother's permission (my parents were separated by that point in 1980), because this had become a common weeknight out. I would just let my mother know that I'd be back by midnight and then I'd slip out of the house and drive through the empty canyons with Missing Persons or the Doors playing and park in a lot off Sunset where I'd pay five dollars to the attendant on North Clark. I would easily get into the Whisky with a fake ID (some nights I wasn't even carded) and in the club I'd ask the Rastafarian by the bar if he knew where I could get any coke and the Rastafarian would usually point to a kid with platinum-blond hair in the back of the room, whom I'd walk over to and gesture at, slipping him a wad of folded cash before I ordered a whiskey sour, which was a drink I favored in high school, waiting for him as he checked something out in the manager's office and then brought me a small packet. Afterward I would drive up the canyons and then cruise along Mulholland—everything was deserted, I was high, smoking a clove cigarette—and descend Laurel Canyon and drive along the neighborhoods nestled above Ventura Boulevard: I'd start in Studio City and then glide through Sherman Oaks slowly in the darkness along Valley Vista until I arrived in Encino and then, past that, into Tarzana, just idly driving by the darkened houses that lined the suburban neighborhoods, listening to the Kings until it was time to head back up to Mulholland. I'd take either Ventura Boule-vard or the 101 and at Van Nuys make the drive up Beverly Glen, and sometimes while heading home catch the green flashes from the eyes of coyotes in the glare of the headlights as they glanced at the Mercedes while trotting across Mulholland—sometimes in packs—and I'd have to stop the car, waiting to let them prowl past. And I could always manage the next morning, no matter how late my nights played out, to pull into the Buckley parking lot, neatly wearing my uniform, minutes before the first class began, never feeling hungover or tired but only pleasantly buzzed.

IF THE SPRING AND SUMMER of 1981 had been the dream, something paradisaical, then September represented the end of that dream with the arrival of Robert Mallory—there was now the sense of something *else* moving in, dark patterns were revealing themselves, and we began noticing things for the first time: a signal we had never heard before started calling out to us. I don't want to make a direct connection between certain events and the arrival of Robert Mallory in September of 1981 after that paradisaical summer but it happened to coincide with a kind of madness that slowly descended over the city. It was as if another world was announcing itself, painting the one we had all safely taken for granted into a darker color.

For example, this became a time when homes in certain neighborhoods were suddenly being targeted and staked out by members of a cult whose purpose was hard to ascertain, the pale hippie hanging out at the end of the driveway muttering to himself, his pacing interrupted by a brief shuffle-dance, and later, in December, there were plastic explosives planted all over town by the cult the hippies belonged to. There was suddenly a sniper on the roof of a department store in Beverly Hills on the night before Thanksgiving, and there was a bomb threat that cleared out Chasen's on Christmas Eve. Suddenly we knew about a teenage boy who had convinced himself he was possessed by a "Satanic demon" in Pacific Palisades and the elaborate exorcism by two priests to rid the boy of the demon, which almost killed him—the boy bled from his eyes and went deaf in one ear, developed pancreatitis, and four ribs were broken during the ritual. Suddenly there was the UCLA student buried alive as a prank by five classmates high on PCP at a fraternity party that a witness blandly said had "somehow gotten out of hand" and who almost didn't make it, ending up in a coma in a darkened room in one of the buildings lining Medical Plaza. Suddenly there were the spider infestations that bloomed everywhere across the city. The most fanciful story that fall involved a mutation, a monster, a fish the size of a small car hauled out of the ocean off Malibu—its skin was gray-white and there were large patches of silvery-orange scales dusted across it and even though it had the jaws of a shark it decidedly wasn't one, and when the thing was gutted by local fishermen they found the bodies of two dogs who had been missing swallowed whole.

And then, of course, there was the Trawler announcing itself.

For about a year there had been various break-ins and assaults, and then disappearances, and in 1981, the corpse of a second missing teenage girl was found—the other one discovered in 1980—and was ultimately connected to the home invasions. Everything might have happened without the presence of Robert Mallory but the fact that his arrival coincided with the strange darkening that had begun to lightly spiral into our lives was something I couldn't ignore, even though others did, at their own peril. Whether it was bad luck or bad timing these events were simply tied together, and though Robert Mallory wasn't the sniper on the roof of Neiman Marcus or the caller who emptied out Chasen's and he wasn't connected to the violent exorcism in Pacific Palisades or anywhere near the fraternity house in Westwood where the pledge had been flung into an open grave, his presence, for me, was connected to all of these things; every horror story we heard that fall, anything that darkened our bubble in ways we never noticed before, led to him.

A WEEK AGO I ordered a reproduction of the 1982 Buckley yearbook from a website called Classmates.com for ninety-nine dollars and it was FedExed four days later to the apartment on Doheny and when it arrived I remembered why I didn't have a copy: I never wanted to be reminded of the things that happened to me and the friends we lost. Our yearbook was called *Images,* and this edition was overseen by a classmate who became a well-known producer in Hollywood and she gave 1982 a cinematic theme: interspersed throughout the yearbook were stills of movies, everything from *Gone with the Wind* to *Ordinary People,* which seemed, in retrospect to what happened, almost unnaturally frivolous and uncaring, a way of forcing a lipstick smile onto a death mask. While slowly turning the pages of the "Seniors" section, where each of us had an individual page to reminisce and thank our parents and add photos of friends and quotations, designing the page to represent who we thought we were at eighteen, our best selves, I was haunted by the fact that out of the sixty seniors from that class of 1982 five were missing—the five who didn't make it for various reasons—and this fact was simply inescapable: I couldn't dream it away or pretend it wasn't true. We were listed alphabetically and after sipping from a tumbler of gin I would tentatively turn to where each of them would have been placed within those sixty pages and notice that they simply weren't there—they had all existed that first week in September but now they were erased. Instead three of them were listed in the "In Memoriam" section at the back of the book.

FALL/1981

1

I REMEMBER IT WAS THE SUNDAY afternoon before Labor
Day in 1981 and our senior year was about to begin on that Tuesday morning of September 8—and I remember that the Windover
Stables were located on a bluff above Malibu, where Deborah Schaffer was boarding her new horse, Spirit, in one of the twenty separate
barns where the animals were housed, and I remember I was driving
solo, following Susan Reynolds and Thom Wright in Thom's convertible Corvette along Pacific Coast Highway, the ocean dimly shimmering beside us in the humid air, until we reached the turnoff that took
us up to the stables, and I remember I was listening to the Cars, the
song was "Dangerous Type"—on a mixtape I'd made that included
Blondie, the Babys, Duran Duran—as I kept behind Thom's car up
the winding road to the entrance of the stables, where we parked
next to Deborah's gleaming brand-new BMW, the only car in the lot
on that Sunday, and then checked in at the front office, and where
we followed a tree-lined trail until we located Debbie trotting Spirit
by his reins around a gated arena that was deserted—she had already
ridden him but the saddle was still on and she was wearing her riding
attire. The sight of the horse shocked me—and I remember that I
shivered at its presence in the late-afternoon heat. Spirit had replaced
a horse Debbie retired in June.

"Hey," Debbie said to us in her flat, uninflected voice. I remember how it sounded so hollow in the emptiness that surrounded us—a
deadened echo. Beyond the manicured stables painted white and pine
green was a forest of trees blocking the view of the Pacific—you could
see small patches of glassy blue but everything seemed ensconced

and still, nothing moved, as if we were encased in a kind of plastic dome. I remember it being very hot that day and I felt that I had somehow been forced into visiting the stables simply because Debbie had become my girlfriend that summer and it was required of me and not something I necessarily wanted to experience. But I was resigned: I may have wanted to stay home and work on the novel I was writing, but at seventeen I also wanted to keep up certain appearances.

I remember Thom said "Wow" as he neared the horse, and, like everything with Thom, it might have sounded genuine, but it was also, like Debbie's intonation, flat, as if he didn't really have an opinion: everything was cool, everything was chill, everything was a mild *wow*. Susan murmured in agreement as she took off her Wayfarers.

"Hey, handsome," Debbie said to me, placing a kiss on my cheek.

I remember I tried to stare admiringly at the animal but I really didn't want to care about the horse—and yet it was so large and alive that I was shocked by it. Up close it was kind of magnificent, and it definitely made an impression on me—it just seemed too huge, and only made of muscle, a threat—*It could hurt you,* I thought— but it was actually calm, and in that moment had no problem letting us stroke its flanks. I remember that I was aware of Spirit being yet another example of Debbie's wealth and her intertwined carelessness: the cost of maintaining and housing the animal would be astronomical and yet who knew how interested she really was at seventeen and if that interest was going to be sustained. But this was another aspect I hadn't known about Debbie even though we had been going to school together since fifth grade—I hadn't paid attention until now: I found out she'd always been interested in horses and yet I never knew it until the summer before our senior year, when I became her boyfriend and saw the shelves in her bedroom lined with ribbons and trophies and photographs of her at various equestrian events. I had always been more interested in her father, Terry Schaffer, than I was in Debbie. In 1981 Terry Schaffer was thirty-nine and already extremely wealthy, having made the bulk of his fortune on a few movies that had—in two unexpected cases—become blockbusters, and he was one of the town's most respected and in-demand producers. He had taste, or at least what Hollywood considered taste—he had been nominated for an Oscar twice—and he was constantly offered jobs to run studios, something he had no interest in. Terry was also gay—not openly but discreetly—and he was married to Liz Schaffer, who was lost in so much privilege and pain that I wondered if Terry's gayness registered with her at all anymore. Deborah was their only child. Terry died in 1992.

THOM WAS ASKING Debbie general questions about the horse and Susan glanced over at me and smiled—I rolled my eyes, not at Thom, but at the overall non-situation. Susan rolled her eyes back at me: a connection was made between us that didn't involve our respective mates. After petting and admiring the horse there didn't seem much reason for us to be standing around anymore and I remember thinking: *This* is why I drove all the way out to Malibu? In order to witness and pet Debbie's dumb new horse? And I remember I stood there feeling somewhat awkward, though I'm sure neither Thom nor Susan did: they were almost never annoyed, nothing ever ruffled Thom or Susan, they took everything in stride, and the eye-rolling on Susan's part seemed designed to simply placate me, but I was grateful. Debbie kissed my lips lightly.

"See you back at my place?" she asked.

I was momentarily distracted by the whispered conversation Thom and Susan were having before I turned my attention to Debbie. I remembered Debbie was having people over that night at the house in Bel Air and I smiled naturally in order to reassure her.

"Yeah, totally."

And then, on cue, as if everything was rehearsed, Thom and Susan and I walked back to our cars as Debbie walked Spirit into his stable, with someone from the Windover staff, uniformed in white jeans and a windbreaker. I followed Thom and Susan along PCH and as they made the left turn onto Sunset Boulevard, which would take us all the way from the beach to the entrance of Bel Air's East Gate, a song that I liked but would never admit to was now playing on the mixtape: REO Speedwagon's "Time for Me to Fly," a sappy ballad about a loser who gets up the nerve to tell his girlfriend it's over, and yet for me at seventeen it was a song about metamorphosis and the lyric *I know it hurts to say goodbye, but it's time for me to fly* . . . meant something else that spring and summer of 1981, when I became attached to the song. It was about leaving one realm and moving into another, just as I had been doing. And I remember being at the stables not because anything happened there—it was just Thom and Susan and myself driving out to Malibu to see the horse—but because it was the afternoon that led into the night where we first heard the name of a new student who would be joining our senior class that fall at Buckley: Robert Mallory.

THOM WRIGHT AND SUSAN REYNOLDS had been dating since they were sophomores—and were now the most popular people not only in our class but in the overall Buckley student body after Katie Choi and Brad Foreman graduated in June and it was obvious why: Thom and Susan were casually beautiful, all-American, dark-blond hair, green eyes, perpetually tan, and there was something logical in the way they had gravitated inexorably toward each other and moved everywhere as a single unit—they were almost always together. They both came from wealthy L.A. families but Thom's parents were divorced and his father had relocated to New York, and it was only on those trips to Manhattan where Thom visited his dad that he wasn't in direct proximity to Susan. For about two years they were in love, until that fall of 1981, when one of them wasn't, which set into motion a series of dreadful events. I had been infatuated with both of them but I never admitted to either one that it was actually love.

I had been Susan's closest male friend since we met at Buckley in the seventh grade and five years later I knew seemingly everything about her: when she got her period, the problems with her mother, every imaginary slight and deprivation she thought she was enduring, crushes on classmates before Thom. She kind of knew that I was secretly in love with her, but even though we were always close she never said anything, only teased me at certain moments if I was paying too much attention to her, or not enough. I had been flattered that people thought we were boyfriend and girlfriend and I did little to stop the rumors about the two of us until Thom stepped in. Susan Reynolds was the prototype of the cool SoCal girl even at thirteen, years before she was driving a convertible BMW and always mildly stoned on marijuana or Valium or half a Quaalude (but functioning—she was an effortless A student) and impudently wearing Wayfarer sunglasses as she walked through the arched stucco doorways to her class unless a teacher asked her to take them off—every Buckley student seemed in possession of a designer pair of sunglasses but they weren't allowed to be worn on campus except in the parking lot and on Gilley Field. Susan seemed to confide everything to me during the middle-school years—in the 1970s they were referred to as "junior high"—and though I didn't quite return that openness I had revealed enough for her to know things about me that no one else did, but only to a point. There were things I would never tell her.

Susan Reynolds became the de facto queen of our class as we moved through each subsequent grade: she was beautiful, sophisticated, intriguingly low-key, and she had an air of casual sexuality even before she and Thom became a couple—and it wasn't because she was slutty; she had actually lost her virginity to Thom and hadn't had sex with anyone else—but Susan's beauty always intensified the idea of her sexuality for us. Thom ultimately took it a step further and Susan's sexual aura became more pronounced once they started dating, when everyone knew that they were fucking, but it had always been there; and even if they hadn't actually been fucking in the beginning, during those first weeks that fall of 1979, when they became a couple, the question was: how could two teenagers *that* good-looking *not* be fucking each other? By September of 1981 Susan and I were still close and, in some ways, I think she felt closer to me than to Thom—we had, of course, a different relationship—but there now seemed to be a slight wariness, not necessarily toward anything in particular but just a general malaise. She had been with Thom for two years and a vague but noticeable ennui had drifted over her. The jealousy that they inspired and that had almost broken me was, I thought, dissolving by then.

THOM WRIGHT, LIKE SUSAN REYNOLDS, HAD started Buckley in seventh grade, transferring from Horace Mann. His parents divorced when he was in ninth grade and he lived with his mother in Beverly Hills when his father relocated to Manhattan. Though Thom had always been cute—obviously the cutest guy in our class, adorable even—it wasn't until something happened to him over the summer of 1979, when he returned from New York after spending July and August with his father, that he'd somehow, inexplicably, become a man; some kind of metamorphosis had happened that summer, the cuteness and the adorability had faded, and we started looking at Thom in a different way—he was suddenly, officially, sexualized when we saw him back at school that September of our sophomore year. Even though I had always sexualized Thom Wright everyone else now realized he was *built*, the jawline seemed more pronounced, the hair was now shorter—somewhat ubiquitous among the guys at Buckley (mostly because of haircut regulations) but Thom's was now something stylish, a moment, a cue to manliness—and when I glimpsed him in the locker room that first week back from the summer changing for Phys Ed (our lockers throughout our time at Buckley were side by side) I hitched in a breath when I saw he had obviously been working out and his chest and arms and torso were defined in ways they weren't at the end of June, the last time I saw him in a bathing suit, at a pool party at Anthony Matthews's house. There was also the paleness around his newly muscled thighs and ass—the place where his bathing suit had blocked the sun from his weekends in the Hamptons—that contrasted with the rest of his tanned body, which shocked me. Thom had become an ideal of teen boy handsomeness and what was so alluring about him was that he seemed not to care, he seemed not to notice, as if it was just a natural gift bestowed upon him—he didn't have an ego. I had repeatedly gotten over any notions that my feelings for Thom Wright would be reciprocated, because he was so resolutely heterosexual in ways that I wasn't.

This inchoate crush on Thom may have come back those first few weeks after he returned from New York that September in 1979 but then he was suddenly with Susan and we effortlessly became a kind of threesome once we got cars that following spring, hanging out on weekends, going to the movies together in Westwood, lying on the sand at the Jonathan Beach Club in Santa Monica and cruising the Century City Mall, and my crush on both Thom and Susan was rendered pointless. Not that Thom would have ever noticed it, though

Susan, I'm sure, had registered my feelings and knew I desired her: Thom was, admittedly, a fairly unaware individual—about a lot of things—and yet there was an intriguing blankness that was attractive and soothing about him, there was never any tension, he was the pinnacle of laid-back and he wasn't a stoner. By the time we finished junior year the only drug Thom liked was coke, and only just a line or two, a few bumps could take him through a party, and he didn't drink except for the occasional Corona. He was so easy to hang with and so agreeable to any option that when I fantasized coming on to him I often dreamt he would have let me, at least halfway, before gently rejecting my advances, though not without a kiss and a suggestive squeeze on my upper thigh to uselessly reassure me. In some of my more elaborate fantasies Thom didn't reject me sexually and these would end with both of us covered in sweat and in my dreams the sex was exaggeratedly intense and afterward, I'd imagine, he would kiss me deeply, panting, quietly laughing, amazed at the pleasure I brought him, in ways that Susan Reynolds never could.

I DIDN'T WANT DEBBIE SCHAFFER to kiss me at the Windover Stables that afternoon in front of Thom and Susan but I hadn't minded either. In a way she was an experiment—I wasn't determined to have a girlfriend my senior year at Buckley except if it had been Susan Reynolds—and yet Debbie had become, somewhat inexplicably, exactly that at the beginning of the summer. We were at another party at Anthony Matthews's house and she just started making out with me on a chaise by the lit pool. I was stoned on a Quaalude, she was on coke, it was midnight, Split Enz's "I Got You" was playing from inside the house (. . . *I don't know why sometimes I get frightened . . .*) and I was at a point where I still tried to be attracted to girls—that hadn't ended yet—and all the requisite elements seemed to be in play. She simply pushed herself onto me and I surprised myself and went with it. I really didn't care about appearances—though I definitely wasn't out as bisexual and I had no desire to lead a girl or a guy on—but I was also fairly passive, and when it came to Debbie Schaffer, whom I had known since the fifth grade, I just went with whatever she wanted that summer, and I thought including her might round out the group of Susan and Thom and myself, make it less painful for me, hopefully inspire one of them to become jealous, which of course never happened. I also wanted to get closer to Debbie so it might bring me nearer to Terry Schaffer, the famous dad, who I'd always been drawn to and yet after all these years never really knew, and I'd known Debbie seemingly forever.

Debbie had transformed from a somewhat awkward-looking girl—though always bizarrely confident, or maybe just entitled, but pudgy with braces and a ponytail—into a kind of slutty teen boy fantasy by the time she reached ninth grade. Her breasts were full and high and she took every opportunity to show off her cleavage. A Buckley girl wasn't supposed to reveal this, the white blouse was supposed to be buttoned to the point where you couldn't see anything, but many of the girls ignored this rule in tenth and eleventh grade and, depending on what adult glimpsed this, it had become allowed— the rules were malleable. Her legs were stunning, long and tan and waxed, and the saddle shoes she wore with ankle-high white socks helped turn her into something fetishistic; the hem on the gray skirt of her uniform was at the highest permissible length so you could see past upper-thigh, and often when she sat down you just as easily glimpsed the light-pink panties she was fond of. By senior year her hair was a shade off platinum, Blondie-inspired, and though makeup was against the rules for younger girls (lip gloss was acceptable), if you were in eleventh or twelfth grade it was allowed minimally, and often girls casually wore understated lipstick though Debbie wore hers defiantly, hot pink and blood red, even though she was often asked by a teacher or our principal, Dr. Croft, to wipe it off. Susan barely wore any makeup at all because Thom didn't like it.

EVEN THOUGH AS A COUPLE THOM AND SUSAN, in my mind, seemed more defined than anything else in the minimalist moment we were moving through in 1981, which was inspired by New Wave and punk—numbness and disaffection, a general rejection of seventies kitsch, everything was clean with sharp angles now— they were a throwback to a distant era despite how up-to-date and effortlessly hip both of them outwardly seemed—they often acted as if they could have been the king and queen of the prom from a movie made in the early 1960s: happy, carefree, untroubled. But I knew at a certain point—by the late spring of 1981, almost two years after they started dating—that Thom was happier than Susan. She had recently confided to me one day near the end of our junior year as we walked through Westwood after school in our Buckley uniforms while Thom was at baseball practice that "Thom isn't dumb exactly . . ." She said this apropos of nothing, and I didn't know how to respond—I just looked over at her. It was true: his grades were good, he kept them up—he had to because of the sports he played and excelled at: football, basketball, soccer, baseball, track—and he read and admired books (as sophomores we bonded over how much we both liked *The Great Gatsby* and *The Sun Also Rises*) and he had become almost as much of a cinephile as I was, often accompanying me to revival theaters like the Nuart, where I would educate him about the differences between good Robert Altman and bad, and why Brian De Palma was an important director. "But Thom *can* be—" Susan started, then stopped herself. I remember she chose the following words carefully as we stood in front of the Postermat, debating whether to go in. *Outland,* a movie set on one of Jupiter's moons, was playing next door at the Bruin, I remember. "Not dim," she said, then pausing. "But uncurious."

Well, Thom didn't *need* to be anything, I argued, kind of joking. He was *hot,* his family had money, Thom would be okay whether he was dumb or not. What was she trying to say?

Susan looked at me strangely after I said this, seemingly bothered that I was overly effusive about defending something so innocuous and vague. "You're hardly not hot, Bret," Susan said as we slowly floated across the sidewalk.

I was swinging a yellow Tower Records bag (Squeeze, *East Side Story,* the Kim Carnes LP with "Bette Davis Eyes") and tried to seem utterly nonchalant when I said, "But I'm not *Thom.*"

This annoyed her. "God, you sound like you want to date him."

"Date?" I said, smirking. "Is that a possibility?" I was joking but I wanted to test her.

Susan glanced at me, smiling at first, and coy, Wayfarers on, lips lightly touched with bubble-gum gloss, and then she said seriously, "No, I don't think so. No, it isn't."

The way she answered this with such a casual finality annoyed me. "Jesus, Susan, I'm kidding," I said, even though, of course, I wasn't.

Susan didn't say anything as we crossed Broxton, just kept looking over at me even though I couldn't see her eyes because of the Wayfarers—she was trying to figure something out.

I asked, "How do you know Thom wouldn't?"

She finally sighed and said, "Oh, Bret, I hope you're happy. I really do. Your secret is safe with me."

I laughed and said, "You don't know my secrets."

But we *were* finding missing pieces and secrets everywhere and I had more than a few and in that moment I wondered which ones Susan knew, which ones she had uncovered, and which ones remained mysteries.

EVERYTHING SPED UP when you got your car at sixteen: you were now autonomous in ways you hadn't been, you could take care of yourself or so you thought—that was the illusion—and now that we were older, and especially if we didn't have siblings—which strangely none of us had, not Thom, not Susan or Deborah, not Matt Kellner, or myself—this encouraged our parents to either work longer hours or travel with less restrictions, many of them to distant movie sets in other countries, or they were simply taking more elaborate vacations, leaving behind empty houses in Bel Air and Beverly Hills and Benedict Canyon and along the cliffs of Mulholland and into Malibu that we took advantage of our junior year. And because of this new autonomy and mobility we were driving over to a friend's house whenever we wanted or hanging at the beach club on a whim, and some of the boys were now openly purchasing porn at the newsstands in Sherman Oaks and Studio City or sometimes driving into West L.A. or Hollywood to flash a fake ID and buy magazines and videotapes.

We also started spending time at the Odyssey, an all-age nightclub on Beverly Boulevard near the corner of La Cienega, which didn't serve alcohol but if you knew your way around you could score

Quaaludes and weed and small baggies of cocaine, and for me, at least, the Odyssey had the added allure that there were gay men in attendance even though it was ostensibly a straight club; and though the gay men were perhaps older than I wanted to pursue, this was the first time I was in close proximity to them and it had been mildly thrilling even though I didn't do anything, just danced with Thom and Susan and Jeff and sometimes Debbie and Anthony and whoever else was there until two or three in the morning on weekends, and with our parents mostly absent that spring we could roll home whenever we wanted, sleep late, and then do it all over again—this was what the cars afforded us.

WE ALSO DIDN'T HAVE TO DEPEND on our parents' driving us into Westwood Village, where we would meet up to watch two or three or even four movies (if we were feeling particularly ambitious), which is how we spent our Saturdays, catching up on everything that opened Friday—the group evolving every weekend depending on what movies were playing and who wanted to see what, usually myself and Thom, Jeff and Anthony, maybe Kyle and Dominic. We would decide on Saturday mornings in a number of overlapping phone calls while going through the "Calendar" section of the *Los Angeles Times* on what to see (the only way in 1981 to find out what was playing where and when) and by a certain point the group scheduled where we'd be exactly throughout the day, so the girls would know where to meet us later. The girls were usually not interested in the two or three matinees we planned on seeing and they would meet us for a light dinner, usually sushi at a place we frequented just below Le Conte Avenue, a half-block from the Village Theater, and the last movie of the night.

The guys would start the day by meeting for lunch somewhere at noon—a favorite was Yesterdays and the Monte Cristo sandwich they served, or we'd take the street-level elevator down into the Good Earth, a modish upscale health-food restaurant where we drank giant glasses of cinnamon-flavored iced tea and ate salads, or we'd crowd into one of the red booths at Hamburger Hamlet for patty melts after buying our tickets for the next movie at the Bruin, adjacent on Weyburn. Dinner was sometimes at the Chart House or the old-school Italian of Mario's, with breaks spent at the Westworld video arcade playing Space Invaders and Pac-Man or browsing the Postermat while sixties girl groups blared or looking for new music at Tower Records or the Wherehouse or leafing through paperbacks at any number of the large bookstores that dotted the streets—there were five or six in 1981, there are none now. The night would end at Ships, a retro coffee shop on Wilshire, situated along the edges of Westwood Village, with a boomerang-shaped roof and atomic neon sign, and where we'd order Cokes and vanilla milkshakes and smoke clove cigarettes, ashtrays and a separate toaster on each table, and stay out until after midnight. We were taking tentative advantage of the newfound freedom that had opened up to us—activating something in our group that made us want to become adults fast and leave what now seemed like the stifling world of childhood behind. *Time for me to fly . . .*

IN LATE MAY OF 1980—May 23, to be exact—*The Shining* opened, and I wanted to see it as soon as possible.

I'd read the novel when it was published in 1977, already a big fan of Stephen King, having practically memorized *Carrie* and *Salem's Lot*, his first two books, and *The Shining* scared me mightily as a thirteen-year-old: the haunted Overlook Hotel, the angry and alcoholic father possessed and driven murderous by the spirits of the place, the frightened son in peril, REDRUM, the hedge animals that came alive. I was obsessed and it remains one of the key novels that made me want to be a writer. In fact as soon as I was done reading *The Shining* for a third time I began writing my own novel in the summer of 1978, which I was still working on in the late spring of 1980, though about to abandon it in favor of what ultimately became *Less Than Zero*.

When I heard that Stanley Kubrick was adapting *The Shining* on a lavish scale I was immediately distracted—it became the most anticipated movie in my lifetime, and I closely followed its troubled production (delays, endless takes, a fire destroyed the main set, the ramping costs), and I don't think I've ever tracked the making of a movie with more interest—not even the ones that were later made from my novels gripped me as much as what Kubrick was going to do with *The Shining*. I was almost paralyzed with anticipation. And then a trailer dropped late in 1979; it was simple, almost minimalist, just an image—how one longs for trailers that didn't lay out the entire movie like today's three-act previews—of an elevator in the Overlook whose doors seem to be slowly pushing open because the cabin is filled with blood that starts pouring out in slow motion and then cascades toward us in waves until the blood crashes against the camera, turning the lens red, the credits of the movie rolling upward in neon blue over this one image. I saw the trailer many times during the fall of 1979 and throughout the first half of 1980 and it never failed to rivet me. I began counting the days—the hours—before I could see the actual movie.

I couldn't go on the 23rd because of school and I didn't want to face Westwood on a crowded Friday night, so my plan was to go the next day—Saturday, May 24—and I wanted to see the 10:00 a.m. showing because I knew it would be less crowded than any of the later screenings. Surprisingly everyone argued for 1:00 p.m. at the Village—it was a Saturday, they wanted to sleep in, 10 was way too early. I argued to Thom and Jeff that the lines would be too long later in the day, since it was an exclusive engagement only playing at three theaters in Los Angeles, but everyone eventually bowed out and said they'd meet me for lunch at D. B. Levy's, a deli we frequented on Lindbrook Drive after the movie was over, and then see *The Empire Strikes Back* later that afternoon at the Avco. I was disappointed—I wanted to see *The Shining* with Thom—but it didn't diminish my excitement. This would be the first time I drove to Westwood by myself to see a movie alone, without the guys, and I felt incredibly adult as I raced across Mulholland toward Beverly Glen on that Saturday morning in my father's hand-down, a metallic-green Mercedes 450SEL, a four-door tank that was hardly the sporty vehicle I longed for at sixteen.

I PARKED IN THE LOT ON BROXTON across from the Village Theater at nine-thirty—listening to a mixtape made up entirely of Joe Jackson's *Look Sharp* and *I'm the Man* with a couple of Clash songs from *London Calling* and Elvis Costello's *Armed Forces* added in—and was relieved that only a short line had formed at the box office then being admitted straight into the theater. I remember, and I don't know why, that I was wearing a fashionable new Ralph Lauren shirt, sea green with the insignia of a purple polo pony, and Calvin Klein jeans with Topsiders—and that I kept my Wayfarer sunglasses on when I bought my ticket. *The Shining* was rated R and I was momentarily worried I'd get carded even though I had a fake ID I barely used, the city was lax, and I didn't need it that morning—four dollars for one adult. Again I was reminded as I moved into the grand lobby—looking at the carved winged lions that sat halfway up the 170-foot bleached FOX tower, which loomed over Broxton and Weyburn Avenues, at night lit by a blue-and-white sign crowning the tower, its shaft illuminated, a beacon—that this was the first time I'd come to Westwood alone and I felt genuinely grown-up and shivered with anticipation at whatever the future held. I bought a box of Junior Mints and moved from the bright Art Deco lobby into the darkness of the gigantic auditorium.

The theater was less crowded than I worried it would be but it was only nine-forty and it was bound to fill up, I thought as I sat and stared at the massive set of curtains draped in front of the 70-millimeter screen. Writing this now, I can't believe that I was left to my own devices for twenty minutes, just idly sitting there, thinking about things, about Thom and about Susan, waiting without a phone to look at, waiting without something to distract me. Instead, I took in the theater—my favorite in Westwood and the largest, with over fourteen hundred seats; it was its own vast world I took refuge in and it was one of the few places I was aware I might actually be saved—because movies were a religion in that moment, they could change you, alter your perception, you could rise toward the screen and share a moment of transcendence, all the disappointments and fears would be wiped away for a few hours in that church: movies acted like a drug for me. But they were also about control: you were a voyeur sitting in the dark staring at secret things, because that's what movies were—scenes you shouldn't be seeing and that no one on the screen knew you were watching. These were the things I was thinking about while I slowly pressed down on a Junior Mint, letting it dissolve on my tongue, glancing at my watch as the hands moved toward ten o'clock. The lights in the theater seemed to slowly darken even though there were still about two minutes before the curtain would rise. The ominous music from the soundtrack began softly announcing itself in the domed auditorium: snake rattles and bird trills and wailing horns. I realized, thrillingly, that there would be no trailers at this showing.

And that's when I saw the boy.

This is the reason why I've never forgotten seeing *The Shining* on May 24, 1980, at the Village Theater in Westwood at the 10:00 a.m. show. It was because of him.

I WAS SITTING in the upper echelon of the orchestra section—above me was a two-tiered balcony that you entered on the third floor of the theater and that hung over the last ten rows of the orchestra without obscuring your sight lines—and I was off to the side, near the aisle, when I saw him: a guy around my age so stunningly handsome that I thought at first he was a movie star or a model I'd fantasized about from *GQ* magazine. He seemed to be looking for someone as he walked up the darkening aisle, everything slowly dimming around us. His face was a series of cut angles, and he had a full head of blond unruly hair, short and brushed back, and it stood up, adding to the angularity of his features; he had full lips and slightly sunken cheeks and an aquiline nose. He was tall, probably five eleven, slim-waisted, broad-shouldered, and as he passed I could see his mouth was working, chewing gum, and he was preoccupied with finding whoever he was looking for, and I could also see the long eyelashes and I pretended his irises were blue and that he was tan everywhere. A wave of lust crested hard in my chest and I suddenly ached for him—the sensation was so immediate and so tidal that I was shocked—and adding this new presence to the anticipation of watching the movie that was finally about to begin forced me to slow down my breathing. The boy aroused something primal in me that I had never felt before—I wanted him immediately, I needed to be his friend, I had to make contact, I had to see him naked, I had to own him. I shifted in my seat

as the curtains in the theater were rising, revealing the giant whiteness of the screen—my hands were gripped into fists and I turned
around and craned my neck, hoping to see where he went.

The Warner Bros. logo headed toward us as the opening credits of *The Shining* began over aerial shots of the family's Volkswagen
heading up the deserted roads toward the Overlook. But I couldn't
get my bearings, because I now watched as the boy walked down the
other aisle. He was farther away this time but I had a better look at
his body: the tightness of his jeans showcased his ass, tapering up into
a long back—this was becoming always the first thing I noticed about
a guy—and I watched mesmerized as this boy, this god, walked the
aisle, disappearing from my sight line. He had to be older than me, I
thought; he was a UCLA student probably, maybe even a graduate,
too manly to still be in high school. I saw him once more, mid-movie,
as he walked up the aisle again, and I had to control what seemed like
every muscle in my body and not follow him to what I assumed was
the restroom or the concession stand, because he had glanced at me
as I watched him pass by—we made eye contact, he noticed me staring at him—and he glanced away but not before a kind of lingering
gaze took me in, and I fantasized that he wanted me, too.

After the movie was over—I was underwhelmed, it was nothing
like the book, I felt cheated but also that I needed to be impressed
because I had waited so long to see it—I walked into the lobby hoping
to find the boy but he wasn't anywhere: not in the line to the men's
room, which I checked out, and then idly waited to see if he had been,
in fact, in there, but he wasn't, and when I walked outside to the front
of the theater he wasn't there either. The crowd for the next show, at
1:00 p.m., was enormous: the line snaking around the block, along
Broxton, and then curving along Le Conte, and then back down along
Gayley and finally to the box-office booth of the theater, creating an
almost unbroken four-block-long square. In addition there seemed
to be hundreds of people outside the Village Theater who weren't in
line, just talking and lingering below the giant FOX tower, and I lingered there too, only momentarily, knowing I wouldn't see that magical boy again but hoping to catch a glimpse of him anyway. And yet I
was glad that I didn't see him: it would have been too overwhelming
and ultimately tinged with disappointment, because I could never be

for him what he ended up being for me. I even included a version of him in a short story I was working on that summer where he became a character I controlled.

AS I FOLLOWED Thom's car across Sunset on that September afternoon before Labor Day, weaving along the boulevard's curves, heading toward Bel Air, I reflected on the summer that had just passed: hooking up with Debbie, the weekdays at the beach club, the late nights at Du-par's after dancing at the Seven Seas mildly wasted on whiskey sours—the drinking age in L.A. was twenty-one but everyone had fake IDs—and we'd already left the teenagers at the Odyssey far behind us; there were the pool parties, usually at Anthony Matthews's or Debbie Schaffer's; we saw *Raiders of the Lost Ark* at a preview screening on the Paramount lot courtesy of Terry; a group of us went to a midnight show of *An American Werewolf in London* at the Avco in Westwood the weekend it opened in August, completely stoned, exaggeratedly laughing and screaming as David Naughton transformed into a monster, and we started seeing New Wave bands in smaller clubs—we were moving away from the Eagles at the Long Beach Arena (where we had watched as they broke up onstage in what would be their last concert for fifteen years) and Pink Floyd performing *The Wall* at the Sports Arena last February—our musical tastes were changing—and instead it was X at the Whisky, the Go-Go's at the Starwood, the Plimsouls at the Roxy. It was the summer that fashions changed: all the boys in our class were wearing Ralph Lauren Polo shirts in bold Easter-egg colors—pink and blue and green and purple—something Thom Wright and I'd started, but now worn with the collar sticking up, and plaid shorts, and cardigan sweaters, and we wore dress shirts with the logo of the Armani eagle as part of our Buckley uniform, and Topsiders and penny loafers replaced the standard buckle-up and tennis shoe. The male fashion in that moment was still streamlined, preppie, at times vaguely Italian, more *The Garden of the Finzi-Continis* than *The Lost Boys*—we were a long way from shoulder pads and mullets and the clownish kitsch from the mid-1980s and most boys kept their hair short and dressed neatly and the girls took their dressier cues from retro classics: Capri pants, bubble skirts, taffeta. We were trying to look stylish, we were aiming for cool, we wanted to become adults. It was the August that MTV started airing videos but none of us had any idea what it would become—the Buggles' *Video Killed the Radio Star* was the first video the channel played, and though we knew the song and had been listening to the album it came from, *The Age of Plastic*, we didn't know what a bold premonition that song and video would ultimately morph into.

As I said, the summer of 1981 had been a dream—I liked calling it *paradisaical*—and because of this I was envisioning a fairly uncomplicated senior year unfolding before us, one I would easily move through as if performing a well-rehearsed part while I figured out my escape, possibly somewhere along the Eastern Seaboard, perhaps farther, maybe across an ocean. What an innocent year it was going to be, I thought, driving along Sunset, so easy and effortless to move through.

BY THE END of that summer I'd found out that even though we'd all known each other at least since seventh grade and we were supposedly such close friends and there were so many innocent truths we assumed, we were also realizing that these supposed truths were not, in fact, real, and I became aware that there were things that happened to me during that summer I was never going to tell my best friends, Thom Wright and Susan Reynolds, or my new girlfriend, Deborah Schaffer. They would never know about the dreamy afternoons swimming naked with our classmate Matt Kellner in Encino or that my hand kept caressing Ryan Vaughn's inner thigh in the Town & Country triplex while we watched *Escape from New York,* floating on the Valium I'd taken from one of my mother's many prescription bottles; it was a film I'd already seen—but I didn't care because I just wanted to sit close to Ryan in the darkness of the movie theater. My classmates would never know that Matt Kellner blew me in the pool house he lived in behind his parents' palatial estate on Haskell Avenue before I slid down and did the same to him, or that Ryan Vaughn, co-captain of the varsity football team, hadn't removed my hand from his thigh in the darkened movie theater on an August night just a few weeks ago.

2

AND RYAN VAUGHN was already standing by the pool in the Schaffers' backyard holding a Corona when I arrived at Debbie's house on that Sunday night before Labor Day.

It was barely dusk and Ryan was backlit, a faint shadow, in front of the glowing blue pool and the drifting pink sky, talking to Thom Wright and Jeff Taylor, all of them wearing Polo shirts and pastel shorts, and somewhere Pat Benatar was singing "We Live for Love"—it wasn't loud, it was just coming from the outdoor speakers, background noise that joined the kids hanging out while Paul, the black butler who worked for the Schaffers, prepped burgers and hot dogs and heated the grill in an alcove next to the pool house. A variety of drinks (sodas, juices, iced tea, lemonade) had been set up on a table next to where Paul was standing but there were also bottles of Corona in a silver tub filled with ice that a few of the guys, including Thom and Jeff and Ryan, had helped themselves to, and then Dominic Thompson, who I hadn't seen all summer—he'd been in Europe—joined them, also holding a Corona. Pat Benatar became the Go-Go's, and *Beauty and the Beat* started in its entirety with "Our Lips Are Sealed" as I began making my way down the stone steps that led to the pool area, where everyone had congregated—it was an album we played all summer long in 1981 and knew by heart. Billie, the Schaffers' golden retriever, was wandering around, occasionally receiving a distracted pet from one of the kids.

Pulling up to the circular driveway at the Schaffers' mansion in Bel Air, already lined with cars—I experienced a jolt when I saw Ryan's black Trans Am—I noted that Thom and Susan hadn't waited for me when they arrived just minutes before and I also knew that Debbie wasn't back yet from the stables in Malibu and that would give me enough time to talk to Ryan before the distraction of her presence. The front door of the house was open and I walked through the foyer beneath a massive chandelier and into the hallway that led past the sunken living room, where I glimpsed Liz Schaffer, Debbie's mom, on the phone, in a loose-fitting robe, holding a glass that I presumed was filled with vodka, and which she raised to me as I passed, smiling, and I gave her a little wave back and then moved through the dining room and into the kitchen and said hi to Maria, the Schaffers' main housekeeper, and grabbed a handful of tortilla chips where two of her associates were preparing the rest of the food that night—fresh salsa, potato salad, coleslaw, corn on the cob—while Steven Reinhardt, the Schaffers' personal assistant, placed tubs of Häagen-Dazs ice cream that had just been delivered into the walk-in freezer. I passed through the open sliding glass doors and walked outside to the vast backyard, which took me to the flagstone path that led down to the pool area surrounded by eucalyptus and pine trees, and beyond that the tennis court. Susan had already settled into a chaise longue, where she was talking to Tracy Goldman and Katie Harris while Thom and Jeff stood next to her nodding deeply to something Ryan was saying, the three of them standing beneath a massive umbrella, its canopy a swirl of blue and yellow, and in the background lit Tiki torches dotted the edges of the property as the Go-Go's played.

MY FIRST THOUGHT as I moved down the steps to the pool area was: Why is *Ryan* here?

Well, my mind landed on, he's a friend of Thom's, and though Ryan barely knows Susan, she's Thom's girlfriend, and Debbie Schaffer is Susan's best friend, and that's why Ryan is here—it made sense, but I was nervous seeing him, especially since this was only a small and exclusive group of maybe fourteen, and Debbie, I'd noticed, had not invited anyone else, it seemed, and though many of our classmates were still away on the final vacation of the summer I'm sure there were many who weren't and I wondered what they thought about not being invited to Debbie's Labor Day Weekend barbecue—

but this was how Debbie operated, on exclusivity, and she enjoyed carefully choosing who she would invite, or not, to hang out with, say, Billy Idol at Madame Wong's or Duran Duran poolside at the Hilton or Fleetwood Mac backstage at the Hollywood Bowl.

Ryan Vaughn and I may have known each other since seventh grade but we'd only become close last May, when we started eating lunch together in the courtyard of the Buckley Pavilion, for reasons that were never really clear at first. Or maybe they were and we both ignored them, embarrassed. I had always paid attention to Ryan since he was, I thought, beautiful in a gay-fantasy way, a cartoon stud, and he was, like Thom, impossible not to pay attention to because of this, but the problem I'd increasingly noticed with Ryan throughout our high-school years was that, while Thom ingratiated himself with everyone, Ryan was aloof and private, especially for someone *that* good-looking and with the potential for the equivalence of Thom Wright's popular-ity, and at a certain point I began to understand why—it was con-nected to how I felt. Ryan was *me*. We were *the same*. I realized Ryan was, in fact, the closeted jock, the classic cliché that I doubt anyone would've believed if I had confided it to them, or if I told everyone what was going to be happening between Ryan and myself the first months of our senior year at Buckley. We had gradually figured some-thing out about each other.

This happened to occur, I believe, because we were driving cars and mobile in ways we hadn't been before, and this activated some-thing; possibilities were suddenly introduced to us, there were narra-tives we could now create ourselves. Maybe it started with the glance Ryan and I had given each other at the UCLA Mardi Gras in May of 1980, when we were both sixteen—an idea that there was sud-denly the promise of sex somewhere within our teenage caution, and we had located each other, like secret agents, without telling anyone, and there seemed to be certain opportunities that neither one of us had admitted to until, finally, that past summer, in June, when Ryan and I were driving around Westwood and he showed me a bruise on his upper thigh he received playing soccer, and instead of hiking up the shorts he was wearing he pulled one side down to show me the bruise, and everything skipped; "Urgent" by Foreigner was pumping out of the radio when I saw the pale skin, the muscled thigh, the taut ass cheek, the tuft of hair that revealed itself at the top of his jockey shorts. It was a dare, of course, and when we made eye contact there was a beat before we both started laughing, and yes, it started in that theater in Encino when we saw *Escape from New York*—we suddenly realized we were available. Though it had actually begun before we saw the movie. He had come over to the house on Mulholland to pick me up and there was no one home and I brought him to my room. He was wearing white jeans and a pastel-blue Polo shirt with the collar up and a pair of Vuarnets hung from a lanyard around his neck and his blond hair was parted in the middle, cut short and feathered back. He eagerly followed me down the deserted hallway to my bedroom, curious, but then he realized something and stopped—I was coming on to him too quickly, we had never discussed this before and he wasn't prepared—and so he simply said, somewhat haltingly, "I want to . . . but not just yet . . . not now."

I was mildly surprised that Ryan, who seemed straight, had in fact finally admitted he leaned toward my proclivities, but he came from a far more conservative and middle-class home than other Buckley students, way out in Northridge, and his family was vaguely religious. I had felt this connection we distantly shared throughout our junior year, but it began to seem obvious when we started eating lunch together in the Buckley courtyard near the end of May, where there had suddenly been so much pointless flirtation, and now Ryan had confirmed it. There was no suspicion about Ryan Vaughn among our peers in the student body because Ryan was a dude, a bro, *chill*. He just resembled a cool loner rather than someone secretly marginalized but I knew that he was playing a game by lying low until he could get out of high school, escape L.A., find a college far away and start over, reinventing himself, like me. That was his plan. That was my plan. Since then Ryan and I had only fooled around once—he had come over in mid-August to show me the new Trans Am complete with a CB radio. No one was home at the house on Mulholland and I finally pulled him onto my bed while we hungrily made out and stripped naked. And though things were finally activated and I wanted to take them further, as the summer ended Ryan went instead to Michigan, visiting extended family until the first week of September, and I hadn't seen him since.

—

RYAN SAID SOMETHING TO THOM, motioned to where I was standing, and Thom turned, and smiled at me, raised his Corona, a jock gesture. Ryan said something else and clamped his hand on Thom's shoulder and walked away from him, leaving Thom to turn to Susan on the chaise, where she ignored him a beat longer than she should have. I watched as Ryan neared me, with what I imagined was a certain purposefulness, and I noted when he placed his half-empty Corona bottle on a table he passed that this was a signal he was leaving. Billie, the golden retriever, walked with him halfway up the flagstone steps and then changed its mind and turned, to bound back to the pool. Ryan came up to me, beautiful and blank-faced, no hint of emotion. He raised his eyebrows.

"Hi," I finally said, aiming for casual.

"Hi." He smiled and it was real and relaxed in close-up.

"How was Michigan?" I asked, even though I didn't care.

"You already asked me that," he said. "Earlier. On the phone."

"Oh. Yeah."

"It was great," he said, noncommittal. He was looking around the yard and then directly at me. We were silent—we hadn't seen each other since that afternoon in my bedroom when we sucked each other off. And now it came back—something got activated by his presence—lust rushed over me in an instant. Ryan noted how I breathed in and then exhaled and realized what I had just silently revealed, and laughed, staring straight at me.

"Easy there," he said in a low voice.

"You're leaving?" I asked, blushing.

"Yeah," he said, glancing around the yard again. I waited.

"I wanted to see you but I don't really want to hang out here," he said.

"Why not?"

"Not my thing," he said. "You know that."

I wondered what that meant exactly but also somehow knew.

"Well, I don't want to stay either—"

"I thought you were going to be home this afternoon," he interrupted me.

"Didn't I tell you I was going to the stables?" I asked, flustered.

"The stables?"

"To see Debbie's new horse?"

"Um, no, I don't remember you telling me that," he said. "Her *new* horse?" Another example of everything Ryan hated about this group.

"Yeah," I said. "Out in Malibu."

"No." Ryan looked around as if continually distracted by something.

"Well—"

"Look, I've gotta go."

"I'll come with you—"

"No, no, just stay here, don't follow me out, it's cool." He glanced over my shoulder. Debbie was coming down the steps—she had changed clothes since Windover, wearing a revealing Camp Beverly Hills T-shirt, and striped Dolphin shorts—and she was barefoot, holding an unlit clove cigarette, her hair pulled back with a headband. The smile Ryan offered Debbie was the opposite of the one he'd greeted me with—it was the fake-genial Ryan, straining for patience. I panicked that Ryan wasn't taking what was happening between us with the same seriousness I was and tried to tamp down my frustration by pretending I didn't care. The Go-Go's were singing, embarrassingly, "Lust to Love" and in that moment I was glad Debbie arrived as a distraction.

"Hey, guys; hey, handsome," Debbie said, giving each of us a hug. She was slightly wired from the coke I was sure she'd just done— she had packets of it everywhere and used it casually, as if she was popping caffeine pills. "Are you leaving?" she asked Ryan with an exaggerated concern that I found annoying. Debbie pushed into me, wrapping an arm around my waist, her breast crushing against my chest—I hated this public display of affection in front of Ryan but he barely glanced at that and then shrugged good-naturedly. "Yeah, I've gotta go—just wanted to say hi."

"Oh, don't go, stick around," Debbie whined. "Did you get something to eat?"

"I'm fine, but thanks."

"Come on, stay," I said.

He made a tiny grimace that Debbie would never have noticed.

"Ryan's leaving! Everybody say goodbye!" Debbie called out over the Go-Go's to the group at the pool even though I was positive she didn't care. I'm sure Ryan knew this as well. No one by the pool reacted.

"I already said goodbye to everyone," Ryan explained.

I just stared at him, wanting him to stay but also thinking hopelessly: what would the point be?

"I'll see you guys Tuesday morning," he said, making it clear, I realized, that maybe we weren't going to see each other tomorrow.

"Senior year, baby!" Debbie said.

"It's gonna be great," Ryan exclaimed—it sounded ironic, fake, but Debbie couldn't tell, suddenly preoccupied with her guests by the pool. "Go, Griffins!" he added. This was manufactured as well—it was the name of the Buckley mascot and the school's sports teams and I knew he said it as a joke, part of his performance. He clamped a hand on my shoulder just like he did to Thom and gave it a squeeze that I invested more meaning in than there might've actually been and then made his way up the stone steps leading back to the house.

Debbie had taken my hand and pulled me down to where the group was. I steeled myself not to look back at Ryan leaving, and I arrived at the pool in a light daze and grabbed a Corona, which Paul opened for me, and then started talking mindlessly to Thom and Kyle and Dominic—a lot of the conversation was taken up with Debbie's horse and the visit to the stables and then Dominic's European vacation and all the countries he traveled through—our faces lit by the pool and the wavering Tiki torches, the Go-Go's singing around us. Susan smiled dreamily up at me from where she reclined on the chaise, and gestured at the house—"Why did he leave?" she mouthed. I shrugged, and turned back to the guys. Why had she asked me that? I suddenly wondered. What did she know about Ryan Vaughn and me?

STEVEN came down to the pool area and started taking photos at Debbie's request. No one really posed—*because we were already posing,* I thought to myself as twilight softly descended; we just glanced over at him and smiled as he quickly took inventory, trying to capture everyone—it was a job ordered by his boss's daughter, not something he might have wanted to do—and Debbie conferred with Paul at the grill, ordering the butler around as she usually did, which he took with a geniality that always relieved me, and Maria was laying out the side salads and the condiments for the burgers, and soon everyone made a plate and sat in a loose, makeshift circle on three of the chaise longues and as the night darkened and the Tiki torches dimmed the pool became brighter and was the only source lighting our faces. At one point I smelled marijuana and looked around: Terry Schaffer had lit a joint while lying on a chaise longue across the pool, near the bar, away from the kids.

I hadn't noticed him, which was strange because Terry was fond of making some kind of awkward pass at either Thom or Jeff or myself, usually in the way of a joke, whenever we were at the house on Stone Canyon—this started, I noticed, once we'd turned sixteen, and found ourselves hanging out at the Schaffers' with a new regularity simply because Debbie had the nicest backyard and threw the most parties, second only to Anthony Matthews, and Terry would sidle up to the boys and ask if we'd like to go swimming, even if it was a gathering that didn't involve the pool—we could always borrow one of his bathing suits, he'd insist, or you could just go *au naturel* if we felt comfortable about *that,* he was *cool* with it—he was somewhat stoned when he suggested this and we always declined. I don't know what Thom or Jeff felt (mild annoyance or sheer cluelessness, I imagined) but I had no problem with Terry lightly flirting with me because it wasn't going anywhere—he was over twice my age and he was Debbie's father (of all people) and nothing was going to happen, and yet by a certain point that past summer I became flattered by his attention and never felt threatened.

That night Terry was wearing Polo shorts and a black T-shirt with the logo of *Thief,* a recent Michael Mann movie that had done okay but less business than was expected when released in March, and though it was night he was wearing Porsche Carrera sunglasses, whose lenses were mirrored by the pool's blue water, and I *knew* he was watching one of us, either Thom or myself, or maybe Jeff, but I'd noticed that Terry had been singling me out that summer—the summer I became Debbie's boyfriend—whenever a group of us was over, probably because he'd figured out finally that Thom Wright wasn't available, and neither was Jeff Taylor (unless Terry wanted to dole out some cash whenever Jeff's erratic, alcoholic dad cut him off—if Ron Levin wasn't around who knew what Jeff was up for), and yet why did Terry assume that I was available, even though I was the one dating Debbie? How had he guessed this about his daughter's boyfriend? What clues had I offered? I'd never defined myself as gay but how did Terry know I could lean toward that? And yet, I wondered, how had I known about Ryan Vaughn during our junior year? I imagined it was just the distant signal that secret agents responded to as I watched Billie sidle up to the chaise longue and nestle below Terry.

DEBBIE WAS TALKING nonstop while smoking the clove cigarette—she hadn't eaten anything—and it all sounded like nonsense revolving around the upcoming senior year and how awesome and rad it was going to be, something a PR person would come up with: Homecoming in October—she already had ideas for the class float—and the senior prom, not until May, already being organized and with, of course, Susan and Thom fated for Queen and King, to be held at the Beverly Hills Hotel, and the after party on Dominic Thompson's father's yacht, and all of this had been eagerly set into motion, including the senior Christmas party, the yearbook Debbie would be co-editing, with the new inclusion of the "Hottest Teachers" page, Grad Nite was scheduled for Disneyland, and there would be a private party for Buckley and Harvard and Westlake students in the Blue Bayou restaurant inside the Pirates of the Caribbean where Tommy Tutone would be performing—Debbie had already booked them. At some point I zoned out and when I refocused noticed a few people had left and it was just the core group of Thom, Susan, Debbie along with Jeff Taylor and Tracy Goldman, who I guess were dating by that time though nothing had been confirmed. Terry was stoned on the chaise across the pool, immobile, maybe even sleeping, and the Go-Go's record repeated itself but the volume had been lowered and I remember that "This Town" was playing (. . . *Bet you'd live here if you could and be one of us . . .*) as Debbie continued with her litany of events when Susan suddenly announced as if she just remembered it: "There's a new guy."

"What?" Debbie asked, distracted by the interruption.

"A new guy is coming in on Tuesday," Susan said.

There was stillness, brief and surprised, until someone asked, "What do you mean?"

"Yeah," I said. "A new guy?"

Susan said, "I mean we have a new addition to the senior class. There's a new kid in the senior class."

"Really? That's a little weird," Debbie said.

"Who is it?" Jeff asked, concerned.

"Yeah," Tracy chimed in. "What's his name?"

"Robert Mallory," Susan said.

This was the first time any of us heard the name. The name didn't register. But because of what happened later I will always remember that moment. The moment his name came out of her mouth. The first time it was uttered. The moment he came alive.

Robert Mallory.

"Do you know anything about him?" I asked.

Susan shrugged. "No. He has a Century City address. He lives in one of the Century Towers."

"That's strange," Jeff murmured. "You never get a new kid senior year."

"Do you know where he comes from?" Debbie asked. "Who his parents are?"

Dr. Croft told Susan that Robert Mallory hadn't been an L.A. resident but was coming in from Chicago. The conversation she had with Croft, which dealt with her duties this year as student-body president and what she would be saying when she addressed the school on Tuesday at the morning assembly, was fast and hazy and she couldn't remember if Robert Mallory was living with an aunt or a guardian or a stepmother. (There were other details Dr. Croft had told her about Robert Mallory that Susan wouldn't confess to us until later.) "I really wasn't paying attention," Susan admitted, glancing over at Thom, who was now lying next to her on the chaise she'd been occupying all evening, the two of them pressed together, squeezing in, accommodating themselves to the size of the chaise; all she got was that Croft confirmed Robert Mallory would be on campus Tuesday.

We might have been surprised by this anomaly but none of us thought it was particularly unusual. It was rare to change schools your senior year but the privilege of Buckley and the overall L.A. private-school world in that moment was exploited by parents with the means to move their kids around based on their own needs or scheduling or convenience, and obviously Robert Mallory's parents needed him in a new place, this one in L.A. for some reason, in order to graduate, and not in Boston or Philadelphia or Chicago, or wherever he was actually from, and his parents, or guardians, or whoever, had decided to land him at Buckley. Nineteen eighty-one was a time before private schools in L.A. had waiting lists thousands of names long and parents lost their minds trying to get their children onto those lists let alone into the schools themselves, and in 1981 if you could afford the tuition you basically got your kid in anywhere—there was no competition for any of the open slots that were available, no testing, no belabored meetings with staff, no gifts; if you could write the check to cover tuition you were in. That's how it worked.

And yet it flashed across my mind that night, unbidden—and I don't know why this suspicion arose—if Robert Mallory was living in Century City he would have been eligible to attend Beverly Hills High because he lived within the appropriate district and there was the added incentive that there was no tuition because it was public, and I suddenly wondered, why hadn't Robert Mallory opted for *that*? I didn't say anything, because it didn't seem warranted and I was ready to leave the Schaffers' because I needed to drive around the city and listen to sad music and smoke cigarettes while thinking about Ryan. I noticed that Thom and Susan were sharing a bowl of strawberry ice cream and that Thom was the only one who seemed to have no interest in the dwindling conversation about the new student—his green eyes just stared lazily into the lit pool, a smear of pink cream on his upper lip, his brown hair combed back from his tan forehead and lightly feathered, and I noticed he still hadn't finished the Corona I first saw him with when I arrived. I had finished three.

"Well, he better be cute," Debbie said. I wanted to say "I agree" but didn't.

The SHARDS

Despite the chill of disappointment I felt about Ryan leaving the Schaffers' earlier I can now attest that Sunday in September was one of the last nights, if not the last night, I was ever fully happy and there was no fear.

"I HAVE TO GO, GUYS," I said, standing up. It seemed no one else was leaving and I realized it was early, only eight o'clock, and I'd forgotten that everyone was staying to watch a new movie in the screening room—*Continental Divide*, a romantic comedy starring John Belushi and Blair Brown, that would be released later in September and that I wouldn't have been able to concentrate on that night, not only because I simply didn't want to be there any longer but because thoughts of Ryan were everywhere, distracting me. After a few muffled halfhearted complaints from Thom and Susan I said good night to everyone, except for Terry, who was comatose on the chaise, and let Debbie walk me out to my car. But when she reached the top of the stone steps, Debbie silently redirected me to the back staircase that led up to her bedroom without having to go through the house and I only resisted once—I said I was tired and needed to get home. She knew that wasn't true or just didn't care—she often mistook me for someone hard to get, a tease, a boy who enjoyed playing a game, a boy who was a challenge, and I let her: she liked being in charge.

The screening was about to start and things happened quickly: once in the darkness of her room I was pushed onto the bed and Debbie slipped off her Dolphins and the pink panties she was wearing and immediately straddled my waist, leaning over me, her plush lips pressing against mine while she fumbled with the zipper on my tennis shorts. I lifted my hips so she could pull them down mid-thigh along with my underwear but I wasn't even half hard. And yet Debbie seemed high, voracious, and after uselessly sucking my dick she guided my hand to her pussy, already slick and wet, and she pushed my fingers into it with her own hand. I still wasn't hard but in that moment I don't think Debbie cared—she simply rolled onto her back, her legs spread, and lifted the Camp Beverly Hills T-shirt, urging me toward her breasts. I remember she smelled of rose oil that night as I sucked her stiffening nipples while she kept guiding my hand along her clit, strumming it, her legs spread as wide as possible, the vulva open and hot, and she would push my hand there, which I would finger roughly before she moved it back to her clitoris. Her breasts were big and perfectly formed and I ran my mouth over them, clamping down on her nipples, which were small and pink and wet with my saliva and now totally stiff. She reached for my cock but it was only semi-hard and even if I'd been able to get an erection it would have been impossible to maintain because everyone was now passing outside Debbie's room below us and I could hear their voices through the window as the group made its way up the stone steps into the house, and this distraction was stressing me out. But Debbie always came fast, within minutes she could thrash out an orgasm, it took barely anything to make her come, and this was happening now. I kept hearing the group moving from the pool up the steps to the house, voices fading and then reappearing, muffled and directly below us in the screening room, where I heard Steven announcing the movie—he was the projectionist. Debbie convulsed, her mouth on mine, and quietly came, whimpering.

And then she asked, panting: "Are you okay?"

"Yeah, yeah, yeah," I assured her, sitting up.

The phone by her bed—pink, rotary, next to a copy of *The Beverly Hills Diet*—rang and she immediately answered. "Hello?" She listened. "Okay, Steven, I'll be right down." She cocked her head. "No, I think he's still by the pool." Pause. "Yeah, okay." She looked at me. "No, he's here in my bedroom." She hung up and without looking over, said, "The movie's starting. Sure you don't want to stay?"

"No," I said. "I should probably go."

"You're silly," she said.

She leaned over and turned on the lamp by the bed, revealing the coral-colored room, which was massive, one wall a series of shelves lined with trophies and plaques and ribbons and photos—all from her participation in equestrian sports the last five years. Another wall was covered with recent posters of new bands whose members Debbie had partied with; a reminder she was a rich groupie from Beverly Hills and seventeen, sexy and sophisticated and just jaded enough to locate and gain access anywhere she wanted. My hand was so wet it glistened as if it had been brushed with oil, and Debbie stumbled off to the bathroom, which was almost as spacious as her bedroom, and closed the door. I heard water running while I grabbed a couple of Kleenex and wiped my hand off, then stood and hiked up my underwear and tennis shorts.

Debbie hurriedly walked out of the bathroom—she had slipped on a pair of light cotton sweatpants, also Camp Beverly Hills, and was holding a small plastic packet and quickly did two bumps, then offered it to me. I shook my head no. She shrugged. "I'll see you later, babe," she said. "Movie's starting."

"Okay," I said. "See you Tuesday."

"Not tomorrow?"

"No," I said. "I've got to . . . get ready for, um, school."

We both paused, silently noting how strange that sounded coming from a seventeen-year-old man.

"Okay, whatever. You're lame." She rolled her eyes—she didn't have time to argue. She kissed me on the lips and then hurried out of the room, this time through the door that took her into the main house and downstairs to the theater.

I FOLLOWED Debbie down the grand curving staircase that led to the foyer until she darted down a hallway where I could hear the movie starting behind the closed doors of the screening room in the silent house. I paused, lingering at the foot of the staircase, reached into my pocket, touching the car keys, and was walking toward the front door when I heard someone call my name. The voice was coming from the living room, adjacent to the foyer, and I steeled myself. It was precise as well as sounding alarmed, as if I'd surprised the voice somehow. I knew who it was; I'd been through this before. I moved slowly toward the entrance to the living room, where Liz Schaffer was sitting in a floral-patterned armchair, hunched over, elbows on her knees, one hand holding the same glass I saw her with earlier—but she looked disheveled now, something had happened in the last couple of hours since I'd first seen her and she had innocently waved to me while on the phone. Liz Schaffer had been a fairly beautiful woman—in 1981 she was only in her late thirties, and a famous model in her teens and early twenties, before she married Terry, but her face tonight was decidedly older and flushed, frozen into a kind of stunned grimace, and the Bijan robe Liz wore was half open and her breasts were visible. Next to her was a white baby-grand piano and a vase filled with an arrangement of flowers so formidable they reached to the living room's beamed ceiling. I just stood there, not knowing what to do while she kept squinting at me even though all the lights in the living room and the foyer were on—but it seemed in that brief period of time she'd forgotten what name she called out. And then she remembered and seemed disappointed.

"You're not staying for the movie, Bret?" Liz asked with mock incredulity, as if my exit was offending her.

"I have to go." I smiled tightly and motioned to the front door. "No, I'm not staying for the movie."

"Where? Where would you *have* to go?" She stared at me, hunched over, motionless.

"I just . . . have to be going," I said, gesturing to the door again, and then as if speaking to a child: "Are you going to watch the movie, Liz?"

"Where's my husband?" she asked, sitting up. Liz wasn't a sloppy drunk exactly—when she drank she seemed too angry to topple over or pass out and she never slurred her words. Everything she said was enunciated with a high level of disdain: in fact she always adopted a light British accent in an attempt to suggest control and aristocratic normalcy. When she realized that I'd just asked her something, she answered with an exaggerated sneer, "No, I am not going to watch *the movie*, Bret."

I aimed for being the polite guest, her daughter's gracious boyfriend, and gently started backing away and said, "Okay, well, I hope you have a, um, good night, Liz, and I'll see you soon—"

"Don't walk away from me," she said, glaring.

I stood still, and very carefully, maintaining my pose, said, "Liz, I think you're tired."

She tried to stand up, staggering against the armchair. I almost made a move to help but thought it might piss her off so I remained where I was. Any sudden gestures could ratchet up her anger. Or she might make a pass, a drunken sexual overture; it had happened before.

"Don't condescend to me," Liz said, gripping the side of the armchair and steadying herself, the robe now draping open and revealing she wasn't wearing underwear. "I've known you since you were ten years old, Bret. Do not condescend to me." Her eyes were closed and she was shaking her head.

"I'm sorry, Liz, I really have to go—"

"Where is my fucking husband?" she said, abruptly. She opened her eyes. They landed on me.

"I think he's down by the pool," I said.

"Down by the pool?" she said, confused. "Down. By. The. Pool?"

There was movement to my left—a figure was in the hall. It was Steven. I looked over at him as he made his way toward the living room: mid-forties, frizzy-haired, wild-eyed, a failed screenwriter, now working as an all-around assistant for the Schaffers. I barely knew him even though he'd been with them since 1977—he was their chauffeur, their secretary, often Terry's traveling partner on business, and lived in a guesthouse adjacent to the mansion. I knew Steven was straight and had girlfriends, so there was nothing going on between him and Terry, and besides he was nowhere near what I found out to be Terry's type. I'd always thought Steven was a weirdo and maintained my distance but I was relieved to see him that night.

"With who is my husband with?" Liz balanced herself against the chair. She now pretended to be legitimately intrigued but she was also vaguely threatening. "I'm surprised he's not down there with all you *boys*—"

It stung whenever Liz referenced Terry's gayness—I was always embarrassed and never said anything. I never wanted to engage her further in order to confirm it. "I have to go," I said. "Steven's coming to help you."

"Where are you going, Bret?" Liz asked, trying to walk forward. "Are you going back to the pool? Are you going to see my faggot husband down by the pool?"

"Hey, you can go, Bret," Steven said to me, and then, under his breath, "I can handle it."

"You know my husband is a faggot, right?" Liz was saying this genuinely, calmly.

"Hey, Liz," Steven said, bounding down the steps into the living room. "How you doing?"

"Bret is just leaving," she said with a theatrical flourish. "He told me that my husband is *down by the pool*. Whatever that means. Is this true, Steven?"

Steven took the glass from her hand while she stared into his face with a pleading expression even though the anger was still pulsing beneath it.

"I think he is," Steven said, and in a series of graceful movements placed the glass down, slid his arm through hers and started moving Liz gently through the living room.

I turned toward the front door. Liz noticed and called out in a scolding tone: "Don't you walk away from *me*. I've known you since you were ten years old. Don't you dare walk away from me, Bret—"

I glanced back. She was trying to wrestle out of Steven's grip but he just kept moving her through the living room in tiny baby steps.

"We're going to bed now, Liz," Steven was saying. "Okay? I'm taking you upstairs now . . ."

Steven nodded, indicating he had the situation under control and that I should leave. The last sound I heard was Liz weeping with Steven trying to console her as I closed the front door behind me.

TOTAL SILENCE IN BEL AIR automatically reminded me of sanity, competing with the loud and absurd complications within the Schaffers' mock–French Tudor mansion, and I realized again that I was moving away from Debbie and Liz and Terry and all the useless friends I'd be abandoning in less than a year. Even though it was only eight-thirty I was exhausted but didn't want to go home—something was pushing me, I felt driven, it was vague and uneasy, a hunger; I wanted to stay awake and wished I'd taken a packet of Debbie's cocaine but I didn't want to go back into the house. In retrospect, this was a fairly typical night at the Schaffers' except for one small detail. The name of a boy, a stranger, a mysterious new student, had now been dropped into the narrative, and it had become a distraction for me. *Robert Mallory*. And then I was startled by Billie barking somewhere in the vastness of the backyard. I was in the driveway, leaning against the Mercedes, sorting through my options, when I looked up at the house as I turned to get into the car. And I noticed a figure, half in shadow, staring down at me from a second-story diamond-patterned window—this would have been at the landing where the staircase began. I thought for a moment it was Terry, finally mobile and heading to bed, to join Liz, who I hoped had already passed out. But it was, in fact, Steven Reinhardt, Terry's assistant, staring down at me.

Startled, I held up a hand, a gesture, barely a wave. For a moment it seemed as if he hadn't registered the wave, and this creeped me out, a reminder of how weird I always thought Steven was. But as if a cue was given, he suddenly remembered his part, and lifted his arm and raised a hand—he was an alien or a robot greeting someone he'd never met before. I stared up at the window—I could barely see him, just make out the frizzy head of hair, the slight build encased in a turtleneck he always wore, the blinding lights of the chandelier behind him, the shadow of the fern he stood next to. But then I realized he was holding a camera and had raised it: he was taking my picture. This pushed me to get into the car and pull out of the driveway and once I drove through Bel Air's East Gate I made a left onto an empty Sunset Boulevard and decided to bypass Beverly Glen, which would have taken me back to the house on Mulholland, and instead headed toward Hollywood, where I'd return to the Valley from the freeways there.

3

BUT THERE WAS A DISTRACTION, a flaw in the paradisaical canvas of the summer of 1981: the disappearance of a girl leaving a party on the outskirts of Encino in late July.

There was very little reported about the disappearance at first and none of us knew her—she might have stayed a rumor or what would later be known as an urban myth, *teenage girl disappears from party never to be seen again*—but she was soon connected to two other cases, one from the summer of 1980 and another in January of 1981, and after Julie Selwyn's body was discovered at the end of September, it was revealed that the victims resembled each other and there were details about their deaths that connected them as well. In 1981 no one knew what had happened *specifically* to Julie Selwyn or Katherine Latchford or Sarah Johnson, or that the same person or persons had killed them—just that they had been abducted and were missing for two months with Katherine's and Sarah's bodies discovered in remote locations, called in by what investigators assumed was the killer in a fake groaning drawl, who wanted to know why the girls, dumped weeks earlier, hadn't been discovered yet—he was *waiting* for his *work* to be *admired*. The matching mutilations that the victims suffered were not fully revealed to the press and it was almost a year after the last girl was found at the end of 1981 until most of these details were ultimately known—in a pre-digital world secrets were more easily kept; in fact, secrets were the norm in a pre-digital world. Before any confirmation was made there were only rumors concerning the specificity of the mutilations and how the girls had been tortured and killed. However, there were leaks, anonymous sources verified, containing details so obscene that if you believed them you quickly realized why the Los Angeles Police Department kept the details of what they called "the injuries" as vague as they did. Because those who knew exactly about them—had perhaps seen the wounds during the autopsy beneath the fluorescent lights in the morgue—didn't want the populace to become overly frightened.

THE PUBLIC DIDN'T KNOW this yet but Julie Selwyn would be the third victim of a serial killer who came to be known as the Trawler—this was a nickname that two investigators in the Hollywood division of the LAPD jokingly came up with in private. It was a lewd joke that involved fishing methods, operating a net, the storage of fish, what had supposedly been done to the girl's vaginas, the contents of Katherine Latchford's own *aquarium* had been missing a week before she was abducted and found sewn into hers—though it was actually rubber cement that the killer used—which meant that Katherine Latchford had been targeted weeks *before* she was abducted. "The Trawler" was a dumb name—it came nowhere near defining the totality of the killer's madness—but a memo had been leaked to the press, and in one line that hadn't been redacted "The Trawler" was clearly referenced and became the name of this nascent serial killer in the few articles that appeared: it hit the right ominous note. But in the summer of 1981 the Trawler had not officially been named yet—the victims were just beginning to become connected and the series of articles in the *Los Angeles Times* confirming this wouldn't appear until late September. No one knew yet that Julie Selwyn would be the third victim of a serial killer that had been operating in L.A. County since the summer of 1980 when Katherine Latchford disappeared mid-June. It wasn't until the third week of our senior year that the Trawler would be named, introduced to us and emerge as a character in the city's narrative.

WHEN I LOOK BACK AT 1980 AND INTO the fall of 1981 we didn't think we knew anything about the Trawler yet: meaning we didn't know his name or how he got his name, we didn't know what his history was and we didn't know he was about to thrive and kill three more people that autumn in L.A., one of whom we knew. But beginning in the summer of 1980 there were a number of signs, of clues, that were an actual and legitimate part of what became the Trawler's pattern, the narrative he was building, the story he wanted to tell, that we *did* know about. Later on it was confirmed that there were explicit warning signs if the Trawler had actually targeted someone but in the early days no one knew any of this yet: the connections hadn't been made.

Beginning in the late spring of 1980 a series of home invasions started announcing themselves in the hills above the San Fernando Valley. There was no pattern—young couples, old couples, a single male screenwriter, a woman who lived alone, families where there were teenage girls as well as teenage boys—and though girls ultimately became the preferred victims of the Trawler, initially boys were attacked during these home invasions as well and one boy was later killed by him. The home invasions that we knew of and read about in the spring and into the summer and early fall of 1980 seemed totally random: since no specific *type* was attacked—gender and age seemed irrelevant, it was girls and it was boys—there was really nowhere to hide, no way to protect yourself against this person who was committing the home invasions, everyone was vulnerable. People began to finally piece together that one of the clues connected to the Trawler (again, not named yet) had to do with animals. The Trawler focused on someone whose family had pets or the victim had a pet themselves (and it didn't matter if it was a dog, a cat, a bird, a snake in one instance, mice, a rabbit, a guinea pig) and the pet would disappear, and not only the victim's pet, but other pets in the neighborhood where the victim resided would vanish as well in advance of the home invasion when the victim was attacked. Before he committed his assaults often *three* animals, in the same neighborhood, would ultimately be sacrificed by the Trawler, and it wasn't until the late fall of 1981 that we learned what the reason was—what he ultimately did with their carcasses and why he needed them.

THE HOME INVASIONS began in May of 1980, when it seemed the Trawler was simply testing things out. The Trawler at this point didn't enter properties and remained shrouded, his presence announced only in the clichéd language of horror movies: someone remembered hearing the wind chimes hanging over the veranda in a house on Oakfield Drive in Sherman Oaks even though there wasn't the slightest breeze on that June night, or there was the shaky beam of a flashlight someone on Woodcliff Road reported in mid-July, held by a figure clad in black who was standing on the deck beside the pool, and in his other fist was the glint of a butcher knife. During the summer of 1980, a time when the Trawler hadn't been named and hadn't killed anyone yet (Katherine Latchford disappeared mid-June but her body wasn't found until two months later), there were increasing reports of an actual intruder and the witnesses who supplied descriptions of this person were vague because of the black ski mask and the matching jeans and turtleneck he wore: he was tall, he wasn't that tall, he was lean, he was built, he was heavy, he had "wild" and "violet" eyes, no one had seen his eyes, they were a piercing blue, they were hazel. Whoever played this character was extremely elusive—a shape-shifter—though he was responsible for twenty break-ins that summer alone in the homes on the San Fernando Valley side below Mulholland, very close to where I lived, and stretching from Studio City through Sherman Oaks and into Encino, and then briefly into Bel Air and Benedict Canyon, and then the home invasions became scattered (Pasadena, Glendale, Hollywood), and then abruptly stopped.

They didn't start up again until mid-December where they continued throughout January of 1981. No one had any idea at the time when Katherine Latchford's body was found in August of 1980 that she was connected to the home invasions that had plagued the city, or that it was connected to the disappearing pets and the actual assaults. Later we would find out that phone calls were often made to a targeted home where the next victim resided days before the attack, coming from phone booths lining Ventura Boulevard or Burbank or Reseda, or across the canyons on Sunset and into Hollywood, almost as if the calls confirmed something for the Trawler—the victim would pick up, ask who was there, the Trawler would say nothing, just listen as the confusion morphed into annoyance, and then fear. Later there would be other clues usually offered when one of the victims' memory would kick back in: someone, it seemed, had entered the house previously, before the night of the attack, something about the kitchen or the contents in a bathroom or the bedroom was "different," leading investigators to believe that the Trawler had familiarized himself with the residence in the days before the assault. Later someone noted that Katherine Latchford—the first of the murder victims, the pretty girl with feathered hair and full lips and sleepy eyes that were half closed in the yearbook photo that became famous—complained that her cat had disappeared in the days before she vanished, and unbeknownst to her two dogs from the neighborhood were missing as well. Katherine had also told her parents that she'd been receiving "strange" phone calls in the days leading up to her disappearance— they weren't obscene but in a way they were worse because of the silence: you had no idea what the person on the other line wanted. It seemed there were limitless possibilities that your frightened mind conjured.

ULTIMATELY, IT WAS NOTED, there was something methodical and patterned about the Trawler's attacks—they were so carefully pre-assembled that a plan was suggested, an actual narrative, something being consciously created; they weren't random or impulsive at all. There was, in fact, an ornate staginess about them. At first it seemed that the attacks were created by someone who was ambivalent, and this was confirmed when certain victims involved in the first wave of invasions during the spring and early summer of 1980 admitted something that didn't line up necessarily with a person who had broken into your home and assaulted you. The victims who survived these initial attacks, the ones in May and early June, before Katherine Latchford was abducted—people who had been roped and bound, prone on their bedroom and living-room floors, sometimes stripped by the figure clad in black and wearing the overlarge ski mask—said that whoever had attacked them was "weeping" when he left the residence after he had apparently been sated: a few of the attacks were sexual in nature but most were not. When the first murder happened, and the home invasions and the assaults picked up in mid-December after the long lull of a three-month hiatus, many people who survived the next wave of invasions commented that the attacker hadn't cried at all; it was almost as if he had gained confidence, a strength, and perhaps by committing his first murder had become *emboldened*.

THE LEAD-UP TO THE Trawler's first victim became the elaborate template: the disappearing pets, the phone calls, the rehearsal break-in—but not an assault. This was true of the second victim as well: Sarah Johnson abducted behind the Tower Records on Ventura Boulevard in Sherman Oaks in early January of 1981. Her body was discovered eight weeks later in a drainpipe at an abandoned construction site on the outskirts of Simi Valley; her cat had disappeared, she complained to her mother that the furniture in her bedroom had been rearranged, and someone was calling her, breathing into the phone, not obscene exactly, just unnerving but she was never assaulted in a home invasion. Sarah had left a party in Tarzana and drove to pick up a cassette on the way back to her parents' home in Studio City but she never made it into the Tower Records on Ventura Boulevard and her remains wouldn't be discovered until the first week in March, found in the same condition and with the same "injuries" as Julie Selwyn had suffered when she was found in September of 1981, rotting on a public tennis court in a park near Woodland Hills; she had been propped up and splayed against the net, her head just a skull with flesh stretched over it but with a full head of hair and empty sockets where her eyes had been gouged out, and what had been inflicted upon the rest of her body—what the hideous mutilations represented—we wouldn't find out until the end of the year when the details were finally revealed in a long article in the *Los Angeles Times*, having only been previously alluded to because of the grotesque and upsetting nature of the injuries.

I HAD MOMENTS WHEN I was afraid of whoever was committing the home invasions and that the house on Mulholland might be its next target but for some reason I thought my odds were okay as a lucky seventeen-year-old—there were so many things I was preoccupied with, and the home invasions never really got covered in the way they would have if everyone knew what the Trawler was ultimately capable of: they never set off a mass wave of panic. It seemed my only point of reference in the summer of 1980, when the Trawler began announcing itself, was trying to figure out Matt Kellner. What had become a mild sexual obsession with a classmate distracted me for about a year, until I realized that Ryan Vaughn was going to eclipse Matt. And on that Labor Day Monday I woke up late in the empty house on Mulholland thinking about Matt as I usually did, even though Ryan was beginning to crowd my thoughts, replacing not only Matt but also Thom Wright and Susan Reynolds in my dreams and fantasies.

MY PARENTS WOULD BE AWAY most of the fall, traveling through Europe on a number of cruises trying to repair their flailing marriage after numerous separations and I had zero interest in the outcome—divorce was preferable to the agonies that the marriage played out, and it became increasingly apparent as I moved through my adolescence that I wasn't particularly close to either my mother or my father. We were all distant from each other even though the public façade, the Boomer narrative, suggested otherwise: the Christmas card with the posed family photo emblazoned on it, the sleepovers I had where my mother acted like a concerned chaperone checking in on us as we watched the Z Channel, the days at the beach club with Thom and Jeff and Kyle that my father oversaw and where he acted as if he was our best friend—all of it seemed fake, performative, unreal. There was no doubt my parents loved me and if pressed I would admit I loved them back but I was becoming an autonomous adult and realized that I didn't need them in the ways I once had.

And alone in the house on Mulholland that fall I felt even more like an adult because I had the entire place to myself, even though my bedroom—huge with a sweeping view of the San Fernando Valley—was its own self-sustaining home I almost solely resided in: I had a separate entrance with a veranda that led out to the pool, and a kitchenette with a refrigerator filled with ginger ale and Perrier, a massive bathroom with its own separate shower and tub, and my room was situated close enough to the garage so that I barely spent any time in the rest of the house. Our Nicaraguan maid, Rosa, was off Labor Day weekend and wouldn't be back until the following Tuesday. Though my parents would be away for twelve weeks my mother wanted Rosa to stick to her schedule anyway—she confided in me when I complained and insisted I could look after myself that Rosa needed the money. Her job while my parents were gone was to basically look after the only child, the privileged son, and make sure the kitchen and my bedroom were kept clean, to wash my towels and launder my sheets, to let in the gardener and the pool boy and the landscape designer my mother had recently hired. Rosa was there to collect the mail, attend to the shopping, prepare my meals, and make sure Shingy—my mom's dog, a Lhasa Apso–mutt mix—was washed and groomed every two weeks while my parents floated across Europe. I would be updated on their location with rambling messages left always by my mother on my answering machine.

With Rosa gone on that Labor Day it was my job to make sure Shingy was fed and let out onto the lawn adjacent to the pool in the yard, overlooking the Valley where it dropped onto a hillside lined with eucalyptus and jacaranda trees, while I idly sat in the Jacuzzi and watched the dog sniff around, keeping an eye on him because of coyotes and where I could faintly hear the occasional sound of a car passing behind the huge boxwood hedge that separated our property from Mulholland Drive. I ushered Shingy back inside, where I debated calling Ryan Vaughn but decided he would perceive this as too needy and called Matt Kellner instead, but no one picked up—he didn't have an answering machine—and so I drove down to Encino, where Matt would be high by the pool, and I remember I didn't masturbate that day because I was sure something would happen with Matt and so before I left I reread pages I'd typed of the novel I was working on while smoking clove cigarettes and listening to Elvis Costello until I got bored and then sped through a third of the new Stephen King, *Cujo*, which had just been published that August.

MATT KELLNER WAS A TALL, GREEN-EYED JEWISH guy with a killer body who was also the class stoner and I, at one point in the fall of 1980, had come to believe that he would've had sex with anybody, boy or girl, if they made themselves available to him in the ways that I did, but no one at Buckley seemed to have found Matt Kellner as intriguing. Part of the reason had to do with the fact that Matt was always too distant, lost in his own world, you could never reach him, he was far away from everyone, it almost seemed as if he'd been wounded by something so profound (though he never revealed what it was) that it altered the way he dealt with people. I'd been watching Matt since he arrived at Buckley in seventh grade, and though he should've been popular he was simply too weird—if he had just acted vaguely "normal" he could have been a star because of how physically hot he was but instead he became a kind of outcast, an increasingly fumbling and awkward dude, a parody of a privileged young Valley stoner, and no one was interested. But I grew to like him and his pothead amiability and it was also the gray Buckley slacks worn just a little too tight, overaccentuating his ass, and a noticeably visible bulge, that became so distracting to me as we got older. Matt seemed to have no capability for basic socializing, and at first I wasn't sure if this was because of how stoned he was all the time or if he was just inherently shy, but I soon realized that he simply didn't care about the social contract we had all bought into—he didn't even seem aware of his *surroundings*—and there was something rebellious and almost punk about this stance even though it wasn't conscious: he simply didn't care about how things worked; in fact he seemed defiantly *un*-self-conscious. I noted how he would walk naked through the locker room, from the bench where he took his sweat-soaked clothes off after running track, to the showers, and back again, just naked, drying himself off completely unaware, shamelessly, and no one, not even Thom Wright or Jeff Taylor, was that easygoing with their body—everything was always slightly shy and muffled, you'd shower quickly and then walk back to your locker with a towel wrapped around your waist, and then hurriedly change into your boxers or briefs. But Matt Kellner seemed to revel in his nakedness and I secretly reveled in it, too.

I HAD BEEN going to Matt's house on Haskell Avenue in Encino ever since a July afternoon in 1980 when we were both sixteen and two of about forty students at the Buckley summer program. I had failed Geometry and Science the previous semester, and Matt had failed them as well, and during breaks in these morning sessions we attended in order to pass those classes so we could move on to the eleventh grade, we started hesitantly talking to each other even though we never had before. Had I seen *Urban Cowboy*, he asked; he'd been to an advance screening of *Cheech and Chong's Next Movie* on the Universal lot a week ago; was I a fan of "Funkytown" by Lipps Inc.? Matt liked that song as well as the new Queen record, *The Game.* And in that first week he invited me to the house on Haskell—his parents were away, we could go swimming, get high—he was so amiable and friendly that it bordered on stoner parody and I wasn't thinking about anything else except sex when I listened to him because I instinctively knew—not that Matt seemed gay at all—there was the possibility for something sexual to happen; it might not have existed in the invitation itself but there was a suggestion about the invite that was going to let me initiate this somehow and the path to Matt's house became familiar that summer. He lived in a pool house in the back of his parents' palatial Encino estate, retrofitted into a kind of hip beach shack with a nautical theme: a shellacked dolphin hung from one wall, pastel surfboards were resting against another, an elaborate aquarium ran the length of the room filled with swordtails and pearl gourami and starfish and multicolored snails, and coral beds lined the bottom of the tank lit in shades of blue and green and purple. The room was complete with a stereo, a large TV that had the Z Channel connected to it, and a refrigerator stocked with 7-Up, Corona and bags of pine-green weed, and sometimes a cat—Matt had named it Alex for some obscure reason—would slink into the pool house and sprawl out in front of the aquarium, staring up at it blankly, licking its paws.

That July afternoon we got high and swam in the pool, first in bathing suits and then naked, and the moment Matt suddenly tugged his off—from where I was wading I saw he was half hard as he rested on a hammock strung between two palm trees, sunning himself—I realized what was going to happen and I hitched in a breath as I pulled my suit off and tossed it on the edge of the pool and began swimming toward Matt. I didn't want anything from him except his full-lipped mouth surrounded by light razor stubble, his muscular thighs, the chest with defined pectorals that tapered into a tier of abs, the small line that crept up from the patch of brown pubic hair and ended at the knot of his navel, and the long cock that jutted out from that patch, and his ass, pale and tight and dimpled, very lightly dusted with blond down. At first it hardly mattered to me what resided within this form.

THESE MEETINGS LASTED throughout our junior year. I would occasionally drive over to Haskell Avenue, park on the street, unlatch the gate to the path that led to the backyard and the pool house, and I usually came unannounced, because Matt never picked up his phone, which added to the erotic suspense of the moment. When I arrived Matt was almost always stoned and usually damp from swimming and either concentrating on rolling a small pile of joints or staring at a movie on the Z Channel he'd watched a few times that week and was still trying to figure out or maybe he was holding a textbook that might as well have been written in Mandarin given the perplexed expression on his face, and sometimes Alex the cat would be lying on his lap staring at me blankly whenever I appeared. Matt was almost always wearing the tight lime-green bathing suit he preferred that year, and though he seemed momentarily distracted whenever he saw me, by a certain point we barely said anything to each other when I'd appear in the open doorway and went directly to sex. Matt didn't know the niceties of small talk—our presence was enough—and he was usually stiff in ten seconds or already rock hard by the time we stripped and shared the perfunctory kissing that led to the sex. I doubt it ever took longer than ten or fifteen minutes to get off unless I forced us to prolong whatever we were doing, which would end up mildly confusing Matt, though he went with it. I suppose you had to be standing on one side of the aisle to appreciate Matt Kellner's beauty, but forty years later, sitting in my office high above West Hollywood, I still find Matt's body the most erotic and beautiful I've ever seen and been privy to, and the fact that I had an intimate and hard-core access to all of it leaves me somewhat stunned as I write this at fifty-seven. And yet Ryan Vaughn, who I later confessed my relationship with Matt, wasn't interested and seemed surprised that I'd been. Not my type, Ryan said. Too Jew-y.

—

The SHARDS

DESPITE THE INTENSITY of the sex and the fact that we could fuck two or even three times on a particular afternoon, there was ultimately nothing to hold on to, no basis to build a friendship, and I'm not even sure, as I said, that Matt Kellner was actually gay, or just a massively horny teenage boy who could go either way depending on what was available. But I didn't care and maybe I preferred the ambiguity: there were no gay signifiers, just like there weren't with Ryan Vaughn—everyone was good at maintaining a pose—and it wasn't self-consciously butch either, it was something more natural and boyish than simply that. Susan Reynolds might have been the only one who knew about Matt—it wasn't in anything specific she asked, but whenever she mentioned him it had a vaguely teasing air, as if she had certain information that she didn't want to divulge. She only knew that I had a "friendship" with Matt (quotation marks hers) but no one else I knew ever asked about him so no one seemed to care that we frequently hung out together in the pool house in Encino. Maybe no one asked because Matt and I didn't interact with each other our junior year—we might acknowledge one another in the hallway by our lockers with a nod, or maybe half-smile if we shared a class or glimpsed each other at assembly or in the parking lot but we rarely hung out in public—we never went to a restaurant or a movie together. Matt didn't seem to hang out with *anyone*—and I began to understand Matt preferred it that way; he wasn't crushed by loneliness or doubt or insecurity—he was simply on another planet. I wanted access to the more popular world that Matt didn't care about, and hanging out with Matt, and only Matt, wasn't going to keep that ambition in play our senior year, and so I became alienated from him. On a sexual level I found him porn-star sexy but I never fell in love, the way I ultimately did, for a brief moment, with Ryan—Matt had become a dissatisfying problem that wasn't worth it. Swimming with Matt in the pool behind the mansion on Haskell Avenue and then stumbling into the guesthouse dripping wet and locking the door behind us and fucking in the lit glow of the aquarium, our bodies tinted blue as we positioned ourselves on his mattress, timing ourselves so that we could come together, were afternoons I found achingly erotic until I didn't.

—

I NOTICED SOMETHING WAS SLIGHTLY OFF about the pool house that Labor Day afternoon—I sensed it almost immediately when I arrived but it wasn't obvious and I couldn't tell exactly what was wrong. Maybe it was due to the distraction that the guesthouse reeked even more pungently of weed than it usually did, or the images of forest fires raging in Riverside I noticed replaying silently on the TV screen, or maybe it was "Ghost Town" by the Specials echoing loudly throughout the space. Matt was wandering around idly looking for something and wearing only the lime-green bathing suit and a string of puka shells collared his neck that I hadn't seen before, and he was deeply tanned, bronzed, his hair bleached lightly by the sun—a boy who lived in the pool. He didn't notice me at first as I stood in the open doorway and when he finally acknowledged my presence it was with one of the blankest looks I'd ever seen. "You didn't call," he said. "You didn't answer," I said. "Ghost Town" ended and Matt looked at the drawer he was rummaging through and when he glanced at me again he finally sighed as I made my way toward him and held his face in both hands and hungrily kissed his mouth, smelling like chlorine and marijuana and suntan lotion. The door was closed. I had already started to undress. Matt slipped off his bathing suit.

I pushed the sex further than it usually went that afternoon, because it might've been the last time it would happen. I wanted to make a final impression on Matt and I wanted him to come *hard* and I kept stopping him from having an orgasm, pushing his hand away from the cock he was stroking, until I was ready, but I wanted him to come first, and then he was clenching up, his legs and ass lifted and spread, panting *fuck fuck fuck* and while rocking on his back exploded across his stomach and chest, streaking them white—and then I pulled out and came quietly, staring at him as he looked up at me, shaking, his face a confused grimace, breathing hard, grasping the wrist of the hand that was stroking myself to orgasm. Afterward he was lying next to me, a knee raised, his fingers lightly strumming his reddened chest, his panting subsided, his stomach spattered with both of our semen. I turned to look at him: his face and neck were flushed, and his forehead glistened with sweat, and I was close enough to make out the very faint traces of acne on his chin. He seemed distracted and lifted his head to scan the room. Again, in the silence of the pool house I noticed an element missing—a sound, a noise, movement that I associated with the room—but I couldn't place what it was. My eyes were drawn to the Foreigner 4 promotional poster hanging on the wall, which I'd never seen before. When I asked Matt where he got the poster, he shrugged and said someone had simply left it in the mailbox and he decided to pin it up, it looked cool, he liked Foreigner. Typical, I thought.

"What did you do this weekend?" I asked quietly.

"Do?" he asked back as if he was mildly surprised. He glanced over at me and then rested his head on the comforter we were lying on and fingered the puka shell necklace.

"Yeah, did you do anything?"

"No," he said flatly. "Nothing. Just hung out."

"I went to Debbie's," I said. "She was having a thing at her house in Bel Air."

Matt stared at the ceiling and realized he was expected to say something, and without any malice, asked: "How's your girlfriend?"

"She's okay," I said. "Thom and Susan were there. I think Jeff and Tracy are seeing each other. I think they started dating over the summer."

I realized the moment I said this that Matt had no interest whatsoever in our classmates' social rituals and dating lives. And he didn't say anything—just lay there, naked, lightly running his fingers over his chest. He reached for a box of Kleenex by the bed and wiped his stomach off. He contemplated the tissue before tossing it at the wastebasket by his desk. He handed the box of Kleenex to me.

"There's a new kid," I said, watching as Matt got up off the bed and wiped his stomach again with a nearby beach towel crumpled on the floor that he also ran through the crevice of his ass and then tossed in the hamper below the recently hung poster of the Foreigner 4 record as he walked over to his desk, where he started rummaging around, his back to me; it was littered with empty cans of soda, comic books, take-out wrappers, frozen-yogurt containers, a soccer ball, a stack of neatly folded T-shirts. I looked around the room trying to figure out what the missing element was and then landed back on Matt. When he turned around I noticed there were traces of our semen lightly draped across his chest that he'd forgotten to wipe off.

"Yeah?" he asked. "What do you mean?"

"There's a new kid in our class," I said. "Robert Mallory." I not only don't know why I said the name, I was surprised that I even remembered it.

"Oh," Matt said. "Cool."

"Yeah, it's just a little weird."

Matt shrugged and then turned around and dropped to his haunches and kept opening the bottom drawers of his desk, staring into them. He stood up, his hands on his hips, and scanned the room again. "Weird?" he murmured. "Why is that weird?"

"Well, it's just weird that someone enrolls *senior* year," I said. "That's all."

"Yeah," he said. "I guess."

"Maybe we should just keep to being friends," I said suddenly.

Matt walked over to a dresser across the room and opened a drawer.

"Did you hear me?"

"Yeah," Matt said tonelessly. "I just have no idea what you're talking about."

"This," I said, gesturing at the messed-up bed, the stained comforter, the half-empty bottle of baby oil. "Maybe we should lay off *this* for a while."

It was too quiet. That *sound* was missing; an ambient noise I was used to was no longer there. I pulled two tissues from the Kleenex box and wiped myself off.

"You don't even need to say that," Matt said, squinting around the room. He reached over to his desk and put on his glasses—he used them for reading but mostly wore contacts.

"Well, I don't want you to think that I don't care," I said.

"I don't think anything," he said, glancing over at me, holding it. "I don't think anything." His eyes returned to whatever he was looking for. "I mean, what are you doing? What do you want?" He asked this in a quietly frustrated, almost pleading voice.

I pretended that I hadn't heard him as I reached for my underwear, slipped the briefs on while lying on the bed and then sat up and grabbed my Polo shirt off the floor, again distracted by the silence in the room. And then my eyes glanced over at the aquarium: it was filled with water and the blue and green and purple lights were still glowing but the cover was missing, and it was empty. All the fish had disappeared. The sound of the filters and the bubbling that had emanated from the tank was gone. The filters had been turned off. That was the missing sound.

"Wait a minute," I said. "What happened to the aquarium?"

He looked over, acknowledged it, shrugged. "I don't know."

"You don't know what happened to the aquarium?" I asked. "You don't know why your aquarium is empty?"

"No," he said, more concerned with what he was looking for than what had happened to the aquarium. "I came back the other day and I noticed they were gone."

"What are you looking for?" I asked, annoyed. "Jesus, Matt."

"My pipe," he murmured.

I saw it resting on the nightstand next to the bed: a brass bowl with an orange glass mouthpiece. "Twenty fish just . . . vanished?"

"Yeah, they're gone," Matt said. "It's weird. I don't know." He reached into another drawer, still searching for the pipe. "I don't remember doing anything to them, if that's what you were going to ask me. All I know is that they're gone."

"Do you think maybe . . . the cat did it?" I finally asked.

He looked over at me and we both started laughing.

"You think Alex ate all my fish?" Matt was cracking up. He threw his head back.

"I don't know," I said, still laughing. "Would Alex do that?"

"I don't think so," he said, convulsing. "But maybe we'll never know."

"Why?" I asked, pulling my Polo shorts on.

"Well, the cat's missing, too," Matt said, catching his breath.

And then we both started laughing again.

I'd like to say that the conversation between the two of us on that Labor Day in 1981 was more consequential than what I've recounted here—that perhaps there was closure, a shared sense that we were both moving on from whatever we'd created and continued for the last year; but despite what turned out to be our final shared laughter, I felt I'd embarrassed myself and wanted to leave, and Matt never seemed to care whether I stayed or left. I noticed it was already dark out—school would be starting tomorrow. "It's there," I said, gesturing to the pipe on the nightstand. He walked over to it and picked the pipe up, grinning, and I was still grinning too about the mystery of the aquarium, and yet it seemed to be just another example of Matt's inability to figure things out—there was nothing proactive about him, he drifted along carelessly, he hung up posters left in his mailbox— and as he filled the bowl with a small pinch of weed that he picked out of an open baggie I realized that I was going to be disappearing soon and that he would care about my absence as much as he seemed to care about the cat, the empty aquarium, the world at large. Matt went over to the stereo, bent down and lifted a needle, and the Specials started singing "Ghost Town" again—*This town is coming like a ghost town*—and I left the guesthouse without saying goodbye.

I DROVE ONTO VALLEY VISTA from Haskell Avenue and glided along the deserted boulevard—there seemed to be no one out on that Monday, the unofficial last night of summer, but through the open windows and sunroof of the Mercedes I could smell the charcoal from various grills and hear the delighted cries of children cannonballing into pools, and every so often I'd catch top-forty songs playing from radios in backyards, and I was reminded that even though we lived in supposedly glamorous Los Angeles this was also suburbia, filled with quiet tree-lined neighborhoods, kids riding bikes in the empty streets, swimming parties and barbecues. I was listening to Peter Gabriel's "Games Without Frontiers" over and over (. . . *Whistling tunes we hide in the dunes by the seaside . . .*) as I moved from Encino into Sherman Oaks, and I found myself mindlessly heading toward Stansbury Avenue and the school located there. I was originally going to drive past Stansbury and make a right onto Ventura and let it take me through Studio City, where the boulevard became Cahuenga, and then head into Hollywood, cruising along Sunset until I hit Beverly Glen—a circuitous route back to the house on Mulholland—because I didn't feel like going home just yet. But I drove up Stansbury until it dead-ended into a cul-de-sac where the closed gates of the Buckley School appeared and the brick wall with the school's name in gold letters greeted its students, carefully trellised with ivy and lit by a streetlamp.

The school spanned eighteen acres and was mostly darkened that night. There were rooms lit in the library and the administration offices as well as the occasional sodium light that dotted the hillside, illuminating the path up to the sports field, which was visible from the top of Beverly Glen when you were looking downward at the campus but not at the end of Stansbury, where only the deserted parking lot, the bell towers beyond the gates, and one or two buildings were within view—everything else was dark. I parked in the curved driveway next to the entrance gates and lit a Djarum. "Games Without Frontiers" kept building as I sat in the car and smoked the clove cigarette: the sliding guitar, the synth bass, the militaristic cadence of Gabriel's vocals, the whistled melody adding an eerie vibe to the darkness of Buckley and the black night. *Adolf builds a bonfire, Enrico plays with it . . .*

And then I noticed something in the stillness of the school.

It was by the library, which was situated adjacent to the parking lot laid out just beyond the school's gates.

I saw the lone beam of a flashlight traversing over the trees that lined the hillside the library was nestled beneath.

And judging from where the beam emanated it was in the courtyard below the second floor of the two-story building and whoever was holding the flashlight steadied it until the light wasn't moving anymore, as if the beam was focused on *something*—I first noticed the light guiding whoever was holding it down the stairs and along the walkway that led into the courtyard, which wasn't visible from where I sat. And I wondered what it was focusing on: the benches beside the koi pond, the statue of the school's mascot, the Buckley Griffin—a mythical creature with the body of a lion and the head and wings of an eagle, a gold life-sized edifice rising up on a stand beside the koi pond—the small waterfall that quietly cascaded into it, the date palms draping over the space.

In the driver's seat I sat up, leaning my head down, pushing the visor up, to get a better look through the windshield. The beam moved again through the darkness, and then settled on a space just a few feet away from where it had originally been. The movement of the flashlight wasn't random—it was precise, as if it knew exactly what it was looking for. Was it a night watchman? I wondered. And then I was confused as to whether Buckley even had a night watchman. I turned and craned my neck and saw the darkened security booth that was always manned during the day and there didn't seem to be anybody occupying it that night—there was only a beige van parked next to it. I thought briefly maybe it belonged to one of the campus groundsmen prepping the school for tomorrow's reopening.

The beam moved again to yet another angle and I turned down the volume on the Peter Gabriel song and almost immediately heard the high wavering cries of coyotes somewhere on the distant hillsides surrounding the school. Whoever was holding the flashlight had heard them too, seemingly at the same time I did. The beam of light, which was slowly moving again, suddenly stopped and then quickly swung across the hillside as if it was searching for what was emitting these sounds—the faint howling that signified the animals' hunger.

And then the light was gone, snapped off.

I thought for a moment I'd imagined it but in the next instant knew I hadn't, and then I realized that whoever was holding the flashlight, searching the courtyard of the library, was probably heading toward the parking lot. This was an assumption my mind made—it was the drama the writer encouraged. But instead of leaving, I waited, hypnotized by the sounds of the coyotes lightly filtering through the silence of the night. The clove was still lit, smoke lightly curling out of the sunroof, and I thought about the movie *Halloween.* I thought about Matt's empty aquarium and his laughter over Alex the missing cat, "Ghost Town" echoing out over the darkened pool, the Foreigner 4 poster pinned above the hamper. I suddenly thought about the deserted house on Mulholland waiting for me and couldn't remember when my parents told me they were coming back—first week of November or was it later? I was worried in a way I hadn't been; a small dark wave crested over me. I actually shivered, momentarily disoriented. And then I couldn't hear the coyotes anymore: their howling had subsided. It was completely silent. I waited but didn't know what I was waiting for.

And then the flashlight snapped back on, blinding me, glaring through the windshield.

The SHARDS

Whoever was holding it stood behind the gates, a shadowed figure, maybe six feet away from where I sat, just a black shape, a mass. I didn't shout or jump in my seat. Instead I simply started the car and quickly drove away, the flashlight trained on me as I turned out of the driveway, glancing in the rearview mirror as Buckley and the beam of light retreated behind me until I was at the end of the block, where I turned off Stansbury and back onto Valley Vista. I immediately headed to Beverly Glen, which would take me to Mulholland Drive and the empty house. I decided not to drive around the city and instead take a Valium from the canister my mother left me, read a few chapters of *Cujo* and drift off to sleep. If the Stephen King book was too creepy maybe I'd pick up my mom's copy of *The White Hotel* and read that instead. These were the thoughts I had as I traveled upward on Beverly Glen, trying to distract myself from the nebulous worry that was floating somewhere vaguely in the distance.

THERE WAS A MESSAGE from Debbie on the answering machine in my bedroom—because of how wired she got from the cocaine she'd stayed up all night and slept through the day and wanted to know where I was; she pleaded for me to call her back, it was so important, her mother was a wreck and Susan's faking it with Thom and she missed me. But I was keyed up and didn't want to talk to her—I was suddenly paranoid, even fearful, about how vulnerable I was in the empty house on Mulholland. I turned on all the lights as some kind of warning to the intruder, positive he was approaching, ski mask on, butcher knife clenched in gloved fist, and would bind me with rope and sacrifice Shingy, and wondered what Matt Kellner would have done if I drove back to Encino and asked if I could spend the night. Shingy didn't want to go outside. Maybe the dog registered the faint howling of the coyotes, which seemed closer than usual, and that's why he was lightly shaking, bent into himself on his pillow in the kitchen, and I kept thinking I heard someone on the patio and, emboldened by the Valium I'd taken, headed out onto the deck, where I scanned the yard and the blue-lit pool and heard the coyotes roaming the canyons on their nocturnal hunt but saw nothing. The Trawler kept vaguely crowding my mind and I made sure all the doors were locked and the alarm activated. I couldn't deny it: the air felt charged, electrified even, and though it was warm out on that last night of summer I found myself shivering again, on the veranda staring into the darkness, with expectation, with dread, with the promise of fear fulfilled. I wanted to relax in the Jacuzzi but I was too afraid to sit outside by myself, and so I took another Valium and fell into bed. I couldn't let go of it: some*thing* had come into the city, a presence had arrived, and this was activated by not only the lone flashlight on the Buckley grounds but also by the mention of a new boy in our class, someone who was going to join us, and participate in our rituals and games, our secrets and evasions, the low-key dramas and the shadowy lies. This was the night before we met that boy, Robert Mallory, for the first time.

4

I DON'T REMEMBER WHEN THE VALIUM kicked in and relaxed me into a deep and dreamless sleep, but I woke up at seven-thirty and, realizing Rosa would be arriving at eight, I reached for the small bottle of Johnson's baby oil I kept in my nightstand and quickly masturbated—at seventeen I always woke up with an aching erection—thinking about what happened with Matt yesterday, and then moving on to Ryan, and then the fantasy went, as it sometimes did, to that boy I glimpsed at the Village Theater when I saw *The Shining* last year: I had built an elaborate porn dream around him and there were certain scenarios and positions involving the boy that my mind would race to and quickly get me off. I hopped through the backyard naked, only holding a beach towel, and stepped into the Jacuzzi, submerging myself in the heated water as Shingy wandered the lawn and quickly defecated, having not gone out last night. I could hear the steady stream of cars traveling along Mulholland behind the boxwood hedge: the morning felt animated, the world was waking up to a new season, and I no longer felt the trepidation and anxiety from the night before while soaking in the Jacuzzi beneath the early-morning sun. Shingy sniffed around the edges of the lawn, occasionally running from side to side, seemingly excited to be alive.

I stepped out of the Jacuzzi, wrapped the towel around my waist and let Shingy follow me across the deck to the entrance of my room, where he raced past the bed and down a hallway into the rest of the house. I switched on *Good Morning America,* then showered. As I usually did when I was younger, I studied myself naked from all angles in the bathroom's mirrors while I brushed my teeth because I wanted to make sure I looked good—this was the summer I'd created a small gym in a room adjacent to the garage where I worked out: free weights, a bench, a treadmill I ran on while listening to my Walkman. I had become overly concerned about how I looked, and it bordered, at times, on anxiety, and in the summer before my senior year I was trying to aim for whatever the physical ideal was in that moment and realized I was somewhat succeeding. That morning Graham Parker was on my stereo, *The Up Escalator* record—I clearly remember "No Holding Back" playing—as I put on my Buckley uniform: tailored gray slacks, a white Armani button-down tucked in with the tiny insignia of an eagle on the chest, a Gucci belt, striped tie, burgundy penny loafers, and I made sure everything was in place—the hair boyishly tousled, the face free from the stubble that had started appearing last year, the eyes rinsed with Visine—before I grabbed the blue blazer with the Griffin insignia on the jacket's pocket from a hanger in the walk-in closet and slung it over my shoulder as I left the bedroom that Rosa would straighten up while I was at school. *We can face the danger baby no holding back . . .*

BY NOW IT WAS eight-thirty and I was running late. Instead of Rosa making me breakfast I just threw some Frosted Flakes into a bowl and quickly wolfed them down while flipping through the pages in the entertainment section of the *Los Angeles Times*, noting that I wanted tickets to the ELO tour that had just kicked off—they'd be at the Forum on the 23rd—and then quickly checked the "Metro" section and was surprised and not surprised to see that there was a home invasion on Sunday night where an unidentified victim was attacked, this one in Century City, in a residence above Santa Monica Boulevard, just a block from where Avenue of the Stars began—this was the first one since June. I read it in a blur, it didn't matter, I just needed the headline on page 4 of the "Metro" section to confirm the assault. I grabbed the paper bag that contained the lunch Rosa had prepared and said *adios* and moved toward the garage. She was making a list for the store—she always headed to Gelson's at the beginning of the week—and asked if there was anything I wanted. I called out *Estoy bien.*

My mother drove a sea-foam-green Jaguar XJ6 and my father had left his cream-colored 450SL when they separated and he moved to

The SHARDS

Mountaingate, a gated development that looked over the 405 freeway, its entrance on a deserted section of Sepulveda not far from the house on Mulholland, and had recently bought himself a silver Ferrari. I wasn't driving the green four-door 450SEL anymore and had taken the top off the SL, a sporty two-door with chestnut interior, and started driving it when my parents left for Europe a week earlier. A seventeen-year-old boy (I'd be eighteen in March) tooling across Mulholland in a convertible Mercedes dressed in a private-school uniform and wearing Wayfarers is an image from a certain moment of empire that I was, at times, self-conscious about—did I look like an asshole? I'd briefly wonder—before thinking: I look so cool I don't care. A mixtape playing Blondie's "Call Me" completed my *American Gigolo* moment as I headed toward Buckley, and yet the excitement of it somewhat diminished because I was soon stuck in traffic backed up along Beverly Glen heading down into the San Fernando Valley. I usually took Woodcliff to Valley Vista but on that first day I drove across Mulholland to Beverly Glen because I'd wanted to show off—and now I was paying the price.

And there were cars backed up on Stansbury Avenue, moving slowly toward the entrance gates of the school, where students were being dropped off—a line made up of Cadillacs and Mercedes, Saab station wagons and Jaguars, along with the occasional miniature yellow van with "The Buckley School" written in black cursive lettering on its sides. If you arrived at Buckley early enough you'd miss the peak traffic backed up on the residential street, or if you timed it so you arrived just before classes began at nine you'd avoid it as well—I miscalculated that morning and this was when my relatively good mood started getting rewired. Once inside the gates I pulled to the left, toward the high school, and slowly drove to the parking spaces set aside for seniors only. Ryan's black Trans Am was parked near the front of the row and he was waiting in the driver's seat, looking at something in his lap while listening to music, probably the J. Geils Band, which was the last cassette that had been in his car when I was in it mid-August, though I was hoping he was simply waiting for me. I blanched when I thought this: the fantasy of a little prince. There was a slight adrenaline rush in seeing him but as I pulled the 450SL into an empty space I became distracted by the police car parked discreetly in the alley behind the library and I immediately wondered why it wasn't parked in front of the building—it didn't want to announce itself, I realized, and it was almost as if it had been hidden so as not to alarm any of the students on that first day of school.

RYAN WAS OUT OF THE TRANS AM and waiting for me as I walked through the parking lot after pulling the top of the Mercedes up: it seemed everyone was there already, the spaces filled with Mazdas, Fiats, Camaros, Jettas, Jeff Taylor's Porsche 924, Debbie's white BMW; only a few were empty. And I wondered which car was Robert Mallory's as I scanned the lot walking up to Ryan. His blue-eyed blond-haired blankness would have soothed me on any other morning but I was suddenly nervous, uneasy about something, a new mood was descending, the jitters from last night had returned, and instead of simply saying hi, coolly basking in his beauty, I had to say, "Why did you leave Debbie's the other night?" His expression changed, became concerned. "Good morning to you, too." He was playing a game, enacting a part, and because he wasn't taking it that seriously he inhabited the role beautifully: you couldn't tell he was acting even though I was the only one who knew he was. It was just something he had to do until he got out of here and escaped our hermetic world. "Please, don't be a pussy," he added.

"I almost called you yesterday," I said.

"I'm sorry but that whole thing—"

"What whole thing?" I cut in.

"The Schaffers. Grosses me out." He shrugged. "I thought I could deal with it but it's not for me."

"Thom was there, I was there—"

"Stop. Don't be a pussy," he said again, lightly pained.

He was leaning casually against the Trans Am, wearing his letterman sweater—burgundy and striped with gold, hanging just below the waist, stylish with brass buttons, something that looked as if you could purchase it at Fred Segal. "Why didn't you call me?" he asked quietly.

"I don't know," I said. "Something stopped me." I paused. "Wasn't sure if you wanted me to."

"Yeah, of course, I did," he said, softening, as he glanced around the parking lot.

"Well, you could have called me."

"I did." He directed his gaze back to where I was standing, just a couple feet away. I noticed that Thom's Corvette was pulling into the lot, slowly nearing us, which was what Ryan had been glancing at. I could see Susan in the passenger seat, checking her face in the visor's mirror.

"When?" I asked, distracted.

"In the afternoon." He added for light emphasis: "Twice."

"You did?"

"Yeah."

I didn't tell him I was at Matt Kellner's, though I doubt Ryan would have cared.

"I guess I was out by the pool," I lied easily. "I never heard the phone."

He straightened up and casually saluted Thom as he drove past us toward an empty space, Styx wafting out of the Corvette.

"Let's talk later," Ryan said.

"Are you paranoid?" I suddenly asked.

"Um, I'm . . . practical, I guess." He watched as Thom parked the car and then he and Susan were heading over to us. "We'll make a plan later. I want to hang out." The way he said this had an erotic finality when he added, "With you," and it lightly jolted me, adding to the general unease I was beginning to feel that morning.

I had already turned to Thom and Susan and even though we'd all seen each other at Debbie's on Sunday night we greeted each other somewhat formally, the guys nodding and ironically saying "Sir" while Susan kissed both Ryan and me on the cheek, and then the four of us started walking toward the bell tower that led into the high-school side of campus. "How was the movie?" I asked.

Thom and Susan seemed momentarily confused.

"The John Belushi thing," I reminded them. "Sunday night."

"It was okay," Susan said. "It wasn't very funny."

"I fell asleep," Thom admitted. "It was a romantic comedy, or supposed to be."

"You should have asked Debbie for some blow," I said.

Thom snickered. Susan rolled her eyes.

"She was totally high. She was whispering to me through the

whole thing," Susan said. "And then she was always leaving to deal with Liz, who I guess was totally trashed upstairs and losing her shit. Just another night at the Schaffers'."

"I know, I ran into Liz on my way out," I said. "Did Terry come in? Did he watch the movie?"

"I didn't see him," Susan said. "Hey, why did you leave?" she asked Ryan.

"I actually had dinner plans with my family," Ryan said. "I was over in Westwood picking up some college info at UCLA and that's why I decided to stop at Debbie's."

These were all lies: I knew that Ryan didn't have a dinner planned with his family and that he had no intention of applying to UCLA, let alone the grades to get in, and I wondered if Thom or Susan even vaguely realized this. Susan glanced over at me and then back at Ryan. "You should have stayed, it was fun."

"Yeah," Ryan said. "I had plans."

"Too bad," Susan said, glancing over at me again.

"Was it really that fun, Susan?" I asked pointedly.

I wanted this to sound like a joke but it came out as if I was scowling.

Susan, unflappable, shrugged, and said, "Well, I had a good time."

I watched as Thom reached for her hand. I noted Susan's slight hesitation.

NONE OF THEM NOTICED THE police car, or said anything, but its presence had altered my mood and as we were heading toward the administration office to go over our individual schedules for the year I had an overwhelming desire to see the library's courtyard—I sensed that something had happened there, and that what I'd seen last night was connected to the presence of the police car. And I don't know why I just didn't act on that desire but instead I remember walking with Susan and Thom and Ryan until we arrived at the door of the high school's central building—like most buildings at Buckley it was a low structure, a bungalow, classic stucco with Spanish tile roofs. Everything at Buckley was outside: there were no hallways, each classroom was, in fact, its own bungalow, with walkways connecting them protected by eaves, and it was the administration office that I drifted into as if in a dream on that first day of school. Senior year was more flexible than any other and if you had problems with your schedule then the first morning back was the time to correct it, make changes, switch things around if you wanted to, anything to accommodate members of the senior class. But I didn't care, it didn't matter what courses I took, I just wanted out, there was nothing to change because none of it made any difference, I was going to be a writer, I was working on my novel, that's what I cared about. People I hadn't seen since June and barely recognized in my distracted state were walking in and out of the office; as with everything else at Buckley the scene was always calm and controlled and orderly, but that morning everything seemed in slow motion, fragmented, haunted, vibrating with low-level anxiety.

I remember Dr. Croft was also there, holding a miniature Perrier bottle, while seniors consulted with various secretaries, and he approached Susan wanting to talk to her about what she was going to say at the mid-morning assembly and they disappeared into his office, adjacent to the waiting area. "Anyone see the new guy yet?" Doug Furth asked Ryan and Thom—both of whom shrugged while comparing their schedules with mine. David Walters, the headmaster, walked into the office—a space laden with furniture from Sloane's and ferns draped across tables and a LeRoy Neiman painting taking up an entire wall and discreetly lit and next to an antique grandfather clock and the huge bouquets of fresh flowers in two massive vases—and he reminded everyone that it was after nine and the first class of the day had already begun, and he would see everyone later at assembly. Stacks of the new roster were lined against the flat top of the counter separating the waiting area from the secretaries and I picked one up and opened it to twelfth grade, and saw Robert Mallory's name between Rita Lee and Danielle Peters, and I suddenly felt as if I was being watched—I had experienced this sensation last night as well, when I left Matt Kellner's and on Stansbury Avenue parked in front of the gates and in the darkness of my own backyard.

I was in a full-blown daze, gripping the open roster, staring at the name, when Debbie kissed me lightly on the lips, materializing like an apparition, clear-eyed, made up, a centerfold, any sign of a druggy weekend now completely wiped away. I recovered slightly and realized that Thom and Ryan were still standing next to me comparing schedules—what to change, what to move around, "maybe move Study Hall to last period so we can leave early"—when Debbie announced excitedly that someone had "desecrated" the Griffin statue in the courtyard of the library.

"Desecrated . . ." Thom said, confused.

"It was vandalized," she confirmed.

"Probably Harvard guys," Ryan said.

"What did they do to it exactly?" I asked.

"No one knows," Debbie said. "They blocked off the courtyard."

"That's why the police are here . . ." I murmured.

"You didn't call me yesterday," Debbie whispered.

"I'm sorry, babe."

"I know." She smiled ruefully. "You were getting ready for school."

The atmosphere was hushed, everything seemed embalmed in that dream I walked into: the flat green carpeting I was standing on could have been a lake, the hum of the air conditioning was the distant wind before a storm, the handsome students in uniform were robots, everyone talking scripted dialogue in low voices. On the surface the room conveyed the elegance and control that Buckley emanated, but it all seemed unreal, as if I was making it up and yet, conversely, couldn't control it. Debbie whispered about a new club, actually a "space" on Melrose, she wanted us to check out this week, maybe Thursday night, it wasn't officially open yet, it played videos in empty rooms, there was a bar, someone named Attila had told her about it. I shrugged as I usually did whenever she wanted me to do something. To Debbie, I had realized over the summer, the constant shrugging on my part suggested a kind of masculinity—a strong, silent type I was supposedly embodying when, in fact, I just didn't care. Something died in me while I stood in the administration office on that first day of our senior year when I realized we wouldn't be graduating until June—there would be ten more months of this pantomime—and a new depression landed on me. I was in a uniform, a costume, pretending to be the boyfriend, taking a year's worth of classes I had no interest in, disguising myself: I was an actor and none of this was real. This was the takeaway on that Tuesday morning in September.

I forced myself to pay attention as Debbie and Thom left for their first class, Spanish III, and Susan and Ryan and I headed to American Fiction, but as we entered the classroom I excused myself, telling Mr. Robbins my throat was dry and I needed a drink of water.

THE WALKWAYS were empty as I made my way to the stairs leading to the courtyard below the library—there was no one out, everyone was either in the administration building or in class, since school had officially begun. At the top of the stairs there was a barricade made up of a sawhorse and two orange traffic cones, blocking the path that led into the courtyard—the only other way was through the library itself, which still hadn't been opened, an anomaly since it was usually the first building everyone had access to, the initial gathering place of the day. I paused, glanced around and then bypassed the sawhorse and the pylons and walked casually down the steps. The space was surrounded by walnut trees and sycamores, and I could hear the songbirds nesting in them, and beyond that the waterfall lightly splashing into the koi pond. The first thing I noticed was Miguel, the head of maintenance, who had been at Buckley since I was in seventh grade, as well as the school's head of security, Angelo, who I also knew, quietly conferring with two policemen, armed and in uniform, and who I later found out were waiting for a crime-scene photographer to take pictures of the desecrated statue. I neared the Griffin before any of them noticed me but I didn't understand what I was looking at. It seemed comical at first—a harmless prank, Kleenex, red dye, a wig—until I got closer.

Blood was splattered everywhere in congealed pools below the statue, and the Griffin itself was streaked with it but there was nothing that suggested where the blood had come from, what its source was—it was simply brought from another location. The koi pond was still filled with water but there were about twenty dead fish, white and orange and black, strewn beneath the statue of the Griffin, all of them gutted with their heads cut off. The decapitated heads had been somehow pasted onto the statue, decorating it in circular shapes, creating a pair of female breasts, and another gutted koi was hanging between the Griffin's legs, mimicking a penis, and clumps from what looked like a wig—blond and shiny and synthetic—had been pasted on the crotch of the statue to resemble pubic hair. Gobs of entrails from the fish had been draped over the Griffin's head, a glistening black-and-pink-and-red toupee, above a face where two white fish heads were pasted on with blood to resemble eyes and another white koi was arranged over the Griffin's mouth, meant to mimic a bloodstained smile, a leer. I had barely grasped the crudely elaborate horror of it when Miguel called out, "You shouldn't be down here, Bret—go back up," and made a motion with his hand. The cops and Angelo stared at me grimly as I obeyed Miguel, backing away, literally trembling, finally noticing the flies and gnats swirling around the statue and the pools of blood.

Ryan was wrong: there was no way this was a group of Harvard jocks—it was too perverse, too disgusting. In my shock I remembered with dread that I had actually witnessed whoever had done this the night before when I sat parked in my car at the school gates and watched the beam from the flashlight traverse back and forth across the darkened courtyard and the adjoining hillside. I remember distinctly thinking that morning—it arrived automatically, there was no hesitation—it would only complicate things for myself if I offered any information to the police about an intruder I saw on the school grounds last night. I didn't want to be a witness, I didn't want to get involved, I was afraid. I automatically decided to stay quiet—this was, I felt, the easiest option for me. The desecrated statue offered a narrative that I didn't want any connection to—I didn't want to be part of the story: it was too awful. And as I walked numbly up the stairs and onto the walkway that would take me back to class I couldn't help but think, again, that there was someone watching me hidden in the hills that surrounded the school, through either a pair of binoculars or a camera with a long lens or the telescope of a hunting rifle. I remember thinking that for the first time in my life I was so disoriented it felt like I was melting, dissolving in on myself, becoming another person, and then disappearing into nothing, the incredible shrinking boy.

THE REST OF THE MORNING I was lost in my own movie—I couldn't pay attention to anything. I only pretended to concentrate on the book I'd just opened or contemplate whatever Mr. Robbins or Miss Sylvan had scrawled across a chalkboard. At one point between first and second periods I asked Susan if she had a Valium but she could only offer a Quaalude, which I didn't want—I wouldn't have made it past lunch if I'd taken it. She asked me what was wrong—she noticed—but I didn't tell her, or anyone else, about what I'd seen. The slow-motion dream that began in the administration office had sped up after I saw the awful damage inflicted upon the statue, and I assumed that not talking about it, not even referencing it, would make it recede from memory—I wanted that image of the desecrated Griffin erased from my mind. But trying to grasp the madness of whoever had done this caused a light fear to start streaming forward, accelerating everything, and sooner than I thought possible we were at the mid-morning assembly and the entire high school—about three hundred students—was congregated in the massive courtyard, the plaza beneath the Buckley Pavilion, where the campus indoor athletic arena was, and concerts and school musicals were staged, and which also contained an Olympic-sized swimming pool and a basketball court. A sea of blue blazers looked up to the American flag as the Pledge of Allegiance was recited followed by the Buckley Prayer. Headmaster Walters and Dr. Croft made short speeches about the importance of leadership and the rigors of challenges, and promised that creative excitement and personal fulfillment lay ahead for all of us.

SUSAN WALKED TO THE MICROPHONE—she was student-body president—and as she overlooked the assembly area the loud applause continued and it was joined by a high-pitched siren of wolf whistles emanating from what seemed like almost every male in the plaza: this would have been discouraged now but in 1981 everyone, especially Susan, took delight in the appreciation of the moment. She didn't read off cards or from a script because she didn't have much to say—this wasn't a pep talk (Susan was too cool for that). She just casually welcomed everyone back; reminded everyone about Homecoming and that the designs for class floats needed to be approved by the last week of September; said that anyone who wanted to sign up to be on the editorial board of *The Buckley Gazette,* the student newspaper, should please contact Doug Furth, or, to work on *Images,* the student yearbook, contact Suzie Todd or Debbie Schaffer; announced that the musical this term would be *Mame* and auditions started next week. Coach McCabe and Coach Holtz invited the captain and quarterback of the varsity football team, Thom Wright, to introduce the lineup this year, announcing Ryan Vaughn as co-captain, while U2's "I Will Follow" burst from a tower of speakers and the eleven guys that made up the Buckley Griffins bounded up the steps and formed a line amidst cheers coming from the plaza. No one mentioned the vandalized statue in the library courtyard that morning.

I noticed Matt Kellner standing on the far reaches of the crowd by himself, and though he cheered with everyone else as each name of the football team was called out by Thom, I knew Matt was going through the motions, following a script like I was, far away from it all, and, knowing him intimately (I had been *inside* him yesterday), I could see the distance in the stoned gaze even though he was grinning. To anyone casually glancing at Matt Kellner that morning the grin might have looked genuine—but to me it was a rictus. Matt, a tan ghost with short brown hair streaked blond from the sun, was another reminder that I'd checked out sometime during my junior year and was performing a pantomime in which I only noticed the edges of things, the fringes of campus, the outlines of people, and this was why someone like Matt Kellner preoccupied me, because he was on the periphery as well. It surprised me that being back on campus reignited my contempt so suddenly and doomed any of the optimism I'd been feeling the past few weeks. This was not going to be the happy year I'd foolishly envisioned and hoped for over the summer; whatever excitement had been caused by my own faulty wiring. I realized too late while standing in the courtyard below the Pavilion on that first morning back, that I hadn't been paying enough attention to the actual script.

THE SOFT CHIMING OF THE BELLS announced it was midday. There was no cafeteria at Buckley, so students brought bagged lunches, and since we resided in Southern California we always ate outside. There was a stretch of table-benches with umbrellas along the side of the building that housed the science labs where most juniors ate, and the seniors always took over the tables in the shadow of the Pavilion that overlooked the assembly plaza where ten picnic tables were lined, evenly spaced apart. And though seniors could basically eat anywhere they wanted on campus there was a kind of hierarchy at play with the seating situation at lunch: seniors got the Pavilion tables, juniors took over the benches in the courtyard, sophomores sat along the tables by the arts-and-crafts bungalow. Small cartons of cold milk were made available for all grades in blue crates left on the steps of the Pavilion right before lunch and I reached for one as I headed to where Thom and Susan were sitting with Debbie, who was saving me the space next to her, at the *center* table, the table that was most visible to everyone and was pulled away from the other nine tables and had the best sightlines of the campus—it might as well have been a throne. Everyone could see us.

Some students were better-looking, a few were more charismatic and athletic, there were a few who had more money and those whose parents were famous, which added its own kind of cachet, but the uniforms we all wore discouraged the idea that someone was "better" or "different" than anyone else—you could deal with *that* unfairness after you graduated, in college, out in *the real world*—and the quietude of the campus aided in this notion that was supposed to protect us. The fact that the number of students in each grade was small— just sixty and no classroom exceeded fourteen kids—also encouraged something other than a popularity contest: the opportunity to show off or fixate on somebody was minimized by the rules and structure of the school. And yet it was unavoidable that certain people captured the student-body imagination in ways others didn't—Susan Reynolds and Debbie Schaffer certainly with their looks, and Thom Wright was our king because of his handsomeness and athletic prowess, his bro-jock amiability, and though this popularity, this high-school notion of *power*, probably mattered more to Debbie Schaffer than to anyone else—she got high on exclusivity—I supposed that Thom and Susan were so used to their status that they didn't know anything else, that they accepted it as a given, their right, and didn't even have to try, unaware that people fantasized about them. My popularity, as someone who didn't play sports and avoided extracurricular activities, was tied into being Thom and Susan's closest friend, that was my *in*, that was how I was seen, the sidekick, the fifth wheel, I was famous because of my close proximity to them, this was how it had been for a long time—but I truly didn't care now, it didn't matter to me, and it mattered even less as I moved numbly toward the center table in the shade below the Pavilion on that first bewildering day of school.

BUT I SMILED AS I SLID onto the bench while the girls shared a pomegranate in mid-conversation with rumors about the statue of the Griffin—no one knew what had been done to it or the ways it was vandalized. Earlier, in the administration office, Dr. Croft told Susan confidentially that they weren't going to mention "the rumor" at assembly—he told her only that the kois in the pond had been "removed," and that was it. I was tempted to describe what I'd witnessed but realized they might not have believed me: the blood, the gore, the dead fish, the gruesome fish-leer, the sexualizing of the Griffin, the dripping koi-penis and the white tits made of fish heads, it was too outrageous. Plus I knew that Susan and Debbie would take me to task for what they saw as my tendency to embellish. Susan had always been fond of chiding me about additional details I'd lace a story with, as well as what I concealed, and she'd often interrupt and explain to the listeners that it didn't really happen in *quite* that way, *Bret's exaggerating.* But I was a storyteller and I liked decorating an otherwise mundane incident that maybe contained one or two facts that made it initially interesting to be retold in the first place but not really, by adding a detail or two that elevated the story into something legitimately interesting to the listener and gave it humor or surprise or shock, and this came naturally to me. These weren't lies exactly—I just preferred the exaggerated version.

I also realized that the desecrated statue had made me forget about the new student, Robert Mallory, and I suddenly looked around to see if I could spot him.

From a distant boom box somewhere, the Clash were singing "The Magnificent Seven"—I looked up to see where it was coming from and felt a pang when I saw Ryan Vaughn eating lunch with Anthony Matthews, Jeff Taylor, Kyle Colson, Doug Furth and Dominic Thompson—just the guys. Ryan was laughing, describing something with his hands, seemingly enjoying himself—he was genuinely animated, and not pretending, and I wanted to be sitting next to him in that moment: when he seemed to be real. What happened to those days last spring when we sat away from everyone else, lost in our secret flirtation, on the verge of sharing how we actually felt about each other? I realized: we weren't eating together because Ryan, after what happened in my bedroom in August, thought we were now officially a secret. I was trying to pay attention to what my table was talking about and not saying much, just staring at the lunch Rosa had prepared for me—the group was accustomed to my silence, they thought it was *writerly*—though I announced that I wanted to see ELO at the Forum and asked if anyone wanted to get tickets and I remember the moment when Thom stopped mid-sentence and looked up curiously, offering his warm, friendly, blank smile to someone, and Susan turned from Thom to glance at whatever had interrupted him, and this was followed by Debbie, shifting beside me. It was very quiet and warm out, pleasant and sunny, Mediterranean almost, and the hum of voices beneath the umbrellas continued, undisturbed by a new presence. Someone had approached the *center* table, the most *popular* table, as if he had intuited this without knowing any of us.

From my vantage point, forty years later and knowing exactly what happened that fall, I could paint something more sinister in retrospect, but there was no reason to do so on that day because the boy standing at our table was calm and dreamy, and seemed vulnerable and innocent. He was hesitantly reaching out to us and needed our guidance.

THE FIRST THING I SAW: Topsiders with no socks. And when I looked up the question for me became: How could the cut angles of Robert Mallory's face, jawline, cheekbones be *more* handsome than Thom? Why was Robert Mallory suddenly so much sexier than anyone else even though, just like Thom and Ryan, he looked all-American hot and belonged in a movie and the pages of a fashion magazine? Maybe, I thought, it was because I'd known both Thom and Ryan for five years and accustomed to the way they looked and Robert Mallory was a *new* presence—he suddenly appeared out of nowhere and this was why he made such a seismic impression.

Robert was six foot and the way he wore his Buckley uniform— everything seemed a size smaller—exaggerated the broadness of his shoulders and the slimness of his waist; his hair was dirty blond, on the short side, parted in the middle, feathered back, the style for most Buckley boys in that moment; the eyes were brown and almond-shaped, long lashed with thick lush brows; there was a classic aquiline nose with a small bump near the top, which added to its perfection; the lips were pink and full—a mouth you noticed and were drawn to; there was a light cleft in his chin, and his skin was tan and smooth, no traces of acne; the cheeks were only very slightly sunken and when he smiled there were dimples. He had taken advantage of his senior status and modified the uniform: besides Topsiders with no socks he'd opted out on the blazer and his tie was loosely knotted, and the sleeves of his white dress shirt (Ralph Lauren, Polo pony on the chest, typical of Buckley guys) were rolled up, revealing tanned forearms, almost hairless and lightly veined. You could softly smell him: it was soap or lotion or shampoo, it came somewhere from his hair, his body, his skin. It was cedar, sandalwood, as if he had just walked through a forest of citrus. There was smokiness to the scent as well, ashy, a simmering bonfire on a deserted beach, the salt air mingling with the evaporating flames. Or this is how I remember it. He was, like Thom and Ryan, a movie star, a friendly Greek god.

"Hey, you're Susan Reynolds," the guy said. "Right?"

"Yeah, you must be Robert," Susan said, smiling, surprised.

"Yeah, hi." He said this with a certain degree of shyness that was appealing. "Dr. Croft told me you'd be here and, um, showed me your picture."

"I hope not the ones he keeps in his desk," Susan deadpanned.

Robert was confused for a moment and then pretended not to be and laughed politely. "Ah, no. It was last year's yearbook." He paused, staring at her. "Nice photo. I recognized you immediately."

"Hey man," Thom said, half standing, holding out a hand. "I'm Thom."

"Robert," he said, shaking it, looking Thom directly in the eyes.

"I'm Debbie," the girl next to me said with an intonation that hinted at exaggerated curiosity. I noted the way her voice became higher on the second syllable of her name. "So you're the mysterious new guy."

"Mysterious?" Robert asked, a little startled. His innocence and polite confusion were beguiling, I thought.

The SHARDS

"Ignore her, she's kidding. I'm Bret," I said, shaking Robert's hand, which I glanced at. The hand was large, the fingernails were short and pale and clean, and he looked away from Debbie and stared at me, smiling and, as with Thom, making direct eye contact; this was seductive, he wanted me to like him and he squeezed too hard before realizing and then his grip lightly softened as he pulled away—a nervous first impression. I had to force myself not to smell my palm—I remember that clearly even though I don't necessarily recall the specifics of the dialogue from that lunch, just the generalities of Robert's story, his supposed outline, the official narrative he wanted to push. Nothing at that initial lunch directly hinted at what would happen to us later that fall but, if I'm looking back, there were clues everywhere.

I REALIZED QUICKLY that it wasn't as if I *wanted* to get to know Robert Mallory as much as a feeling I *already* did; that I'd seen him before but I couldn't tell from where and I was too disoriented by his magnetic presence to figure it out right away, or guess about this undisturbed. And I became even more quietly frazzled when Thom and Susan invited him to join us and slid over on the bench so Robert could sit down—he was now directly across from me and I had to breathe in and compose myself while smiling mindlessly at him. But a question forced its way through and I couldn't help it—there was something about him I couldn't shake off: I knew this boy. I asked, before anyone said anything, if we had met at a party or a club, was he ever at the Seven Seas or the Odyssey, the Starwood or the Whisky. Robert glanced at me, again a little startled, and said, "No, man, I don't think so." And added: "I really don't go out much. I really don't know anyone in L.A." I believed Robert, because everything about him seemed momentarily authentic and there was no reason not to—why would he lie about being at the Seven Seas before graduation? And he really was so disarmingly handsome I drifted away from interrogating him. I had imagined that whoever Robert turned out to be was probably going to get marginalized because he wouldn't have enough time to become close with anybody in the hermetic world of our senior class, but I automatically realized upon meeting him this wasn't going to be the case: His looks would open every single door. They would also hide any flaws he might be harboring. His beauty would let him get away with anything. I just stared at him.

There were about twenty minutes left of lunch until the next class began.

Robert started telling us why he was late that day—he arrived at LAX last night, he overslept, he'd barely unpacked, he couldn't find his uniform, he got lost coming from Century City because he over-shot both Benedict Canyon and then Beverly Glen and ended up on the 405 at Sunset before realizing he had to get on the 101 and take the Woodman Avenue off-ramp.

Thom interrupted and asked Robert if he'd ever been to the school before.

"No," Robert said. "This was all kind of a last-minute thing." He threw that line out as if it didn't warrant an explanation. It landed and he moved on.

When he arrived at Buckley it was already eleven-fifteen and he had an orientation meeting with both Dr. Croft and Headmaster Wal-ters, and once he got his schedule figured out they told him he should meet the student-body president, Susan Reynolds, who would be by the Pavilion, at the senior tables, and handed him a map and showed her photo instead of walking Robert themselves because they were late for a quick lunch with generous alumni at Ma Maison in West Hollywood, a hot spot on Melrose with an unlisted phone number, and whose sous-chef would murder a young actress a year later, an acquaintance of Susan's and Deborah's—all of which will, I suppose, give a sense of the empire world we inhabited and the men who ran it in 1981.

I also remember very clearly that Robert had become distracted by my uneaten sandwich and admitted that he mistakenly thought there was a cafeteria at Buckley so he didn't bring lunch. I gestured at the sandwich—*sure, you can have it*—and he grabbed half of it and brightly said "Thanks" and took a bite without inspecting what it was, mimicking relief and chewing hungrily, the muscles in his jaw clenching, unclenching, and he complimented whoever made the sandwich—it was delicious, he said with a full mouth. While he ate the sandwich and then absentmindedly reached for the opened bag of Lay's potato chips, I realized that Debbie, pressed next to me, was probably thinking about the ways she might be able to use him—she didn't flirt, she was just amused and trying to figure out the limits of Robert's malleability. He would definitely be included in everything Debbie planned because of his *newness*, of how exotic he was, and she began throwing out questions, keeping it light and casual, while Susan seemed to retreat into a private place within herself, suddenly guarded and quiet; by comparison Thom seemed to be paying complete and devoted attention to Robert, staring at him as if he was a potential friend and not a rival, which to me, for some reason, he so obviously was.

ROBERT LAID OUT HIS background for us as if it was a job interview he needed to pass: he again confirmed that he arrived from Chicago only last night and even though he had regularly been visiting Los Angeles, off and on, since the summer of 1980, and staying with his aunt, his father's sister, at her condo in Century City, he'd never fully familiarized himself with it and always felt a little disoriented—he knew Century City, Westwood, Beverly Hills and the beaches but not Hollywood or the Eastside or the Valley; and this was the reason he was late today. The last time he'd been in L.A. for any sustained length of time was ten months ago, when he came out for the holidays in December and stayed with his aunt through mid-January before returning to Chicago in order to finish out his junior year at Roycemore, a prep school in Evanston.

"Why are you living with your *aunt*?" Debbie interrupted.

He explained that since his parents' divorce Robert had been living with his mother in Lincoln Park but when she died—in what he only referred to as an accident—Robert moved in with his father, who lived in Forest Glen with a wife Robert had never gotten along with, and their "crazy" teenage daughter from the wife's first marriage, and the acrimony between Robert and the three of them was reaching an explosion until his aunt intervened, suggesting Robert relocate to Los Angeles and live with her and she would enroll him somewhere for his last year of high school. Robert's father, who wanted to send Robert to a military academy, initially vetoed his sister but this past May had a sudden change of heart and acquiesced.

"And here I am," he said, shrugging, making eye contact with each of us, smiling, showing off a row of impeccably straight white teeth.

Robert had gone through this quick backstory, filled with undercurrents of pain and loss, rejection and a dead parent, almost good-naturedly, as if it happened to someone else. The info might have been presented earnestly but it seemed, by one point, rehearsed—as if it was something Robert remembered but hadn't necessarily lived through. He offered this information in a weirdly emotionless way that verged on the hollow. On one level Robert was intriguing enough to make me momentarily forget about the Griffin streaked with gore but something unsettling about him had announced itself and was a reminder of the strangeness of that day: the police car parked in the alley behind the library, the congealed pools of blood and the mutilated koi scattered around the statue in the courtyard, a new boy materializing before us.

I suspected there was something wrong with Robert Mallory almost as soon as I met him. But it was just a feeling. I had no proof.

THOM AND SUSAN REACTED TO ROBERT in different ways: Thom seemed to like him though he was slightly disappointed when Robert said he didn't plan on playing any sports that year, which quieted Thom with an "Okay, man." Susan listened patiently—not withdrawn exactly and it didn't seem as if she was trying to ignore Robert because we were all part of the conversation, he was talking to all of us—but at times it seemed as if she was hoping he would go away precisely because Thom and Robert had immediately bonded, which had to do with how welcome Thom made Robert feel. Thom always gave everyone the benefit of the doubt, Thom always liked everyone, Thom always trusted people, it was part of his charm, Susan knew and should have expected this. And there was a subtle thing happening that I noticed and no one later commented on: Robert was trying, it seemed, not to stare at Susan, even though the principal and headmaster told him to seek her out and introduce himself to her. Maybe it came down to shyness on Robert's part: I don't think Susan ever looked more dazzling than she did on that September afternoon when she was seventeen and at the height of her prom-queen beauty—and this was simply too intimidating. Susan, I thought, was completely oblivious to Robert's glances and lost in her reveries but in her own quiet way, often just demurely studying the seeds in the pomegranate she and Debbie were sharing. I'm not sure if Thom noticed this but at one point he moved closer to Susan, almost as if it was a protective gesture, maybe even a mild warning to Robert Mallory: she's hot, she's mine, we've been together two years, we're going to get married, it's cool, dude, it's *okay, man.*

I kept looking at Robert while moving closer to the answer as to how I knew him but our world in that moment was still a distraction, and though my head was clearing and I was beginning to figure this out, the question hadn't been answered yet.

For some reason I looked over at Ryan two tables away: he was sitting very still, making his jokey *What's up?* face at me, a parody of tense helplessness, his lips pulled back, his eyes bugging a little, a punk visage—a joke we would make in reaction to our surroundings ever since we started hanging out at the end of junior year, a silent acknowledgment of how alarmed we were by what passed for normalcy in the fake enclaves of the world we were moving through. But I didn't make the face back. And then everyone was getting ready to go to the next class—the bells chiming signified the end of lunch. Robert stood up and unfolded his schedule along with a map of the campus. Now, forty years after the events of 1981, writing about this initial meeting with Robert Mallory, I look back at that lunch filling in the gaps, somewhat clarifying the evasions, because I know what ultimately happened: I know the secret narrative.

THE FIRST THING I GLEANED that afternoon in only twenty minutes: Robert Mallory, on the surface, was one of the most charming people I'd ever met; handsome and intelligent with good manners, likable and sexy. And the other thing I gleaned: he was a total and complete liar. He hadn't proven this yet, it was just a feeling I had— but there was something too rehearsed about him that was the tip-off, even when he tried to cut loose with a joke about an ex-girlfriend also attending Roycemore last term and who he broke up with in June. (It turned out there wasn't an ex-girlfriend who attended Roycemore, because Robert Mallory didn't spend the last term of his junior year at Roycemore either.) Instead, there was a carefulness that bordered on a bogus formality behind what he'd hoped was a casually hip and loose façade—*Hey, I'm just another dude like you guys.* In retrospect, I realize now, Robert made so many slipups that week, so many evasions that bordered on lies, and none of us were paying attention to them because we were so unnerved and delighted by him, blinded by his newness and beauty. Robert felt he needed to make as much of an impression as possible in those initial days because he needed everyone to perceive him as *normal*—that was his plan—but it also seemed to me, and later to Thom Wright, when it was too late, that Robert Mallory was already playing a kind of game with us. And it didn't help that his beauty made *me* feel as if I was collapsing inside—it didn't offer pleasure, it just created confusion and caused a faint, dull pain in my chest. I was the only one, I believed then, who intuitively understood that Robert's handsomeness was going to alter everything around us: I wasn't going to be its only victim, there would be other casualties.

Later, I found out that Susan intuited this as well, but didn't know that day in September she was going to be its main target.

AND THEN THERE WAS the moment as lunch ended when I realized with an almost near certainty where I'd first seen Robert Mallory and why I knew him.

This was also the first time in my young life that I remember going *cold* inside. I'd read about this sensation but I'd never felt it until that moment in the courtyard beneath the Pavilion—it was as if an icy wave had quickly been flushed through my system, freezing my body, jolting me into awareness, and I shivered because I knew *exactly* where I'd seen him.

Robert Mallory, in the late spring of 1980, walked the sloping aisles at the Village Theater in Westwood searching for someone as the opening credits of *The Shining* began.

The boy who had been sitting across from me during lunch that afternoon was the same boy I'd glimpsed in the theater.

I was so dumbstruck by this revelation I couldn't help but blurt out a question.

"Did you see *The Shining* at the Village Theater in Westwood when it first came out?" I asked.

The SHARDS

Robert turned to me, clutching his crumpled schedule, and said with a complete blankness, "No," and nothing else. I would get used to this blank look: detached with a barely concealed insectile urgency whirring behind the innocent gaze.

"Are you sure?" I asked. "I'm positive I saw you there."

"Really?" Robert asked, bewildered, then amused. "Positive?"

"Yeah, I'm almost totally positive I saw you there."

Robert looked at me, now only a little confused. "Why would you remember me there?" he asked. "Did I do something to you—"

"No, no—"

"Did I say something to you—"

"No, no. I just saw you a couple of times in the theater." I became bolder. "You, uh, just made an impression." I left it there.

"I haven't seen that movie," Robert said. "So, yeah, I'm pretty sure it wasn't me."

"Well, I'm almost positive I saw you there," I murmured. "In the theater. On a Saturday."

"No," Robert said. "That wasn't me." There was blankness and detachment, yet his eyes seemed worried, as if I'd found out something about him that he didn't want anyone to know.

"Weird," I murmured. "Very weird."

"Were you, like, following me or something?" he asked.

It was a strange question even though it made sense later, after everything happened, but in that moment the only concern I had: how to process the fact that he was lying and I knew he was. And yet I didn't correct him or ask once more, *Are you sure?* I didn't describe to him what he'd been wearing or that he'd been chewing gum or that he went to the restroom about an hour into the movie and made eye contact with me as he walked up the aisle—but it was the same boy, there was no doubt. The boy I'd fantasized about in a variety of ways since that May morning in 1980 was the boy who turned out to be Robert. And on that first day of school we didn't know anything about how his mother really died, or the rape of his stepsister, the suicide attempt, or Robert Mallory's stint, during what should have been the last term of his junior year at Roycemore, in a mental institution outside Jacksonville, Illinois.

5

THE REST OF THE AFTERNOON happened, I suppose, and then the bells were chiming and the day was over. I say "suppose" because I was so distracted by Robert I remember nothing of the remaining three classes. I suppose I walked the pathways and neared a bungalow and opened a door, I suppose I stepped into an air-conditioned room and placed my textbooks on a desk and scanned the chalkboard, I suppose I glanced outside the tinted windows when someone walked by and everything moved within the orderly mandate Buckley imposed. Nothing comes back to me until I remember meeting Susan beneath the bell tower in front of the library, where she was waiting for Debbie, the two of them were going to drive over to Fiorucci and then Debbie would drop Susan off at her place in Beverly Hills since Thom was at football practice. Susan, on that Tuesday afternoon, seemed slightly melancholy and a semi-fake smile greeted me as I neared her, leaning against the stucco base of the bell tower—and maybe this supposed sadness accentuated how beautiful she was becoming as she moved through seventeen, the gravity of it placing her into another realm of beauty. Beyond us kids were getting picked up by a long line of cars that snaked past the gates and onto Stansbury Avenue, and a train of miniature yellow buses and vans exited the campus in a row, driving past the palm trees that bordered the gates, two of the security guards directing traffic.

"Hey," we said to each other.

"Sure you don't want to join us?" Susan asked.

"What am I gonna buy at Fiorucci?" I said. "I want to get home and work on my book."

"Okay." She sighed, resigned. "You're lame."

"Is everything all right?" I asked. "You seem kind of bummed."

"Bummed?" she asked. "Really? I'm not bummed."

"I thought I noticed something at lunch," I said vaguely.

"I think you're making things up," she said. "I'm definitely not bummed."

"I thought something threw you off," I said, wanting her to comment on Robert Mallory without mentioning him.

"Really? At lunch? No. Why?"

"Okay," I said. "Maybe I'm wrong."

"No, in fact, I've been thinking that I want to throw a party," she said. "That's exactly what I was thinking before you showed up. A party."

"Bummed girls think of throwing parties all the time," I said.

"I'm not bummed, Bret," she said, smiling widely as if to prove this.

"When are you going to throw this party?" I asked.

"You'll see, you'll get an invite," she said, purposefully coy.

"Well, then, *why* are you throwing a party?"

She paused, then cocked her head. "To. Bring. Everybody. Together," she said in a sickly-sweet voice.

"You're scaring me."

In that moment I thought of the supposed dissatisfaction with Thom that Debbie had hinted at and my mind flashed on his hand reaching for Susan's while she reclined on the chaise by the pool the other night and her hesitancy in taking it both then and this morning in the parking lot as we walked toward the bell tower. I wanted to ask about Thom but instead we watched Mr. Collins, a young intense Irishman with the prerequisite fiery green eyes and ginger goatee who taught junior-high English, pass us on his way into the library, neatly suited and holding a briefcase—Mr. Collins was one of the reasons Debbie Schaffer wanted to add a "Hottest Teachers" page to the yearbook. I seemed to be the deterrent as to why Mr. Collins didn't stop and talk to Susan and just nodded at us.

"You know, he hit on me a couple of times last year," Susan said. "He's extremely flirtatious."

"I know," I said. "You told me."

"Sometimes I flirted back," she said. "Did I tell you that?"

"You're crossing boundaries," I said. "You're taking it all in stride."

"I'm the girl in the Police song."

We were playing a game. "I always knew it."

"Sometimes it's not so easy to be the teacher's pet." She said this ruefully.

"And I know how bad girls get." We were quoting the lyrics to the song.

"Do you think I should let him fuck me?" she asked casually.

"What would Thom say?" I thought I was playing along.

She looked away from the library doors Mr. Collins had just disappeared behind. Something hard creased her features. "What do you think he'd say? Jesus, Bret." She was suddenly annoyed.

"Why are you asking me that? What's wrong?"

"Because I'm pretty sure you'd already know what Thom *would say*, so why are you asking me—"

"Hey—"

"I was *joking*, Bret—"

"Maybe I just wonder if you're still happy with Thom," I said. "Debbie thinks you're faking it."

"That's Debbie's story," Susan said. "I don't know. I'm pretty happy. Thom's great. I'm just . . . ansty, I guess."

"So what did you think of the new guy?" I asked.

She froze a little and then, hesitating a moment, asked: "What did *you* think about Robert?"

"I don't know," I said. "He seems . . . nice." I was vague again, as if directing this answer to someone else, the air, a vacant space, the hillsides surrounding the campus. The way she hesitantly said his name made it seem so strangely intimate.

Debbie's BMW pulled up to the curb where we were standing. She was behind the wheel, wearing Wayfarers, a scrunchie in her hair, and Romeo Void blared out of the sunroof. Debbie leaned over the passenger seat as Susan walked away from me and said through the open window, "I'll call *you* later, baby—and I want to talk to *you* and *not* the answering machine," and pouted her lips. I nodded and gave a little wave of reassurance. Susan headed toward the car and reached for the passenger door.

The SHARDS

"Hey," I said.

"Yeah?" She turned around.

"You didn't tell me what you thought of Robert," I said.

She mimicked someone pondering a great mystery, cocking her head again, two fingers at her chin, and then casually tossed off in a mock-British accent: "Well, I thought he was rather electrifying." She looked at me. "Be honest. Didn't you?" And then she slipped into the car and shut the door and Debbie made a quick U-turn and drove through the parking lot and past the gates, leaving me momentarily stunned.

BUT I PUT MY SUNGLASSES ON and headed toward the 450SL and noted in the distance Thom's Corvette and Ryan's Trans Am just a few spaces away from each other, and a wave of melancholy struck me—Thom was with Ryan at practice on Gilley Field, I was not. It was three-thirty and the lot was less than a quarter full, most of the remaining cars belonging to members of the varsity football team. I suddenly wanted to know which car Robert Mallory drove to Buckley that morning and, scanning the lot, landed on a black Porsche 911 and guessed this was his: I hadn't seen it before. Jeff Taylor rolled alongside where I was walking and pressed his head against the driver's window, making a zombie face, the muffled sounds of the B-52s playing from inside the car, and I just nodded coolly back, carrying a couple of textbooks in one hand and my keys in the other. Even though it was only the second week of September autumn skies were arriving and in the very far distance, where the senior parking lot ended at a series of spaces below a concrete wall pushed up against the hillside, everything was bathed in a faded yellow light that announced the changing season, and I noticed Matt Kellner.

Matt was standing by his car, a red Datsun 280ZX, and he'd changed into a T-shirt and tennis shorts for the drive back to Encino—Matt was never comfortable in his Buckley uniform, or clothes in general, and he kept squinting since he faced the sun, engaged in a conversation with a student whose back was to me. Matt was trying to explain something and made a sweeping gesture with his arm, arching it over his head for emphasis. Based on his expression he was in a mild state of confusion, but since Matt always seemed semi-bewildered it didn't mean anything serious to me. And yet there was something different about him—I noticed a bristling anger in his expression as I walked closer—but I was too far away to hear anything Matt was telling the other person. I remembered yesterday in the pool house—Matt naked on his bed—and I twitched, immediately turned on. Horniness destabilized me and I stopped at my car, standing behind it, and took off my sunglasses, breathing in. Matt looked away from whoever was talking to him and then glanced back guiltily. He half-smiled at something the person told him, and then became resigned. I realized the two boys were standing very close to each other, which suggested a pronounced intimacy that surprised me, something almost sexual in nature, and I was struck by the back of the boy talking to Matt, by the snugness of his gray slacks hugging a shapely ass—and even though I was done with Matt (or maybe not) I was suddenly jealous, because the fact that Matt was talking to *anyone* surprised me since he was such a loner, but maybe there were acquaintances I didn't know existed.

I was about to put my books in the Mercedes and start walking toward Matt when I stopped and realized who Matt was talking to.

This was when the person turned their head, startled by a car horn that briefly blared across the parking lot. And I caught the profile.

I stared uncomprehending, and noticed I had gone cold for the second time that day.

I'd only seen Robert Mallory in close-up during lunch. That's why I hadn't recognized him from across the parking lot. In that moment the idea that Robert and Matt would be engaging with one another bordered on the outlandish to me.

What could they have been talking about? Robert had given the impression that he knew no one here. That he hadn't even been to the campus before. So how did he know Matt Kellner? Why was he talking to him? When had he introduced himself?

Robert's hands were on his hips and it seemed like he kept quietly interrupting Matt. This wasn't an angry conversation—there just seemed to be a misunderstanding that both boys were trying to work out, a debate, some kind of disagreement. Robert shook his head as if he was hearing something that disappointed him, and then Matt listened to what Robert was saying and looked at him with suspicion but nodding. I couldn't even begin to imagine the topic of this conversation and landed on maybe Robert had heard that Matt easily scored the best weed available, but anyone in our class would probably have directed Robert to Jeff Taylor and not Matt. Neither of them noticed my presence in the distance from where they were talking.

I opened the door to the Mercedes and quickly sat in the driver's seat. I would have usually pulled the top down but I didn't want Matt or Robert to see me. When I started the engine music blasted— "Don't Touch Me There" by the Tubes from their *Young and Rich* record. I turned the volume down and waited.

Matt and Robert walked away from each other and it seemed, maybe, that something had been clarified, resolved.

Matt got into his Datsun and just sat in the driver's seat looking at something in his lap. I knew the ritual: he'd get stoned while listening to the Specials before heading back to Encino, it would make the ride so much more bearable, and then he'd spend the rest of the afternoon naked in the pool, wasted.

I watched through the windshield as Robert walked over to the black 911 and opened the door. Robert scanned the campus as if he was in a contemplative mood, his handsome profile gazing at the library, and then across the forested hillsides, thinking something through, before slipping into the car.

I had to compose myself—because in that moment I was genuinely upset about this intimate conversation that involved Matt and Robert and which forced me to make a decision. I drove onto Stansbury Avenue, where I pulled over halfway down the block and waited as my car idled against the curb. And when Robert Mallory sped by in the black Porsche I followed him to Valley Vista Boulevard, where he made a left turn, and I started trailing him.

ON VALLEY VISTA I ASSUMED he was going to make a left onto Beverly Glen, which would take him back to Century City, where he supposedly lived with his aunt, but Robert instead turned *right* onto Beverly Glen, which took him five blocks down to Ventura, where I noted he was going to make a left onto the boulevard. I didn't know why Robert was heading into the Valley but in my vague panic I assumed that, right now, it was tied to Matt Kellner and whatever they had talked about in the Buckley parking lot. I was directly behind his car but I really couldn't see him, because the Porsche's rear windshield was so small. There was one car in front of the Porsche when the light turned green and they both slowly wheeled forward to make the left onto Ventura and I was the third car in line and worried that I wasn't going to be able to make the left at this light and would lose Robert. But there was a break in the traffic crossing Ventura and streaming up Beverly Glen and I was able to make the turn with the Porsche as it headed west, curving past the Casa de Cadillac dealership on the corner and coming to a stop at the red light on Van Nuys. I waited there, too.

The light at the intersection of Van Nuys and Ventura turned green and I followed Robert past the Sherman Oaks Newsstand and farther down, at the end of the block, Tower Records (where Sarah Johnson was abducted from the parking lot one night in early January, eight months ago) and the grand Art Deco marquee of the La Reina Theater (*Body Heat* was playing) as the Porsche kept moving down the boulevard. Was Robert heading toward Encino—to Matt Kellner's house on Haskell? Had they made a plan? A date? I imagined showing up at the guesthouse by the pool and confronting them as they smoked Matt's weed in just bathing suits, wet and high, but then realized, embarrassed: confront them about . . . *what*? I was so keyed up—this supposed meeting between Matt and Robert I dreamt up had so disturbed me—my mind was childishly racing around, barely able to focus, vibrating with suspicion and unease. I might have ended it with Matt but I still felt a certain propriety: he was *mine*, even though seemingly no one else desired him the way I did. Robert's handsomeness was also a factor in my building panic— would Matt get sucked into the liar's world and the three faces that operated as one, the fake face of Robert, the face whirring behind the façade, and then the face taking everything in from another angle before figuring out what the best play was? This was what con men did: Robert had lied about being at the Village Theater and this drew me to him immediately, it was a seduction. And if there was no way I wasn't going to get sucked into whatever he was planning and if this was happening to me—the watchful, observant *writer* who now knew what Robert Mallory was capable of—then what could possibly be the outcome for dumb, clueless, vulnerable Matt Kellner? "Going Under" by Devo was playing on the mixtape and I heard, *I know a place where dreams get crushed . . .*

I KEPT FOLLOWING HIM, UNAWARE of how close I was to Robert's car, lost in my fantasies, not realizing I was pressing down on the Porsche, making myself obvious, not enough at a distance, and just past the Sav-On Drugs he suddenly swerved over to the curb to let me pass and I panicked—why had he done that? What was he doing? But when I looked in the rearview mirror I watched as the Porsche immediately pulled away from the curb and started following me, pressing up on the Mercedes, exactly what I had unconsciously been doing to Robert, but now it was an antagonistic gesture, an alpha move. I gripped the wheel and kept driving, pretending to be oblivious, not giving any clues that I knew Robert was now following me, but I was so startled by the abruptness of this maneuver I almost rolled through a red light at Kester Avenue. I managed to brake hard and waited, the black Porsche looming behind me. And that's when I finally realized Robert thought that whoever was in the 450SL had been actually *following* him and wasn't just a clueless driver who was grazing the bumper of his car, and so he decided to switch it around by following them instead: he was playing a game.

As we waited at the light I glanced into the rearview mirror and couldn't see his face through the windshield. The visor was down and only the white Polo shirt and the red-and-gray-striped tie were visible, his head obscured. The light turned green and we started moving together, in unison, the Porsche following too closely, teasing me, and I tried pretending that I didn't notice but it wasn't acceptable by a certain point and it pissed me off that Robert knew it wasn't acceptable and a couple of blocks before Sepulveda I said "Fuck you" and abruptly swung over to an empty spot against the curb in order to let Robert pass.

But the black Porsche pulled over immediately, swerving to the curb behind me as if it knew this was exactly the maneuver I'd planned, and the Porsche timed it perfectly. And now it simply idled, revving its engine, waiting.

I said "Fuck you" again, this time louder, and waited until the traffic started moving forward from the light that had just turned green two blocks behind us. Looking in the side-view mirror, I gauged when I'd be the only car able to merge back onto Ventura, swinging onto the boulevard without giving the Porsche enough room or time to follow, blocked by the oncoming stream of cars.

I gripped the steering wheel and braced myself and then the Mercedes lunged away from the curb.

And yet the Porsche veered in front of the first car in the oncoming traffic, which uselessly blared its horn, and resumed tailing close behind me.

Robert played this reckless move in order to prove something—Robert was tailing the Mercedes to simply fuck with me, to tell whoever was driving it that the dude in the Porsche was *in charge* and that he was going to follow them wherever they went, there would be no escape, because *I am relentless.*

I looked in the rearview mirror again when I came to the light at the intersection of Ventura and Sepulveda, where the interchange of the 405 and the 101 freeways towered above us, but the afternoon sun bathed the Porsche's windshield into an orange block of light and I couldn't see anything inside the car. How long could I keep this up? I wondered. How far could I drive? Tarzana? Woodland Hills? Where was I going to escape Robert, the boy who was fucking with me? Devo became Public Image and I had to lower the volume on the jangly madness of the music in order to concentrate when I noticed the white mass of the Sherman Oaks Galleria across the intersection and decided I wasn't going to keep up with whatever game Robert was playing. I'd become offended by his actions even though I was the one who had started following him, and I looked back at the Porsche and then at the Galleria and when the light turned green I actually revved the car and gunned it, racing across the intersection. A half-block past Sepulveda and beneath the overpass of the 405 was an alley on the right side of Ventura that took you to the multi-level parking lot of the Galleria, and I abruptly swerved into it. I braked hard and glanced quickly in the rearview mirror as the Porsche sped past me beneath the shadow of the freeways.

I WALKED THROUGH the second floor of the May Company, situated at the north side of the mall, and out onto the Galleria's concourse: it was three levels surrounding an open space and the entire ceiling was made of glass, an atrium, where natural light flooded through, giving it a bright center and the faint impression that it was, in fact, an open mall. The carpeting was mauve, and chrome railings lined each level and staircases connected the floors along with two escalators anchored in the center of the mall along with a pair of glass-walled elevators. My first stop was always B. Dalton's—browsing through bookstores calmed me—and as I looked over the latest bestsellers on the front display table I realized whatever annoyance— even anger—I'd felt about Robert Mallory was dissipating because it was just a joke, a guy thing, nothing sinister, I was the instigator, it was all my fault, no big deal, we'd laugh about it later: everything seemed to float away in the fluorescent-lit temple of the bookstore.

In 1981 I was in a major Joan Didion phase, a writer that Mr. Robbins, my English teacher, had introduced us to when he taught *Slouching Towards Bethlehem* our junior year, and soon I was taking almost all of my cues from those essays as well as another collection, *The White Album,* and her Hollywood novel, *Play It As It Lays,* and the particular style and tone she achieved was what I aspired to as a writer, trying to mimic her prose in the fiction I was working on. But in the summer of 1981 I was also reading commercial writers like Martin Cruz Smith and James Clavell, Joseph Wambaugh and Ken Follett, and I was reading *Cujo,* which was the number-one bestseller that week, and my mom's copy of *The White Hotel* by D. M. Thomas, also a bestseller, and I soon realized I had enough to read and there was nothing I really wanted and I was determined to work on my own novel, waiting for me in the bedroom on Mulholland, where I kept notebooks and journals stacked next to an electric Olivetti that helped flesh the novel out, and so I left the bookstore and took the escalator to see what was playing at the Pacific 4 multiplex even though I wasn't sure I wanted to watch a movie that afternoon. When I got there I realized I'd already seen everything: *An American Werewolf in London, Private Lessons, Heavy Metal, Hell Night.*

IT WAS FOUR. Schools had been out for an hour and yet there weren't a lot of kids around. This was the first day back for many of us, and it might have been too early in the season for kids to head immediately to the Galleria once classes were done for the day. Any of them who were at the Galleria seemed to be at the food court, which was the main hangout because of its proximity to the arcade and the multiplex. The northern side of the food court started with Chipyard Cookies and then passed along to places like Hot Dog on a Stick and Kaboby, Mexican Dan's and Perry's Pizza, and ended with an Orange Julius. (A McDonald's and Taco Bell were located on the second floor of the mall.) That Tuesday mostly teenage girls in pairs were dotting the red-topped tables on the overhang that looked out on the mall, private-school babes from Westlake and Oakwood, pretty and seventeen and SoCal tan, all of them in their uniforms and lounging under the atrium as the lingering afternoon sun lit the space. There was a hushed quality that day even though this was a world made up of adolescence—teens worked the food court as well as congregated there—but the electric rowdiness that hummed through the mall's social scene on busy afternoons and weekends was absent. Everything was quiet and subdued. I'd turned away from the ticket booth of the Pacific 4 when I suddenly realized I was hungry since I hadn't eaten my lunch (Robert had) and my stomach was growling. I wandered away to the railings and looked down at the ground floor of the mall three stories below me—no one was there. I glanced up at the other side of the mall and scanned the vendors at the food court and nothing really appealed to me—my scan confirmed this. And when I was about to turn away from the railing I froze and involuntarily gripped it.

Robert Mallory was leaning against the Swensen's Ice Cream counter.

—

The SHARDS

HE WAS TALKING TO the lone girl working there: generically pretty and blonde and wearing the Swensen's antique uniform, which made her look as if she was presiding over an old-fashioned ice-cream parlor. The first thing I noticed: she was smiling widely—it was completely genuine, almost dazed.

Robert's head was cocked raffishly, as if he was doing an impression, saying something that made her laugh.

I imagined she was trying not to look at him in awe as she handed Robert the ice-cream cone he'd ordered: one large scoop, pink. He paid for it and she just stared at him as he walked away pocketing the change. Robert seemed to know what effect he had on the girl: judging from the expression on his face he was pleased. He just ambled along the food court, licking the ice-cream cone, and I realized he had followed me into the Galleria. This was never his destination—I was the reason. He had turned around on Ventura Boulevard—made a U-turn—after my car dived into the alley, and I was almost certain he'd driven through the parking structure until he found the Mercedes and slid in next to it. When I left the mall this was confirmed: the black 911 Porsche was parked directly beside the 450SL on the lot's deserted third level, where there was only a beige van parked in the distance.

Robert stopped, looked around the food court, and seemed to make his decision on what direction to head based on where the most girls were hanging: this was the seating area. Two girls passed him as he shuffled across the orange-tiled floors and then clutched each other, giggling, whipping their heads back to gawk at the hot guy in the Buckley uniform eating an ice-cream cone. It played out as an almost-parody of teenage lust. He wasn't oblivious to it either when it happened again with another pair of girls—he looked over his shoulder when he heard their laughter and smiled and just continued walking in an aimless way through the food court, where he passed a table of four girls and confidently ignored them as they all leaned in and whispered to each other, their eyes following him. There was no hint of the hesitant outsider at lunch beneath the shadow of the Pavilion and I had an awful premonition about Susan Reynolds, and what would happen to Thom Wright, and all the potential drama involved, ruining senior year, but I also hoped in that moment that it was just the writer imagining this and that I was worrying over nothing. Robert made it to the steps of the seating area, the ice-cream cone half finished, casually checking the tables out. It all seemed so innocent.

I was standing behind a column across the mall, watching him. My heart was actually beating fast and I felt flushed, semi-dizzy from Robert's presence and my hunger. I was also aware with a faint embarrassment that I'd been reduced to this—hiding behind a column, in the Galleria, staking out the new boy, hoping I wouldn't be seen.

He walked down the steps into the seating area and just wandered around until two girls sitting at a table were brazen enough to ask him something. Robert stopped, pretending to be surprised by their attention, and leaned in, suddenly inquisitive. He listened to what they said and then laughed, nodding, which caused the girls to become animated. They talked for only a moment and then Robert gestured he had to move on, and held up the hand not holding the ice-cream cone to show them his watch. He walked away from the table and one of the girls mock-fainted—and when I witnessed that, the dizziness suddenly evaporated and I became slightly angry. Three girls sitting at the far edges of the food court motioned him over to their table, and he strode to it, grinning lazily, lapping at the ice-cream cone—and I realized he was doing it so he could make them focus on his mouth, his lips, his tongue. The girls made gestures at each other, probably introducing themselves, and Robert nodded, listening as they talked, and he answered their questions in a friendly, gracious way that was undeniably, even from where I stood, flirtatious. It became apparent that Robert didn't need to hit on anyone, because he had an innate confidence—he wasn't a creepy stalker—and he was never rebuffed or rejected by any of the girls he chatted with in the food court. He never approached anyone—in fact the opposite would happen, because the girls said hi, the girls waved him over to where they sat, the girls made the first move, while he innocently licked the pink ice-cream cone, reducing it to a small pale mound. The girls were delighted by Robert's presence and his boyish nonchalance and they were almost swooning as he walked away from them, their faces collapsing into mock grimaces of love-struck pain and longing.

The SHARDS

I slowly moved from behind the column when Robert stepped out of the seating area and noticed two girls he started following toward the Time Out arcade and then the three of them disappeared into the darkness of its entrance. I realized I hadn't been breathing and finally exhaled loudly, a faint pang repeating in my chest.

I would have found a way to intervene if I'd known how dangerously ill Robert Mallory actually was. But I didn't know this yet.

I HEADED TO LICORICE PIZZA and stared at a display in the front window for the new Rolling Stones record, *Tattoo You,* and there was a poster for *Belladonna,* the Stevie Nicks album that had been released in June, as well as posters still up for the *Endless Love* soundtrack, which had the number-one song all summer, as well as the soundtrack for *Arthur,* and there was also a poster for the ELO album *Time*—a reminder to call my dad's ticket broker and get seats for the concert at the Forum. I didn't feel like going into the record store and instead walked over to the Gap, next to the entrance of Robinson's, which anchored the south end of the mall—I wasn't hungry anymore or maybe I was too stunned to notice. *Down under where the lights are low*—the Devo song was still in my head as I stared into the Gap, not knowing where to go or what to do. I'm not sure how long I stood in front of the store, dazed and immobile, trying to formulate a plan for the rest of the afternoon and that night, when I realized a floating presence in the near-empty mall and I reoriented myself: Robert Mallory materialized behind me, his image reflected in the window I was staring into. I don't know why I wasn't afraid or didn't recoil. I simply turned and faced him.

"Oh, hey," Robert said, feigning surprise at seeing me. "I thought that was you."

"Hey," I said, playing along, keeping everything even.

"And that was *you,* right?" he asked grinning. "Following me?"

"I wasn't following you," I said, innocently. "I was heading to the Galleria and I happened to be behind you, I guess." I pretended to be confused. "You were in the Porsche, right?"

"I know, yeah, that was me," he said. "I was just fucking with you."

He reached out and lightly punched me on the shoulder. I refrained from flinching. "I don't like being followed."

"Yeah?" I asked. "You don't like being followed?"

"Yeah," he said, looking around the mall. "It freaks me out."

"What are you doing here?" I asked, trying to sound natural.

"I need to buy some clothes," he said, gesturing at the Robinson's entrance, and with the mock formality of a game-show host asked, "And what brings *you* to the Galleria on this Tuesday afternoon?" Without waiting for me to answer he added, lowering his voice, almost conspiratorially, "There are a lot of hot girls here."

I floundered and landed on: "I was going to see a movie."

"Oh yeah?" he asked, briefly animated. "What movie?"

"Well, turns out I've seen them all, so—"

"Maybe *The Shining*?" he asked in a fake ghoulish voice, raising his eyebrows, grinning wolfishly.

I had to admit this disarmed me—the fact that he brought this up made me trust him. It was part of the seduction—he was a con man. I smiled even though I didn't want to. "You sure you weren't there?" I felt helpless asking this—but the desire overrode rationality.

"Dude, you've got to let that go—"

"But I'm pretty sure I saw you, Robert." I uselessly stood my ground.

"I might have been in L.A. but I haven't seen that movie," he said, bewildered by my insistence. "Was I that unforgettable?" he asked, mimicking someone fey, a pansy, lifting a limp wrist. But then he was grinning like a movie star, and though the question was supposed to make fun of me it was said without any real malice. It was just because his handsomeness was so unnerving that briefly suggesting something about me that he didn't know—that I might be gay and desired him—was painful. And yet the pain emboldened me.

"What were you talking to Matt Kellner about?" I asked. "Do you know him?"

"Who?" He appeared to be genuinely confused.

"Matt. Kellner," I said. "You were talking to him in the parking lot after school."

"Oh. Yeah?" Robert paused. "You saw that?"

"Yeah," I said. "As I was walking to my car."

"Are you guys . . . friends?" He asked this with a barely pronounced slyness.

"Is that an innuendo?" I asked and realized I sounded too defensive. "Yeah, we're friends."

"Is that a *what*?" Robert asked, again confused.

"Nothing, forget it."

"Innuendo about?"

"Were you implying something?" I asked. "About me and Matt?"

"Implying?" he asked, and then changed direction. "Why didn't you come over and say hi?"

"Didn't want to interrupt the conversation," I said, trying to act casual. "It seemed like you guys were really into it, having a deep talk about something."

The three faces suddenly appeared, lured by me, and I saw the manic cycling behind Robert's eyes. There was the mask, and then there was the dangerously ill person behind the mask that we didn't know about yet and then there was the face that was looking at the scene from a wide angle, a master shot, trying to figure out what would calm this nervous and inquisitive boy standing in front of him.

"Yeah . . ." he started haltingly. "We have a . . . vague family connection."

"Really?" I said. "A family connection?"

"Yeah, but he didn't know anything about it," Robert said. "My aunt's ex worked with his dad. Matt seems like a pretty confused guy."

"He's just very easygoing, laid back," I said lamely.

"So, wait, Thom is Susan Reynolds's boyfriend?" he asked. "They're seeing each other?"

Something dropped in me. "Yeah," I said, suddenly freezing.

"How long?" he asked, staring.

"What?" I asked, staring back at him, shocked that he'd be asking me this.

"How long have they been dating?" he asked. "How long have they been together?"

"About two years," I said in a hollow voice.

He took this in, nodded to himself while scanning the mall, contemplating the information. "So," he started, looking back at me, "she's serious." He paused. "About him." It wasn't a question.

Actually I wanted to say Thom was more serious than Susan, but I didn't say anything, just nodded my head slowly affirming this. I didn't want to prolong the conversation but I also couldn't stop myself.

"Why are you asking me this?" I said. "They've been serious for two years now."

He shrugged. "She's hot," he said. "Quite the little honey."

I remember those words and the way he said them exactly. I had never heard a girl referred to in that way: *the little honey.*

"Yeah, she's very pretty," I said. I felt like I couldn't breathe. I had to get away from Robert Mallory and everything emanating from his presence. "Okay, well, I gotta go."

"Yeah." He thumbed the entrance to Robinson's. "Gotta get some threads."

"Okay, yeah," I said. "Well, okay, I gotta go."

"Are you all right?" he suddenly asked with a concern that felt— like everything else about him—borrowed, fake.

"Oh yeah, yeah," I said. "I'm fine. See you tomorrow."

Robert wasn't ready to say goodbye yet. He was staring at me, try- ing to understand the individual in front of him —was I a friend, was I an enemy, could I be trusted, would he have to play games with me, what was my story exactly. He wasn't offended or angry—just curious. I made a motion with my hands: *Is there something else?*

"I just figured something out about you," he said, nodding slowly. "Yeah, I just figured something out about you, Bret."

I tried to smile. "Yeah? What did you just figure out?"

He paused for emphasis. "When you talk to me you're really talk- ing to yourself, dude," he murmured and then quickly smiled as if this was a casual and natural observation even though it was clearly meant to unmoor me—it was a tease. But I laughed politely, because I had nothing left to say. Confused, I immediately walked away from him and thought I was going to pass out from hunger and went straight to McDonald's on the second floor of the mall and ordered a Big Mac and large fries and ate them ravenously while sitting alone. When I headed out of the Galleria about fifteen minutes later I saw Robert

The SHARDS

Mallory in the deserted mall, just a lone figure with a blank expression, a handsome teenage boy in a private-school uniform, standing in front of a particular storefront on the first floor and staring intently into the glass windows: it was the mall's pet shop, called Vince's Pets.

AT THE EMPTY HOUSE ON MULHOLLAND I waited for Ryan Vaughn to call me but he never did. So I called the house in Northridge and hung up when his father answered—I realized I'd need to schedule with Ryan during the day so he'd know when to pick up my calls, though I'm sure he'd want to know why I didn't just ask George if I might speak to his son—*Please, don't be a pussy*, I heard Ryan admonish me yet again. I couldn't really concentrate on anything because of Robert Mallory—lust mixed with dread—and I ignored two phone calls from Debbie and zoned out in the Jacuzzi, muttering to myself, and then took a scalding shower. *When you talk to me you're really talking to yourself, dude,* repeated in my mind as I sat at my desk, the Olivetti humming in front of me, while I stared out the bay window at the San Fernando Valley beyond the backyard framed by eucalyptus trees. I finally shook off the stupor and was rereading the pages I'd typed when the phone rang. It was after nine and I thought it was Ryan and since I knew he would never leave a message I picked up. *Happy Days* and then *Laverne and Shirley* had played, and now *Three's Company*, all with the sound turned off because they were reruns due to the recent Writers Guild strike. Instead of Ryan I heard another voice.

"Bret, it's Steven Reinhardt," the voice said. "I hope it's not too late but I have Terry Schaffer calling."

"What?" I asked, confused. "You mean Debbie."

"Um, no, Terry's calling you," Steven said. "Hold, please." And then I heard: "Hey, Bret, it's Terry." He said this in a casual way, as if Terry calling at nine o'clock on a school night was cool, and immediately asked in a low voice, "What are you wearing?"

I was shocked but used to it. "Very funny," I said, blushing. I could have told him I was wearing only jockey shorts but decided against it, afraid of where that might take the conversation. "Just joking, just kidding," he said. I heard ice clinking in a glass and noted the nasal quality of Terry's voice as he commanded something to Billie, the golden retriever, who barked lightly twice in the room Terry was in, and then quieted down. He asked, "How are you?" He sounded smoothly professional, on top of things, despite the alcohol and what I supposed was cocaine.

"I'm fine, I'm fine," I said. I stood up from the desk and began nervously pacing the room. My face was reddened and I had to contain the wavering in my voice. I did this by lowering it. I couldn't figure out why Terry was calling me.

"What are you doing?" he asked.

"I'm . . ." I stammered. "I'm doing homework." I shrugged to no one else in the room.

A pause. "Well, I hope I'm not interrupting—"

"No, no, not at all, Terry—"

"Look, I heard that Liz accosted you the other night," Terry said. "And I'm very sorry about that. Steven told me. I'm mortified."

I was suddenly relieved. "Oh, it's fine," I said. "I hope she's okay."

"Well, we all want her to get better," Terry said diplomatically. "But she has to want that herself. And she doesn't seem to think there's a problem." He paused. "As of yet."

I stayed silent. I didn't know what to say.

"Steven told me you were very gentle and understanding with her," Terry said. "And I appreciate that."

"She didn't really accost me . . ." I murmured.

"And I'd like to show you my appreciation," he said, not listening. "I'd like to get to know you a little better. Debbie tells me you're a writer. I didn't know this. She says you're working on a book."

Everything—all the tension—dissolved. I was flattered. My face was burning.

"Would you be interested in writing scripts?" he asked casually.

I heard the clinking of ice in the pause that followed.

"Yeah, sure," I said. This suggestion—I rewrote it as an offer—immediately excited me.

"You like movies, right?" he asked. I could hear the flirtation in his tone.

"Yeah, definitely."

"Well, I'm always looking for fresh voices," Terry said. "It's an exciting time for young people," he offered blandly. "But their stories aren't told well enough. Slasher flicks, sex comedies. Dumb stuff."

"Yeah," I said though I liked sex comedies and slasher movies. "I guess."

"Maybe you can come up with something," he said. "If you have any ideas maybe we could meet." He paused. "And you could pitch me something."

"Yeah, sure, Terry," I said. "That would be great."

"Okay," he said. "And again—thanks about Liz."

There was a pause that indicated the conversation wasn't over yet and then Terry lightly cleared his throat and said, "Deborah doesn't need to know about this."

"About what?"

He stopped, as if he had overstepped a boundary, as if he was making a mistake.

"About me calling you," he said, clarifying. "You don't need to tell Debbie."

"Oh, yeah," I said. "Oh, right, of course. Yeah." At first I didn't know why Terry thought this was important but I went along with it. I didn't want to displease him. And then I wondered if Steven Reinhardt was on the phone, listening in.

"Yeah?" Terry asked, relieved. "That's cool?"

"Oh yeah, yeah," I said. "I won't say anything."

"Good night, Bret," Terry Schaffer said.

There was a click and then the phone call was over.

I WAS TOO keyed up to concentrate on homework or read the Stephen King book or watch lame sitcoms I'd already seen, so I looked through a couple of straight porn tapes I occasionally jerked off to that I'd bought from Jeff Taylor. I played them on the Betamax beneath the TV directly across from the king-sized bed, where I'd prop myself up against the pillows masturbating while under the spell of a young Joey Silvera, who had a lean and handsome face with wide brown eyes and a slightly sleazy mustache but with an idealized body—tall and bronzed, a flat stomach and abs, a tan line and a big cock with a brown bush. The three tapes Silvera starred in were from the late 1970s:

Babyface, Extremes and my favorite, *Expensive Tastes,* where a group of men, along with a woman, plot and execute a series of rapes. It was directed by a woman, which might be why Joey Silvera was, at least to me, so idealized as a physical object—he's by far the hottest guy in the movie and whoever was shooting this knew it. There's a scene where one of the rapists, all in ski masks, sucks Joey off during the gang rape of Silvera's own girlfriend and it was agonizingly erotic for me when I first watched it even though we find out later that it's actually a *woman,* and that Joey Silvera is actually part of the group as well: this is just a ritual that turns them all on and the masked, supposedly male, cohort sucking him off gives Silvera a reason *not* to go to the police because he's too ashamed to admit he was sucked off by a dude—he argues to his raped girlfriend, seemingly anguished. I masturbated that night to images of Joey—there were two that almost always got me off—and then took a Valium, which moved me into a fast and dreamless sleep but not before I fantasized about Terry Schaffer and my future. I knew he wanted something from me and there would probably be a *quid pro quo* I'd have to deal with when the moment came but I'd worry about that when it happened. I was seventeen and the future had opened up considerably that night— Terry Schaffer wanted me to write a script for him. There was a way out of the trap, I realized. This was an escape from the pantomime. Terry's call confirmed I had plans, I was mapping out my own destiny, I was a writer.

6

THAT WEEK IN SEPTEMBER passed in a blur—Wednesday, Thursday, Friday remained hazy and indistinct. We all followed the rules and acted accordingly, wore our uniforms and attended classes, arrived at school and wheeled our cars into parking spaces and walked across the pavement to the bell tower and entered the campus beyond it, but I was self-imprisoned in my own world, creating a new narrative for myself, even as I tried to be positive and upbeat. For example, that week I got used to the idea, the belief, that whatever happened to the statue of the Griffin was a harmless prank that simply took a ghoulish turn unintended, and that whoever held the flashlight in the courtyard of the library on that Monday night realized things had gotten out of hand and regretted it, and I believed that Robert Mallory was sane and no less stable than anyone else in the senior class, and that we were all innocent and safe, protected by privilege and linked together by status and class and our parents' ambitions for us. But I also had increasingly *not* been a part of Buckley and I was resisting the integration of myself into the stream of high-school life. I felt a profound disconnection for the first time that lightly touched everything I came into contact with. And I realized I was no longer the tangible participant in not only the life of Buckley but in the outside world as well. Nothing seemed to affect me. I had become numb.

FOR EXAMPLE, I didn't care that Ronald Reagan had been elected president last November—this meant absolutely nothing to me at seventeen and politics have stayed that way for the rest of my life.

I'd paid attention when he was shot in March, returning to his limousine after a speaking engagement at the Washington Hilton, by John Hinckley, who had committed the assassination attempt to impress the actress Jodie Foster, but like everything else it didn't really register. It was empty excitement. I knew the details but didn't attach anything to them: feelings or meaning.

For example, I might have been too young to fully appreciate John Lennon's artistry as a Beatle or a solo performer but his murder at the hands of a deranged fan didn't have the same shock effect on me as it did to my older classmates and last December I *pretended* it upset me far more than it actually had and acted appropriately melodramatic, playing *Double Fantasy* more than I wanted to—I always thought it was mediocre even though devastated mourners assured me there was greatness in it now that Lennon was dead.

For example, that following January of 1981 I drifted through a trip to New Orleans with my father and Thom Wright to attend the Super Bowl though I had no interest in football (Thom Wright did, of course, being the Griffins' quarterback) and I didn't even know what teams were playing against each other in the Louisiana Superdome that Sunday afternoon. Thom's dad, Lionel, had flown in from New York and the four of us stayed at the Ritz-Carlton, where I shared a room with Thom, and though I was alienated enough not to be able to tell you what teams played (it was the Oakland Raiders versus the Philadelphia Eagles) I can remember with the intensity of a brightly lit snapshot Thom changing in front of me in the suite we shared and briefly glimpsing him naked, coming out of the bathroom in a Ritz-Carlton robe after taking a shower, and just idly talking to me as he slipped the robe off, turning demurely so I wouldn't see his dick when he slipped on a pair of jockey shorts as I watched the white cotton stretch over his perfect ass—I had seen a variation of this many times in the boys' locker room at Buckley but it seemed so much more intimate in a hotel suite far from Los Angeles—it felt, just very briefly, something could have happened, though I wasn't delusional enough to pretend my desire would be reciprocated by Thom. But I remember that image more than the game itself, where we sat high above the field in a VIP booth complete with a full bar and where Thom and I ordered shrimp cocktails and were allowed to drink Michelobs and a number of men came up to say hello to both my father and Lionel Wright. The Iran hostage crisis had just ended—there was a pregame ceremony honoring this—and the Superdome had been wrapped in a giant yellow ribbon to show solidarity with the hostages (the country had been strewn with yellow ribbons for what seemed like years) and yet I was more interested in the perfection of Thom Wright's ass than anything else on that trip. Though I remember we met the NBC anchorman Dick Enberg, and then Bryant Gumbel, who would be interviewing me on the *Today* show four years later, the summer *Less Than Zero* was published. I was numb to everything except for a flash of nudity in an anonymous hotel suite.

For example, celebratory events that meant something to the world at large failed to ignite my interest: The royal wedding between Prince Charles and Lady Diana happened in July and I never watched a minute of it as the ceremony aired across the globe—Susan and Debbie were hooked to the spectacle. The lack of engagement from the no longer tangible participant, I noted, was vast and spreading. Sex and novels and music and movies were the things that made life bearable—not friends, not family, not school, not social scenes, not interactions—and that was the summer when I watched *Raiders of the Lost Ark* every other week but barely had dinner with my separated parents even twice. I had no stakes in the real world—why would I? It wasn't built for me or my needs or desires. And I was reminded of this almost constantly since I was locked in a teenage horniness skyrocketing into the stratosphere and constantly activated by things I found erotic—and yet could never have. This was my only point of reference. This was what contributed to the no longer tangible participant.

MAYBE I DON'T REMEMBER that first week because I realized that senior year was going to become a struggle and that I'd need to resort to a kind of cunning to get through it and this distracted me further from my day-to-day reality. But it was really just a quiet week: students were adjusting to a new year back, and Buckley made it easy for everyone—it pampered you and made you feel safe and that you not only mattered but were important. The days just evaporated. I only went to classes. I hadn't joined the Buckley literary magazine (two issues a year) or *The Buckley Gazette* (biweekly) and there was an endless list of extracurricular activities I never neared: the drama club, the backpacking club, the biology club, the dance club, the cooking club, among dozens of others. I remained the proud under-achiever. The things that happened the first week that I remember had nothing to do with me—there was fallout from a racist skit that had been performed by Doug Furth and David O'Shea in Señora Ipolita's Spanish III class; we found out that the Algebra teacher, Mrs. Susskind, was getting a divorce; one of the bus drivers died at her home from a heart attack; there'd been a fire in a utility shed on the sports field. I also remember that Robert Mallory didn't join us for lunch at the center table beneath the Pavilion that first week—he was testing out other groups, sizing up their possibilities, and it also seemed to me as if he was purposefully staying away from Susan Reynolds. I glimpsed Robert eating with Matt Kellner on that Thursday but neither of them was saying anything to the other: Matt was wearing a Walkman, sunning himself, eyes shut; Robert cross-legged next to him reading a paperback. It wasn't until Debbie demanded that we hang out Friday night at my place with Thom and Susan that I suddenly woke up, and paid attention to the reality of my situation: I had to get un-numb, I had to play the part better.

BUT DEBBIE HAD TO MOVE the get-together with Susan and Thom from Friday to Saturday because a rockabilly band called the Stray Cats was playing at the Roxy on Friday. I had no desire but not because I didn't like the band: we'd listened to their U.K. import produced by Dave Edmunds a lot that summer before their American debut was released the following year. Even though the song "Rock This Town" was being played on KROQ the Stray Cats didn't have a record deal in the United States and I didn't go to the Roxy that Friday night—even though Debbie promised me there'd be a lot of celebrities and we'd hang out upstairs after the show—because this gave me the opportunity to see Ryan Vaughn instead. I didn't call Ryan that Thursday afternoon I found out about the Stray Cats concert because he was at football practice and instead waited for the allotted time we'd agreed upon earlier that day, when we were having lunch, and he picked up the phone at seven, amused that I was so prompt. I'd hoped Ryan would want to get together and spend Friday night at the house on Mulholland with me, but there was "something" the following morning with his mom and dad and younger brother he couldn't get out of and he didn't tell me what it was and I didn't ask—I imagined it was religious, church-related. "What about Saturday night?" he asked. "Your parents are out of town, right?" This suggestion put me into an automatic erotic trance. "I could be there around six . . ." He trailed off. And then I realized that the plans with Debbie and Susan and Thom had been moved because of the concert so I invited Ryan to come for dinner and hang out with us on Saturday night and when everyone left he could stay over and the two of us could spend Sunday together, maybe he'd even sleep over on Sunday night as well. Since there were no new movies that weekend Westwood wasn't really an option, so we could spend all day lying by the pool. How did that sound?

"That's a little . . . ambitious," Ryan said cautiously, as if he was glancing around the room he was standing in. "That's a little too much. And I don't really want to hang out with that group." He added this quietly, in a low voice.

"You like me, you like Thom," I said. "It would only be for dinner."

"Thom's okay," Ryan said, noncommittal.

"He thinks you're great," I said, trying to soften his hardness.

"He's not that smart."

"That's not true."

"Maybe Sunday. We can hang out." Ryan paused. "I want to see you. I think about you."

"I think about you, too."

"But for this to work . . . uh, requires a certain amount of, um, subterfuge," he said slyly, as if this was a game we were playing. "Do you understand?"

"Why do you sound like a spy from a 1940s movie?" I asked.

"I'm just . . . practical," he said. I liked the subtle sexiness in his voice.

"Yeah," I said, nodding to no one, alone in my bedroom. "I get it, but—"

"I gotta go," he said. *"Talk. To. Ya. Later."* He made a reference to the Tubes song that had been popular earlier that year. There was a click.

I thought I had fucked up. In my frustration I was going to cancel Saturday night with Debbie and Thom and Susan and then call Ryan back, when Thom suddenly called and told me that instead of going for sushi at the Japanese place in the Glen Centre, about a mile down the road from the house on Mulholland (I didn't even know that had been part of the plan), Susan and Debbie decided to order pizza from Santo Pietro's—and that's what we'd be doing Saturday night. "But *why* are we doing this?" I blurted out, frustrated. "What do you mean?" Thom asked. "What is this get-together about?" I wailed. Thom said that Susan wanted to talk to us about something, a party she was throwing—didn't I know about this, she thought it would be fun if we all planned it together, that's all, what's your problem? "Is everything okay, Bret?" Thom's calm, almost plaintive question, filled with an innate sense of care, made me realize that everything was, in fact, fine and that I actually did want to see everyone, my friends, Saturday night and I was relieved they were coming over. I'd deal with Ryan on Sunday, I hoped.

And on that Friday night I typed up five pages of *Less Than Zero* (though these pages wouldn't appear in the published version) and then heated up the enchiladas Rosa had prepared for me, finished reading *Cujo* (the kid died—I was impressed and shocked; Stephen King had balls) and then watched Joey Silvera in a scene from *Expensive Tastes.* The two new premieres on the Z Channel were *Flash Gordon* and Roman Polanski's *Tess,* and I'd already seen both in theaters last December. I couldn't sleep and I ended up driving through the canyons while playing a song I'd become haunted by, B-Movie's "Nowhere Girl," which always put me in a strange and heightened mood, a kind of spell, I entered a film—it was a piano-driven minor-key New Wave song, faraway and ethereal, doomy and lightly propulsive, and it would aid in whipping me along the desolate streets in the Mercedes convertible, making the loneliness of my world seem thrilling, something to embrace and covet. The emptiness and the numbness I felt were *feelings* whenever I heard the song, and the song also applied to Julie Selwyn and wherever she had disappeared to that summer, twirling on the dance floor at the Seven Seas, in a video, fading into the strobe. I drove late that night listening to "Nowhere Girl" over and over while I traced Mulholland and a deserted Sepulveda, zooming up Beverly Glen and back to the lit house on the cliff side overlooking the Valley, until I was tired enough to finally fall asleep and dropped onto the bed exhausted, ignoring the messages Debbie left on the answering machine whenever her calls awakened me in the middle of the night.

IT WAS FOUR O'CLOCK on that Saturday in September when I heard the doorbell. Since Debbie and Thom and Susan weren't coming over until six I walked to the foyer with mild trepidation—for a flash I imagined hopefully that it was Ryan—that he had changed his mind, he'd come to surprise me—and the fantasy was momentarily exciting until I thought maybe it was the Trawler, someone wearing a black ski mask in broad daylight clenching a knife in a gloved fist, not caring, waiting for me to open the door, slavering, I was next. But when I looked through the viewing hole I saw Debbie, alone, wearing Wayfarers, impatiently standing there, grim-faced, the BMW in the driveway behind her. I paused before opening the door, realizing something was wrong. I wondered where Susan and Thom were. Debbie rang the doorbell again, startling me. I opened the door. Debbie didn't say anything as she passed across the foyer and into the kitchen, where she pulled a pink can of Tab out of the refrigerator and then opened the sliding glass door and walked out to one of the chaises arranged by the pool. Shingy followed her and was jumping around excitedly as she just sat on the edge of the chaise, ignoring the dog, and contemplated the blue, still water through her sunglasses.

"O-kay," I said to myself as she lit a clove cigarette, not looking back at the house.

Debbie expected me to follow her but I was resentful that she'd arrived on Mulholland earlier than she told me. I had planned to work out in the makeshift gym next to the garage and then jerk off, go for a swim and reread what I had written yesterday before Thom and Susan and Debbie arrived. But that was not going to happen, I realized sourly as I stared at Debbie through the sliding glass doors, knowing she was in a bad mood and I was the target, and I resented it. Instead of going outside and playing her version of the scene I walked through the kitchen and down the hallway to my bedroom. I turned on the TV and sat at my desk thinking things through. The door leading out to the deck was open and there were no sounds coming from the yard, which contributed to the annoying suspense of the moment. I waited fifteen minutes, until I finally heard footsteps on the veranda leading to my room. I realized futilely this had been a contest that I won. Debbie walked across the deck, sunglasses pushed up against her forehead, Shingy following, still curious and excited by her presence. Debbie sounded confused, low-level angry. "Hello? Bret? *Hello?*"

"I'm in here," I called out. She finally stood in the doorway but didn't come in. I remained at my desk, in front of the typewriter.

"Why are you in here?" she asked. "Why didn't you come outside?"

"I thought you . . . wanted to be alone," was how I played it.

This ticked her off. "Why would I come over here if I wanted to be alone?"

"You're early," I said. "Is something wrong?"

"You're not happy to see me?" she asked. "You're not excited to see me? You're asking your girlfriend if something's *wrong*?"

"You're just early," I shrugged. "I wasn't expecting you until six."

"We've got to clear something up," she said. "I need to know where you are."

"Where I am?" I pretended to be confused even though I knew exactly what she was getting at.

"Do you like me?"

This came out hard and fast, more of a declaration than a question, and I didn't have to act surprised because I legitimately was.

"Very much," I said, stunned. "But if you're asking that you must think I don't and that's a problem."

She wasn't convinced but she softened, and from where she was standing she looked around the room as if searching for something. Rosa didn't come on Saturdays, so my bed was unmade and a T-shirt and a pair of tennis shorts and a towel were strewn next to it. And then she saw what she was looking for: the answering machine blinking on the nightstand next to the bed. Debbie shifted her stance and looked at me accusingly. I knew the messages were hers because I heard Debbie leaving them at midnight and one o'clock and two-fifteen, but I hadn't picked up, just groaned, pushing a pillow over my head, and fell back asleep. But the blinking light proved to her that I hadn't played them yet and therefore confirmed I hadn't heard her when, in fact, I actually had as she was leaving the messages. She bit her lip, contemplating something.

"How serious are you?" she asked.

"Why are you asking me this?"

"Because you've been a frigging zombie this past week."

"No, I haven't," I said automatically. And then, realizing, "I'm sorry."

"A zombie. A fucking zombie. I really don't know what's wrong with you."

She realized she was being uselessly harsh, so she softened again. "Talk to me." She paused. "I need you to be honest with me."

"Honest about what?"

"I need your reassurance. No bullshit."

"You need my reassurance?" I asked. "About what?"

"About us," she said. "God, you're such a zombie."

"You're just saying things," I said. "You're just talking. None of it's making sense. You need my reassurance?"

"I need your reassurance, Bret, about us."

For a very brief moment I was on the verge of admitting something to her—a truth, my real feelings. But then I realized with an acid awareness that I didn't want to complicate the year because everything had been set up, the narrative was in play, we were already enacting our roles; there was nowhere else to go—and I wanted to keep hiding the real Bret. I intuited this year was going to be a bummer in so many ways that I actually needed the pretend safety of Debbie's structured world so I could get to June. In that moment it was simply the easiest path: there wasn't another alternative. I was going to be the attentive boyfriend. The pragmatist was going to try and become the tangible participant once again. "I really like you," I told her—and this was true, this was real and not a lie. "You know how I am," I said, shrugging.

"Susan says you have secrets."

"That's just a game we play."

"Are we playing a game?"

"I'm not playing a game."

"You're either with me or you're not," she said.

"I'm with you."

"I don't want to trap you but I need to know."

"You're amazing. You're beautiful. I'm just distracted. I'm just out of it, you know that—"

"I hate asking this, Bret. I hate being put in this position—"

"You're putting yourself in this position—"

"—because you should just, I don't know, be into me, Bret. Or not. Maybe you're into someone else. Are you into someone else?"

"No, no—"

"Because if you are just tell me."

"I swear I'm not."

She stared at me—the anger was replaced with longing.

"Hey, baby," I said. "Come here."

She pouted, it was both real and exaggerated, like so many aspects of Debbie, and then she walked over to me and automatically slid onto my lap. I wrapped my arms around her tightly in an embrace.

"You know I get distracted," I said softly. "I get lost in my own world. I get lost in my book. You've known this about me since we were kids—how spacy I can get. You've always known this about me."

"You just seemed so totally spacy this last week," she said quietly. "We've barely hung out." She kissed me. I gave her my tongue and then pulled back but not in a teasing way.

"Hey," I said softly again. "How was the show last night? How were the Stray Cats?"

"Fun," she said. "I wished you'd come. They're going to be big. They have a deal with EMI," I remember she said before trailing off and kissing me again.

We led each other to the unmade bed and fell onto it and my lips became sticky with strawberry gloss and then I was on top of her and she wrapped her legs around my waist, grinding into me, while I tried concentrating on the sex and focused on what I was supposed to be doing, making sure my actions and movements were tinged with the requisite lust. But I was distracted because Debbie liked to move fast and she took over quickly, as she usually did, and then I was lying on my back and pulling my T-shirt over my head while she pulled my shorts and underwear all the way off and flung them to the floor. She lifted her Camp Beverly Hills T-shirt, revealing those incredibly perfect breasts, pink and firm with small stiff nipples the color of cotton candy, while riding me, hands pressing down on my chest as she balanced herself, leaning over and kissing me again, and then she maneuvered out of her shorts and panties until she was fully naked above me, riven with lust. The fantasy we were creating almost cracked for me because of how real it seemed to her. And I realized that in order for this to work I had to stop thinking Debbie deserved someone better. I had to believe that she deserved me.

THE KNOWN FACT: Debbie Schaffer was the hottest girl at Buckley—she wasn't the classic beauty that Susan Reynolds embodied but she was the fantasy boys jerk off to, dream of naked, fucking. She was *Penthouse*, a Vargas Girl, the cover of *Candy-O*, she was the teen boys' ideal, a porn star, any guy would've been extremely lucky to have her, to the degree that I believed someone would kill in a testosterone-fueled rage to be *able* to have her and only once, to instill the memory of that one fuck in order to save their own pathetic life and give it meaning. Add to this she was smart—Debbie wasn't an airhead, as if this even mattered compared to the power of her physicality. So why was I her boyfriend? I had gone through the usual adolescent problems: I'd never had braces but I gained weight after eighth grade while staying with my grandfather in Nevada that summer: too many unsupervised vanilla milkshakes and cheeseburgers in the coffee shop at one of the hotels he owned in Elko and visits to the drugstore on Main Street to buy a bag of candy that would take me through the night. I didn't lose it entirely until the end of ninth grade and then regained it briefly in tenth, until I lost it again in eleventh, but the proof would always be there in terrible yearbook photos taken at the beginning of our junior year. I'd had a few awkward haircuts, light acne that luckily vanished completely before tenth grade began with the help of an expensive dermatologist in Beverly Hills, but I had insecurity issues even after my transformation junior year because I never felt I was in Thom Wright's league or as good-looking and athletic as Ryan Vaughn or even as hot as Matt Kellner. But it turned out that into eleventh and twelfth grade I was actually quite close—though I realized this fully much later on. I just hadn't liked myself enough, and the attendant aloof attitude never endeared me to anyone. In retrospect I realized—in fact I was told—that there were many girls who liked me whenever I shed the weight but the elusive vibe I gave off was intimidating. *Don't touch me there,* the Tubes sang out in one of my favorite songs—the mock-1960s parody lyrics were about a woman who wasn't ready for sex, but to me it had become a metaphor about my own alienation.

What did Deborah see in me that she didn't see in anyone else during that moment, I kept wondering—did she see a version of Terry and was she trying to figure something out about her father through me or was that overly complicating her simple desires? I realized early on that my distance and supposed spaciness implied to Debbie that I was just another clueless dude and this had worked to my advantage over the summer. I had assumed, on a certain level, that I was cooler than everybody; the truth was that Debbie made me cooler than I really was. But I was confused: Debbie was a rich girl who took advantage of her wealth and seemingly did whatever she wanted, completely ignoring and unencumbered by the realities of the world (even though she was aware that her mother was an alcoholic and, I supposed, that her father was gay), and as she increasingly moved toward the edges of, I don't know how else to put it, the trappings of a rock-and-roll lifestyle and the bands and men that attracted her, I was, by comparison, a fairly clean-cut option, a preppie WASP, almost square. I could have easily passed as a dude in a fraternity or a member of the Young Republican National Federation; in fact *all* the guys at Buckley our senior year resembled this: Thom, Ryan, Jeff, Matt. And I was surprised Debbie found *me*, of all people, as sexy as she did. Debbie was actually hip and hungry for experience in ways that I simply wasn't and I knew so little about her, I realized over the summer of 1981. I never wanted her to come off as desperate and needy but I now had to take responsibility: I had created this version of Debbie Schaffer in the summer before our senior year and I hated the way she transformed because of her feelings for me—her desire and frustration were real and intertwined and it was all my fault, the false vibes I emanated only encouraged her lust. I was the secretive and not entirely trustworthy boyfriend, the cad, not the bad boy exactly, but the boy who wasn't there, the incredible shrinking boy. She deserved someone better than me.

DEBBIE HAD TAKEN COMPLETE CONTROL and was grinding on my dick, which unlike Sunday night in her bedroom had gotten fully stiff. My hands reached for her breasts and she encouraged me to lightly run my palms over her nipples, and she was moaning how good it felt. She guided me in—we never wore condoms—and it amazed me how quickly she came: it was within minutes of me thrusting into her while she fingered her clitoris that I felt her clenching around my cock. And then she urged me to come as I kept thrusting, straining to ejaculate, and anxiety that I wasn't going to be able to maintain the erection caused me to pull out and start jerking myself off, eyes closed, thinking about Matt Kellner naked and wet, on his knees sucking my cock as I leaned against a wall in the pool house, while Debbie kissed me, massaging my balls as I kept stroking myself. And then she pushed my hand away and started deep throating my penis until it was slathered with her saliva and I saw Ryan's spread ass above my face as we sucked each other off in a 69 position while I tried to tongue his smooth pink butthole on that afternoon in August, and then it was Matt again and I remembered how intensely I'd made him orgasm on Monday. I started breathing harder, tensing up, I didn't think I was going to be able to come but I found myself lifting my head and nodding at her, unexpectedly climaxing while thrusting into her mouth, my legs wide open, ejaculating as she kept jerking off the shaft, half of the penis in her mouth, swallowing the semen that shot out of me. She was grinning, pleased, and kissed me, and I smiled groggily at her and tasted my own semen, remnants of it on her lips, on her tongue. What did it matter, what did anything matter, nothing mattered, I realized, panting.

We walked naked to the Jacuzzi and sat in it quietly, listening to the traffic on Mulholland while watching Shingy roam the expanse of lawn as the light above us very slowly started changing, receding into a softer light, and soon it was nearing six, the time when Thom and Susan were supposed to come over.

We stayed silent in the Jacuzzi, and the only noise was just the sound of the jets set on low, causing the water to lightly bubble, until she asked, "What do you think of Robert?"

I thought about how to answer this and asked, "The new guy?"

"Do you listen to yourself?" she said, pretending to be shocked. "Do you pay attention?" She moved closer to me, grinning. "Are we in the same conversation?" She stared at me, amusingly bewildered. "Who else would I possibly be talking about? Yes. Robert. The new guy, Bret."

"Okay, okay," I said, trying to smile back. "I'm sorry."

"Don't be sorry," she said. "Just be, I don't know, more present, babe."

"Okay, the new guy, yes." Debbie was straddling my lap, facing me, half floating in the warm water. "What about him?"

"What do you think of him?" she asked.

"I don't really . . . know him," I said, not wanting to get into a conversation about Robert Mallory.

"I think Susan likes him," Debbie said, hoping to surprise me, pressing lightly down on the word *likes*. I didn't want to take the bait, I didn't want to go through that door with Debbie, and I ignored the comment.

"What about you?" I asked playfully, teasing her. "Huh? What about you? What do you think of the new guy?"

She looked into my eyes, trying to figure something out, perhaps why I wasn't more curious with what she was suggesting about Susan. "Not really my type."

"I think he's probably everyone's type," I said.

She pushed off me and floated on her back in the lightly bubbling water.

"I wouldn't want to go out with a boy who was that much better-looking than me," Debbie said.

"Hey, thanks a lot," I said, splashing at her.

"You know what I mean," she said, squinting up at the fading sky. "Like a model or whatever." She paused. "It's not my thing."

The SHARDS

"Susan likes him?" I asked. "How do you know?"

Debbie shrugged. It was evasive and held a meaning that she wanted me to pursue and decipher but I didn't want to follow through on that particular story and so all I said was "I hope she behaves herself."

Debbie, her eyes closed, smiled, nodding her head as she floated in the water, her blond hair splayed out, and only said, "Let's hope."

I GOT DRUNK THAT SATURDAY. It started early on with beer and then moved to champagne and by the end of the night I was doing shots of tequila and snorting bumps of Debbie's coke. But when Thom and Susan arrived I was only mildly buzzed on a couple of Coronas Debbie and I were sharing while listening to music in the living room—the Motels' first record, with "Total Control" on it—and then we were waiting for the pizza from Santo Pietro's to be delivered; Thom had ordered it about half an hour after they arrived at six. There were two bottles of Mumm's in the refrigerator, one that Debbie and Susan opened; they poured themselves glasses and then walked to the pool as the sky slowly faded into sunset, and smoked clove cigarettes, talking quietly to each other, the Motels playing over the yard from outside speakers, while Thom talked about when he would be leaving L.A. to look at colleges with his dad during two bye weeks in the middle of football season. The doorbell rang at around seven-thirty and Thom paid for the delivery and brought it into the kitchen, where we prepped everything: I stacked some plates and dumped the two salads into a wooden bowl while Thom opened the pizza box and placed it on a tray we were going to take outside. I quickly drank a glass of champagne and poured myself another, finishing the first bottle off, and then opened the second. I looked out at the girls, now just in silhouette against the pool's blue light, misty tendrils of steam rising from the Jacuzzi, and asked Thom, "What do you think they're talking about?" Thom glanced outside. "Probably us," he said, with his brand of low-key confidence. The girls didn't want to eat by the pool—it was too warm, they complained, and there were mosquitoes—so we decided to eat within the air-conditioned comfort of the kitchen, where we sat around the large circular table in the middle of the open room. Before we sat down Susan wanted me to bring out candles and dim the lights, I guess to set a mood, and because of this request I became uncertain about everything. I was a little tipsy from the two glasses of champagne I'd quickly drunk and felt dizzy and nervous, and I told Susan I wanted to keep all the lights in the house on. Someone asked why.

"The home invasions," I said. "The break-ins. There was another one last Sunday night. In Century City." I paused. "And two more this week." I paused again. "One in Rancho Park." I breathed in and swallowed. "And one in Culver City."

Everyone was silent. No one had reached for the pizza yet. I noted their confusion.

"Are the houses . . . *dark* when the home invasions happen?" Thom wanted to know. "I mean is that why?"

I realized something. "I don't know," I said. "I guess not. I don't know."

"So—what difference does it make if the lights are on or off?" Thom asked, hesitantly. Susan and Debbie were staring at me.

"Well, I'm assuming, with the lights on it's a deterrent," I said, dumbly.

"I haven't heard anything about that," Thom said. "I don't think it matters to whoever's doing it. I mean if the lights are off or not."

"They say people are targeted," Debbie said unfazed, reaching for the salad. "Do you feel you've been targeted, Bret? Do you think someone's coming to get you, baby?" She was humoring me but I was still slightly afraid of what she was suggesting. Susan noticed that I flinched as I looked nervously from Debbie to her and then back to Debbie.

"I know, it's kind of scary," Susan said, but she was lifting a slice of pizza to her mouth and didn't seem frightened at all.

"The last one was back in June," I said, trying to explain something. "And before that, January. I don't know why they stopped for almost six months. But now they're happening again. Animals are missing." I paused. "Whoever's doing it steals people's pets, their cats, their dogs. It's fucked up."

The SHARDS

"That girl is still missing, too," Deborah said, spearing a small wedge of tomato. She looked up at all of our faces, blankly. "I mean I think that's a little more upsetting than someone's missing cat."

"Julie Selwyn," I said. "It's been almost eight weeks since she disappeared," I murmured, nodding to myself. "They've found nothing." I wondered aloud: "Do you think it's connected?" I asked. "The break-ins and Julie Selwyn?" I swallowed.

"What do you think happened to her?" Thom asked.

"Well," I started, "I was hoping she ran away but the longer she's missing—"

"Guys, let's stop trying to creep ourselves out," Susan said, cutting me off. "I want to talk about my party." She laid her slice down after every bite and then wiped her mouth, before picking the slice up again.

"Your party?" I said, trying to seem amused that this whimsy could replace the dark seriousness of the home invasions, and forcing myself into a different mood. I had already wolfed down a slice of pizza before the girls came in and was just pouring myself another glass of champagne and I should have been legitimately relaxed—the blow job, the orgasm, the Jacuzzi, making up with Debbie, the Coronas that initially put me in a mellow mood as well as being with my three best friends drinking my parents' expensive champagne—but I was keyed up, expectant, there was something wrong about the tenor of the night, and what Susan and Thom brought with them into the house on Mulholland. And then it was confirmed.

"Yes," Susan said demurely. "I'm going to throw a party to welcome Robert Mallory."

She smiled at me and added, "It's going to be at my house and I think we should all throw it together. The four of us. To welcome him. We'll invite everyone in the senior class."

I stared at Susan and felt strangely distanced, as if I was floating above the kitchen, watching myself in a movie where I didn't know the story, or who my character was, what my lines were or how I was supposed to react to the dialogue other people were reciting—I was just lost in it with nowhere to go. I glanced over at Debbie, who was staring at Susan, waiting for her to continue, looking a little bored. Thom was chewing a slice and washing it down with Corona. "Yeah," he said, confirming he was down with the party while wiping his mouth with a napkin. I wanted to appear both completely neutral and yet also aligned with the group. Since I was buzzed the possibility to convey this emerged. "Totally awesome," I said, but I couldn't help myself and asked: "Why?" And then I asked, "Why don't you just throw a party and invite him? What? It's going to be, like, a theme party? Like a Welcome Robert Mallory to Buckley party?" I hoped the confused expression, bordering on a grimace, was registering without being too insistent or overdone.

"It's not exactly a theme party, Bret," Susan said. "It's not like he's going to know it's for him."

"I don't get it," I said.

"I think we should make him feel welcome," Susan said. "I think he's had some hard times and I think he needs to feel welcome here."

"What are the . . . hard times?" I asked with an inquisitive and caring voice that I hoped hid the light level of disgust I felt about Susan throwing a party for Robert Mallory.

She paused. She looked over at Thom, who nodded, and then at Debbie, who shrugged. I realized uneasily that they all knew what the supposed hard times were and that this information was now going to be directed at me and that I had somehow missed it because of my lost week as a zombie. "I want to keep this between the four of us, okay, Bret?" Susan said. She had eaten the slice down to its crust and placed it on a napkin by her plate. Debbie was helping herself to another serving of the salad. Thom swigged from his Corona again and reached for the pizza, which was now a half-circle.

"Why?" I suddenly asked. "What's wrong?"

Susan was addressing me, not Thom or Debbie, because, of course, they already knew. "Dr. Croft, um, wanted me to relay that everyone should be friendly to Robert and to encourage us to include him in things and just make him feel that he belongs here. At Buckley. With us."

"Why would Dr. Croft ask you this?" I stared at Susan while I gulped down half a glass of the champagne I'd just poured, controlling the hand holding the bottle so it wouldn't shake.

"Well, it seems that Robert wasn't exactly up front when we first met him . . ." Susan started. "He wasn't at Roycemore last spring."

I just stared at Susan while Thom and Debbie casually ate.

"Where was he?" I asked.

"He was in Illinois," Susan confirmed. "But he just wasn't in school. He was actually in Jacksonville."

The silence in the kitchen from Thom and Debbie was almost maddening and I suddenly looked over at both of them with an alarmed expression.

"Doing what?" I asked.

"He spent last spring being treated at a . . . developmental center," Susan said vaguely.

"A developmental center?" I asked, making a face. "What's that?"

"Yeah, a developmental center, that's what Dr. Croft called it," Susan said. "Being treated for . . . depression and . . . other issues Robert was having."

I realized something. "You mean he was institutionalized," I said. "You mean he was put in a mental institution." I looked to Thom and Debbie and then back at Susan. "That's what you mean." I stayed calm but I felt sick, heavy. I was on the verge of getting drunk but in that moment I pulled back, because I needed to steady myself and maintain control.

"Dr. Croft called it a developmental center," Susan corrected me, as if subtly admonishing a child, reprimanding them so they wouldn't make the same mistake again. "He was discharged in May," she added.

"Why don't we just call it what it really is," I said in a condescending way. "An asylum." I looked around the table. "Right? I mean 'developmental center' is just a fancy term for 'mental institution' and 'mental institution' is just a fancy term for 'asylum.' So Robert Mallory was in an insane *asylum* last year. That's what you're telling me, Susan. And you want to throw a party for him?"

"'Asylum' is a little dramatic, Bret," Susan said and then sighed. "But we're used to you embellishing things, so—"

"You can call it whatever *you* want," I said, holding my hands up. "Developmental center is fine. I just want us to all know what we're dealing with here."

"What *we're* dealing with? He had some psychological issues," Susan said. "And took care of them. I don't understand what's wrong. What's your problem?"

"I think you've had too much to drink, babe," Debbie said to me. "Maybe cool it a little bit."

"What were his psychological issues?" I asked, ignoring her.

"Well, I don't really know. I assume his parents' divorce, his mother's death, Dr. Croft mentioned there were drugs. Nothing hard-core." Susan immediately clarified, "Marijuana, and Croft said hallucinogens." She was looking at me for a reaction. "But he's clean now."

"Or so he says," I said.

"What does that mean?" Thom asked in an attempt to defend Susan.

"He's a liar," I said. "Obviously he lied to us. He's lied to me."

"About what?" Debbie asked, turning, suddenly paying closer attention to the conversation now that I had placed myself in the narrative.

"I saw him somewhere, here, in L.A., a year ago, at a movie theater," I said. "It was absolutely him. And he denied it. He's a liar. And he lied about Roycemore. And if he lied about Roycemore then he lied about the girlfriend—"

"I don't even know if he was a full-time patient—" Susan said.

"He had a girlfriend in the mental institution?" I asked. "If he was discharged in May, Susan, that means he was a full-time patient."

"It was the first time we met him," Susan said. "He was probably nervous. He was probably embarrassed. What? He's going to announce this automatically? I think we'd all couch the truth." She stopped and then pointedly said, "It's not like you haven't made up stuff before."

"Oh, come on, Susan," I said, raising my voice, frustrated. "It's not the same. I might embellish something but I don't fucking lie. I might give things a spin but I don't make up a girlfriend I didn't have or lie that I wasn't in a fucking insane asylum—"

"Oh, stop it," Susan said. "You're doing it now. Insane asylum? Give me a break."

"Have you talked to him about any of this?" I asked. "So you could, y'know, clarify what he was in there for exactly?"

"No, I'm not going to ask him," Susan said. "Croft told me not to mention it to him. And I'm not. There's no point. If Robert wants to bring it up and tell us, fine. But he doesn't know we know." She looked at me sternly. "And I want to keep it that way."

"So you don't know how severe his problem was—"

"Bret, it's just a party," Susan said, pleading.

"No, it's a validation," I said. "Actually, Susan, it's a validation."

"I think it'll be the cool thing to do," Thom said, stepping in again.

"But we don't know him *at all*," I stressed hard.

Susan and Debbie started at the same time defending Robert, overlapping each other. "What are you talking about? What's your problem, Bret? What's wrong with you?"

"How did he move on to his senior year if he was in this developmental center and wasn't discharged until May?" I interrupted. "How did he get into Buckley?"

"Croft told me that he had a tutor there," Susan said. "And after he was discharged in May he went to summer classes and yes at Roycemore. And he worked hard. He caught up. He's smart. I don't know." Susan stopped. "It's not that hard to get into Buckley, Bret. And he's smart. What?"

"I think a rather sizable donation was probably made, Susan," I said. "Let's not be more naïve than we already are." I let out an exaggerated sigh. "Yeah, you can easily get into Buckley after spending six months in a mental institution. Right."

"What is wrong with you?" Susan asked, staring at me. "I don't get it."

And then the table was silent again. I had turned the night around from where it was supposed to be heading—with friends ordering pizza from Santo Pietro's and having fun planning a party, the music, the food, who else to invite outside of the Buckley circle—into what everyone now assumed was my own paranoid cave, creating a scenario that didn't connect with the facts they thought they knew. I realized I had to defend myself, so I brought up what happened Tuesday afternoon on Ventura Boulevard.

"First, the guy lied about something to me that I know is real, and then he followed me like a maniac, fucking with me on Ventura Boulevard, and then he's stalking girls at the Galleria—"

"He said you were following him," Susan said quietly, interrupting me.

"What?" I asked.

"He said *you* were following *him*," Susan said again but this time with an emphasis on those two words.

My gaze moved from Susan's face and started scanning the room we were in: my parents' house had an open layout and the entrance past the foyer led into an uninterrupted space, there were no walls, and off to the left was a huge living room, minimally decorated with floor-to-ceiling windows that constituted the entire side of the house overlooking the San Fernando Valley, and this space flowed into the kitchen, where we were sitting, and I could hear the music coming from the stereo in the living room—it was the Motels' second album—and as I glanced at the half-circle of pizza I realized that Robert Mallory had spoken to Susan and obviously to Thom as well, which meant that Debbie knew this, too, about something I had supposedly done. Robert had already told them something I wasn't going to tell anybody. They looked at me blankly, wanting me to confirm this or explain what really happened, what my version of events was compared to Robert's. The information they had been given refuted my memory of that afternoon. But still, the worst thing was that Susan Reynolds and Robert Mallory had talked about me.

"What?" I asked again. "That's not . . . true," I said.

"He said you were following him first." This was Thom's voice.

"Yeah," Susan said. "That you followed him from Buckley."

"I was going to the Galleria," I said. "I didn't even know he was in the Porsche." I fumbled around. "It was so aggressive on his part. It was so weird." And then I asked, "Did he say he ran into me in the Galleria? That he *followed* me into the Galleria? And that he was *stalking* girls there?"

"He said that he went to Robinson's to buy some clothes," Susan said.

"Yeah, I-I-I know, he-he told me that, too," I stammered. "But I saw him—"

"Look, are you with us?" Susan said, reaching a hand across the table. "It's just a party. It's not a validation of anything. It's just a party, Bret."

"He's drunk," Debbie said.

"I'm not drunk," I said. "In fact I'm extremely sober."

"Right." Debbie snickered and leaned over and kissed me on the cheek.

I was stunned and yet I pretended not to be and I visibly relaxed as I took Susan's hand in mine and squeezed it. "Yeah, of course, whatever you want."

Thom grabbed my shoulder. "There he is," he boomed. "He's back! Bret is back!"

I turned and smiled at his handsome face, which was beaming and made me feel, foolishly, as if I had accomplished something by making Thom Wright happy. Everyone was suddenly relieved. You could feel the tension exit the space because I'd conceded or pretended to. I realized the only option was to get obliterated. "Anyone want to do shots?" I quickly asked, standing up, clapping my hands together. I had to push the slight panic I felt about Susan's party and Robert Mallory and the conversation the two of them had about me out of my mind and discard it somewhere as far away as I possibly could or I was going to hurt somebody.

MY PARENTS ONLY DRANK tequila in margaritas, so we didn't have any top-shelf brands in the house (nobody really did in 1981), but there was a bottle of Jose Cuervo on the liquor shelf in the wet bar off to the side of the living room. The girls wanted rum-and-Cokes— actually Debbie made herself a rum-and-Tab—and so I brought out a bottle of Bacardi hidden behind two Smirnoff bottles and filled up an ice bucket. Thom and I did shots and I sliced a lime and sprinkled salt from a shaker on the side of my wrist and licked it off. Thom usually didn't drink alcohol but it was a Saturday and he didn't have to get up tomorrow and Susan would only be having one drink and she'd be the designated driver even though Thom said he'd be fine driving if he only had just a shot or two but instead we got drunk fast and I was bringing out my records and soon Thom and I were blasting the Dickies (Chuck Wagon, who played keyboards and saxophone, had shot and killed himself in June; I had a crush on the bassist, Billy Club) in the living room while the girls watched as we air-guitared and moshed to "Stuck in a Pagoda with Tricia Toyota" and I remember at some point Debbie offered a couple bumps of cocaine so I could semi-clear my head and then Susan did a small line and so did Thom and the girls kept going outside to smoke while Thom and I played songs we wanted to hear, slightly wired by the small amount of cocaine we'd done, jamming out to tunes and lip-synching while I kept going back to the bar to do shots until the Cuervo bottle was nearly empty.

We started hopping around to the drumbeat of David Lindley's version of "Mercury Blues" and then it was "Somebody Got Murdered" by the Clash, where we took turns singing the verses (I was Mick Jones and Thom was Joe Strummer) and as the song was ending I sung bug-eyed, "Sounds like murder!" and then Thom shouted out, leaning in to me, "Those screams!" and then we'd both sing "Are they drunk?" Beat. "Down below?," which then led to an actual duet: "From a Whisper to a Scream" where I sang along to the Glenn Tilbrook vocal and Thom did Elvis Costello, both of us joining in on the chorus, and then it was "Turning Japanese" by the Vapors and "What I Like About You" by the Romantics and "Pretty in Pink" by the Furs and after that it was "Skateaway" by Dire Straits and after about twenty songs I staggered down the hallway to my bedroom so I could pass out. I was too wasted to have sex with Debbie, who draped herself on top of me, kissing my face and purring as the room spun and I was groaning and she thought it was from drunkenness but it wasn't, because no matter how wasted I got I couldn't erase the fact that someone was watching the house on Mulholland—had been watching *me,* in fact, all summer long—and that *I* had been targeted and the person who targeted me was the new boy from Chicago racing after my car on Ventura Boulevard, who spoke intimately with Matt Kellner and Susan Reynolds and was probably—and I didn't have a doubt about this even though I had no proof—the person holding the flashlight in the library courtyard who desecrated the statue of the Buckley Griffin on the night before school began.

I WAS NAKED ON MY stomach under a sheet and someone was gently rubbing my back, purring into my ear, Debbie's plush lips grazing the lobe, the familiar smell of rose oil acting like a smelling salt, an ammonia, helping me regain consciousness. I didn't remember taking off my clothes before I fell into bed last night and I was so hungover that it took me a long moment to figure out where I actually was. I squinted at an unfamiliar wall I was facing and then saw the Elvis Costello poster hanging on it and realized I was in my bedroom. I slowly turned my neck and looked up at Debbie, who laughed softly, sitting next to me, as she tallied the damage based on my swollen face, my half-shut puffy eyes, the pained expression caused by the headache and dehydration.

"Poor baby," she said, leaning down and kissing me lightly on the lips, and when I exhaled she backed off, waving her hand. "You still smell like tequila. You okay?"

I couldn't say anything—I was paralyzed by the hangover. I never drank the way I had last night and I could only blame myself: not Robert Mallory or Susan, who was throwing a party for him, or Thom Wright, who I'd so badly desired last night while the girls were outside, or how I wanted to drown the actor I'd become who salvaged his relationship with Debbie Schaffer with one quick fuck yesterday afternoon. The clock on the nightstand said, inexplicably, it was one-thirty. I squinted back at Debbie, who looked completely radiant— she had washed and blow-dried her hair in my bathroom and put on light makeup and was dressed and she seemed so much more relaxed than yesterday afternoon, when she arrived at the house on Mulholland—she was drained of the rigid insecurity and the black frustration. She was calmed by the knowledge that I'd assured her about us and I was momentarily relieved.

I was unable to fully open my eyes and my mouth and throat were so dry I could only croak: "Where are you going?"

She was heading to Malibu to ride Spirit and she preferred Sundays in the late afternoon since she wouldn't be going out that night to see a band or check out a club. It was still so incongruous: Debbie in a bikini teasing John Taylor by the pool at the Hilton while we were hanging out with Duran Duran last summer also owned a horse named Spirit and had for a number of years competed in equestrian sports—the disconnect always suggested a lingering innocence to me. She'd been riding since seventh grade and even though other interests had started occupying her—mainly music and concerts and bands and she had stopped competing—she could never shake off the pleasure she got from horseback riding—it was comforting, it touched me.

I was burrowing my head back into the pillow when she said, "Matt Kellner called."

I knew Debbie was wrong. I knew this was an impossibility. The odds of this happening were nonexistent. In the fourteen months since we started having sex Matt Kellner had never called the house on Mulholland, not even once. It had simply never happened and it was unfathomable that he knew my phone number and picked up the receiver and dialed it that morning. But I became worried almost immediately, when Debbie repeated this, as I processed that Debbie wasn't lying.

"You're friends with Matt Kellner?" Debbie asked. "I didn't know that."

"Kind of," I said. "Not really." I paused. "Did you talk to him?"

"He seems a little strange," Debbie said. "Yeah, I picked up."

"Oh, yeah?" I said, trying to act casual. I sat up and winced. "Did he say what he wanted?" It seemed unreal that I was even asking that. "Are you sure it was Matt Kellner? You're not getting him mixed up with someone else?"

"Yes, it was Matt," Debbie said. "I just find it weird that you guys are friends and I never knew."

"I wouldn't say we're friends exactly . . ." I started, and then realized that sentence could open two or three doors for Debbie and I wanted to keep them all shut. "I know him," I said vaguely. And then I decided on: "Sometimes I buy weed from him."

"That's what I thought," she said. "Anyway he just wanted to know if you were here but I said you were asleep."

"Did he tell you I should call him back?" I asked tentatively.

"No. Nothing. Didn't leave a message." Debbie looked at her watch and then at me—she was relaxed and smiling. "I'll talk to you tonight, handsome." And then she left.

The moment I heard the front door open, then close, I hobbled into the bathroom and peed with a hard-on, splashing urine all over the rim of the toilet seat. Wincing, I walked quickly, gingerly, to the pool, where I simply fell into the deep end and sank to the bottom and stayed there until I couldn't hold my breath any longer and pushed to the surface, feeling less pain and the horniness mildly abated. When I was slightly clearheaded, I hauled my body out of the cool water, but I stumbled where the concrete surrounding the pool met the grass, stubbing my toe, which seemed more painful than it actually was because of how sensitive I felt due to the hangover—everything, in fact, seemed heightened, dramatic, over-scaled. In my bedroom I dried off quickly and immediately threw on a pair of tennis shorts, a Polo shirt and my Topsiders and hurried to the garage, where I pulled the 450SL out of the driveway and made a left onto Mulholland and then another left onto Woodcliff and raced down the canyon to Valley Vista then to Haskell Avenue—it took maybe ten minutes.

I PARKED on the street, jumped out of the car, unlatched the side gate, and walked the pathway to the backyard directly to the pool and the guesthouse beyond it. The door was open and when I walked in I didn't see Matt. I looked around an empty room—it seemed barren but that could have been because it was finally clean. My first thought: furniture was missing, and yet maybe the room was simply rearranged by Matt. The aquarium was now fully drained, the TV was on but the volume was turned down and fires raged silently somewhere in the distant hillsides, the room still smelled of weed but not as strongly as usual and there was no sign of Alex the cat. And then I looked at the Foreigner 4 poster above the hamper, which was neatly tamped down with clothes, and walked toward it: the record had been released in July and the poster was a simple black and white image of the number 4—frozen on the countdown of an old-fashioned film leader. The poster was completely minimal with the logo of the band's name at the top in blood-red lettering. It was a large and mostly off-white-and-gray image except for the bold black number 4, which took up the center. As I moved closer I noticed that someone had drawn what looked like a star off to the left corner of the poster and it was large enough for me to know that the star hadn't been there on Monday: it was a new decoration. But when I peered at it I realized it wasn't a star: someone had drawn a pentagram. I remember Matt had told me he found the poster rolled up and sticking out of the mailbox—something promotional, and he didn't know who had left it. I then looked over at the dolphin mounted on the wall, shellacked and dead-eyed—in my hungover daze I imagined it was staring at the boy standing in the middle of the guesthouse.

"I'm here," someone said behind me.

I WHIRLED AROUND. Matt was reclining on the bed, propped against the wall, in the tight lime-green bathing suit he favored and a faded Dodgers T-shirt and wearing sunglasses. I hadn't seen him when I walked in because the bed had been moved to the side of the room next to the entrance and I'd passed unaware that a person was on it. I just stared at Matt, not knowing what to say. He looked pale as he sat there unmoving, diminished somehow, less sexy than he'd been only a week earlier, but I suddenly desired him with a ferocity that was impossible to manage—the hangover made me desperately horny. I couldn't help it—I became excited and started getting a hard-on since I solely associated the room with Matt and sex. The hangover was aiding in the arousal but so were Matt's bare thighs, his biceps, the full-lipped mouth. For a moment I wished it away and focused on the pipe and the bag of weed sitting next to him on the bed. What had he wanted when he called that morning? I kept wondering, on the verge of panic. But he spoke first.

"Why do you keep calling me?" Matt asked flatly.

A mixture of confusion and surprise altered my focus. "What are you talking about?"

When he slowly repeated this, spacing out the words for emphasis—"Why. Do. You. Keep. Calling. Me?"—I realized he was pissed off. I had never heard this tone from Matt before.

"I'm . . . not calling you," I said.

Matt took off his sunglasses and his green eyes were hard and blank as he assessed me. "You're not calling and just breathing into the phone?" he asked.

"No, I'm not doing that," I said, confused. "Why . . . would I call? You never pick up anyway. Why are you picking up the phone now? Who's . . . calling you?"

"You've been rather insistent, Bret," Matt said, resembling a bad actor in a mystery where he thinks he's found out who the murderer is—the "rather" sounded completely unlike him, as if he thought it was a word that would make him seem smart. I realized he'd probably been practicing exactly what he was going to say to me all morning and rehearsed his lines in such a precise way that I would have to admit what I was being accused of even though he had no proof and was wrong.

"That isn't me," I said. "Whatever the fuck is going on that isn't me."

"Well, you're here now." He gestured at the green rotary phone on his desk. "And it isn't ringing."

"I got wasted last night and I was asleep until an hour ago."

Matt just stared at me in a way that confirmed he was unconvinced.

"I was with Debbie. She spent the night. She can vouch for me. I didn't call anybody." I initially liked the way I could offer this information to Matt and he knew it was true because he spoke briefly to Debbie that morning. I also realized that Debbie would never make Matt Kellner jealous or draw him closer after I wondered what he thought about Debbie and me as a couple. I was someone who had so eagerly sucked him off a hundred times and endlessly played with his asshole, fingering and fucking and tonguing it, and kissed his mouth while talking dirty, and yet I was now with Deborah Schaffer. I realized in that moment he must have thought I was a fraud, an impostor— that how I reacted to him was passionately real and whatever I was doing with Debbie was tied to pretending because I wasn't as sexually attracted to her as I was to him. It was connected to what Matt saw as the fake social world of Buckley that I thought I'd wanted to be at the center of our senior year, which was why I ended up with Debbie Schaffer. I'm certain he had nothing but disdain for this person I turned out to be instead of the loner lost in summer school he perhaps thought I was when he invited me to Haskell Avenue in July of 1980. "Whoever's calling you isn't me," was all I said. And I couldn't believe amiable-stoner nice-guy Matt was convinced that it was.

"It has been going on all week, Bret," Matt said, barely keeping it together. "The phone calls. You haven't called six times this morning, just letting the phone ring and ring until I have to pick it up and you just don't say anything?" He couldn't help it: he had reverted to the boy he really was, confused, scared, and completely untethered to the reality of the world. And then, even more sadly, I realized that of course he thought it was me: I was the only friend he had, and was I even a friend? The confusion I felt mixed with the stress of Matt being angry at me and my horniness and the hangover became overwhelming and I remember that I needed to lean against something or sit down but I didn't because I was positive Matt didn't want me to.

"And you haven't been coming over here?" he asked. "Going through my things?"

"Matt," I said, my eyes closed. "Please, stop it. What are you talking about?"

"Well, I didn't do this," Matt said, and raised his hand to gesture around the room.

"Do what?"

"Put the furniture like this."

I paused, thought it through, didn't exactly believe him at first.

"Did the housekeeper or maybe your mom—" I started.

"My *mom*?" he cut me off with an incredulity that suggested I existed on another planet. "You didn't come over here and move my bed one afternoon this week—"

"Matt—"

"—and push all that shit to the other side of the room?"

"Matt, I'm sorry," I said, and then I couldn't help it. Suddenly I blurted out: "What did you and Robert Mallory talk about the other day?" In that moment I needed to know this. It was more important than anything that had happened in the pool house: the rearranged furniture, the empty aquarium, the pentagram on the Foreigner poster, the phone ringing endlessly.

"Yeah, that's another thing," Matt said, staring at me. "What did you tell him?"

I was losing my patience and I shouted out, "What did he want? What did he say to you?"

"He introduced himself to me," Matt said, glaring. "He heard that my dad knew his aunt."

"And that was it?" I asked.

Matt's face clouded over with suspicion. "What did you tell him about us?"

"I didn't tell him anything," I said with an urgency that surprised me. "You're stoned, and drugged out, you're smoking too much fucking weed, you're disoriented. You don't know anything. This is crazy."

"Does Robert Mallory know something happened between us?" Matt asked with a steady calmness that belied his anxiety.

Dizziness swept over me again. I needed to sit down. "What are you talking about? What did he say? I didn't talk to him about us."

"He didn't say anything exactly," Matt said in a steely voice. "But he hinted at it."

"Is that what you were talking about in the parking lot?" I asked. "What was he telling you that day in the parking lot?"

"Yeah," Matt said. "He asked a couple of questions about you."

I panicked. I felt fear. "Like what?"

Matt didn't say anything until: "I didn't know the answers to the questions."

"Are you sure you're not making this all up, Matt?" I asked, and then began to completely ramble. "Because I think you're making this all up. I think you got fucking stoned and did something to the aquarium and that you rearranged the room and drew the fucking pentagram on the poster because you were fucking high as fuck and that's what I think." Matt just stared at me with his incredulous stare, unwavering. "Look, I'd stay away from Robert," I said, and I didn't care if Matt told him I said this. In fact I wanted him to. "I think there's something really wrong with him and I don't think he's . . . all there. I think there's something very wrong with him." I stopped, even though I was tempted to tell Matt about the mental institution in Jacksonville I'd promised Susan I wouldn't tell anyone else about and in that moment it really didn't seem that pertinent. "What was he telling you that day in the parking lot? What was he asking about me?"

Matt was now just looking at my face dully. "Stop calling." And then: "Don't come over here anymore."

I didn't realize I'd moved closer to the bed; my hard-on was so stiff it was painful—the hangover had electrified me with lust.

"Matt," I said reaching out to him.

The expression on his face when he realized I wanted to have sex was the worst moment I ever shared with Matt Kellner. He looked at the hard-on jutting up and making a tent in my tennis shorts and then back at my face as if he were appalled. I'd never seen this expression before. It was almost a parody of fear and overexaggerated disgust.

"This was never a serious thing," Matt said, looking at me, stunned. "What are you doing?"

"Matt—" I was about to sit on the bed next to him.

"What the fuck are you doing?" Matt asked, backing away. "What do you want to be? Boyfriends? You think we're gonna be *boyfriends*? Are you fucking crazy? Get away from me."

I was so close now that he was able to physically push me back. Matt stared at me with disbelief, furious. This was the Matt I never knew existed—real and emotional, conflicted, angry and alive—and who I'd wanted to know since I met him, and who finally revealed himself to me on that Sunday afternoon in the minute it all ended. And it was heartbreaking that I would never be coming back again and this fact wounded me to such a degree that when I stumbled out of the pool house I could barely control myself until I got to my car on Haskell Avenue and once I closed the door burst into tears, falling against the steering wheel, hyperventilating, and it was a release so intense that it was almost orgasmic. I drove home carefully because I kept crying so hard: Matt had never felt about me the way I'd felt about him, which would be a recurring theme for the rest of my life though, of course, I didn't know this yet on that September afternoon in 1981, when I was seventeen and still navigated on hope.

7

BUT STEVEN REINHARDT called Monday morning as I was getting ready to leave for Buckley and because of this everything about
Matt Kellner and my subsequent pain and desire began vanishing. The
gray slacks were zipped up and the white Armani shirt buttoned and
the blue blazer had been freshly ironed and I had just finished knotting the red-striped tie when the phone in my bedroom rang. Rosa
was in the kitchen making my lunch and I had piled the textbooks
I was taking to school next to the Olivetti, reluctant to pick up the
phone because I couldn't figure out who'd be calling at eight-thirty
on a school day. Steven Reinhardt started leaving a message but I
grabbed the receiver in time and said, "Hey, Steve, it's Bret. I'm here."

"Oh, hey," Steven said. "I'm calling because Terry wanted to know
if you were available for lunch this week."

I was surprised, and then bolted with excitement: I hadn't spoken to Terry since Tuesday, when he thanked me for dealing with a
drunken Liz the night of Debbie's barbecue—I'd been mild with her,
I hadn't made a scene, I didn't freak out—as she stood naked beneath
her opened robe and berated me, suggesting I was doing something
sexual with her *faggot* husband. Terry wanted to reward me for this
even though I'd encountered Liz drunk a few times and that night's
outburst was mild by comparison. Only Steven had witnessed me and
relayed my gentle reaction, which led Terry—gave him a reason—to
perhaps offer me a job writing a script while also telling me, pointedly, not to mention this to his daughter, my girlfriend, for reasons I
wasn't quite grasping, though in the back of my mind I probably knew
exactly why. Steven asked if I was free for lunch on either Wednesday

or Thursday. I thought Terry would have chosen a Saturday since I had school and I remember asking, "Um, can't he do it on the weekend?"

"No, sorry, Bret," Steven said. "It has to be during the week. Terry's schedule this weekend is pretty packed."

"Oh, okay," I said. "Let me see." I pretended I was perusing my own packed schedule but of course there was nothing on it and so I simply said, as if I was deciding decisively: "Okay, I can swing either Wednesday or Thursday."

"Let's mark down Wednesday," Steven said. "Trumps at one?"

"One o'clock," I said. "Trumps."

"Do you know where that is?"

"Yeah, I know where that is."

"Okay, the reservation is under 'Schaffer' at one on Wednesday at Trumps," Steven confirmed.

"Thanks, Steven," I said. "I'll be there."

"Yeah, one more thing," Steven said. "You'll be coming straight from school, right?"

"Yeah. Why?"

"You don't need to change out of your uniform," Steven said matter-of-factly. "You can just stay in your uniform."

"Oh," I said, thinking at first this would make everything easier since I wouldn't have to take the time to go home and change, but then realized there was something *performative* about this request and, of course, Terry wanted me in my Buckley uniform because it accentuated something for him—my youth, my boyishness—and suggested a narrative he might take advantage of even though I wasn't going to do anything with him. This was simply, I thought, a fetish, something that would amuse Terry and turn him on. The uniforms were stylish enough so I had no problem wearing one in public and yet I blushed deeply at the unapologetic weirdness of the request as I stood in my bedroom. "And, of course," Steven added, "Terry asked me to remind you not to say anything to Debbie about meeting him for lunch."

"Yeah, right, of course," I assured him, wanting to please both Terry as well as Steven in that moment. It was our secret and there were reasons why Debbie didn't need to know that I was having lunch with her father. I might not have been privy to them exactly but I believed that Terry, and to a lesser extent Steven Reinhardt, knew how to handle things, because Terry was an adult, he was a man, he was successful—he must know exactly what he was doing. I was only seventeen, I didn't have a teenage daughter, my wife wasn't an alcoholic, I was just finding out how the adult world worked, what its rules were, how to comport myself within it, I needed guidance and I was beginning to select the adults I'd take my cues from and Terry Schaffer was one of them.

AND ON THAT WEDNESDAY in September I left the Buckley campus at twelve-thirty without telling anybody.

The group was sitting together at the center table beneath the shadow of the Pavilion: Susan, Thom, Debbie, Ryan, along with Jeff Taylor and Tracy Goldman, and Robert Mallory. I stood in the distance, below the courtyard, obscured by a stucco column, and glimpsed Debbie looking around for me, distracted, with Ryan and Thom and Jeff all trying to talk over each other, vying for everyone's attention, while Robert Mallory and Susan Reynolds listened silently on opposite ends of the table with Tracy occasionally leaning in to Robert and laughing about something—he just smiled politely. I didn't see Matt Kellner in the plaza, where he was usually splayed during lunch, though I'd seen him earlier that day walking from the parking lot to the bell tower when I was sitting on the bench with Susan and Thom—we were hanging out waiting for Debbie before first period began—and Matt passed by and managed a nod, and we silently acknowledged each other throughout the week. Despite what happened we didn't pretend the other one wasn't there—we were slightly more mature than that, and the school was too small to encourage that kind of brush-off. And this helped me move on and erase the humiliation of Sunday afternoon even though I kept thinking: *Move on from what?* I wasn't as embarrassed as I might have been about Matt's rejection now that it was Wednesday because I was on my way to meet Terry Schaffer, and it also helped that Matt Kellner simply didn't look as vibrant and sexy, the nerdy hot surfer, as he had that past summer— something seemed to be draining him. He looked diminished.

—

TRUMPS SAT ON THE CORNER of Robertson Boulevard and Melrose Avenue, across the street from Morton's, which was the primary restaurant frequented by people in the film industry—Trumps was less formal, less business-attire, more relaxed and decidedly gayer, and, pulling into the driveway where the valet stood, I realized I was early—it had only taken fifteen minutes to arrive in West Hollywood from Sherman Oaks—and I thought about driving around the block until the allotted time I was supposed to meet Terry. But I decided to leave the car with the valet and have a drink at the bar while waiting— something to relax me, a cocktail to help mellow out. The majority of the cars at Trumps were parked in back of the restaurant but there seemed to be a kind of selective VIP section next to the valet where the Ferraris and Bentleys and Porsches were lined that day. I pulled one of the massive double front doors open next to where the name of the restaurant was written in small pink handwritten neon, a playful touch hinting that Trumps didn't take itself so seriously; Trumps was about L.A. and artifice and a new kind of freewheeling California Cuisine—it was supposed to be fun. I'd been to Trumps twice but only at night, once with my mother for dinner, and with Thom and Susan for drinks, when the space was dimmed with candles. During the day it was a shock: a high-ceilinged oversized room filled with light and lined with wheat-colored stone tables beneath an atrium— a huge white space that sat roughly a hundred people, and it was dramatic and modern, yet also whimsical and unpretentious.

Nearing one o'clock it was already packed and when I told the hostess who I was meeting she was very apologetic: Terry hadn't arrived yet and I was welcome to either sit at his table or wait at the bar. I was going to be way too self-conscious sitting alone at Terry's table—it was Table One—so I told the hostess I'd wait at the bar for Mr. Schaffer instead. The hostess walked me over and leaned toward the cute blond bartender and pointedly said, "This is Terry's guest," as if to let him know I was important, part of the scene, a young player.

A SERIES OF ED RUSCHA PRINTS lined the white wall above the bar and continued across the lounge and into the front of the dining room, adjacent to where I took a seat and scanned the restaurant, shocked to see Jerry Brown, the governor of California, sitting at a corner table near the back with two men and a woman whose face was blocked by another diner—I hoped it was Linda Ronstadt, who Brown had been dating and whose New Wave record *Mad Love* I played over and over last year, but I wasn't sure if they were still together. I saw Erik Estrada, the star of *CHiPs,* at one table, and Elizabeth Montgomery—Samantha on *Bewitched*—at another, and Allan Carr, the producer of *Grease,* in the banquette with two hot young guys, and even though I was seventeen I knew who the painter David Hockney was and immediately recognized him sitting at a table facing the bar, owlish and smoking a cigarette, and staring at me, registering the schoolboy uniform in a very thoughtful and intrigued way, and I turned back to the bartender, who was acknowledging my presence with a patient smile. I ordered a Greyhound, vodka and grapefruit juice, and the bartender asked to see my ID, which I showed him, and he studied it a beat longer than I was comfortable with. He looked away from the ID and then at what I was wearing: I left the Buckley blazer with the insignia of the Griffin in the Mercedes, so I could've been any dude wearing what looked like the semblance of a prep-school uniform: gray slacks, white button-down, striped tie. "Cute," he said, and then proceeded to make the drink—I loved the fact that the Greyhound at Trumps was made with freshly squeezed *pink* grapefruit juice: it was festive, it was fun, it was gay. And of course, I now realize, the bartender let me order whatever I wanted because I was Terry Schaffer's guest, regardless of how old I was.

After two large swallows of the cocktail I got up the nerve to glance around the dining room again and saw that David Hockney's companion, who I didn't recognize, was now turning around every so often to get a look at the bar to glimpse the boy in the school uniform while Hockney grinned mischievously. I understand, and it's really only now, as a much older man, seventeen in L.A. had a special power that I hadn't fully grasped, the age when I started noticing that men of a certain demo, like Terry Schaffer and a few of the fey male teachers in the arts and music divisions at Buckley—the *flamers* Jeff Taylor sometimes referred to—began engaging in flirtatious ways that I thought I wasn't quite worthy of. But looking at photos of myself from that senior year I now realize I actually was cute enough to warrant their attention, and this was the afternoon in 1981, at the bar in Trumps on a Wednesday, sipping a Greyhound cocktail, when I began to fully sense its formation, and when this consciousness about myself—that never really bloomed because of so much insecurity and self-abnegation—was beginning its struggle to accept itself and grow.

IT WAS NOW a little after one o'clock and Terry still hadn't shown up but the cocktail put me in a calmer space and I breathed in, breathed out, vaguely floating, but Steven Reinhardt was suddenly standing next to me and even more off-putting in the brightness of Trumps compared to a week ago at the Schaffers' house: here in the airy light he was too thin, the wispy blond mustache and the permed hair adorned what resembled an emaciated face, a skull with deep-set wide eyes, and he was wearing a ratty brown turtleneck and jeans that barely clung to his bony frame and sandals but he had taken his expensive sunglasses off, and was swinging them around as if he was the hippest guy in the room. The fact that Steven thought he was a player because he was Terry Schaffer's personal assistant was a reminder of the constant desperation flooding Hollywood and how the town made everyone completely delusional.

"Hey Bret," Steven said. "Terry's across the street, over at Morton's, just finishing something up. He should be here shortly."

"Oh, okay," I said. "Thanks, Steven."

Steven eyed me up and down, taking note of the uniform, and then the near-empty cocktail on the napkin in front of me and said nothing—just acknowledged it as a detail that would be reported back to Terry, and I realized this was one of the reasons why Steven remained an assistant and was never going to be a successful screenwriter or filmmaker. I was learning about how the world worked from the ways adults acted and presented themselves, what they noticed and thought was important, and what they ignored or took in stride, and it confirmed to me that afternoon in Trumps, and more clearly than ever before, that Steven Reinhardt was a loser. I couldn't explain exactly why—it was just a feeling I got from the way he looked at the empty cocktail glass. "Thanks, Steven," I said again, turning away.

"Terry really appreciates this," Steven said.

"There's really nothing to appreciate," I said, staring at the shelves of liquor, the Ruscha prints. "I understand that Liz has a problem and she needs help. That's all. I was just being nice to her."

"Yeah," Steven said. "She's got to recognize that there's a problem but y'know . . ." He trailed off.

I wasn't sure what to say, so I idly glanced at my watch: a cue, a hint, for Steven to leave.

"I would, um, be . . ." Steven started, and then stopped. He considered finishing the sentence and then decided to. "I would just be, ah, careful, Bret."

"Pardon me?" I said, turning to him and leaning in. I didn't think I'd heard him correctly.

The bartender interrupted and asked Steven if he wanted anything to drink and Steven shook his head no.

"I'd be careful about, y'know, Terry." He said this shrugging, in an almost apologetic way, and yet the seriousness of it broke through the buzz of vodka and scared me.

"I will," I said automatically, trying to placate him, while I thought: why in the hell would I placate Steven Reinhardt? And I asked, "What's that supposed to mean?"

"It means . . ." Steven leaned against the bar, then pushed himself away, gripping the stone counter, trying to stay casual, trying to aim for hip and loose, and failing. "It means everyone has an agenda."

"Yeah?" I said.

"Terry has one, I have one." He paused. "You have one."

"Really?" I asked. "What's my agenda?" Steven just stared at me. "What's your agenda, Steven?" I played it cool but I was getting revved up inside.

"I meant generally," Steven said, weaseling out of defining whatever he'd hinted at, and backing away from this threat he'd tossed out. "I didn't mean specifically." He paused. "Sometimes these agendas don't connect with what we actually want or what we're going to get. That's all." He paused again. "Just be careful."

I felt daring, in a place above him, and I was going to remind Steven that he was only an assistant and that he was dismissed—I'd wait for Terry alone at the bar and if I wanted another fucking Greyhound I'll order it and down it in one gulp, you stupid bastard. "Just don't take it so seriously," he said, leaving *it* undefined, though I knew at some point Terry was going to hit on me and test how far he could push things and I was going to have to make a decision about what my boundaries were. But I went in knowing what could happen: this wasn't an ambush or an assault. I walked into the room realizing a number of unwanted narratives could present themselves and I'd have to deal. And then I realized Steven sounded as if he was talking about himself in some abstract way and it reminded me of what Robert Mallory said while we stood in front of the Gap at the Sherman Oaks Galleria last week: *When you talk to me you're really talking to yourself, dude.* It sounded like the ominous hippie nonsense Charles Manson might have uttered and I shivered at the memory of Robert telling me this.

"I can take care of myself," I said. "Don't worry."

"I'm not worried about you so much," Steven murmured, and then, "I think I've got you figured out." And then he said it: "I guess I'm more worried about Deborah." And now his eyes landed on mine and he just stared. I stared back. Things were veering out of control and I had to steady the narrative.

"You've got me figured out?" I asked. "That's interesting. I barely have myself figured out. What have you figured out?"

"Well, you're here to have lunch with Terry," he said. "I didn't think you were going to do it." He paused. "For many reasons." He paused again. "And yet here you are."

"Yeah, here I am," I said, turning on the bar stool. "What do you really want to tell me, Steven? What do you really want to say?"

Suddenly he glanced behind me and fake-smiled, raising his eyebrows. Terry had just walked in.

"I think you need to watch it," Steven said. "I think you need to be careful." He paused before he moved away from the bar and then said, "Modulate yourself."

"Fuck you," I muttered under my breath, but I was safe because I knew he couldn't hear me.

I REMEMBER TERRY SCHAFFER WAS WEARING jeans and a collarless Pierre Cardin shirt, the top three buttons undone, and the Porsche Carrera sunglasses he favored. He held the hostess's hand as he kissed her on the cheek and then smiled as he saw Steven and myself moving toward him and I noticed that every gesture of Terry's was efficient and immaculate, something to emulate and aspire toward—he was a professional, an adult, someone I wanted to be. I was shown to Terry's table while Terry and Steven conferred by the hostess stand for a moment and I couldn't bear to look around the dining room—I was too embarrassed. I just concentrated on the menu until I glanced up and saw Terry walking toward me—he stopped twice, talking to two tables on the way to his. He noticed someone else across the room and raised his hand as he took a seat—it was Jerry Brown, who raised a hand back.

"Hey, how you doing, Bret," Terry said, draping a linen napkin over his lap. "You look nice. But you're seventeen, you always look nice at seventeen."

He still had the Porsche Carrera sunglasses on and I was afraid he wasn't going to take them off, but when he glanced over the menu and then looked at me, he removed them and slid the temple into the neck of the Pierre Cardin shirt. I realize, in retrospect, how handsome Terry was for someone forty, which was certainly not my type in that moment (it's rarely my type now, I regret to say), but he was also aiming for younger than forty—a short boyish haircut, a lean build he maintained because of a personal trainer (before this was a thing yet), the casual attire. He seemed very pleased and didn't say anything for a moment as he took me in with barely contained amusement—I was being stared at and appraised. And then a waiter in a string tie and a white apron brought Terry a bottle of Perrier and asked me what I'd like and I said just a ginger ale, and that's when Terry and the waiter exchanged a bemused glance—and I was reminded, in that moment, yet again, that Trumps had a gay vibe—I knew that the chef was gay, the big investors were gay, the designer of the space was gay, all or most of the waiters were gay, even the location was gay: smack in the middle of what was known as Boystown. The entire aesthetic had an undercurrent of fuck you to the straight status quo and I suddenly felt slightly uncomfortable being there at the center of it. Terry ordered a couple of appetizers: the grape-and-Brie quesadilla that the restaurant was famous for and the salmon tartar, which was served exactly nowhere yet in Los Angeles.

THE TALK QUICKLY went to movies and Terry asked me what I'd seen this year that I liked and I remember the conversation initially landed on the filmmaker John Boorman, who had rebounded after a couple of expensive flops with a moderate hit this past spring, *Excalibur*, a violent R-rated retelling of King Arthur and the Knights of the Round Table, and Terry had liked it too and asked if I'd seen Boorman's L.A. noir from 1967, *Point Blank*. I hadn't even heard of it, though I'd now be searching for the movie on the monthly calendars from the Nuart and New Beverly, the two revival theaters I frequented—Terry assured me it was great, Boorman's best film. I was a John Waters fan and a group of us had gone to a sneak preview of his latest movie, *Polyester*, in Westwood over the summer, starring Divine and featuring a gimmick called Odorama, where you could smell what was on the screen in certain sequences with a scratch-and-sniff card handed out in the lobby (the movie's ad line was "It's Scent-sational!"), but Terry hadn't seen it. I also liked *Stripes*, the Bill Murray army comedy that was a big hit that summer, and Terry did as well. However, he balked when I told him I liked a little-seen Barbra Streisand movie called *All Night Long* with Gene Hackman and an impossibly sexy young actor named Dennis Quaid and Terry laughed and made a dismissive gesture with his hand and said, "Sue's husband made that picture!" and then "It was terrible!" He was talking about Jean-Claude Tramont, the Belgian husband of Sue Mengers, a fairly big talent agent who represented Streisand. Terry thought the movie was awful and couldn't stand Barbra even though he "adored" Sue, and yet I wasn't embarrassed by my opinion because I liked how honest he was—how adult he treated me. It felt like there was a new kind of grown-up respect burgeoning between Terry and myself. Terry mentioned that he had just been to a screening of a movie he thought was going to do "quite well" called *Chariots of Fire*, which would be opening at the end of the month. I barely noticed that the appetizers had arrived and neither one of us had touched them.

The SHARDS

—

TERRY ORDERED AN ENTRÉE OFF THE MENU, an omelet with tomato and avocado for himself, and suggested I have either the lobster in vanilla sauce or the potato pancakes and goat cheese. "Neither are as crazy as they sound," Terry said, before giving the order to our waiter, choosing the lobster for me instead of the pancakes. Allan Carr came over to the table as he was leaving and shook Terry's hand and said hello—he seemed high and looked haggard. Terry didn't introduce me as Debbie's boyfriend when Allan Carr inquired as to who this "handsome young gentleman" was, but instead said, "This is Bret Ellis, he's going to be writing a script for me. About . . . young people." "Ooh, young people," Allan Carr said, "I love it." An executive who Terry didn't introduce me to replaced Allan Carr and I took this as an opportunity to excuse myself to the men's room, where I focused on the boy in the mirror and studied him. I was expecting to see someone older but in Trumps the Buckley uniform looked dumb: I resembled an oversized child pretending to be an adult, or an adult pretending to be an oversized child, which was even worse. When I sat back down, deflated, Terry was in the middle of eating the omelet that had quickly appeared and the lobster tail was waiting for me. I draped the napkin over my lap.

"Debbie told me you want to be a writer," he said. "I never knew this about you."

"Well, yeah," I said. "I've been writing stories and stuff since like fifth grade."

"Really?" Terry said, forking a slice of avocado. "That's very impressive."

"Yeah," I said. "I, um, enjoy it."

"So—what are you working on?" he asked while concentrating on his plate.

"I'm working on a novel," I said, suddenly thinking how absurd this all sounded.

"A novel, really?" Terry asked, glancing at me, surprised, eyebrows raised.

"Well, it's something I've been working on for about a year

and . . ." I started, not sure I could fully explain the process. I changed course. "Actually I began with an outline and that took a long time, but, um . . ." I trailed off. A long pause ensued. Terry took another bite of the omelet.

"So you do an outline?" Terry asked, encouraging me to continue.

"Yeah, but I'm now writing the prose and, um, yeah . . ." I felt completely inarticulate, broken, that I didn't belong here, that I was a child aspiring to become an adult but wasn't ready yet. I looked at the pink flesh of the lobster on my plate and realized even if I'd been hungry I wasn't comfortable enough to eat anything in front of Terry.

"What's it about?" he asked.

I didn't know exactly how to describe *Less Than Zero*. And I didn't want to: it was about *me* but there was no story, there were *scenes* but it didn't have a narrative exactly, there was just this drifting numb quality that I was trying to perfect. How could I possibly explain this amorphous *feeling* to someone? Terry waited, glanced up from the omelet, wondering why I paused. I was trying to figure out how to synopsize whatever it was I'd been typing dutifully every day at the Olivetti in my teenage-boy bedroom for the past year, and came up with: "I guess it's about me."

"Yeah?" Terry asked. "So it's autobiographical? A coming-of-age story?"

"Well, it's set here in L.A. and . . ." I remember what Terry said to Allan Carr. "It's about young people," I confirmed.

"What do they do?" Terry asked, glancing up at me as he kept eating.

I didn't know how to answer this because it didn't matter to me what the characters *did*. They existed, and I just wanted to convey a mood, immerse a reader into a particular atmosphere that was built from carefully selected details. What did the young people *do*? This suggested there was a plot, a story that was going to resolve itself. They hung out, they listened to music, they had sex, they went to clubs, sometimes they consumed drugs, they attended parties in mansions where there were pools and tennis courts and screening rooms, they drove aimlessly around the city at night, their parents were absent, they went shopping along Rodeo, they moved through the world alone, they stared at chandeliers high on acid. How could I sum this up in a plot? It was, I imagined, about Jeff Taylor letting Ron Levin blow him—this had, in the book, bloomed into the one tragic thread, what would become the main incident that would close out the final chapters: a male prostitute owed money to a drug dealer, or so I planned in my outline. The name was now Julian, which I cribbed from Richard Gere's character in *American Gigolo*.

"I'd rather not talk about it just yet, Terry," I said, trying to mimic how an adult would evade describing the particulars of what he'd just been asked. "I feel a little awkward about it, I guess."

"Don't worry, no pressure," he said. "I was just curious." He finished the omelet and slightly pushed his plate away and sat back in the chair, appraising me again. I hadn't touched my plate. Terry didn't encourage me to eat the lobster, or seem distracted at all when the waiter came and whisked his plate away. Terry ordered a glass of white wine, and when the waiter asked me if I wanted anything else I shook my head.

"The ice cream is pretty good," Terry offered.

"I'm fine," I said, blushing.

The waiter gestured at my plate and looked at Terry, who nodded, and the waiter took it away.

"What writers do you like?" Terry asked.

"Well, I've been reading a lot of Joan Didion," I said. "I'm really influenced by her work."

"Oh, I know Joan and John quite well," Terry said. John was John Gregory Dunne, Didion's husband, and also a bestselling writer. "Maybe I'll invite them over and you can meet her."

I really wasn't that surprised at how casually Terry offered this—the opportunity to meet Joan Didion, of all people, my favorite author, in Terry's world was completely possible. I knew this but "That would be awesome," I said, while trying to figure out what I was doing in Trumps at two o'clock on a Wednesday afternoon with a forty-year-old man and bailing on school—it was starting to seem surreal and this was confirmed when Jerry Brown materialized and shook hands with Terry, who stood up and didn't introduce me—I blanked on what they talked about. After the governor walked away Terry sat back down and studied me while I just glanced around the restaurant, which was slowly emptying out. The waiter brought Terry the glass of white wine. I suddenly wanted to leave.

"So," he started, after taking a swallow of the Chardonnay. "How serious are you about Debbie?" he asked. "I'm just curious. You started dating at the beginning of the summer, right?"

"Um, yeah, in June, at a party, Anthony Matthews's, um," I confirmed vaguely. "Yeah, we're pretty serious, I guess."

"As I said, I'm just curious," Terry said. "There's no need to look so alarmed."

I hadn't realized that was my expression. "Oh, I'm okay," I said.

Terry stared at me and took another swallow of wine, and then swirled it around the glass. There was something in his tone that seemed to suggest unasked questions: is there an alternate history, a secret one, what are you really doing with my daughter, is this legit or is this suspect?

"It's very serious, Terry," I said.

"Come on, you can be honest with me," Terry said. "I won't tell anyone."

"I am being honest with you," I said. "Why are you asking me this?"

"Well, I want her to be happy," he said, taking another swallow of wine.

"I understand that," I said. "I want her to be happy, too."

"Good," he said, and then suddenly asked, "Do you like guys as well?"

I sat very still, and started slowly shaking my head, reddening. "What?"

"I think you heard me," Terry said. "Do you go both ways? I'm just curious."

This was something you asked an adult. I felt that with this one question I was now effortlessly crossing to the other side of the room, where the grown-ups were hanging out—but I wasn't ready: I thought I'd been but I wasn't. I also realized I had to rise to the question and try to tell the truth. "Well, I'm not limited," was how I answered with what I thought was the right touch of diplomacy. "I mean, it depends." I tried to appear casual, offered a little shrug, and then nervously sipped my ginger ale in the gayness of Trumps.

"Depends on what?" Terry asked, still slightly smiling, staring at me.

"I guess it depends on . . ." And then I found myself admitting: "I certainly wouldn't kick Richard Gere out of bed, if that's what you want to know." I was trying to sound tough and butch when I said that but I really sounded evasive and lame.

"Yeah? What about Thom Wright?" Terry asked. "You find him hot?"

This was the beginning of the game Terry was proposing, the warm-up, and if I wanted to get anywhere I had to at least try and play it. "Do you?" I asked, staring back at him.

"Thom? Yeah, of course," Terry said. "In fact I'm very jealous that you get to spend so much time with him." He thought about something. "He's pretty fetching, though I'm fairly sure his tastes are more . . . limited than yours."

"Sometimes I can't tell if you're joking around or not, Terry."

"What do you mean?" Terry said. "I'm being totally serious."

"I mean how do you know Thom's tastes are more limited than mine?" This came out the wrong way and suggested something I hadn't intended.

"That's interesting." Terry sat up a little. "Come on, tell me, you ever fool around with Thom, a little drunk, a little high, a sleepover, you guys get horny and need to—"

"That's not what I meant." I tried to laugh but it sounded as if I had just lightly coughed. "Thom is so not what you're picturing."

"Come on, what do you think of Thom?" Terry asked me. "What about Jeff Taylor?"

"Terry, what do you think I think?" I asked.

He was enjoying himself, toying with me, making everything lightly pervy. "I think that if your tastes, as you say, Bret, aren't that limited then I think you probably would want something to happen with Thom or Jeff."

"Yeah, why them?" I asked.

"Because I think you're all quite attractive young men," he said. "You go to school together. You share a locker room, I assume. You . . .

shower together. That's all. They're available." He sipped his wine again.

"They're not available," I stressed.

"Okay, whatever you say," Terry said, and then, "Richard Gere? Really?"

Terry had just confirmed his homosexuality to me that afternoon—something he had never admitted before in so many words; it was always just innuendo, a dumb joke or suggestive phrasing, there had only been rumors. *What are you wearing?* Terry asked me over the phone last week and we'd just laughed it off. He'd never made a move or touched any of us inappropriately as far as I knew, and he didn't seem, in the parlance of today, a predator—and if he was, so what? I could probably handle it even though I didn't want to. But Terry seemed to feel something was now allowable—I had met him for lunch and he'd admitted something about himself and didn't have to pretend anymore. But my curiosity was clouding the situation. It became unavoidable.

"What about Liz?" I asked.

"What about her?" Terry asked back.

I shrugged, looked down at the table. "What does she think?"

His tone didn't change when he said, "You're smarter than that, Bret."

"I don't know what that means."

"She has her suspicions, of course," Terry said. "But I'm under the impression that we have an understanding." Terry tossed this off casually, and then, tinged very lightly with irony, enunciated, "An arr-ange-ment."

"That's cool" was all I could think of to finally say, and I didn't ask how this explained away her drunken outbursts concerning Terry's sexuality.

"What about Debbie?" Terry asked me, grinning. "Does she know about your proclivities?"

"My proclivities?" I asked. "You mean that I'm not limited?"

"No, that you're probably . . . bi," Terry said. "As if such a thing exists. Though I guess for the right price . . ." He looked at me when he said: "I heard a rumor about Jeff Taylor."

I noticed that David Hockney and his companion had gotten up from their table and were looking over at Terry, who smiled and held up a hand. That's when I decided I needed to get out of Trumps. I looked at my watch. "I should probably be going."

"Why?" Terry asked. "Don't you want to meet David?"

"I have a class," I said. "And some after-school stuff back at Buckley."

"Okay." He watched as I stood up.

"Thanks for lunch, Terry," I said. My heart was racing as I tried to act super-casual but I was so disappointed. What had been accomplished? What was the purpose of all this? The answer was: nothing.

"You barely ate," Terry said, touching the stem of the wineglass, swirling what was left of the Chardonnay. "Though I heard you had a cocktail at the bar before I arrived."

"Yeah, well." I shrugged, then reached into my slacks for the valet ticket.

"Please don't say anything to Debbie," he reminded me, looking up.

"Isn't that a little weird?" I couldn't help but ask.

"Isn't *everything*?" Terry said. "Oh, tell her, don't tell her. I don't think you will."

"Thanks for lunch," I said again and turned away.

And then suddenly Terry grabbed my wrist. I stopped, stunned, and looked down at him, my arm stretched out between us.

"I'll have Steven call you and we can set up a time to start talking about that script I want you to write for me," Terry said quietly.

8

I'M GOING TO RECOUNT an incident that occurred in a space on Melrose, the one Debbie mentioned the first day of school when I stood dazed in the administration office realizing what the future entailed for me our senior year: it was the space that didn't have a name, the space that someone called Attila had recommended, the space that just showed videos. And for the longest time I connected that night to Robert Mallory, because it seemed to exactly precede the series of events that began to alter and consume our lives in the following weeks, a kind of macabre prologue to what ultimately happened to us in the fall of 1981. I suppose I could now look at that night in the space on Melrose from a different angle and not connect it directly to the presence of Robert Mallory, and consider, rather, that this was an incident solely about the deranged cult that drifted in from the high deserts southwest of Los Angeles and began materializing on the streets and in the neighborhoods of L.A. But in the end it didn't matter what the angle was, since the two—Robert and the cult—were ultimately intertwined.

THAT WEEK I'D BEEN reading an article about the cult in the *Los Angeles Times*. A group of young, barely articulate hippies, formed out in the Mojave, acolytes of a leader only referred to as "Bruce"—who turned out to be a high-school English teacher from Lancaster, fired due to "sexual improprieties" with a number of female students—and it would normally have sounded absurd and been dismissed as junior-level Manson stuff, but their persistence in making themselves known and visible in L.A. was becoming slightly chilling in its aggressiveness; many of them had been arrested for trespassing, climbing over a gate to the backyard if no one answered the front entrance, or if the bell the hippie eagerly pressed was ignored they'd walk around the property, peering through windows, and then try the sliding glass doors, banging on them until someone appeared in the kitchen and called the police; sometimes they were found in someone's pool or on a chaise longue in Hancock Park and Silver Lake, tripping on acid, wreaths of leaves garlanded as crowns around their heads, or sometimes they were hiding in the garage wedged into a trash can, and a few of the men were involved in physical altercations with people exiting grocery stores and movie theaters, restaurants and parking lots, demanding money, berating anyone who wasn't willing to offer a few dollars. I remember there were three or four photos of various cult members in the *Los Angeles Times* article and they looked slightly cleaner than members of the Manson family and so young and harmless—but maybe Los Angeles became more invested in this cult because of how wounded it had been by the Tate-LaBianca murders and the damage inflicted on the psyche of the city—and there was the same general ragtag scruffiness, the dead-eyed youth, a kind of psychotic apathy behind whatever brainwashed mission they conjured up. It was vague: unify, bring together, utopia, erase pain, destroy status quo, the same tired slogans. They also believed in aliens who could "heal" them and they were enthralled with peyote and *Love is everything, everything is nothing.* This was the first time I'd read about the cult, self-named Riders of the Afterlife; they'd been encountered from Beachwood Canyon all the way to Ojai, but I'd never heard of them before.

And in that same issue of the *Los Angeles Times* there was a report of another home invasion last Monday night in Woodland Hills. It was the familiar narrative: phone calls in the preceding week, furniture rearranged, a dog in the neighborhood missing for a few days; the victim was assaulted by a figure in a black ski mask, the victim was tied to a chair and knocked unconscious, a pattern was completed, the victim unaware that they had found themselves in a pattern; otherwise they would have gone to the police earlier. And for a moment I began to connect the home invasions with the cult. I remember putting the paper down on that Thursday night and going back to my novel, distracted and worried about the Riders of the Afterlife, and wondering if they were responsible for the break-ins and the disappearances that were haunting the city instead of just a lone intruder. Maybe it was the eeriness of the article about the cult that activated my imagination that night, because I kept thinking I heard someone in the house. I was at my desk, working on the novel, and whenever I stopped typing I would suddenly sit very still, positive that a presence either was lurking outside the house or was actually somewhere within it. I'd try and push it out of my mind but a number of times I thought I heard the doorbell or the chiming that announced the garage doors were opening. I crept through the house clutching a butcher knife, but no one was there.

AT NINE O'CLOCK on that Thursday night I jumped in my chair when I heard a car pulling up the driveway and my heart started racing before it took me a moment to calm down and realize that it was Debbie who had come to pick me up and remember we were heading to the space on Melrose. I grabbed my wallet and jogged out of the bedroom and down the hall and walked straight out of the brightly lit house to where the BMW was parked in the driveway. Debbie had just gotten out of the driver's side and was standing with the door open when she saw me bounding down the front steps. I was wearing jeans, a white T-shirt and a burgundy V-neck sweater with a gold Armani eagle emblazoned on its chest and Topsiders with no socks. It was warm out.

"I was going to come in," she said.

"Let's just go," I said, hurrying toward the car.

"Well, I wanted a drink."

"Let's just have one when we get there," I said. "I want to get out of the house."

"Is something wrong?" she asked.

"No," I muttered. "I just want to get out. It's already nine."

She waited a beat and decided not to push it. I opened the passenger door and slid in. The car smelled of clove cigarettes and roses and when she started the ignition "Tainted Love" blasted out, startling me and I jumped in my seat—the second time that night. Debbie turned to me, amused. "You're . . . a little tense." I forced myself to relax and smile lazily at her. "I'm fine, babe," I said in as suave a voice as I could muster. She turned the car around and started pulling out of the driveway that led down to Mulholland, deserted at nine on a Thursday night. She looked over at me before making a left as if to confirm something. Annoyance briefly flared and I said, "Come on, I'm fine." She breathed in and said, "I didn't say anything," then turned onto Mulholland, and soon we were passing Beverly Glen as we listened to a mixtape I'd made (obscure tracks from Talking Heads' *Fear of Music,* and David Bowie's *Scary Monsters*) and then we passed Coldwater Canyon, and made a right onto Laurel, where Debbie raced down the winding road—barely another car passed us that night—until we crossed Sunset and Fountain and Santa Monica and finally hit Melrose.

It was now nine-thirty, and past Fairfax, Melrose was mostly a dark and deserted stretch of storefronts—this section of Melrose hadn't become totally gentrified and except for the occasional retro clothing store there really weren't any other shops or restaurants, so it wasn't hard to find an empty parking spot on a Thursday night. I wondered how close the club we were going to was located as Debbie did a couple of bumps from a small plastic packet and then offered it to me—I declined. I couldn't handle cocaine like Debbie or even Thom Wright was able to—I couldn't just do a bump or two and let that take me through the party. I always craved more, which is why I said no that night; there was never enough and we had school the next day. When I got out of the BMW I looked both ways down the empty street and had no idea where the space was: there was nothing to signify this "happening" and "underground" location only a few knew about—no lights, no sign, no people milling out in front—and though this was Debbie's first time at what came to be known only as "the space" she knew exactly where it was and I walked with her until we came to a darkened storefront in the 7200 block. Debbie simply opened a metal door and walked in and I followed, accompanied by the lone sound of a helicopter somewhere in the overcast night sky.

—

THE OPENING OF "RAPTURE" BY Blondie was playing as we moved down the entrance hall, where only a couple of bare lightbulbs illuminated a concrete floor and Pepto-Bismol–pink walls, the paint peeling away in great patches of black and silver, and Junior, a tall, thin Jamaican wearing a black suit with a white shirt and a black tie and a porkpie hat, was sitting on a high wooden stool and hugged Debbie while the dreamily ominous first verse of "Rapture" played out softly past the doorman—I remember this so clearly and I remember looking behind me to see if anyone was following us down the hallway. I was introduced as "This is my boyfriend, Bret," and then she took my hand and led me into the room beyond the hallway, our movements seemed to be choreographed by the song itself. It was so dimly lit that the few people in the space, maybe only four or five, were just silhouettes, shadows, you couldn't fully see them—the only light source came from the soft orange neon thinly piped along the bottom of the walls, giving the room just enough of a faint glow to make sure you could navigate the space without losing your equilibrium. Flat gray carpeting covered the floor and made it feel as if you were moving across a darkened landscape through a heavy mist. The other faint light came from six smaller rooms off to the sides of the main space, each of them playing different videos. A green neon palm tree and a pink neon flamingo affixed to the wall gave off the only light at the bar situated between them and it was manned by a lone bartender, waiting, immobile. "Rapture" kept playing as Debbie swayed to the music while we ordered drinks—I had vodka-and-grapefruit and Debbie had a glass of champagne and then lit a clove cigarette and said something to the bartender, who she seemed to know and who gestured toward the darkness as I paid. Debbie took my hand and wanted me to meet Jon, who had opened this space and was in the back room, but I didn't want to meet Jon, so I told her I was going to check the space out, maybe watch some videos in the space, just hang out in the space.

"Is that, like, okay?" I asked when I made out her expression in the green glow coming from the palm tree. "Rapture" kept playing somewhere softly above us, and Debbie shrugged and simply said, "Okay," and headed to the back of the space. It annoyed me that this disappointed Debbie but not enough to accompany her to meet Jon.

The SHARDS

I moved toward the door I was closest to and "Rapture" faded behind me, replaced by the tom-tom-ing of Mick Fleetwood's drum intro to "Tusk," which was the video playing in that room. There were no chairs, no furniture, just a couple of ashtrays dotted the flat gray carpeting that lined the room illuminated only by the video projected on the wall. Lindsey Buckingham's low ominous voice was asking *Why don't you tell me who's on the phone?* as I sat on the floor and sipped my drink, watching the video, which was footage of Fleetwood Mac recording the USC Marching Band in the summer of 1979 at a deserted Dodgers Stadium, palm trees set against the faded white sky beyond the empty black scoreboard, and you glimpsed Christine McVie holding a glass of white wine and Stevie Nicks looking hungover and puffy, twirling a baton, and there was a cardboard cutout of John McVie propped in the stands since the real one was in Hawaii, and the Spirit of Troy were in their Roman gladiator attire. I sat up a little when I realized that Lindsey Buckingham, in a new phase of his career, cleaned up, shaven, short-haired, New Wave—the seventies were over—and wearing a white T-shirt and sunglasses resembled almost exactly someone I knew and suddenly while watching the video for what must have been the hundredth time without ever noticing this before, I realized that person was Terry Schaffer. And I suddenly found Terry Schaffer sexier in a new way because of how sexy I now found Lindsey Buckingham.

I was so unnerved by this connection that I got up and quickly left the room, muttering to myself. The same face, the same smile, the same color hair, the same build—in the "Tusk" video Lindsey Buckingham resembled Terry Schaffer in such an unsettling way that it changed my perception of everything. And then I realized Terry Schaffer had actually introduced me to Lindsey Buckingham backstage at the after party when Fleetwood Mac played the Hollywood Bowl on the final night of the *Tusk* world tour, when Terry and Debbie and Liz and Thom and Susan and I all sat in a box and ate takeout from Pioneer Chicken and drank Taittinger from plastic flutes. Why had I never made the connection before? I wandered through the main space recovering from this realization; a few more people had arrived but you couldn't make anyone out, maybe when someone lit a cigarette, and then just briefly. The only lights that guided you through the space were the flickering doorways, where videos played, and the entrance, where Junior sat, which acted like a beacon in the darkness. Someone brushed against me, then disappeared into the mist, and it could have been a ghost.

I PASSED INTO ANOTHER EMPTY room, where Kim Wilde was about to sing one of the pop glories from that year "Kids in America" and I sat on the floor looking up at the video projected on the bare wall. It was so simple: a synthesizer, a smoke machine, Kim Wilde's blank blue-tinged face staring straight at us, and like so many songs of that era it was an anthem, something about being the kids in America, where everybody lives for the music-go-round, but Kim sang it with a quiet determination, a girl who could handle anything with her cool indifference: she didn't get excited by the excitement of the song. This is what gave the song an added tension: Kim remained unsmiling through the soaring chorus—she was withdrawn, dead-eyed, even drugged. Maybe she knew where she was, or maybe she didn't know, maybe she could have been anywhere—this was what became so suggestive in the video. She was offering an invitation but she didn't care if you came or not, because she could always find somebody else. She was radiating that numbness-as-a-feeling aesthetic I was so drawn to and trying to perfect in *Less Than Zero* and I was thrilled seeing it embodied in the poppiest of artifacts. And she also reminded me of Susan Reynolds to a degree—Susan was far more beautiful than Kim Wilde; she was gorgeous by comparison—because Susan also, increasingly, had a faraway demeanor that wasn't indifference exactly; it was really numbness as a come-on, something alluring, something that Susan had developed for years and that was now flowering. They both had it in their eyes, the way their mouths were set, their overall non-expressiveness—and it was hot. I also knew that someone as earnest as Thom Wright would never survive it. But someone like Robert Mallory might thrive.

I suddenly thought again: as a writer, you're always hearing things that aren't there.

And then I flashed on: *When you talk to me you're really talking to yourself, dude.* I was still haunted by it.

The SHARDS

I looked away from the video and stood up and walked back into the main room. But I immediately stopped because, as if on cue, I saw Jeff Taylor with Robert Mallory talking to Junior at the end of the lighted hallway before you descended into the darkness of the space, and the doorman was checking a list even though I had the feeling that Jeff knew him and, of course, I realized, it was Debbie who had invited Robert Mallory and I thought: *God, he's really a part of us now.* Watching him from my hidden vantage point, I also thought about how sometimes he filled me with dread and other times there were flashes when I wanted to kiss him and have him fuck me and the fear and the sex were rarely separated. And then there were the darker moments where I imagined how insane he really was even though none of us knew anything yet; this was just the writer's intuition, the writer's hunch, based heavily on one lie he told—we didn't know the other lies yet.

I WATCHED as Jeff and Robert walked past Junior and into the space and were subsumed by the misty darkness—it concealed everything. They couldn't see me—I was just a few feet away—as Jeff led Robert toward the bar and I turned and went into another, random room, where I fell to the floor, prone on my stomach, and finished my drink. On the wall Roxy Music was singing "Same Old Scene" and I laid my head down on folded arms and could smell how new the carpet was as I waited—there were still so few people in the space that I knew it was only a matter of minutes before Jeff and Robert would locate me. And then I wondered if Thom and Susan were coming and realized I hadn't even asked Debbie, because it never occurred to me that they *wouldn't* be coming, but now I had my doubts and—because Robert was here—I hoped they weren't. I remembered I hadn't asked because I was just so relieved to be in Debbie's BMW moving away from the empty house on Mulholland and concentrating on the mixtape I'd made her in August, the car's air conditioning lightly causing my breath to steam, my eyes fixated on the road outside the windshield, hoping Debbie wouldn't say anything.

I rolled onto my back because suddenly Jeff was standing over me prodding my shoulder with a Topsider. "You wasted already?"

I smiled at him, just lying there, and nodded even though I wasn't.

"Cool," he said approvingly. "Where's Debbie? It's dark as fuck in here."

"She's in back," I said.

"With Jon?" Jeff asked.

"I guess," I said, and then noticed Robert's head over Jeff's shoulder. He offered a little wave and a goofy smile.

"Take care of this guy," Jeff said to Robert. "I'll be back."

A wave of apprehension crashed over me at being left alone with Robert and I was suddenly paralyzed as he smiled and sat down in a lotus position; he was holding a Corona and sizing me up. I felt vulnerable and tried to sit but I couldn't, something wouldn't let me, so I simply rolled onto my stomach and stared as another video started: "I Got You" by Split Enz, the song Debbie and I made out to the night she initiated our relationship at Anthony Matthews's house at the beginning of summer, and when I glanced over, Robert was looking up at the wall, bopping his head to the ominous thumping beat that opened the song and played throughout. He then lay down next to me so that we were side by side and I instantly became distracted—he was close enough to kiss, for me to reach over and run my hand over the rise of his ass, I could smell him. This feeling wasn't remotely pleasurable—it was just a basic hunger that couldn't be waylaid or stopped. The lead singer, Neil Finn, at the height of his twenty-year-old beauty, was in a suit and heavily made up, singing in a room, standing by a pair of French doors, the curtains lit blue and lightly billowing, and shadows patterned the wall where a "painting" hung of the band, everyone dressed in the New Wave suits of that moment, and the band would come alive when the soaring chorus played after the eerie minor-chord verse—it was another anthem, yet this one was tinged with fear.

"What are you doing here?" I finally asked, without looking at him.

"Debbie invited me," I heard him say.

"Oh yeah? Cool," is all I said. I could smell the lotion he used, the shampoo, cologne, cedar and sandalwood, it seemed adult, something a teenager wouldn't wear.

"Yeah, Thom's coming, too," he added.

"Is Susan?" I asked apprehensively.

"No," he said and then turned to me. "Just Thom."

We watched the video. Pairs of eyes were superimposed over Neil Finn, who was trying to hide, and then he joined the band in the painting while also standing in the room and for some reason I was never entirely sure of he starts to collapse with dread—because he sees himself entrapped in the painting while he's still standing in the room, I always guessed, even though I also thought: *What's so bad about that?* The volume was low enough that I could hear Robert say something as the song faded out. And then the video started playing again.

I turned to look at him. "What?"

"Why didn't you end up with her?" he asked, staring up at the images projected on the wall.

"Who?" I asked back, blinking, confused.

"Susan," he said softly.

"Because Thom did," I automatically answered. "What?" I was annoyed—I didn't want to talk about Susan with Robert. And then I wondered: who else did he talk to about her?

"Yeah, but why didn't you?" he asked. "I mean Thom's not the most scintillating dude."

I was shocked that Robert said this about Thom. "He has other . . . attributes," I said lamely, defending my friend.

Robert mimicked me, laughing. *"He has other attributes."*

"Are you okay?" I asked him.

"Yeah, I'm fine," he said, glancing at me and then back up at the video.

"Really?" I asked. "Are you?"

"Yeah. Why? Thought you saw me somewhere again?" he asked with a wink.

I was so close to telling him we knew about the "developmental center" in Jacksonville where he was a patient in the spring of his junior year but I couldn't because of the promise we'd made to Susan—the secret we shared. I looked back up at the video. Just to do something, I lifted the plastic cup and tossed some of the ice at the bottom into my mouth and started chewing, acting casual, pretending Robert wasn't upsetting me with the direction he was taking this conversation. And then he asked, "Are *you* okay?"

"Oh yeah," I said. "I'm good."

"Really?" he asked. "I heard you had a . . . falling out."

Despair flushed through me. "A falling out?"

"Yeah," he said. "With your buddy Matt."

Tendrils of panic started drifting out from the despair, creating their own unique sensation. I kept chewing the ice, trying to remain casual.

"I asked him the other day why he seemed . . . freaked out," Robert said. "Well, not exactly freaked out. But, yeah . . ." He reconsidered but then decided not to. "Freaked out, I guess."

"And what did he say?" I asked tonelessly. Robert always made you aware that ignoring him wasn't allowed as an option.

"That he had a falling out with a friend," Robert said.

"How do you know that's me?" I asked, with a slight shiver of relief. No name. *A friend.*

"I just assumed," he said softly.

"No, not at all," I said. "I don't know what you're talking about."

Robert realized something: he intuited I was lying. "That's how you're going to play it?" he asked softly.

I remember nodding to myself, riding along with the game, and forcing a smile. "Yes, that's how I'm going to play it."

"Oh," he said. "Okay."

The video was suddenly ending again, the song was fading out, the wall became white. We waited for another video to begin. He turned onto his side.

"You never answered me," Robert said. "Why you didn't end up with Susan."

"What do you want to know?"

"I heard you were there first," he said.

"Because Thom came around."

"But why weren't you with her instead?" he asked.

I realized something and swallowed hard.

"I didn't want to lose a friend," I said.

"But didn't you lose Matt?" Robert asked softly.

I didn't say anything, just stared at him. I was disoriented, dizzy. I needed another drink to blot out the pain that suddenly shot through me.

"I don't get it. About Susan," Robert said. "Didn't you want to? I don't get it." He positioned himself on his back, a leg crossed over a knee.

"Didn't I want to *what*?" I asked, completely unnerved, sitting up.

He shrugged. "Squeeze those titties? Suck and bite those titties?" he asked softly. He waited. "I bet her wet pussy tastes pretty sweet."

I sat there and looked at him blankly. But he wasn't looking at me. He was just lying on his back, surrounded by the flat gray carpeting, and staring up at the ceiling.

"I don't know about you, Bret, but I'd love to put my tongue up that tight little pussy, all pink and wet," Robert murmured, lost in his own reverie. "Little honey pot."

I became aroused hearing Robert talk like this but also repelled because he was talking about Susan.

"Yeah," he was saying. "I'd really like to fuck her in the ass. Really fuck that ass hard. Make her scream for it."

At this point I just pushed myself up and walked out of the room.

"Hey, where are you going?" I heard Robert calling out.

I wasn't a prude: I was drawn to porn and sometimes talked dirty to Matt Kellner while we had sex and I knew someone who fooled around with Ron Levin for cash and made no judgments but I'd never been part of a conversation where someone detailed what they would do to a friend of mine sexually and what made it so awful was that Robert was someone I barely knew. A young actress or a pop singer was usually the norm, the target, for this kind of guy talk, rather than a girl you knew, but never bragging about what you'd do to them in the particularly explicit way Robert had, because it was trashy and low-class. And it wasn't as if I even cared about decorum or rules or propriety—I was a writer: I believed everyone had a voice and could say whatever they wanted, and sometimes I'd wished that Thom talked more about sex than he ever did or that Ryan wasn't so circumspect or that the conversations in the boys' locker room were rowdier and more gleefully obscene, but Buckley didn't encourage this, and that night in the space on Melrose I was *glad* it didn't. The way Robert Mallory said this about Susan—it was only two or three lines—*relieved* me that we were all somewhat apprehensive about expressing ourselves in such a grotesque way. I also remember thinking that I should have stayed in the room with Robert and talked him through this so I could have a better inkling of what his plans for Susan Reynolds actually were, because I knew he was going to act on them and I was afraid for Susan and I wanted to be prepared. But I also knew: she was going to throw a party for him, she had found him *electrifying*, she was going to let herself get lost in his madness, and everything would get ruined. I was shaking, furious, when I left the room.

I MOVED into the space and walked up to the bar and asked the bartender where the bathrooms were and he pointed to a barely illuminated EXIT sign at the back of the room and I made my way past a few clusters of shadows, the orange ash from the tips of cigarettes the only props that confirmed people existed in the darkness, because you couldn't see faces and everything was vaguely hushed, even with Madness singing above us. I remember that I didn't get what the point of the space was: on one level, I supposed it was cool—because Debbie Schaffer knew about it—but what was the point if you couldn't see anyone and there was no dancing and the only thing to do was sit in an empty room on the floor and watch videos from 1980. And I remember being annoyed that I would have to confront Debbie about inviting Robert because of how unstable he was and yet I remember pausing when I planned to do this because Robert's instability hadn't fully proven itself yet to anyone else and I didn't know what could set him off. *I don't like being followed,* he told me in the Galleria—I had taken note of that.

I remember that once I'd parted the black curtain below the EXIT sign I suddenly heard Debbie's faraway voice and the muffled sound of male laughter, coming from wherever Jon's office was—I heard Jeff Taylor's hyena giggle as well. I moved down a hallway lined with windows that looked over a small parking lot where an alley traversed parallel to Melrose and the hallway was lit by the streetlamps that illuminated the alley. There were no cars in the parking lot except for a beige van situated in the last parking space and no one in the hallway waiting for the one unisex bathroom. A white candle was lit next to the sink, so you could only make out the toilet and the urinal but nothing else, and it smelled as if it had been recently cleaned. I couldn't find the light switch to brighten the space, so I closed the door and locked it and walked over to the urinal illuminated by the candle.

Another question I almost immediately asked myself: why would a mirror in a bathroom be almost completely ensconced in darkness at a nightclub for young people—girls who wanted to touch up their makeup, boys who wanted to check out their hair? But maybe there was a point to the space that I wasn't grasping yet, maybe it was partly a prank, the *anti*-scene, the wry commentary on how you could make anything seem fashionable to L.A.'s young and hip if you just made it exclusive enough. Maybe the space was performance art conjured up by older hipsters taking advantage of the naïveté of the city's youth. But then I doubted this, because Debbie was so plugged in and would have told me the space was a joke, not real, something to be amused by, a one-shot, and she hadn't.

I unzipped my jeans and stood at the urinal, and sensed that the bathroom, despite the darkness, was much larger than I even first presupposed—when I initially flushed the urinal its sound echoed farther into a darkness than I originally imagined. It was completely silent as I contemplated my shadow wavering against the wall and tried to relax—I couldn't hear anything from the space, no music, no muffled sound, and I should've been relaxed enough to urinate, but Robert Mallory had hyped me up and I was still tense from our encounter. I remember that I breathed in and thought about how much progress I'd made on the novel and looked forward to new movies I wanted to see, Ryan Vaughn, calm blue ocean—but these thoughts were interrupted by: should I tell anyone that I thought the desecration of the Buckley Griffin was connected to Robert Mallory—that *he* had vandalized it—and that he was planning on fucking Susan Reynolds in the ass until she screamed? I exhaled, relaxed, tried again.

And then I realized something. I wasn't alone in the bathroom.

—

I REALIZED THAT SOMEONE was also in there, with me, in the darkness.

And I remember how I froze when I started hearing a faint whispering coming from one of the darkened corners behind me, and it sounded low to the floor, as if whoever the whispering emanated from was crouched down.

"Hello?" I asked with a jolt of adrenaline. I immediately zipped up.

I remember that I turned around but couldn't see anything—just the area illuminated by the candle. There was a larger room beyond that lit area, I now realized.

The whispering continued.

"I'm sorry," I said. "I didn't know someone was in here."

No one answered or said anything.

Instead a voice began whispering what sounded like an incantation, repeating phrases over and over, almost as if they had to eagerly convince themselves of whatever it was they were desperately incanting, a series of garbled sounds, in a language I didn't recognize, but in the five seconds I stood there in the darkness I realized that it wasn't a language—it was just gibberish, nothing. I don't know why, but I was bold enough to pick up the candle and near the voice in the darkness—it kept breathlessly incanting and then wheezing inward and there was another rush of infantile rambling and I remember it became daunting how deep the bathroom seemed. I had walked maybe eight full steps, holding the candle up, until I saw a shadow crouched in the corner.

"Hey. What are you doing here?" I asked, my voice managing to stay calmly inquisitive.

I moved the candle closer until a pale young face was looking up at me, bearded, grinning, floating in the darkness, and his hair was matted blond, dusted with what looked like twigs and dead leaves, and his eyes were crinkled shut as he kept grinning and incanting, like an idiot, swaying back and forth on his haunches, and he was barefoot. I thought this was someone legitimately retarded or severely handicapped but then he stopped whispering and his face bolted up at mine completely serious and I remember his eyes opened and widened and the smile turned threatening. I saw his hands were dirt-stained and the nails were so long they resembled yellowed talons. I remember backing away, and then dropping the candle, which cracked on the floor and sputtered out, plunging us into darkness, and on instinct, I quickly slammed myself against the wall, clawing toward the direction of the door, grabbing for the handle and unlocking it, and raced out of the blackness of the restroom.

I REMEMBER THAT I walked straight back into the space, where I told the bartender there was someone—maybe a homeless guy—who had crashed the club and was in the bathroom. "Some freak is in there who doesn't belong" was how I put it exactly, spitting this out—and what a strange way to word what had happened, I now realize, sounding more pissed off than scared. I remember a song by a band called Spider, "New Romance," was playing lightly throughout the space as the bartender disappeared into the sparsely populated darkness and reappeared where Junior was standing in the light. The bartender relayed what I'd told him and then the two of them crossed through the darkness to the bar and the three of us headed toward the black curtain below the EXIT sign.

And I remember the moment we parted the curtain we heard a scream.

In the hallway a blonde girl was nearing us, her hands held up, her face lightly streaked with blood that was quickly spurting from a thin line drawn across her forehead as she staggered down the hallway, the door to the bathroom open behind her, the gibbering now a kind of elongated screeching. "He's in there!" I remember whisper-yelling, pointing. Junior gently took the girl's arm, guiding her away from the bathroom and asking what happened. She said she didn't know: she went into the restroom, wondering where the lights were, and felt something swipe across her face, scratching her.

I watched the bartender walk to the open door with no trepidation and reach in and find the light switch. Immediately the bathroom was illuminated and the hippie rushed at him, the gibbering now incensed and high-pitched. I remember that Debbie had appeared behind me with Jeff and a guy I assumed was Jon, everyone gasping with confusion as the bartender easily pushed the hippie against a wall and then put him in a headlock and dragged him out of the bathroom. The hippie was squealing and thrashing around until he landed in the hallway, where the bartender threw him to the floor. The bartender told Jon to call the police: there was an intruder, get an ambulance. I remember the girl realized something and said she was okay and didn't need an ambulance. And even though it was just a very thin scratch from where the hippie's nail had swiped at her in the darkness it wouldn't stop bleeding as Junior kept pressing paper towels against her forehead that quickly became stained red. "It doesn't hurt," she said, as if annoyed. "But it doesn't hurt," I remember she kept saying. Debbie and Jeff were asking me what the fuck happened and Jon had already called the police and then conferred with Junior and the bartender, who had his foot on the hippie's back, waiting for the police to arrive. I remember that the hippie was looking up at us, pressed against the floor, still whispering incantations, drool slathering his chin, his yellowed teeth bared like he was some kind of animal, and yet what bothered me was that no one seemed particularly frightened of him.

DEBBIE REALIZED SHE VAGUELY KNEW the girl and went over to where she was standing and asked who she'd come with, and then Debbie left to find the friends as Junior kept pressing paper towels to the girl's forehead. Red and blue lights flashed through the windows of the hallway and Jon let the two officers in from the back door and the hippie was handcuffed and hauled out to one of the squad cars in the parking lot and then it was simply over: a girl had been scratched by an intruder who climbed in through an unlocked window, that was it. I remember that the bleeding finally stopped, and the girl was soon standing in front of the mirror, her two friends had joined her, and you could barely see the thin red scratch above her eyebrow—the bleeding had stopped but one of the friends urged her to go to the ER because the scratch might be infected. The girl didn't want to—she seemed annoyed and just asked if anyone had coke. I drifted with Debbie and Jeff through the black curtain and out into the space, which was completely undisturbed by whatever happened in the bathroom and hallway. I remember music was still playing but louder now—Tim Curry, "I Do the Rock"—and the space was filled with more shadows, some of them swaying in the middle of the semi-deserted room, and seemingly no one knew what had happened in the hallway at the back of the space. The bartender was making drinks again as if nothing had occurred and I grabbed a vodka-and-grapefruit and Debbie disappeared into the darkness with another friend, who wanted to do some blow, and I found a room where I sat down and I remember being calmly elated: this was something I could write about, this was an incident I could place into the narrative of the novel I was working on, and I began to think of ways to embellish it—paint it darker, give it an eerier vibe, push evil. I thought about adding the stench of shit from the pile of excrement the hippie had laid out, the knife he was now clutching, a deeper wound inflicted upon the girl, more blood. I wasn't even looking at the video projected on the wall because I was dreaming a different one.

I DIDN'T KNOW THAT someone had been trailing me in the darkness but then Thom Wright pushed me over and I fell onto the carpet, where he playfully tackled me, Jeff Taylor urging him on—this was how Thom sometimes showed affection when he was a little high. He had downed a couple of tequila shots and snorted two bumps of Debbie's coke, and I wrestled with him while he kept trying to tickle me. We were both laughing, his hard body writhing over mine, when he suddenly lifted himself off my chest, panting—Thom had no idea I was getting an erection—because suddenly one of our favorite videos started playing and we looked up to it projected on the wall. The video was mostly in black and white and it was a song about a brief love affair in Vienna and minimalist, with just the slow beat of a drum machine and a mournful piano and synth bass. We had seen the images hundreds of times and they still entranced us: a horse moving through the fog on a cobblestone street, flashes of lightning, the lead singer in a trench coat, an empty city, Vienna in the off-season but also North London, gargoyles. There were the eighties video staples that hadn't become clichés yet: a fancy party in an embassy, a candelabra on a white baby grand beneath a chandelier, martinis drunk by grotesques shot in fish-eye lens, a tarantula crawling across the face of a passed-out guest, an ominous child playing a violin. There were lovers discovered by paparazzi, and someone shot to death on the grand curving staircase of an opera house. *The feeling has gone,* the singer cried out. *It means nothing to me. This means nothing to me.* The final chorus climaxes with a cymbal crash and it always gave me chills. *Oh, Vienna.*

The song was too slow, it was too long, and yet it moved us and like the best pop songs it was an abstraction, poetry that could mean anything to anyone—it was a launching pad for our separate longings but it was obviously a metaphor about loss, and this was something all of us shared, whether it was the pain Thom Wright's parents' divorce caused him, with the father he was closer to now long gone across the continent, or the alcoholism that was destroying Jeff Taylor's father, or my own defeats tied to the actor I often played and didn't want to and who my own father still ignored even as I kept trying to enact the part of a son I thought he wanted. This particular Ultravox song seemed to, obliquely, sum everything up and it defined us in that moment no matter what the lyrics or the video was actually about. We all stayed silent until it was over.

The last thing I remember from that night in the space was Thom Wright and Robert Mallory lying side by side in one of the rooms, where I joined them. The video for Duran Duran's "Girls on Film" was playing and I was standing in the back and watched Robert leaning over and whispering to Thom Wright—who was gripping a Corona bottle, nodding at whatever he was being told, high and innocent— and I imagined he was urging Thom on to the same dark wavelength Robert Mallory himself resided.

9

AFTER THE HORROR OF 1981 the numbness I had found exhilarating during my sophomore and junior and into my senior years hardened ultimately into a remote coldness that took decades to finally thaw. I was never really the same after 1981—there was never a recovery period—and I can now mark the moment when I was last happy, or more specifically where the last traces of happiness, even a warmth, actually existed before I tripped into fear and paranoia and began to understand how the adult world actually operated compared to my adolescent fantasies of how I supposed it worked. And it was the weekend that Ryan Vaughn spent with me at the house on Mulholland when it was mid-September and we were seventeen, a weekend before Matt Kellner disappeared, a weekend before Julie Selwyn's body was found, and everything changed. This weekend with Ryan, flat and uneventful and resolutely peaceful until it briefly wasn't, became the demarcation between innocence and, for lack of any better word and trying not to sound too dramatic, corruption. It's not as if there weren't other weekends in my life that possessed a calmness or even verged on the blandly pleasant—days where I forgot about that year long enough to enjoy myself—it's just that they were always tinged with the knowledge of what happened to us that fall.

For example, in the late summer of 1982, after I graduated from Buckley, I spent the last weeks of August on the shores of Lake Tahoe in a house my aunt had rented and where I remember walking through forests every day, mentally preparing to leave Los Angeles behind—finally, excitedly—and start a new life back east, beginning with Vermont and a small liberal-arts school in the town of Bennington, and then to Manhattan: this was the plan and I spent those weeks in August clearheaded because of the ensuing escape (. . . *time for me to fly* . . .), but I was always aware that someone was watching me, that Robert Mallory was somehow back, and I could soon feel his presence whenever I roamed the empty trails with my Walkman on or swam alone in the lake or was tanning on the deserted deck that led out to the pier. A weekend I remember so clearly because of the freedom that was being promised became a weekend, instead, shrouded with doubt: I would always remember a wall streaked with blood in a high-rise condo and the adjacent balcony splashed with it, I realized.

THERE WAS A WEEKEND soon after that, in October of 1982, when my parents met me in New York. My father had just completed a real-estate deal that moved him into another realm of wealth and he had flown up from Pittsburgh, where the sale had been conducted, while my mother flew in from Los Angeles to celebrate and aim for reconciliation—they had been separated on-and-off for two years— and I took the train down from Bennington so we could attempt to become a family again. We stayed at the Carlyle, we saw *Cats* in previews at the Winter Garden, my father's newly hired art adviser encouraged him to check out the show of a young painter named Julian Schnabel in SoHo, we ate at Le Cirque. I remained drunk most of the time, presenting the new identity I'd formed at Bennington to my relieved parents, and through that whirlwind weekend, filled with musicals and restaurants, shopping at Gucci and flitting through art galleries, my parents' presence was a constant reminder of Los Angeles, a place I wanted to forget. And again I had become fearful I was being watched, whether I walked through Barneys or along the edges of Central Park or at the crowded bar in P. J. Clarke's—I never got over the feeling that Robert Mallory was somewhere, holding a pair of binoculars, or looking at me through a telescope, constantly locating and monitoring me, from *somewhere*.

There was a weekend that still haunts me from the summer of 1991, when I rented a cottage on the beach in Wainscott. I'd embarked on a relationship—really, my first—with a Southern lawyer who worked on Wall Street only a few years older than me, and it seemed happiness might finally announce itself, after I'd tried to forget about that autumn a decade behind me, and it came close mainly because of the distraction of endless sex while "Losing My Religion" strummed constantly throughout the cottage, REM's *Out of Time* being the record we played most that summer, but I ran into someone from L.A. at a party in Amagansett that third weekend in the Hamptons who recognized me and knew about the events at Buckley in 1981—the guy was my age and had graduated from the Harvard School for Boys the same year—and drunkenly asked about what really happened to Robert Mallory, and Thom Wright and Susan Reynolds, and everything immediately got ruined. I knew I would never forget a dead girl found mutilated in a soundproofed basement or the blood-splattered condo in that Century City high-rise where everything ended up devolving into ruin, and certainly not the faint pale scars that crisscrossed my chest I was so self-conscious about. The lawyer and I left Wainscott earlier than planned, as if there was someplace else to escape.

THERE WERE TWO weekends in 2008 that in my mind thematically led into each other, and one played out more as a metaphor than something tangible and tactile. The first was spent at the Hearst Castle, where I had accepted, along with a dozen other guests, an invitation from Jay McInerney and his wife, Anne Hearst, to spend the weekend and where I drove up the coast from Los Angeles to San Simeon on Friday, September 12, with a younger guy I wasn't serious about who I met in West Hollywood. Once you were there it was almost impossible to get phone reception and after a while you just stopped looking, so the weekend, lavish and decadent, spent swimming in the Roman Pool at sunset while drinking Dom Pérignon and eating beluga caviar, passed by with us having no idea what was about to happen in the real world. As we drove down the coast on Monday the 15th we learned that Lehman Brothers had officially gone bankrupt and financial markets across the globe were collapsing— the disconnect between that weekend spent in a gilded bubble and the actual reality of the messy world acted as a metaphor for me as a writer that I haven't been able to shake off. And I mention it only because, strangely enough, it led to the following weekend, which I spent in Palm Springs at the behest of a producer I was writing a script for who put me up at the Parker, where I was one of only three or four guests because of what happened with the financial markets—everyone had fled. The Parker was kept open and ghostly, the grounds entirely devoid of life, and I would sit in the empty dining room after spending a day with the producer at his home in the movie colony working on a script that would never be made, months wasted on a project that hadn't even paid that well but I was promised I could direct (this was the added incentive), and all I could think about that weekend in 2008 was running into Susan Reynolds at Las Casuelas, a Mexican restaurant on North Palm Canyon Drive, at one point during the fall of our senior year and how I'd made a promise to her there about a secret she needed kept, something I could never tell Thom Wright.

And I remember the weekend with Ryan Vaughn in September of 1981 at the empty house on Mulholland, because it was the last weekend untainted by the past. The basic reason why the weekend *happened* was, I realize in retrospect, sex, and the hope tied to the sex. It was about desire in its simplest form, and a purity that I would never experience again.

IT HAPPENED SO easily, with no drama, none of the "subterfuge" that Ryan had hinted at, and no planning. Ryan and I were by the lockers on that Friday afternoon and he simply said, "I'm going to spend the weekend at your house," and I responded with "Yeah, that's great." He looked at me and then made the *What's up?* face, our parodic expression of tense helplessness—bug-eyed with surprise, lips pulled back, something we might have seen in a Devo video— and I lightly laughed as I lifted a book from the locker and then he said, "I'll see you sometime tonight," and turned and walked away. That was it. I don't like to admit this but I started shaking in front of the opened locker and it took more than a moment to control it—the trembling came from lust and the fact that I knew what was going to occur, finally, between the two of us, something more than just the quick blow job and jerk-off that happened in August. On one level very little actually occurred that weekend: we barely left the house, there was not a lot of conversation, the NFL season had started and there were football games on Sunday that Ryan wanted to watch, we went to the market at the Beverly Glen Centre only once, to pick up two six-packs of Corona and a couple of steaks, which we grilled Saturday night, mostly relying on the premade food Rosa had left in the refrigerator. The weekend was, however, mostly devoted to sex and everything else seemed to revolve around it. Each day was punctuated by sex; sex was what defined the weekend.

Ryan arrived around six on Friday, parking the Trans Am in the driveway and carrying a duffel bag over his shoulder as he walked toward the house. I remembered how strange it always seemed to look at Ryan Vaughn not in his Buckley uniform—it was how I was used to him—but also on that Friday it was even stranger to see him finally reduced by desire and the nervousness in trying to hide it and I could feel something strained between us as I walked him into the house, which he had only been to twice before. And I was nervous too—you could hear the nervousness in our voices and the distant ways we were dealing with each other. He put the duffel bag down and petted Shingy, who was leaping around Ryan, the dog wagging its tail frantically, uselessly excited by Ryan's presence, and it seemed that Ryan was grateful to have this distraction for a moment while he figured out where this was all going, and then said he wanted to take a swim. This was the prelude to sex, I realized: the removal of clothes, the cleansing of the body. I was already in a bathing suit and a T-shirt and I walked out to the backyard with him as he kicked off his Topsiders and pulled the Polo shirt over his head and then unzipped his jeans and tugged them off, leaving the white jockey shorts on. He gracefully dived into the pool and quickly swam its length, smiling at me as just his head sliced across the water until he turned around and glided across the pool with another lap. I was now sitting in the Jacuzzi watching him, hoping the warm water would calm me, because I was too keyed up, too horny, and I realized one of us was going to have to make that first suggestion so we could move past this almost intolerable state of expectation, and I doubted Ryan was going to initiate it. I got out of the Jacuzzi and told Ryan I was going to take a shower.

He silently swam to the edge of the pool, rested his arms on the tiled coping and nodded, just grinning blankly.

"Okay, I'll be there in a minute," he said.

I WAS HAVING TROUBLE controlling my breathing as I walked across the lawn to the deck that led to my room, where I opened the door and stepped in and just stood still for a moment, staring at the bed and the light-gray comforter stretched tight over the king-sized mattress. When I came out of the shower Ryan was in the doorway pulling off his wet jockey shorts and I walked up to him, a towel wrapped around my waist, and our mouths locked together in a sudden hungry kiss and I dropped the towel. He pulled back, trying not to trip over the wet jockey shorts entangled around an ankle, and when he finally kicked it off, he briefly stood still, tall and casually muscled, not bulky but lean, almost completely smooth except for the tufts coming from his armpits and the light blond hair on his forearms and the bush where his pink cock was sticking straight up almost parallel to the abdominal muscles that ran up his taut, hard stomach. I reached for his cock and he reached for mine. The sex wasn't based on anything except an overwhelming need and that's why it was so intense that weekend: it just had to happen, there was a physical logic to it—it wasn't about dreams or friendship or love or romance. It was, in fact, methodical and we were prepared. We knew this wasn't a fantasy: beach towels were laid across my bed so we wouldn't stain the sheets with baby oil, this was the first time I showed Ryan how to use an enema, we took turns fucking with a small vibrator I'd bought at the Sex Shoppe on Ventura Boulevard before we carefully guided our own cocks into each other. The one time Ryan and I'd been together had been exciting but rushed, and on that Friday in September we took our time.

The surprise, for me, was not how horny we were but how badly we wanted to give each other pleasure—unlike with Matt, sex with Ryan was an unexpectedly sensual experience, he was curious and relaxed and the sex played out longer because we wanted it to, there was no need to hurry and get it over with, because we had all weekend, there was no time limit. And there was nothing but the sex: there was no domestic situation playing itself out, no guilty conversations about what we were doing, no one was racked with anxiety, neither one of us inhabited a particular role, no one was only passive, no one was only dominant—I fucked Ryan the same amount of times he penetrated and fucked me and often we switched off, took turns fucking each other in the same session until both of us were aching to ejaculate and couldn't hold it in any longer. And I was amazed looking down on his muscled back flexing with a sheen of sweat while he was on all fours, his pale ass spread open, allowing my cock to slide in and out of him while he muttered obscenities urging me on, that Matt Kellner didn't exist anymore—Ryan had erased him.

RYAN PLAYED BOB SEGER'S *Against the Wind* that weekend and Bruce Springsteen's *The River* and we watched *Flash Gordon* on the Z Channel, making sexy jokes about Sam Jones, who we both thought was and wasn't hot—we went back and forth, we couldn't tell, something about the hair, a debate about his costume. We lived in the bed and in the pool and in the living room that weekend, just the two of us, and I ignored phone calls from Susan and my mother, who was somewhere in Greece. Debbie called and we only talked briefly—she threatened to come over after I told her that I wasn't feeling well and I'd see her Monday morning at Buckley, but this only worried her: "You're not feeling well? Do you know what's wrong? Are you okay?" I assured Debbie that everything was fine but that I wanted to go back to sleep and finally got her to hang up, and then realized something, and I remember pulling my mom's Jaguar out of the garage and backing it onto the driveway to let Ryan park his Trans Am in her space instead, and closing the garage door, in case Debbie came by unannounced. "That was a good idea," Ryan said, pulling me into the hallway, and kissing me deeply as I became instantly erect. We stumbled toward the bedroom. Later, we were soaking in the Jacuzzi, slightly buzzed from Coronas, and we were about to make dinner but languid from the sex, and were just staring at each other, only Ryan's head and shoulders above the bubbling water, his blond hair wet and darkened and slicked back. It was night now and Ryan murmured he was getting hungry and then I asked him something, genuinely curious how he would answer. I remember "Thunder Island" by Jay Ferguson was playing from the outside speakers.

"What do you think of Robert Mallory?"

"The new guy?" Ryan asked. "He's a good-looking guy, why?"

I hated the way he said this as if it wasn't something he had to think about or process. It was apparently so obvious that this response came out of his mouth automatically. I breathed in. "Yeah, I guess."

He noticed the way I sighed. "What? Is something wrong?" He tipped his head back until he was floating, one of his feet brushing against my chest; he kept his toe pressed against a nipple, smiling as if he was proud of himself—Ryan's confidence was a turn-on, animal and masculine.

"No, nothing, yeah, he's pretty good-looking," I said quickly, and then, after a prolonged beat, where I grabbed his calf and held it in both hands, said, "I think Thom is maybe getting too close to him." I wasn't sure if this was exactly true but I was haunted by the way Thom and Robert lay next to each other on the carpet below the Duran Duran video in the space on Melrose and I threw this out there to see how Ryan would react.

"Too close?" Ryan asked, raising an eyebrow, pulling his leg away. "What does that mean?"

I paused, looked up at the night sky, and then back at Ryan. "Nothing."

"Thom likes everybody, Bret," Ryan said quietly. "Thom would become friends with a head of lettuce if he could. A taco. A raccoon." I smiled at Ryan, letting him know that I knew this too about Thom. And yet I couldn't let it go.

"Yeah, but I think there's something wrong with him," I murmured.

Ryan was losing the thread of the conversation. He asked, somewhat confused, "Who? Thom?"

"No. Robert," I said. "I think there's something wrong with him."

He looked at me, concerned. "Like what?" He floated off the bench he'd been sitting on and started to step through the water toward me. I realized I couldn't tell him what I knew—about the developmental center in Jacksonville that Robert had been a patient at—because of the promise I'd made to Susan, the secret I told her I'd keep. In the silence that ensued I drifted off.

The SHARDS

"I'd do him," Ryan said, nearing me. The light in the Jacuzzi was off but the adjacent pool was glowing aqua blue and illuminated his features, and with his hair slicked back the details of his almost perfectly symmetrical face were more pronounced and I even noticed for the first time that a very light span of freckles dotted his nose and cheekbones. I hated that he said this about Robert but I was so relaxed and so dazed by the sex that a kind of calmness mitigated the flair of emotion I suddenly experienced when Ryan said that. And I had to agree with him about Robert Mallory. "Yeah, me too," I said. "I'd do him too." Ryan was directly in front of me, on his knees, staring into my eyes as I felt a hand on my dick, and then he said in a low voice, heavy with lust, "What would you do to him?" He was so close to me our lips touched and I could feel the tip of his erection as it pressed against my thigh.

"Tell me," he said. "What would you do to him first?"

THERE WAS A MOMENT NEAR the end of the weekend when things slightly veered off course and this was early Sunday night. Ryan had been watching football games all afternoon in the living room and drinking Coronas since around two o'clock and I kept wandering in and out, working on my book in the bedroom, going over an essay I was late with, joining him for an occasional pool break—we'd already had sex when we woke up—and at one point Debbie called, wanting to know how I was feeling and if she needed to come over: maybe she could bring me something, chili from Chasen's, Double Rainbow ice cream—and I spoke to her in the kitchen, mid-morning, in front of Ryan, who was eating a bagel with smoked salmon while reading the "Sports" section of the Sunday *L.A. Times* and said nothing when I had to reply, "Love you, too," and then hung the phone up. Ryan simply accepted that Debbie Schaffer was something that I was going to pursue and took another bite of the bagel and turned a page, but not before glancing at me with a grin and an exaggeratedly cocked eyebrow. I shrugged. "It's okay," he said. "I get it." But when Debbie called again, later, on the main line after I hadn't picked up the phone in my bedroom, while we were in the living room, and I didn't pick up, she left a long message on the answering machine and

I watched as Ryan seemed jolted with tension, slightly writhing, raising the volume on the TV, holding the remote with his arm pointing straight at the screen, trying to drown out Debbie, and he shook his head when she finally hung up but didn't say anything. When she called a third time, around six, Ryan was still slumped in the armchair in front of the TV, a number of empty Corona bottles on the floor next to him, and he howled: "Jesus Christ—what does she fucking *want*?" He craned his neck to see where I was. "What is she expecting from you?"

I was in the kitchen looking to put out something for dinner. "She just wants to know how I am," I said, shrugging.

"Your imaginary illness?" Ryan asked, rolling his eyes. "She just wants to know if you're recovering from your imaginary illness?" He made a noise. "Smart girl. Can't she take a hint?"

"She doesn't know it's not real," I muttered, pulling a bowl covered with Saran Wrap out of the refrigerator, inspecting it—penne with mozzarella and tomatoes, Rosa's bland specialty.

"She's a spoiled fucking mess," Ryan said, quietly staring at the TV: halftime somewhere was starting, a commercial appeared.

"She's not a mess," I said, finally moving toward him and standing by the armchair. "She really isn't. She just cares . . . about me."

"They're all spoiled fucking rotten," Ryan said quietly, and then, lightly exasperated, "Jesus, Bret, come on."

This was the first time there was any tension, an opposition to what we'd shared during those days, and I suppose I could have let it go and moved back into the kitchen and continued pulling the premade dishes Rosa had left for that weekend, but instead I just stood there and finally asked, "Who is they?"

He paused, made a face, turned to look up at me. "Really?"

"Yeah," I said. "Who is *they*?"

He looked back to the television. "Well, Debbie Schaffer, your girlfriend, for one, with her fucking horse and her beyond-entitled attitude. Tony Matthews, Jeff Taylor—"

"What are you doing?" I asked.

"—Dominic Thompson traipsing around fucking Europe all summer, Tracy Goldman—"

"What about Thom?" I interrupted him.

A pause. "Of course he is," Ryan said quietly. "He's probably the worst."

"The worst what?" I asked, and then, "How can you say that about Thom?"

Ryan waved a hand at me. I realized he was drunk. "They're all spoiled and they do whatever they want and there are no consequences for any of them—"

"Consequences about *what*?" I asked, straining.

"Being a disgusting rich kid," he said, staring at the TV, using the remote to move across channels. "Kyle Colson. Susan Reynolds. Doug Furth. Clueless. That fucking new kid, Robert, with his fucking Porsche 911. Who gets their kid a Porsche 911?"

"What about Matt Kellner?" I ventured.

Ryan just shrugged at the name, didn't say anything.

"You're hardly poor, Ryan," I said finally. "You certainly pass pretty easily."

"Thanks a lot," he muttered.

"You can't possibly care about this," I said. "Come on, you're joking. You don't really care." And then, "I thought you liked Thom."

"I like Thom Wright," Ryan said patiently. "But Thom Wright is also a wuss. A wussy little rich kid who doesn't have a clue."

"Thom Wright thinks you're one of his best friends."

I had been staring at the TV and when I looked down at him from where I was standing I could see that his face was tensed with spite. "Thom Wright is clueless. He doesn't know anything about anything except his stupid little world—"

"I think Thom knows more than that," I said. "I think Thom knows about pain."

"How? Everything is given to him. How do any of our so-called classmates, Bret, know about pain when everything is given to them?" He paused. "They're all spoiled fucking robots, protected in their mansions and given everything they want."

"Thom's parents divorced—"

"Oh yeah, Daddy had to move to New York and get a better job to keep little Tommy and his mom all gussied up in Beverly Hills—"

"Thom is a nice guy, Ryan, and he's a friend of ours."

"I didn't say he wasn't a nice guy." He suddenly sat up—alarmed that this was my takeaway. "I said he was a disgusting little rich kid. But I didn't say he wasn't a nice guy."

"You're drunk," I said. "You sound crazy."

"Maybe," he said, shrugging. "Maybe I'm totally crazy."

"Why do you have so much contempt for Thom? Or for Susan?" I stopped, and then asked, "What about me?"

He shrugged again. "You all just protect each other."

"Protect each other?" I asked. "From what?"

"Reality." Ryan said this in a purposefully spooky voice, making it echo away from him, as if he spoke it in a vast and empty cave.

I DIDN'T PUSH IT further because there didn't seem to be any point—Ryan was mildly drunk and something about the message that Debbie Schaffer had left annoyed him, which led to this quiet tirade about our classmates—that was all. Ryan may have lived in Northridge, which admittedly wasn't as desirable as Beverly Hills, and his father might not have been a famous movie producer or a studio executive or a wealthy real-estate developer and, unlike just about all of his classmates, Ryan usually held down a summer job, but I always thought of him as one of us, and he had something very few students at Buckley possessed, in fact only two or three, and that was a pronounced physical beauty—whatever else eluded Ryan that he may have longed for this one tangible and hard fact about him remained: he was beautiful. And I doubt Ryan would have traded that for Debbie Schaffer's mansion in Bel Air or Dominic Thompson's yacht or Robert Mallory's Porsche. I just blamed this weird petulance on five or six Coronas, since I'd never seen Ryan drink alcohol before and I believed that this was what stoked his quiet outrage, and I let it go. I had never really heard a hint of this class-consciousness in any of the conversations that we'd had last spring or over the summer. But maybe, I thought, he actually had shared this with me at one point and I just hadn't noticed, too lost in his beauty to fully hear him and grasp who Ryan really was besides just a body, a form, an erotic trophy I wanted to win.

Before another football game started Ryan stumbled up and collected the empty beer bottles on the floor next to the armchair and carefully walked into the kitchen and after placing the bottles by the sink pressed against me where I was standing by the island and wrapped his arms around my chest, lightly grinding against my ass. He murmured an apology as his lips grazed my ear and then he turned me around and dropped to his knees—this was the sixth time we'd had sex that weekend, and the last, it turned out. We fell asleep together but he knew that the housekeeper was going to be here at eight the next morning and made me set the alarm. When it went off at seven-thirty, I bolted awake and turned over, but he was already gone. The empty side of the bed was the first hint that maybe Ryan Vaughn wouldn't be taking this as seriously as I was—he hadn't woken me when he'd left, he hadn't said goodbye, he hadn't kissed me. The second hint was the flash of sadness and panic when I realized: I doubt I touched Ryan in quite the same way he touched me.

10

KATHERINE LATCHFORD WAS FOUND in a dumpster in the back of a gas station near Redlands that hadn't been emptied for a month, and Sarah Johnson's body had been stuffed in a drainpipe at an abandoned construction site on the outskirts of Simi Valley, but Julie Selwyn's remains were "presented" in a much more public place when they were finally found—discovered on a tennis court at the Shadow Ranch Park in Woodland Hills by two high-school guys who went to Taft and wanted to play a few sets early that morning—and this suggested that the Trawler was getting increasingly comfortable with the story he was creating, and that perhaps he wanted to make a more immediate impression. The boys from Taft thought that what they were approaching on the green asphalt was a mannequin, someone's idea of a perverse joke, until they smelled a faint rancidness and noticed the clouds of gnats swarming over the desiccated body propped up against the net, legs splayed: there was the skull with the full head of hair and the empty sockets where the eyes had been gouged out and newspapers had been stapled to her body, acting as a kind of wrapping paper, concealing the mutilations—what were later called the "alterations" and the "remakings"—inflicted upon Julie Selwyn. These "alterations" were not known until a series of articles about the Trawler was published in the *Los Angeles Times* later that year, filling in gaps and answering questions people kept wondering about, though it didn't go into a full and complete description and remained somewhat vague because the details about the "alterations" and the "remakings" and the "assemblages" were too obscene and upsetting for what was deemed a family newspaper.

The SHARDS

—

THE WEEK JULIE Selwyn's body was found the LAPD confirmed they had received two phone calls from the suspect or suspects ("the groaning drawl" of the suspect's "fake" voice, the voice that promised it had committed the crimes, and would commit more, was confirmed in the articles that followed) and the nickname that was connected to the suspect was—twice cited as a joke in the redacted file from the Hollywood division of the LAPD—the Trawler. Later, in the *L.A. Times*, there was a photo of a letter scrawled in childlike handwriting from the suspect, the obscenities deleted in black, admitting that he "and his friends" had abducted Julie Selwyn when she was walking to her car, leaving a party on a hillside street in Encino—not far from Haskell Avenue, I noted. What wasn't shown was the letter detailing the damage the Trawler had done to her, something only he would have known—confirming his guilt—and what the two boys from Taft hadn't been able to see beneath the newspapers stapled to what was left of the girl's body. The only thing leaked—and this was never verified that first year—sounded so outlandish as to have been made up, an urban myth, something akin to the quarts of semen that were supposedly pumped out of Rod Stewart's stomach, but even more ghastly: the fish from Katherine Latchford's aquarium, missing a week before she was abducted (and after a poster for the Madness record *One Step Beyond* was left at the doorstep of her parents' house off Coldwater Canyon in Studio City), had been inserted into Katherine's vagina which was glued shut with a liberal amount of rubber cement.

The questions that week in September had become numerous: Where were the bodies kept during those eight weeks between abduction and discovery? How had they been preserved to the degree that they were? When were the girls actually killed? What was the actual cause of death? The *Los Angeles Times* also confirmed that the home invasions that began plaguing the city during the summer of 1980 and the early winter of 1981 and resumed in the late spring of that year and then stopped and began again in the second week of September were definitely connected to the murders, since it was confirmed all three victims in the weeks leading up to their disappearance had complained of the silent phone calls, the rearranged furniture in their bedrooms, the mysterious gifts left for them—in Sarah Johnson's case a poster for the Public Image Ltd double-LP *Second Edition* and in Julie Selwyn's a promotional poster for the Cure record *Three Imaginary Boys*—and, most ominously, the number of disappeared pets from the surrounding neighborhoods that were later sacrificed. But it was also noted that none of the three girls, the murder victims, had been previously attacked by whoever was committing the home invasions.

I BECAME MILDLY FREAKED out that week even though there was an element about the announcement of the Trawler—a confirmation of evil—that made everything vibrate softly with melodrama and I almost became excited in the atmosphere that was playing out: heightened, lightly dangerous, somewhat sexualized. There was an initial narrative that I was creating against the backdrop of these sickening crimes that felt like being in a movie, especially when I'd play Fleetwood Mac's "I'm So Afraid" in the empty house on Mulholland high on Valium, wandering along the veranda, imagining someone was watching me, accompanied by Lindsey Buckingham's wailing guitar solo echoing over the cliff side and the eucalyptus and jacaranda trees, but it couldn't sustain itself and soon I was buying weed from Jeff Taylor in order to fall asleep more easily, numbing myself from the fear that would descend in the moments after I got into bed and turned off the lights, imagining sounds everywhere, the Trawler breaking in, *because it was your turn now,* the ski mask above me would say in that awful drawling voice, eyes wide with madness.

And then I was both surprised and disturbed that the discovery of Julie Selwyn and her connection to the two other murdered girls wasn't much talked about or given the weight that I thought it deserved at Buckley. It seemed to me that people weren't paying attention; maybe people knew that Julie Selwyn had been found and maybe there were others who'd heard about the connections between her and Katherine Latchford and Sarah Johnson but Susan and Debbie weren't as interested as I was and this disappointed me. When I'd ask them about what I called "the case" or what they thought about the Trawler, at first they didn't know what I was talking about, both of them preoccupied, and they deflected my interest by moving on to the planning of Susan's party or a band Debbie wanted to check out downtown or the mysterious Robert Mallory (but only if Thom wasn't around, I'd noticed), and both of them wondering if I'd fully recovered from the weekend when I'd told Debbie I wasn't feeling well enough to hang out with her—days I had spent mostly naked with Ryan Vaughn. I deflected their deflections.

DEBBIE AND SUSAN AND I were sitting beneath the Pavilion during lunch—Thom was at another table, crowded with members of the Griffins, including Ryan, and I hated that Ryan wasn't glancing over here just a table away, at least halfway acknowledging me, and Debbie was busy concentrating on a late assignment, her pen quickly scanning across a sheet of college-ruled paper while she checked the open textbook in front of her, and Susan was turning pages in a recent *Rolling Stone* with Jim Morrison on the cover ("He's hot, he's sexy and he's dead" was the headline) and even though he'd died over a decade ago, the Doors had been rediscovered by us and we all owned their *Greatest Hits* and the soundtrack that summer and fall was dotted with "Light My Fire" and "Break On Through" and "L.A. Woman." I remember that day I noticed Robert Mallory in the distance, walking into the courtyard plaza, my eyes trailing him until he stood over Matt Kellner, who was wearing a Walkman, sunning himself as usual, and simply nodded at Robert, who sat down, rummaging through a white-and-black-checked lunch bag and brought out a sandwich. Matt, looking pale, almost gaunt, just leaned back against the wall and slipped on his Ray-Bans, which suggested without saying anything: I don't want to be bothered. In retrospect, once certain details about what preceded the murders had been publicized it occurred to me—too late—that Matt's aquarium had been tampered with and his furniture moved and his cat had disappeared but I was trying so hard to stop thinking about Matt Kellner that I simply didn't put it together at first, mostly because the Trawler had only killed women and Matt didn't fit that profile and I was too lingeringly obsessed with Ryan Vaughn, who had erased Matt, as well as Robert Mallory, who was eclipsing everything else.

I was perusing that morning's issue of the *Los Angeles Times* and mentioned again Julie Selwyn and this *thing* that suddenly appeared who was taking responsibility for the home invasions and the missing pets, besides the three murders, and the girls just didn't react in the ways I'd expected. Yeah, they both murmured, looking over at the photos in the paper—"She was a pretty girl," Susan said, both of them confirming that they knew who Julie Selwyn was—and yet Debbie went back to her homework and Susan's eyes darted to the article about Jim Morrison in *Rolling Stone,* something else more interesting occupying her mind in that moment. When I mentioned the Trawler again they didn't know what I was talking about—they knew a body had been found on the tennis court at the Shadow Ranch Park but they didn't go further into the story, or acknowledge that whoever had killed Julie Selwyn had also committed two other murders. I felt as if I was floating above everybody, alone, the only one of us who cared about these crimes, as my eyes kept being drawn to Robert Mallory innocently sitting beneath a walnut tree on a warm September afternoon, concentrating on his lunch, Matt Kellner beside him. And I wondered why Robert hadn't joined us, why he wasn't sitting with Debbie and Susan and myself at the center table beneath the Pavilion. It was as if there was a presence that he didn't want to disturb and I thought: it was Susan. I almost called him over—Matt wouldn't have cared—but realized that I didn't want him sitting with us, because there was something wrong with him and I had a terrible premonition that Susan Reynolds was falling in love. I looked back at the article in the *Los Angeles Times,* frustrated that no one but me seemed to care.

But maybe in Southern California we were burned out by the number of serial killers roaming the landscape throughout the seventies and into the eighties, crisscrossing each other on the freeways and through the canyons and boulevards, hunting for victims hitchhiking at the beaches and waiting at bus stops, hanging out at gas-station diners up the coast and stumbling drunk out of bars, from Glendale to Oceanside, Westminster to Redding, Cathedral City to Long Beach, strewing mutilated corpses, extravagantly tortured with steel pipes and broken glass, in dumps and sand dunes and forests and along Highway 395—a time before video surveillance and cellphones and DNA profiling, when serial killers were allowed to be cavalier and bountiful: the number of murders committed by just one or a duo could hit twenty or thirty, fifty or sixty, during that particular decade. (Mass shooters have replaced them.) Maybe the Trawler didn't seem threatening enough with only three confirmed kills and maybe everyone around me just felt so young and invincible and that's why the initial news of the Trawler's victims failed to ignite the conversation that I thought it deserved. But it really didn't interest anyone yet, not even after the press conferences, or that weekend when new ghoulish details emerged in a long piece in the *Los Angeles Times*. Susan kept busily planning the party at the house in Beverly Hills on North Canon Drive that, as only Susan and Debbie and Thom and I knew, was really being thrown for Robert Mallory. To maintain a kind of frazzled innocence I did whatever Debbie wanted that week and accompanied her to wherever she went, because this calmed me—at Buckley she was all over me, ruffling my hair into place and straightening my tie and leaning in to lightly kiss my lips at the mid-morning assembly, where she had the largest audience watching us, and always holding my hand as we walked to class or up to lunch at the tables below the Pavilion, where we'd sit with Susan and Thom, and occasionally joined by others, usually members of the football team, while I became even more acutely aware that no one talked about the Trawler.

THAT WEEK I could feel something had changed between myself and Ryan—we had created a hard-core history in just two days when there was nothing about each other we hadn't felt or seen or tasted but he seemed shyer and less emboldened than I thought he'd become. I never assumed Ryan was going to metamorphose into a brash, uncaring punk because of what we'd experienced—the *breakthrough*—but I was surprised at how subdued and evasive he became on campus, as if he was paranoid someone was watching us, studying our interactions, finding clues in the ways we looked at each other, and the usual knowing glance in the hallway by our lockers or beneath the bell tower became a fixed smile that turned into blankness—there seemed to be a new anxiety about even looking at me because this would give something away to whoever was watching us, our secret stalker, or maybe Ryan was being, in his words, "practical" and "pragmatic" and making sure the movie we were in streamed forward smoothly and that his evasion was simply for Debbie's benefit and therefore mine, and on that level I should have been grateful. And yet that week he eagerly came over to the house on Mulholland after school and even with Rosa preparing my dinner in the kitchen or folding towels in the pantry he felt no trepidation to walk with me to my bedroom, where we locked the door, shut the thin gray venetian blinds, stripped fully naked and then fucked quickly with both of us coming within minutes, my mouth pressed against his, muffling the sounds he made while his body strained at orgasm.

The sex that occurred that week replaced us hanging together during lunch and Ryan never joined me anymore, preferring to sit with Dominic and Doug and Kyle while I sat with Thom and Susan and Debbie and sometimes Jeff Taylor and Tracy Goldman, and Jeff would watch Thom and me play backgammon while the girls planned Susan's party with Tracy. There were always new details, new setbacks, endless tiny dramas about nothing—they had decided on inviting the junior class as well, they were going to order sushi, they were adding songs to the mixtape. No one mentioned the dead girls. When we were standing at our lockers I asked Ryan what he thought about the discovery of Julie Selwyn and the announcement of the Trawler and he looked at me blankly and muttered that he didn't know what that was. Our eyes caught after he answered and in that moment lust flashed in the space between us and he breathed in and just nodded and I did the same, almost involuntarily. He muttered, "I want to come over again," and as I placed two textbooks into the locker I muttered back, "Yeah, I want to taste your cock," and he was briefly jolted, then quietly asked, "Yeah, you want me to fuck you again?" and I couldn't speak, just nodded, busying myself with something in my locker. And then he drifted away to another class without saying anything else. My face always reddened and I always had to control my breathing.

THERE WAS ALSO SOMETHING HAPPENING, I noticed, to Susan Reynolds during that week in the fall of 1981. Another kind of beauty began to announce itself; something was glowing within her, it seemed, a new radiance, and I couldn't pinpoint exactly where it was emanating from: she just seemed more beautiful as she passed through seventeen; there was an effortless confidence about her movements that was riveting. She wasn't reactive or surprised or disturbed by things—she was just gliding calmly through our world vaguely stoned and this gave her an even more pronounced sexual aura. She had done something to her hair and I couldn't tell what and I hadn't asked but it was slightly shorter, and the makeup she wore might have been more pronounced—around the eyes, her lips—but still subtle. She almost never wore the Buckley blazer—most girls and a lot of the guys didn't once classes began because it was too warm to wear year-round and instead kept them hung in their lockers—but it was actually required of everybody during the mid-morning assembly, where the Pledge of Allegiance and the school prayer were intoned, and that's where I noticed that Susan, even below the Buckley blazer, was wearing a new variation of the white blouse that was part of the girls' uniform, and that Susan's was gauzier and more stylish than her classmates'; now, with two or three buttons left open (unlike just the top one), you could clearly see the cleavage of her breasts, which I realized she wanted us to. But this wasn't for Thom Wright's benefit: this was something Susan was doing, I realized fearfully, for someone else, and though it wasn't proven yet, I sensed it was for Robert Mallory, as was the higher hem of the gray skirt, which she was now wearing upper-thigh, like Debbie Schaffer.

When this hit me, on the Wednesday after the weekend I spent with Ryan—I was talking to Susan beneath the bell tower in front of the library—I momentarily zoned out and missed whatever she'd been saying to me, staring at the tops of her breasts, and then forced myself to pay attention, and nod thoughtfully, agreeing with whatever she had just proposed. But she stopped, looked at me quizzically and asked, "Really? What did I just say?" I didn't want her to know that I'd lost the conversation at least a minute ago but when I made eye contact and looked at her blankly she just sighed.

"Oh, Bret," she said. "What are we going to do with you?"

"What are we going to do with me?" I asked, shrugging. "You have any ideas?"

"You okay?" she asked. "What happened to you?"

"It was just a flu," I said. "A bug. It was nothing."

"You disappeared," Susan said.

"I was in my bedroom the whole time—"

"Why didn't you want Debbie to come over?" Susan asked. "Bring you stuff, take care of you?"

A flash of annoyance woke me up, because Susan knew something she wasn't admitting—this inquiry felt like a tease, as if she sensed I was hiding Ryan Vaughn. Mild anxiety lightly danced around my chest while I stared at her and then I shook my head, shrugging, playing a part. "There was no need," I said. "She didn't need to bother. I didn't want her to waste her time." I then added, "I was fine."

"I hardly think she would have seen it as a waste of time," Susan said. "Considering that you're her boyfriend, right?"

I stared at her, wondering what she was doing. The "right?" punctuating that sentence created a negative dimension, made it seem as if Susan knew I really wasn't Debbie's boyfriend; it was a challenge. I thought about helping her speed along to wherever she wanted to go with this conversation but realized there were too many pitfalls and I didn't want either one of us to trip into them.

"Yeah, I just wasn't feeling it," I said casually, looking past her to the parking lot. I spotted Robert's black Porsche as if my eyes were inadvertently drawn to it, darkly gleaming in the sun.

"Well, *she* was feeling it," Susan said. "Coming to see you. I mean did you consider that?" She paused. "How hard would it have been to let her come over on Saturday or Sunday?"

I stayed silent and just stared at Susan. She was staring back at me with blank green eyes, the lashes very lightly mascaraed, waiting for me to say something, and I suddenly felt a hopelessness that could never be eradicated. It seemed so vast there was no reason to even try. I breathed in, just staring at her. And she kept her gaze fixed back on mine, patiently, waiting for an answer. Where was the tangible participant, the willing boyfriend, I had decided to become for the rest of the year? Where was the actor going along with the pantomime? But I managed it effortlessly—I breathed in and grinned, even though I now saw this conversation as some kind of confrontation, and breezily said, "I didn't want her to catch what I had so I was, in fact, the caring boyfriend, Susan."

"What were your symptoms?" Susan asked, concerned. "What was wrong?"

"Why?" I said, flinching. "I had a headache. I was nauseous. I thought I was coming down with something." A long pause followed and it was filled with so many things unspoken. How had we arrived at a point when what we wanted to say to each other was now floating in the pauses that dominated the conversation?

"Anyway, I'm glad you're feeling better," Susan said. "Thom and I were worried when you weren't picking up the phone over the weekend. I mean I know Thom doesn't really like to talk on the phone but you and I usually do."

"Yeah, I know, but I got your messages, so . . ." I said and then left it at that. I had nowhere else to go.

"Why didn't you pick up?" she asked. "When I called? Or when Thom called?"

"Susan," I said. It came out as a warning, which is maybe what she wanted.

"It was kind of a strange weekend," she said. "Everyone seemed gone."

"Yeah?" I asked. I started walking with her into the parking lot. "What do you mean?"

"Well, Jeff had gone out to Malibu with Tracy, Robert was in Palm Springs with his aunt and Thom couldn't locate where Ryan was. Tony and Kyle weren't around either." Susan paused as we neared her car. "Ryan's dad said that he was going to spend the weekend with a friend but he didn't know who it was. Do you have any idea?"

Robert was in Palm Springs with his aunt. Why would Susan know this? Why would she place Robert in this list of our absent friends? Why would she reveal this to me so casually? But she had asked me about Ryan and where I thought he might have been and I had to answer her.

"Why don't you ask Ryan?" I said. "Why would I know?"

"I thought you guys had become friends," she said.

"Well, I certainly don't know," I said. "I don't know where Ryan was."

She paused and this silent beat meant she was processing what I had just told her. A lie.

"Anyway, I'm glad you're okay—"

"Susan—" I started, my eyes closed. "Just let's drop it, okay?"

"Drop what?" she asked, seemingly innocent.

"I have my own life," I said. "If I want to spend the weekend alone, working on my book or just hanging out by myself, I really, really hope that's okay with you and I don't have to answer to anyone as to why I want to be alone." I stopped, and then blurted out: "Maybe I wasn't even sick! Maybe I was feeling fucking fantastic and just wanted to be alone. Is that okay with everyone? Or did I do something bad?" I jutted out my lower lip like a child who'd been chastised and talked in a baby voice. "I was a bad boy, Susan? Did I do something bad?"

"No." I heard this in the same soft unwavering tone—if she was perturbed it didn't register. "Not at all, Bret."

"Whatever I did this past weekend has nothing to do with Debbie," I said.

"Yeah, that's pretty obvious," she muttered, walking in front of me to the white BMW.

"Hey, hey—" I said, reaching out to turn her around.

She pulled her shoulder away from my grasp and put her books on the roof of the car before facing me.

I was about to say something when she reached up and pressed a finger against my lips. This had been a dramatic gesture we often made to each other indicating we didn't need to hear what the other person was going to say because we already knew the answer and it wouldn't make a difference anyway, or it meant that the other person should stop asking questions that were never going to be answered. It always amused us and we both smiled at our awareness of this, something lovers did in a bad movie.

"You don't need to say anything," she said in a hushed voice. "I'm fine, Bret, with whatever you want to do. I was just curious but you don't need to say anything."

Her cool finger pressed against my lips disarmed me totally and any anxiety I was feeling or the anger that had formed around me lifted away in seconds and I exhaled as she lowered her hand, removing the finger.

"I don't have anything to say," I finally said. "Maybe that makes me guilty."

The SHARDS

"Do we have secrets?" she asked suddenly. "We never used to, or so I thought, maybe one or two. But do we have secrets now?"

Your secret is safe with me, I remember Susan told me this in Westwood last spring and I never asked her what she meant. And then I automatically thought of Robert Mallory and Susan's supposed feelings for him—something I had, admittedly, only heard about from Debbie Schaffer and no one else. There was nothing to base it on except for what Debbie told me when she was floating in the Jacuzzi two weekends ago when she hinted to me that Susan liked him. And though it was embarrassing that Robert had told Susan and Thom I'd been following him along Ventura Boulevard on the afternoon of the first day of school, I actually never saw Susan and Robert together those initial weeks in September, so there was no proof that this was in fact a real thing. Sometimes I had to calm myself whenever I thought I was creating this narrative in my head and the light paranoia Robert Mallory conspired to swirl around me. *You hear things that aren't really there* . . . This was what a writer did.

"Why are you throwing a party for Robert Mallory?" I asked in a small voice.

"Oh, stop it," she muttered. "Really?"

"Is that part of a secret, Susan?" I asked.

She opened the driver's-side door and slid into the BMW and again I noticed how short her skirt had become before she closed it and I fell back into that anxious state tied to her supposed feelings about Robert, which, for me, were totally confirmed by the party she was so meticulously planning for him. And then she looked at me after she unrolled the window and simply said as she started the car, "It's only one more year, Bret." I just stared at her blankly. "We're only here for one more year," she said.

AND A WEEK LATER ON the following Wednesday I ended up talking to Robert Mallory—he approached me, otherwise this wouldn't have happened, meaning I would've never started a conversation with him willingly. It was the first time we spoke since I saw him at the space on Melrose, where he casually told me what he wanted to do with Susan Reynolds—lick her pussy, fuck her ass, *make her scream.*

This took place during Phys Ed, which was third period that year for the senior class, in the hour before lunch, and it was the only class of the day the entire twelfth grade shared, but with the boys and girls usually separated. On that day the guys from the senior class were on Gilley Field, while the girls were in the Pavilion, either swimming or playing volleyball or maybe listening to records and just hanging out. Phys Ed senior year was casual and participation only irregularly enforced compared to the lower grades, when it was a more structured class and participation was mandatory. Seniors were left alone to do whatever they wanted—you could work out with weights, you could play tennis, if a group of guys wanted to put together a soccer scrimmage or a touch-football game then whoever wanted to join could do so, and some of the guys just sunned themselves in the massive stand of bleachers that rose above the giant rectangular grass field bordered by an oval track and beyond the track was a baseball diamond complete with two dugouts, the San Fernando Valley, smog-baked and endless, spread out below us. Coach Holtz or Coach McCabe—both resolutely heterosexual though that didn't stop me from fantasizing about them—usually monitored everything from the sidelines, hanging out beneath the goalposts that towered above the soccer nets at the ends of the green field, whistles around their necks, holding clipboards, a few guys conversing with them about the NFL games that aired over the week. Above us forested hillsides surrounded the field leading all the way up to Mulholland, and the only movements were cars silently driving along Beverly Glen, which curved through the landscape overlooking the school.

On that particular day when I talked to Robert Mallory I was situated near the top of the stands after running a few laps, my shirt off, lying on one of the tiered rows of benches—there were exactly forty of them rising toward the announcer's booth—and I was mostly distracted by Ryan Vaughn wearing a Griffin T ripped into a half-shirt and tossing a football to Thom in red Griffin shorts, shirtless. Doug Furth and Kyle Colson were lazily jogging along the track and Anthony Matthews was goofing off with Kevin Kerslake; for some reason they were ducking each other on the baseball diamond, where the American flag hung from a tall silver pole. Tom Petty and the Heartbreakers played from a boom box next to one of the goal posts and "Here Comes My Girl" sounded echoey and faraway from where I sat, marveling at Thom Wright's athleticism as he leapt and threw a football with balletic grace to Ryan, who ran backward, caught it, and then threw it back at Thom, who captured it while still in motion. Earlier that day Ryan had mentioned coming by after school and my body tightened with lust when I thought about him naked in my bedroom and I watched intently as he placed his hands on his knees, panting, and then looked around the field until his eyes reached the top of the bleachers, where he spotted me and turned abruptly away when someone called his name—no smile, no wave, the new distance he imposed upon us in public clearly obvious to me, and I felt a soft pang mixed with arousal along with images of his stiff pink penis, wet with my saliva and jutting upward. I realized I hadn't seen Matt Kellner that day and I hadn't noticed him at assembly—I glanced over at the tennis courts, then back to the baseball diamond, then over to the coach's office, confirming that he definitely wasn't there. "Tusk" was now playing from the boom box and it made me think of Terry Schaffer and his resemblance to Lindsey Buckingham and I smiled to myself as I watched Dominic Thompson mock-marching to the song with Jon Yates and David O'Shea, wondering when Terry or Steven Reinhardt was going to call me to set up a meeting about the screenplay that Terry wanted me to write, and I shivered with anticipation.

WHEN I REFOCUSED after rereading a few pages from *Slouching Towards Bethlehem*, I saw Robert Mallory conferring with Thom and Ryan, the three of them standing in the middle of the field, hands on their hips, occasionally nodding to one another, Thom always smiling widely, beaming, so innocent, so beautiful, and Ryan just staring at Robert, and I remembered the things he whispered that he wanted to do to him in the Jacuzzi on that Sunday night, his erection pressing against mine as we shared our sexual fantasies about the new boy. I tensed up when I realized Robert was walking away from Ryan and Thom and crossing the field, heading toward the stands. And then Robert was confidently heading toward me and up the steps, his red shorts provocatively hiked up, accentuating his bulge, and he was squinting as if he couldn't see me while he climbed the bleachers, swinging his arms uncaringly. Coming from the distant boom box Pete Townshend was now singing "Let My Love Open the Door" and because of where I was at seventeen I realized I hadn't seen Robert naked yet in the locker room and I badly wanted to despite the mild revulsion he inspired but his locker was on the other side of the divide and this was the reason. He just nodded as he stood on the bench below mine, looking out to where the Valley came up against the San Gabriel Mountains, and he stretched, taking the view in. I could smell him—that particular scent of sandalwood and cedar and ash wafted over me and acted as a narcotic. The Griffin T was tight and promoted his tan biceps and I could make out the rippled abs and pectorals beneath it and my eyes casually traced the muscled thighs very lightly lined with brown hair and I averted my gaze when I caught the whiteness of his underwear beneath the red shorts as he sat down.

"Nice up here," he said. "Quiet. No one around."

He paused, scanning the field and the small figures scattered about on the vast green lawn. I played it cool and didn't say anything. I felt self-conscious in his presence and was going to put my T-shirt back on but worried this would start a conversation that I didn't want to have—*you don't have to be shy around me, Bret.* My nipples stiffened as if a cool breeze had suddenly drifted over the stands and I put down the Joan Didion paperback and was now leaning forward as if concealing something. Robert always managed to put me in an apprehensive mood.

"What are you doing up here?" he asked innocently. "All alone?"

"Plotting my next move," I said flatly.

At first he seemed shocked that I said this and then looked briefly confused, as if I'd insulted him. I never wanted Robert to think anything negative about me or that I'd purposefully avoided him. I actually wanted him to be calm and realized I'd been careless with that particular greeting and yet I was surprised he assumed it was connected to him. *Plotting my next move.* For me: sometimes Robert was around, sometimes Robert wasn't and that was fine. I hadn't gotten up and left the lunch table when he sat down and I never looked away when we made eye contact passing each other at the lockers or on the walkways under the eaves, and we always managed a smile. He was in two of my classes (Senior English, European History) even though he sat in the front row and I sat in the back in both, and we never acknowledged each other there. The only times he truly alarmed me at Buckley were when I saw him talking with Matt Kellner at the mid-morning assembly or eating lunch with him in the courtyard below the Pavilion. Otherwise I just tried to pretend that the Robert Mallory who lied to me about being at the Village Theater a year ago, and the Robert Mallory that desecrated the statue, and the Robert Mallory who had spoken obscenely about Susan Reynolds, simply didn't exist. He was just part of the overall erasure that I was enacting: the eradication of my real self into the tangible participant who saw everything as normal. The fact that he was sitting in front of me and it was just the two of us at the top of the bleachers overlooking Gilley Field and I hadn't walked away was, I hoped, proof that I accepted him.

"I'M JUST HANGING," I said, sitting up, correcting myself. "I ran a couple laps." And then: "I'm not plotting anything."

"I was wondering where you've been hiding," he said, stretching his legs out.

"I haven't been hiding," I said, meeting his gaze. My answer came out as a challenge and I hated that Robert always seemed to make me react this way. "Why would you say that I've been hiding?"

"Maybe you've been avoiding me," he said.

"Why would I be avoiding you?" I asked.

"I don't know," he said, leaning back. "Maybe I said some things you didn't like."

I paused. "Like what?"

"Maybe I said something the other night at the space," he said, stretching. "That space on Melrose."

I decided to be honest. "Oh, that?" I asked, without being specific. "I guess I'm not used to people talking about my friends that way."

"What way?" he asked, with a genuine curiosity.

"Things you said about Susan," I muttered, gesturing. "All that sex crap."

"Dude. Really? You were offended?" He sat up and looked at me, confused. "I'm sorry you're so sensitive." And then: "I'm just a guy."

He smiled: dimples. In a movie I would have instantly desired him but in the flesh his supposed innocence was overwhelmingly menacing because it was so rehearsed and didn't seem natural. This is what made everything tense whenever he was around: I could see through the act and it was maddening that no one else did. I was afraid of him—he scared me, and except for the desecration of the Griffin, I didn't know exactly why this fear existed. Maybe because he had spent time in a developmental center outside of Jacksonville his junior year and what chilled me: no one knew what the reasons were. Maybe the reasons were innocent but maybe they weren't. And yet we'd promised Susan that none of us would bring the topic up and ask him about it. We had to pretend we didn't know in order to protect Robert Mallory: just another absurdity in the fake world of Buckley life that the tangible participant had to accept.

"And there's other stuff," I said, finally.

"Like what? Let's hear it," he said, amused, and then with slightly more concern, "Wait. You're not mad at me, are you?"

"Mad at you?" I asked. "No. Why would I be *mad* at you?"

"Well, you just walked away from me at the club—"

"I'm not mad." I said this as gently as I possibly could.

"Well, what are you, then?" he asked, mimicking my gentleness.

"I'm not anything," I said, raising my voice slightly, looking away from him.

"Well, I think we should try and be friends," he said coolly. "I mean, don't you?"

"Oh yeah, yeah, for sure. Everything's fine," I said. "Yeah, we should try and be friends." I paused. "I mean there's no reason not to, right?"

"Good." He nodded.

There was a pause. He seemed satisfied. He stretched again and lay back, letting the sun wash over him, bleaching his head and body, and I could hear Bruce Springsteen's "Hungry Heart" playing from the field. I didn't admit this to Robert but I'd gotten pissed off and felt trapped in a totally fake conversation—he had won a contest he put into play by coming to the top of the stands and asking me why I'd been avoiding him even if I hadn't. He locked me into something I didn't want to be a part of, starting a nonsensical conversation that put me on the defensive. I sat very still while I looked down at him, displayed like a teenage Greek god, and I couldn't help thinking that Robert knew he was taunting me, and in ways that were different from how he was probably taunting Thom Wright and Matt Kellner. I resented the paranoia he inspired and yet I also found him undeniably erotic, an unparalleled object of teen boy desire and lust, and I hated the fact that these two opposite feelings coexisted within me. I simply stared at him silently, wondering what he looked like naked. He opened his eyes and stared back at me, his head resting in the hands that were folded above his head, and said nothing; he just kept staring at me with a half-smile. If it had been any other boy I would have thought this was a come-on.

"Matt Kellner told me you were asking about me, asking, like, questions," I said.

"Oh yeah?" he said, just gazing at me. "Really?" he asked softly.

"Why don't you just ask me?" I said, noticing my voice was slightly tremulous. "Don't talk to Matt, just talk to me."

Robert continued to lie there in the sun, and a hand absentmindedly reached under his T-shirt to scratch himself and I caught a glimpse of his hard tan stomach, the abs and the trace of hair leading up from the shorts to his navel, lightly pushed out, pronounced. His eyes were closed again and he seemingly took what I said in stride.

"Really? Matt told you that? Like, what was I asking?"

"He didn't say," I said softly. "But what did you want? What did you want to know about me?"

"I think Matt's a little strange," Robert said, eyes still closed. "If you ask me."

I paused, staring at him. "Strange is . . . relative."

"What does that mean?" He was smiling when he asked this, but curious, and yet his eyes were still closed.

"Well, people . . . probably think I'm a bit strange." I paused, not knowing where I was going with this. "And . . . people probably . . . think you're strange." I paused again. "I don't know. I mean, strange is . . . relative."

He shrugged. I had lost him. "Yeah, I guess, but I think Matt has . . . crossed a line." He paused and then said, "Into. Utter. Weirdness." His eyes were still closed.

"You don't know him, Robert." I inadvertently said his name, wanting to make a point. I immediately regretted it.

Robert opened his eyes and squinted at the sky before sitting back up. "But you do, right?" He paused. "You do know Matt."

I shrugged. I didn't know what to say or how much to admit.

"You should talk to him," Robert said. "See what's wrong. I think he's depressed." He paused. "I haven't seen him. He's been absent a couple days."

"I think . . . he just smokes too much weed," I said, carefully. "I've never known Matt to be depressed exactly."

"But, then, you don't really know him, do you?" Robert said. "Right?"

Robert crossed his legs, and then moved his hand into his shorts and adjusted his genitals so he'd be more comfortable in that position. "He said you guys had a falling out," Robert murmured. "If you guys had a falling out you must've . . . known each other . . ." He trailed off suggestively. "Right?"

"What would we have had . . . a falling out about?" I stared at the hand that had just touched his cock and balls and felt another quick flash of desire.

He shrugged. "You want to tell me?"

"I don't know what he's talking about," I said quietly, and then, "Did he really say that to you?" I paused. "Did he really tell you we had a falling out?"

Robert looked at me without saying anything until, "I don't know, Bret, I just don't know." Robert said this shaking his head, his gaze fixed up at me.

"What . . . don't you know?" I asked.

"If you're being real with me," he said softly.

"I feel no obligation to be real with you, Robert, whatever that means." I paused. "What were you asking Matt? About me?"

"I don't really remember," he said, staring. "Maybe I just wanted to get a feel for everyone. It's kind of hard being the new guy. Plus I don't know if I made the best first impression. With you." He paused. "About the fact that you thought you saw me somewhere that I wasn't."

"Forget it," I murmured. "It doesn't matter." I felt completely unmoored from everything in that moment.

"I'm just trying to be nice to you," Robert said softly. "Even though . . . I heard you have problems with me."

This was a conversation one had in a dream, I thought. "Who did you hear this from?" I managed in a mild, calm voice, but a light, glancing fear started swirling. I wanted to end this conversation and yet his presence kept me bolted to the bleachers.

"Well . . ." he began, hesitantly, "Matt said that you told him something was *wrong* with me." He said this grinning. "Would you like to tell me what that is?"

I froze.

"Matt said that you told him he should probably stay away from me." Robert cocked his head, curious. "Really?"

I just sat on the bleacher above him, momentarily paralyzed until a distant anger started reanimating me, bringing me closer into the reality of the moment we were sharing.

"I also heard from Susan," Robert was saying. "And from Thom."

"Heard . . . what?" I asked, keeping calm, but my fists were clenched, my nails biting into my palms.

"That I don't tell the truth," he said quietly. "That I'm a liar."

A rage I'd never felt before flared and left me speechless. I stared at him, hoping I looked uncaring, as if none of this bothered me in the slightest, that I was too cool to give a shit about the pitiful mini-dramas and gossip of my classmates, but I was legitimately enraged at Susan, at Thom, at myself, and I felt ashamed sitting in front of Robert—they had talked about me to Robert, they had told Robert that I mistrusted him. And maybe Robert could sense this shame and anger, as much as I tried to hide it, because for the first time since I'd met him something in Robert softened and he became vulnerable in ways that took me back to the moment we'd first met him, below the Pavilion, when he shuffled up to the table we were sitting at, clutching his schedule and a rumpled map of the school, resembling a lost child.

"I mean, look, I don't know," he started gently. "I guess I probably need to tell you things but . . . I can't just yet," he said. He left it there. It was my turn.

"You don't have to tell me anything," I said, barely breathing, trying to control myself.

"Okay, cool, that's cool," he said. And then there was a pause before he asked, "But do you think I'm a liar because I said I wasn't in that movie theater?" He paused again. "The one you thought you saw me at?"

I snapped and stood up. "Look, Robert," I said, wanting the conversation to end. "I'm just . . . distracted this week. None of this really matters. I don't care about any of this bullshit. I'm just distracted by other things. Okay? It's not you."

"What are you distracted by?" he asked. "By Matt?" He paused. "Do you know where he is?"

"No, not by Matt," I said. "Other things." I gestured vaguely.

"About what?" he asked. And this was the gentlest I'd ever heard him: he was concerned and seemed to care about what distracted me. Vulnerability was emanating from him and it didn't seem forced or rehearsed now—it was genuine. There was a real person sitting on the bleachers waiting for me to explain myself, my worries, my fears, wanting me to open up about Matt Kellner and what I'd become so distracted by last week and this week, the things that haunted me.

"About that girl who was found in Woodland Hills," I said, suddenly lost. "No one seems to care."

There was a long silence while he processed this.

"But why should they?" he finally asked. "Did . . . people know her?"

"Do you know what I'm talking about?" I asked, barely noticing him, transported into another world. "Julie Selwyn?"

"Are you asking me something?" he said. "I don't understand."

I froze again. The atmosphere got instantly complicated in that moment and it was as if a new person suddenly possessed Robert and all the traces of warmth and vulnerability that had manifested themselves only seconds before were now gone and replaced by the three faces behind the whirring eyes. There was the innocent face that was squinting up at me trying to figure Bret out, and there was the face that was looking at everything else in a master shot, wide-screened, where all the pieces were visible and in play and offering a number of paths to navigate from this vantage point, and then there was the increasingly hostile face of a dangerously ill psychopath who had been institutionalized and was trying to contain himself and really didn't care about anything. This was the person who was suddenly staring up at me when Coach Holtz blew his whistle, signaling it was time to hit the locker room and get dressed for lunch.

"I was just asking if you know what I'm talking about." I pulled on the T-shirt and then leaned down to pick up the paperback. "That's all."

"Not really." His voice was strained. "Do you want to tell me about it?" His expression was slightly twisted with confusion.

And for a moment I wanted to tell him, but it passed and we were interrupted by Thom and Ryan calling out across the field, waving for us to come down from the top of the bleachers, and without saying anything Robert simply followed me as I jogged the steps toward the edge of the dirt track where the two of them were standing. And as we neared I made a sudden run for Thom and tackled him, the two of us falling onto the grass bordering the track—after that I didn't know what else to do with my rage. But when Ryan shouted out "Hey" and tried to pull me off Thom, he soon realized that Thom was wrestling me, and that Thom had taken control, and that Thom was laughing as he pinned me to the lawn—Thom thought I was horsing around and that this was payback for him tackling me in the space on Melrose the other night. When his sweaty armpit became pressed against my face, covering my nose and mouth while Thom steadied me, coiled in an embrace, his face just an inch from mine, so I could smell his milky breath, that's when I stopped struggling and tapped out and went limp. I could tell from the look on Robert's and Ryan's faces that Thom had misread my move—my rage reinterpreted as just clowning around. And a secret narrative started playing itself out on Gilley Field in that moment as Thom and I untangled ourselves, and this fake narrative about what really happened was carried with us as we walked down the hill back to the locker room, where three of us pretended that something else had happened instead of what really did.

11

DURING LUNCH MY DESIRE to confront Susan and Thom about confiding in Robert Mallory what I'd said about him was interrupted by the faint, lightly gnawing apprehension I experienced whenever I noticed Matt Kellner's absence that week, which was confirmed when we were sitting at the center table beneath the Pavilion. Susan walked over about fifteen minutes into lunch after a private meeting with Dr. Croft and Headmaster Walters just ended, looking confused in ways that were totally unlike the blank-faced, utterly unworried girl she'd been enacting, and for the first time that term seemed slightly perplexed when she told us that Matt Kellner was missing—"officially missing" were the words she used, as if there was any real difference. Simply "missing" sounded more ominous to me without the "officially" attached to it.

I realized that this information supplied by Susan, through Dr. Croft and Walters, verified that I really hadn't seen Matt for the past few days and not only that the red Datsun hadn't been at its usual space in the senior parking lot: this confirmed that the 280ZX wasn't in the parking lot at all. I hadn't distractedly imagined any of this: the car definitely hadn't been there, Matt hadn't been to Buckley in two days, he was now officially missing, and this was going to be announced tomorrow at the mid-morning assembly. The moment Susan said this as she sat down—Debbie, Thom, Ryan and Robert were sitting at the table with us—I thought I was going to be sick. I dropped the sandwich I'd been eating onto the paper bag and stared at it while trying not to turn away from everyone; in fact I had to restrain myself from stumbling up from the table and quietly collapsing in the boys' restroom located off the lobby in the Pavilion. But no one noticed that I'd dropped the sandwich or that my body was suddenly rigid with tension. Everyone was looking at Susan, wondering what this meant: Matt Kellner was missing? Yeah . . . and? Even though I was automatically encased with dread when I heard this, the fear I initially felt also seemed too dramatic at first, because no one knew what happened yet—Matt might be playing hooky, lounging on a beach somewhere up the coast, taking in the last rays of summer, high and peaceful, crashing into waves and scoring weed. No one knew yet—it was a mystery still tinged with hope.

I ALSO REALIZED I couldn't appear too concerned or overly alarmed, or so I felt, because that would open something up, it would give away a secret, and if I broke down into a panic attack (because I was always assuming the worst—I never thought Matt was going to be found alive) it would be the beginning of a complicated narrative that might ultimately wreck everything that had been put into play and that I was trying to save: maintaining boyfriend status with Debbie, having secret sex with Ryan, getting through senior year, carefully monitoring Robert Mallory from a neutral perspective. I remember that in that initial moment after Susan told us Matt was missing I looked over at Robert, who somehow intuited I was going to do this and glanced back at me with a blank expression that lasted too long before looking back at Susan, who was telling us what she'd been told by Croft. The initial confusion creasing her features had reverted to that casual and sullen beauty as she now simply recited the information to us, and yet I noticed that Susan kept inadvertently glancing over at me, her eyes softly worried, while talking about the few facts concerning Matt Kellner's disappearance that she knew, until I was glaring back at her, wishing she'd stop looking at me. And then it seemed she forced herself to quit and, like an actress, addressed a table that seemed relatively calm, even unconcerned, about the disappearance of Matt Kellner.

—

WHEN IT WAS NOTED IN THE ATTENDANCE records that Matt hadn't been at Buckley for the past two days, Dr. Croft's secretary called the Kellner residence in Encino and wanted to know when Matt was coming back to school, and Matt's parents, Ronald and Sheila, neither of whom I'd ever seen, let alone met, were unaware of Matt's absence. And I knew why: Matt was more autonomous than any of our classmates, the only one living by himself in a pool house with its own garage in the back of the massive property on Haskell Avenue. At this point in his adolescence Matt was rarely watched over by his parents anymore—in fact I'd never heard Matt mention either one of them and had no idea what his father did for a living. The reason that Ron and Sheila Kellner didn't know that Matt hadn't been to school for two days was precisely that he'd often be completely out of their sight, and sometimes a week would pass without either of them glimpsing their son. What this dynamic suggested was perhaps a more extreme example of what many of us experienced as teenagers in the late 1970s and into the next decade, whereby not engaging with your parents for days on end didn't seem particularly weird or abnormal—my parents, for example, were absent for more than two months on a European cruise throughout the autumn of 1981, when I was seventeen, and neither they nor I had any issues or trepidation about this whatsoever.

One of the reasons Matt Kellner was given such particular leeway was that his GPA was okay, his SAT scores were serviceable (and weren't going to get any better—he wasn't going to retake them, unlike me in late October) and he never got into trouble—Matt was just an avid purchaser of marijuana who looked old enough to buy his own beer illegally and never got carded at any of the liquor stores he frequented along Ventura Boulevard. In fact no Buckley kid had ever gotten into any real trouble during those years and I could count on one hand the number of physical altercations between the boys in our class starting from seventh grade onward—I couldn't even remember the last time two guys in our class got into an actual argument; this just didn't happen at Buckley, the atmosphere was too controlling to allow it, everything was too constrained. I may have been impressed that Matt never got busted for buying—and smoking—as much weed as he did but, then, everyone's mild drug use was fairly under control in 1981 and there was no such thing as rehab—at least for teenagers like Debbie Schaffer or Jeff Taylor or Matt Kellner—it wasn't ubiquitous yet. In fact I don't think any of us knew a single individual who was prescribed meds. (Robert Mallory, we would find out, was the first.) There were also no DUIs, there were no overdoses, there were no suicide attempts, and of course, there were no school shootings anywhere—all of this would come later. And Matt Kellner, even though he might have been numbed with marijuana and was having a sexual relationship with me for over a year, was deemed a good kid with decent grades who kept to himself, living in some kind of underwater fantasy world: stoned in the pool was where he resided in a marijuana haze and that was all he ever needed; this was what gave Matt sustenance, the late-afternoon sun, the scent of chlorine, the shade of the palms above the hammock he rested in, the Specials singing "Ghost Town" coming from a pool house lined with surfboards and an aquarium that stretched along a wall he zoned out on while stroking Alex the cat.

RON AND SHEILA KELLNER ASSUMED that Matt's schedule was as routine that week as it had always been since he moved into the pool house in the middle of tenth grade, which coincided with when he got his driver's license: he would get up early, he would swim some laps, sometimes one could hear reggae faintly coming from the pool house at that hour, before Matt left for school, and then he'd pull the red Datsun out of his garage and head to Buckley. Matt would rarely come up to the main residence to grab breakfast even though the housekeeper always laid something out in case he did; he usually preferred to stop by the McDonald's in Sherman Oaks before school. For Matt school lasted until three, since he wasn't involved in sports or any extracurricular activities, so he was often back at the pool house by four at the latest. On weekends he would sometimes drive to the beach alone, down the coast to Newport and beyond, and—this is key—he always left a note on his desk in the pool house telling whoever came across it where he'd gone and when he'd be back. On some nights Sheila Kellner would glimpse the guesthouse from the windows in the second-story master bedroom and the only light would be coming from the aquarium or from candles Matt had lit, lined against the pool, where Matt swam until he went to bed, but she rarely saw him, as if Matt was keeping himself purposefully invisible to his parents. Sheila noted that she realized over that weekend there was no aqua glow emanating from the windows of the guesthouse since the aquarium had been drained, and she didn't see any candles or hear sounds coming from the pool. The Jacuzzi hadn't been used either.

AT LUNCH SUSAN TOLD US that the Kellners began cooperating with the Los Angeles Police Department once it became apparent that no one had seen Matt for at least three or four days, possibly six—Ron Kellner hadn't seen his son since late last week and it was now Wednesday—or knew where he was and that's when he became officially missing. The last time Ron Kellner had seen Matt was the previous Thursday, when he walked down to the pool house to ask Matt if he had replaced the headlight on the 280ZX and Matt told him he never drove it at night so what was the hurry—he'd do it next week. Frustrated—and seeing how stoned his son was while he complained about how much homework he had to complete—Ron took the Datsun to the Nissan dealership in Encino, where they quickly replaced the headlight, serviced the car and adjusted the suspension and then washed it while Ron sat with the owner of the dealership in his office—and because it was Ron Kellner it took under an hour instead of leaving the car at the dealership overnight. Ron returned the car to the pool-house garage, told Matt that the headlight had been replaced and that if he wanted to keep the car he needed to take better care of it, and Matt muttered his thanks. It was confirmed that Matt had been at school the previous Friday and the last person who had seen him at Buckley was Angelo, the head of security, who had been directing traffic in the parking lot and remembered Matt driving past him and out the school gates at roughly three-fifteen—Matt was alone in the car and wearing sunglasses and Angelo confirmed that there was nothing strange or unusual about the sighting. The Kellners' housekeeper saw Matt when he returned to Haskell Avenue that afternoon.

No one saw him Saturday or Sunday, which, again, wasn't unusual, and there wasn't anything off about Matt not showing up at Buckley on Monday morning—maybe he wasn't feeling well, maybe he felt like skipping a day, maybe he slept in late and decided to hit the beach instead. But he had probably slipped away sometime that weekend, though no one was even vaguely certain of this because the Kellners never checked the separate garage where Matt kept his car—at least not until Wednesday morning, when Dr. Croft's secretary called and asked when Matt was returning to school and Ron Kellner first noticed the red Datsun was missing, and Sheila Kellner realized she hadn't seen any lights in the guesthouse all weekend—and it was odd that the pool was never lit on Saturday or Sunday night. It was also odd that this time out Matt hadn't left a note or a message telling anyone that he was leaving or where he was going or that he wouldn't be attending school for the next few days. It became easier to locate how long Matt Kellner had been missing because of the details Sheila supplied about the lights, even though she admitted that they didn't really know precisely if this absence was "typical" of their only child or not. It wasn't something that would have concerned or even worried them otherwise, until they found out that Matt hadn't been to school for three days and then the fear set in.

THE THING THAT SCARED ME most about Matt's disappearance was that I knew it wasn't random and that something had been leading up to the disappearance; there were specific details in a narrative that was being carried out by someone, and on that day Susan announced the disappearance, it started forming in my mind that maybe Matt had become the fourth victim of the recently named Trawler, the person who had been responsible for the home invasions and the abductions and three murders because a similar pattern had been closing in on Matt: there were the anonymous silent phone calls, there was the rearranged furniture within the residence, there were the fish that disappeared, there was the missing cat—we didn't know the significance of the posters yet—but I kept forcing myself to calm down because Matt was male, and so he really wasn't part of the pattern, and why, then, should I be so worried about that particular narrative? But my mind wandered restlessly to the question: What if there *wasn't* a pattern? What if *we* assumed that there was a pattern and there actually wasn't—that it was more random than what it looked like? After all, the home invasions targeted both women and men—both genders had been bound and assaulted—which hinted that the Trawler never really adhered to a standard narrative in the first place when it came to his targets. And what if there had been other victims—adolescent, male—that no one knew about yet, and not just the three pretty teenage girls that occupied the media with their youth, their freshness, their smiles in the photos flashed on the local news as a stinging reminder of how doomed they all were? I also wondered in the initial days of the disappearance if Matt was just an unstable dude I never really knew who fled down the coast for a week just because he didn't give a fuck and would be back by next Monday—shake the paranoia that had been gripping him, take a break from the classmate who'd become obsessed, get out of Encino and head to Manhattan Beach, Newport, San Diego, wherever.

AT THE ASSEMBLY THE FOLLOWING MORNING both Dr. Croft and Susan mentioned for the first time the disappearance of Matt Kellner in their separate addresses to the student body and asked anyone who had information about Matt to please come to the administration office—and no one did. I noticed that Ryan glanced over at me in the packed courtyard, his blond hair newly cut and brushed back, looking remarkably composed even while he kept clenching his jaw. (Or maybe he was just chewing gum, I hoped. I was turning everything into a drama and trying to pull back from doing so.) And then, afterward, by the row of lockers the seniors shared, Ryan asked in a low voice, "Do you know what happened?" He asked me this, of course, and in such a way, because he was the only one who knew my history with Matt. I didn't say anything, just shook my head. Ryan stared, leaning against his locker. "Well, where do you think he is?" he asked. I grabbed a book and stared back at Ryan, keeping it together, trying to play everything casually, Ryan being the last person I wanted to notice how frightened I actually was by his questions and how they implicated me: *Do you know what happened? Where do you think he is?* "I think he'll be okay," I said in a steady voice. "I think he went up to Santa Barbara or Ojai." Ryan nodded reluctantly, and then asked me if Matt had ever done anything like this before— just split without telling anybody. I thought about the last year—the period between the summer of 1980 and this past Labor Day—and realized, no, Matt had never done anything like this before. This was, in fact, very unlike him.

I didn't tell Ryan that but simply said again, "I think he'll be okay."

SOMETHING WAS BUILDING WITHIN me and I didn't know what to do with it. My mind kept flashing on the phone calls Matt accused me of, the empty aquarium, the missing cat, Matt's furi- ous paranoia. What kept weighing me down with fright was that I knew that something had been happening to Matt that caused him to disappear—I believed there were forces beyond Matt's control that led to his disappearance and had been circling him weeks before he was "officially" missing. There was no other angle from which I could look at what happened to Matt Kellner: he had been targeted, and these forces entered into his life and before it became too late to figure any of this out they had simply taken him. The nights after I heard of Matt's disappearance, and before the body was found, I smoked the weed I bought from Jeff Taylor to get me to sleep but it was too strong and caused me to vividly dream until I woke up doused with sweat, paralyzed. What made the fear that caused the need for the marijuana so maddening was that there was no one to talk with about the fear or to tell my dreams to or talk about Matt with: my own girlfriend, who I'd committed myself to, was under the innocent assumption that Matt had only been my weed dealer and hadn't asked me anything else about him since she answered the phone on that Sunday he called while I was passed out.

When Susan *did* ask me about Matt after the assembly where she announced that Matt had disappeared—purposefully not in front of any of our friends—I just brushed her off. She asked me if I knew anything and when was the last time I saw him and how close were we really and I hated everything this intimated and how her ques- tions, like Ryan's, seemed to implicate me in Matt's narrative. My anger about Robert Mallory—that Susan and Thom talked to him about me—had faded and the only thing I said to Susan was that Matt had been freaking out about *something* and I didn't know what. But you guys were close, right? Susan asked, insisting. Didn't you hang out all the time? Didn't you spend weekends with him? Weren't you good friends? Didn't he tell you what he was freaking out about? I realized while we were standing beneath the eaves, about to walk into a classroom together, that we were talking about an angle that she was presupposing—that I knew Matt Kellner better than I'd ever revealed, and that this constituted an intimate relationship Susan was now acknowledging and that she was certain about and that I was now confirming by answering her. I don't think Susan was necessarily intimating that Matt and I were having actual sex—I had never admitted it to her, she had never flat-out asked—but she would joke teasingly about our friendship and maybe I confirmed something by going along with it, never denying the jokes, in fact making another joke to link with hers. But in the scope of things none of that mattered—it all seemed small—because another day passed and Matt Kellner didn't appear at Buckley on Thursday. And I somehow knew that something awful had happened to him, and even worse, I thought: if it was at the hands of the Trawler it might be months before his body was found.

AND THEN WE HEARD THAT A BACKPACK was discovered by a ranger down the coast in a parking lot in Crystal Cove State Park, above a bluff overlooking the ocean—and it had a name and address tied to it on a small ID tag that proved it belonged to Matt Kellner. The only reason the backpack was brought to the attention of the Orange County Police was that there was blood all over it and the name checked with the missing-person report that Ron and Sheila Kellner filed with the Los Angeles Police Department. This was what Susan was told by Dr. Croft, who warned her that the information was considered too upsetting to reveal to the school at large, especially the students in seventh and eighth grades, and so Susan just reiterated at the mid-morning assembly on Friday that Matt Kellner was still missing and that anyone who had information should please come to the administration offices, adding that anything offered would be kept completely confidential—whatever that meant. Was that a message to me? When I wondered this it made me almost physically sick. There were moments when I imagined I could walk into the administration office and control the answers to the questions I'd be asked but I also knew that there was no way the questioning *wouldn't* lead to the sexual nature of our friendship—it was an inevitability that I didn't want to face, plus I had no real info about the disappearance anyway, only my fearful dreams and fantasies, my writer's intuition and sense of drama, the things I heard that weren't there. But then the fear would ratchet up when I realized I was perhaps the only person who knew about the aquarium and the rearranged furniture and the missing cat—it would hit with a queasy force that Matt probably hadn't told anyone but me. I'd calm myself with the fact that no one really knew anything yet and that Matt could totally be fine, lying on a towel somewhere, glistening with suntan oil, lounging in the autumn heat, stoned, listening to Foreigner on his Walkman.

BUT THE BLOODSTAINED backpack found in the parking lot at that beach in Orange County was sufficiently ominous to ramp up the fear level. It simply seemed like the prelude to discovering another death even if no one was admitting this yet, and after Susan confided in us that she had just learned this detail that morning questions were asked by our group for which there were no answers: what was he doing in Crystal Cove State Park, did Matt inflict a wound upon himself, was that why the backpack was stained with blood, how much blood was on the backpack, what was in the backpack, did anyone see if Matt was with someone, why had the backpack been left in a parking lot, where was his car? But the questions were just perfunctory, a kind of mimicry I thought the group felt they had to perform, and there was no real urgency or concern behind any of the questions tossed at Susan—not from Thom or Debbie or Jeff or Tracy— and since she didn't have the answers to any of them the questioning drifted away. I noted that Robert never asked a single question about Matt, and neither did Ryan. I was the only one in a state of disbelief that no one seemed to really share—it might have been "eerie" that a student was missing and "freaky" that the backpack had been found and "the missing kid" got people mildly excited if only for a moment, and then school life went on.

Classes weren't canceled, the parking lot was filled with cars, we went up to Gilley Field for PE, on that Friday I ate lunch at Du-par's in Studio City with Thom and Susan and Debbie, and Matt Kellner's name didn't come up once as I tried not to become that zombie Debbie accused me of playing. I maintained some surface semblance of pretending life was normal but I was dying inside and everything was a blur as I sat with Debbie nestled into me across the booth from Thom and Susan in the diner—just two clean-cut couples, Buckley kids, ordering grilled cheese sandwiches and vanilla milkshakes in their preppy uniforms. I had tried to concentrate on my homework in the empty house on Mulholland but I was relying too much on the weed I was buying from Jeff Taylor, and getting stoned was now laced with a new paranoia, it was sharper and more intense and left me completely in shambles, and I just opted for Valium so at least I could focus on the assigned reading and complete papers and sit at a desk in an air-conditioned classroom and fill out the answers in a pop quiz that Mrs. Susskind surprised us with on Friday afternoon and that I barely managed to pass. Ryan didn't come over that weekend—he had intimated earlier that week he would—and I don't think I masturbated for six days, from the moment I heard Matt was missing to when the body was finally found I didn't want to touch myself.

AND THEN IT HAPPENED. Early Saturday morning the gardener arrived at the Kellners' address on Haskell Avenue, having heard nothing about Matt's disappearance. The gardener walked the side path up from the street and unlatched the gate that led him to the backyard. There was a utility closet next to the pool house where trash bins and rakes and hedge clippers were stored and there was a small window that looked into the garage of the pool house, where the red Datsun was now parked, though the gardener wouldn't have noticed the blood spattered across the passenger seat and dashboard. The gardener dragged a trash can along the lawn, passing the guesthouse, when he stopped and smelled something. It was silent in the backyard but there was the distinct whirring of insects coming from close by and the gardener couldn't tell where the odor of rot was emanating from. And then he saw the body of a cat nailed to one of the wooden columns of the pool house—but he wasn't sure if it was the cat the gardener had usually seen prowling the property because this animal was decapitated. It was tied mid-column with a belt and oversized nails had been driven into each paw, crucifying the animal, splaying it out. The cat was eviscerated and a bundle of dark-red, pink and white intestines hung from where someone had gutted it, gathered between the cat's hind legs, where a swarm of flies congregated.

The gardener turned and saw something floating in the pool. It was a body. It was naked. It wasn't moving. The arms were extended in front of the body as if it was in mid-swim and the legs were stretched into a slight V and the hair was wavy in the blue-lit water, which was lightly rusted with blood. The build, the color of hair, the height—the gardener recognized it as Matt; he had seen him enough times over the years to know exactly who this was. And then the gardener noticed a small object sitting at the edge of the shallow end, where the steps led into the water. And that was the head of the missing cat—the cat that was now nailed to the column—its eyes gouged out, its ears sliced off, and its tongue pulled so far from its mouth that it draped obscenely across the tile surrounding the pool. The head had been placed in the center of the coping so that it was directly in line with the corpse suspended in the water. The pool was very still, the boy in the water was frozen in place, the only noise the sound of flies. The gardener started running up the lawn toward the main house, away from the body in the pool and the mutilated carcass of the cat. This was at eight o'clock Saturday morning, a week after Matt had probably disappeared.

THE LOS ANGELES POLICE DEPARTMENT called the school by the time mid-morning assembly started on Monday and Dr. Croft addressed the student body after the Pledge of Allegiance and the prayer and intoned there had been an "unfortunate" event: Matt Kellner, the missing student, had died over the weekend and every-one's prayers should be sent to his family. Matt's death was referred to as an accident, the student had drowned *accidentally* in the pool,

Matt had slipped, Matt had hit his head on the pool's ledge and then drowned, there was the hint of drugs. This was the official version on that Monday and Croft did not remind everyone that Matt Kellner had been missing for a week before this happened or that a blood-stained backpack belonging to him had been found in a parking lot an hour outside of L.A. On that Monday they were making it simple, open and shut, not too disturbing: Matt disappeared, drove around the coast for seven days and then returned to the house on Haskell Avenue in the middle of the night and tripped into the pool and accidentally drowned—this was the clean version. This was the story being pushed, for now, and there was no reason for anybody not to accept it. On that morning no one knew Croft was going to announce this—none of us had heard anything about Matt's death until that moment—so the surprise of it eradicated any kind of reason to be suspicious. Not even Susan Reynolds as student-body president had been briefed beforehand. I was too stunned to feel anything except relief that it didn't seem to be connected to the Trawler: it was an accident, Matt had done this to himself, no one else seemed to be involved. For me, the tension broke that day because of this.

It was as if everything momentarily dissolved—all the worry, all the fear. Matt was gone, as I knew he would be, it was so inevitable as to be preordained, the suspense was over, hopefully he was at peace. I had been expecting a dark and violent outcome, and though I was shocked by the news I didn't cry out, I didn't collapse, I stayed remarkably calm. I simply gasped quietly and held a hand to my mouth and felt nothing except a mounting confusion began building on that Monday because after I got over the shock I didn't quite believe in the surface narrative of this particular story that was being offered to us—something started gnawing at me, something was off. After assembly I skipped Phys Ed, along with most of the senior class, and drove back to the house on Mulholland and sat in a chaise in the backyard, completely numb. I didn't want to see anyone at lunch and I didn't want to be asked any questions by Susan or be comforted by Debbie and I didn't want to be anywhere near the person Matt had become closest to in the days before his death: Robert Mallory.

—

The SHARDS

IN THE DAYS AFTER THE ACCIDENT the talk shifted to suicide pretty quickly in the revolving rumor mill concerning Matt's death but I believed this even less than the accidental-drowning theory. There was no way Matt killed himself: it was completely improbable that he had purposefully ingested a variety of drugs (weed, 'ludes, acid) and then decided to drown himself during a psychotic break, no matter how frazzled he was when I last saw him. The story I began to believe was that Matt had gotten scared: he realized there was something "wrong" about the phone calls and the rearranged furniture and the missing cat and left Los Angeles because he felt targeted—his paranoia was full-blown, I had seen it and I believed this was what caused him to leave Encino on that weekend without telling anyone, so no one could find him. He didn't leave a note because he didn't want to risk getting tracked, and he drove down the coast and probably paid cash for everything and slept in his car—it was certainly warm enough that September to do this comfortably and it sounded like Matt. There was, however, the mystery of the bloodstained backpack found at Crystal Cove, in addition to knowing that Matt never took opiates or hallucinogens. I began to believe that the death wasn't accidental or a suicide but that someone else was involved and helped cause it or actually *staged* it. Large sections of the narrative about Matt Kellner's death were simply missing and on some nights I'd think maybe logic or coherence didn't play a part in any of this—and I was haunted by what Terry Schaffer had said in Trumps when I asked him if something was weird. "Isn't *everything*?" he had asked back, lightly mocking me.

In the end it played out as an accident that was too banal, boring even, there wasn't anything about it to fully engage people—there wasn't a real story, no drama, no mystery—and so Matt's death barely made the news: one item in the *Los Angeles Herald Examiner* with a small headline, "Encino Boy, 17, drowns in pool," and just a brief obituary in the *Los Angeles Times* complete with Matt's junior yearbook photo appearing within the hundreds of other obituaries from that week spread over two pages (1964–1981), his face lost in a sea of old people; there was no funeral or memorial service.

—

A STUDENT DEATH—which had never happened at Buckley while any of us were there—should have been an occasion. Or at least a bigger moment than Matt Kellner's death became, and since it wasn't an occasion I processed and accepted it far more easily than I ever could have imagined, because *no one seemed to care*—there may have existed the surprise of it but because it was Matt Kellner it just didn't carry the weight it would have if someone more popular had died. If it had been Thom Wright I believe the campus would've shut down for two days so everyone could grieve and recover, or even Jeff Taylor would have merited some kind of memorial. But Matt had disappeared into himself and was so invisible over the past few years that it didn't seem like such a big deal—he was a stoner, he went missing, he drowned, he was a weirdo, so what. I ended up being more shocked than saddened by the way this played out and I never cried, because I had already cried over Matt Kellner and everything that was lost when I drove away from the house on Haskell Avenue that hungover Sunday afternoon. The death struck the campus in a mild, even muted, way because no one had known Matt.

Even worse, Matt became a punch line, a joke, and, walking through the hallways between classes, I overheard the occasional comment in those first days of October after Matt was found dead, with guys mimicking Cheech and Chong and Mr. Bill ("Oh no, Sluggo! Don't push me into the pool, Sluggo!"), and the person who became most activated about Matt's death was the one person I wished hadn't and that was Debbie Schaffer, who didn't believe I was okay when I told her in fact I was.

Matt had called the house on Mulholland and only briefly talked to Debbie but she now created a deeper connection between Matt and myself after Susan inadvertently told her Matt and I were closer than she might have thought and Debbie overblew it because she "felt bad" that she had wrongfully assumed he'd only been my dealer— which is exactly what he was, I argued. Debbie became "worried" and she didn't want to let me out of her sight and canceled a session she booked at Windover so she could follow me to the house on Mulholland and comfort me, assuming I wanted to lose myself in sex because of the "friend" I had tragically lost. I didn't know what to do with her, so I went with it, using the sexual imagery with Ryan as a way to get through sex with Debbie, but I couldn't sustain this for more than a couple of afternoons and soon I was using Matt's death as an excuse *not* to have sex with Debbie, reiterating that I really was okay and the charity event she'd been training for was so much more important since there was nothing anyone could do now: Matt was gone.

There was one person I wanted sex from but Ryan was fading away and after the announcement of Matt's death stopped suggesting he should come over to the house on Mulholland. "You're not freaked out?" Ryan asked at the lockers one afternoon that week the body was found. I shook my head because I didn't know what else to do. "Well, I'm freaked out for you," Ryan said. Ryan hadn't known Matt—only whatever I had told him—but I realized increasingly that maybe I hadn't known Matt either: if it was true he had a psychotic break after disappearing for a few days and then returned only to accidentally or purposefully drown himself while on hallucinogens then I really didn't know this person. I knew his body intimately—I'd memorized it—but if this narrative about his death was real then I had to accept that he'd been a ghost the entire time. But the fact remained that I didn't believe in the official narrative: I increasingly believed that someone else was involved with the death of Matt Kellner and there was a point that week where I began to suspect that Robert Mallory had something to do with it—that on some level he had put it into motion.

SUSAN REYNOLDS POSTPONED THE PARTY she was throwing for Robert Mallory until the third Saturday in October, and she told me this as we sat in her car in the senior parking lot, where moments before we had shared what should have been a relatively normal scene leading up to getting into the BMW—we'd been talking about Thom's upcoming trip back east to visit colleges and how I hadn't even met with Mrs. Zimmerman, the school's college adviser, let alone planned to visit any campuses yet. Susan believed she was probably heading to her first choice, UCLA—in fact it was inevitable, there was no way she wasn't going to get in. "Yeah, the same with Thom," I said. This caused Susan to break out of the pose she'd perfected and look over at me warily. "We don't know if Thom is going to UCLA," she said. "Why not?" I asked, surprised. "I just told you he's going to look at places back east," she said. I reminded her that the only reason Thom was going back east was that Lionel, his dad, could take time off to accompany him to the colleges Thom was supposedly looking at—Syracuse, University of Connecticut, Boston— even though Thom's first choice *was* UCLA and the trip was to please his father, who was hoping that Thom would attend school on the East Coast so he could be nearer to him. "You *know* that," I said to Susan. The conversation, which should have been tinged with excitement, I remember, had become sullen and resigned, and I noticed bitterly that this mood didn't have anything to do with Matt Kellner; he seemed to have already been forgotten—Susan was distracted by something bigger, or so I presumed. And then she leaned over and turned up the volume on the car's stereo.

THERE WAS A SONG Susan and I shared, sung by a group called Icehouse, from Australia, and it was now playing in the car as we sat there after school while she smoked a clove cigarette and stared out the windshield and I just looked at her, struck by how beautiful she'd become—this new beauty which seemed to have blossomed almost overnight. *Why didn't you end up with her?* Robert Mallory asked me in the space on Melrose—a night that seemed a thousand years ago. I remembered the first time I noticed Susan—it was at a party Anthony Matthews (always trying to be the most popular boy in our class) threw in the first weeks of seventh grade where she suddenly appeared in Calvin Klein jeans and a halter top and walked down the steps toward the pool just as the opening riff of "Saturday Night" by the Bay City Rollers blared from the outside speakers as if she was a girl in a movie we were all standing in, and later we watched her blithely gyrate to "Boogie Fever" with Jeff Taylor, who we thought she was going to end up with, but nothing happened. And I remember the following year, when I was allowed to join a sleepover at Debbie's, Susan and I finally connected and became closer than we ever had, while the group watched *Carrie* on the Z Channel, and then for some reason I remember a few years later touching her thigh while watching *Fame* at the Cinerama Dome after school, a movie Thom didn't want to see, just to test her, to gauge how serious Susan was about Thom, who she'd been dating for almost nine months by then—this was in May of 1980—and she didn't push my hand away and I finally removed it myself. And I thought of all the corny songs that Susan and I bonded over, and that Thom and Debbie didn't like: Neil Diamond and "If You Know What I Mean" and Barry Manilow and "Tryin' to Get the Feeling Again" and "Weekend in New England" and everything by the Carpenters. *Why didn't you end up with her?* I knew why and yet I also didn't know—it shouldn't have happened but it could have happened—it wasn't because I also liked boys. There was something that seemed unattainable about Susan and I guess in the end I preferred her that way—the inevitable reality would have been too crushing.

WE'D BEEN PLAYING THE ICEHOUSE song since it came out—it was the first track on the band's debut—and we had bought it together at the Tower Records on Sunset one day in the last week of school our junior year and then drove around that afternoon listening to it and rewinding the cassette so we could experience the song over and over, surprised at how much we liked it since we'd never heard it before. Susan had bought the cassette for the single that was being played on KROQ, the upbeat pop song "We Can Get Together," but this other track became a song only Susan and I knew; Debbie didn't know it, Thom didn't know it, Ryan didn't know it. The song was something Susan and myself shared, referencing it secretly, as if it was a coded message only the two of us found meaning in. It was a ballad about a girl outside an icehouse where the rivers never freeze, and the singer tells us that the girl is dreaming of a new love but she has to wait so long for him because he needs another year, and in the second verse we learn that the devil lives inside the icehouse—he came with the winter snow, the singer tells us—and the girl is dreaming through the summer and hoping through the spring and she can't remember getting any older. The vocals were wavering and slightly robotic behind a drum machine and a minor-chord synthesizer melody but it became warmer when it moved into a new key—it sounded ominous until it wasn't. There's a break, a bridge, where the tension is heightened and then it flies into one last chorus as the synth hook keeps cascading over the song. It had an aching, dreamy quality and it soared—it was like all the songs from that year, an anthem, and it appealed to the dramatic ways we saw ourselves ending with the narrator who has been watching the girl through the trees outside the icehouse singing, *Now it's colder every day.* It ends with a simple admission—*There's no love inside the icehouse*—and the song doesn't fade, it just ends.

I remember the power the song had the first time we played it in Susan's car as we drove across Sunset Boulevard and through Beverly Hills and the vocals were yearning for something better than what the lyrics offered and the chorus was about dreams, about hope, which were intensified by the doomy romanticism of the overall track itself. I realized the song was about Susan and it was about Thom, because this was the moment Susan was revealing to me that her feelings for Thom had fissures, a crack was appearing—she had first admitted this only two weeks earlier, in Westwood, before we even heard the song. *Thom isn't dumb exactly* . . . and the song seemed to sum up Susan in that moment. She was the girl outside the icehouse dreaming of a new love and Thom was the love the girl hopes will be there soon, but what made it so sad is that Thom was already there and it was obvious that Susan was waiting for someone else, and the devil was the reason this was happening—but who was the devil? (I thought for a while it was me, but it turned out to be Robert Mallory.) The song saddened me and gave me hope—the best combination for a pop song—and as we listened to it throughout the summer it kept confirming something about Susan and her mild dissatisfaction, the way she had consciously been numbing herself, and why she had brought up Thom's trip back east to visit colleges, as if she thought this was proof things might end by the time senior year was over, or maybe even before. But I also knew: there was no way Thom Wright was feeling the same narrative.

THE SONG ENDED—it had put me in a solemn mood and I was still briefly emotional because of it. I realized I was staring at Susan's breasts beneath her unbuttoned blouse and then I focused on anything else: the tin of Djarum cigarettes and the Tic-Tacs on the dashboard, various cassettes: the Go-Go's, the Clash, Stevie Nicks, Pat Benatar, the Psychedelic Furs. And then I focused on Thom's Corvette through the windshield and, beyond it, a few spaces away, Robert Mallory's black Porsche gleaming darkly in the parking lot. Our world would die, I suddenly thought: it was inevitable.

"Can I ask you something?" Susan said.

"Yes," I said.

"What was going on between you and Matt?" she asked softly. "Can you tell me? Can you be honest with me?"

I didn't say anything, just stared straight ahead. Another song began but Susan turned down the volume. And I was briefly touched when I realized that Susan actually had been thinking about Matt in that moment and that I'd been wrong in assuming she wasn't. I didn't say anything because I had no idea what to say.

"It can be a secret," she finally said. "I won't tell anyone."

"Why would it have to be a secret?" I asked.

She sighed. "Okay. Whatever."

"What do you want to know, Susan?"

"I just want to know . . . what he meant to you, I guess," she said. "What was your friendship like?" She stopped and then tentatively asked, "Was it more than a friendship?"

"Meaning what?"

Carefully, she said, "Were you hooking up?"

I wasn't shocked. I wasn't surprised. This was simply the moment when I could go either way—it was an offer to come clean. I could maintain a lie, and keep everything evasive, and make sure the world kept running smoothly in our little group at Buckley, or just finally admit it to her and let the drama pour out of me within what I assumed was the safety of our friendship, and yet I didn't know if I trusted Susan in the way I once had—because of Robert Mallory—and in that same moment she asked me the question I realized I couldn't tell her the truth and this revelation was so sudden and landed with such force that any hope of relief was wiped away. I could only be half honest with her—I had known Susan for a long time and I loved her in such a way that meant I could never fully lie to her and up to that point I never had. But we weren't there anymore.

"I didn't really know him," I started. "We hung out and some-times something happened. I don't know why or how. But, yeah, we hooked up a couple times."

"Only a couple?" she asked, unfazed that I'd admitted this.

I calmly shrugged and didn't say anything else.

"So it wasn't . . . a serious thing?" she asked.

"It was an . . . experiment. I was experimenting." I looked straight ahead through the windshield, completely drained, when I said this. "Susan, if you tell anybody, if you tell Thom or Debbie or Robert, I swear I'll—"

"Stop it," she said, cutting me off. "Of course I'm not going to tell anybody. Why would I want to tell Thom or Debbie or Robert this?" She was looking at me. "This is a secret, I get it." She paused. "It was between you and Matt. It's nobody's business."

I remember I felt nothing admitting this half-truth—even a quarter of the reality, denying the passion of it on my part—and this was proof that I was moving away from Susan, from the group, from everyone. She had told me in so many ways that she knew some-thing had been going on with Matt, not at first, but obviously we were closer than I'd let on. It was a friendship we sometimes joked about, but then, I only realized now, the joking had stopped. At a certain point Susan started understanding there was something else going on with Matt Kellner.

"I really didn't know him," I said. "I mean I don't know what was going on with him." I stopped, and lamely gestured with my hands. "I guess we were friends, but maybe not." I stopped again. "It was . . . confusing, I guess." I looked over at her. "It was an experiment."

"But you liked him?"

"I didn't know him."

"What does that mean?"

"It means I didn't know him," I said. "It means I don't know what happened to him. If I had known him I think his death would've made sense. But I guess I didn't know him because this wouldn't have happened to the Matt I thought I knew." I was rambling, confused, blushing.

"But I didn't ask you that," she said quietly. "I asked if you liked him."

"What do you mean?" I asked. "Like, was I in love with him? Jesus." I turned away, pretending to be disgusted.

Susan was quiet, contemplating what I'd just told her.

"Someone told me you guys had a falling out," she said.

The shock I felt in that moment—the betrayal—was massive and it hit immediately. I had to grip my fists to combat a wave of anger that slammed against me.

I almost got out of the car but I controlled myself. "What do you mean?" I asked once again in a flat, low voice.

She sighed, uncertain if she should go on, but then decided to.

"Robert told me that you and Matt had a falling out," she said. "But a falling out about what?"

"Why would Robert Mallory tell you this?" I couldn't help but use his full name when I asked her that.

"I don't know," she said. "Why would Robert tell me that? I guess he had talked to Matt and Matt told him." She paused. "What was the falling out about?"

"Well, didn't Robert find out and tell you?" I asked, continuing to control myself so I didn't spit this out at her, so my features wouldn't become twisted with rage, so that my hands wouldn't gnarl into claws, so I wouldn't let her see what I was really feeling in that moment. Instead my mood remained placid, my face blank.

"He said he didn't know," Susan said. "Just that Matt said he had this falling out with you over something and it kind of bummed Matt out."

Hearing this killed me. I kept steady. "Well, I don't know what that would have been," I murmured. "I mean, I told Matt that he was smoking too much weed and I couldn't deal with his paranoia and stuff like that and if he was going to get so high all the time what was the point of us hanging out."

Susan listened to this lie and nodded. "Did you, like, break off the friendship with him?"

I shrugged. "Yeah, I guess, but not really. I just . . . um . . . admonished him."

"Admonished him?" she asked, confused. "Admonished?"

"Yeah, about, um, how much, um, weed he was smoking," I said haltingly.

"Do you think this had anything to do with him not coming to school and disappearing—"

"Susan—" I warned.

"No, I'm serious—"

"Susan—" I warned again, this time louder.

"Was Matt upset enough to—"

"Kill himself?" I asked. "Are you fucking kidding me?" I turned around in the passenger seat and was facing her. "It was an accident. What are you implying?" I asked. "You can't start making up shit like this—"

"Why are you so defensive?" she asked, reaching over and grabbing my hand.

"Because you're implying whatever happened to Matt I had something to do with and that's bullshit," I said, pulling my hand away.

"Bret, please, I'm not suggesting that," she said. "I just thought maybe you knew why Matt thought you guys had a falling out."

"No, I don't," I said, calmly. "I have no idea what he was referring to. And by the way Robert already asked me about this and I told him I had no idea. What are you talking to Robert Mallory about? You're talking to him about me? He's a fucking freak, Susan—"

"Bret," she said softly, reaching again for the hand I'd pulled away. "I'm sure Matt's death was hard to deal with . . . for you . . . and I'm not implying anything." She paused. "And this has nothing to do with Robert."

"But he's the one who made this shit up—"

"What did he make up?"

"Oh, fuck it, I'm okay," I stressed. "I'm really okay." I pulled my hand away from her again. "It's all fine, Susan. It's all fine."

"Are you sure?" Susan said. "You can tell me, you can talk to me."

"Susan," I said. "What do you want to hear?"

"Whatever you want to tell me," she said. "It's just us."

"You think I had something to do with Matt's death—"

"That's not fair!" she exclaimed. "I never said that! Why are you such a fucking drama queen?"

"You're implying it!" I raised my voice. I was almost shouting. "Robert Mallory is implying it!"

"Bret, you've got to calm down," she said. "You don't need to get angry with me. I'm just trying to help. I'm the only one who seems to care about Matt. I'm the only one asking you these things." She paused. "And you're so resentful . . ."

"You're right, you're right, that's not what I meant."

"Jesus, Bret," she muttered.

"But why was Robert so interested in Matt?"

"I don't think Robert was *so* interested in Matt—"

"He was always hanging out with him," I said. "He was hanging out with him more than I was."

"That's because you had a falling out, right?" she exclaimed, looking at me, her eyes wide with disbelief. "That's because *you* 'admonished' him." She kept staring as if she couldn't understand me. "You abandoned a friend and yet you're upset with *Robert* for trying to meet new friends and trying to be friends with Matt?"

"Susan," I said, "Robert didn't want to be friends with Matt—"

"How do you know that? You don't know that—"

"I'm sorry I'm not a member of the fucking Robert Mallory fan club but I don't believe Robert wanted to be *friends* with Matt Kellner—"

"I just want to know one thing," Susan said, cutting me off.

"Okay," I said. "Yeah?"

"When did it stop with Matt?" She paused, then clarified. "The two of you fooling around."

"Why?" I asked. "What does it matter?"

She thought about it and then measured her words carefully. "It matters to me because Debbie is my best friend."

I slowly nodded when I realized what she meant, what she was really asking, the time line.

"I think it was May," I said, and then continued haltingly. "Nothing . . . happened over the, um, summer."

"So nothing happened between you and Matt when you started dating Debbie?"

I hated the way she asked this. I hated that this mattered to her. I hated the way she used the word *dating*. It suggested a different Susan than the numb, uncaring beauty I had become so enamored of in the past few weeks. It suggested that there were rules we needed to follow and a kind of propriety I thought Susan had abandoned. She was confirming we were in high school, where there were football games and assemblies and prom kings and Homecoming queens and boys didn't fuck each other and everyone was faithful and abided by the laws we set up and conformed to. A year ago I might have admitted this disgust to Susan when she said this and I could have told her I felt this way over the summer. But something had changed since then and now I couldn't.

"Yeah, that's right," I said. "I didn't want anything to happen." I stopped. "I was with Debbie. And I think . . ." I realized a different narrative, a new take, and I went there. It formulated quickly. It solved everything.

"Yeah?" Susan asked, waiting.

"And I think . . . that was something that really upset Matt," I said. "I think that was what started driving us apart." I paused for emphasis. "Debbie. It was my relationship with Debbie." I nodded as if realizing this for the first time. "That she had become my girlfriend . . ."

Susan thought about this and nodded slightly as if she understood. And what made the moment so much worse was that she exhibited relief and relaxed. This lie caused a small wave of nausea to crest over me but then it dissolved when I realized it was all going to play.

"You can never tell her, Susan. Please." I turned to her, desperate. "She can never know. It would fuck everything up."

"I know, I know," she said, thinking things through. "I won't say anything, I won't say anything," she said, reaching for my hand. "I promise."

"Thank you" was all I could say. "Thank you," I said again.

She looked back at me and tried to lighten the moment by saying, "Your secret is safe with me," but now it sounded ironic, not lightly joking like all the other times she'd said this, and I suddenly realized there was bemusement intertwined with her relief and I reacted to the irony by mimicking a shy schoolboy smiling bashfully and turning away. This made her laugh.

12

I LEFT SUSAN'S CAR and walked over to the Mercedes and opened the door and sat in the driver's seat and knew automatically I would be heading to Matt Kellner's house without having any idea why I was doing this. There were simply no other thoughts. I was completely calm as I nodded at Miguel, who was directing traffic in the Buckley parking lot that afternoon, and then drove past the gates and onto Stansbury. I drove along Valley Vista in a daze, heading toward Encino, but when I turned onto Haskell and arrived at Matt's house I was suddenly struck with a fear I had never experienced before—it was adrenaline that acted as a warning for me to save myself but also mixed with an over-whelming compulsion to move forward no matter how I felt, and find out whatever I thought I needed to know. I parked where I usually parked; the street looked the same, the house looked the same. The only difference in this section of the movie: Matt was dead.

I walked the path to the gate, surprised to find I could unlatch it as easily as I had a hundred times before—it wasn't locked, as I'd expected. I walked the pathway as I had a hundred times—usually in a heightened state of erotic excitement, of which I was now uncomfortably reminded—to the back of the property and stopped when I saw the pool house and involuntarily took in a deep breath: the sight of it caused me to start panicking about some vague and nameless thing. But then I realized the panic was simply connected to the fact that this was the place where Matt and I had *existed,* the only place I ever saw him except Buckley, and the pool house itself held just as much meaning to me as Matt actually had—and now it was tainted by death, a haunted place. The fear and adrenaline and panic were suddenly engulfed by an ache I was surprised I felt, like the moment you suddenly heard sad music playing over a particular image in a movie, even though I realized "Ghost Town" was the last song I heard here—decidedly not a sad song. I drifted toward the front door not knowing what I expected but the yellow crime-scene tape crossing the entrance I'd anticipated wasn't there (because Matt's death wasn't a *crime,* right?) though I noticed a column wrapped in what looked like a sheet of blue plastic that offered the suggestion something criminal *had* taken place (I knew nothing yet about the cat nailed to the column) and then I was touching the doorknob. I was surprised, again, that it turned, and the door opened, and I was allowed access. And I just stood there in the fading afternoon light, realizing at seventeen that I was already staring into my past—that the past had a meaning that would always define you. I remember this being one of my first moments nearing adulthood, when I realized how powerful memory was—or at least it was the first time it hurt the most. And there was nothing I could do about the pain of the past—it just settled over me. The pool house and Matt were a part of my life that had *happened* and now they were gone. That was all. No one else knew about it. No one cared.

THE ROOM SEEMED even more barren than it was the last time I'd been in it, when Matt, in the lime-green bathing suit and the Dodgers T-shirt, recoiled from me reaching out to him. My eyes scanned the space—I had never seen it this clean before. I quickly averted my eyes from the bed, which was really now just a mattress, the cardigan sheets had been stripped from it. I noted the surfboards stacked against each other (just a decorative touch—Matt never surfed) and the shellacked dolphin curved and mounted above the empty aquarium that ran along the wall as I moved deeper into the room—it smelled musty, unaired, as if no one had been in it for a long time. I had noted the stereo and the records neatly lined on the floor next to one of the speakers when I saw the Foreigner *4* poster above the hamper and it inexplicably chilled me—the poster that had been left in Matt Kellner's mailbox by someone. I moved forward until I was standing in front of it, gazing at the image as if it held a mysterious meaning that needed to be deciphered, but none existed. I opened the refrigerator: the weed was gone; only a couple of Corona bottles and a lone can of Cactus Cooler remained. I went to his desk, where schoolbooks were neatly stacked next to a Smith-Corona typewriter: the drug paraphernalia—the bongs, the pipes, the rolling papers— were nowhere in sight. I started to pull open the drawers, which were mostly empty except for the occasional notepad and pen, a stapler and a small box of paper clips, a pencil sharpener, a calculator, a ruler (I had used it once to measure our erections), and I was surprised to find an issue of *Hustler* in the bottom drawer and wondered why no one had gotten rid of it when everything else seemed so studiously cleaned. I had just picked up one of the pads when I noticed on the top page a phone number and the letters *RM* jotted down in Matt's oversized, looping handwriting, and I froze. I don't know why but I immediately picked up the green rotary phone on Matt's desk to dial the number, and nothing happened—the line was disconnected. RM was Robert Mallory—there was no doubt. I tore the piece of paper from the pad and slipped it into the pocket of my slacks. I assumed Matt had a school roster that contained Robert Mallory's phone number, so why would Matt need to write it down? And then I thought: maybe Robert Mallory had *another* phone number, maybe he had a *separate* number, a *private* number, and this was the one he had given Matt. Or maybe this *was* the number in the roster and I was hearing things that weren't there because I was the writer.

I BECAME DISTRACTED when I noticed a stack of neatly folded clothes on the bedroom bench pushed against the stripped mattress— they had been washed but I wondered when they had been left out. Had they been cleaned while Matt was missing that week and stacked and folded for him when he returned from wherever he was, or had they been washed after his body was found in the pool—part of a continuing schedule in the rituals enacted by the Kellners trying to maintain a façade of normalcy in the face of their son's death. I found the Dodgers T-shirt and lifted it up to smell it but there was no trace of Matt's scent. And then my eyes landed on three pairs of white jockey shorts next to the T-shirts and an overwhelming signal of lust pulsed within me and I picked one of them up and pressed it to my face, inhaling deeply, pushing it into my mouth, tasting it, chewing on it—I couldn't help myself. They were clean: there were no stains, no odor, no hint of Matt, everything about him washed away. I immediately stopped, embarrassed, and shoved the underwear into my pants pocket, where I tried to flatten it out so it wouldn't bulge. I checked the pool-house garage and it was empty: the red Datsun was no longer there. And as I walked out for the final time I realized something I hadn't noticed when I first arrived: the pool had been drained—it was completely empty and totally dry, and it looked diminished without the water, just a small hole of white concrete. My heart stopped when I saw the hammock tied between the trunks of the two palm trees and remembered the first time I saw Matt naked there, on that July afternoon in 1980.

AS I LEFT THE POOL HOUSE the sprinklers were spraying across the lawn that led up to the main residence—a massive two-story English Tudor, impossibly wide and probably built in the mid-1960s—and I saw someone sitting at a table in the gazebo off to the side of the lawn that ran up to the house and surrounded by flowers, blue-violet and golden yellow. I had noticed the gazebo before—it was large and white with an ivied roof—but I'd never seen anyone sitting in one of the patio chairs situated around the small table at its center. And there was a woman in one of the chairs, smoking a cigarette, wearing a tennis skirt mismatched with a flower-patterned blouse, her long tan legs crossed, and she was barefoot, blankly assessing me as I decided to move across the lawn toward her because I felt caught and needed to explain who I was. I realized this was Matt's mother, Sheila.

I supposed I must have seen her at various school events but her face didn't remind me of anyone I'd met before. I'd only known Matt, and even though I'd been coming over to Haskell Avenue for about a year I was never introduced to Sheila or his father, Ronald. I actually had never been inside the main house. Sheila's brown hair was shoulder-length and a pair of sunglasses were pushed above her chic blunt bangs and she looked older than most of our mothers—a woman probably in her late forties. I knew nothing about Sheila: Matt didn't complain or say anything complimentary about his mother—he never mentioned her. I wasn't wearing the blazer but I had the rest of the

Buckley uniform on—the striped tie was loosened, my sleeves were rolled up—and I supposed my youth was what caused her to remain calm at the appearance of this stranger walking toward her, though I realized almost immediately as I moved halfway up the steps leading into the gazebo that she was sedated and this was what caused her stillness and kept everything calm and light; as I got closer I saw that she looked, in fact, dead-eyed and stunned. The only movement was when she crushed the cigarette out in an ashtray next to a pack of Pall Malls. She waited as I stood there not knowing what to say.

"Yes?" she finally asked. "Can I help you?"

I didn't know how to explain that something had compelled me to drive to the Kellner residence and why I was standing in front of her in this moment. I was suddenly shocked when I realized that she had probably watched me walk into the pool house from the pathway and emerge moments later and that I was going to have to give her some kind of reasonable answer as to why I was standing there even though I didn't have one myself.

"I'm a friend of Matt's," I said softly, then realized. "I was a friend of Matt's."

Her head slightly tilted when I said this, and in the same stunned voice asked, "A friend?" She paused. "Of Matthew's?"

"Yes, I'm Bret," I said. "Bret Ellis. I'm in Matt's class." I paused. "At, um, Buckley," I mindlessly clarified.

The silence that followed suggested she had no idea who I was but raised her eyes involuntarily as if surprised.

"We've never met," she said, looking me over with a blankness that seemed completely natural under the circumstances but unnerved me anyway.

"No, we never have," I said. "But I came over often." I paused. "To see Matt." I paused again. "To swim and hang out."

"Oh," she said. "So that was your car I always saw? The green sedan?"

"Yeah," I said, and then, "I'm sorry. I'm so sorry about what happened—"

"But what happened?" she asked in the same toneless voice. She asked this too quickly—it overlapped with my condolences.

"I'm . . . Excuse me?" I automatically asked dumbly, confused.

"But what happened?" she asked again, reaching for another cigarette, which she slipped out of the pack and placed between her lips, and the flame from a gold lighter quickly lit it. She exhaled as she continued staring at me. I noticed the half-full glass of orange juice next to the ashtray and the burgeoning alcoholic in me wondered if there was vodka in it.

"What do you . . . mean?" I asked, trying to sound sympathetic though my features were creased with confusion. The scene had reduced me to an actor and I was struggling with my lines, trying to hit the right notes and get on her level.

"I mean," she began in that toneless voice with the blank stare, "we don't know what happened to my son." She paused before adding, "Exactly."

There was a silence between us, just the sound of the sprinklers spraying over the vast lawn, their rhythmic click-clacking occasionally adding to the soundtrack of the movie we were in.

"I don't know . . . what happened," I said, aware that a pair of Matt's jockey shorts were in the pocket of the gray slacks I was wearing, pressed against my thigh. I shifted and took a step back on the stairs leading up to where Sheila Kellner sat in the center of the gazebo and glanced at the empty pool and the barren guesthouse. "He had . . . an accident. It was an accident. I mean, right?" I asked tentatively, looking back at her but barely meeting her gaze.

She was obviously in pain and confused—you could sense it in her eyes and her stillness as if there was an aura of bewilderment surrounding her, but whatever medication she had taken blunted this to the point where she could talk about Matthew without breaking down. And then she asked, "Do you know if he got into a fight with anybody?"

This was something so out of the range from what I expected that I had to wait a moment to collect myself, and then asked, "A fight?"

"Yes," she said, inhaling on the cigarette. "An altercation?"

"What do you mean?" I murmured.

She answered with a stoned nonchalance. "He was bruised," she said. "He was very bruised. The side of his face was bruised."

Again, I didn't know what to say. "Maybe that happened when he fell?" I made a gesture with my hands, hopelessly. "Into the pool. And, um . . . hit his head?"

"No," she said, and then, clarifying, "he had bruises on his chest and back. His legs."

I wasn't prepared for any of this. I hadn't expected to see Sheila Kellner. I had no idea I would be having a conversation with my dead friend's mother. Standing on the steps of the gazebo was almost intolerable. Bruises? There were *bruises* all over Matt? This was a movie I was totally lost in. I retraced my steps, found myself back in the scene and improvised my lines. "Does anyone know where . . . he went that week? Maybe something happened wherever . . . he went." I paused and for a moment was genuinely scared. The bruises? No one had mentioned anything about bruises. "Maybe . . . the bruises happened then?"

Sheila said nothing. She looked from me to the faraway pool house and then at my face, completely expressionless.

"I mean, didn't they find his backpack at . . . that beach," I said quietly, "in that parking lot?" I was speaking so softly I could barely hear myself. "At . . . Crystal Cove."

"Matt didn't play sports," she said, as if she hadn't heard me.

"Not that I know of—"

"So that wasn't it," she said, exhaling smoke. "I think it was maybe from surfing," she said quietly. "I think he went surfing and maybe that's when the bruises happened." She paused and looked at me but it was without conviction. "The bruises seemed so odd but it was probably from surfing." I just nodded, trying to placate her. I knew Matt didn't surf and yet Sheila thought her son was a surfer and I realized with a shocking and intimate finality that Sheila Kellner really didn't know her son. But I was reminded that I hadn't known him either—no one had. And then it was as if Sheila had suddenly floated into a new area of sedation—she seemed even further away from me when she asked, "Why did you come here?" It wasn't chilly and there was nothing accusatory about the question—it just came out like a dull inquiry, as if she really didn't care about my answer. I was surprised that she was able to hold the cigarette as steadily as she did—she smoked with her left hand, I noticed, and I glimpsed the diamond wedding ring on her finger. The movement of the hand lowering to the ashtray and rising back to her mouth was completely robotic, aided by whatever was sedating her.

"I came over . . ." I started, then stopped. "I came over because I wanted to find out what happened to Matt." Sheila Kellner stared at me for a long time with an unstinting gaze.

And after I left Haskell Avenue that afternoon, I realized, chillingly, in that moment, she was thinking: *No, you don't. You don't really want to find out what happened to my son.* But I didn't know that then, while I was standing on the steps of the gazebo. She finally said, "You can talk to my husband. He's in his office."

THE SLIDING GLASS DOOR leading into the kitchen was halfway open and there was a Mexican housekeeper in a maid's uniform wearing rubber gloves up to her elbows silently scrubbing the stovetop as I walked in and quietly closed the door, uncertain if I should. She turned her head to glance at me but without surprise. She took note of the school uniform and knew who I was: a friend of Matt's. But she was grim-faced and didn't say anything. She picked up a spray can of Easy-Off and was now heading toward the open oven as I tentatively moved through the kitchen—"I'm looking for Matt's . . . I mean, Ronald, Mr. Kellner, Señor Kellner . . ." was my halting explanation. The maid shrugged, and said something in Spanish that meant he was in *la oficina* and turned back to the oven. Past the kitchen a hallway led into a dining area, where I walked by a chrome-and-glass table with a potted fern in the middle of it and that sat on an expanse of off-white shag carpeting, which flowed into a sunken living room situated at the front of the house, where bay windows revealed the circular brick driveway and a view of Haskell Avenue. Once in the living room I could hear a voice somewhere within the house and moved to the staircase in the foyer, where my hand rested on a polished red-oak railing until I could locate exactly where the voice was coming from—it wasn't upstairs, I realized, and then turned toward a hallway that took me to the other side of the house.

—

The SHARDS

THE HOUSE MIGHT HAVE BEEN SPRAWLING but so silent it was easy to locate Ronald Kellner—I followed his voice down another hallway. The voice was quiet and tired, often muttering to whoever he was on the phone with. I turned into a large room that I assumed was Ronald's office, lined with the same off-white shag carpeting, and the generic pseudo-impressionist paintings my father also bought from the Wally Finley Gallery in Beverly Hills, and there was a kaleidoscope and an opened backgammon board on a low coffee table that sat in front of a wine-colored sofa and above that a panoramic view of the backyard. I later found out that Ronald Kellner ran one of the most powerful legal firms in L.A. (I'm not going to name it or make up a name for it) and the offices were based in Century City and represented, again I later found out, a group of clients in the real-estate and entertainment industries and the law firm had fifteen lawyers on its payroll in a number of suites in the Century Plaza Towers. But I didn't know any of this yet on that afternoon when I visited the Kellners.

Matt had never mentioned his father or what he did, because I guess I'd never asked, or maybe I had and didn't remember during all the long and aimless conversations over our year together, in which topics never got personal until the final week, when I'd pushed it, so of course I didn't know what Matt's dad did for a living and I never cared—when I was with Matt I often just got on his wavelength, talked about whatever he was interested in and then used him for sex, I realized while standing in the doorway of Ronald Kellner's office. He was in his early-to-mid-fifties—reminding me again that this was an older parent than those of most of our classmates in twelfth grade—and he was tall with thinning gray hair and a neatly trimmed beard. What struck me most about Mr. Kellner was that he appeared normal— nondescript beige slacks, a Polo shirt tucked in, he was wearing a belt, he was wearing loafers—and I wondered briefly why he didn't look like a mess, stomping around in pajamas and tear-faced, anguished and gripping a half-empty bottle of gin because his only child had just died. Ronald Kellner was capable of presenting himself as if this dreadful event had never happened. He looked completely professional on that afternoon despite the death of Matt.

—

RONALD KELLNER HELD the receiver to the side of his head as he stared out the bay window, the chord of the phone reaching from his desk to where he stood, looking out at the gazebo his wife was sitting in. I wasn't even listening to what Ronald was occasionally muttering into the phone because I was glancing at various mimeographed photos on his desk, which was strewn with papers and files and manila envelopes beneath a large metal Tensor lamp—the only instance of disorder within the neat and lavishly decorated office. He noticed me when he turned around and just stared blankly, unsmiling, as he continued the call. Again, I don't remember what he was saying, but it was quiet and strained, and when he walked over to the desk to hang the phone up his expression became lightly curious as his eyes scanned the uniform and then my face and asked, "Are you Robert?" I suppose I wasn't as shocked as I want to remember being when he asked that—if I was *Robert*—because I was able to calmly say, "No, I'm Bret." I paused. "I'm Bret Ellis. I go to Buckley. Mrs. Kellner told me you were in your office and that I could come in."

"Who are you?" he asked again, confused.

"I was a friend of Matt's," I said.

"A friend?" he asked. "His friend?"

"Yeah, we're in the same class at Buckley."

"You're Matt's friend from Buckley," he asked, just standing there.

"Well, yeah, we hung out," I said. "Sometimes I came over and . . . hung out."

He stared, large hands on his hips, studying me with a new grimness that hardened his expression. "How well did you know him?" he asked.

"Well, I've known him since seventh grade," I said. "When he came to Buckley." I paused. "But we became friends last year."

"You became friends with my son?" he asked. "Last year?"

I nodded.

The grimness turned into something else: a kind of suspicion joined it and Ronald cocked his head. "How well do you think you knew him?" he asked. "Matthew."

I realized I had to tell the truth. "I don't know." I sighed. "After what happened I really don't know."

This truthful admission softened Ronald—the grimness and suspicion left his face and he looked down. "What are you doing here?" he asked too softly. "What do you want?"

I don't know why I expected affection from him or even a kind of removed emotional response because of my presence but he seemed slightly exasperated that I was in his office—a stranger who admitted that he'd been friends with his son but didn't really know him. This wasn't exactly true, because I knew Matt in ways more intimate than any person I'd ever met up until that moment in my life, but I couldn't admit this to his father.

"I cared about Matt" was all I said.

"You cared about my son?" Ronald asked. "That's why you're here?"

"I just . . . I just wanted to find out what happened."

He was staring at me again with mild suspicion. We didn't say anything—we just kept looking at each other blankly until it became too uncomfortable and I finally said, "I'm sorry I bothered you," and then, "I'm sorry about Matt." I waited a beat before I turned to exit, aware again that Matt's jockey shorts were pressed into my pocket.

"You wanted to find out what happened?" Ron asked flatly.

"Yeah." I paused. "It was an accident, right? It was an accident in the pool."

Ron looked at me, deciding something, and then walked over to the cluttered desk, where he put on a pair of reading glasses. "Well, you haven't come to the right place, because we don't know what really happened." Ron sat down in a brown leather high-backed swivel chair and slowly scanned the papers strewn across the desk. He looked over at me, then motioned. "Please. Come here. Maybe you can try and explain this to me."

I slowly walked over to the desk and stood beside him.

"These were taken by the crime-scene photographer I called in," I heard Ronald say as I looked down at the desk. He picked up a stack of photos, eight-by-tens.

"A crime-scene photographer?" I asked quietly, suddenly filled with dread.

The first thing I saw was a body, carefully positioned, lying by the pool on a sheet, drowned, naked, the penis shrunken into nothingness. Matt's head wasn't in any of the photos Ronald Kellner was showing me—the first photos I saw had all been taken below the neck—but I recognized every inch of this body, every place I had licked and kissed and inhaled. There were a number of photos shot from different angles documenting the bruises Mrs. Kellner had mentioned, as if Matt had been pummeled by someone or something—they were lightly purple and immediately noticeable. There was a photo of Matt on his stomach in which the bruises continued along his lower and upper back, and there were two on his muscled ass. I couldn't help but automatically think I had been in that ass—my cock, my tongue, my fingers—and I had to resist any notions of arousal it inspired, a kind of necrophiliac lust that shocked me with its suddenness. There was a photo of Matt's left arm gashed open, the wound wide and pink, deep enough so you could see muscle and sinew. And then Ron showed me another photo. This one was of Matt's head. He looked peaceful, his eyes closed as if he was sleeping and I could almost detect a smile in the way his lips slightly arched up. But one side of the face was purpled with bruises and there was a large wound on the left side of his forehead, another gash, skin had peeled off and you could clearly see the white bone of his scalp.

"Do you think this happened when Matt hit his head when he fell into the pool?" Ron asked without any emotion.

I was so horrified by what I was looking at I became paralyzed. The pictures of Matt were so traumatic that one part of my life was now over and I had entered into another world, where I would remain forever. There was no going back to innocence or childhood—this moment was my official introduction into the realm of adults and death. I swallowed and looked away, closing my eyes. I heard Ronald shuffling papers around, and then sliding something out of a folder. I wanted to say: I didn't know your son but I loved him anyway. I opened my eyes because they were tearing up. I clenched my jaw hard to keep from crying in front of him.

"I'm supposing my son was a drug addict," Mr. Kellner said, looking up at me.

"No," I murmured. "No, I don't . . . It was just . . . pot, just weed. I . . ."

"So he wasn't into acid or Quaaludes or anything like that? Pills? LSD?"

"No, no," I murmured, shaking my head. "I never saw that. He never saw him do anything except . . . smoke weed . . ."

"You never saw him tripping on acid, you never saw him taking any pills?" he asked.

"No, I didn't. He never talked about any of that."

"Hallucinogens?" Ronald asked. "He never talked about that?"

Again, I shook my head, numbly.

"Quaaludes?"

"I never saw any Quaaludes around," I said. "Matt never talked about . . . that . . ."

"Well, then, how do we explain the six thousand milligrams of methaqualone that were found in his system?" Ronald Kellner asked me. I suddenly felt we were in a courtroom and I was on trial and Ron was a prosecutor trying to gauge whether I was innocent or guilty.

I was totally numb but managed to ask, "What is that?"

"Quaaludes," he said. "Six thousand milligrams of Quaalude were found in my son's system."

I just kept shaking my head. There was nothing to say. The power of the pictures had reduced me to a shell. I felt completely empty inside. I didn't care about anything anymore and I was so frightened I could barely move.

"I'm trying to piece together where my son was that week," he said. "Do you know anything?"

"Well," I started, "didn't they find that backpack at the parking lot?" My voice sounded like that of a little boy.

"In Crystal Cove?" Ron asked. "You mean in Crystal Cove State Park. In Orange County."

"Yeah," I said. "Didn't they find the backpack in that parking lot, so, um, didn't he drive there and maybe . . . maybe . . . I don't know . . . something happened . . ."

"He didn't drive anywhere," Ronald said flatly.

"How . . . do you know?" I asked—the dread kept expanding.

"I spoke to my son before the weekend he disappeared," Ronald said. "I told him he needed to get the headlight replaced on the Datsun. I'd told him to do this for weeks but he was always . . . distracted"—was the word Ronald Kellner landed on, replacing the more obvious choice: *stoned*—"and he hadn't done it. I know the head of the Nissan dealership in Encino and so I took it in myself and got the car serviced." Ronald stopped and then looked up at me. "He didn't drive one hundred and forty miles to and from Laguna Beach."

"How . . . do you know this?" I asked quietly.

"Because when I had the car serviced I noticed what the mileage was. I had seen what the mileage was at the dealership." He stopped. "I noted the mileage on that Thursday, and a week later, when the car was driven back and parked here in the garage at the guesthouse, I checked it again."

I just stared at the photos on the desk, listening to Ronald Kellner as if he was telling me this while we were standing on a faraway planet.

"My son drove that car barely ten miles the week he was missing," he said.

I looked over at Ron as I exhaled.

"No one drove that car to Crystal Cove," he said, confirming this information again. "No one drove that car anywhere. Oh, maybe over the hill and back, but no one drove that car to Crystal Cove." There was another silence in the office. I stared out the window onto the expanse of lawn that led to the empty pool. Sheila Kellner was still sitting, frozen, in the gazebo. I had nothing to say.

"There was blood all over the front seat of the Datsun and the dashboard," Ronald said, pointing to the photo of Matt's arm. "This is where they say he sliced himself open." He paused. "A suicide attempt during a psychotic episode, they say."

Ron started looking through a sheaf of papers he picked up from the desk.

"They told me my son probably took too much"—he glanced at the page he was holding—"tetra-hydro-cannabinol," was the word he carefully pronounced. "Marijuana," he clarified flatly. "They can't find marijuana levels in an autopsy but they assume that, because of all the drug paraphernalia found in Matt's backpack, this was what led him to ingest 'a massive amount of Lysergic acid diethylamide.' LSD." Ronald said this in the same flat voice. "And then, according to them, he probably had a psychotic break and then took the Quaaludes and fell into the pool, where he drowned. That's what they pieced together.

That's their official story." I realized the paper he was looking at was part of the autopsy report. Ronald started to say something and then paused, unsure if he should admit what he was going to say next. And then he did. "Also found in Matt's stomach were the mostly undigested contents of what had been in his aquarium, which he apparently ingested during this supposed psychotic break." Ronald looked back at me as if I could somehow explain how this might have possibly happened.

I wanted him to stop talking. I wanted to leave the room. I knew the aquarium had been empty for weeks. I knew Matt had no idea what happened to the fish. And then, because of what I'd just been told, I wondered if he had placed the contents of the aquarium in another location before ingesting them during the supposed psychotic break. But this sounded ludicrous. I didn't know what to say. The whole scenario had become so surreal compared to what we originally heard and yet there was proof that this narrative had actually happened. It was typed on the papers that Ronald Kellner was holding. It was in the autopsy report filed by the L.A. County Department of Medical Examiner-Coroner, their title stamped at the top of each page Ronald held.

Ronald sighed and then said, "And he supposedly also did this."

Ronald showed me another photo—there was a series of them. I took the photos in my lightly trembling hand and at first I didn't know what I was looking at—something was hanging from the column now wrapped in the sheet of blue plastic. It was the column you passed as you entered the pool house. My eyes adjusted to the photo: there was some kind of animal hanging from the column but I couldn't tell what kind because it didn't have a head. A belt had secured the animal midway up the column and then someone had crucified all four of the animal's paws with nails so that it was splayed out like an X. And it had been eviscerated: a pouch of intestines hung between its legs and the bottom half of the column was darkened with blood. I started realizing something and it was confirmed when I looked at the next photo: it was the head of Alex placed on the edge of the pool's shallow end. The cat's eyes had been gouged out and its ears sliced off and someone had pulled its tongue so far out of its mouth that the tip was draped over the edge of the coping. I tried to process this but my mind was shrieking with horror: I was supposed to believe that Matt had somehow found Alex—or Alex had reappeared—and Matt decapitated the cat and then nailed its body to a column and placed the head at the edge of the pool and then fell, hit his head and drowned, tripping on a psychotic break in which he ingested six thousand milligrams of Quaaludes in a supposed suicide attempt. I had seen Matt wasted numerous times and I knew what he was and what he wasn't capable of—only lightly stoned, he still couldn't get up from the bed to grab the remote control on his desk to change the TV channel. I'd never seen Matt on acid but the amount of Quaaludes in his system would've rendered him paralyzed if what Ronald Kellner read to me from the autopsy report was correct—he wouldn't have been able to move. None of this made sense. Ronald sat in the swivel chair, his head bowed, lifting papers, adjusting his glasses, dispassionately looking for clues, a narrative that would add up.

"You knew Matt for how long?" Ronald finally asked.

"About a year," I mumbled, unable to stop staring at the pictures of his dead son that sat on top of all the other papers on Ronald's desk.

"Do you really think he would be capable of this?" Ronald looked up at me.

"I don't know," I murmured. "I don't think so." And then: "No, I don't."

"I think someone struck him with something," Ronald said quietly. "I think he was with someone that week. I think they fed him drugs and then I think they struck him with, I don't know, a hammer, a hammer or something, while he was high and then placed him in the pool." He stopped. "And then they did that to the cat."

"The cat had been missing—" I started but Ronald was talking over me.

"And I think the whole thing was staged," Ronald was saying. "By someone Matt knew or met. And I think they drove him out to Crystal Cove." He paused. "Or they drove out there and dumped the backpack there." He paused again. "When you first walked in I thought you were Robert," I heard Ronald Kellner say.

"Why did you think that?" I managed to ask.

"Because he mentioned something about going over to Robert's house the day I got the car serviced," he said. "That he might be hanging out with someone named Robert. I assumed he was a friend of Matt's." A pause. "Do you know Robert? Robert Mallory?"

"Yes," I said, carefully putting the photos of Alex back on the desk. The desk was so cluttered with files and reports it didn't seem to matter where I laid it. Ronald automatically turned the photo over, as if he didn't want to be reminded of what it depicted. "He's a classmate of ours."

"I know that," Ronald said tiredly, rubbing his eyes. "I found out I have a vague connection with his aunt's ex-husband."

"Does anyone know if Matt . . . was with Robert?" I asked. "I mean . . . that week?"

Ronald looked up at me with an alarmed expression. "What do you mean?"

"I mean . . ." I started carefully, ". . . does anyone know if Matt went to . . ." I swallowed. I realized I had a headache. "If he went to see Robert."

Ronald looked at me with an immediate disdain. "I'm not implying one of your classmates had anything to do with this, Bret." He landed hard on my name. I was surprised he remembered it. "Is that what you're implying?"

"No, no, I mean, I was just . . ." I trailed off. "I was wondering if maybe he hung out with Robert that week."

"We called Robert," Ronald said. "We spoke to him. He was in Palm Springs with his aunt the weekend Matt disappeared." He looked at me questioningly. "Didn't you see him at school during that following week? I really don't know what you're implying about Robert."

"Nothing, nothing," I muttered quickly.

"He told us he had never hung out with Matt," Ronald said, still staring at me as if I'd revealed something about myself that he distrusted. "Are you really implying that you think Robert Mallory had anything to do with what happened to my son? Are you serious?" He looked disgusted. And it immediately was a reminder of Matt recoiling from me in the pool house that Sunday afternoon. It was almost as if I was replaying a variation of that scene with Matt's father. But I was too numb with fear to be embarrassed.

"I think I should go," I said, backing out of the room. "I'm sorry, I'm really sorry about . . . everything."

Ronald had already turned away from me because the phone was ringing, and he reached for it quickly, as if awaiting information that would explain this nightmare he'd been forced into. I kept backing out of the office until I was in the hallway while Ronald muttered, "I don't know," into the phone at evenly spaced intervals, responding to a series of questions that didn't have any answers. I made a decision to leave through the front door, because I didn't want to move through the house again and walk down the lawn and pass the stoned woman sitting alone in the gazebo, or the covered column where the cat had been hung, or the empty pool where a boy had supposedly drowned during a psychotic episode, my friend, who I look back on while I write this as my first love though I didn't fully realize it then, in 1981. I walked across the brick driveway to Haskell Avenue, where my car was parked, and drove away from Matt Kellner's house for the last time.

I WAS DRIVING SO CAREFULLY, so slowly, that I had to keep pulling over on Valley Vista because other cars were blaring their horns behind me, until I finally made it to Woodcliff and then sped up the canyon to Mulholland in a suddenly desperate state, and back at the house I immediately swallowed two Valiums, washing them down with a glass of vodka I threw some ice into while Rosa was in the pantry folding clothes she'd just pulled from the dryer, and then I took the bottle of Smirnoff with me and, alone in my room with the door locked, started smoking Jeff Taylor's weed from a small yellow pipe—I wanted to obliterate myself. I poured another glass of vodka and got wasted quickly. I called Susan, drunk and high, and just started rambling and then hung up on her while she was in the middle of a sentence—I have no idea what I said or what I told her or what she asked back. There was a beat and then the phone immediately rang and I grabbed it, knowing it would be Susan, and told her, "I'm okay, I'm okay, I gotta go, I gotta go," and then hung up on her again. There was a moment of silence while I lay on the comforter in the bedroom, in my school uniform, my shoes kicked off, imagining patterns in the smooth white ceiling I was staring up at, and then looked over at the Elvis Costello poster on the wall. *TRUST* is what it blared. I was surprised that Shingy was in my room, but lying under the desk had become one of his preferred sleeping areas since my mother left, and he jumped onto the bed and was sniffing and licking my immobile face before cradling himself against me. The phone rang again. I didn't pick up. No one left a message—I realized it was probably Susan. I was becoming paralyzed by the combination of vodka and weed and Valium and when the phone rang about five minutes later I thought there was no way I would be able to pick it up or form a sentence and it didn't matter who it was—the world was lost to me.

But it was Debbie, who Susan had obviously called, and I heard her worried voice: "Bret? Are you there? Pick up. Bret? Pick up." I found out later that Susan had actually called the Windover Stables in Malibu and paged Debbie and then Debbie called my number from their main office. "Susan says something's wrong. That you're wasted, Bret. Pick up. Pick up the fucking phone." I finally reached over, panting from the effort, and fumbled with the phone until I muttered into the receiver: "Please, please, please, I'm fine. Just leave me alone, I'm fine." I kept reassuring Debbie everything was okay in my increasingly slurred voice and she kept saying how wasted I sounded until I shouted: "I *am* wasted! *I want to be wasted. IS THAT FUCKING OKAY?*" There was a brief silence and then she said, "You don't have to yell at me," and asked, "Why the fuck are you getting wasted at four in the afternoon?" I was becoming enraged but realized the anger couldn't actualize itself because of everything pumping through my system and so I gently told her: "I'll see you tomorrow, babe. Don't bother coming over. I'll be passed out, babe. I'll see you tomorrow." I was seriously fading when I hung up the phone. The need to erase the information about Matt Kellner and what really happened to him— and the fact that no one else knew: the photos of his naked corpse, the bruises, the slashed-open arm, the dead cat—was immense and the alcohol and the Valium and the weed were aiding quickly in locating an erasure of facts. I wanted to lose consciousness and I eventually did. At one point I heard Rosa knocking on my locked door, calling out that she was leaving for the day and that she'd see me tomorrow. I called back a muffled "Okay" and returned to darkness.

13

WAKING UP THE NEXT MORNING at six-thirty, I realized I'd
slept through the entire night—I had moved through the trauma of
the previous afternoon and somehow survived.

Shingy was scratching on the door leading out to the backyard,
and I stumbled up from the bed still in my Buckley uniform and
opened it and watched as he scurried onto the deck. I made a decision in that moment: I was going to pretend that everything was normal and that yesterday hadn't happened. I removed the uniform I'd
passed out in and masturbated for the first time in what seemed like
weeks and came so hard that it blew apart any remnants of the hangover and I felt such immense relief I was able to sit up and clearly
orient myself and create a schedule I was going to follow daily and
embody a new attitude. I looked at the near-empty bottle of Smirnoff
on the nightstand and the yellow pipe next to the bag of weed and
the canister of Valium whose contents were dwindling and something
resolved within me: fuck the fear. I was exhausted from being afraid.
No more weed, no more Valium, drinking kept to a minimum and
on weekends only. I would set the alarm and wake up to an allotted
time and jack off thinking of Richard Gere or Dennis Quaid or Hart
Bochner or David Naughton or whatever movie star was on my radar
in that moment, but never Matt Kellner again or Ryan Vaughn, and
then I'd work out before school, either lift weights or swim laps or
run on the treadmill, and then I'd shower, put the uniform on, tell
Rosa to prepare something healthy for breakfast, and while waiting
at the island in the kitchen I'd scan the "Calendar" section in the *Los
Angeles Times* and make a list of new movies I wanted to see, their

theaters and show times, and I'd ignore any news about the Trawler. I'd drive to Buckley, get there early, smile at everyone, kiss Debbie on the lips when I saw her in the parking lot or waiting for me on the bench beneath the bell tower, intone the Pledge of Allegiance and the Buckley Prayer, run laps on Gilley Field, play tennis with Thom, read Joan Didion in the bleachers and calmly think about my novel, eat lunch with the gang at the center table below the Pavilion, join the conversations—no more writerly silences—and concentrate on my afternoon classes, take better notes and ask questions, drive back to Mulholland, and finish all reading and homework assignments before working on *Less Than Zero*—maybe there would be a movie on the Z Channel I'd have time to watch and then I'd promptly go to bed at eleven, and sleep through the night easily because I was pushing all the useless trauma out of my mind.

I'd also be committed to focusing on another priority: I was going to track Robert Mallory. This actually moved to the top of the list and everything else followed, and this new discipline would clarify my days. I was going to start paying attention to Robert and not resist him anymore: this was number one on the schedule I was laying out. I pushed myself off the bed, and in the bathroom washed the drying semen from my stomach and chest and penis, and stared at my face in the mirror above the sink until I forced a smile—I tried several on before I turned away.

I WAS STARVING—Rosa hadn't arrived yet and when I walked into the kitchen I grabbed a yogurt out of the fridge and some blueberries and raspberries and threw them into a bowl, rummaged around the cupboard for some almonds, tossed those in as well and ate the whole thing in a matter of minutes while standing behind the glass door, contemplating Shingy roaming the lawn. I looked around my room and decided to actually make the bed—even though Rosa usually did—because I had to stay busy. I couldn't just sit around waiting for school to start, thinking about what actually happened to Matt Kellner, and kept the TV on *Good Morning America* just to have some noise float through the space—words and information, headlines and interviews—because I didn't want to hear any music that might move or depress me or become a reminder about Matt. I wanted to stay neutral and not only on that particular morning but *all* the mornings that followed until I graduated. I was usually fairly neat anyway so there was never a lot of clutter around but I needed something to do so I mindlessly rearranged the books on a shelf next to my desk and then noticed an unused Gucci backpack, a gift from my dad before my parents left for Europe that had been lying in the corner for a month beneath the Elvis Costello poster, and decided to put all my textbooks in it—I liked it, it looked cool, it was stylish, it represented the new me. And then I slipped on a bathing suit and swam sixty laps in about twenty minutes—swimming them fast and hard. When I got out of the pool Rosa had arrived and seemed surprised, almost concerned, when I walked through the kitchen, toweling myself off, and asked her to make me an omelet *por favor* while I showered and got dressed—I almost never asked Rosa to make me anything for breakfast and she was often knocking loudly on my door at eight-fifteen to make sure I'd be up in time to get ready for school. But not today: the tangible participant appeared, ready to engage with the world and track the new boy that had entered our lives: the psychopath.

IN THE BATHROOM I stood in front of the mirror again and realized I needed a haircut—my mother usually had her hairdresser, Allen Edwards, cut mine at his salon in Encino and she always made the appointments, but I marked down a note to find the number and call the salon myself—maybe this week. Staring at myself, I thought it was remarkable how composed I looked—the intensity and relief of the orgasm, the swimming of the laps, making a new schedule, embracing a new outlook, the thought of tracking Robert Mallory and keeping an eye on him, it all aided in this calmness. On that morning in early October I believed it was all going to work out but there was one small glitch: as I picked up the clothes I wore the day before I felt a bulge in the gray slacks and found a pair of white jockey shorts in the pocket and stared at them, mystified, as if I didn't know where they'd come from. And then I realized I'd taken them from the pool house on Haskell Avenue yesterday afternoon. I breathed in and my chest tightened as I remembered the photos

The SHARDS

Ronald Kellner showed me and I had to erase Matt completely from my mind—and I did—but I was conflicted by this item of clothing and instead of distracting myself by spending the time to figure out what to do with it I simply tossed the jockey shorts into the bottom drawer of my desk, one I rarely, if ever, opened. I now realized about Matt Kellner on that morning: there was *nothing* I could do. There was nothing *anyone* could do. He was gone—the photos I'd seen in Ronald Kellner's office proved this unequivocally. But the new schedule would offer a way to erase memory and offer a semblance of control, which is what I really craved, and allow me to wipe away the past. Everything was now about the future. And then I noticed the piece of paper I'd taken from Matt's desk at the pool house yesterday afternoon and stared at it—the initials *RM* and a phone number. I forced myself not to moan and before slipping it into my jacket I briefly flashed on: the new attitude might be more elusive than I thought.

BUT ATTEMPTING THIS NEW ATTITUDE for the first time worked: it made everything easier. I drove to Buckley that day in silence—again, I didn't want to hear music, songs that would remind me of Matt, or make me *feel* something, and distract me from the schedule. I wanted to remain emotionless, and climb onto that vaulted tier of numbness that Susan Reynolds resided on. That was the plan. I waited patiently without the usual annoyance in the line of cars on Stansbury Avenue before driving past the Buckley gates. I parked the Mercedes in its usual space and I saw Debbie and Susan on the bench beneath the bell tower, both of them watching me carefully as I stepped out of my car—they were *concerned* about me and didn't know what to expect and yet this wouldn't be an annoyance—and then I saw Ryan and Thom standing by Ryan's Trans Am and they waited as I slung my new backpack over my shoulder, and neared them, happily draped my arms around their necks and smiled widely as we walked toward the girls. This gesture made Thom really happy—he was the human equivalent of a golden retriever, I had realized a long time ago—and he asked, grinning, "How you doing, buddy?" and I said, "Great, dude, everything's great," and Thom said, "That's awesome."

Ryan pretended this was all acceptable even though I knew he was continuously flinching inside, stiffening up as the three of us walked together, my arms around his and Thom's shoulders. Thom was loose, Ryan was uptight and that was okay.

When we got to the girls, who'd been silently watching us approach, I hugged Debbie as she stood up and gave her a kiss and apologized for yesterday afternoon's outburst and the worried expression on her face morphed into a smile and I took her hand—all of this right in front of Ryan Vaughn, who, in the spirit of the new schedule, could go fuck himself, I thought, you fucking homo—and walked with Debbie through the pathway that led into the heart of the school, Thom and Susan behind us murmuring to each other, Ryan following as well, until we got to the administration office and it was almost nine and time for the first class of the day, which I shared with Susan and Ryan, American Fiction, taught by Mr. Robbins. Debbie and I kissed goodbye—it was ridiculous she needed this when she would be seeing me in only forty-five minutes but I was going to supply the public displays of affection she wanted so badly and keep my fucking mouth shut—just do whatever she wanted, that was part of the plan, these were details in the new attitude I'd be adhering to. I was the tangible participant once again.

Susan and Thom shared a similar kiss but Susan turned away a little too suddenly after the kiss and Thom's smile faltered. I caught his fleeting confusion—it was something only I noticed, and still remember to this day because it was about a rare thing: Thom Wright's disappointment. I held the door open for Ryan Vaughn, who passed me into the classroom and muttered, "You're ridiculous," and I didn't say anything back. I didn't let it bother me—I might have fallen in love with him but there was no way for this to *happen,* to actualize itself in this particular time and place, in the atmosphere at Buckley, in high school, in 1981, so fuck it, go with the counter-narrative. Who cared anyway? It was all bullshit. It felt so cleansing to look at things from this angle. I wanted to be where Susan Reynolds was. And I wanted to write like this as well: numbness as a feeling, numbness as a motivation, numbness as the reason to exist, numbness as ecstasy.

—

The SHARDS

AND ROBERT Mallory was in the courtyard below the Pavilion at the mid-morning assembly, looking immaculate, reading a paperback, and it all seemed so manufactured: the dimples when he fake-smiled at someone who passed by, the model good looks that disguised—or maybe accentuated—the darkness, the mannequin that pretended it was human. I was standing with Debbie, who was talking to Susan and Thom about Homecoming, while I noticed Robert's thick brown hair, wavy and streaked with gold, his tan, the cleft in his chin—Thom had the same cleft, so did Ryan—and I imagined a big cock below that slim waist because he was so fucking confident. Without excusing myself from Debbie I headed toward Robert, who was standing alone, and noticed a group of ninth-grade girls huddled nearby whispering about him as if he was a movie star they'd just glimpsed at a mall, and I pretended to walk casually around the plaza filling up with students, deciding where to stand during the assembly, idly passing in and out of kids grouped in clusters, when, in fact, I was heading toward Robert, who automatically noticed me when he looked up blank-faced from his book—*Rabbit, Run,* by John Updike, the current assignment in American Fiction—and then smiled widely as I approached, but I located the worry in his eyes.

He said, "Hey, dude," in what sounded like a practiced line reading and I said, "Hey, dude," back and matched his smile and he asked, "How you doing? You doing okay?" and I said, "I'm doing great. Everything is gonna be okay. I'm just moving along. Taking it easy." He nodded approvingly. "That's rad, man, that's the way to do it, man. Just go with the flow."

And then I said, also nodding, "Yeah, the flow, that's what I'm going with, dude. It's rad. Take it easy."

Robert noticed I was studying him, almost peering at his perfect features—the slightly hollowed cheeks, the lips that verged on thick, the perfect nose, the row of white teeth visible whenever he offered a fake smile. He tried not to seem startled.

"Yeah? Is anything wrong?" he asked, lightly concerned.

I didn't give a fuck anymore and I asked him, "Have you ever modeled? Or auditioned for something? Like a commercial or a movie?"

He looked at me quizzically, or pretended to, because there was something—a madness—now whirring behind the eyes that I so easily activated, and this gratified me. He thought there was something wrong with my question yet didn't know what to say.

"Have you ever wanted to be a model?" I asked him. "You look like you could be a model. Ever done any modeling when you were in Chicago?" I asked. "You're a pretty good-looking guy."

He tried not to stare at me as if I was crazy and just accept the compliments but it was obvious that my approach disturbed him.

Before Robert could say anything the assembly began and I sensed his relief as Dr. Croft walked to the microphone and the Pledge of Allegiance was about to be dully intoned, and I glanced at Robert as he placed his hand on his chest and noticed I almost decided not to— maybe I wasn't going to say the Pledge of Allegiance that morning, standing next to him, inhaling his scent, cedar and sandalwood, as it drifted toward me.

But then I smiled pleasantly and looked up at the flag hanging from the steel pole high above the hundreds of students dully inton- ing the pledge, and placed my hand over my heart. He glanced at me again when the Buckley Prayer came next and seemed mildly sur- prised when I hesitated to clasp my hands and bow my head. But it was just a pause, a kind of warning, to destabilize him, to let him know that I was perhaps as unpredictable as he was. He had no idea that a phone number with his initials next to it was in the pocket of the jacket I was wearing and that I had torn it from the pad a dead boy had kept in his desk drawer and I wondered what would happen if I brought the slip of paper out and asked Robert if it was something he recognized, if those were his initials, if that was a number he knew, and then innocently inquired why he had given it to Matt Kellner.

BOTH DR. CROFT AND SUSAN REYNOLDS offered their reminders that Homecoming was next Saturday, and there would be a pep rally on Friday where the Queens and Kings would be announced, and which team the Griffins were going to be playing against in the Private School League; it went without saying it would be a team they could easily beat—that was one of the rules about Homecoming, and the visiting team knew this going in, and though no one threw a game just so that the Buckley Griffins could be declared victors, a team was agreed upon they could lightly trounce and everyone was a good sport—the Griffins and whatever visiting team they played (odds were it was going to be Brentwood). Susan reminded the student body that each class could begin decorating their Homecoming floats on Thursday starting at three o'clock on Gilley Field and juniors and seniors would be allowed to stay as late as ten-thirty on both Thursday and Friday if they felt more work was required.

"Escape from Buckley High" was the announced theme of the senior float that year and it was a take on *Escape from New York*, the popular John Carpenter movie released that summer, a futuristic thriller set in 1997 where the island of Manhattan had been converted into a giant maximum-security prison—and the senior float was going to replicate the poster's main image: the fallen head of the Statue of Liberty lying in the middle of Fifth Avenue. It was a dystopian choice we thought would be funny—and since the hero, Snake Plissken (played by Kurt Russell), wasn't on the poster there would be an enlarged image of Thom Wright's scowling, lightly stubbled face superimposed over the Statue of Liberty's head complete with an eye patch. We'd replicate our take on the title in blood-red lettering and rework the ad lines promoting the movie. Instead of "1997. New York City is a walled maximum security prison" we'd replaced 1997 with 1982, and New York City with Buckley. And we'd keep the rest: "Breaking out is impossible. Breaking in is insane." This was surprisingly punk for Buckley in 1981 and we were surprised that the administration's unusually conservative decorating-approval committee had accepted it. By comparison, the junior class was playing it safe and their float was simply a replica of a box of Junior Mints.

Saturday would start off with the football game and a parade of floats during halftime, a mini-carnival with booths set up on the elementary-school field on the other side of campus, and then the annual Homecoming dinner would commence in the Pavilion, catered and with an orchestra; tickets could be purchased at Mrs. Strohm's desk in the administration office and there was the reminder that seating was limited. I paid close attention to Susan as she dully read this information almost as if she was lightly mortified by it—she was in another world far beyond this one, floating on a cloud of numbness, but it was different than before, something was off. And though I realized later where this hesitancy was coming from regarding Home-coming, it seemed odd standing in the crowded courtyard hearing her even more resolutely unenthusiastic than she'd already become—she was taking her alluring numbness into a new place that was tinged with what I sensed was embarrassment.

I turned slightly to see Robert Mallory looking up at the girl behind the microphone and I had never seen Robert as seemingly calm as he was in that moment, staring serenely at Susan—he had transformed into another boy. He realized at a certain point that I was gazing at him and he just blankly stared back, almost daring me, until he finally fake-smiled and I looked away. I couldn't help but note—it broke through the new attitude I was adjusting to—that no one men-tioned Matt Kellner anymore and on that morning I had to accept: this was okay. It had already happened, it was in the past, Matt was over. This was what the new attitude demanded. But my central ques-tion was still connected to Matt: why had Robert Mallory killed him?

I REALIZED I HAD unnerved Robert and I apologized to him after assembly and said, "I'm sorry if I weirded you out." He made a gesture, a sympathetic shrug, and said, "You didn't weird me out. It sounded pretty gay but it didn't weird me out." And as he turned to walk toward the Pavilion, where the boys' locker room was located, said he'd see me up on the field. But I skipped Phys Ed that day and went instead to the administration office and asked one of the sec-retaries, Mrs. Stanley, if I could take a look at the Buckley roster. I needed to check something, I explained, as she reached into a drawer and handed it to me, red and with a sketch of the bell tower on its cover. I hadn't been able to find the roster at the house on Mulholland that morning but it wouldn't have been in my bedroom anyway, since I already had the five numbers I needed memorized—Susan, Thom, Debbie, Ryan, Matt. I wanted to compare the number I found on the piece of paper I'd taken from the pool house with the number listed next to Robert Mallory's Century City address. The phone number at that residence, of course, did not match, which is what I expected.

But not dreaded, because dread was not part of the routine any-more. Dread was a waste of time. Dread didn't get things done. Dread stalled you. I might have assumed that Robert had something to do with Matt's death—yes, without any proof this is what the writer does: he is *always hearing things that aren't there*—but I wasn't going to let it fill me with dread, because then I wouldn't be able to figure things out. And yet what was there to figure out? I imagined someone asking me. There was no proof, there were no connections, Robert had supposedly been in Palm Springs the weekend Matt disappeared, or so Ronald Kellner had been told, and I *had* seen Robert at school various times during that week, so what the fuck were you thinking, Bret? I could imagine someone gently reprimanding me.

I sat downstairs in the near-empty library and tried answering two essay questions for European History and then "studied" for my retake of the SATs in late October; my combined score was barely 1100 even though a tutor had come over to the house on Mulholland twice a week for a month before I took the exam—and that score, of course, minimized the number of colleges I could get into, but I never cared what college I got into and I had never been particularly invested in what my SAT scores were: I just wanted out of Buckley, I wanted out of the house on Mulholland, I wanted to get away from Thom and Susan, I wanted out of Los Angeles, the sprawl of which allowed a dozen serial killers to coexist, a place where the Trawler thrived and disappeared girls. But the new attitude I embraced that morning made me realize I *should* care about the SATs and what my college options were because if I wanted to get out and not end up at USC (the University of Southern California, often jokingly referred to as the University of Spoiled Children)—which at the time seemed like my one decent option and even then only because of my father's connections—I had to pull myself together and *care more*.

I REMEMBER very little about the rest of that day except certain and specific images when I met the group for lunch. Instead of extending the drama about Matt and sharing the reality surrounding his death, which I so easily could have done, eagerly giving them the horrible information I discovered in Ronald Kellner's office, I just went with the flow of conversation, which was all about Homecoming, and it was hard to follow because there were few things I cared less about at

Buckley than Homecoming, and I struggled to keep up with the conversation and happily participate in it—instead offering the writer's cynical perspective on the event and making everyone laugh. This was part of my job, I realized—making fun of Buckley—and it was a character I was expected to sometimes play and the group always seemed to enjoy it: I made fun of stuff and people laughed. Even Robert Mallory threw his head back and laughed when I said something especially scathing about one of the gay art teachers, a *flamer*, but the one thing I remember most intensely is how Susan and Robert barely interacted with each other at the center table we were all sitting at in the shadow of the Pavilion and it wasn't just because Thom and Jeff and Ryan commanded the conversation and kept deciding on which direction it would go, but it was as if a genuine shyness had enveloped both Susan and Robert, and they seemed muted compared to the rest of the group. But they didn't ignore the conversation and Robert asked perfunctory questions about what the usual Buckley Homecoming was like—it seemed so lavish and nothing like what he had experienced at Roycemore—and sometimes Susan answered one or two of his inquiries, but more often Thom would explain what the day entailed, finally adding that there was an after party at someone's house—this year Anthony Matthews's, because he lived closest to the school—and "expect to get wasted, dude," Thom promised, while Debbie pushed into me and I suggestively placed a hand on her bare thigh: I could feel goose bumps rising across her flesh while I tried not to stare at Ryan.

THE THING THAT HAUNTS ME from the day I embraced the new Bret was, I remembered Thom and Ryan had football practice after school and Debbie had driven to the Windover Stables and I asked Susan if she wanted to head into Westwood and see a movie—there was one that had opened at the Plaza, co-written by Joan Didion and John Gregory Dunne, an adaptation of Dunne's bestseller *True Confessions* starring Robert De Niro—but Susan demurred and said she didn't want to see that movie. I then suggested a Ryan O'Neal comedy at the Mann triplex or *Mommie Dearest* at the Village—I had made a list that morning with late-afternoon show times on it—but

The SHARDS

Susan seemed vaguely withdrawn in ways I hadn't witnessed before: the numbness was different now, it was in a place I couldn't locate, an area I wasn't allowed into. Susan said she was going to drive back to Beverly Hills and get as much homework done as possible and she wanted to finish reading *Rabbit, Run*. I immediately noted I had seen Robert Mallory reading the same paperback at the midmorning assembly but why had I rushed to *that* connection? We were *all* assigned to read it—I was reading it. I automatically made *that* connection and found a hidden meaning in it—Robert and Susan reading the same book—because it had slipped through my new attitude. Why would I care? Because: *You hear things that aren't really there* . . . That connection was coming from the dramatist I'd been trying to erase and I had to let him go.

And I admitted happily, and graciously, that this sounded like the better and more practical idea as Susan and I walked toward the parking lot together. We hugged at her car and then I walked to mine and sat in the 450SL while Susan sat in her car. And yet she wasn't going anywhere. The BMW remained in the space for what seemed like twenty minutes while I tried waiting her out but my new attitude wouldn't allow this—I was wasting time and I wanted to stick to the schedule. I imagined Susan was probably listening to Icehouse, smoking a clove cigarette, thinking about Thom's trip back east, contemplating the party she was throwing postponed due to Matt's death and then Homecoming. Finally, Susan won out and I tried not to curse when I pulled the Mercedes out of my spot and drove by her sitting alone in the BMW and as I steered the car toward the gates leading out of Buckley I glanced in the rearview mirror, and on cue, Robert Mallory appeared from the afternoon shadows of the bell tower and stepped carefully off the curb, as if he had been waiting for my departure.

THE NEXT MORNING I got behind the wheel of my mother's Jaguar XJ6 and carefully pulled left into the traffic racing along Mulholland and drove to Buckley, where I parked the car in the first available space on Stansbury Avenue and walked up past the gates and into the entrance to the school. This was the second day with the new attitude, the new Bret—and it had worked the night before: I ate the quesadilla Rosa had left for me to reheat, I completed all my homework, I swam laps, I wasn't afraid, I tried to finish the Updike novel but I found myself too tired and so I set the alarm and fell into an easy sleep because I hadn't let anything distract me. I had kept focus on the essays and the calculus homework, which I could never make sense of, often just zoning out on the textbook with the logarithmic spiral of the nautilus shell on the cover—but that night I at least tried. And I typed three double-spaced pages of the novel before I picked up *Rabbit, Run,* and went to bed. The next morning I woke up before the alarm and masturbated to a fantasy about the two stars from *Gallipoli*—Mel Gibson and Mark Lee—having sex with each other, in character; few actors, I felt, were more beautiful than Mel Gibson, and I didn't want to think at all about Ryan Vaughn, and definitely not Matt Kellner, but suddenly Martin Hewitt, who had starred in *Endless Love* that summer, took over the fantasy and I came hard thinking about him, briefly naked, on top of Brooke Shields, on top of me, and I was gripping his ass, urging him on. I showered and dressed after realizing I'd be running laps on Gilley Field that day instead of working out in the makeshift gym next to the garage. Rosa hadn't arrived yet and I ate a bowl of Frosted Flakes while I watched Shingy frolic mindlessly on the lawn. I didn't open the *Los Angeles Times* that was sitting folded on the island.

On my way to the library I nodded at Miguel, who was directing traffic, and noticed that neither Thom's car nor Susan's car nor Debbie's BMW nor Robert's Porsche was in the parking lot and I realized that I'd arrived at school far earlier than I planned when I looked at my watch. I walked into the library and sat in a wood-paneled cubicle and unzipped the Gucci backpack and read *Rabbit, Run,* until just before nine, when I headed to American Fiction and saw that the class was filled. I nodded to Ryan in the front row off to the side and then sat down next to Susan, who casually leaned over and said "Hi." She was so lovely in that moment that I simply stared into her face shocked by its beauty, but she located something besides the shock and asked, "What's wrong?"

I shrugged and said, "Oh, y'know, everything."

She smiled with an exquisite blankness. "Debbie was looking for you," she said quietly as Mr. Robbins placed his briefcase on the desk in front of the long black chalkboard he rarely used.

"I was hiding in the library," I whispered.

"Hiding from who?" Susan asked, amused and expectant.

I paused and then said, "Everybody."

She sighed as the class began and I wanted to ask her what she talked to Robert Mallory about yesterday afternoon when I drove out of the parking lot and saw him approaching Susan's car. But the new attitude, the new Bret, restrained me from inquiring about this.

THERE WAS A FOOTBALL game that afternoon at Buckley and though I can remember who I masturbated about on that early October day (I wrote it down—I kept lists, a jack-off journal) I can't remember what team the Griffins were playing though I knew Susan would be in the stands, mildly cheering Thom on as quarterback, and I took a chance and assumed Robert Mallory wouldn't be attending the game. I walked down to my mom's Jaguar and waited for the black Porsche to roll out of the gates and onto Stansbury Avenue, passing a car Robert had never seen before, unlike the 450SL, which he now completely associated me with. And the black Porsche appeared at about three-fifteen and I didn't repeat the same mistake I'd made when I followed him on the first day of school. I intuited that Robert would be heading home to Century City as he drove along Valley Vista until he hit Sepulveda and made a left and then another left, driving up the on-ramp of the 405 freeway, and I trailed him three to four cars behind while moving in and out of lanes as we zoomed through the Sepulveda Pass until the Porsche steered down an off-ramp to Santa Monica Boulevard, where we passed the Nuart, the revival theater I haunted, and then the Porsche headed toward Century City and the condo Robert shared with his supposed aunt.

I traveled three cars behind Robert as he turned right onto Avenue of the Stars and passed the fountains of the ABC Entertainment Center and my father's offices located above the Shubert Theater, where my parents took me to see *Evita* that past year (they had ended up getting into an argument in the lobby during intermission), and after their second or third separation I'd browse through the Brentano's bookstore waiting for my father's day to end, and we'd meet for a movie at the Plitt or dinner at Harry's Bar. Those painful excursions with my father seemed lighthearted and innocent compared to where I was now, I realized bleakly as I followed the Porsche past the sweeping crescent of the Hyatt Regency Hotel and then finally arrived at the Century Towers on the corner of Pico, the last buildings on Avenue of the Stars, where Robert made an easy left into the driveway as the Jaguar passed the two towers that mirrored each other, both twenty-eight stories and overlooking the Hillcrest Country Club and the golf course at Rancho Park. The avenue was fairly empty and I easily made a U-turn and then drove slowly past the driveway, where Robert was now leaving the Porsche with a valet and entering the tower closest to Pico. I thought about spending the rest of the afternoon at the Century City Mall but I was too keyed up and that wasn't part of the new schedule. *The French Lieutenant's Woman* had opened at the Plitt and I was tempted to see it after driving away from the Century Towers but the new schedule allowed movies only on weekends—afternoons and evenings during the week were devoted to homework and planning, swimming and sleeping, taking care of yourself so the useless dread wouldn't come back and haunt your dreams. *Being afraid is so lame,* I kept telling myself. *Being afraid is so lame and you're not a pussy,* I kept telling myself.

THE NEXT MORNING I DID the same thing. I drove my mother's Jaguar to Stansbury and found a parking space on the street. I followed Robert again that afternoon—he left at the same time and drove across the same route—always two or three cars behind: Valley Vista to the 405, through the Sepulveda Pass, the off-ramp at Santa Monica Boulevard, the right turn at Avenue of the Stars, and then I'd slow down as he made the left through the gates of the Century Towers, where he pulled the Porsche up to the valet. I made the same U-turn from the day before and watched again as Robert walked past the fountain and into the building he'd entered yesterday, while never noticing the Jaguar pulling past the gates. Everything Robert did seemed perfectly normal—boring even—and yet I hesitated as I looked for a place to park so I could wait and see if Robert was coming out again, if he had changed out of his uniform into something more casual and would maybe drive over to the Century City Mall and prowl the pathways, looking for girls from Beverly High. But I had a new schedule and I was adjusting myself to it. I realized I was becoming addicted to following Robert Mallory after school. He apparently had no clue that someone was tailing him. He never seemed to notice or gave any indication that he knew one of his classmates in a sea-foam-green Jaguar XJ6 was following him from Buckley to Century City, and this excited me.

THE NEXT DAY I parked the Jaguar on Stansbury again and then walked through the gates as I had the previous two mornings. I was early—per my new schedule—and headed straight for the library, where I sat in the same wooden cubicle and finished *Rabbit, Run*, nonplussed, not really caring one way or another about it. I realized that what I really cared about the last three days was: *waiting*. I was *waiting* to follow Robert Mallory again. As the day crept by I was *waiting* for three o'clock. Because I wasn't participating with the "real" world of Buckley as *myself*, I don't remember a lot of what happened: I just played a part that seemed to make Thom and Debbie happy, and it relaxed Robert—it didn't affect Susan because seemingly nothing now did. And, of course, Ryan knew all about the act because he was playing it, too, and there were a few times where we acted our parts *with* each other, especially if other people were around—at lunch or hanging out in the minutes before one of the three classes we shared started. Sometimes an uneasiness appeared within the pantomime—a kind of stage fright—but you could work through it if you just smiled passively and continued enacting the nice and trustworthy boyfriend, the best bud, the platonic relationship, the denial of lust.

I LEFT SCHOOL hurriedly after the last class. Debbie had already headed for the Windover Stables in Malibu, and there was another football game, so Susan wouldn't be available to anyone. I lowered myself behind the steering wheel of the Jaguar waiting for the black

Porsche to glide past and hiding until I felt the moment to pull away from the curb and follow Robert to Valley Vista, where he made the same right turn as the previous two days and where I would follow him on the same route to Sepulveda. But on that day Robert didn't stay on Valley Vista—he made a left onto Beverly Glen instead of a right, which was difficult to maneuver since traffic was continually flowing in both directions during the late afternoon. But the Porsche made the turn aggressively with almost no concern for the drivers on Beverly Glen, who braked abruptly and blared their horns as the Porsche interrupted the flow of traffic. And it took me about a minute to make the same left and I pressed hard on the accelerator, revving the car, pushing the Jaguar to catch up with Robert as I curved up the hillside. When the Porsche came into sight about nine cars ahead of mine, where Mulholland interrupted Beverly Glen and the stoplight there, the relief overwhelmed me to a point I found embarrassing. And then I was momentarily horrified by the thought that Robert was heading to my house but the taillight on the Porsche was blinking, indicating he was making a left, in the direction away from the empty house on Mulholland.

I WAS ABLE TO make the left along with three other cars behind me, and stayed far enough away from the Porsche so that Robert wouldn't suspect someone was following him. I watched through the windshield as the Porsche turned off Mulholland and onto Benedict Canyon and then I had to slow down when only one car was between us. As we maneuvered down the canyon I wondered if this was simply a new route to Century City or if Robert was going to visit someone but I couldn't imagine it being anybody we knew. Suddenly, from out of nowhere, like an anxiety attack, the dread returned, taking over any curiosity I was tinged with, because I realized I shouldn't be doing this—tracking a classmate—and I was failing to reassure myself that Robert Mallory was dangerous and capable of ruining everything and what I was doing had been justified. I only caught flashes of the black Porsche curving down the winding road, until it straightened out as the canyon flattened. I was the only car traveling behind the Porsche—the car behind him and in front of mine had made a left into the gated community of Wallingford Estates—and I kept my distance as the Porsche slowed and then swerved left about six houses up from the stoplight at Hutton.

I pulled over to the side of the road and waited for five minutes, then carefully drove past the place Robert had pulled into. He had parked the Porsche in the stone driveway of a two-story house pushed deep away from the canyon road and there were no other cars visible in the driveway except his—and that's all I quickly glimpsed as I drove to Hutton, which was the only stoplight on Benedict Canyon until you hit the flats of Beverly Hills. Instead of turning left onto Hutton and heading back home, I made a U-turn and drove toward the house and braked slowly, parked about five houses up and waited, glancing into the rearview mirror. The stereo was off and when I switched it on the Eagles blared—what my mother had been listening to before leaving for Europe. And I quickly turned the sound down, waiting. Robert was only at the house for about ten minutes before the Porsche pulled out of the driveway and swerved left onto Benedict Canyon, speeding away in the opposite direction from where the Jaguar was parked. I had no desire to follow Robert any longer that afternoon.

I MADE ANOTHER U-turn and drove toward the house and, lightly electrified with adrenaline, steered up the driveway and past the wrought-iron gates, which had been pushed open, and where a mud-streaked WARNING: NO TRESPASSING sign, in red letters, hung crookedly. The driveway was gravel until it smoothed out into the curved entranceway made of stone. The house was white with green shutters, traditional and anonymous, probably built in the late 1960s or early 1970s; it was somewhat featureless—the second story was crested with a sloping rooftop adorned with gray shingles and there was an arched entryway that led to a white door with green trim and a squared bay window and the house was shaded by oaks and sycamores and appeared to be empty, the canyon hillside rising behind it. I debated exiting the car but the compulsion was too strong and so I parked the Jaguar and stepped out. It was eerily quiet and from where I stood I noticed that a line of trees actually hid most of the house from the canyon road. I was breathing too hard and realized there was no way I could last here longer than a minute—I was keyed up and exhausted. Sweat caused the white button-down shirt to stick against my back.

I quickly moved toward the bay window but it was curtained and when I tried the front door it was locked—this was all happening so fast that I didn't even process what I was looking for or what I'd expected to find. I hurriedly moved around the side of the house and into the backyard, where there was a tennis court with a sagging net, strewn with leaves, and an empty pool—it reminded me of Haskell Avenue except this one was half filled with brackish water. I scanned an ancient red brick patio situated above the pool and overlooking the tennis court, confirming there was nothing that suggested anyone was living in the house. I looked up to the second story and all of the windows were shaded. Everything was shadowed by the steeply rising hillside behind the house and I imagined there were only a few hours where the sun could hit the pool and the tennis court, otherwise the light was blocked out everywhere by the hillside and the towering sycamores, and it was so silent.

AND THEN I felt it: there was a presence, someone on the hillside, hidden, watching me. I stood still, imagining what the presence, the thing, wanted from me as it kept staring so intently from its secret vantage point. I imagined it was breathing heavily, drooling, as it stared at me through a pair of binoculars it held in gnarled hands tipped with yellowed talons. It was someone from the Riders of the Afterlife, it was the Trawler, it was the ghost of Matt Kellner. And then I heard a rustling on the hillside as if the thing was making its way downward to where I stood beside the dilapidated tennis court. The presence forced me to quickly leave the backyard. But as I rushed to my car I stopped, bolted by a sentence someone had said to me, and breathed in, trying to calm myself. I took another step, then stopped, confused, and waited a moment before regaining my composure and walking back to the Jaguar.

The dread I'd been trying to avoid had returned and even though I hadn't witnessed anything ominous somehow my mind told me that I had. And this feeling was enveloping the world because of one thing

The SHARDS

Ronald Kellner said about Matt's Datsun. This was why the dread returned with a sickening intensity, the dread I'd been ignoring as the tangible participant, the new Bret. I suddenly believed the house I was standing in front of was the house where the phone number that Matt Kellner had written on a notepad and that I found in his desk was located somewhere inside. And my mind raced toward: the mileage on the Datsun. *Oh, maybe over the hill and back,* Ronald Kellner said, *but no one drove that car to Crystal Cove.* I convinced myself, in that moment, trembling next to the Jaguar, that this house was where Matt Kellner had disappeared into during the week before he died. And maybe this is where he had been *kept.* I tried to calm myself with the usual mantra—*you hear things that aren't really there*—but this time the signal was too strong to ignore, because it was pulsing and sending out shivery waves of panic, and I was drawn to them, like a zombie.

14

ON GILLEY FIELD it was still warm out at 10:00 p.m. on the Thursday before Homecoming and we were having problems and only twelve of us stood around the half-finished float. Most of the high school had come up at three o'clock that afternoon and the seniors were the only class left on the field—everyone else had gone home—because we'd hit a snag and now time was running out and Devo's "Beautiful World" sounded throughout the hushed air and Angelo was soon going to come up and usher everyone off the field and Jon Yates was muttering that we had thirty minutes left and we all knew that we'd be here tomorrow night as well, reconfiguring the float, because it just wasn't working. We had become overly ambitious with our "Escape from Buckley High" design and though the Statue of Liberty's head, painted a muddy green with the spikes done up as gelled hair (punk-style), looked good, we were having trouble with the rest of the float, especially the street the head was lying on, as well as the houses we built from plywood and wallboard imitating a facsimile of Stansbury Avenue complete with palm trees, and hanging above this a banner announcing the title of the float in the exact same lettering as on the poster for *Escape from New York*. Something was off: you couldn't tell it was Stansbury Avenue and the giant black-and-white photo of Thom Wright's head pasted over the statue's face complete with Snake Plissken's eye patch and the stubble we'd drawn on it with Magic Marker wasn't recognizable as Thom—this could have been anyone.

—

The SHARDS

THE FLOAT WAS getting too complicated—we were over-scaling it. Above the statue's head, ESCAPE FROM BUCKLEY HIGH didn't fit within the banner we'd created and "HIGH" had to be removed. Someone suggested maybe sparkling the entire float with glitter and things were looking bleak and the flatbed truck the senior class had chipped in to rent was parked at one end of the vast green lawn by the bleachers and the tagline that would run across the side of the float just wasn't coming through—Tracy Goldman stood at the top of the stands, which were going to be packed with roughly five hundred people on Saturday, and couldn't make out what the words said, so we went back to the pile of red cardboard and started cutting out bigger letters, a tedious job. To make it legible for people in the stands we had to lose the word "MAXIMUM" and instead the tagline would read 1982: BUCKLEY IS A WALLED SECURITY PRISON and then beneath that BREAKING OUT IS IMPOSSIBLE. BREAKING IN IS INSANE. and we had to remove the "IS" in both sentences to make the tagline fit, using colons. Those of us who stayed were still in our uniforms and became hungry quickly when it all looked hopeless and Doug Furth and Anthony Matthews drove down to Barone's, an old-school Italian restaurant on Ventura Boulevard, and brought back four large pizzas sometime around eight and there was a cooler filled with Cokes and Tabs and 7Ups nestled in melting ice by the tennis courts to help fortify us. The hillsides surrounding the partially lit field were darkened, with only the glow from houses situated within the forested canyon and the headlights of an occasional car cruising up Beverly Glen. The smell of weed came from Kyle Colson and David O'Shea standing near the bleachers—another sign that the float was a mess: they'd given up and gotten high. Jon Yates, who had meticulously sketched the float with Doug Furth, kept walking around it, clutching his drawings and staring at the measurements in quiet disbelief: the reality wasn't matching up to his designs. And then Jon had a mini-breakdown when someone asked if *Escape from New York* had even been popular enough to warrant such an elaborate re-creation of the poster.

—

BUT PEOPLE KEPT diligently working: Jeff Taylor was standing on a stepladder next to Robert Mallory, affixing green tassels on the cardboard trunks of trees to resemble palm fronds, as Doug Furth kept busily walking around the float, constantly making new suggestions. We were going to have to move the statue's head up to the front of the float to make it more visible or else scale back one particular side of Stansbury Avenue, because the head was being hidden—endless conversations ensued between Doug and Jon, and ultimately one side of Stansbury Avenue was removed so the statue's head could be plainly seen and there was a pathetic relief palpable among my classmates that made me just want to go home even though it was Robert Mallory's presence that forced me to stay—I'd thought about following him that night once we both drove out of the parking lot but knew I probably wouldn't, because I was exhausted and tinged with disgust. That some of my classmates seemed to care more about the float than the death of one of their own was what bothered me the most: Matt Kellner might have never come up to Gilley Field to decorate the Homecoming float, so it's not as if his presence was missed, but the fact that no one talked about him anymore was disturbing—just two or three busy days of shock and then a few Mr. Bill jokes and now nothing: he was completely forgotten by mid-October. This hardened something in me as I stapled the new and bigger red cardboard letters beneath the main bulk of the float and I suddenly thought Homecoming was so dumb and this float was just one half-turn around an oval track. What were we doing? Why were we wasting our time? I was ostensibly there because Thom and Susan wanted me to help and I'd demurred—the novel was always a good excuse—but once I found out that Robert Mallory would be decorating the float as well I changed my mind. The juniors had finished their float hours earlier and the white Junior Mints box glowed with white and pine-green tassels lightly taunting us across the field with its Warholian simplicity.

DEBBIE SHOWED UP late, having spent the afternoon at the Windover Stables riding Spirit, training for the charity equestrian event, and when she arrived on Gilley Field kissed me hungrily with her tongue and I pulled away too quickly, but Ryan Vaughn had already left hours ago. As co-captain of the football team he had to make an appearance and he also had an excuse to leave early and he really hadn't helped out: he stapled a couple of boxes together but really just stood around and watched the unraveling proceedings, amused, then split, promising he'd be there tomorrow night if the float wasn't finished, and I realized he never would've cared if he had seen the French kiss with Debbie Schaffer—he'd probably just feel sorry for me. Debbie noticed my reticence but didn't say anything, preferring to ignore it, just stayed near me as she kept stapling the red cardboard letters I was handing her to the bottom of the float spelling "BREAKING OUT: IMPOSSIBLE. BREAKING IN: INSANE." while Doug was worriedly trying to figure how to improve Stansbury Avenue with Jon.

But I was actually distracted by something that had nothing to do with the senior float or Homecoming or the absence of Matt: a call from Steven Reinhardt that morning set up a meeting with Terry Schaffer to talk about the script Terry wanted me to write on Sunday at the Polo Lounge in the Beverly Hills Hotel; it had ended with a reminder not to tell Debbie and I eagerly confirmed that I wouldn't and that I'd meet Terry there at four o'clock. I occasionally glanced over at Debbie and realized she had no idea I'd already met her father for lunch, when he'd become openly flirtatious, and that I was prepared for the same behavior when having drinks with him in the Polo Lounge on Sunday, and then I stared up at the hills listening for coyotes but the Devo cassette coming out of the boom box was the only soundtrack. What was the Trawler doing tonight? I wondered, infusing myself with a useless shiver of dread, a feeling that occurred whenever I looked over at Robert Mallory, whose mad green eyes were fixed intently on the cardboard palm tree he was busily decorating.

AT ONE POINT I realized neither Thom nor Susan was helping with the float and that they were standing across the empty field under a stadium light, just the two of them, and Thom was gesturing while Susan stood there and listened—she wasn't saying anything, she was just staring at him. Thom was finally rendered helpless because of

Susan's numb neutrality and whatever anger was emanating from him seemed pleading and confused—he was frustrated and had become enraged by her passivity. Seen from the distance of our vantage point, Susan was coy and elusive, her arms crossed, listening to whatever Thom was saying, but her patience was increasingly frayed—we could tell as she kept shifting her stance. Thom was visibly upset, though we couldn't hear what he was talking about—we could hear a voice but not the words. No one knew what they could possibly be fighting over but that small sense of dread started building within me again and I started making my own connections, even though I didn't know the real reason for Thom's anger. I looked over at Robert Mallory standing on a stepladder, holding a wreath of green tassels—he was the only one of us who wasn't looking over at where Thom and Susan stood, almost as if he pretended it wasn't happening or, I thought darkly, knew exactly why it was happening. Thom kept gesturing and Susan's arms remained crossed against her chest defensively. And then we heard her. "Tell me, Thom," she suddenly shouted, loud enough for us to hear across the field. "How does this matter? What does it fucking matter?"

"What the fuck is wrong with you?" Thom shouted back. "What the fuck is wrong with you?"

"Why does it matter?" she shouted at him.

"It matters because I love you," he shouted back, red-faced.

"That's not it!" she shouted. "That's not what I'm talking about!"

"It would look fucking complicated if you weren't with me!" Thom shouted. "How about that? It would look too fucking weird if you weren't with me!"

As Susan started stalking away Thom grabbed her arm and whirled her around. And then: she slapped his face.

Everyone on the float watching this altercation gasped. You could hear it from where we were: the palm of Susan's hand making contact with Thom's jaw. The slap stunned Thom so badly that he automatically let go of Susan's arm and watched, humbled, as she made her way across the field, moving through the patches of darkened lawn, in and out of the stadium lights, until she got to the float and walked past us to the restrooms by the tennis court.

You couldn't overestimate the shock of this moment—the ten of us standing by the float who had watched this fight and the subsequent slap went silent, and then turned away embarrassed as Susan walked by us without saying anything—she was scowling, muttering to herself. I looked at Debbie, who didn't say a word. And I realized that she had this wary expression on her face, as if she knew something that no one else did—she was the only one of us who didn't seem shocked. Even Robert Mallory's eyes were widened with surprise. No one had ever seen Thom and Susan get into a fight, and it was something seismic, a revelation, an explosion, a rift that split the calmness of Buckley and its traditions raggedly open: there was never any hint of tension between them, they both seemed so easygoing, so cool, so blessed with a general good-naturedness. I knew Susan could be brittle and sarcastic and see through everything, yet she always kept it together, and I also knew that Thom had been sufficiently wounded by his parents' divorce that he saw the world from a more jaded angle than he had before the separation, but he rarely showed it and only privately, never in public. This rising tension between Susan and Thom had happened gradually and so it was something that no one had ever noticed; it had taken two years for it to play out on Gilley Field that night. It was as if she had finally arrived at that place through her relationship with Thom where she now resided in a completely different world and was ready to blithely leave him somewhere behind. I thought of the Icehouse song and how I always knew it sounded like an omen. But that night on Gilley Field the omen was confirmed; the omen had become actualized.

ROBERT MALLORY jumped off the stepladder and jogged across the field to where Thom stood alone, head down. Robert placed a hand on Thom's shoulder and Thom just slowly nodded after Robert said something. Debbie and I left the float to find Susan—everyone murmuring behind us as I followed Debbie to the girls' restroom. Susan was leaning against a sink, smoking a clove cigarette, and though her hand was lightly shaking her face was blank—the neutrality and numbness had returned after that flash of anger. The girls' bathroom was softly illuminated with a dim fluorescent light and I was surprised how large the space was—there were at least ten stalls with their own corresponding sinks and mirrors. I caught my reflection in one and turned away, disturbed by how frightened I looked.

"I can't do it," Susan was muttering. "I won't do it."

Debbie just stood there not saying anything, as if she expected this.

"Do what?" I asked, completely confused.

"Homecoming Queen," Susan said evenly. "Sit in that stupid car and wave for three minutes as we crawl by the bleachers." She moved the cigarette to her lips: inhaled, exhaled. "It's so stupid. I won't do it. I told Thom. I told him all week. I told him I don't want to be Homecoming Queen this year. Last year was fine. But I don't want to do it this year and I'm not going to do it this year."

I just stared at her. "But you're going to win tomorrow."

She didn't look at me when she asked, "Win?" She smiled ruefully to herself. "Win? What am I going to *win*, Bret?"

Debbie wasn't saying anything. She just stared at Susan.

"I told you *you* could take my place," Susan said to Debbie. "Why don't you just take my place? You're probably coming in second anyway."

I realized this was true: Debbie would come in second place, though we'd never know. There was no short list for Homecoming King and Queen and the secretaries in the administration building privately tallied the ballots, because the school didn't want anybody's feelings hurt. And I also realized with a humbling clarity that even though Debbie Schaffer would come in second place for Homecoming Queen, I probably wouldn't rank in the top five for King. I was popular because of my connection to Debbie and Thom and Susan but this didn't mean I was well liked enough to be anywhere near this particular coronation.

"I don't want to take your place—" Debbie started.

"Jesus, Debbie," Susan muttered.

"I told you that, Susan—"

"I'll just tell them that I can't make it to Homecoming this year," Susan said over her. "I'll just make up an excuse—"

"Oh, don't be ridiculous," Debbie said. "Don't do this—"

The SHARDS

"And *you* can be Homecoming Queen—you'll probably come in second place," Susan said again, repeating this as if it was some desperate truth that would change Debbie's mind.

"Susan, you have got to get real and calm the fuck down," Debbie said harshly, and then, "Do you have anything to take? Because you're acting crazy."

"What's so crazy about the way I'm acting?" Susan asked, glaring at Debbie.

"There's the game, there's the parade, there's the dinner, and there's Anthony's party." Debbie was listing these events as if they were an inevitability Susan simply had to partake in.

"What are you saying?" Susan asked, daring Debbie to admit something private, as if I wasn't standing in the restroom next to them. "What does any of that mean?"

And then I suddenly got angry. "It's only one more year, Susan, right?" I actually spat this out at her. "Where did that attitude disappear to? You told me it's only one more year. Why don't you stop being such a bitch to Thom and suck it up like everyone else does and just do Homecoming. I mean, Jesus, how hard can it be, sitting in a fucking float?"

Susan looked at me hard. "When I said that, I was referring to *you*, Bret, and *your* situation." She inhaled on the cigarette and then exhaled. "I was referring to *you*. Not me. Not us. But *you*." She said this with a casualness that was still pointed and direct.

I was so deflated by this response that I just wanted to limp out of the restroom.

"Look, let's be diplomatic about this," Debbie was saying.

"I'm sick of what Thom wants!" Susan suddenly screamed. "I'm so sick of it!"

Debbie and I backed off—we actually physically moved away from her. I had never seen Susan as frustrated and angry as she was on that night in October. There was obviously a secret narrative unfolding that I knew nothing about—something that I was left out of, something that was supposedly none of my business, something that was arousing this rage within her.

"I didn't want my name to be eligible," Susan was saying in a rush, "and I told Thom that maybe we should let someone else be King and

Queen, let Jeff and Tracy or Jeff and Debbie, or whoever. It's so stupid, I argued. The whole thing is so stupid." She paused. "He didn't get it. He didn't understand how dumb it all is. I just told him: Let someone else have a chance. Who gives a fuck?"

If I look back I would have married Thom Wright. He seemed to be the perfect guy—genuinely intelligent, world-weary but optimistic, just damaged enough to be interesting, beautiful and athletic, so nice, so hot, his face, his body, his kindness—but I realized in that moment how someone could tire of him over the course of two years and I was shocked that this had so obviously happened to Susan. How could anyone not want to keep having sex with Thom Wright, to bask in his concern, to be in his presence daily, to have him love you unconditionally? I realized on that night this might easily happen—that Thom Wright's charms could wear off. That someone else could replace him. And then I thought of Robert Mallory. I was suddenly dizzy, because everything was going to get ruined. Thom was going to get hurt. Robert was going to get what he wanted. I was going to get nothing.

"And then he got desperate and he said, Okay, I get it, but let's just go through the motions—I'm the fucking quarterback, he said, he actually said, 'I'm the captain of the football team and you're my girlfriend and you don't think it's going to look strange if we win and you don't do it?' And then I said I don't care how it looks! That's the problem, I told him. You care. I don't. And he just couldn't really understand this, or he could but said we had to do it anyway." The hand holding the slow-burning cigarette was still lightly shaking but her voice softened. "I know that when this is announced tomorrow at assembly it's going to be my name and his and I'm not going to do it—I'll give it to someone else." She paused, glanced quickly at both Debbie and myself with a slight desperation. "We won't make a big deal about it. I'll come up with an excuse. My grandmother is sick or—"

"Baby," Debbie interrupted softly, "there's no reason to cause this kind of drama right now. You know that. You know how it works."

"The fact that I would be causing drama because I don't want to be Homecoming Queen is indicative of something, Debbie, don't you think?" Susan asked with venom in her voice.

Debbie just shrugged and stared at Susan. "No, not really. I don't. I don't think it's indicative of anything."

The SHARDS

Silence fell across the restroom. I didn't know what I was doing there with two girls who obviously knew something that they thought I didn't have a clue about and that was tied to Robert Mallory and being kept from me. I wasn't the gay best friend you could confide everything to for Susan and Debbie, and yet in reality I actually was, but they didn't know this. And I might have been exactly that if I'd played things differently or if we were in another world. Here, in this situation, in the confines of Buckley, I was, in so many ways, an impostor.

"Do you really want to be standing on that hideous float waving to the crowd?" Susan asked Debbie. "Do you really want to do that?"

"No, I don't," Debbie said calmly. "But I'm not in your position. And, I'm afraid, you're going to have to do it—"

"Fuck off," Susan muttered.

"No, I'm serious." Debbie glanced at me for some reason and then back at Susan before admitting, "Look, I get it. I know what's going on but—"

This startled me and I blurted out, "What's going on?" And then in a high voice asked accusingly, "Is there something going on that I don't know about?"

Debbie rolled her eyes and made a gesture. "Bret, just, y'know . . ." She trailed off, concentrating on Susan, expecting me to excuse myself. I realized again: they knew something that they thought I didn't know.

"Of course, it's your decision, it's your life, it's whatever," Debbie was saying. "But at this point you have to play it a certain way. I'm sorry, babe, you just do. It's too late. You agreed to be student-body president because Thom asked you to—I mean what did you expect? It's not as if anyone held a gun up to your head. You went along with it. You're a couple. And now this is happening. It's really happening and you're going to have to do it."

Susan stared at Debbie as if I was invisible.

"Do you want me to be happy?" Susan asked her.

Debbie sighed and cocked her head. "Don't be so dramatic. It's dumb."

I was utterly lost standing there, listening to the two girls having this coded conversation in front of me.

"And you shouldn't have hit him," Debbie said. "Jesus, Susan."

"He couldn't get it through his dumb skull—"

"Susan, stop it—"

"And he grabbed me, Debbie," she said. "And it hurt."

"Stop it—"

"Are you saying it didn't hurt when he grabbed my arm?"

"What did you expect him to do?"

"Oh, fuck off—"

"Okay, look, what does it fucking matter?" Debbie asked, taking the cigarette from Susan, inhaling and blowing a thick stream of spice-scented smoke into the air. "I mean: what does it really matter? It just makes you look like a bitch." Debbie paused. "I mean, tell me. What does it matter? Just do it. What does it matter?" She handed the cigarette back to Susan, who didn't say anything.

I realized one last time I shouldn't have been there because I wasn't wanted in that particular moment. This was really between Susan and Debbie and I knew they weren't mentioning something because I was standing there. And so I backed away, and neither one of them said anything as I quietly left the restroom—and then I could hear their urgent muffled whispering behind me. Finally they were allowed to speak freely because of my absence. I was momentarily enraged that this drama superseded Matt Kellner and that more emotion was being poured into whether Susan wanted to be Homecoming Queen or not than his mysterious death—a death that none of them really knew about or cared to know about. This was what sickened and exhausted me as I left the restroom and walked back to the field.

THOM WAS WALKING WITH ROBERT to the float, which everyone had started working on again, pretending nothing had happened. I could see Angelo's flashlight nearing us in the distance—it was ten-thirty, time to go home, and there was no point working on the float any longer. We were shaken and distracted because we'd witnessed something that never occurred before: the fantasy couple revealed there were problems in the relationship, something that had happily lasted for over two years because they were so in love was now fractured, the slap was the proof of damage, there was now doubt. I shuddered as I watched Robert walking closely next to Thom, their heads bowed down, Thom listening to whatever Robert was telling him, and occasionally Thom would nod while staring at the lawn he was crossing, both dressed in their gray school slacks and white shirts. I just stared at Robert and Thom and became so envious of this momentary intimacy between the two of them that I briefly got dizzy again and then felt shame—I desired both of them and it was never going to happen. That's just something you'll have to accept, I told myself, and another thing hardened within me: the world isn't going to work out that way for you—get over it. I was still staring at them when I was knocked out of my reverie, as Thom looked up, blank-faced but also yearning, and then smiled sadly. Debbie and Susan had come out of the restroom and were walking toward Thom and Robert standing by the float. Susan's face was also blank and I had no idea what she was going to say as she walked up to him—Robert had already gently backed away from Thom. Susan's pragmatism kicked in, aided by Debbie, and she sincerely uttered an apology to Thom and said, "Of course, I'll do it," and then Thom, his face slightly crinkled with emotion, hugged her and lifted Susan up, before placing her back on the lawn. He was so relieved it was almost embarrassing—this was a different side to Thom, which I'd never seen before. I now knew he was weak. They kissed.

Everyone surrounding the float started clapping, including Robert, and Anthony Matthews whistled his approval. It was dumb, something out of a movie, but I pretended to get caught up in the moment and started clapping too, and then I noticed Debbie standing next to me, leaning in, but she wasn't smiling even though she was clapping as well, and her eyes weren't fixed on Susan and Thom—instead they were on Robert Mallory, who was smiling broadly. The applause only lasted ten to fifteen seconds but it aided in our overall relief—it was the representation of our relief. And then we started leaving the field and headed down the hill to the parking lot, still lit below the darkened campus, and a light sense of defeat hovered everywhere: we'd have to finish the float the following afternoon, maybe even start from scratch, Doug Furth muttered hopelessly to Jon Yates. We trailed past the science building and I watched as Thom clasped Susan's hand while we moved through the darkness of Buckley. And then realized Debbie was reaching for mine.

AND I WAS standing in the courtyard of the Pavilion the following morning while the campus cheered when Thom Wright and Susan Reynolds were announced Homecoming King and Queen of the senior class. They walked up to the mic and thanked everyone who voted for them and Thom was beaming obliviously, as if nothing had happened the night before, and Susan had reverted to her dreamy and numb self, alluring as any girl at Buckley, her cleavage clearly visible, the hem of the skirt near the top of her thighs, an almost slutty idealization of teen-girl sexuality. I looked over at Ryan Vaughn, who was clapping, and then got distracted by Robert Mallory, who wasn't clapping—he just stared at the couple behind the mic at the top of the stairs below the shadow of the Pavilion, a gaze tinged with what I imagined were sadness and rage. He turned to look at me and stared back, as if I was a reminder for him to start clapping, which he then did. There was, however, a feeling in the courtyard on that Friday morning before Homecoming that the night before, on Gilley Field, was the beginning of the end for Thom Wright and Susan Reynolds's reign as Buckley's golden couple. And only a few of us knew that the beginning of the end had happened far earlier than that.

SATURDAY: I woke up and stared at the ceiling in the empty house on Mulholland and tried to summon the spirit of the tangible participant but I was too distracted by the meeting with Terry and depressed about the motions that were expected of me at Buckley that day. And then I realized that the promise of Terry Schaffer at the Polo Lounge was reason enough to get out of bed and pretend to be excited about Homecoming and my participation in it, on the sidelines at least—*Turn it around!* a voice inside my head exclaimed—and just stay positive until the meeting on Sunday, when Terry and I would talk about the script he wanted me to write, and perhaps find me an agent, and then I imagined maybe Sue Mengers would represent me as a favor to Terry and we'd celebrate by having dinner at Ma Maison with Joan Didion and John Gregory Dunne. It all seemed possible. After jerking off and letting Shingy out, I decided, while trying on various smiles in the bathroom mirror, that I would "happily" walk up to Gilley Field with my girlfriend and cheer Thom Wright and Ryan Vaughn and the rest of the Griffins and I'd say hello to friends' parents whom I hadn't seen in *ages* and Debbie and I would stroll through the carnival, hand in hand, and buy cotton candy, and laugh and lean in to each other while I won her a Smurf doll after a game of darts, and I forced myself to feel: it would all be good. But my meeting with Terry was the drug motivating the actor.

I REMEMBER THAT Debbie wanted to pick me up from the house on Mulholland so we could arrive at Buckley together. I argued there was no need for her to pick me up because I had to come back to the house on Mulholland after the football game in order to change for the dinner in the Pavilion. I then told her she sounded ridiculous when she suggested I bring a change of clothes to Buckley, as she was doing so she didn't have to drive back to Bel Air—we could change clothes in the locker rooms—this suggestion automatically put me into a state of annoyance. When I said that I didn't want to bring a suit and a pair of dress shoes to Buckley, Debbie offered to drive me back to Mulholland after the football game and the carnival and "help" me change into a suit for the Homecoming dinner, which I couldn't believe I was actually attending. "Maybe I should take my own car, babe," I said, when I realized she was also suggesting maybe we could fool around before the dinner, maybe take a dip in the Jacuzzi, maybe I could go down on her, maybe she could suck me off—she didn't actually say this, it was all intimation. I should just take my own car, I argued. What's the big deal? I asked. I'll meet you underneath the bell tower or by the science building and we can take the elevators up to Gilley Field together, what's the big deal? But my voice lacked conviction. Debbie won out. She was a force. I caved.

I DIDN'T WANT Debbie coming into the house on Mulholland, so I waited outside, wearing jeans and a Polo shirt and Topsiders, Wayfarers on, holding a garment bag that contained a suit my dad bought for me at Jerry Magnin, a dress shirt, and a tie from Brooks Brothers as well as a pair of penny loafers. I kept muttering to myself: get excited, stay excited, fake the excitement, Robert Mallory doesn't exist, Matt Kellner didn't die, you're in a committed relationship with Debbie Schaffer, Ryan Vaughn is a great dude, you love Thom Wright and Susan Reynolds and not even the hate you sometimes feel will ever change that.

Debbie pulled up and after I hung the garment bag in the back seat we kissed and then she drove down Woodcliff and on Stansbury Avenue a line of cars with VIP parking passes were slowly moving toward the open gates of the school. Shuttles were picking people up at the empty lot across from the Ralphs on Ventura, or you could try and find parking along Valley Vista, which was, I noted, packed with cars lined on either side of the boulevard's curb. We dropped the car off with the valet set up by the bell tower and Debbie and I slung our respective garment bags over our shoulders and headed to the locker rooms to drop them off before going to the field. Walking with Debbie, our sunglasses on, I suddenly felt I was a model in a commercial, we were a couple in a travelogue who barely knew each other, which led to the notion that I was actually being watched, that everyone was looking at me, whether they were or not, or that someone hidden, from a vantage point I couldn't see, was monitoring my movements. Debbie disappeared into the girls' locker room and I could hear the activity emanating from the boys' locker room as I was about to enter and then changed my mind and called out to Debbie if she could hang my bag with hers—I didn't want to see the Griffins suiting up or get distracted by them, and I didn't want to say hi to Thom or Ryan. Debbie took the garment bag from me and hinted slyly that there was no one in the girls' locker room if I wanted to join her—the cheerleaders were already up on the field. I smiled and went along with the innuendo, to a point, and instead suggested the game might be starting soon. Her smile couldn't mask the faint disappointment she felt, or so I intimated. Maybe Debbie Schaffer actually expected me to fuck her in the girls' locker room before the Homecoming game or maybe this was only what I imagined. I'm not sure I could tell anymore.

Instead of walking up the steep road to Gilley Field we waited in line at the elevator banks and rode up in the large lift with who I suspected in the thirty seconds it took to arrive on the field were George Vaughn and his wife, Lois, and Ryan's younger brother, Laine, who resembled a fourteen-year-old miniature Ryan—this suspicion wasn't verified until later that day, when I saw Ryan with this family after the game. The only other parent I remember who arrived at Homecoming that day was Thom Wright's mother, Laurie, who was with a good-looking guy about her age, roughly late thirties, whom I'd never seen before, and the way they carried themselves suggested he was more than a friend, and since I really hadn't hung out with Thom this semester I had no idea what was going on in his mom's life—I usually did. Laurie spotted Debbie and me as we took our seats in the first row of bleachers and waved, smiling through her sunglasses, while her date was leafing through the program, and we waved back. Liz and Terry Schaffer were never going to show up to Homecoming, and neither were Don and Gayle Reynolds, Susan's parents, especially since their daughter had probably begged them not to.

IT WAS in the mid-sixties and the sky was clear and blue, a mild afternoon, the smog usually floating over the Valley only visible far away, lightly shrouding the San Gabriel Mountains, but I became uncomfortably warm sitting beneath the sun in the stands as the Griffins were announced and bounding onto the field to greet the varsity team from Brentwood (they'd be having their own Homecoming the following week) and I just sat idly next to Debbie, who was talking to Susan and Tracy in the two seats next to hers as I pantomimed the expected cheering. I was on the aisle—I had requested this to Debbie when she bought the tickets, warning her I wouldn't go if I didn't have an aisle seat. Two yearbook photographers were covering the stands, while Mr. Richards, the photography teacher, was taking pictures of the action on the field, which I scanned uselessly—I knew no one in the marching band, I didn't really know any of the cheerleaders from the junior and senior classes, meaning I hadn't been to any of the games that semester, so I was surprised, I guess, to see that Karen Landis and Rita Lee and Katie Harris were all jumping around flinging red-and-white pom-poms into the air. One of the yearbook photographers took a photo of Susan and Tracy and Debbie squeezing in to each other smiling while I shifted away in my seat, disappearing myself, and then everything passed quickly as I watched the figures on the field scrambling after each other while I started to outline the pitch I was going to offer Terry Schaffer the following afternoon at the Beverly Hills Hotel, sitting with him in a large green booth, and I'd be wearing a blazer (it was required in the Polo Lounge) and explaining what I had in mind—a boy, his friends, young people in L.A., sexy, a little bi, drugs, someone is killed, there's a chase, violence and bloodshed, a mystery the boy solves or maybe not, I preferred the downer ending but we could make it upbeat as well, I'd offer, we could negotiate that.

I WAS JOLTED BACK into paying attention when halftime was announced. Susan was no longer in her seat and the first float appeared on the track—it was a miniature bell tower the seventh-graders had built, and there were two students, a boy and a girl, both blond and very cute, sitting on a replica of the bench beneath the bell tower and waving. And then I felt a curdling as the second float passed and there was sustained applause and cheering for a massive autumn leaf festooned with a thousand strands of red and orange and yellow tissues slowly drifting across the track with the two most adorable eighth-graders waving from where they sat below the leaf. I was shifting in my seat—I needed something to take the edge off: it would be unbearable to see Susan faking it on the float. I wished I had brought what was left of the dwindling supply of Valium my mother had given me before leaving for Europe but the tangible participant had denied this. The ninth-grade float of an American flag with pastel stars and flowers wheeled by and I was gripped by a new sense of dread—it was compounded with the idea that I was *again* being watched from somewhere in the hillsides surrounding Gilley Field, and I realized I hadn't seen Robert Mallory anywhere and turned around and scanned the hundreds of people filling the stands above me. When I turned back to the field a float of the Buckley Griffin wearing a football helmet slowly passed, with two sophomores flanking it waving, and I was dreading the following moments. My hands clutched at my jeans.

Debbie noticed and turned to me. "Are you okay?"

And I involuntarily asked, "What's going on with Susan and Thom? What's wrong with Susan? What's going on? Can you please fucking tell me?"

The Junior Mints box wheeled itself across the track—cheers and laughter as Dean McCain (admittedly hot) and Alison Garner (less so) waved from where they sat.

"You're asking that now?" Debbie said grimly while clapping.

"Forget it, forget it," I muttered as the senior float appeared.

It was modified, fixed—we had spent Friday night making it cohere and it paid off. There was the Statue of Liberty's head with a much clearer photo of Thom Wright's face, and behind the head sat a replica of an L.A. street complete with palm trees—not exactly Stansbury Avenue but no one noticed or cared—and there was the banner that could be clearly read from the stands, ESCAPE FROM BUCKLEY HIGH, as well as the tagline. I wasn't surprised that the float got a big laugh, and cheers followed as Thom Wright, in his football jersey, and Susan Reynolds, in a skirt and a Buckley blouse, stood on the slowly moving float being driven by Jon Yates and waved to the crowd. Thom's smile was genuine and excited as he took it all in, and Susan's smile seemed to be as well, even if it was less emphatic. I noted that Debbie watched the float coldly. And then it was over and my dread evaporated. Nothing bad had happened.

The Kings and Queens hopped off their respective floats, which were driven off the field to be parked at the bottom of the hill so people could admire them as they sat near the lane leading into the school's parking lot. The cheerleaders aligned into formations while the marching band played what sounded like a medley of Queen's "Another One Bites the Dust" followed by "Believe It or Not," the theme from the TV show *The Greatest American Hero,* and capped off with Neil Diamond's "America." And then the game resumed and the Griffins won and Brentwood took the whole thing good-naturedly—the game meant nothing, it was just fun, seventeen to seven—and while Thom was propped up on the shoulders of his ten teammates, and tossing his sweat-soaked hair back, basking in the manufactured delirium of the moment, I just scanned the hills, waiting for the sniper to locate me within the scope mounted on top of the rifle, but I wasn't afraid anymore, because the bullet would actually save me from the rest of the day.

And yet, I thought hopefully, there was Terry Schaffer and the screenplay to live for, and I became an optimist again.

SUSAN went to the lockers to wait for Thom while Debbie and I walked down the hill to the carnival on the field that ran across the hillside of the elementary school—it was basically for the kids who didn't want to watch football. There was a miniature Ferris wheel, a merry-go-round, a haunted house, and booths with games, and tents selling food. Debbie and I shared a Häagen-Dazs ice-cream cone and we were in that commercial again, that couple in the travelogue, interrupted by various parents who said hello to Debbie and the tangible participant while my main distraction was looking for Robert Mallory, wondering if he was ever going to show up—since I hadn't seen him in the stands I imagined he'd be at the carnival we were strolling through. Susan and Thom finally found us and Thom was jazzed and freshly showered and in the suit he was going to wear at dinner and Susan had changed into a black cocktail dress and she reminded us that drinks were starting in the Pavilion's lobby at six and I was suddenly relieved at how fast the day was passing so I could stop *waiting* and get to the next day and present myself and the movie I wanted to write for Terry Schaffer, whose daughter's hand I was holding as we walked through the crowded carnival. I spotted Ryan with his mom and dad and younger brother, confirming that the trio in the elevator were indeed the Vaughns—and felt nothing.

I went with Debbie to the locker rooms and Susan came with us but everything the girls talked about in my presence was pleasant and vague—they would talk privately when Debbie was changing. Susan brought out my garment bag and her eyes caught mine and we held a gaze for a moment but said nothing, and then I changed in the boys' locker room, which was now empty, yet there was still the lingering scent of teen bodies and soap, sweet and stale, that always connected me to vague erotic longings. Once I was dressed and knotting my tie in front of a mirror I found myself fighting that particular brand of hopelessness that was again invading the cloud of positivity the tangible participant was trying to float within. *Why are you so upset?* the tangible participant asked. *What is so upsetting?* it asked. *None of this is real.*

MANY OF THE PEOPLE who streamed out of Gilley Field that afternoon and walked through the carnival were not staying for the dinner in the Pavilion and most of our class had opted out—the dinner was open for juniors and seniors and their parents as well as alumni, of which there were many, but only a smattering of people from our class sat at the two large banquet tables that lined the Pavilion's auditorium where the basketball and volleyball games were played, and each table sat about one hundred attendees below the stage, where a small orchestra performed standards, and though every seat had been sold, they were mostly filled with older alumni, none of whom I recognized. There was a full bar set up in the lobby and waiters from the catering staff fetched drinks for parents and the aging alumni, and there were bottles of wine dotting the banquet tables, which were candlelit and decorated with autumn flowers and displays of corn husks. Debbie and I sat in the same general area as Susan and Thom, next to Laurie Wright and her good-looking new friend, and Ryan was sitting with his family across from Coach Holtz and his wife at the other banquet table, but it was apparent that most of our classmates were skipping the dinner and would meet at Anthony Matthews's in Studio City, up Coldwater into Fryman Canyon. I barely said a word that night: just kept scanning the Pavilion for a glimpse of Robert Mallory, who never appeared.

AT ANTHONY MATTHEWS'S, DEBBIE and Susan and I situated ourselves on chaises by the lit pool, where we lay for the duration of the party. Tony's parents were staying at the Sportsman's Lodge that night, just down the canyon on Ventura Boulevard, so we were unsupervised, but it turned out very chill: kids from other private schools showed up and the party turned out larger than expected but nothing got rowdy; in fact it was mellow, with the soothing smell of gardenias drifting through the night air and kids only drinking Coronas. Drugs were done discreetly and Debbie abstained, because she had to be at the Windover Stables from three until six tomorrow, and I realized that Terry had timed my arrival at the Beverly Hills Hotel to coincide with her being unavailable. Only Tony and a couple of the guys spending the night at the house in Fryman got trashed, and I remember very few specifics of what happened at the party because I was just waiting and waiting and I didn't want to drink; I didn't want anything. I was just preoccupied with *waiting.*

And then an *absence* announced itself when I heard "Dreaming" by Blondie: shadows were standing next to the pool and one of them was wearing the same puka-shell necklace Matt Kellner wore and I realized again that Matt had been alive and now he was dead, as if in a dream that had dematerialized, and I was homing in on the pool, the bright square of light in the backyard, and I kept staring deeper into it until I located the drain and I imagined the swirl above the drain filtering the pool, and a vortex appeared in my mind, and it was the spiral nautical shell on the cover of my calculus textbook, and the vortex became a tornado but there wasn't a vortex, there wasn't even a swirl—this was something the writer was imagining as he *waited* on the chaise longue next to the two girls who were keeping a secret from him, and it was only the occasional helicopter flying above us in the night sky that distracted me from the vortex that wasn't there.

DEBBIE DROVE ME HOME after it became apparent the party wasn't ending anytime soon. She thought I was tired, because I started feigning an exaggerated yawn every two minutes, and in the driveway of the empty house on Mulholland she started making out with me, insisting we go inside, but my resolve was too strong and so I gently backed off and told her I'd speak to her tomorrow, when she got back from the stables—I would have already returned from the meeting with her father by then. I got out of the car and grabbed my garment bag from the back seat and walked up the steps to the house and then disappeared without waving goodbye. I waited in the foyer until I heard her car pull out of the driveway while Shingy danced around my legs, pawing at my feet as he followed me to the kitchen, where I let him out onto the lawn and waited, making sure there were no coyotes scrounging the hillsides. I just waited by the open door until he was finished, and when I called his name he froze, mid-lawn, listening to something I couldn't hear, and then scampered back into the kitchen. I slid the glass door closed and walked slowly to my bedroom.

But I couldn't sleep and it was barely midnight and so I drove the Mercedes through the canyons, listening to "Nowhere Girl," until I hit Benedict and neared the house that Robert Mallory had visited for approximately ten minutes last week and where I prowled the back-yard until I remembered what Ronald Kellner told me on Haskell Avenue about the mileage on the Datsun. *Oh, maybe over the hill and back, but no one drove that car to Crystal Cove.* The gates were closed and I could barely make out the WARNING: NO TRESPASSING sign that crookedly hung from them but there was a faint light coming from one of the rooms on the second floor and it seemed to be waver-ing, as if several candles were lit, but in the overall darkness I couldn't see if Robert's car was in front, because none of the lights circling the driveway were on. And then, as if someone realized a car was idling on the canyon road below the house, the wavering lights went out, the second-floor window darkened and I drove quickly away.

15

A VALIUM WAS ESSENTIAL TO move me through the meeting with Terry Schaffer. I realized this when I got into the convertible Mercedes at three-thirty to head down the canyon to the Beverly Hills Hotel and I had one in my pocket.

I never expected to get so keyed up as the day progressed but the waiting became unbearable and nothing could soothe it: not working out, not swimming, not another soak in the Jacuzzi, not another jerk-off session. I kept changing my mind about what to wear: I had a dark-green-and-brown tweed jacket I decided on that basically went with any color dress shirt I owned. I finally opted on just a white Ralph Lauren and then refolded all the shirts I had tried on. I called the hotel and told them that I had a meeting in the Polo Lounge at four o'clock and asked if jeans were allowable and was told yes. I paced the length of the bedroom. I paced the hallway, muttering to myself, and then into the kitchen, where I opened and closed the door of the refrigerator a number of times. I wanted to appear as if this meeting was just another confident yet casual moment in my hip adolescent life. I wanted Terry Schaffer to be impressed by me. I didn't want him to desire me exactly—though I knew that could be the path the narrative took—but instead I wanted him to take me seriously enough so we could make a deal for the script. The waiting and my fantasy about the real reasons Terry wanted to meet me at the Beverly Hills Hotel were an example, I realize now, of how naïve I could be at seventeen despite my surface cool and the air of jaded knowingness I was aiming for and worked so hard to project.

The SHARDS

—

I KNEW it would only take me fifteen minutes to get to the hotel from the house on Mulholland but I didn't care if I was early—and I no longer cared if this made me seem slightly desperate, because I had to get out of the empty house and I didn't want to risk driving around when I was this jittery and distracted. I hoped the desperation would be reread as eagerness, as respect, as a way of pleasing Terry. I timed the Valium and placed it in my mouth as I turned down Benedict Canyon, letting the small yellow tablet melt under my tongue, and I already imagined its calming effects before the pill actually hit. I didn't even glance at the house that was connected to Robert Mallory as I sped past that flat section of roadway a minute later and through the light on Hutton, just six houses below it. Everything was quiet on that Sunday in L.A. and I rarely passed any cars until Benedict brought me to Sunset Boulevard, where I turned left at the light, drove the length of the block the massive pink building was situated on, and then made another left and drove past the pine-green sign announcing the Beverly Hills Hotel at the entrance, where an American flag was waving high above the front of the driveway lined with towering palm trees that led upward to the valet that dropped you in front of the entrance to the lobby.

I had been to the Beverly Hills Hotel about fifteen times when I was thirteen, the year it seemed every bar mitzvah was held either in the Crystal Ballroom or the Sunset Ballroom or the Rodeo Ballroom and inevitably had a *Star Wars* theme, but I'd only been on the grounds beyond the ballrooms twice before, both times when my grandparents visited L.A. from Nevada, but they ultimately preferred the Bel Air Hotel, and so I'd never spent any time at what was referred to as "the Pink Palace" as I got older. I had seen the hotel in a few movies, most prominently *California Suite* and *American Gigolo*, but the Polo Lounge had been stylized into a reconfiguration in the Richard Gere movie and though it was certainly beautiful and worked for the film's aesthetic it didn't resemble the current reality—it was dreamt up by the visual consultant, Ferdinando Scarfiotti. I knew things like this at seventeen. I pulled the car up to a young blond valet, dressed in a uniform of dark-green slacks and a sea-foam-green short-sleeved Polo shirt with a black bowtie, who opened the driver's-side door and handed me a ticket as I stepped out and told him I was meeting someone for a drink. I noted there were only three cars idling in the four lanes of the valet stand on that late afternoon—a convertible Bentley, a Cadillac and a waiting limo with tinted windows—and even though the valet had handed me a ticket I was worried that I wouldn't be allowed in, that I wouldn't pass. But I apparently did: the 450SL, the tweed jacket, the clean-cut looks—it all seemed to work, because the valet nodded and didn't make me feel like the impostor I could warp myself into becoming if I'd given myself the right dosage of self-loathing.

I WALKED BENEATH the pink-and-green-striped canopy that led to the entrance doors, which a doorman pulled open, and then I entered a deserted lobby, completely devoid of people. A fire danced in the hearth behind a metal grate but there were only three men in suits manning the front desk off to my right and seemingly no guests. I looked around, mildly confused, having no idea where the Polo Lounge was located. I checked my watch—I was about ten minutes early. I walked tentatively to the concierge desk and asked where the Polo Lounge was—I told the concierge I had a meeting there at four o'clock, trying to sound as official as possible. The concierge told me that it was right around the corner and, gesturing with his hand and slightly bowing, referred to me as "sir." I thanked him and made my way across the sea of green carpeting and turned left, where I saw the entrance of the Polo Lounge but not before I glanced down an impossibly long corridor lined with banana-leaf wallpaper—completely deserted, reminding me of something out of *The Shining* if it had been set in Southern California. But it was a Sunday and checkout was probably at twelve and this must have been the reason why it was so quiet and there were no people anywhere—the weekend was over. When I told the host who I was here to meet he asked me to take a seat at the bar and he would call Mr. Schaffer and let him know I'd arrived. I automatically wondered what that meant: *call Mr. Schaffer?* But I didn't say anything.

The small bar directly next to the entrance sat six and all the stools were empty and the room was dotted with only a few couples talking softly to each other in the hazy light of late afternoon. The bartender asked me what I'd like and I ordered a ginger ale, explaining that I was waiting for someone, suggesting that I was important. After the bartender served the ginger ale he placed a small bowl of light-green dip surrounded by tortilla chips next to the glass, and that I didn't touch. Why would the host have to call Terry? I wondered. Was he staying in the hotel? Was he driving in from somewhere else? The Valium had kicked in and these questions floated away as I drifted into a vague, soothing calmness and sipped the ginger ale. While I kept waiting, however, I started thinking about the house on Benedict Canyon that Robert Mallory had disappeared into and the candlelit window I passed by last night and the things Robert did to Matt in that house the week Matt was missing. The thought was interrupted by a familiar voice. "Hey, Bret." I tightened up. It was Steven Reinhardt.

I turned on the stool and pretended not to be surprised. "Hey, Steven."

I HADN'T SEEN HIM since the lunch at Trumps and nothing had changed: the same turtleneck and the extra-small jeans that still hung baggy on his bone-thin frame, the deep-set eyes locked into an emaciated skull topped with a frizzy mop of blond curly hair. He was grinning at me but there was no friendliness within the smile. I always sensed a desperation emanating from him and yet he was Terry Schaffer's assistant, his right-hand man, and I always tried to defer to him until I couldn't. There was something unbearable about Steven Reinhardt and he filled me with a light disgust that I simply couldn't hide anymore.

"Where's Terry?" I asked. "Is he going to be late?"

Steven kept grinning at me, and then he shook his head slightly, as if in mild disbelief. "So—you made it," he said. "You actually came." He paused. "I almost made a bet with Terry that you wouldn't."

"Why wouldn't I come?" I immediately asked, confused. "Why would you make a bet?" I asked.

Steven raised his eyebrows, the grin disappeared, and he glanced around the empty room. "I don't know. I guess I'm always surprised by a person's level of, um, propriety or lack of it, I guess. Or self-interest. Or self-delusion." He said this calmly and with no rancor but it sounded like the insult he intended. "How badly they want something. La la la." He paused again. "I'm always surprised what they think they're capable of. What they think they're going to get away with." He paused once more. "I guess I shouldn't be, but I am."

My face had become a scowl. "What does that mean?" I grimaced. "What are you talking about? Terry wanted a meeting with me and I came. What are you fucking blathering on about, Steven? You set this up."

Steven registered my displeasure and innocently opened his arms and said, "It means absolutely nothing, Bret, calm down." He reconsidered. "Or it means whatever you want it to mean." He paused. "I wasn't necessarily talking about you." He cocked his head slightly. "You're more innocent than that, right?"

"It means whatever I want it to mean?" I asked. "It doesn't mean anything, Steven. It means that Terry set up a meeting about a script and I'm here."

"Whatever, whatever . . ." Steven said gently. "No need to get pissed."

"I'm not pissed. You just seem surprised that I'm here," I said. "Why should you be? Terry set this meeting up. Why would you be surprised that I would show up to a meeting?"

"Well, I thought you might've been hungover from Homecoming," Steven said. "You went to Homecoming, right?"

I stared at him. I didn't say anything. He stared back.

"What does Homecoming have to do with anything?" I asked.

"Was it fun?" he asked. "Did you and Debbie have fun?"

I didn't say anything. I wanted to look anywhere else but at the death mask that was Steven Reinhardt's face. I kept calm, though a twisting anger was trying to break through the Valium haze. "Yeah," I finally said with no emotion. "It was fun."

He gestured to the bar. "Did you have . . . a drink?"

"Um, I just, um, had a ginger ale," I stammered. "I'm fine."

"You should've probably had a drink," he murmured.

"I didn't want a drink, Steven," I said, calmly.

"Hey, Gene." Steven motioned to the bartender. "Put it on Terry's tab."

The bartender shook his head while wiping a glass. "On the house."

This was my cue to stand and I did so hesitantly. I suddenly realized something. "Where are we going?" I asked.

Steven just said, "I'm taking you to Terry."

"Aren't we having the meeting in the Polo Lounge? I thought we were having the meeting in the Polo Lounge."

Something slightly snapped in Steven and in retrospect I realize that it was my naïveté that annoyed him. "No, you're not having your *meet-ing* with Terry in the Polo Lounge, Bret." He started walking out into the lobby. I followed him.

"Where are we having the meeting?" I asked as Steven pushed open a glass door that led to a pink pathway just outside the entrance of the Polo Lounge next to a pair of elevator banks locked in the wallpaper swathed with banana palms, and just around the corner was that endless and deserted corridor.

"Your 'meeting,' your 'meeting,'" he said. "What do you think your meeting is about, Bret?" He turned his head, smiling, as he glanced at me.

"I think it's about a script Terry wants me to write," I said. "I've got an idea."

The pathway kept winding and flora was draped everywhere and vines of bougainvillea exploded across the banana leaves. Steven didn't say anything, just kept walking forward along the pink path.

"Where are we going?" I asked again, this time trying to sound casual—the Valium helped but I was realizing not only that there had been a change of venue but also perhaps what the meaning of the meeting itself was and there seemed to be a new sense of purpose about what I was doing at the Beverly Hills Hotel at four o'clock on a Sunday afternoon. Or maybe I was hearing things that weren't really there.

"Terry wants to take the meeting in the bungalow," Steven said.

"What bungalow?" I asked.

We had suddenly stopped in front of what looked like the façade of a faded pink cottage. A simple set of steps led to a white door with green trim.

"Is this normal?" I asked. "Does Terry usually do this?"

Steven was facing me when he asked: "Is there something wrong?" He stopped. "You seem confused."

"No," I said. "But I didn't think we were going to have a meeting in a hotel room—"

"It's a bungalow," Steven said. "It's not a hotel room—"

"If I had been told this I would have worn something more casual—"

"You look fine," Steven said. "A little overeager but fine."

"Why doesn't he just take the meetings at Stone Canyon, then?" I asked.

"He always books a bungalow on weekends instead," Steven said. "And because Debbie and Liz are in the house on Stone Canyon—"

"But Debbie is at the stables today—"

"Bret—" Steven warned quietly.

"What about the offices?" I asked. "On Wilshire?"

"It's the weekend." Steven shrugged. "It's a Sunday," he said pointedly, as if this meant something I couldn't grasp.

"Quite a little chatterbox today, aren't you?" Steven said. "Got your big movie idea all ready for Terry? You going to pitch your new script?"

"I have an idea," I said defensively. "I just don't understand why we're not in the Polo Lounge."

Two older men wearing tennis shorts with sweaters tied across their shoulders were walking along the pink path and checked me out as they passed us. I should have been flattered but in that moment I was just grossed out. Steven waited until they were out of earshot and then said: "Look, you're at the Beverly Hills Hotel on a Sunday afternoon meeting Terry Schaffer. You got yourself all dressed up. You're so eager. You're so willing. I warned you not to take any of this seriously. And yet you're still here." Steven shrugged. "I really thought that you wouldn't show up. That you understood something."

I just stared at him. "Like . . . what?" I asked, completely confused. "Look, Steven, I don't want any problems between us. I'm just trying to figure something out."

The SHARDS

"What are you trying to figure out, Bret?" Steven asked and perhaps for the first moment of that afternoon was genuinely curious as to what I was going to say.

But I realized that I was very relaxed due to the Valium and that not only did I have no idea what I was trying to figure out but I also didn't care. In that moment I understood I was going to have to let it play out—whatever it was. This was suddenly so funny to me that I couldn't help but laugh. Steven stared while I put my hands on my hips and looked around, laughing softly to myself. I was laughing at me, at Steven, at the implausibility of the new location, the situation itself. I had opened a door and I was going to walk through it and I knew what the possibilities were and I went in anyway.

"You think this is funny?" Steven asked. "Good. That's good."

Steven waited for me to say something and I didn't and then he turned and led me to the door of the cottage, which I realized was the bungalow that Terry was waiting in. "Terry's on the patio, probably still on the phone," Steven said. "Make yourself comfortable." And then he added, before turning away, "Go with the flow."

I MOVED SLOWLY into the bungalow and shut the door behind me. The room I walked into was spread out with thick white carpeting and the walls were painted a pale green. There was a room-service cart with an opened bottle of champagne in an ice bucket, Dom Pérignon, along with three crystal flutes. Pink curtains patterned with the trademark banana-palm fronds were draped over the windows, darkening the living room, which was softly lit with recessed lighting, and where two sofas sat across from each other, lined with pastel pillows, divided by a glass coffee table on which a vase of pink roses sat, and then past the living room was a dining area I moved through, brightly lit because the windows were open, and then I was peering into a room, where there was a king-sized bed and a TV on a stand—a football game was playing with the sound off—and the bedsheets were the same pale green as the satin headboard, and the shutters were closed and latched but the slats were open, allowing a faint breeze in. I remember that I noticed there were ashtrays everywhere though Terry didn't smoke: on all the tables, on the nightstands in the bedroom, on the bar, on the desk, on the small dining table. I moved down another hallway, where I could hear Terry's voice more clearly, and followed the sound, passing through a kitchen where a door opened onto a patio. Terry was on the phone, the cord trailing behind him, wearing sandals and a very short robe that almost resembled a white toga, and his Porsche Carrera sunglasses were on even though the patio was shaded by the tropical flora that draped over it blocking out the sun and he was smoking a joint, a half-empty flute of the Dom in his other hand. He noticed me, smiled as if surprised, held the receiver away from his mouth, and said quietly, "Help yourself to a drink."

I nodded and then moved back through the kitchen and into the living room and switched on a chrome lamp with a white shade by the bar and sat on one of four stools lining the marble countertop, where a bowl of chrysanthemums glowed dimly. I looked over the shelf of bottles and realized I didn't want a drink—I didn't need any alcohol, the Valium was enough. Why was Terry wearing that robe? I thought to myself. It really sucked that he thought something was going to happen with me, and yet Steven Reinhardt was correct in his assumptions: I was here, I drove myself here, I walked with Steven to the bungalow, I closed the door behind me. *Go with the flow.* I eventually poured myself half a glass of the champagne and took a single sip while my eyes scanned the room: a painting of a peacock, a drawing of lilies. And then I realized that Terry had followed me in when I looked up at the mirror behind the bar, and he was watching me intently, still on the phone, listening to whoever was on the other end of the line. I became self-conscious and though I wasn't actually going to drink the champagne I downed the glass and poured myself another, tipping the glass as my parents had taught me so the flute wouldn't foam over. I drank half that as well and started getting buzzed. I'd known automatically that something was off about the setup—the bungalow instead of the Polo Lounge, Terry's robe, the open bottle of champagne—but I didn't leave because I was moving into the world of adults and I wanted to find out what would happen to me.

—

The SHARDS

TERRY MOVED BACK into the kitchen to hang up the phone and then he was gliding toward the middle of the living room. He took me in and smiled, stoned. "You made it, I'm glad. You look great." Terry held his empty flute with a steady hand as he poured himself another glass of champagne and then sat down on the couch facing the bar, where I was now standing and gently lowered myself back onto one of the stools, across the room from him. And then I realized where this afternoon was supposed to land in Terry's mind when I saw that he wasn't wearing a bathing suit or a pair of underwear beneath the robe. Terry had taken off the sunglasses and smiled boyishly at me—he wasn't faggy or fey but the robe and the somewhat visible genitalia were not bringing me over to his side of the aisle; they had the opposite of the intended effect and I became briefly angry at myself for being there, but I was mildly high on Valium and, along with the champagne, I felt a kind of peace in letting go.

"How are you doing, Bret?" Terry asked. "Everything okay?"

"I'm . . . okay," I said. And then realized that I was going to play the sympathy card to disarm him and it came so easily because it was genuine: if I wanted to in that moment I could have easily burst into tears about Matt Kellner. I was suddenly emotional and I said his name. I told Terry that I'd been thinking about him while waiting in the Polo Lounge. And that it was hard.

"Who?" Terry asked. He was busy relighting the joint. "Matt?"

"Um, Matt Kellner. He was in our class," I said. "At Buckley. He recently died."

"Oh, right, right," Terry said, realizing. "Debbie mentioned that to me. He overdosed? What happened?"

"Actually, I think he drowned. I don't know—"

"Drowned?" Terry asked, taken aback. "How did he drown?"

"Accidentally," I said. "Or so they think." I paused. "Maybe it was an overdose," I muttered. "No one knows."

"Well, let's not be a downer, because that's not what we're here for," Terry said. "It happened. I'm sorry. But you need to focus on the future."

"Well, that's why I'm here," I said, sipping from the flute.

"You want a real drink?" Terry asked.

"I really don't even want this one," I said, placing the flute on the bar.

"You want a hit?" he asked, offering me the joint.

"No, I'm okay." I was scanning the living room of the bungalow. "This is nice."

"Yeah," Terry said. "My home away from home."

"Why didn't we take the meeting in the Polo Lounge?" I asked.

Terry stared at me with a slight grin as if this was a question he hadn't expected, and didn't say anything until, "I like it here, more comfortable, more privacy."

"Terry, let's just talk about the script," I said. "Because nothing's going to happen. I know you think it might happen but it's not." I looked around the room and then landed on him. "I'm here to talk about a script."

"Really?" Terry asked, seriously. "What's not going to happen?" He mimicked someone confused.

I sighed theatrically. "I thought you wanted to talk about a script. I thought that was what the meeting was about."

"I do, I do," he said. "Let's talk about it."

"I mean if I made a mistake and you want me to go . . ." I trailed off, leaving the sentence unfinished.

I stared at him and he stared back and then he started laughing. "I'm sorry, I'm sorry," he was saying. "It's just that I don't know what you were expecting." He paused. "I don't really know what you're talking about." I just stared at him with an utter blankness. "I mean, I guess this was a bit of a dare on my part. But I didn't really think you'd think . . ."

A blush had swept across me, and it felt as if my entire body had reddened.

"You didn't really think what?" I asked.

"I guess I was just fooling around and I didn't think you would take it so seriously," he said.

"You thought this was all a joke?" I asked.

"No, Bret, no, not at all," Terry said, registering my hurt. "Of course, I'm interested in a script—"

"But, then, what's the problem?"

"There's no problem . . ." Terry stopped. "Okay, tell me what the script is about."

"You don't really want to hear it, do you?" I said, sighing.

"You're in a kind of self-defeating mood," he said, and downed the champagne. "Look, we're here, I'm here, we're having a meeting, I want to hear about the idea you have for the script." He paused. "But come over here. I can barely see you." He gestured at the couch across from the one he was sitting on. I hesitantly pushed away from the stool and started walking across the room, but before sitting down poured myself another glass of champagne. Terry had crossed his legs and pulled the hem of the robe tight over his thighs so that nothing was visible. "I'm listening," he said gently. "Tell me a story."

I WAS CALM ENOUGH to start telling Terry about the movie I'd been envisioning in my mind for the past few weeks but realized about five minutes in that I actually hadn't fully thought it out to the degree where I could coherently tell it to someone. The Valium and champagne emboldened me to start thinking out loud as I moved the characters from the beginning of the movie until its violent ending but I kept going back and re-explaining incidents from different angles, and what made this worse was how authoritative I tried to sound, almost as if I was the director and suggesting particular ways scenes should be shot and how I pictured certain camera movements. Terry listened to the whole thing, occasionally nodding, or pointing something out that contradicted what I'd said previously. There was the moment when I tried to explain a dolly shot and realized Terry had zoned out and was patiently waiting for me to wrap it up, but I hadn't thought about how to wrap it up and I started punctuating the pitch with "But maybe this could happen instead" and when I glanced at my watch I was embarrassed to see that I'd sucked up thirty minutes of our time with this gibberish. I might have been thinking about this idea for weeks—and at some points I thought what I'd constructed would make an amazing movie—but now, sitting on the sofa across from Terry in a bungalow at the Beverly Hills Hotel, I realized that the whole thing was preposterous, a truly lame idea, and I quickly ended the pitch—I actually said, "The End." Terry was frozen with boredom and slow to react—it seemed as if he was politely trying to think of something nice to say. I had finished the champagne and needed to use the restroom—an escape. Terry just sat there, smiled tightly and said there was one around the corner in the bedroom.

I stood up, my legs wobbled, and then I walked through a hallway and into the bedroom, where I stood still in front of the breeze coming through an opened slat from the shutters. In the bathroom it seemed like I pissed endlessly, and then flushed the toilet and washed my hands while looking at myself in the mirror. You did this to yourself, I thought. You ended up here. No one forced you. No one held a gun up to your head. You wanted to come.

WHEN I LEFT the bathroom Terry was standing in the doorway of the bedroom. I stopped. Again I felt the breeze touch my face as it floated through the slats of the opened shutters.

"Okay," he said flatly. "I like it. You want to make a deal?"

I was stunned, then flooded with relief. "You liked it?"

"Yeah," Terry said. "There's something there."

"Really?" I slowly nodded.

"So—do you want to make a deal or not?"

"Yeah, sure," I said, hoping I didn't sound too eager.

"That was thirty minutes of my time," he said. "And now I want thirty minutes of yours."

There was a silence. "What does that mean?" I mumbled. I knew exactly what he meant but I just wanted to postpone the reality of the situation.

"*Quid pro quo.*" He shrugged.

"What does that mean?" I asked again, staring at him from across the room.

"Why don't you get comfortable," he said—it wasn't a suggestion.

"I . . . am comfortable," I said.

"Why don't you lose the jacket," Terry said flatly.

I automatically took the jacket off and tossed it onto an armchair I was standing next to. I realized I'd been sweating during the pitch and my underarms and back were damp with perspiration.

"And you can take off the shirt, too," he said.

The SHARDS

He took a step into the room, watching me.

I unbuttoned the shirt and tossed it onto the jacket.

Terry dispassionately looked me over as if inspecting a delicate object that he wasn't quite sure he was interested in and then took another step into the room, closer to the bed. He kicked off his sandals. I waited. I just stood there, my arms hanging limply by my sides, not knowing what to do next. I could have made this more playful—flexed, laughed, jumped on the bed, eager to consummate the deal—instead of coming off as, Terry intimated earlier, a downer, but I just wanted to get it over with and I didn't want to hear his voice instructing me what to do. I kicked the Topsiders off and then unzipped the jeans and tossed them onto the armchair with the shirt and the jacket, until I was just standing in my jockey shorts in front of Terry. He walked over and untied the belt of his robe and I averted my eyes so that I was only looking at his face—I didn't want to see his body, his chest, his dick. Without saying anything, he pulled me up against him and roughly kissed my mouth and I let him at first but, tasting an acrid combination of weed and champagne, I pushed him firmly away. He grinned, and placed his hands on my chest, lighting squeezing my pecs, and then playfully shoved me. I lost my balance and fell onto the bed, where Terry pulled down my underwear and I accommodated him, lifting my feet off the floor so he could remove them completely, and then he immediately got on his knees as I stared at the ceiling—I hadn't felt any real excitement even though I got fully hard as Terry kept sucking and stroking my cock. I lifted my head and glimpsed his body—he was thin and tan and basically in good shape and, writing this now, I realize he looked younger than he actually was. On a surface level he was attractive for his age but he was just too old for me to even contemplate as a realistic sex partner when I was seventeen, and yet there I was: lying on the green sheets as he devoured my cock, slapping it against his face, deep-throating and inhaling it. After what seemed like a couple of minutes he grabbed my hips and rolled me onto my stomach and then lifted my ass up and I felt the stubble around his mouth and then his tongue. This went on for what seemed like minutes as well until he suddenly pushed a finger deep inside me and I reached around and grabbed his wrist, which slipped from my grasp as he stood and began rubbing his cock against my asshole, trying to push it in, pressing it against the anus he had just wetted with his saliva, and then Terry slipped two fingers deeply into me and it hurt and I grabbed his wrist again and forced him to pull his hand away. I rolled onto my back. He pushed my legs up until my knees were suddenly touching my chest and I said "No" and kicked away.

It was completely silent except for the breeze teasing the trees outside the bungalow as I looked over at the football game playing on the TV until Terry repositioned himself on the bed and started sucking my cock while he rammed himself down my throat—we were in a 69 position. He was pumping too hard or maybe he was too excited and couldn't help himself or maybe this was how older guys did it—roughly, dispassionately—I'd only been with Matt and Ryan. I grabbed his hips to steady him so that I could breathe but then he was ejaculating and I felt, then tasted, the semen shooting down my throat and coating my mouth, his balls pressed against my nostrils. He groaned deeply with my cock in his mouth as he came and then continued sucking me off as I pulled my head away and his already softening penis slipped out, and then I surprised myself as I started climaxing—my orgasm had come from nowhere, it hadn't built, I barely knew it was arriving, my legs were spread and Terry had two fingers pushed deep inside me. And then it was over. Terry swallowed all of it.

He rolled off me onto his back and waited until his panting subsided. Terry wiped a hand across his mouth and started laughing good-naturedly and looked at me as he said, glassy-eyed, "That was intense." I tried to sound enthusiastic when I responded, "Yeah," as I pushed myself off the bed and walked to the bathroom, where I closed the door, then sat on the toilet and wiped Terry's saliva off my asshole. When I looked at the piece of tissue I noticed there was a small streak of blood from where his fingernail had scratched my rectum. I dampened a Kleenex and wiped again until there was no more blood. I washed my mouth out with warm water and then stared at my face in the mirror. I looked not only remarkably composed but as if I'd actually accomplished something—it wasn't what I wanted but it wasn't so bad. I was okay. I took a deep breath and walked back into the bedroom naked, relieved that Terry wasn't there. I could hear his voice from outside—he had returned to the patio and was on the phone. I picked up my jockey shorts off the floor and pulled them on and after getting dressed walked through the hallway to the kitchen and leaned out to where Terry was sitting at a table: the robe was on, there was a fresh glass of champagne, another joint had been lit, Herb Alpert's "Rise" was playing from somewhere. I offered a wave and a smile, gesturing that I had to go. He nodded and said, "We'll talk soon, Bret, thank you," and then I was walking through the darkened living room and out the front door to the pink pathway that would take me back to the lobby of the hotel. I passed the Polo Lounge, then moved under the canopy to the valet, tipped him, and then drove aimlessly until I returned to the empty house on Mulholland. It was barely five o'clock by the time I left the hotel. Everything had happened within the space of an hour.

Neither Terry Schaffer nor I would know what was happening outside the window of the bedroom while the two of us had sex that afternoon in early October: we didn't know that somewhere deep in the flora on the grounds of the Beverly Hills Hotel I'd been photographed walking into Terry's bungalow and neither of us could hear the rapid clicking and the whir of a camera that was aimed at the bed Terry and I were lying on through the open slats of the shutters that lined the bedroom's windows. We would find this out later, as the fall of 1981 moved inexorably toward its ironic and tragic conclusion.

16

THE PARTY SUSAN REYNOLDS was throwing "secretly" for
Robert Mallory became the main distraction that following week at
Buckley. The party was coming up on Saturday after having been postponed twice: once because of Matt Kellner's death and the other time
for Homecoming. But when that night in mid-October finally arrived
I'm not sure if Robert Mallory was completely unaware that Susan
was throwing the party for him, which she had told Thom Wright and
Debbie Schaffer and myself weeks ago, in early September, when she
mentioned throwing a party specifically for him as a way of making
this new student feel comfortable and accepted by his classmates.
The party seemed like a plot to disarm Robert Mallory, since we'd
found out that he spent six months in a mental institution outside of
Jacksonville, Illinois—and for me, and not Susan or Thom or Debbie,
the party suggested that Robert was too *delicate* and we needed to
be so *careful* and we should *placate* him even though we didn't quite
know what was wrong with him yet. Why had he been in the developmental center? What had he done that placed him there? Was it
only depression and mild usage of marijuana and hallucinogens? Was
it due to the aftermath of his mother's death and the frustration he
felt toward his father and the new wife? Or was it something darker
that Robert could never admit to us and that we would never fully
know? And yet the inner voice of the tangible participant argued:
how bad could it have really been if he'd only spent six months there
and been released last summer and was now wandering among us in
sunny L.A.? The rest of the senior class, I'm supposing, didn't know
anything about this angle, and yet I think Robert sensed something

about the party by the time it finally happened and maybe he had already *learned* about it from someone in particular, confirming that this was, indeed, the case: the party is being thrown for *you,* Robert, by Susan Reynolds in order for *you* to feel accepted because—and here was the dark truth—she has feelings for you.

Why would anyone, at this point, think that Susan Reynolds would be the cheerleader for a charity event when the community had already embraced Robert Mallory? The semester was flying by and in the six weeks since Robert arrived at Buckley he *had* been accepted, even desired, by the entirety of the twelfth grade and admired by all the other classes even though, I noticed, he did absolutely nothing to encourage this—he just passively accepted it. In mid-autumn he was simply very popular: besides his handsomeness—like Thom Wright he could look rugged and masculine and then, depending on an expression or emotion, sensitive and almost boyish—there was a quiet mystery about him that girls were almost instantaneously attracted to and gossiped about, and it also helped that Thom Wright actually liked Robert and it seemed they were becoming friends in ways that I might have expected—and dreaded—when they first met on that Tuesday in September, but this burgeoning friendship that I really hadn't been paying attention to had suddenly happened, and it gave off a signal to the rest of the student body, confirming: Hey, if Robert's my friend he's okay. *He's just another God, like me.* That week before the party I kept calling the number I'd found in Matt Kellner's drawer with the letters *RM* next to it and nobody ever picked up and there wasn't an answering machine where I could leave a message.

THAT WEEK FOUND ME in another dazed moment and it had nothing to do with what had happened at the Beverly Hills Hotel with Terry Schaffer, which hadn't bothered me in any substantial way, and I wasn't shocked how easily I could compartmentalize it: yes, I was technically "underage" but no one had hurt me, I hadn't been assaulted, I let it happen, I made it easier for Terry to take my underwear off and bring me to an orgasm, and I really had no feelings either way about what transpired in the bedroom of the bungalow on that Sunday in October. I simply hoped it would lead to a scriptwriting gig but there was the possibility that it wouldn't: that the offer had been ephemeral, a tease, a ploy to let him taste my cock and rim me, suck me off and fuck my mouth. I wasn't going to get pushy about the *quid pro quo* of it or use what I thought was my advantage over Terry by threatening to relay it to his daughter if he didn't acquiesce to my demands, because I soon realized Terry and I had a shared list of *dis*advantages to worry about if Debbie was ever told or found out about the relationship between myself and her father. And I needed Debbie my senior year and I *was* going to try harder to be that caring boyfriend she so badly desired, though there were parts of that other boyfriend—the colder, distant one—that I think she also responded to. But I had to keep track of my aloofness because sometimes I could so easily slip into the role of the zombie she'd identified that week in early September and had called me out on even though there was something about my cold disregard that I knew excited her as well. I would play the role as best I could in order to please her and become the tangible participant whenever she was around. But in that dazed week before Susan's party Debbie was always at the Windover Stables training with Spirit and I don't remember seeing her that much in the days after I'd met her father at the Beverly Hills Hotel.

I may have barely made it through the week without collapsing but by Friday afternoon the rest of my classmates were excited and buzzing over the party. Susan's parents weren't going to be there. Susan had invited a group of good-looking and popular juniors. Susan told people to bring their bathing suits if they wanted to dip into the pool or Jacuzzi. Susan was having the party catered: chopped salads from La Scala, platters of nigiri delivered from Teru Sushi. A few people were going to spend the night, including Thom, even though his mom's house was also in the flats of Beverly Hills, barely ten blocks away, and so was Debbie, and Jeff and Tracy were invited as well as myself, and Robert. But I was noncommittal and told Susan "Maybe." I heard nothing from Terry or Steven Reinhardt that week and I barely noticed Ryan Vaughn or the absence of Matt because something else happened that erased everything and it became my focal point in those days leading up to Susan's party: another girl had disappeared.

—

The SHARDS

IT WAS ON MONDAY MORNING that I found out about the missing girl in an article in the *Los Angeles Times*. My alarm had gone off at seven-thirty and I stared at the ceiling in the empty house on Mulholland, and realized after several minutes passed while I lay immobile on the king-sized bed that I was allowing myself to creep closer toward that widening despair I could so easily fall into if I didn't combat it by becoming the tangible participant. I heaved myself off the bed and opened the bedroom door. Shingy scrambled onto the lawn and I swam a number of laps, letting the pool's cold water awaken and distract me from the gathering ennui. I took a long hot shower and got dressed, mentally preparing myself for the day—the weeks, the endless months—ahead. I didn't turn on the TV or play any music as I looked over whatever homework I'd completed the night before— despite what went down in the bungalow I was decidedly calm and easily concentrated on the assignments that were due the following day—and then placed my textbooks in the Gucci backpack and walked down the hallway to the kitchen, where I greeted Rosa with a smile I hoped wasn't too forced. She was standing in front of the opened refrigerator compiling a list when I asked her if she could make me an omelet *por favor.* The *Los Angeles Times* was sitting on the island along with a stack of magazines she'd retrieved from the mailbox at the end of the driveway: *Time, Newsweek, Rolling Stone, Vogue, GQ*: on its cover Michael Schoeffling's handsome face briefly distracted me.

I poured myself a glass of orange juice and unfolded the *L.A. Times* and immediately saw in the bottom right-hand corner on the front page a photo of a local teenage girl and the announcement that Audrey Barbour, age seventeen, had been missing for three days. It took a stunned moment for the light chill of dread to get activated when I realized this was probably the Trawler's next victim, and I automatically wondered where she was right now, if she was already dead or being kept alive somewhere, bound and tortured and bleeding out. I became lightly nauseated when I smelled the omelet that was now being prepared on the stove adjacent to the island where I stood and realized there was no way I'd be able to eat it. I heard something pop out of the toaster and then a plate was placed next to the paper I was staring at as Rosa told me about all the things she needed to get done today, but I could barely hear her as my eyes scanned the article.

AUDREY BARBOUR HAD BEEN with a group of friends at the Promenade mall in Woodland Hills on Friday night when she announced she was leaving. She wanted to go home and watch the fifth-season premiere of *Dallas*, which would reveal the identity of the dead woman floating in the Southfork swimming pool that ended the fourth-season finale last spring, and Audrey didn't want it taped— she wanted to watch the episode as it aired. She left the group and apparently walked through the lot behind the mall where her car was parked, at around nine. A couple entering the Robinson's that anchored the south end of the mall told the police they had passed by the girl as she was leaving, which corroborated a time line established by the group of friends. Audrey didn't make it back to her parents' house in Calabasas by nine-thirty, which they thought was unlike her since Audrey stressed she would be home by then to take a shower and get ready to watch *Dallas* at ten, and yet she hadn't called from the Promenade telling them she would be staying out later than she initially thought and asking her father to tape the show for her. Audrey Barbour was pretty in the same generic ways Katherine Latchford and Julie Selwyn and Sarah Johnson were but on that Monday, in the article I read, she hadn't been "officially" tied to the girls and linked to the Trawler, even though later that week it would be discovered that two dogs had gone missing in the Bell Canyon neighborhood, near where she lived, days before her disappearance, but Audrey's parents didn't remember anything about furniture being rearranged or the sense that anyone had entered the house or that their daughter had been targeted by someone, and the only home invasion and subsequent assault that matched the Trawler's style in that general area had happened in the faraway summer of 1980.

However, later that week Audrey Barbour's friends confirmed that Audrey had told them about the phone calls she was receiving on her private line because Audrey had been so curiously compelled by them; her parents knew nothing about the phone calls. It was rare but not unusual in 1981 for certain teenagers to have their own phone lines; Matt Kellner had one, Debbie Schaffer had one, as did Susan Reynolds and Thom Wright and myself, as well as Robert Mallory, I suspected. Audrey had been annoyed by the phone calls at first, the silences punctuated by heavy breathing and sighs, but once the irritation subsided she started to actually talk to the silence on the other end of the line, admitting things, chatting about guys she thought were hot, sometimes mentioning a sexual fantasy to whoever she was now flirting with on the other end—and she admitted to her friends that she thought she could hear the person masturbating because of the wet sounds and the animal panting, and sometimes she thought it was two people. Audrey Barbour's friends said that there were no actual conversations, because the person on the phone never spoke. Often Audrey would waste an afternoon just waiting for the unknown person to call so she could tell it about her day and talk about cute boys and tease it with insinuations.

IN THE *LOS ANGELES TIMES* article there was the first mention of a poster, but no one had connected the meaning of the poster Audrey Barbour received with the other posters and it became an odd detail hanging there—so specific that it seemed meaningless to add into an article where so much was unknown and unresolved: a "gift" had been left on the front porch of the house in Bell Canyon, a poster for the record *Entertainment!* It was by Gang of Four, a band that Audrey hadn't even particularly liked and only knew a song or two from; she thought, according to her friends, that the "secret admirer"—this was what she now called him—had left it for her. No one had found out that this was part of the targeting: the delivery of the posters to homes of potential victims. When I read that detail about the poster I immediately wondered: who left the poster in the mailbox on Haskell Avenue for Matt Kellner? And then I asked myself: if you received a poster did that mean you died? Or were there teenagers all over L.A. the Trawler was targeting and leaving the posters for regardless of whether he was going to kill them or not? When Audrey hadn't made it home to watch *Dallas* that night her parents called all of her friends but it was a Friday and none of them were home, and when the Barbours finally drove out to the Promenade, long after it closed, they found their daughter's white VW Rabbit sitting alone beneath the sodium glow of an arc light in the vast parking lot. Audrey Barbour had never made it to her car.

I REALIZED at a certain point I hadn't touched the omelet or the piece of buttered wheat toast next to it and when I tried to take a bite I just gagged and spit it into a napkin. I pushed away from the island and walked slowly to the garage without saying goodbye to Rosa and sat in the driver's seat of the 450SL and waited until I became motivated to switch on the ignition and pull the car out of the driveway and pass the boxwood hedge and merge with the traffic racing along Mulholland and focus on the road taking me down into the Valley and the gates of Buckley. But the disappearance of Audrey Barbour kept distracting me and it changed everything that week. As did the fact that Robert Mallory wasn't on Gilley Field last Friday night. He had left around six o'clock, when it was getting dark, and I'd seen him leave. I watched from the other end of the senior float as Robert said something to Thom Wright, who was on a stepladder realigning the buildings that were supposed to replicate Stansbury Avenue, and the two of them talked softly for half a minute and then Robert left after Thom nodded. Thom turned his attention back to the float and after a moment looked up. I hadn't realized I was still staring at Robert over Thom's shoulder as he walked across the baseball field to the hill leading down to the parking lot. But Thom thought I was staring at him and just flashed a Thom Wright smile at me, white and beaming with reassurance, while he adjusted a papier-mâché palm tree. Why had I thought in that moment—and the thought arrived instantly, unbidden—Thom Wright was doomed?

IN THE WEEK LEADING UP TO SUSAN'S PARTY I kept reading various articles about the disappearance of Audrey Barbour in both the *Los Angeles Times* and the *Herald Examiner* and was automatically aware of the connection the media were making between the Trawler and the missing girl even though the Trawler never called anyone that week—not the LAPD or the *Los Angeles Times*—to own responsibility for the disappearance, which wasn't necessarily unusual, because the self-described monster and "his friends" usually called *after* he dumped their bodies at a specific site—though both the LAPD and the *L.A. Times* admitted that week there had been phone calls from the suspect during the weeks Julie Selwyn and Sarah Johnson were missing, but not Katherine Latchford. The local media convinced themselves that Audrey Barbour was the fourth victim of the serial killer and this was more or less the confirmed narrative the week after her disappearance even if the LAPD said they were not "leaping to that particular conclusion at all," because there was still hope she would be found, and they reminded everyone that it was very early in the investigation. And yet it seemed so plausible that the Trawler had caused this girl to vanish and was out there somewhere torturing her to death if she wasn't already killed. I don't know why I was naïve enough to assume that the disappearance of Audrey Barbour would in some way distract or worry my classmates at Buckley. But no one talked about it. No one seemed to care. Another girl had disappeared, but girls were disappearing all the time, some of them ran away, some of them were found dead, some never came back—another missing girl just didn't have the effect I thought it would, especially among the females I knew who were the same age. They were seemingly invincible at seventeen, just as I'm sure Audrey Barbour and Katherine Latchford and Julie Selwyn and Sarah Johnson had felt. Our odds looked good: we were young and alive and strong and nothing could hurt us, and there wasn't anything clouding this perception, a fable about our place in the world, and we ignored the intrusive notions of fate and horror and hideous death that might kidnap us from the golden dome of adolescence we resided under.

THAT WAS THE WEEK I became reminded how astrology affected the populace, when one of Audrey Barbour's friends said Audrey's "rising sign" indicated "danger perhaps" in the ensuing days after the disappearance, and it was revealed that Audrey Barbour was a Libra and obsessed with astrology and wore a gold ankh around her neck, which was visible in the junior yearbook photo that was printed everywhere. These believers also included Susan Reynolds and Debbie Schaffer, who both dabbled in Sydney Omarr's annual paperback forecasts and often referred to these yearly charts' confirmation of the luck of certain dates with an alarming frequency—or so I thought—even though both girls admitted there was a campy element to astrology they didn't take too seriously. It *was* an entertainment, they stressed. But I also thought, at times, it actually guided them, as well as many other students in our class: there was, in 1981, an Astrology Club at Buckley. Other people I knew from that era heavily invested in astrology included my father, who also believed in biorhythms, which, like astrology, was a kind of pseudo-science about how our lives were significantly affected by rhythmic cycles and there was a calculator you had to purchase that prefigured where your physical and emotional and intellectual states could potentially land after you entered certain info into the calculator. My father was an atheist and yet enamored by the religion of astrology and it suggests something about him that I thought I'd never seen but now realize, writing this, was always visible: a childlike lostness.

Susan and Debbie bought into the notion that the seventeenth was a "positive" night to host an event because of something foretold in Susan's copy of the Sydney Omarr Cancer forecast for 1981—and yet they never spoke about the disappearance of Audrey Barbour. The relative positions of constellations and lunar cycles indicated it had been a bad week for Audrey Barbour and yet a good week for Susan Reynolds, who was throwing a party for the boy who, in my mind, had abducted Audrey from a parking lot in Woodland Hills.

MEXICAN FAN PALMS animated by ground lamps lined the pathway made of bluestone steps leading up to the tall black-enameled doors of the house on North Canon Drive, brightly lit, with music faintly emanating from somewhere behind it. The living room was made up entirely of white marble and I saw it behind me as I caught a glimpse of myself in a massive gilt-framed mirror that hung in the foyer. The living room was entirely white—the couches, the armchairs, the coffee table, the wet bar lined with four leather stools—and gave off an immaculate sci-fi vibe, as if it was a movie set no one inhabited. It embodied a starkness that was incongruous with how friendly both Donald and Gayle Reynolds always seemed to me throughout the time I'd known Susan, but the house, which they'd moved into three years ago and which was specifically redesigned by Gayle, suggested something about Susan's mother that I'd never quite grasped previously and Susan had always hinted at: her mother could be a cold bitch. The upstairs of the house, by comparison, was warmer, even old-fashioned, with plush green shag carpeting and playful wallpaper and framed posters of movies that Donald, an entertainment lawyer, had worked on and five homey bedrooms, which always reminded me that the house was too large and ostentatious for a family of three— Susan used one of the extra bedrooms as her closet. Donald and Gayle had departed for Palm Springs on Friday to spend the weekend with Susan's grandparents who lived in the Canyon Estates, not far from my aunt's house on South Toledo near the Indian Canyons Golf Resort, so the party that night would be unsupervised by adults, which had begun to seem necessary as we neared the cusp of becoming seniors that summer. And so far nothing bad had happened at the parties that weren't chaperoned by adults. We had become the chaperones. We were becoming the adults.

I MADE MY WAY from the empty living room to the kitchen after reminding myself the party was taking place in the backyard and passed the long granite counter lined with tequila bottles where Bruce Johnson and Nancy Dalloway were busy making margaritas in two blenders and filling plastic cups rimmed with salt that they placed on a tray Michelle Stevenson took outside to the backyard. On the kitchen table were the boxes of chopped salad waiting to be dressed and mixed, along with platters of glistening sushi. I opened the refrigerator to find a soda but it was almost completely stacked with Coronas and I didn't see any Coke or 7Up, and after opting for a beer I said hi to Bruce and Nancy, who hadn't noticed me previously, and then stepped into the backyard. The Tom Petty and Stevie Nicks duet "Stop Draggin' My Heart Around" which had been so popular that summer was playing from outside speakers and there were only about twenty people standing around and even though it was mid-October you could still sense traces of night-blooming jasmine, and the massive bougainvillea that sat off to one side of the yard was now dotted with a multitude of white Christmas lights and since it was a cool autumn evening the pool was heated and steam from its surface kept rising upward in tendrils toward the eucalyptus trees that bordered the brightly lit rectangle of blue water and obscured the darkened tennis court beyond it.

ROBERT MALLORY SIMPLY APPEARED first in my line of vision: like me, he had gotten a haircut, and was wearing a sky-blue Polo shirt with the collar up tucked into a pair of tight Calvin Klein jeans and Topsiders. He stood with Thom and Susan and Jeff and Tracy, and looked so innocent that his handsomeness was a force, something pure and undeniable—this was a truth people responded to regardless of what he was hiding. I was again reminded that I never had a casual reaction when I saw him: I was always jolted whenever he appeared, fear mingling with lust, horniness blinding me to the awful possibilities of this person, this form, and it was something I realized would either go away (which was a lie, because I had similar feelings about Thom and I'd known him for almost six years) or I'd have to accept Robert and get used to the fear and desire until we graduated. Thom was saying something to the group, gesturing with his arms, and this was making everyone laugh except Susan, who seemed to just smile politely, slightly dazed, wearing a skirt from Fred Segal and a tight pink Lacoste shirt accentuating her breasts and unbuttoned so that the deep line of cleavage was clearly visible. And then Robert was adding onto whatever Thom was saying and the group laughed again and it sounded real and not fake, as if everyone had fully bought into the idea of Robert Mallory—the idea he had *sold* them on—and I realized I'd been too preoccupied to notice how close they'd all become in the past few weeks because I was lost in my own daydreams.

I watched Debbie walk out from the opened French doors by the side of the house, near the laundry room, where a small guest bathroom was located, lightly wiping her nose, eyes glittering, and joining the group beneath the massive bougainvillea. I turned away, almost tripping over a silver tub filled with Coronas lodged in a small mountain of crushed ice.

THE PRETENDERS' "Brass in Pocket" started playing after the Tom Petty and Stevie Nicks duet—Susan and Debbie had compiled the mixtape played at the party—and during the first verse I saw Ryan Vaughn sipping a margarita while standing by the fire pit talking to the two hottest guys in the junior class, both holding Coronas: Dean McCain, the eleventh-grade Homecoming King, undeniably handsome with thick wavy brown hair cut short, a strongly defined jawline and piercing blue eyes and tan complexion, and Tim Price, another sexy jock from that class, blond-haired and chiseled, vaguely surferish, both of them straight, but, then, everyone was and everyone thought Ryan was, so what did it matter if I noticed this *thing* about them: maybe they weren't straight at all, I fantasized, and just faked it like everyone else was supposed to. I was wondering what Ryan Vaughn was thinking about Dean McCain as I walked up to them and how he was sizing him up sexually (there was no way he wasn't) when they all turned and Ryan suddenly grabbed me in a playful headlock with one arm and a frozen smile and growled good-naturedly, "Look who turned up." He let go of me and I patted my hair back into place, mildly turned on by how strong he felt, and with the same frozen smile he said to Dean and Tim, "You know Bret, right?" They both nodded and said, "Hey, dude." Ryan didn't bother introducing them and they deferred to us because we were seniors and even if I wasn't particularly popular this status bestowed upon me a kind of unearned respect I wouldn't have received otherwise. Mindless jock banter followed before Dean and Tim headed off when they saw a group of girls from their class walking out of the opened doors of the kitchen and into the backyard. I noticed the flames from the fire pit were wavering in the same direction as the steam that was drifting off the pool behind Ryan and I focused on that. Ryan just stood there.

"So you showed up," I said without looking at him. "You can deal with this?"

"Yeah, I told you I was going to show up," Ryan said, somewhat defensively. "But I'm leaving after I finish my margarita."

"Yeah, you're here to support Robert," I ventured, turning to him. "Right? Say hello to the birthday boy?"

"Yeah, I said hi." Ryan shrugged, noncommittally. "I guess, whatever." And then he softened slightly. "How you doing?"

"I'm okay," I said, and then, "I came."

"Did you hear anything else about Matt?" Ryan asked quietly. "About what happened? Any other info?"

I stared into his beautiful face, lit orange from the flames of the fire pit, and just shook my head.

He sipped his margarita. He looked around the yard. He didn't say anything. I couldn't believe Ryan and I had come to this moment when we simply had nothing to say to each other. I stared at him, wonderingly, almost daring him to stare back: what had happened to the person I spent that weekend with in the empty house on Mulholland and whose body I explored so relentlessly, while we hungrily and endlessly kissed and licked and sucked until our lips and chins were chafed and our tongues were sore? He looked back at me and both of us silently assessed each other. The staring became a kind of comic dare and we tried not to smile until Ryan finally made the *What's up?* face we used to share and a pathetic relief washed over me and I laughed but didn't make the face back. Ryan relaxed and was studying me while every so often glancing at the group on the other side of the yard.

"So what's going on?" he asked. "What's happening? You and Debbie okay?"

"Yeah, well," was all I said.

"That's what I thought," he said.

"You're doing okay?" I asked.

"Oh yeah, I'm fine," he said with a breezy confidence I envied. "Just biding my time, just smiling and biding my time."

"Biding your time until?" I asked. He let the question hang between us longer than I thought he would. And I realized he knew what I knew he meant—this secret between us—his longing to get out of Buckley and move away from everything. Sustain the illusion for another year, until graduation, when he would finally be free.

"You know," he started, "you don't have to make things so difficult," he said, in a low and soothing voice, almost as if he was a sales-
man letting me in on a secret about how I could get a better deal. "It's
not that hard."

"What do you mean?" I asked, suddenly embarrassed but too
curious to stop from asking. "What do I make too difficult?"

"You need to relax, take it easy," Ryan said. "You don't have to
make things so difficult for yourself. For whatever's happening."

"What's happening?" I asked.

Ryan rolled his eyes and shook his head. "Forget it. I don't want
to talk about it here."

"No, I want to know what you mean."

"No, you don't," he said. "You want to turn everything into a
drama."

"I don't, I really don't," I stressed. "Have I been doing that? Have
I been turning everything into a drama?"

"I think it's something you can't help," he said. "Look, I don't want
to talk about this here."

"You've been avoiding me, and I'm . . . okay with that, I guess," I
said. "But I kind of want to know why."

"See. This is the problem," he said. "I haven't been avoiding you."

"Bullshit," I said. "We used to be a lot closer."

He flinched and quickly scanned the backyard to see if anyone
had heard me but the grounds were vast and we were far away from
anyone else and the party had gotten larger and a louder song started
playing—"Planet Claire" by the B-52s suddenly announced itself.

"But I'm the same person," he said. "I'm the same person I've
always been. And that you've always known. Nothing's changed." He
paused. "And yet you think I have changed." He paused again. "That's
kind of the problem."

"But you have changed, Ryan," I said in a low steely voice, averting his stare by looking over at the flames of the fire pit. "You're no
longer friends with me."

"Why would you think that?" he asked. "I really don't want to
have this conversation here, Bret." He said this as a warning and
scanned the yard again. He noticed that Debbie Schaffer realized

I was here and excused herself from Thom and Susan and Robert and started making her way over to the fire pit. "Jesus," Ryan muttered and downed the rest of the margarita. "Look, I am your friend. I'm closer to you than just about anybody else in this fucking place. But whatever you think was going to happen just can't. I'm not saying something won't happen again but I can't get involved in your drama. Whatever your, I don't know, expectations are." He looked at me blank-faced when he said this in order to make a point. "I don't want to hurt you."

"Okay, okay," I said. "I understand. I'm sorry."

"Cool," he said, smiling at Debbie as she immediately kissed me open-mouthed, deeply, a lingering French kiss that I went with in front of Ryan. "Hey, handsome," she said, smiling, pulling back, wasted already. Sometimes cocaine made Debbie tight and jittery, her body tensed with the pleasure the drug gave her, and other times, depending on the coke, she might act slightly sloppy, as if she was drunk on four vodkas instead of simply high. She was wearing a plaid miniskirt and a button-down Polo shirt with a Camp Beverly Hills sweater tied across her shoulders. "Whoa," I finally said, pretending to be stunned by the kiss. There was a silence and then Ryan started laughing and then I started laughing and finally Debbie started laughing, but she was confused as to why we were all laughing. "That was quite a greeting," Ryan explained, good-naturedly. Debbie pushed into me. "I can't help it," she said. "He drives me crazy." I placed an arm around her waist, wanting Ryan to notice. "When did you get here?" she asked me. "Why didn't you come say hi?"

"Just a few minutes ago," I said. "Ryan waved me over," I lied. "How's everything going? The place looks great." Ryan wasn't looking at me any longer—he had finished the margarita and was planning his escape.

"Fabulous," Debbie intoned theatrically. She suddenly looked from me to Ryan. "Hey." She wanted his attention. He looked back at her. "Does anyone want a bump?" she asked casually.

Ryan immediately shook his head. "No, I'm fine."

Debbie turned to me. I pretended to be conflicted until I said, "Maybe later."

The SHARDS

"Okay," she said. "Just let me know," she whispered into my ear before she kissed it, tonguing the lobe, lingering. Ryan stared at the two of us amused, as if he thought we were daring him into a reaction.

AND THEN WE noticed Thom and Susan and Robert walking to where we stood. Susan floated between them in the semi-darkness of the backyard as "Clubland" started playing over the party—I'll always remember that moment, her movements somehow synched with that particular song and its inherent drama and Elvis Costello's voice, that beautiful numbness radiating out of her—that enviable detachment—and she had never looked more desirable, especially when her face neared mine in the wavering flames of the fire pit and she kissed my cheek. "I'm happy you're here," she said, her breasts grazing my chest. "I'm glad you made it."

I suspected she was high but you could never really tell with Susan: she might do a line or two and act just as casually as if she had sipped a Perrier; she never got wired like Debbie.

"Hey, man," Thom said, only a little wasted on tequila.

Robert greeted me with that strange wave he'd sometimes offer, suggesting he was dealing with a child, I always thought, and I don't think I'd ever seen him make this gesture to anyone else. I offered my hand and he looked at it questioningly before taking it.

We shook and as I pulled back I said, "Congratulations."

He stalled briefly, the mania now whirring behind the eyes, and said, somewhat confused but not wanting to pursue what I meant, "Thanks."

I just wanted to fuck with him—no one else noticed the exchange because everyone was murmuring how cool the party was and how great the yard looked and Robert turned away and started nodding his approval and then Thom and Ryan were talking about an upcoming game and then the oddest exchange happened: Michelle Stevenson walked over with a tray of margaritas, and though I declined, Debbie took one as did Susan, and when Robert reached for a plastic cup rimmed with salt and garnished with a lime slice, Susan quietly said, "You shouldn't be drinking that—I thought you weren't going to drink."

I was so shocked by the simple intimacy of the comment that I barely registered it when Robert shrugged and said, "I'll be okay, babe." The way he said "babe" confirmed something I didn't want to confront that night, and as Robert chugged the margarita the girls turned away and Debbie said something about maybe hitting the beach this week, after school one day, before Thom left to look at colleges back east—he was flying to New York on Friday. Thom heard this and turned away from Ryan and said that sounded totally awesome—the beach, let's do it—and a plan formed while Susan explained to Robert where the Jonathan Club was and how everyone's father was a member, except for Terry Schaffer—but Terry, Debbie told us, was throwing a party in two weeks, and we were all invited, and she mentioned the stars who were dropping by: Sigourney Weaver, Mel Gibson, Jane Fonda, Richard Gere, Chris Reeve.

I WAS MOSTLY WATCHING Ryan's face while this conversation played (his father wasn't a member of the Jonathan Club either) and since I knew exactly what he thought about everyone—Thom was a spoiled wuss, Debbie was clueless, Susan was entitled, he'd wanted to suck Robert's cock and then fuck him in the ass—something within me started churning with sympathy for Ryan Vaughn even though he had rejected me and when everyone decided to head into the kitchen for sushi and another margarita I felt that familiar pang as Ryan said he had to leave and get back to Northridge. I was the only one who understood this was what Ryan actually preferred. It was a Saturday night. There wasn't a curfew. He wasn't secretly meeting friends to catch a movie in Westwood. No one was waiting for him at home. He *wanted* to leave the party and the house on North Canon Drive. Thom made exaggerated attempts to get him to stay and there was a general protest from the rest of the group but not from me. Ryan eventually said good night as people began to circle the table in the crowded kitchen and served themselves—though it seemed only the guys were hungry, with Thom and Robert and Jeff piling their plates with chopped salad and handfuls of sushi, while the girls sipped their drinks and chatted among themselves.

I waited for a beat and when the group was busy pouring themselves fresh margaritas from one of the blenders Bruce Johnson was still manning—he was high on coke as well, I'd find out later, and *into* the idea of being that night's bartender—I slipped away and walked quickly through the backyard beneath the bougainvillea tree and onto a pathway that lined the side of the house and then across the front lawn toward North Canon Drive, where Ryan was already sitting in the Trans Am—the engine was running, the headlights were on, I could hear Bob Seger singing "Beautiful Loser"—and I tried to open the passenger door but it was locked and when I crouched down and rapped on the window, Ryan turned to see who it was and his expression became creased with concern and he shook his head twice—no—and pushed the car into drive and quickly glided away from the curb.

IN THE KITCHEN I GRABBED a margarita and then passed by the adjacent dining room, where I glimpsed Thom and Susan and Jeff and Tracy but couldn't see enough of the room to know if Robert and Debbie had joined them, and then I walked outside and moved through the expanding crowd hanging on the lawn—"Mirror in the Bathroom" by the English Beat echoed over the yard—and headed toward the darkened tennis court, where I pulled out a pack of Marlboros I brought for the party and lit a cigarette while wandering back and forth along the net, sipping the margarita and contemplating my place in the world and wondered where Audrey Barbour was, the week after she disappeared from the Promenade parking lot in Woodland Hills. From where I was hidden I had a full view of the lawn beyond the steaming pool and into the house and both the downstairs and the upstairs were flooded with light. It seemed that by nine o'clock the entire senior class had arrived along with a disproportionate amount of the junior class and the kids I didn't recognize were, I guessed, from other private schools in the city—girls Susan and Debbie knew from Corvallis and Westlake and guys who Thom knew from Harvard and Beverly. Thom and Dominic and Jeff were standing before a half-circle of girls while people kept walking up to Robert Mallory, who was standing beside the Buckley crew, to shake his hand and say "Hi" before engaging in the small talk I so dreaded and then moving off so another person or couple could replace them, coming up to Robert and saying "Hey" and repeating the ritual that had just transpired moments earlier, as if they were all introducing themselves to him, or in some cases reintroducing themselves.

At one point this seemed so fake that it became legitimately disconcerting and I had to look away. Susan's knowing that Robert shouldn't be drinking suggested to me that this was somehow connected to his problems from the past—the mental institution he'd spent time in—and yet obviously it wasn't bad enough for her to actively discourage it: Robert drank the margarita anyway.

AND WHEN I LOOKED back I noticed that Robert was drinking another margarita and that once it was finished he was looking around for whoever was passing them until a group of younger girls that I didn't recognize interrupted him and looked as if they were nervously approaching a movie star about to ask for his autograph. The backyard was now packed and as I crouched on the darkened tennis court the party became permeated with the smell of marijuana; from where I was hiding I could actually see a haze of smoke float over the crowd and just hang there as if a light fog bank had descended above the backyard. And inside the house lines were forming for the bathroom adjacent to the kitchen and the one by the laundry room—kids in groups of three and four squeezing into the small guest bathrooms to share coke. I smoked another cigarette, masked by the darkness, and kept watching the house, trying to forget about Ryan and my useless feelings for him—I had gotten a haircut for him, I thought I looked hot, nothing mattered—and realized that what I felt wasn't sadness anymore but a rising anger.

WHEN MY EYES LANDED ON Thom and Dominic and Jeff I noticed that Debbie had interrupted whoever Robert was talking to—Robert was buzzed and gesturing excitedly with the hand holding a fresh margarita sloshing over the rim—and Debbie whispered something in his ear that caused him to freeze and then nod. "Gates of Steel" by Devo began playing as Robert excused himself from the group and let Debbie guide him through the crowd to where the French doors of the dining room opened into the house. Robert kept leaning in to her, asking things or explaining something, while he followed her out of the kitchen and disappeared from my sight. I stayed fixed on the house, wondering where they were going; then I suddenly looked upward and saw Susan standing by the window in her parents' bedroom, partly hidden in silhouette, partially lit by the lamp on the bedside nightstand. She was staring down at the party and I imagined she was looking at Thom, who was craning his neck searching for someone, interrupted by a high-five. I also knew the following was about to happen and waited impatiently until it occurred: the door of the bedroom opened and Debbie and Robert appeared and then Debbie turned and locked the door behind her. Susan immediately walked over to Robert, who just stood by an armoire, staring at Susan as she took the half-empty margarita out of his hand while Debbie sat on the side of the bed and pulled out a small packet from her skirt and tapped out a line on the nightstand. Susan was standing too close to Robert and whatever she was telling him caused his face to slacken with exaggerated disbelief and then he was gesturing to himself as if he was creating a manic defense against whatever Susan was accusing him of. And then he tried to touch her face.

I LOOKED BACK AT Debbie but she had leaned over the nightstand and I couldn't see her. Susan had paced away from Robert, her arms crossed, shaking her head, pissed. But then Robert said something that caused Susan to turn around and after a beat she started laughing, because Robert, I guessed, had disarmed her, and then I looked over to Debbie, who had sat up and was wiping her nose while laughing too. And then I watched as Robert walked over to Susan and gently touched her arm and explained something to her and then she said something and he nodded. Debbie stood up and was listening to them until Susan jokingly pushed Robert away and then Debbie started walking toward the door, and Susan and Robert followed her, moving out into the upstairs hallway, and then the door closed. That was it. Nothing else happened. Robert didn't stroke Susan's face. They didn't kiss. And nothing that I witnessed from my vantage point on the darkened tennis court seemed as intimate as that one line Susan said: *You shouldn't be drinking that—I thought you weren't going to drink.* And yet a narrative about Susan and Robert confirmed itself to me that night when I watched them interact in her parents' bedroom.

Wasn't there a moment when I would have been in Don and Gayle's master bedroom over the summer, just a few months ago, and I'd be sharing a couple of lines with Debbie Schaffer and Susan Reynolds instead of Robert Mallory? And now I wasn't. I had been replaced. Nothing mattered anymore. *It means nothing to me. This means nothing to me.* I finished the margarita in one gulp—it was strong, my eyes watered, peace briefly blanketed over me and then disappeared. *Oh, Vienna.* When I looked back at the yard my eyes landed on Thom Wright, who was still distracted, scanning the party. There would only be one person he was looking for: Susan. His girl-friend. Thom stood on his toes to get a better view around the yard but she wasn't there.

I JUST TURNED AWAY AND HID in the darkness of the tennis court, where I kept smoking cigarettes and putting them out in the empty plastic cup. I was muttering to myself while walking along the length of the net when I heard my name over the sounds of the distant party. "Bret?" I heard it again. I looked up. There was a shadow standing beneath one of the eucalyptus trees that bordered the court. "What are you doing here?" the voice asked. Something in me deflated and yet I took a deep breath and summoned the tangible participant. "Are you okay?" It was Debbie. I later found out that she'd been looking for me and had actually gone outside to Canon Drive, where she located my car still parked at the curb and quickly checked the house until she surmised I'd drifted away from the party and was alone somewhere and that's when she decided the pool or the darkened tennis court was where I'd be.

"Yeah, I'm fine," I said. "I was just having a cigarette?" It came out like a question.

"What are you doing here?" she asked again. "In the dark?"

"I just wanted to . . . take a break," I said.

"Take a break from what?" I heard her ask. She was still a shadow, just a voice.

"From the party," I said monotonously.

"Why would you want to take a break from the party?" she asked.

"Because I wanted to," I said with a slight tinge of defiance.

"Is something wrong with the party?" she asked.

At this point I thought she was purposefully fucking with me and I got pissed. And then I realized there was no other option except to approach this scene with an optimism that I might have lacked but knew I could fake. She appeared out of the darkness and was now visible. I turned to see if Thom had found Susan yet but he was semi-obscured behind the thick sheets of steam coming up off the pool.

"No, the party is great," I said, smiling, turning around. "You guys did a great job. Who decorated the tree? The white lights. The sushi. The mixtape . . ." I trailed off.

"You don't look like you're having fun," she said. And then, "But you never really do."

"That's not . . . true," I started. "Debbie, I . . ."

I don't know what I was going to confess—certainly nothing about her dad, because whatever happened with Terry had nothing to do with her or anything else, and this was true of Ryan Vaughn and Matt Kellner as well. I just wanted to explain myself in some vague way that Debbie Schaffer could grasp and finally understand that I never wanted to hurt her—just like Ryan Vaughn didn't want to hurt me—and that I was as lost as anyone she knew and this was fucking me up and that she deserved so much better than this seventeen-year-old zombie who was pretending to be someone he wasn't. But I couldn't form the words because I saw a future that seemed even more desolate than the present I was trapped in if I admitted any of this. Debbie kept moving closer and it appeared as if my presence had a calming effect: she didn't seem jittery or high and I thought maybe she'd taken a few hits off one of the joints it seemed everyone was passing around, but I realized she was simply calm because she'd found me. She asked for a cigarette and I offered her the pack of Marlboros and then she leaned in and I lit the tip. She inhaled, then exhaled. She looked up at the night sky bordered by the glossy green leaves of the eucalyptus trees and then past me at the party on the packed lawn. "Tainted Love" by Soft Cell was playing—we all owned the U.K. import—and she asked if I wanted some coke. I didn't. She handed me the cigarette and then pulled out a baggie from the pocket in her skirt and with the pearled nail of her index finger snorted a bump.

"What were you all doing upstairs?" I asked, watching her.

"Who?" Debbie asked, startled.

"You and Susan and Robert."

"How did you know—" She looked over at the house and realized that from my vantage point I could easily see into Don and Gayle's bedroom. It was a tiny moment but Debbie had to compose herself because of my question. "Were you spying on us?" she asked, taking the cigarette back from me.

"Yes," I said. "I'm always spying on you."

"That's not very nice," she said, teasingly. "But it's kind of sexy."

"What were you guys doing upstairs?"

Debbie quickly made a decision, because what lie could she tell me? I had watched the entire scene even though I hadn't heard it.

"Well, Susan was upset about something—"

"What?" I interrupted. "What was she upset about?"

Debbie looked at me curiously, and then took another drag off the cigarette. "She was upset because Robert was—Robert is—drinking too much tonight. That's all."

"Why would Susan care if Robert was drinking too much?" I asked.

"Well," Debbie started, "it seems that Robert is taking . . ." She stopped. ". . . some medicine and it might not interact well with alcohol."

"What kind of medicine?" I asked. "For what?"

"I . . . don't really know," Debbie said.

"Really?" I asked. "You don't know? You don't know what kind of medicine Robert is taking?"

"Why do you care?" she asked. "Why do you care what kind of medicine Robert takes? What difference could it possibly make to you?"

I didn't say anything, just stared at her, and she met my gaze and kept it.

"And . . . ?" I let the word hang there. "Is that your answer?"

"Are you trying to ask me something?" Debbie said. "Because if you are: just say it. Don't play this stupid game with me."

"I'm just asking what's going on," I said, casually. "I just wanted to know why you had to bring Robert upstairs to Susan." I paused. "Why couldn't she get him herself?" I paused again. "Was it because Thom was there?" I asked.

"I didn't have to 'do' anything, Bret," Debbie said. "You're turning something into something it's not." She paused. "It's not a big deal."

"I just asked a question," I said. I looked back at the party.

In a break from the steam rising off the pool I glimpsed Thom craning his neck, distracted, not listening to the voices surrounding him—he still couldn't locate Susan in the crowd. I scanned the party and didn't locate Robert either. They were both somewhere inside the house, maybe talking, maybe leaning in to each other, maybe Susan was quietly pleading with him not to drink another margarita, maybe Robert was assuring her he'd be okay; *Kiss me,* one of them was saying. I was becoming angry and I didn't want to lay it out on Debbie so I just said, "Let's go." I paused before I muttered, "This is fucking ridiculous."

"So now you want to go back to the party?" she said, sighing, as if she hadn't heard me. "After I've got you all to myself you want to go back to the party? Jeez, Bret."

"Yeah," I said, ignoring what she insinuated. "I want another margarita."

My fury consumed me and I was going to tamp it down with tequila—there was no option except to get drunk. Debbie saw where I put the cigarettes out and crushed hers in the same empty cup. And then she walked up to me before I turned away and kissed my mouth. I expected it. I steeled myself. But I didn't push her away—I simply let her kiss me and it only took a few seconds until I kissed her back, suddenly overwhelmed with horniness, and I realized it had been building all night, ever since I saw Ryan talking to Dean McCain and Tim Price and probably even before that, when I was again reminded how handsome Robert Mallory was and how I had always loved Thom Wright and suddenly it wouldn't have mattered who was kissing me on the darkened tennis court—I would have fucked anybody in that moment, boy or girl, old or young, handsome or ugly. Debbie murmured her surprise at how passionate I'd become and it shocked her when I pulled her face away from mine, roughly clutching a handful of hair in a fist, and this activated something and she immediately fell to her knees and we both unzipped my jeans and pulled out my cock, which was aching—I realized I hadn't jerked off in days—and when she began swallowing it expertly a kind of relief spiraled through me.

Debbie wasn't high enough to be completely impractical and just have me fuck her on the green asphalt—though if she kept blowing me I would've come easily in the next minute—and she pulled me even farther into the darkness on the other side of the tennis court, where we tumbled onto an inflatable raft, a pool toy, and I couldn't believe how hard I was. My erection was sticking up out of my jeans like some kind of absurd fertility symbol, and yet I realized that rage was what excited me—and it was aimed at everyone: it was directed at Robert Mallory, of course, but it was also directed at Thom Wright, who had let Robert become his friend while I was slipping away, and it was directed at Susan and at Ryan and at Buckley, and maybe in that moment it was directed at Terry Schaffer, but mostly it was directed at myself and the futility I was feeling, fed with images of imagined sex with Thom and Robert that would never happen or the *reality* of the sex that I experienced with Ryan and Matt and that was never going to repeat itself. Everything that had once given me hope was taken away and this was tied to the rage I was unfairly directing at Debbie.

BUT SHE LIKED IT. She enjoyed herself. I had never fucked her like this before. Lying on the raft, she had slipped off her panties and raised the miniskirt—I just pulled my jeans down to my knees and she was so wet I easily slid in. It lasted barely two minutes, during which she came twice and I just kept fucking her, just ramming my cock in, cursing until I exploded inside her and immediately collapsed, panting, the rage finally diminishing. "Jesus," she muttered. "Where did *that* come from? Fuck." I rolled off her and half fell off the raft, still panting, my dick hard and wet and sticking up. I felt like I was burning. I couldn't catch my breath. My heart was beating so fast. She was laughing with relief—this had proven something to her: I really was her boyfriend. I really liked her. I had desired her so badly and in ways she never supposed—the fuck was the proof. As I pushed myself up off the raft I could clearly hear "Pulling Mussels (From the Shell)" and realized that the din of the party had quieted down—only the song played, no one was talking. And then I heard someone yelling. It was Thom Wright's voice, which had somehow silenced the hum of the crowd. I moved hesitantly toward the pool and Debbie walked over to where I was standing and suddenly cursed when she saw Thom leaning over Susan—he didn't seem wasted, just racked with fury. Everyone at the party was silent and staring at them.

"Where were you?" he was shouting. "I asked you where you were?"

"Stop screaming at me!" Susan shouted back.

"Where were you, Susan?"

"You're drunk," Susan shouted. "Stop it."

"Where in the fuck were you, babe?" Thom was red-faced, standing over Susan in a threatening stance. I had never seen Thom Wright this angry before—it didn't connect with the boy I'd grown up with. Jeff Taylor was whispering in Thom's ear, trying to pull him back.

"I was in the fucking house!" Susan was shouting.

"With who?" Thom yelled. "Doing what?"

"With Debbie, you fucking idiot," she screamed. "What does it fucking matter?"

"You're lying!" he shouted. "You're a liar. You lie. You lie all the time now!"

Debbie rushed away from me and across the darkened tennis court, then along the side of the lit pool, until she was on the lawn, pushing through the party. I pulled up my jeans and then slowly moved forward, suddenly exhausted from the sex, my Topsiders trudging across the asphalt until I reached the edge of the pool.

"Thom, stop it!" Susan was shouting. "You're being such an asshole."

"When did you become such a bitch?" Thom yelled. "Why have you become such a fucking bitch?"

"You're being ridiculous," Susan said.

"I'm not being ridiculous," Thom shouted.

"You're drunk!" she shouted back. "You're wasted!"

"Fuck you!" Thom suddenly roared. "Fuck you, Susan! Tell me where the fuck you were?"

"What do you fucking want from me?" Susan cried out.

Debbie appeared and said something to Susan as she pulled her away from Thom, who was struggling with Jeff and Dominic, and then I froze as I watched Robert Mallory walk up to Thom. Robert's presence seemed to momentarily relax him while Debbie ushered Susan into the house. Robert eased Thom away from Jeff and Dominic and then the four of them were walking toward the pool, the crowd parting for the quartet of guys. Thom was muttering, shaking his head, a clearly wasted Robert whispering in his ear as the four of them crossed the lawn. My gaze shifted to Debbie conferring with Susan in the kitchen as other girls surrounded them—Susan tossed back a margarita that Michelle handed her. By the fire pit Robert drunkenly hugged Thom, with Jeff and Dominic briefly acting as sentries to ward anyone away.

"RESPECTABLE STREET" BY XTC started playing and the collective voice of the party hesitantly sounded up again once the actors in this particular drama had exited the stage. Thom collapsed on a chaise by the pool, Robert leaning over and murmuring to him as Thom nodded, and I noted the way Robert's hand was rubbing Thom's shoulder, and then Anthony and Doug walked over with a tray of margaritas and a full bottle of tequila. I couldn't hear what anyone was saying from where I stood in the darkness on the edge of the tennis court. I might have remained hidden for the rest of the party but there was something unbearable about the way Robert was touching Thom and how close he was to him that enraged me. And I quickly revealed myself, walking over to the group of guys lounging on the chaises by the pool. I ignored everyone but Thom and Robert and stood over them and asked hollowly, "Is everything okay?"

It was Robert who turned to me and said, "Yeah, everything's okay, Bret."

But I wasn't looking at him. I was staring down at Thom, who finally looked up at me, smiling sadly.

The SHARDS

Jeff and Dominic, and Anthony and Doug, stopped talking and everyone waited for Thom to say something.

And then Thom apologized and started rambling. It was Susan's party. She had to deal with guests. Thom was on edge. He overreacted. He probably drank too much. He did a line. But I could barely hear what Thom was saying because Robert was sitting so close to him on the chaise and I wondered if I had ever sat that close to Thom Wright. Had he ever let me? Had I ever dared myself? Their thighs were pressing against each other. Thom kept talking and I intuitively looked over at Robert, who was now staring at me. There was something off—he wasn't as in control or fake: his eyes were half closed and he was loose, tired, woozy. He was looking past me and when I turned I watched as Susan and Debbie made their way across the lawn to the edge of the pool. I turned back, distracted by Robert pushing himself up and falling into a nearby patio chair, presumably to make room for Susan. And then Thom was looking up at Susan and reached out a hand and Susan automatically took it and crouched down and they lightly kissed, quietly apologizing to each other, and I could feel everyone relaxing as Susan sat next to Thom in the space where Robert had been sitting. I downed the margarita I was clutching in one gulp and then reached for another.

EVERYONE GOT WASTED that night. A group had formed around the King and Queen, and Bruce Johnson and Michelle brought out more margaritas, and then Kyle Colson and David O'Shea and Kevin Kerslake joined us, along with Tracy and Katie and Rita Lee, and cocaine was being openly passed around in small packets. A phone call had been made and someone met a dealer in front of the house on Canon around midnight and stronger margaritas were blended to go with the coke and I sat with Debbie on my lap—she was purring with happiness about the fuck we shared earlier—and after my third margarita I was drunk enough and decided to do a couple of bumps and kept a small packet Debbie handed me so I could sustain my high uninterrupted—the supply was seemingly endless. Thom had only done another line—that's all he needed—but Susan, lying next to him on the chaise, was calmly doing small bumps every five minutes, occasionally inhaling on a clove cigarette, which I knew Thom didn't like—she usually refrained from smoking around him but not that night. Robert had been slumped in a chair next to them and he was one of the few people not partaking in the coke because of the "medication" he was supposedly prescribed, even though he was already hammered. At a certain point I noticed he'd disappeared while I was engaged in a nonsensical conversation with Jeff and Tracy.

Someone making whooping noises startled us, and it took a moment to realize they were coming from Robert, dashing out of the pool house and stumbling toward the lit block of water. Robert had discarded his jeans and he was pulling the Polo shirt over his head and only in his jockey shorts by the time he stood at the edge of the pool. And then he stepped out of the jockey shorts and was completely naked—this was the first time I'd seen Robert's body and though I only glimpsed it quickly I was paralyzed: it was exactly as I imagined in my fantasies. Tan except for the whiteness across his thighs and ass, Robert had a similar build to Thom and Ryan, the body of an athlete, tall and broad-shouldered, lightly sculpted with defined pectorals and a flat tier of abs lowering to his penis, which was long and thick and pink with a bush of brown hair above it. Robert cannonballed into the pool and swam sloppily to the shallow end, where he stumbled up the steps and padded over to the diving board, completely wet and naked, and I homed in on his tight, smooth ass and I was suddenly unable to breathe. He dived in again. Thom and Jeff were laughing but Debbie had shifted on my lap and said "Susan" as if it was a warning but Susan had already stood up and was watching with a concerned expression. Thom and Jeff stopped laughing when they watched Robert just splashing around in the middle of the pool, flailing incoherently, smacking the water with his arms in what seemed like a drunken, spastic rage, steam billowing around him.

And that was the moment when everyone realized this wasn't a joke: there was something wrong with Robert.

Susan said quietly, "Thom, will you get him out of the pool." It wasn't a question—it was an urgent demand.

Thom looked up at her, confused.

"Do something, Thom," Susan said. "Get him out of there. He's wasted. He's going to hurt himself."

The SHARDS

Robert disappeared under the water and wasn't coming up for air. Thom finally realized something serious was happening but didn't know what exactly—just that this went beyond a drunken joke. He staggered up and kicked his shoes off and pulled his shirt over his head and quickly unzipped and stepped out of his jeans. The body I had glanced at in the locker room all these years was more noticeably muscled because of football season: lighter and leaner. Only wearing the plaid Polo boxers Thom now favored, high and tight, accentuating his thighs and ass. I watched as Thom walked quickly to the pool's shallow end, where he waded in and then dived under the water and swam to Robert, pulling him off the floor, where Robert had sunk, and up to the surface, and though it looked as if they were struggling, Robert seemed lost in another world, the whooping sounds replaced with gibberish, something incomprehensible, and he kept splashing water at Thom, who was reaching out to him, smiling as he tried to get Robert calm enough to follow him out of the pool. And then Robert went underwater again.

"Is he okay?" I remember Jeff asking.

"I told him not to drink," Susan said quietly, still staring at the pool. "He's on Thorazine and three other medications." I looked at her after she murmured this to herself.

THOM DIVED to pull Robert up and dragged him to the surface again. But he kept struggling with Robert, who giggled maniacally and splashed at the steaming pool as if he was impersonating an angry child, and soon Thom was getting on Robert's level so he'd follow Thom out of the pool, by splashing along with him. With a growing impatience Susan watched this game Thom was now playing until she snapped.

"Jesus," she muttered, and unzipped her skirt and pulled off the Lacoste and in just bra and panties walked steadily toward the pool to help guide Robert out. Something in me shrank as I realized she cared enough about Robert Mallory and his insanity to strip down in front of us and help rescue him from her own pool, and I shuddered and quickly downed what was left of my margarita. Debbie removed herself from my lap and stood next to the chair I was sitting in and watched the pool intently. Thom brought Robert to the surface again, his arms wrapped around his chest, Thom's biceps bulging with the effort, as Robert kept pounding the water with his fists—something primal was happening that he wanted to express. When Thom noticed Susan in just her panties and bra walking down the steps into the shallow end, he groaned, "Aw, come on, babe, I got this, put your clothes back on." Susan ignored him and waded into the warm water, moving quickly over to where Thom was embracing Robert, and when Robert saw Susan he stopped struggling and stared at her with what seemed like drunken wonderment, suddenly babbling about how pretty she was, and then Robert looked at Thom and told Thom how handsome he was and that he was such a beautiful dude. "Come on, buddy, you need to get to bed," was Thom's response. "We need to get you out of this pool."

I kept noticing the way Thom's biceps were bulging with the effort it took to steady Robert as Susan neared them and then Robert stopped struggling for a moment, as if stunned by the sight. And as Robert stared at Susan he became immobile, which allowed Thom's grip to loosen, and then both Thom and Susan were guiding Robert out of the pool as he kept turning to each of them, babbling nonsensically. At one point Robert tried to kiss Susan, who pulled back, and when Robert suddenly turned to Thom and tried to kiss him Thom didn't pull back fast enough, letting Robert's mouth make contact with his but Thom took it in stride, laughing. "Come on, buddy," Thom said. "Let's get you outta here." Robert kept trying to kiss both of them, turning from one to the other, as they guided him toward the steps that led out of the pool, and soon both Susan and Thom were just letting Robert kiss their mouths, their faces, because it was easier than fighting him—he was finally relaxed.

Thom kept laughing and Susan seemed annoyed. The kissing didn't carry a sexual vibe because Robert was too wasted to distinguish them; they were both the same to Robert in that moment, and since the goal was to get Robert out of the pool without any hassle they just let him keep kissing them, as if he was a puppy, eagerly licking one face and then the other, desperately searching for affection from either Thom or Susan. (Robert's mouth repeatedly making contact with Thom's has remained an indelible image during the rest of my life.) Robert limply put both arms over Susan's and Thom's shoulders as they helped walk him up the steps and out of the pool. Robert slipped, pulling both Susan and Thom down with him, and then they were crouching over his prone body. Robert was on his back, totally naked, his legs spread, his knees slightly raised, and I was focused below the tight ball-sack, where the crack of his ass was visible, and Susan told Thom, "Get a towel." And Thom asked, "What? Where?" looking utterly confused. "They're over there," Susan said harshly, gesturing. Robert lying on the wet concrete was in a trance, shivering, lost and naked, an exhausted child. "Take him into the house, Thom," Susan quietly commanded after Thom trotted over with a beach towel he draped over Robert and then leaned down and easily lifted Robert up, quickly carrying him across the lawn into the kitchen. He had already passed out by the time Thom placed him on the couch in the living room.

SUSAN STOOD AT THE EDGE of the pool, wet, her bra and panties now translucent because of the water that stained them, her breasts and pubic hair clearly visible, and she grabbed a towel and wrapped it around herself and silently followed Thom as if she was ashamed about what had happened. Debbie and Jeff and Tracy realized the night was over: from Robert diving into the pool until Thom carrying him into the house took only a few minutes and it was the catalyst for the party to end. I finally kissed Debbie goodbye and assured her I was sober enough to drive home and raced through the canyons to the empty house on Mulholland, where I took two Valium and tumbled into sleep. I later heard that Thom passed out in Susan's bed, and Tracy and Jeff fell asleep in the guest room, and Robert slept through the night on the white couch in the living room, huddled in blankets that Susan had arrayed over him while she and Debbie stayed up doing the rest of the coke and cleaning the house, and occasionally keeping an eye on Robert, who, according to Debbie the following day, didn't stop shivering, and occasionally moaning, lost in what seemed like an endless flow of nightmares.

17

IF I COULD PINPOINT THE BREAK, the collapse, the reordering of our world, I remember an afternoon on the beach at the Jonathan Club in October of 1981 as the beginning of the end to something. The secret story about Matt was my loss of innocence, my first moment of adulthood and death, and I never moved through life again unaffected by the trauma this caused, everything changed because of it, and, even more painfully, I realized—and this was the truer, starker loss—that there was nothing I could do. This was life, this was death, nobody cared in the end, we were alone. And so, in some ways, Ronald Kellner's office on Haskell Avenue is the crux—everything leads up to it, everything falls away after it. On that cold day at the beach club the narrative sped up and I began to see more clearly what was about to subsume us—where the probable outcome was going to land.

WE HAD DECIDED to take Robert to the beach club before school let out on Thursday afternoon, the day before Thom left to look at colleges back east. When we proposed this to Robert on Wednesday he agreed eagerly—any reminder of what happened Saturday night seemed to have been eradicated by Monday morning, when I first saw him at assembly in the courtyard, mingling with classmates and grinning. Thom and Susan, and Debbie as well as myself, along with Jeff Taylor and Tracy Goldman, were the only people who witnessed Robert's freak-out at Susan's party: everyone else had left, and none of us mentioned it to anybody in our class; it hadn't become a story, gossip one of us told by the lockers or the tables beneath the Pavilion in a lowered voice the following week at Buckley. We stayed silent. Robert couldn't recall any of it—he only remembered the party until a certain point and he didn't know about the fight between Thom and Susan, or that he gently guided Thom past the fire pit to the chaise by the pool afterward. The party dimmed somewhere while he was greeting the people who wanted to say hi and though he remembered at one point Debbie touching his shoulder he couldn't remember anything after that. All Robert knew, or so he said, was that he woke up around ten o'clock Sunday morning on the couch Thom Wright had placed him on in the living room with no idea where he was before he stood, wrapped a sheet around himself and heard Debbie and Susan still awake in the kitchen from the previous night. And they relayed what had happened—the mania, the removal of clothing, the dive into the pool, sinking to the bottom, splashing mindlessly at Thom—and Robert, Debbie told me, seemed humiliated hearing this and started to silently cry, tears running down his "surprisingly blank face" (Debbie's description), which he urgently wiped away. Susan told him not to worry: they wouldn't tell anyone. Jeff and Tracy and Thom were still sleeping upstairs and they were the only other ones who'd seen the episode from the night before—for some reason she failed to mention that I witnessed it, too. Susan assured Robert they wouldn't say anything either. *Your secret is safe with us,* I imagined her promising him.

WE LEFT BUCKLEY DURING LUNCH, taking the rest of the afternoon off—we could do this infrequently as seniors if we were caught up on homework and assignments—and Susan and Thom took the Corvette, and Debbie had picked up the tangible participant from the house on Mulholland that morning in her BMW and we followed the Corvette, as Robert followed Debbie's BMW in the Porsche, and since the early-afternoon traffic was light we breezed through the Sepulveda Pass until we veered off the 405 and merged onto the 10. The Jonathan Club was on the beach about a mile from where the Santa Monica Freeway morphed into the Pacific Coast

Highway. Membership was invitation-only and by 1981 the club had been accused so often of discrimination that the complaints weren't even registering anymore and had become something of an open joke: everyone supposed it was anti-black and anti-Jew (one reason Terry Schaffer wasn't allowed) and no women could be members, and though we were aware of the club's purported racism we just hadn't attached a deep or real meaning to it, because 1981 wasn't asking us to. To say that any of us were politically engaged was stretching that notion into fairy-tale territory: we were teenagers distracted by sex and pop music, movies and celebrity, lust and ephemera and our own neutral innocence. The fact that Ronald Reagan was president meant almost nothing to us—if anything, like the purported racism of the Jonathan Club, it was kind of a joke, absurd, nothing to take too seriously, because it was so abstract, but of course we could afford to look at everything through this prism of numbness.

The beach club was built in 1927 and the original architecture hadn't been tampered with since—it had a grand old-fashioned feel to it, rococo almost; everything seemed over-scaled to me as a child, since I'd been going there in the mid-1970s, when my father first joined, and we'd spend weekends in the summer; the young and handsome all-male staff set you up with fold-out chairs and oversized towels and as many giant teal-colored umbrellas as your party needed on the private beach. The parents lounged on the sand with the latest bestsellers while their kids explored the Olympic-sized indoor pool, the tennis courts, the Ping-Pong tables, the glimmering sea. This was all pure empire: careless sunburns and endless sugary soft-serve ice-cream cones from the cafeteria—you just signed for everything—and re-enacting scenes from *Jaws* with friends in the shallows of the Pacific, Elton John and Rod Stewart playing from tape decks and transistor radios, the towering bluffs of Santa Monica looming as a backdrop, the California Incline winding above us. There were the prerequisite hot SoCal lifeguards I studied intently and in the men's locker room you could always casually wander around—it was high-ceilinged and vast, unchanged from 1927—and catch sight of older teenage boys changing in and out of bathing suits or taking showers, where they would wash the sand and salt water from their tanned, lithely muscled bodies.

The SHARDS

—

THAT THURSDAY the parking lot at the beach club was almost completely empty and the lone valet wearing a Jonathan Club cap and shirt walked over and though the attendants usually wrote down the make and license-plate number of the vehicle, today the valet didn't, and just opened the doors as we got out of our separate cars.

"Where is everyone?" Thom asked.

The attendant, a blond lifeguard with a Valley drawl, said, "Oh, we had some problems with that cult."

We gathered around him carrying our respective beach bags and stared blankly—I seemed to be the only one who was aware of the cult.

"Riders of the Afterlife, y'know?" the valet said. "They broke in two nights ago, vandalized something, took food from the cafeteria, and they keep coming around, harassing people leaving the parking lot, and they come in from the beach. It's a private beach and we've got lifeguards but they can only keep so many of those freaks out."

The valet wasn't handing us tickets for the cars because, I realized with a chill, there weren't any other cars in the parking lot.

"They've been all over Santa Monica and Venice this week," the valet said. "A lot of break-ins. Vandalism. Missing pets."

Thom looked around the empty lot, his Wayfarers hanging from a lanyard around his neck, and muttered, "Jesus."

The valet said, "I understand if you want to head out. It's been pretty quiet today. We're probably going to close up early, so . . ." His voice trailed off.

We all looked at each other until Debbie made the decision by simply saying, "We're already here."

I reminded her about the intruder at the space on Melrose a month ago and what the cult was capable of and Debbie waved me off. "Some dumb hippie scratched a little girl," she said dismissively. "Please."

This answer caused Susan to automatically turn toward the desk leading into the club and sign in for the group using Donald's account number, and the valet didn't ask for any ID to check if the last names matched with the roster because it didn't seem to matter that day.

And then the five of us headed to the steps that took us to the walkway leading to the locker rooms as a cold gust of wind whipped the American flag above the entrance. Everyone was silent, as if the deserted club acted as a warning, an omen, a portent—we needed to be on guard and conversation was the distraction that could get us hurt. Because of the silence I could tell that something had changed in the vibe between Susan and Thom since we'd left Buckley only thirty minutes ago. There was a new distance—you could feel it in their body language and in the way they weren't acknowledging each other: something had definitely happened on the drive over to Santa Monica, which Debbie seemed coolly oblivious of, but she probably knew exactly what was going on. Robert was following her. I lagged behind and watched as he glanced at the empty tennis courts, which were usually filled, the reservation list almost always packed, but not that day. The wind caused the canopy leading into the club's main building to ripple and snap loudly, startling us out of our respective reveries.

THOM AND I HEADED to the men's locker room with Robert following us, a large black duffel bag over his shoulder, where we'd change out of our Buckley uniforms and into bathing suits. There was no one around except a manager at the front desk, who handed us our keys, and the lockers were located next to each other, imposing a kind of intimacy on the three of us that was perhaps unwanted by the other two guys. Robert kept talking about how impressive the club was and he thanked us for bringing him regardless of whether anyone else was there, while Thom just kept muttering how cold it would be on the beach and if he ever saw one of those fucking freaks from the cult approaching us he'd kick their butt. We started changing in front of each other—Thom and Robert seemed less hesitant and self-conscious than I was—and I took sidelong glances at them as we casually talked to each other while stripping off our uniforms. Thom turned around when he slipped off his underwear and quickly stepped into his bathing suit, unaware that I wanted to see his smooth pale ass more than I wanted to see his dick, and Robert took his cue from Thom and also turned as he slipped off his underwear, momentarily naked; the whiteness of his taut ass cheeks contrasted with tan quads lightly blanketed with sparse brown hair made me hitch in a breath. We were all wearing the Polo swimsuits in Easter-egg colors that had become so popular that summer: Robert's was purple, mine was bright green, and Thom's was hot yellow. We decided to keep T-shirts on because of how cold it was, and maybe, Thom said hopefully, we could take them off once we hit the sand. Yes, hopefully, I thought to myself. Hopefully.

WHEN WE STEPPED OUTSIDE to wait for the girls I looked out at the empty vista and shivered: it seemed so warm in the Valley that morning and during lunch, and I'd expected throngs to crowd the private beach and help make this afternoon an occasion. "Jesus," Thom muttered, looking at his watch, annoyed that the girls took as long as they always did, and then Susan and Debbie appeared minutes later, wearing bikinis with cardigan sweaters that draped to their knees, and they didn't take off their sunglasses when they silently greeted us. "Finally," Thom muttered and then strode over to two staff members waiting at a cabana where towels and chairs and umbrellas were stored. We each took one of the oversized beach towels they handed to us and Thom trudged through the sand, the two staff members following him, one of them holding a teal umbrella that Susan requested and the other carrying five fold-out beach chairs. Thom finally decided on a spot midway between the shore and the club—it was where he always preferred. As the two staff members dug the umbrella into the sand and laid out the five folding chairs I noticed that the beach was almost completely deserted in either direction and there were only faraway figures in the sun-blasted distance. A lifeguard booth, unmanned, sat off to our side. Another gust of cold wind rose up off the Pacific.

WE SAT IN A ROW on the sand, facing the ocean, seemingly none of us happy to be there: we had made a mistake. Thom and Susan were at one end, Robert was in the middle, and Debbie and I sat at the other end. Someone had brought a boom box and we were listening to KROQ as the sun beat down (only Susan and Robert wanted the shade from the umbrella), and though it wasn't overcast—only a lone bank of massive cumulus clouds floated above the flat sheet of sea where it met the horizon—we occasionally complained that it was freezing. Susan and Thom weren't talking or even acknowledging each other, sharing the same bad mood: Susan never took off her sunglasses and Thom barely spoke. While pacing the sand considering a dip in the ocean, I asked Thom about his upcoming trip and he made a dismissive gesture before taking his T-shirt off and oiling himself with suntan lotion, and I felt slightly wounded as I sat back down. Robert was the only one of us who couldn't sit still and kept getting up: he wanted to check out the indoor pool, maybe take a quick swim—and then he made a joke about how he didn't need anyone to watch him, he could be unsupervised today. No one laughed, though I looked up at him and politely smiled.

Thom lay back in the sun immobile, his pectorals and small brown nipples and abdominal muscles gleaming, while he held up a copy of *Sports Illustrated* with Wayne Gretsky on the cover. Debbie was leafing through an issue of *Interview*, an oversized pastel drawing of Diana Ross staring out at me. I was holding a Joan Didion paperback rereading the first essay in *The White Album* and Susan was just staring out at the sea behind her Ray-Bans. KROQ played only downbeat songs that afternoon: David Bowie and "Ashes to Ashes" and the Rolling Stones' "Emotional Rescue" and a new Police single called "Invisible Sun" and the Doors' "Riders on the Storm." At one point Thom stood up and said, "It's too fucking cold," and asked if anyone wanted anything from the café as he slipped the T-shirt back on—he was hungry. Susan murmured no and Debbie decided to go with him. Susan and I didn't say anything to each other the entire time they were gone. Robert hadn't returned. The sad songs kept playing. Thom came back with a club sandwich and fries, and Debbie handed Susan an iced tea even though she hadn't asked for one. I was thinking about Audrey Barbour, the missing girl from Calabasas, and, glancing at Robert's empty chair, I wondered what else was in the black duffel bag he was carrying—I looked for it but didn't see it and guessed he had taken it with him when he went to the pool. The waves crested gently across the shore and I stared back at the book I was reading and came across the words *Petals on a wet black bough* and a reference to "The Wichita Lineman" and someone being unable to drive across the Carquinas Bridge as I kept drifting away.

WHEN I FINALLY LOOKED UP the light had changed. I saw someone approaching us in the distance and I became frightened it was one of the cult members from Riders of the Afterlife, but I recognized the purple bathing suit. Robert Mallory was walking aimlessly along the shore and I saw a figure approach him in the frame, compact yet broad-shouldered, someone male, maybe a surfer, and I sat up, interested, and then realized it was Thom. They met and stood on the sand looking out at the ocean, shirtless and lit orange by the fading sun, teenage Greek gods standing on the shores of Santa Monica talking to each other, even though it was too far away to hear what they were saying. It took me a moment to realize that Susan was looking over at them as well, and the only sounds seemed ambient but heightened: the movements of the sea, the DJ on KROQ, the traffic on PCH, the gulls squalling. Thom and Robert stood facing each other as the waves foamed white against their ankles and Thom seemed to be listening intently to something Robert was telling him and nodded, understanding him, assuring him it was all cool, similar to what I'd witnessed in the parking lot at Buckley when I watched Robert talking to Matt Kellner on the first day of school—it was the same scene but a different location, and I felt vaguely sickened, as if a premonition had washed over me. This was maybe the only moment that afternoon when I noticed Susan Reynolds lower her sunglasses while she stared at the two boys in the faraway distance. Thom and Robert contemplated the skyline and then Thom reached down to feel the temperature of the water. He said something to Robert and they laughed. I looked over at Debbie but she wasn't paying attention, lying back in the fold-out chair tanning herself, eyes closed. Susan still had her sunglasses lowered as she watched Thom and Robert continue talking and I could feel her fear rising and expanding around us, but why would there be fear? "Whatever," Susan said curtly to no one, turning away from the two boys on the shore.

—

AT A CERTAIN POINT Thom and Robert ambled to where we were lying and then Robert said he was heading back to Century City and we murmured our goodbyes as he swung the duffel bag over his shoulder. Susan was numbly subdued to the point of catatonia and barely registered him. I stood up and pretended to stretch but really wanted to watch as Thom walked with Robert to where the sand turned to pavement and they gave each other a slight bro-hug and Robert disappeared into the entrance of the locker room and Thom turned around and jogged back to where we were, the light falling around us as the ocean slowly darkened. Thom flopped down on the fold-out chair and picked up the copy of *Sports Illustrated*. And no one said anything for ten minutes, until Susan finally suggested that maybe we should probably get going—it was too cold, she was tired, Thom needed to pack for his trip. "I'm already packed," he snapped, not looking at her. Debbie reluctantly agreed with Susan, which over-rode everything—the girls always won. I picked up my Gucci back-pack and said I was going to take a quick shower and Thom told me we'd meet by the entrance. It was over between Susan and Thom, I thought to myself as I walked away from the friends who were slipping into the past. Something had happened.

THE MANAGER WAS GONE. I noted his empty desk as I entered the locker room.

The space was too vast to be completely silent even when empty, and the slightest impression echoed everywhere, and when it was filled with males, young and older, the noise could be deafening. I heard the late-afternoon traffic on PCH but it was muted and the sound of water dripping from the shower stalls was the central intonation—but who had taken a shower? I wondered. There was no one here, right? I thought. "Robert?" I said tentatively. No one answered. I walked past a row of lockers to the open blue-tiled stall, which had fourteen separate showerheads sharing the same space and because of its empti-ness suggested no one was in the locker room. I'd planned on taking a shower because it was so cold and not because I wanted to wash water and sand off myself—it would simply warm my body—but instead I headed to my locker, noticing that Robert's was hanging open, empty, as I shoved my Buckley uniform into the Gucci backpack, and then heard a toilet flushing and was surprised that anyone else was in the locker room—I assumed I'd been the only person. And then I waited for follow-up sounds but all I could hear was just the echoing drip coming from the shower stall. "Robert?" I asked again.

I walked slowly through the space, which was usually lit by fluorescent bulbs, but because no one was there that day most of them were darkened and just the light coming in from the panel of windows below the high ceilings offered any illumination. The locker room was always filled with sons and brothers and fathers, men of all ages, and I'd never been there when it was empty, even remotely, and when a stall door swung open, and a toilet flushed again, I jumped, startled. I could only hear the dripping echoes from where the showers were located. I took a deep breath to calm myself and turned a corner and walked to where twenty toilet stalls were lined against a wall, their blue doors mostly closed. I hesitated before I moved toward the one stall where the door was fully opened and swallowed whatever apprehension I felt and decided not to be a pussy and see if anyone was still there. *Some dumb hippie scratched a little girl. Please.* "Robert?" I suddenly asked again. There wasn't an answer.

I also moved closer because there was a glow emanating from the open stall, I realized and when I turned to face the stall I saw a small candle flickering on the lid of the closed toilet—it was white and lightly melting and situated directly in the center of the seat. I was confused until things began to clarify themselves.

ON THE WALL ABOVE the toilet was a drawing I couldn't make out in the faded light. I looked around to see if anyone was watching me as I moved into the stall—everything was completely silent—and I saw what the drawing actually was: a pentagram painted red and dripping with what seemed like blood. And then I froze when I saw the dead seagull, crushed and smashed into the corner, folded in on itself, mangled, its white feathers stained red and purple with blood, its neck twisted, its yellow beak opened in mid-cry. Someone from the cult had gotten into the Jonathan Club locker room *while we were there*. And a flash of anger hit, mixed with the sudden and very real fear I felt in that moment: the blood illustrating the pentagram came from the seagull, and the candle was supposed to represent a meaning. The sandals I was wearing pressed down on a hard object near the toilet, beneath its bowl. I thought at first it was something dead, another animal, another sacrifice, but when I lifted my foot and looked down I saw it was only a mask. And I couldn't help myself: I lowered my arm and reached to pick it up. It was hairy, there was some kind of fur on it, and when I brought it up to the light of the candle I stared at the face of what I guessed was a werewolf, a cheap Halloween mask, something a child would wear, lightly spattered with blood from the seagull.

It felt dirty in my hands—the snout, the fangs, the lupine eyes squinting into a growl—as I fingered the tight string where you secured the mask around your face. I kept staring at the mask, wondering what its purpose was, its meaning, how it tied into what the cult believed. I knew that the werewolf mask had been purposefully placed there—it was supposed to complete the meaning of the tableau, complement the dripping pentagram and the dead seagull—but I didn't know what it was supposed to add. Just that it was a warning of some kind. And then I flashed on: maybe Robert Mallory had done this.

In that silent moment someone suddenly touched my shoulder. I screamed and whirled around.

IT WAS THOM, so startled by my reaction that he began laughing. I brought a hand to my chest, and sagged against the stall door clutching the werewolf mask. "Goddamn it, Thom," I said.

Thom looked at the mask, curious, and leaned into the stall, glancing behind me, his eyes darting from the pentagram to the seagull. "Jesus, they got in while we were on the beach?" he asked in disbelief.

I just nodded, trying to control my breathing. And then he noticed something and looked at me as if I was to blame.

"It's just a dumb cult," he said.

"I know," I muttered.

"Why are you shaking so badly?" he asked while I walked away from him.

"Let's get out of here," I said.

In the empty parking lot we told the attendant about what we found in the men's locker room and he took the news with an unnerving nonchalance. "Yeah, they've been doing shit like that," he confirmed. "Animal sacrifice and shit. I'll see if security can come in." And then he left to get Debbie's car first. While Thom rifled through his wallet to give the valet a tip, Susan finally responded to the world. She removed her sunglasses and gazed at me and then Thom, and asked, "Are you okay?" But it was with a numbness that almost rendered the question futile, and for the first time I realized Thom had finally perceived this numbness and wasn't happy about it—in fact, on that cold afternoon at the beach club, it seemed as if he was genuinely appalled. He just stared at her hard, his green eyes devoid of their usual friendliness, his jaw clenched with rigid concentration. But it became a pose—he broke it down with fake relief and smiled, touching the side of her face, and said soothingly, "Yeah, babe, of course we're okay."

Later that night Thom called me at the empty house on Mulholland and asked if I'd drive him to LAX the following morning.

18

I WAS SO SURPRISED BY Thom Wright's request to drive him to the airport that I didn't have a contemplative moment to hesitate or use school as an excuse or to tell him I didn't want to—I just automatically said yes, even though I later wondered why Thom's mother or Susan wasn't driving him instead. That night Thom called my number on Mulholland and we had a brief conversation back and forth about what happened at the beach club before he asked if I could drive him to the airport, and after I agreed he told me to pick him up at ten—the flight was at noon—and he'd see me tomorrow morning. That was it. Driving to LAX wasn't a hassle in 1981 and I wasn't going to miss anything important in my morning classes at Buckley, and besides I would have probably done anything Thom Wright asked me to. I wanted to be around him, to be of use to him, to be his servant, and I gladly accepted the offer to drive him to the airport. This might sound somewhat absurd and adolescent but I felt *special* that Thom had requested this from me as I drove over to Laurie Wright's house on North Hillcrest Drive, between Sunset Boulevard and Elevado Street in Beverly Hills to pick up Thom at 10:00 a.m. on that Friday morning to take her son to LAX for an American Airlines flight that left at twelve. Lionel had purchased the ticket and was flying Thom to New York first class, which Thom waved off as being excessive, a little desperate, and totally reeking of guilt—Thom mentioned he'd be fine in coach but Lionel insisted, and I knew that Thom would've been excited either way, because first class didn't really matter to Thom Wright, or so I assumed in my fantasy of him, which ended up getting slightly cracked that morning.

The SHARDS

—

IT WAS A HOPELESS TRIP in many ways, because Thom knew he would be going to UCLA, but it gave him time to spend with his father—Thom being one of the only guys I've ever met who had a closeness with his dad that approached the brotherly. When Lionel moved to New York during the separation from Laurie, I knew this wounded Thom profoundly but everyone understood why Lionel did it: an opportunity too financially rewarding to ignore, and Lionel needed the money, considering how expensive the divorce turned out to be. Thom weathered it stoically, refusing to let it affect him to the degree where he was distracted from school or sports, and in crucial ways the separation and subsequent divorce intensified Thom's dedication, striving toward a certain kind of excellence while gaining a new knowledge of the world—he had learned something terrible about adults and marriage and moved through it. Lionel relocating to New York also brought Thom closer to Susan in many ways and it brought Thom and me closer to each other than we'd previously been. I admired everything about Thom Wright and, despite his obvious physical beauty, what I loved most was really his attitude and the way he cared about things and how he always put a positive spin on any potentially negative situation: you fall down, you get up; self-pity is for losers; don't be a pussy.

But this was easy to do when you were rich and handsome, and except for Lionel's abandonment Thom had never faced any hardship—he was, as we all were in today's parlance, a white privileged male, a king of the system, but Thom didn't flaunt it the way Jeff Taylor or Anthony Matthews did, bragging about their freedom while strutting along the pool's edge or peeling their Camaro out of the Fred Segal's parking lot, a what-the-fuck entitlement I also admired, especially as a writer, just as I was drawn to the outsider on the fringes like Matt Kellner or the insider with a secret like Ryan Vaughn, but that all floated away and seemed lost and disingenuous beside Thom Wright's earnest amiability, something that he was able to connect with more easily because of his physicality and wealth.

—

WHEN I PICKED HIM up he was dressed for cooler weather: corduroys and a navy-blue Polo argyle vest and a tweed blazer. Laurie Wright was in a pink robe, hugging her son in the front doorway of the white two-story colonial, and then Thom walked the stone path dividing the lawn, wheeling a large piece of gray Samsonite luggage with a carry-on bag slung over his shoulder, Wayfarers on, his hair still slightly damp from a shower and freshly shaven. Laurie waved to the car and I waved back, turning down the stereo. The mystery that hung everywhere as I drove from Mulholland to the flats of Beverly Hills was: Why isn't Susan Reynolds taking Thom to the airport? Why wasn't that happening in the narrative? I wondered this again as I popped the trunk and Thom heaved the Samsonite bag in. But soon Thom's presence erased any questions, because he was sitting next to me in the 450SL, in the flesh, and I could smell the shampoo and deodorant and whatever soap he used and the light scent of Aramis, the cologne Thom preferred—all of this mattered more. We weren't in a rush: in 1981 Thom could just check his bag and amble to the gate after I let him out at the curb in a semi-deserted midday LAX minutes before the plane took off—there were no checkpoints, you could go anywhere you wanted in an airport then, flights were often half filled, everyone dressed up. I was used to Thom's presence, having known him since 1976 and whenever I was alone with him—either driving around or sitting together in a movie theater or with our knees pressing against each other at lunch or with him showing me something in his notebook while just wearing his tight jockey shorts and standing close to me in the locker room—I never failed to experience a distracting erotic thrill, but it was faint and distant because there was no way to act upon it. What would Thom have done if I'd lightly rested my hand on his thigh as we drove to Westwood on a Saturday? How would Thom have reacted if I'd leaned over and kissed him as we sat side by side in the Nuart?

Thom immediately fiddled with the radio and landed on KROQ—Depeche Mode, "Just Can't Get Enough"—as I pulled away from the curb and started heading down Hillcrest.

"How you doing, buddy?" Thom asked.

"I'm good, man," I said. "I'm doing okay."

"Yeah?" he said. "I was worried about you a little bit there."

"Really?" I asked, startled. "When?" And then realized what he was referring to but didn't confirm it for him. "Oh. Yeah?"

"Everything's gone by so fast," he said, easing the seat back to accommodate his legs. He then rummaged through the leather carry-on: I glimpsed a Walkman, and a thick paperback, *The Stand.*

"I know, we haven't gone to the movies or hung out, in like forever," I said. "Just us."

"I know, I know, it's crazy," he said. "But you're okay?"

"Yeah." I paused. "Why do you keep asking that?" I said, knowing what the reason was. "I'm good."

"I just thought about what happened to Matt and I know you two were closer than I realized . . ." Thom said this without any sense of secrecy or judgment. "I mean I don't think I knew the guy at all but I feel bad that you lost a friend." Thom paused. "Why didn't you ever tell me you guys were close?"

"Tell you what?" I asked. "What was there to tell?" I paused. "We hung out sometimes," I said as I braked at the stop sign on Santa Monica. "I bought weed from him."

"I thought you didn't smoke weed," Thom said. "Or if you did I thought you'd buy it from Jeff."

"I guess you never knew." I shrugged. "I bought from both."

"What really happened?" Thom finally asked. "Do you know anything?"

"I guess he had some drug issues and um . . ." I suddenly couldn't concentrate, making the turn onto the boulevard, thinking about Matt. "It was an accident," I said, hoping this would wrap things up, waiting for the passing traffic to flow by. "Just this freak thing."

"Jeez," Thom said softly. "That's crazy."

"Yeah," I said. "I know." And then: "It sucks."

I started driving along Santa Monica, cruising through every light until we came to Rodeo, where Thom said, "I've missed you, man," turning toward me. Only Thom Wright could say something like that without it sounding scripted and cloying and I was touched and I turned back to him and smiled. "Yeah, I know, we've got to hang out when you get back." "For sure," Thom said. We started heading toward Wilshire Boulevard and were just listening to music—New Order, the Cure—when I asked him if he was looking forward to the trip, suddenly eager to find out Thom Wright's state of mind, where he was floating emotionally; everything about him was interesting to me. He sighed, trying to formulate the best answer for my question without lying. "I'm just doing it for my dad," Thom admitted.

"Yeah?" I asked. "I guess I knew that."

"I mean I'm going to UCLA, dude," Thom said. "And he knows it. The places we're looking at? I mean I can get into all of them but I don't want to leave L.A. I mean I don't know what my dad is thinking, it's kind of sad—I want to hang out with him but I'd rather just stay in New York for a week." Thom stared out the window as the Beverly Hills Park passed by. "But it'll be fine," he said, reassuring me as if I needed it.

"I know it will," I said. "Lionel is cool."

"Yeah," he said, sighing. "My dad's cool."

"Is your mom still seeing that guy?" I asked, just wanting to make conversation so I could hear his voice.

"Who?" he asked, surprised. "David?"

"Yeah, I guess," I said. "Whoever that was at Homecoming."

"David," Thom said, distractedly. "I don't know how serious it is. He seems nice. I want my mom to be happy. She's been pretty miserable." He paused and then added, "The last ten years."

I laughed and then he laughed as well. Thom wanted everyone to be happy, everyone deserved the best, life was unfair and you had to snap out of it and make it happen for yourself. He had been through something punishing—his parents' separation, his father's abandonment, the drawn-out divorce—and exited the other side, stronger and unscathed, so why hadn't Laurie? Thom turned to me. "You know what? She makes herself miserable. But she always has. So—I want her to be happy but I don't know if she's capable of it." I had nothing to say: there was nothing to fix, it was too vast a problem for me to offer advice, I'd known of Laurie Wright's unhappiness for a long time, Thom had his own coping mechanism to deal with it. We were now heading along Wilshire, curving through the corridor of apartment buildings, heading toward the 405, when Thom suddenly asked me something as he lowered the volume on the radio, fading out a Human League song.

"Can you do me a favor?"

"Sure, man," I answered automatically. "What is it?"

He crossed his legs, shifting in the passenger seat, trying to get comfortable.

"Can you kind of keep an eye on Susan, um, while I'm gone?" he asked.

I went cold inside—it was as if someone had turned off a switch—but I managed to ask casually, clearly, "Keep an eye on? What does that mean exactly?" I may have thought I wanted to perform any task Thom Wright requested but realized in that moment, as we cruised past Westwood and toward the freeway, that this wasn't true any longer. There was a suggestion in that request of something distrustful and perverse. He wanted me to be a secret agent and make sure his girlfriend was behaving—or at least that's what the request sounded like in the cabin of the Mercedes. There was something childish and weak about the request—something a loser would ask, not Thom. The day was getting wrecked, but softly, in a hushed way. This was the moment when I started looking at Thom Wright from a different angle. I was surprised and disappointed.

"Just hang out and make, I don't know, a concentrated effort to hang out with her a bit more." Thom paused, unsure if he should admit what he wanted to tell me so he could explain the meaning behind this request. "I don't know what she's going through exactly . . . but if you'd just, y'know, keep an eye on her. Go to the movies. Stuff like that." I was silent and stared out the windshield, contemplating what Thom just asked me, and how I should answer. The tangible participant suddenly arrived and had one idea of what to say, but the real Bret had another.

"You mean spy on her," I said. "You want me to spy on your girlfriend."

"No," he said, and then laughed. "I don't want you to spy on my girlfriend."

"What are you worried about?" I asked.

"I'm not worried about anything," Thom said but he sounded unconvinced.

"Really?" I asked. "You're not worried about something?"

He sighed. "Bret, just do what you usually do—whatever, keep an eye on her," Thom said, slightly frustrated. "That's all I'm asking."

"Is that what I usually do?" Thom was dragging me into something that I didn't want to deal with—everything about it seemed tinged with betrayal and bad faith and suspicion and all the things that I didn't know and others did: whispered secrets, the girlfriend who desired another guy, the girlfriend who had become numb and wanted to break away, the real reasons a classmate was prescribed Thorazine and spent six months in a mental institution outside of Jacksonville. Thom was silent, thinking things through, before he asked, "Do you . . ." He changed his mind. "Oh, forget it. It's nothing."

"What?" I said—I was completely cold by then, steeling myself, gripping the steering wheel so tightly my knuckles were white. "Ask me."

"What do you think of Robert now?" Thom asked. "I mean . . . after he's been here a couple months? Have your . . . feelings changed about him? Do you . . . like him now?" Thom was asking this in an uncharacteristically halting manner I'd never heard before. This suddenly seemed like a test I had to pass, and I started answering as the tangible participant but kept getting sidetracked by the real Bret, who argued: Why would you have to hide your feelings about Robert Mallory? Just be upfront with Thom Wright—you've known him for almost six years—and tell him what you really think. *Don't be such a pussy.* But this didn't happen: because what could I tell him? That I thought Robert Mallory was somehow connected to Matt Kellner's death? That I thought that he was responsible for the hallucinogens and the blood on the backpack and the drive out to Crystal Cove and that Matt probably stayed at a house on Benedict Canyon that week, wasted on drugs, while Robert attended Buckley, acting out a role, pretending nothing was happening, as a boy slowly went mad in a locked room on the second story of that house, surrounded by candles lit in a ritual?

"Oh . . . um, yeah," I stammered, the tangible participant was disappearing from me, waving goodbye as the rain swept across the vista he was standing on and I needed to bring him back in order to continue the conversation. "Yeah, I guess." And then I paused. "I don't really know him, Thom." I stopped again. "Obviously, he has . . . issues. He's on medication, he spent time in, um, that place in Jacksonville. I hope he gets better . . . but whatever happened at Susan's party was fucking crazy, though." I had to stop before I went on a tangent and offered a litany of things I thought were wrong about Robert Mallory. "Why are you asking me this?" I tried to camouflage my worry and annoyance with a soft, almost pleading voice. Thom was silent for a long time as I sped up the on-ramp of the 405 and merged into the light mid-morning traffic zooming along the freeway toward LAX.

"I don't know," he finally said. "Do you think he's a nice guy?"

"A *nice* guy?" I asked. "What does that even mean?"

"Bret," Thom warned, and then he asked again, "do you think he's a nice guy?"

"Are you going to tell him my answer?" I couldn't help but ask back.

Thom looked at me, and then, sounding shocked, asked, "What?" He realized something. "No, no, of course not. I'm not going to tell him anything. You can be honest with me, dude." He stopped, concerned, and worriedly asked, "I hope you always are."

"Nice guy?" I asked. "Maybe." I dreaded having this conversation. It was the last thing I thought Thom would want to talk about and it had already ruined my mood. "Do you?" I asked, both daring him and being evasive. "Do you think Robert's a nice guy?"

I noticed he had turned to me again, gauging my features as I was about to form another answer explaining who I thought Robert Mallory really was while concentrating on the lane I was speeding across. "I can't tell," Thom said, as if something had finally stumped him—a plotline Thom couldn't figure out. "It's weird."

I breathed in, pretending to play dumb. "What does that mean?" I asked. "You can't tell? You can't tell what?"

"It means sometimes I think I'm dealing with one person . . ." Thom started. "And then I feel I'm dealing with . . . an actor." He shook his head. "I'm not explaining this right, but someone pretending to be something . . ."

"No," I said as relief started flooding through the coldness and dread. "I feel that way about Robert sometimes, too."

"Yeah?" he said in a hopeful voice, and then, after thinking things through, admitted in a rush: "I mean, I know you probably don't like him. I know your feelings probably haven't changed. I don't know why I'm even asking you. I'm sorry."

"What was he talking to you about on the beach?" I asked. "Yesterday?"

Thom was now looking through the windshield—we were sharing the same view.

"Well," Thom started, "he was telling me about how grateful he was that he had friends here." Thom stopped then started again, unsure. "And then . . . he started telling me about how . . . he thinks he's being followed and—"

"He's being followed?" I asked—I automatically thought of myself but I knew that wasn't what Robert was referring to when he told Thom this yesterday on the beach.

"Yeah, he said it'd been going on for a while and that—these are his words—'some freak' is out there and has been following him ever since he first started coming to L.A. a year or so ago. Stalking him. Sometimes." Thom paused. "That's what he was telling me on the beach yesterday and that's when I realized that he's still, I don't know, maybe a little mental?" This came out as a question that Thom wanted me to answer in a reassuring voice that I just couldn't muster: *No, he's not, Thom. Hey, come on, buddy, he's our friend, he's not mental, he's cured.*

"Some . . . freak?" I asked instead. "What does that mean? Did he say who it was?"

"Yeah, like someone stalking him, that's the word he used, stalking, and he doesn't know who it is," Thom said. "I didn't know what to say. Y'know, being in the . . ." Thom looked over at me and tried to lighten the darkness that had descended on the conversation. ". . . the loony bin."

"You mean *the developmental center*," I said sternly, trying to amuse him. But none of this was funny and neither of us laughed.

"Yeah," Thom said tentatively. "So . . . I don't know how much to believe, because, I mean, he . . . could be making it up, right?" Thom asked in a tone approaching bewilderment. "But he says there's this person out there who has been, like, watching him and sending him stuff. I didn't know what to say. Maybe there is. Or maybe he's . . .

imagining it, I don't know." Thom stopped. "Anyway, that's what we were talking about on the beach."

In the pause that followed I realized we were almost at the off-ramp for the Howard Hughes Parkway and I started moving across lanes to reach it.

"But I know Susan cares about him," Thom said. "And I know that she thinks he's a kind of cause, someone to help out . . ." He trailed off as I looked over my right shoulder.

"Thom, what's happening between you and Susan?" I asked, once I veered down the curve of the off-ramp. "You can tell me. I won't say anything to her."

"I don't know," Thom muttered. "I think she's questioning a lot of stuff and we're all gonna be graduating and I think she's just preparing herself . . ."

"Preparing herself," I repeated. "For what?" And then I inhaled. "Thom," I said, "she's been a bitch. Come on. Get real, dude. She's turned into a total bitch."

When I said this Thom flipped open the passenger-seat visor to study himself in the mirror, checking for something on his face. He didn't find it. He pushed his fingers through his hair. He closed the visor: a useless gesture to deflect what I'd just said.

"Why don't you tell me what you really think," he said flatly.

"I just want you to be happy, man," I said. "I've never seen you guys fight. And now I've seen it twice in the last week and you guys were totally silent on the beach yesterday and—"

"We're good, dude, we're good," Thom insisted.

"Why isn't she taking you to the airport?" I asked.

"Because I wanted to talk to you," Thom said.

"Because you want me to spy on your girlfriend?"

"No, no—"

"Because you think she's going to do something with Robert Mallory?"

"Do something?" Thom asked, dubiously.

"Yeah, do something," I said.

"What?" Thom said, honestly shocked. "Why in the fuck would you think that?"

"Because I think he's capable of something," I said.

"But . . ." Thom stopped and thought about what he was going to say.

"But what?"

"But don't you think he's gay?" Thom asked.

"Who?" I asked back, completely confused.

"Robert," Thom said, looking at me strangely when I turned my head to face him. "Don't you think he's probably gay?" Thom stopped. "Don't you think that's his real problem?" Thom was looking at me but I had turned back and was staring out the windshield as I glided onto Howard Hughes Parkway and then to Sepulveda. "That's what he's hiding from us," Thom said. "Right?" He paused. "That's why he was in the institution."

My mind was riveted with confusion. I was so frustrated with Thom in that moment that I almost started writhing in my seat, but I kept cool.

"What in the hell are you talking about?" I asked quietly. "Why would you think this?"

"Well, I . . . suspected it," Thom said. "I think it was confirmed the night of Susan's party. Trying to make out with me, dude—"

"Thom, I think that was just the combo of booze and the Thorazine and whatever else he's taking," I said. "He was also trying to kiss Susan—"

"So then he's bi—"

"I don't think Robert Mallory is gay," I said carefully. "Has he hit on you?"

"No," Thom said. "But I get the gay vibe from him. You don't?" And then he asked, "Did he ever make a move on you?"

"What's the . . . gay vibe?" I asked. "No, he hasn't."

This was the first moment that I can look back on in my life when I can locate the cluelessness of heterosexuals about gay men. If Thom Wright assumed, based on nothing, that Robert was gay, then what did he intuit about me? About Ryan Vaughn, his co-captain of the Buckley Griffins? About Jeff Taylor, who occasionally accepted cash for sexual favors from Ron Levin? This absurdity took every muscle I had to refrain from saying, *Dude, he wants to bang your girlfriend*

what the fuck are you talking about how could you get this so wrong?
But instead, I just murmured, "I don't think Robert's gay, dude." We
were now on Sepulveda and I veered right onto Skyway. The Theme
Building—its crossed arches, the iconic space-age structure, a flying
saucer with four legs—was in view. The traffic was sparse in Depar-
tures, and there were just a few cars in front of the American Airlines
terminal as I parked the 450 at the curb and Thom and I got out. I
opened the trunk and helped him lift the tightly packed Samsonite.

"I'll be back in a week," Thom said. "Thanks for the ride."

"You okay?" I asked.

"I'm great, buddy," he said, smiling, seemingly completely unfazed by the conversation we'd just had. "You'll keep an eye on her?"
he asked once more. I nodded and then watched as he disappeared
past the sliding glass doors and into the terminal. This was the last
time I ever saw Thom Wright happy.

I WAS SHAKING when I got back into the Mercedes and started
driving toward the city. Everything crashed around me after the conversation with Thom Wright on that morning in October: my notions
of him became rearranged, altered—I no longer looked at Thom in
the same way after he asked me to keep an eye on Susan Reynolds,
or that he assumed his biggest romantic threat was actually gay. And
yet he asked me about Susan because he must have suspected something about her and the uncertain possibilities floating in the air or
maybe, the other voice argued, Thom simply *cared* and was worried
about leaving his girlfriend unattended for a week because she might
miss him too much and act out. And none of this had anything to
do with Robert Mallory because, according to Thom, maybe Robert
was gay, without realizing you had to be gay to understand that Robert Mallory most definitely *wasn't* gay, and Thom had started paying
attention to another narrative that he *thought* was unfolding—*Thom
isn't dumb exactly*—and this would be, in the end, his downfall,
another painful life lesson, this one about girls and relationships and
love, the first heartbreak, a year of sadness that Thom would have
to push through while both he and Susan attended UCLA, trying to

avoid each other on the tree-lined paths and the green quads and the streets of Westwood.

But maybe this all added up to nothing, I thought, trying to console myself. Maybe the writer was creating yet another scenario doomed with disillusionment and pain—and because of this the tangible participant suddenly reappeared and interrupted: of course I'd keep an eye out on Thom's girlfriend and plan a few events for the weekend. Maybe we'd go to the Windover Stables and watch Debbie ride Spirit; a number of horror movies had opened I wanted to see— *Galaxy of Terror, Strange Behavior, The Pit*—or maybe we'd go to the Seven Seas on Saturday night and dance to Siouxsie & the Banshees and Soft Cell and Adam & the Ants and drink whiskey sours and do bumps of Debbie's cocaine, lose ourselves in the last year of youth. I steadied myself as I drove to Buckley because I now had a plan. Who was I kidding? There was no way I wouldn't help Thom Wright and if this meant spying on Susan Reynolds then it was a job I'd embrace, not only without complaint but eagerly, so I could please the king.

I ARRIVED AT BUCKLEY about thirty minutes before lunch began and sat downstairs in the library, thinking I was going to dutifully study for the SATs I planned on retaking at the end of the month, but I was just fooling myself and bored and I walked upstairs to check out the *Los Angeles Times,* which I hadn't read that morning because I woke up late and headed over to Beverly Hills to pick up Thom—I knew I wasn't going to school on time and didn't set the alarm. There were usually two or three copies of the *Los Angeles Times* in the magazine rack by the front desk that the school librarian, Miss Crumbrine, presided over. I nodded to her as I took a copy from the newspaper holder and she simply greeted me with "Bret" in her carefully controlled and modulated voice—it always sounded like a put-down—and then I carried the *L.A. Times* over to a dark-wood-paneled cubicle and sat, unfolding the paper. Something started screaming at me from the front page: a row of black-and-white photos of Katherine Latchford, Sarah Johnson, Julie Selwyn and Audrey Barbour accompanied an article about the serial killer haunting the San Fernando Valley, who

The SHARDS

had sent a detailed letter to the *Los Angeles Times* last week that was verified by both the paper and the LAPD as coming from the Trawler. Everything disappeared around me.

MY EYES SHOT UP to the first paragraph of the article and I barely breathed when I turned to the "Metro" section, where it continued, blasted across an entire page with photos of where the girls' bodies were found as well as excerpts from the letter itself—some of it typed and redacted, some of it scrawled in different-color pens—which detailed a day only last week where "I and my friends" spent the afternoon wandering through an abandoned mill looking for the "appropriate dumping ground" and then stealing another dog last night from a neighborhood where an upcoming target was located—"the sacrifice" is how the Trawler referred to the target, who would ultimately be left to "the God." The article was a jagged piece of insanity and I had no idea why the *Los Angeles Times* was quoting so liberally from this madman's letter—it was repellent, ghastly, and yet I inhaled it like I was starving because it confirmed something for me and I located the hideous truth being expressed: the secret madness of the world was revealed. And it was, admittedly, fascinating to read details that clarified this monster's life and try to uncover what the motive might have been. The article quoted how he and "his friends" lived in motels and moved across the city by night, "following the moon," hitting on certain neighborhoods, looking for houses with the easiest access or perhaps finding out where potential victims they'd already "targeted" resided, and then "tracking" them to judge which ones were suitable for "sacrifice" and which ones were not, the ones they would be able to leave for "the God." The letter detailed how the Trawler and "his friends" watched young women jog alone on empty streets through a pair of binoculars, or maybe they shuffled after them through a mall's food court or were waiting for them in a public parking lot by the beach, hoping to find a target who was "appropriate" for "the God." The bodies were referred to as "paradises" that were needed in order to show off "the alterations," and the Trawler confirmed that he had been "altering" for years before he arrived in Los Angeles and that this city was just a next step in "the continuum."

—

THE PAPER WOULDN'T CLARIFY what the "alterations" were and they avoided listing the materials the Trawler used, only confirming that the alterations would begin before he had "removed the life from the body," and that "its blood" was tied to what he referred to as "The arousal" and once the arousal was maintained then the removal of "tissue and muscle and flesh" would happen so the alterations could begin. These were also referred to in the letter as "the remakings" and "the assemblage." There were a few details—the bleach poured into buckets, the hacksaw that went dull, the collection of Polaroids—that were rendered with even more horror because of what was left out. The mind automatically went to: What were the buckets of bleach for? Why was the hacksaw dull? What were the Polaroids of? And, confused, the mind answered these questions in the most gruesome ways. There were the "lonely spaces" between the murders, where the "blood lust washed" toward him, and that's when the home invasions would begin again and what the Trawler called "the rearrangements," which were actually "tests" to see "how viable" the "target was"—if they were suitable for "sacrifice" and "the God." There was the admission that he'd never "sacrificed" a target he had physically attacked—those were two separate things—and that so much of his time was spent "waiting" and that following people was what kept him "in control" and "the rituals" were part of a repeating narrative that was highly structured: the driving around, the selection of a particular neighborhood, the selection of the house based on the selection of the teenager who resided there, usually a girl, the stalking of the residence, the search for animals. This narrative, the Trawler admitted, aided in quelling his paranoia—he was distracted from "the pain" with "the project." The screaming of the victims, which the Trawler says he recorded, was the climax of the "ultimate annihilation": the larynx was crushed to stop the screaming and "the orbital sockets" were gouged so no one could see "me and my friends anymore" and the entire ritual could take up to a week by the time the final "assemblage" had been completed. There was nothing confirmed about Audrey Barbour in the article and there was no mention of Matt Kellner or any male victims.

The SHARDS

—

MY MIND WAS shrieking with horror when I finished the article, which had the force and intimacy of an interview even though it was mostly made up of excerpts from a madman's letter, and I was suddenly exhausted—the article was so unnerving that I pushed away from the cubicle feeling sick and knew I could no longer stay at school and concentrate on the rest of the day—I wouldn't even be able to sit at lunch and follow a simple conversation without a wave of fear cresting over me—and so I walked to the parking lot and got back into my car and drove to the empty house on Mulholland, where I walked past Rosa, who didn't seem surprised to see me, and went to my room and smoked what was left of Jeff Taylor's weed and lay in bed watching TV the rest of the afternoon, until it started getting dark, floating in and out of reality, wondering what Thom was doing on the flight heading east, and I suddenly envied his escape from Buckley and Los Angeles and the Trawler and Robert Mallory and the girlfriend who was going to leave him. I hauled myself off the bed and slowly removed the school uniform in a daze and slipped on a bathing suit and walked outside to the pool, where I waded in and slowly swam its length until I was tired enough to just sit in the unheated Jacuzzi and stare at the darkening sky. I got out, dried myself off and padded into the kitchen, where Shingy scrambled to attention and raced over and leapt up on his hind legs as I searched through the refrigerator looking for something to eat. Rosa was about to leave for the weekend and we had a brief conversation about *el perro;* she reminded me to feed Shingy the prepared food and not the dry dog food in the pantry, which I guess I had mistakenly done last weekend, and I nodded at her, blank-faced.

I took a shower and sorted out my homework and decided to call Susan at seven, which arrived surprisingly quickly.

I SAT ON THE EDGE of the bed and dialed Susan's number but she didn't pick up—I got her answering machine instead. I was annoyed and left a message, but the need to talk to her was overwhelming and I called the other number at the house on Canon and waited while the phone rang until Gayle picked up.

"Hey, Mrs. Reynolds, it's Bret—is Susan there?"

"Oh, hi, Bret," Gayle said. "How are you?"

She sounded slightly tipsy, overenthusiastic about my presence on the other end of the line. I imagined her standing in the middle of the cold ice-white living room holding a glass of Chardonnay she was pouring from an almost empty bottle.

"I'm fine," I said. "I called Susan's number and she didn't pick up. I thought maybe she was downstairs."

"Oh," Gayle said, sounding disappointed for me. "She went out to Palm Springs after school—didn't you know? She's staying with her grandparents."

I stood up and started pacing. "She did?"

"Yeah, she came back from Buckley and left around four—I told her to wait so she wouldn't hit any traffic but she insisted."

"Palm Springs, really?" I asked.

"Yeah, to see her grandparents," Gayle reiterated. "She didn't say anything? She'd been planning this for weeks. And with Thom gone and all . . ." She trailed off.

"Did she go with anybody?" I managed to ask.

"No, I don't think so," Gayle said. "Why?"

"I guess she told me," I said, confused, and then: "Did Thom know she was going to Palm Springs?"

"I assume so," Gayle said coolly as if somewhat offended by my question. "Is . . . anything wrong?"

"Oh, no, I'm fine, I'm fine," I said, regaining my composure. "I guess I'll see her on Monday."

"Yeah, she's coming back Sunday night," Gayle said. "You sure you're okay? You sound a little confused."

"No, I'm fine; thanks, Mrs. Reynolds," I said. "Have a nice night."

"You too, Bret." And then she clicked off.

I IMMEDIATELY walked out of my room, down the hallway, through the kitchen and the living room to my mother's bedroom and headed straight to her nightstand, where I opened a drawer and found the red cover of the Buckley roster. I hesitated only a moment and then walked to the wet bar to get a drink so I could steady myself and realized the tequila was gone, as were the rum and the two bottles of Smirnoff, and remembered with a pang that everything had been drunk since my parents left. I found myself steeling up as I walked back to my room and sat on the bed, opened the roster to twelfth grade, located Robert Mallory's number and waited, thinking through what I was going to say when I asked for him. I tried to come up with a reason but one wouldn't materialize. Fuck it, I thought, and just dialed the number listed in Century City.

Adrenaline lightly hummed through me as I waited for someone to pick up while I paced the room. And then a woman's voice answered the phone, saying, "Hello?"

"Hi, I'm calling for Robert," I said. "I'm a friend of his from Buckley. I'm Bret. Bret Ellis."

There was a brief pause suggesting a slight moment of confusion. "Oh, hello, Bret," the woman said as if she was composing herself. "Robert has mentioned you. You went to the beach with him yesterday." There was an unmistakable uncertainty to her voice, as if the woman was quickly trying to process both who I was and the reason why I was calling and somewhat bewildered by both.

"Yes, yes, that's me," I said.

"I'm Abby, his aunt," the woman said with a caution that was easy to locate.

"Nice to meet you, Abby," I said, rolling my eyes, impatient. "Is Robert there? Can I talk to him?"

"Actually, he's not here," Abby said tentatively. "He's . . . away for the weekend."

I closed my eyes and reached behind me to find the bed so I could sit down.

"Hello?" she said when I didn't respond.

"Oh, I'm sorry," I said. "I didn't know." And then I asked, "Where did he go?"

It took her a moment before she said, vaguely, "Out to the desert."

"I guess he didn't tell me," I said in a calm and casual voice. "I thought maybe we could go to a movie tomorrow, but, um, okay . . ." I didn't know what else to say until, "Did he go with anybody?"

She paused, deciding something. "Not that I know of." She answered in a coolly diplomatic fashion.

"Do you, um, know where he's staying?"

Another pause. "He told me he's staying with a friend in Rancho Mirage." I heard her say this, again, in a vague and offhand way. But the answer also had a finality to it that suggested: Don't ask me anything else.

"Okay, well . . ." I trailed off.

"Should I tell him you called?" she asked.

"No, there's no need," I said, finding my voice. "I'll see him on Monday. Thank you, Abby." I waited for her to say something else. She was silent too long.

"Not a problem, Bret," Abby finally said, and then she seemed to hesitate until I hung up first.

I FOUND THE NUMBER of my aunt in San Francisco and called to ask if I could stay at the house in Palm Springs that weekend and, surprised, she said yes and told me where the key was hidden but warned that it had been closed in early May and a housekeeper hadn't been to air it out since the last week of September—my aunt wouldn't be opening it up for "the season" (as she called it) until the end of October. I said it didn't matter and thanked her and then quickly packed a few things—I'd leave tomorrow, it was too late, I was tired and didn't want to drive at night, I'd leave Shingy enough food and water, I'd only be gone a day. I kept asking myself as I lay in bed before the Valium hit: how many people were involved in a lie and how long could they keep it going before everything cracked open and the truth spilled out?

19

THE 111 MERGED INTO North Palm Canyon Drive and, passing the huge wing-shaped roof of the visitors' center on the edge of town, I realized I hadn't been out to the desert since Spring Break, in the first week of April, when I went with Susan and Thom—Debbie wasn't quite in my narrative yet, at least we weren't dating—and the three of us stayed at my aunt's house on Toledo Avenue.

The towering San Jacinto Mountains loomed over the city in the darkening late afternoon, blocking out the sky, shadowing the boulders and sand dunes, palm trees and cactus that lay spread out beneath it. I opened the window of the Jaguar and the air smelled of brush and sage and it was warm but mild compared to the astonishing heat of the summer months. And I thought about how different things were now—bleak and death-haunted—contrasted to those few days the three of us spent as juniors during Spring Break, how innocent it seemed by comparison to where we'd arrived only a few months later: a dumb, rowdy party at the Hilton; another at someone's house on Rose Avenue in a mid-century modern that once belonged to the Kennedys, margaritas with fake IDs in the cantina at Las Casuelas, lying by the pool listening to the Doors and Sinatra, going to see *The Omen III*, horseback riding along the trails behind the Smoke Tree Stables, glimpsing Thom removing his bathing suit in the outdoor shower below the ficus tree and so bronzed that it looked as if his perfect ass and muscled thighs were painted white, hanging with Susan in the mornings beneath the umbrella by the Moroccan-tiled fountain, splitting a Quaalude while Thom slept in the master bedroom until he would walk groggily out in just his jockey shorts, the teenage Greek god yawning and rubbing his eyes, leaning in to give Susan a kiss, which she accepted with a smile, before he sank into the Jacuzzi, still lost in the dream that their relationship would move forward through UCLA and beyond. That week Susan mainly wore a chic white bikini—even picking up groceries and tequila at the Ralph's we frequented on Palm Canyon Drive—and I eyed the stares she got from so many men, young and old, blatant and charged with lust, and wondered why she was dressed so provocatively, revealing so much of her admittedly luscious body to the world. But it didn't matter, at least not then. I always brought my own tensions to wherever I went but they dissipated that week in Palm Springs, where the three of us lived together peacefully in the house on Toledo and our futures seemed to be moving along the paths that were promised to us, as we were arriving at the beginning of that paradisaical summer of 1981.

I HAD MADE IT in under a hundred minutes on Saturday afternoon, uselessly speeding across the freeways, not knowing what I was going to find, blankly staring out the windshield until I crossed the city limits—the "Welcome to Palm Springs" sign took me out of my trance—and then I was pulling into the curved driveway of the empty house on Toledo Avenue as dusk settled over the desert.

I found a key beneath one of the terra-cotta pots that sat on the raked gravel on either side of the entranceway and opened the doors that led into the foyer. In the musty darkness I reached toward the wall for a switch and the Sputnik chandelier lit up. I walked deeper into the house, turning on another set of lights, revealing a massive high-ceilinged sunken living room decorated in white and mustard with faint traces of purple, where a wall of floor-to-ceiling windows were interrupted by a white marble fireplace flanked by two of the many floor lamps with flower-patterned shades traced violet and yellow that stood on a wide expanse of white shag carpeting. I walked across the terrazzo floors in the kitchen and opened the refrigerator, which was empty but still working. I looked through the sliding glass doors that led out to the pool, and the backyard seemed barren, since the yellow umbrellas and lounge chairs were now stored in the garage, and though the pool was filled it was just a flat black surface lit only by the lights on the patio.

I moved through a hallway until I arrived at the master bedroom and opened the sliding glass doors to air it out. I sat on the bed and reached over and turned on the nightstand lamp and waited, deciding what to do, the numbness rendering me both calm yet clueless, as if I couldn't figure out exactly what it was I'd traveled to Palm Springs to find. But then I thought about Matt Kellner, and then Audrey Barbour, and that none of us really knew how dangerous Robert Mallory was—I seemed to be the only one who suspected this—and the danger motivated me to get off the bed and drive to Susan's grandparents' house, the main incentive being that it was only two minutes from my aunt's on Toledo; if it had been anywhere else I might not have gone.

IT WAS NOW NIGHT and there was no one out on Toledo Avenue: just a long stretch of wide and open highway that was only ever lightly traveled and completely deserted on that Saturday. I drove for a few blocks and then made a left onto Sierra and then a block later made another left onto a cul-de-sac called Silverado, where I saw a white Cadillac and Susan's BMW parked in the driveway of a mid-century modern, ground lamps situated on the shiny green lawn lighting an array of palm trees, and I felt a palpable relief that broke through the numbness and faint dread because it meant Susan actually was at her grandparents' and not staying somewhere else. I slowly pulled my car into the cul-de-sac, and as I made the turn that would take me back onto Sierra I stopped. And though I knew this was always a possibility I was now shot through with the fear that had been trailing me since the beginning of September, because a black Porsche was parked next to the curb leading up to Susan Reynolds's grandparents' house.

I TURNED off the headlights and parked on the other side of the street, away from the house, and waited even though I didn't know what I was waiting for. I just sat there in the driver's seat staring through the windshield as an hour passed and then another one began. Nothing moved within the cul-de-sac—I couldn't tell if the other houses were occupied, there didn't seem to be any cars in the driveways, there were no shadows or muffled voices behind the bay windows of the living rooms or on the patios of the backyards. The only light came from Susan's grandparents' and an ambient silence surrounded everything, broken by the words I was muttering to myself within the cabin of the Jaguar. There was something so brazen about what Susan and Robert were doing—were they really so childish (or ill) as to think they could get away with this? And then I thought: Was Robert actually staying with Susan? Or was he really staying with a friend in Rancho Mirage, as his aunt had suggested to me, and was only visiting Susan that night?

And then they stepped out of the house as I watched from the darkness of the Jaguar.

They arrived at the car and Robert opened the passenger door for Susan. As he walked around the Porsche to the driver's side he stopped before getting in and quickly scanned the neighborhood, as if he was purposefully looking for someone, but didn't seem to notice my mother's car parked in relative darkness—or it didn't interest him. The Porsche revved up and slowly pulled away from the curb and made a right onto Sierra. I waited a beat and then started the Jaguar and followed them.

ROBERT DROVE INTO TOWN, where he pulled the Porsche into an open parking lot situated in the middle of North Palm Canyon Drive at La Plaza and found a space. I drove by and circled the block and then parked the Jaguar at the opposite end of the lot, next to a hedge of pink bougainvillea, and carefully made my way toward the street. There was only one place where Susan and Robert would be going and that was Las Casuelas Terraza, the town's most popular Mexican restaurant, just a block up from where Robert had parked. I breathed in, dizzy, as I moved along the sidewalk, drifting past various people, just shapes, featureless to me, until I was where the restaurant announced itself—I didn't want to walk by the open patio that faced the street, so I crossed to the opposite side of Palm Canyon Drive and moved along the sidewalk there while keeping an eye on the restaurant, which had been a fixture for me since my childhood.

It was almost overly familiar: the arched doorways, the adobe roof, the mission bell in the stucco tower, the green shutters that framed the second-story windows and the baskets of flowers hanging below them, the lanterns that glowed on the patio, the palm trees looming in the darkness above. When I looked up at the waving fronds and the twirling weathervane atop the mission bell, I noticed the warm wind lightly gusting around me, the first wave of that season's Santa Anas, and I stared up at the San Jacinto Mountains, which were now just a black mass overlooking the town, and shivered. I could hear the mariachi band inside the cantina softly playing "Hotel California" as I jogged across Palm Canyon and moved to the entrance of Las Casuelas and walked up the steps through the open wooden doors, and across the tiled entranceway, where I passed an empty hostess stand beneath an iron chandelier and took a seat at the deserted bar that led out to the cantina, which was where I assumed Robert and Susan were sitting. A bartender startled me and asked what I'd like. I said "Just a water" before changing my mind and ordered a Pacifico and then asked if I could have a basket of complimentary chips and salsa. I needed to eat something or else I was going to be sick. Once I downed the beer and ate a handful of the tortilla chips I moved toward the arched entrance of the cantina, where the mariachi band was playing, and which seemed crowded compared to the rest of Las Casuelas that night—a slow Saturday in the off season. I motioned to the bartender that I was going to move to the cantina, and he asked if I wanted to order something to eat. I said no and laid down cash for the beer.

I WALKED through the arched doorway with "La Cantina" written over it next to a large-scale painting of a multicolored parrot and immediately sat at the end of the curved counter, somewhat hidden by the trunk of the date palm that rested in the middle of the bar, which was lined with shelves of alcohol beneath a thatched hut dangling with white Christmas lights, and I saw them.

They were at a green-tiled table for two that overlooked Palm Canyon Drive, a candle and an unopened menu between them—only one, because Susan knew it so well. She had already ordered a margarita and it looked as if Robert was having a Coke and the tableau seemed so innocent. She was talking and he was listening, a Spanish-mission lantern hanging from the column next to the table suffusing it with a dim orange glow, and a ceiling fan rotated slowly above them and the mariachi band was on the stage bathed in pink light, still quietly playing another Eagles song. I felt calm watching Susan and Robert—a kind of relief instilled me with hope, because the mystery of Susan and Robert seemed answered, and sighting them confirmed something that had been gnawing at me for weeks that I could never figure out. There was a truth now, and yet the numbing calm was diffused with a distinct and sudden sadness. I stared at them while I was hidden at the bar and realized it almost didn't matter that I was there: the two of them were so locked into each other they could have been anywhere, another country, another planet—they only noticed each other, everyone else was invisible, only the other one mattered. Susan was relaxed and Robert was suddenly laughing and it was genuine—he seemingly wasn't playing a role for her and he looked happier than I'd ever seen him. And it was obvious they were a couple—this was a date and not just two friends meeting up in Palm Springs for a drink—there was a pronounced intimacy connecting them.

But what had I been expecting? Susan and Thom were never going to be together forever in some kind of rosy fairy tale we had collectively dreamt up: the cliché of an aspirational high-school romance starring the quarterback and the most beautiful girl at Buckley. Susan had been moving away from Thom for months now and Robert Mallory was simply the catalyst for her to actually make the break. A version of this notion first struck me on that day in Westwood last May when Susan said, "Thom isn't dumb exactly . . ." and I had seen so many instances even before Robert Mallory entered our lives: pulling a hand away, an unfinished kiss, the Icehouse song, the bikini in the supermarket—these had been clues emerging within a widening puzzle. The sadness I felt was tied to Thom's impending pain and it was something I didn't want to process: Thom didn't deserve this. But, then, I thought, as the fear started overriding my sadness: who *deserved* anything? We get what we get.

SUSAN SAID something to Robert and he nodded, picking up the menu as she pushed away from the table and stood up. I immediately slipped off the stool and quickly headed back through the restaurant, and went to the pay phone situated in a corridor where the restrooms were. I closed the door but kept it ajar so the overhead fluorescent light wouldn't reveal me and waited. I briefly turned my face away when I saw Susan walking past the hostess stand and toward the *baño de mujeres,* my heart beating fast, the adrenaline I'd become used to that autumn shooting through my system, freezing me into a heightened alertness. I was clutching the receiver and bowed over as Susan passed by and then turned my head and watched as she entered the women's restroom. I hung up the phone and waited before I opened the door of the booth and as if I was floating just landed in the middle of the foyer. A couple walked in and were seated by the woman at the hostess stand while I zoned out on a row of sombreros hanging on the wall and then looked up at the swaying black iron chandelier and through the open doors I heard the wind gusting along Palm Canyon, people lowering their heads as they walked against it, and a tumbleweed flew across the highway, followed by another one.

And in that moment I thought about leaving: just walking into the night and getting in the car and driving back to L.A. and playing the tangible participant and calling Debbie Schaffer and pretending that none of this ever happened. It wasn't my narrative anyway—it was Susan's and Robert's and ultimately Thom's. And yet I felt invested—weren't we all connected as classmates, and if something affected one of us then wouldn't the others feel the reverberations of our suffering and therefore console and protect us? But in that moment I realized this wasn't true. Because no one had been affected by Matt Kellner's death and my anguish. Everything was futile. There was no hope. The world didn't notice your pain. That familiar tide of anger crested against me—the anger was actually a motivator—and I suddenly didn't care if Susan thought I was interfering with her secret life. On one level I understood what she was trying to do—move away from the simplicity of Thom, make herself happy, find another world, freedom, numbness as a feeling. On another level it made me sick.

"What are you doing here?" I heard a voice ask.

—

I TURNED AROUND. Susan was facing me, staring blankly even though there was a new hardness creasing her features. I didn't know how long she'd been standing there.

"Oh, hey," I said, lamely pretending to be surprised. "I was just, um, meeting my aunt for dinner and—"

"What are you doing here?" she asked again, interrupting me, stone-faced. She waited for an answer.

"Susan . . ." I finally said. It wasn't entirely implausible that we would both be in Palm Springs for the weekend but she knew there was something wrong.

"Why are you here?" she asked, but it didn't sound like a question anymore. "What are you doing here?"

I stood in place, staring at her, frozen.

"Are you going to pretend you just ran into me?" She asked this in a soft voice but I could tell from her eyes that she was furious.

I lifted my hands up and could only say her name again. "Susan . . ."

She hadn't moved. She was standing very still, composing herself, a statue, as she glared at me. "How did you find out?" she asked.

"Find out . . . what?" I asked back, dumbly.

"That I'm in Palm Springs," she said in a flat voice.

"Susan, I . . ."

"Oh, fuck it, Bret." Her eyes had watered and she raised a hand to the side of her neck and held it there as if it was a position that would calm her. "What are you doing? Do you want to ruin everything?"

"How long did you think you could keep this up?" I asked softly.

"Keep what up?" she asked with a visible annoyance.

"Whatever you're doing here with Robert," I said tonelessly in a hollow voice. "Hiding this from Thom." The moment suddenly seemed so intimate that I was almost embarrassed for myself but I couldn't turn away from her. Susan suddenly looked shocked by the mention of Thom's name and then realized something and asked, "What did he tell you on the way to the airport yesterday?"

I paused, staring at her, stuck, and then mumbled an answer.

"What?" she asked, glaring. "I couldn't hear you." She said this as if reprimanding me, a teacher scolding a student.

"To keep an eye on you while he was gone," I said, making my voice clearer.

"Jesus," she muttered. She kept the tensed hand on her neck.

"Susan, what's happening—" I started.

She took a step forward. "Please don't tell Thom." The numb hard woman suddenly morphed into a pleading little girl. "Please, I'm begging you not to tell Thom." She said this in a strained voice barely above a whisper, and the way she asked this activated something in me.

"Tell Thom what?" I asked loudly. "What shouldn't I tell Thom? That you're out here with Robert Mallory? Spending the weekend with Robert Mallory? Susan, what in the fuck are you doing?" I stepped toward her.

"Don't yell at me," she said, glancing around, but there was no one near us.

"What are you doing?" My voice also had a horrible pleading quality to it now.

"Just promise me you won't tell Thom," she said, still glancing around the foyer, and then back at me, guiltily.

"Promise not to tell him what?" I asked. I realized I was livid and that I wanted to lash out and hurt her. "That you're fucking Robert Mallory—"

"Oh, stop it," Susan said, suddenly disgusted. "You don't know anything. You don't know what you're talking about. You sound like an idiot—"

"What? I'm wrong?" I asked, incredulous. "You're not?"

"Stop it—"

"Is he staying with you? Is he really staying with your grandparents? Who do they think he is?" I asked. "A *friend*?"

"Yes," she said. "Because he is. He is a friend."

"I think he's dangerous," I said quietly. "I think he's going to hurt you."

"Why are you here?" she asked again, ignoring what I'd just said. "Why do you want to ruin everything?"

"*You're* ruining everything!" I shouted without realizing, then turned to see what Susan was looking at: the hostess had returned to the stand and was staring at me wide-eyed, shocked, and then shook her head before glancing away. I stepped closer to Susan.

"I love you," she was saying. "Do you understand that? I love you. I've always loved you. I don't know why I care so much but I've been feeling so lost and . . ." She stopped, and waited, before she asked, "Do you love me, too, Bret?"

"Yes, of course, yes," I said, faltering. "You know that."

"Then please promise me you won't tell Thom," she said.

"I hate Robert," I said in a rush. "I hate him. I don't understand why. But I hate him. And I hate that you're here with him. It makes me sick, Susan. It makes me sick for Thom. It makes me sick for you. I hate him." I was on the verge of weeping. I could feel my face crumpling. I couldn't control myself. It just poured out of me.

"Bret, this isn't about you," Susan said calmly. "It doesn't matter."

"I hate him," I said. "I think he did something to Matt—"

"Did something to Matt?" she asked, recoiling. "What are you talking about?" This was the pleading voice again. "You sound crazy. You sound so crazy when you say that."

"But *he's* crazy," I said, unable to control my rambling. "I'm not the crazy one. Robert is. He's dangerous. He's sick—"

"Shhh, Bret, please, you have to stop this," she said. "You don't know anything. I can't talk now but please just . . ." Desperation caused her to trail off.

I closed my eyes and shook my head and helplessly acquiesced. "I promise. I promise I won't tell Thom."

"I love you," she said again.

"Don't say that anymore," I scowled. "He's ruining everything. This is going to wreck Thom—"

"Thom will be fine," she said in a hushed voice.

"And it's going to wreck whatever we had—"

"No, no Bret, it isn't," she said. "I have to go."

I was losing it and I just wanted to end the conversation when I realized it was actually over. I finally said, "Don't tell Robert you ran into me. Don't tell him you just saw me. Don't tell him you talked to me."

Susan paused and then reached for my hand. I let her lift it up as she clasped it.

"I don't know if I can do that, Bret." She said this in a controlled voice—gentle but steady. "I'm with him—"

"If you tell him, then I can't keep my promise," I said, looking hopelessly around—at anywhere but Susan in that moment. "I'll keep your secret. I won't tell Thom that you were here but you can't tell Robert you saw me. Can you do that?" My eyes landed back on her.

She slowly nodded. "And you'll never tell Thom?"

"If you don't tell Robert you saw me . . ." I stopped, remembered something. She waited. And then I said, echoing her, "Your secret is safe with me."

She quickly drew me into an embrace—it was tight and fierce—and then let go and walked quickly away without saying goodbye and back toward the cantina. I stumbled across Palm Canyon Drive, the Santa Anas guiding me as I blindly walked into the parking lot, passing Robert's Porsche, and then got into my mom's Jaguar and, through a scrim of tears, started driving to the house on Toledo. I'd leave early the next morning and get back to L.A. before noon.

AT SOME POINT on the drive from Las Casuelas to the house on Toledo—which took only about ten minutes—I noticed a pair of headlights behind me on East Palm Canyon Drive and I began to suspect someone was following the Jaguar. The only reason this notion occurred: there was no one else out. When I made a right onto La Verne Way, and it made the same turn, I realized that the headlights belonged to a beige-colored van; I caught a glimpse of it beneath a streetlamp in the side-view mirror. The paranoia was so heavy that night that my mind began to trick me into thinking that the beige-colored van was, in fact, trailing after me and that it wasn't headed anywhere else—that it was homed in on the Jaguar and it wanted to know where I was going, where I resided, where I'd be sleeping for the night, where it could find me later, so someone could wear a ski mask and hold a butcher knife while standing over the bed and in a groaning drawl ask me if I wanted to die, the eyes wide with madness and hunger.

I was paying attention to the rearview mirror and barely looking at the road, only concentrating on the headlights behind me, when I veered into the oncoming traffic lane. But there was no one out, and as I veered back into my lane another wave of dread overcame me and I felt nauseous and I needed to take a Valium to quell the panic and, nearing the house on Toledo, I started wishing away everything that had happened that night—I was actually praying. I looked back into the rearview mirror: the van was still slowly gliding behind me. *Don't be a pussy*, I heard Ryan Vaughn's voice, and my heart cracked. As I turned into the driveway of my aunt's house I expected the beige-colored van to slow down but it didn't—the van just simply drove by as I sat there in the Jaguar, a mess, on the verge of tears, wiped out by the dread my paranoia had activated, and by Susan, and by Robert, and what was going to happen to Thom, and by the dead girls, and the Trawler, and Matt Kellner. The van just kept driving forward, moving along Toledo, fading away from me, and I watched until its taillights disappeared. *You. Had. Imagined. Something.* I almost whimpered with relief as the wind gently rocked the car. I was so sickly exhausted that I trudged to the master bedroom without turning any of the lights in the living room or patio off and closed the sliding glass doors leading out to the pool and took two of the Valiums I had brought and started to fall asleep listening to the wind outside gusting over the desert.

And before I drifted off I realized I had seen the beige-colored van a number of places during the fall of 1981: in the Buckley parking lot the night the Griffin was desecrated, on the third floor of the Galleria's garage on the first day of school when Robert followed me across Ventura Boulevard, in the alley behind the space on Melrose the night the girl was scratched by the hippie. These three remembered sightings led my mind to flash on many more, a few that I thought were real, but some of these flashes weren't verified, they were imagined. That night in Palm Springs was the first time I became aware that there was something sinister about the beige-colored van and that its presence was a reminder, another example, of everything that was careening out of control that fall. And it was the first time I vaguely connected it to Robert Mallory. I don't know why—there was no proof that linked them—but somehow, I knew, the beige van was *about* him. There was a link—I just didn't know what it was yet.

A FAINT CRASHING SOUND woke me up. Something had tipped over outside and shattered. I thought maybe the wind had toppled one of the large and empty terra-cotta pots in the backyard onto the concrete patio—the Santa Anas were louder than earlier, occasionally screaming as they swept over the desert. I looked out through the sliding glass doors of the master bedroom and realized everything was black—the lights I had left on were out, and there was no glow emanating from the hallway leading into the master bedroom or spilling onto the patio, which meant that the lights I'd left on in the living room and the foyer were off as well. And I knew that I hadn't turned them off before I fell asleep. The Valium helped me remain calm as I reached for the phone next to the lamp—but the line was dead, and just a hint of the familiar dread drifted over me. My first thought: a power outage caused by the winds had darkened the house. But when I got up and slowly moved toward the living room, running a hand along the wall to help guide me through the darkness, I could suddenly see past the panels of glass on either side of the front door that the streetlamps and other entranceways on Toledo were lit. I had fallen asleep with my watch on, and when I pressed the side of the face the digital numbers lit up and told me it was three-thirty. I stood in what was an almost total darkness—the only light was faint and either coming from Toledo and through the panels of glass or from the high desert moon that dimly lit the house, forming shadows and silhouettes once my eyes adjusted: I could see the outline of the large ficus in the backyard bending in the wind, the hedge behind it that separated the house from the desert, the dark rectangle of the pool, but there were no colors, nothing was distinct. I moved from wall to wall, finding various light switches and uselessly flipping them up and down: nothing. Everything was dead. The sound of the wind would ratchet up, boom across the desert and then fade away into a momentary silence before sounding again.

I gave up and turned and headed to the bedroom, where I knew I could easily fall back into a hazy Valium sleep, but froze when a beam of light slowly started moving across the living room.

SOMEONE was by the pool holding a flashlight and making their way across the windswept patio and the beam continued traversing across the walls of the darkened living room, occasionally stopping on a piece of furniture as if it had landed on something it thought was important. The beam moved across the glass coffee table and the white shag rug and then moved along the bookshelves that were connected to the hallway I'd stepped back into, which led to the master bedroom. The beam left the living room and from my vantage point at the end of the hallway I saw the light slowly appear again, enlarging as it moved across the patio and then crawled along the floor of the bedroom, until it landed on the bed and stopped suddenly, as if it was surprised that the bed was empty, that there was no one in it, that whoever had been in it was gone. The light then moved back and forth over the bed from one side of the room to the other, like it was searching for something, and then it stopped, confused, when it landed on the Gucci backpack I'd brought with me.

Whoever was holding the flashlight moved away from the sliding glass door of the master bedroom and started creeping through the yard toward the patio and back to the side of the house where the kitchen was. I moved into the living room, following the light, and watched as it suddenly waved across the walls and traversed the bookshelves again.

My mind was fumbling: I thought it might have been a security guard from the Canyon Estates, but they would have rung the doorbell and they wouldn't have been prowling the backyard. The light remained still and then suddenly jerked over to where I was standing, and I instinctively ducked to the floor, hiding from it.

The beam paused, lingering, and then I watched as the light slowly moved from across the living room wall, traveling toward the kitchen, sometimes stopping before it started moving again, trailing the floor, then the ceiling.

Through the Valium and sleep daze I finally realized with a sickening jolt: whoever was out there was looking for the person in the house. There was a car in the driveway. There was an unmade bed. They were wondering: where was the person residing here? There were dozens of empty houses lining Toledo that night waiting to be robbed, but this person had chosen this particular house *because someone was in it,* my mind screamed.

The beam of light crossed the living room again, purposefully lingering in corners where the terrified victim might be pressed against a wall, hiding. I was still on the floor, shaking so hard I couldn't control it. But it was more frightening not to know where this person was, and I slowly lifted my head so I could keep my eyes on the flashlight.

—

The SHARDS

THERE WAS NO other light from the backyard—not from the patio, not from the pool—and I kept wondering who this person could be and what they wanted and why they had chosen this house. It was just a barely discernible shape behind a white beam of light—I couldn't see anything else. The wind was suddenly battering the sliding glass doors, screaming again, and then, just as suddenly, it subsided.

The light was now moving back to the bedroom—it changed course on its way to the kitchen. The beam scoured the pool and ran across the outdoor shower, the ficus trees, the Moroccan-tiled fountain.

I realized I'd been so afraid that I hadn't even known it—the fear had been so massive and abstract—and now it was specific, and this caused me to stand, hunched, and glance over at the front door, figuring out an escape.

It was totally silent in the house as the light returned to the living room and started scanning it again.

I dropped and crawled to a space behind one of the sofas and in my fear shouted out something—not a word, not for help, not a warning, just a sound, garbled and high-pitched.

The beam froze and then the light frantically moved across the shag carpet and along the couch, trying to locate where the sound came from. The light immediately landed on the sofa, but I was behind it and couldn't be seen, and then the light stopped, as if it realized something.

I was pressed against the back of the couch, breathing raggedly, paralyzed, barely able to contain the fear—I looked over at the front door again. The wind momentarily picked up and then it was silent. I waited, uselessly hoping this was a dream that I'd be waking from soon, but knew with an awful certainty it wasn't. I didn't know if I'd been targeted and if this person was an actual threat and I didn't want to find out by provoking them. But I couldn't help myself and I emitted the strangled cry again.

I STARTED SLOWLY CRAWLING across the living-room floor toward the hallway leading to the master bedroom, everything shrouded in darkness, and then I stood up and stumbled along the hallway toward the bedroom's entrance, again using my hand to guide me.

I just needed the keys to the car—that's all I was focusing on. They were on the nightstand by the bed. I didn't need anything else. I'd drive back to L.A. in just the T-shirt and underwear I'd been sleeping in if I had to.

The beam of light from behind the sliding glass doors was now tracing the headboard and then the wall above the bed, and I dropped down to the floor just before the doorway that led into the master bedroom. I was shaking so badly I couldn't stay still, but I forced myself to wait. And in those moments the beam disappeared.

I kept waiting. Just the sound of the wind could be heard. And then the beam reappeared, aimed at the ceiling, and I could hear another noise besides the wind and I didn't know what it was at first.

It was just a tapping sound, even and rhythmic, but slow: something was tapping against the glass of the sliding doors.

When I looked up at the round beam of light moving forward and backward across the ceiling I realized that the person outside was slowly tapping the flashlight on the glass door that led into the master bedroom.

It was teasing, it was a warning, they were waiting for me to show myself and make a move for the keys.

I was so frightened I shouted out "Robert!" and then I shouted it again: "Robert!"

I'm not even sure I thought it was Robert Mallory at that point— it was just what I landed on in the moment, it was just panic. Because of this the light automatically clicked off—the beam disappeared. Suddenly it was gone. I waited for it to come back but it didn't appear again.

I couldn't move for what seemed like an hour, just listening to the wind, trying to calm myself down. When I looked back at my watch I was stunned to see it was only three-thirty-seven. The entire ordeal— from when I awoke to the moment I looked at the watch—had lasted barely seven minutes.

I grabbed the backpack and the car keys and ran from the house and drove out of Palm Springs only wearing my T-shirt and underwear and arrived back in L.A. at dawn, as the sun began rising over the city.

20

WHEN I PULLED UP to the empty house on Mulholland early that Sunday morning I immediately noticed that the mailbox at the bottom of the driveway was open and there was something inside it: a Maxell cassette. I first thought it was left there by Debbie Schaffer—a mixtape filled with songs that she imagined meant something to me, music that commented on our relationship, and what we had supposedly built together since June, the girlfriend-boyfriend thing. A pang of apprehension and guilt flowered within me as I pulled the cassette out of the mailbox and tossed it onto the passenger seat, and then continued up the driveway, opened the garage and parked the Jaguar. I could hear Shingy's excited barking from within the house as I got out of the car and slumped against it, imagining the messages waiting for me on the answering machine from Debbie, left on Saturday night, asking where I was and why I wasn't picking up. I wondered if, by now, she knew I'd been in Palm Springs, if Susan had called her when she got back to the house on Silverado and told Debbie about the confrontation in Las Casuelas. I also, in that moment, in the garage, truly didn't care. The Santa Anas rattled the garage door and I realized I had zoned out and needed sleep.

I WATCHED AS the dog ran circles across the lawn in the morning light, seemingly delighted by the hot winds that gusted across it—leaping and barking at them—as much as he was by my return. I left the kitchen door open so he could come back inside and then walked tiredly to my bedroom, where I placed the cassette on my desk and dropped the Gucci backpack by the bed and almost immediately fell asleep. When I woke up it was two in the afternoon and my thoughts were about Susan and Robert, as if I was still dreaming about them— fucking each other, naked, in one of the guest bedrooms of her grandparents' house, the winds howling, Susan's breasts, the nipples stiffened and wet with Robert's saliva, Robert's pale ass pumping into her, their mutual cries of ecstasy; my hard-on was throbbing and I jerked off quickly to these images to get rid of them—but I couldn't, even after I came. I was dreading Thom's return, and frightened about the following day at Buckley without him there, the endless pantomime of it all: pretending we were in someone else's dream, a place where I hadn't seen Susan in Palm Springs with Robert that weekend. I reached over and pushed PLAY on the answering machine: Debbie leaving two messages on Saturday night—disappointed, then perturbed—along with one from my mother, who was somewhere still in Greece, and a number of hang-ups. I lay back and stared at the Elvis Costello poster adjacent to the bed: *TRUST.*

There had been a point along the line in the last seven weeks where Susan had fallen in love with Robert Mallory and I couldn't have imagined anything more hopeless happening than this—at least socially—because it could only be hidden for so long and once it was revealed everything would get altered, everyone's relationships would become rearranged, sides would be chosen and this would completely change the mood of our senior year, and I was afraid it would ruin Thom, no matter how sunny and strong he appeared on the surface. There was a widening crack that Thom hadn't paid attention to—and it was going to swallow him up. Everything would curdle, become bitter, it would be our only point of reference, the world would die. The one person who had known about this so far was Debbie Schaffer, and as I lay there in bed on that Sunday afternoon I suddenly resented her because she had seen what the outcome was going to be at a point long before I did and hadn't warned anybody. She had known that everyone was going to find out and this made her guilty in my eyes; she was so entitled and so careless. What did she expect from me? I thought angrily as I wiped the semen off my dick and stomach with a Kleenex. Had she really spent hours creating a mix-tape that would detail her feelings about me in twenty-four songs and did she really expect me to be touched by this? And then the flow of emotion stopped and my eyes landed on the cassette across the room on the desk that she had left for me while I was in Palm Springs and I realized something: I had only assumed it was a mixtape Debbie had made, but there wasn't a case with a listing of the songs on side A and side B along with the geometric shapes Debbie favored, which often dotted the title of each track, and I only then noted that there had been something else wrong. I pushed myself off the bed and walked to the desk and looked down at the Maxell cassette.

Someone had misspelled my name with two "T"s. BRETT. And it wasn't Debbie's handwriting.

I STARED AT THE CASSETTE for a long time without picking it up because I suddenly didn't want to touch it if it wasn't from Debbie. I thought hopefully, uselessly, for just one moment, that it was from Ryan—that maybe he'd had a change of heart about us, that maybe the extra "T" was a private joke, a cassette filled with Bob Seger and Springsteen songs—but knew that was impossible. There was something wrong about the cassette. When a wave of hunger-induced nausea hit me I realized I was starving and left the bedroom and walked to the kitchen, where I looked through the fridge and pulled out a bowl of pasta Rosa had prepared and picked at it while looking at the Santa Anas rippling the pool and Shingy splayed on the lawn beneath the afternoon sun, his fur tousled by the winds, and I just stood in the kitchen, standing in place by the island, for a very long time, slowly eating the penne with my fingers, before I realized I had to walk back to the bedroom—something forced me to—and immediately picked up the cassette and slipped it into the tape deck of my stereo. I pushed PLAY and then sat at my desk and waited.

I had expected a song but there was nothing at first—just silence—then a gradual buzz, a humming, and I thought maybe this was the beginning of the first track. I leaned over to adjust the volume but couldn't hear anything else, and I was distracted by the wind from outside, until I realized the wind was also coming from the speakers in my bedroom. The wind had been recorded. But there was no other sound and the wind didn't seem to be announcing a song. I sat very still, listening, leaning forward, my ear tilted toward one of the speakers, and I could barely make out the other sound: distant waves crashing across a shoreline somewhere. And this was soon accompanied by something else that I couldn't quite make out and that I first thought was static, before I changed my mind, and realized it was the sound of a fire crackling. But the wind outside my bedroom was competing with the sounds coming from the speakers and I looked around for my Walkman, then remembered it was in the makeshift gym, on the tray of the treadmill, where I retrieved it and pulled a Billy Idol cassette out. When I walked back to the bedroom the sound of wind and waves was still emanating from the speakers. I pressed STOP and pulled the Maxell cassette out and placed it in the Walkman and situated the earphones carefully over my head and listened. Three minutes passed and there was nothing except waves cresting along a shoreline, distant and faint, and the wind occasionally gusting, dominating the soundtrack, and the muted crackling of a fire. And then finally there was what sounded like a voice and I thought at first it was saying *"See it . . . see it . . ."* but I couldn't hear it clearly enough to make sure if those were the exact words. The sound got clearer on the Walkman and I realized that the voice wasn't saying *"See it . . . see it . . ."* but actually *"Eat it . . . eat it . . ."*

THIS VOICE WAS horrible, and even though it sounded as if it was coming from a young man it was also a pretend voice, groaning and quavering, a Halloween voice, someone trying to scare you. It kept instructing whoever it was with to *"eat it"* and then paused so you heard what sounded like someone weeping, trying to contain themselves, but failing and then collapsing back into the weeping, and then they were trying to speak, as if confused or under the influence of some monstrous thing that left them blasted and weakened. "I . . . don't . . . want . . . to . . . eat . . . it . . ." the other voice said, strained with tears, between intakes of breath. *"Eat it, eat it,"* the pretend voice hissed, a man mimicking an exaggerated crone—the voice was slightly mushy, as if the mouth was filled with food—and when there was a pause it was just the waves and the wind and the sound of burning logs until the horrible voice said approvingly *"Yesshhhh, thasssh good, yesshhh,"* and then the mic was moved so you could hear the scared person chewing on something and the chewing was interrupted by crying and then another sound could be heard—the microphone passing over the crackling of the fire, and then the waves were crashing again. I tried to imagine who these people were and where this was being recorded: they were on a beach, it was windy, they were sitting next to a fire, so it was probably night, and why was this exchange being recorded. Was it written? Was it staged? Were these actors following a script?

The fake monster voice kept urging the other person again to *"eat it . . . eat it . . ."* and the boy's voice said, while weeping, "I'm afraid . . . I'm . . . scared . . . what are those lights . . . oh, man . . ." There was a pause where you could just hear the boy groaning until the thing urged, *"Eat . . . thish . . . one . . ."* The boy's crying continued and then he started pleading, haltingly, as if he was struggling to get the words out: "Take off . . . the . . . mask . . . please . . . take the . . . mask off . . . ," and after a deep and choking intake of breath pleading again, "Please . . . take off . . . the . . . mask . . ." *"Eat it . . . Eat thish one . . . ,"* the Halloween voice commanded, as if it was offering the boy something outstretched in a claw. I could hear the chewing sounds again and then the weeping as the boy said something, his mouth filled with whatever he was eating: "I'm scared . . . I'm so cold . . ." *"EAT IT,"* the voice shrieked, *"EAT IT."* There was a retching sound, followed by coughing, and then the boy wept, "I'm sorry . . . I'm sorry . . ." and then ". . . please . . . please take the . . . mask off . . ." And then the boy's voice was racked with convulsions as if he was shivering uncontrollably, "I-I-I'm s-s-so co-cold . . ." he said. I realized at a certain moment, in the chair at my desk, that this was real—this wasn't something acted out. It wasn't a joke. Whatever had been recorded was genuine: there was too much fear in the boy's voice. And I was suddenly afraid as well, more than I'd ever been.

A LONG SILENCE BETWEEN THE VOICES FOLLOWED— just the crackling of the fire, the waves in the ocean, the booming wind—and I realized that whatever was sitting across from the boy had handed him something that the boy was now eating and chewing on, and that was the moment I realized it was the fish from Matt Kellner's aquarium. I clutched myself, completely frozen, listening as Matt kept weeping and the pretend voice kept telling him to *"eat it . . . EAT IT . . ."* This back and forth went on for twenty minutes, while Matt gradually got higher, like he was tripping and the intensity of it was frightening him, reducing him to a child. I stared out the window through the slats of the venetian blinds and onto the lawn in the backyard and I kept stopping myself from fast-forwarding to the end, because even though I couldn't bear it I had to hear the thing play out. "Take . . . off the . . . mask . . ." Matt kept asking, sounding helpless, bewildered. *"Eat it,"* the voice insisted. Matt said something I couldn't hear and I rewound the tape and pressed PLAY again. Matt, sounding increasingly like a child, was saying, "But . . . it's still . . . alive . . . please . . ." *"EAT IT!"* the voice commanded. The mic was adjusted so you could hear Matt chewing on the fish that the thing kept handing him. And then there was a click and music started playing, an elaborate piano riff that was automatically familiar—I knew it but couldn't place it at first. *"Sing the song . . ."* and Matt, weeping, tried to sing, encouraged by the awful voice. The wind died down, the waves paused, and only the crackling of the flames could be heard, and then I recognized "Year of the Cat" by Al Stewart and the ghastly voice asked *"Did . . . you like the cock?"* Matt just wept. "It's so cold . . ." *"Did you like inserting the cock in your anus?"* the voice wheezed. Matt kept crying.

"*Sing the song . . .*" the voice gurgled. Matt started singing in a light voice and you could hear him trembling and the shaking got worse so it sounded like he was vibrating as he was singing along with the song but he couldn't sing the lyrics coherently, he didn't know the lyrics, he was just making noises, trying to hum along with it. "I'm afraid," he said again, and you could hear the tears. "I'm s-s-scared." *"Did you like sucking the cock?"* the voice asked. *"Did you like the cock in your asshole?"* There was an interruption and the mic was adjusted again. And then I heard the first slapping sound but Matt wasn't protesting or crying out because the "massive amount" of lysergic acid diethylamide finally swallowed him up and he was lost in the fear of another world now, hypnotized by it. "Year of the Cat" kept playing, interrupted by the slapping sounds—this was the noise of something striking Matt, across his back and face and chest, along with his calm weeping. I realized that Matt was naked and that something flat and smooth was making contact with his flesh—these were where the bruises came from. The waves kept crashing in the background, rhythmic and timed with the slapping sounds, the water crested along the shore, and then ebbed out, and there would be a silence, and in the pause where another wave formed, the slapping would sound out again. This was Matt naked by a bonfire on Crystal Cove beach, the ghoul next to him recording this. "The lights . . ." Matt finally wept. "Oh God, the lights . . ."

And then the tape abruptly ended. I was so mesmerized and frozen with horror that it took me longer than it should have to realize I was going to be sick. I ripped the Walkman off my head and lurched away from the desk, knocking the chair over, and stumbled to the bathroom.

21

MY INITIAL THOUGHT on that afternoon when I first heard the tape—a recording made on the last night of Matt Kellner's life—was to burn it. I thought about this even before I contemplated taking it to the police. At one point that afternoon I drove to Haskell Avenue and was going to slip the cassette into Ronald and Sheila Kellner's mailbox—wipe my fingerprints off it and let them deal with this— but by the time I pulled up in front of the house I'd changed my mind. I couldn't figure it out but there was a reason why I didn't want anyone to hear it—there was something tainted about this piece of evidence that stopped me from going to the authorities or to the Kellners. Instead, I called Jeff Taylor from a phone booth on Ventura Boulevard that Sunday afternoon and asked if he had any weed or Quaaludes and Jeff confirmed he had both and he'd bring them to Buckley the following day, but I needed them now and told him I'd drive out to Malibu. I made my way across Topanga Canyon until I hit Pacific Coast Highway and sped out to the Colony, where Jeff met me in front of the gates—he would've invited me in, he said, but his dad was watching football games totally wasted and warned he didn't want any guests around when Jeff mentioned I was coming over. I could barely maintain a casual façade in front of Jeff for even the moment it took to make the exchange and I just nodded and quickly said, "It's okay, dude, I gotta run." I threw the bag of Quaaludes onto the passenger seat next to the cassette.

I never wanted to hear the tape again but I didn't want it out of my sight either and it started to dawn on me why I didn't want anyone else to hear it, at least for now. I was positive that Robert Mallory had recorded it and that he had been playing a kind of game with Matt— Robert manic, Matt wasted—and somehow this game got out of hand as it kept escalating until Matt was dead, with Matt never knowing that Robert had been institutionalized or having any idea how unstable he was. The only solace I felt was that, at one point, I had warned Matt about Robert. Procuring the drugs relaxed me enough so that I could drive steadily from Malibu with a minimal amount of anxiety, and once in the empty house on Mulholland I smoked a few bowls of grass and then took a full Quaalude and everything got erased and I was able to fall asleep without thinking about the horrible sounds coming from my Walkman earlier that afternoon. I dreamt about nothing that night and woke up groggy as Rosa knocked on my door the following morning, reminding me I'd be late to school, and it sounded like such an innocent concern compared to what had happened over that weekend I almost smiled.

MONDAY. I PARKED THE Jaguar on Stansbury. I already knew what my plan was for that afternoon as I listened to the rest of "Time for Me to Fly"—still stoned from the Quaalude I had taken last night and the weed I'd smoked that morning, and, walking up to the gates of the school, I stumbled on the rise leading into the parking lot. I was late—too long in the shower, zoning out while getting dressed, traffic on Beverly Glen—and tried to walk more quickly but then just relaxed into an easy stride, thinking: who cared if I was late? I didn't want to be there anyway, nothing mattered; yesterday I'd listened to a boy being tortured on a beach. There was a cassette tape in a drawer in my bedroom that eradicated everything: why should I have to be on time for an English class, why should I take notes or study for the test, why should I care about the novel assigned? I made it to Mr. Robbins just as the bells were chiming and stopped for a moment after I opened the door, about to enter the classroom. Susan Reynolds was sitting at her desk and next to her was the desk where I usually sat but today I didn't want to sit next to Susan, who looked up from her notebook and was staring at me blankly. Another realization: I didn't want trouble. I didn't want to break the dream of the pantomime. I tried to transform into the tangible participant and smiled. I noted that, two rows over, Ryan Vaughn hadn't looked up from the paperback folded in his hands.

"Mr. Ellis?" Robbins asked hesitantly. "Could you please take a seat?"

"Sure," I said, and walked over to the desk next to Susan's and smiled at her. She subtly cocked her head and smiled back: it was natural, and numb, and totally guileless.

"Hey," she said blankly as I sat down.

"Hey," I said, still smiling, placing the Gucci backpack on the desktop.

"You okay?" she asked.

"Yeah," I said, glancing at her. "You okay?" Her eyes gave away nothing. She was utterly calm. Saturday night in Palm Springs had been erased between the two of us.

"I'm fine," she said.

"Okay," I said, pulling out a notebook from the backpack.

The dream was put into play—we helped in its creation—and I floated along with it. Both morning classes passed by quickly, and then I joined Susan as we walked up to assembly in the courtyard below the Pavilion. Debbie kissed me lightly on the lips and all I could register: Thom Wright's absence wasn't even that noticeable. After assembly the three of us chatted—that's the term, *chatted;* that's what it was, *chatting*—until Susan left for the girls' locker room to suit up for Phys Ed. Debbie wanted to talk and I patiently held back while noticing Robert Mallory and Ryan Vaughn walking toward the boys' locker room together, talking animatedly; Ryan gestured as if something was exploding, making a face; Robert laughed. An acid pang flowered in my chest but I didn't let it distract me from focusing intently on Debbie, who reminded me about her father's party on Saturday night at the mansion on Stone Canyon, and I assured her I would definitely be coming, and then she asked what I did over the weekend and why hadn't I answered any of her phone calls or called back. I stared at her before formulating an answer. She became impatient.

"This is a difficult question, I know," she said, with a whisper of sarcasm. "Remembering what you did this weekend."

I realized in that moment that I wasn't sure if she knew I'd been to Palm Springs and that I'd seen Susan with Robert there. I realized:

Debbie would have confronted me with this if Susan had told her. Or she was testing me. We were lost in the maze of the pantomime.

"Well, if you want to know the truth—" I started.

"No, I want the lie, Bret," she said, again sarcastically, and then, "Of course I want to know the truth."

"I worked on my book and got stoned," I said simply. "That's all I did this weekend."

She studied my face before she asked, "Really?"

"Yeah, just got wasted all weekend long," I said. "I bought a bag of weed and some 'ludes from Jeff and just got wasted and wrote." I shrugged. "It was fun. I like having weekends like that sometimes."

"You didn't go anywhere?" she asked in a faraway voice, thinking things through. ·

"No, I didn't," I said. "Why?"

She just stared at me not saying anything.

"Come on, we're going to be late." I reached for her hand so we could end the conversation before it headed into specifics. She took the hand hesitantly.

"Bret . . ." she started.

"Yeah?" I waited, my arm outstretched.

Debbie forced a smile and said, "It's nothing."

I pulled her forward and we walked to the locker rooms together.

AFTER CHANGING into the red shorts and a Griffins T-shirt for PE, I waited in the boys' locker room until I was sure Debbie had already walked up to Gilley Field because I wanted to be alone. I didn't want to interact with the script Susan and Debbie had devised, so I waited ten minutes sitting on a bench—all the guys were already gone—staring at Thom Wright's locker and I involuntarily reached out to touch the small silver padlock that hung there and understood that he would never grasp my tender feelings toward him. I trudged up the steep hill leading to the field rather than taking the elevator and as I walked toward the track I saw Ryan jogging lazily around it, by himself, and then noticed that today was coed and Debbie and Susan and Robert were standing by the tennis courts just talking casually, as if it was last month, as if there was nothing signifying that a dramatic event was forming itself among the three of them, as if they were all actors in a play; Thom was gone but they were still careful. Katie Harris and Tracy Goldman were playing tennis behind them, and I looked up at the bleachers, where I was going to sit and read Joan Didion for the remainder of the period, and spotted Michelle and Nancy and Rita lying on the first tier of benches, sunning themselves. I realized it would look strange if I didn't walk over and say hi to Debbie and Susan even though the thought of getting close to Robert Mallory made me dizzy with apprehension mixed with an awful desire that still pulsed within me despite everything I knew about what he had done to Matt. I watched as Anthony Matthews and Doug Furth tossed a football and I must have zoned out standing in place, because I suddenly noticed Ryan was in front of me, lightly panting, his face misted with sweat. The last thing I'd remembered was a boom box playing something off Pink Floyd's *The Wall*.

"Hey," he said. "You okay?"

"Um, yeah," I said, looking up at him, dazed.

"You were just standing there spacing out," he said. "I thought maybe something was wrong."

His presence activated me. "I wanted to talk to you."

"Yeah?" Ryan said apprehensively. "About what?"

"Yeah," I started. "I just want to let you know that I'm totally fine with everything and I don't—I really don't—want to cause any drama and I'm sorry if I have." I paused. "I thought I was more cool than that but I guess I'm not so—"

"Oh, that's okay," Ryan interrupted quickly.

"No, really, I don't want there to be any problems between us," I said.

Ryan glanced around the field, but we were far away from everyone and no one could hear us.

"So, you know, I get it, we're friends and that's how it should be," I continued. "So from now on we're cool, right?"

"Yeah." Ryan nodded. "Thanks."

"Do you want to see a movie or something?" I suddenly asked.

"Yeah, that would be great." He said this with a genuineness that briefly delighted me.

"Want to do it this afternoon?" I ventured.

"Um, I can't this afternoon," he said. "But what about tomorrow?"

"Great, yeah," I said. "Tomorrow."

"Cool," he said.

"Okay," I said. "I'll look and see what's playing."

Without saying anything else, he jogged away, leaving me standing by myself, and I started walking across the field to where Susan and Debbie and Robert stood, and soon I noticed that the conversation suddenly stopped while I neared the tennis courts and the three of them just looked at me and benignly smiled as I got closer. They were all wearing the red shorts and the Griffin T-shirts and Wayfarers—and so good-looking they could have been the popular teen villains in a high-school exploitation movie. "Hey, guys," I said, loose and, I hoped, engaged, joining them. "What's going on?" and then added, "Everyone's looking really hot today." This didn't land in the right way and Robert took off his sunglasses and smiled at me quizzically. "What were you talking about?" I asked, trying to appear both casual and as if I was actually interested, but feeling neither.

"Oh, just talking about Terry's party Saturday night," Susan said, pushing her sunglasses up onto her forehead. "Who's going to be there, y'know." She stared blankly at me. "You coming?" she asked.

"Oh yeah, it's gonna be cool," I said. Debbie leaned in to me and I let her.

"That is, if you're not too wasted to show up," Debbie teased, nudging my side.

"What did *you* do this weekend, Bret?" Susan asked with a jokey knowingness that was supposed to have me confirm what I'm sure Debbie had already told them.

"I had fun," I said, shrugging, and then, staring at Susan. "It's a secret."

"Apparently not," Susan said, without a beat, smiling at me.

"I worked on my book," I said, explaining this to Robert. "I took drugs and worked on my book." He looked at me, confused. "I do that sometimes."

"Oh," Robert said, not knowing what else to say, then hesitantly added, "Cool."

I drifted away from the ensuing conversation—I was just studying faces. If I was required to say something I did. If I was required to react to something I did. I laughed when required. I agreed with something when I was supposed to. I offered a similar opinion about something that the three of them agreed on. I was able to look into Robert Mallory's beautiful face on that day and there was no one hiding behind the eyes and yet I was electrified standing so close to the person who had essentially helped, I thought, kill Matt Kellner, and it took all the strength I possessed not to confront him and let Robert know what I suspected. His nonchalance and his handsomeness were even more distinct when contrasted with his madness—this was the normal boy who made the horrible voice taunting Matt, this was the popular boy wearing some kind of mask that Matt wanted him to take off, this was the boy in love with Susan Reynolds making Matt eat the fish that were ultimately found inside him, this was the boy slapping Matt with some kind of object that left the bruises. I tried picturing the scene that played out at Crystal Cove in front of the bonfire and was verified on the cassette but I couldn't imagine visually what had happened—and what made it worse was that I had to guess, and that's when the writer's fantasies were more alarming than what mundane reality probably offered and I had to shut it out.

You couldn't tell that Susan and Robert were a couple that morning on Gilley Field because they'd cast themselves and were now performing in different, more innocent roles, and yet because of this the fake rapport between the four of us eased into something that seemed almost genuine. This happened even though I knew Debbie and Susan and Robert were liars and it ignited my increasing disgust at the girls for protecting a maniac but especially at Susan for having fallen in love with him, and this was going to cause her to break up with Thom. This fact simply silenced me: it was too big to fight and there was nothing to win. It was already happening. For about five minutes the volume was lowered and I only concentrated on their faces and then I heard Debbie talking about Spirit and the equestrian event at the Windover Stables and again who was slated to show up at Stone Canyon on Saturday night, and Robert was relaxed and mostly just nodding as the girls talked, his particular scent drifting toward me—sandalwood and cedar—and I imagined licking his armpit—and when Susan admitted she'd been in Palm Springs for the weekend, staying at her grandparents', this seemed to be only for my benefit. And then I couldn't help myself.

"You were in Palm Springs, too, right?" I asked Robert casually.

"How did you know?" Robert asked, trying to downplay his surprise—not that I knew he'd been in Palm Springs but that I actually asked this in front of Susan and Debbie.

"I was going to see if you wanted to go to a movie and your aunt told me you were in Rancho Mirage," I said.

"Right," Robert said, nodding. "She told me you called." He said tonelessly, "I would've totally gone to a movie with you."

Susan was just staring at me, not saying anything. Debbie knew that they had been in Palm Springs together and yet seemingly didn't know that I had been there as well, and Robert was also unaware of this fact, or so I thought—if Susan had kept her promise to me. Maybe it was better this way, I was thinking, at least for now: play it dumb, just keep the pantomime revolving, admit nothing, say your lines, move offstage, wait for another cue. But I still couldn't help myself.

"You talk to Thom?" I asked Susan.

"No," she said coolly without a pause. "I haven't."

The dream continued throughout the rest of the day. It carried over into lunch, and there was something so much easier about following the rules of the dream rather than confronting the reality of the situation, and I just sat with both girls at the center table below the shadow of the Pavilion and tried to eat the lunch that Rosa had prepared for me and that I kept trying to concentrate on—the tunafish sandwich on wheat bread, the Lay's potato chips, a few Famous Amos cookies, an orange—but there was another moment when I saw Robert and Ryan Vaughn conferring by the steps leading up to the courtyard, and the sight of them together completely unnerved me and it was a reminder of all the times I saw Robert with Matt Kellner and I shuddered when I envisioned a similar fate for Ryan. Robert bounded up the steps to our table and sat next to Susan and again the four of us engaged in the kind of useless banter the pantomime encouraged. It was then, during lunch, at the center table, below the Pavilion, overlooking the courtyard, that I felt Thom's absence even more strongly, and I looked around at the other senior tables and realized maybe no one felt this way except me—I was the only one who truly missed him and I was also the one most concerned about his happiness, his outcome, his future. Thinking about Thom was too wrenching and I decided to compartmentalize everything and place Thom elsewhere in my thoughts. I started to think about, instead, what movie Ryan Vaughn and I would see the following afternoon and was mildly surprised that I could actually look forward to something besides what I was going to be doing after school that day.

WHEN THE bells rang at three o'clock I was the first to leave class and went directly to Stansbury, where I got into the Jaguar and waited for Robert Mallory's Porsche to appear, though I wasn't entirely positive it would. And when it cruised down the street roughly twenty minutes after school ended for the day, quickly enlarging itself in my side-view mirror, I slid down as it passed by. I immediately sat up and started the car and followed the Porsche onto Valley Vista. On that Monday afternoon Robert made the left onto Beverly Glen instead of continuing across Valley Vista to the 405, which meant he was stopping at the house on Benedict Canyon. I kept my distance as I followed two cars behind and then pulled over and parked six houses up from where the Porsche turned into the driveway. Robert got out and pushed open the gate with the WARNING: NO TRESPASSING sign hanging lopsidedly from it and stood still for a moment, looking around as if he thought he was being watched. On that particular stretch of Benedict Canyon a few vehicles were parked along the sides of the road—the trucks of gardeners and pool cleaners—but none that caught Robert's interest, and then he got back in the car and it disappeared from view. I waited. It took about fifteen minutes for the Porsche to pull out of the driveway and back onto Benedict Canyon. I continued to wait until a car passed and then I followed Robert until he stopped at the light on Sunset Boulevard and then drove into Beverly Hills, as Benedict Canyon turned into North Canon Drive, and I realized that he was going to glide past Susan Reynolds's house even though her car wasn't in the driveway, confirming—my heart beating fast—that she had definitely stayed at Buckley that afternoon. What was Robert doing parked in front of the house if he already knew this? The Porsche backed up and then moved forward as if the driver was angling to get a better look at something, trying to solve a problem that the house offered, hoping it would give him answers to the questions he was asking.

I was parked at the end of the block watching as the car idled in front of the Reynolds residence for about five minutes. And then I resumed following Robert as he pulled away from the house, and I stayed at least a thousand feet behind but I wasn't worried about losing him, because he never varied from his ultimate destination. Robert made a right onto Santa Monica Boulevard and I trailed him until Century City loomed into view and then he made a left onto Avenue of the Stars. I made the same left and followed him until he made another left into the driveway of the Century Towers, where he pulled up to the valet and hopped out the driver's side, carrying a black duffel bag and hurriedly walked into the tower closest to Pico.

ON THAT MONDAY in October I sat in the Jaguar longer than I usually did parked across the street from the entrance of the Century Towers and had finally decided to go home when I saw a car I recognized pull into the valet and I watched it, slumped in the driver's seat, barely cognizant of anything but my own private thoughts, and then suddenly very aware of something else—the switch from one state to another happened so fast it was electric.

A black Trans Am entered the driveway of the Century Towers and I watched it brake in front of the valet and the tension within me kept rising until my entire body felt pressurized. The valet opened the door of the Trans Am and Ryan Vaughn got out of the car, still in his Buckley uniform and letterman's sweater, and he asked something of the valet, who gestured to the building Robert Mallory had entered thirty minutes previously. I stared out the windshield; the passing rush of traffic coming up from Pico and flowing down from Santa Monica Boulevard flashed by, jump-cutting my image of Ryan as he walked into the tower. I was frozen. I was literally so cold with the shock of seeing Ryan that I started trembling, even though I wasn't sure what I'd actually seen or what any of this meant. What had I missed? What hadn't I been paying attention to? Why hadn't I noticed that Robert and Ryan had become friends? And what made it so much worse was that I knew how attractive Ryan found Robert Mallory. Regardless of Robert's heterosexuality and his love for Susan Reynolds, Ryan had admitted the weekend he'd spent in the house on Mulholland that he wanted Robert to suck his cock and that he wanted to get Robert on all fours and fuck him—Ryan told me this in the Jacuzzi while we fantasized out loud about the new student and what we'd do to him sexually if we could, if he would ever let us, or later on, as the fantasy got more heated, if we forced him to. I felt as if I was being crushed. Panic started consuming everything. I realized I needed to go to the bathroom and I quickly pulled away from the curb.

And as I made a wide U-turn across Avenue of the Stars I noticed in the rearview mirror another familiar vehicle, which I couldn't quite place at first and then in a rush I did.

It was the beige-colored van that followed me through Palm Springs on Saturday night.

I don't know how I placed it so quickly but it was slowly gliding by the entrance of the Century Towers and I kept staring at it in the rearview mirror until I almost rolled through a red light and had to brake to a sudden stop, lurching forward. I watched as the beige-colored van flashed its lights twice—as if it had confirmed that it had seen me though I could have completely imagined that—and then made a U-turn and headed in the opposite direction back toward Pico Boulevard.

ROSA WAS ALREADY GONE when I arrived at the empty house on Mulholland. I didn't linger in the car after I closed the garage, as I sometimes did. I went straight to my bathroom, where I tried to pee but couldn't—I was too wired with tension and unable to relax and let the urine stream out. I smoked three bowls of weed and relaxed enough so I could finally urinate. The jealousy that inflamed me was lightly minimized by the weed, and the half of the Quaalude I took sent me into the fuzzy realm of simply not caring—"SNC," I imagined emblazoned on a tight T-shirt that Susan Reynolds wore—and soon I was high enough to walk into the kitchen and look through the fridge to see what Rosa left for dinner. But I wasn't hungry and simply started to look through the *Los Angeles Times* folded on the island in the kitchen, searching for traces of the Trawler and new info about Audrey Barbour. I stopped when I realized that if I found anything it would alter the high and potentially interrupt the calmness I finally felt, which made me forget about Ryan Vaughn and Robert Mallory and everything else except my own inner peace.

I floated back to my room and sat down at the desk and lifted books out of the Gucci backpack and then I stopped and leaned over and opened the bottom drawer and stared at the cassette I had listened to yesterday, placed next to the pair of jockey shorts I'd taken from the house on Haskell. The Santa Anas had picked up that night and it was the only noise I heard: the wind crashing over the canyons and swirling outside the empty house, booming against the windows. But when I picked up my European-history textbook the winds had died down and I heard another sound—or thought I had. It was the chime of the garage door opening, announcing itself throughout the house, and I froze. If it hadn't been for the Quaalude flowing through me I wouldn't have been able to stand and move slowly toward the hallway that would take me into the rest of the house. I would have hidden in the bathroom and locked the door.

I went to the kitchen and opened a drawer and calmly pulled out a butcher knife and then made my way to the door that led to the garage. I opened it and the lights above the cars automatically flickered on. The garage door, I noticed, was halfway open, banging lightly in the winds that were gusting across Mulholland. I just stood in the doorway and stared, trying to remember if I had fully closed the garage with the remote or if I'd been too distracted because I had to use the bathroom. I walked through the garage and passed between the three cars parked in a row: the Jaguar, the 450SL and the larger sedan. Everything looked as if it was in place. Nothing had been rearranged. No poster had been left for me. There was no intruder waiting, crouched below the cabinets. I placed my hand on a panel and pressed it with my fingertip and the garage door slowly lowered until it was fully shut. I waited a beat and then turned and stepped back into the silent hallway. Either I hadn't fully closed it or the wind had activated some mechanism that opened the garage. I didn't know. Or was it something else? I pushed the thought away because what other reason could there have been?

You're hearing things that aren't there.

But I wasn't sure about that anymore, I told the writer.

Maybe we've moved into another realm, I told the writer.

Still clutching the knife, I walked slowly into the living room, calmed by the drugs, and headed trancelike toward the other side of the house, toward my mother's bedroom. I stood in the doorway and turned on the light and it didn't seem as if anything had been rearranged—everything was neat and untouched. I told myself, again, that I was imagining things. I was hearing something that wasn't there. *Don't be such a pussy.* And yet the sight of Ryan Vaughn entering the Century Towers and the beige-colored van gliding across Avenue of the Stars were *real*—they materialized and had *happened.* I saw it—I was a witness. And then the colliding thoughts stopped because I realized something was missing. I moved back into the kitchen and slowly scanned the space.

"Shingy?" I said and waited. "Shingy?"

THERE WAS NOTHING: no barking, no excited whimpering, no scrambling of paws clicking along the kitchen floor—just silence. His food dish was full, as was the bowl of water next to it. I walked back to my bedroom, moving slowly down the hall, clutching the butcher knife. I scanned the space—like my mother's room it looked neat, nothing was out of place, nothing had been rearranged, it was clean, almost untouched. But Shingy wasn't under my desk or lying at the foot of the bed. I opened the door that led out to the deck and tentatively walked across it as the wind blasted through the trees in the backyard. I was still wearing my Buckley uniform and the striped tie blew into my face when I called Shingy's name again, straining my voice over the sound of the wind, and waited. I lowered the knife to my side and stood on the deck shivering. The backyard was brightly lit and the lawn was a shiny dark green and the pool was a glowing blue rectangle, the water rippling in the wind, the sudden black drop onto the cliff side cutting a straight line between the light of the yard and the darkness of the canyon that lay beyond it. I called the dog's name again and moved closer to the edge of the cliff, the eucalyptus trees above me thrashing in the wind. There was a full yellow moon hanging over the lit blanket of the valley, which seemed a hundred miles away that night, and reminded me how alone I really was and always would be. I called the dog's name again—I actually yelled it, my hands cupped around my mouth: "Shingy!"

I waited.

In a break in the Santa Anas I heard something rustling through the brush on the hillside and the sound made me instinctively back away to the deck, but when Shingy emerged from the darkness of the canyon he saw who had been calling his name and barked excitedly. Relief flooded through me as the dog attempted to race across the lawn to where I stood but Shingy was limping and I saw something wrong with his right front paw. I knelt down as he jumped around me, whimpering, and I tried to get him on his side so I could inspect the leg. It was lightly wet with blood and when I tried to push the hair back to see the wound Shingy growled and snapped at me and then stood and limped to the kitchen door. I walked across the lawn and opened the door and he limped toward the food waiting for him. I watched as he ate quickly and then settled into his pillow and started licking the injured paw. I knelt down and tried to move his mouth away from where his tongue stroked the wound but he growled, warning me, baring his upper teeth. It didn't look so bad in the light of the kitchen and I stood up and placed the butcher knife back in the drawer and floated to my room.

Nothing else happened that night after I took the other half of the Quaalude. I finished my homework in a peaceful daze and kept the TV on for company and when the phone in my room rang at eleven and then at midnight and then at one o'clock and I picked it up all three times the Quaalude minimized any thoughts that might have occurred to me about the half-opened garage, and the injury Shingy suffered, the question that I might be a target and the fact that no one said anything each time I answered the phone in the middle of the night.

22

I DECIDED on the five o'clock showing of *Chariots of Fire* at the Bruin in Westwood as the movie Ryan and I would see on that Tuesday in October, and when I suggested this Ryan agreed and said cool. We were by the lockers after Mr. Robbins's class and he seemed completely open in the moment—his clear blue eyes alert and homing in on me, the smile natural, his whole vibe looser than usual—and I realized he was no longer uncomfortable in the way he had been: we were just friends now and he didn't feel the pressure of my desire anymore. I didn't ask Ryan Vaughn where he had gone the previous afternoon—if he was hanging out with Robert Mallory—or mention that I had seen him in Century City: there was no way to ask about this without looking like a freak. If I told him I knew about this I was certain it would ruin everything and any hope of getting closer to Ryan would be lost. Ryan betrayed nothing and just exhibited his usual low-key swagger and mentioned that it was a movie about runners, right? Yeah, I said, and stopped myself from adding: there are supposedly a few hot guys in it. The plan sounded fine to him and he suggested maybe dinner after the movie at Hamburger Hamlet, next to the Bruin. We'd have to meet in front of the theater at four-forty-five, since he'd be coming from school. There were no games scheduled that week, because of the bye week when Thom Wright was away, but Coach Holtz expected Ryan at practice that afternoon, only an hour, and he could easily make it to Westwood by the time the movie started. I was looking at Susan Reynolds and Robert Mallory talking to each other on a walkway beneath the eaves when Ryan said this and then I was staring back at his face, and noticed that he'd glanced at them as well, and in that moment I realized I didn't trust him anymore, if I ever really had, and that there was nothing to save, things were already ruined, there was nothing to hope for. But I just smiled and said I was looking forward to the movie.

I WAITED UNDER the giant curved blue neon Deco marquee of the Bruin as the chilly sky over Westwood darkened, holding my ticket, constantly checking my watch, nervous. I paced across the terrazzo floor leading into the lobby, quiet at five o'clock, and watched as a few people bought tickets and two guys in UCLA sweatshirts were the only ones at the concession stand. I looked at the posters encased in glass for movies opening later that fall—*Ragtime, Venom, Absence of Malice*—and lingered in front of them. Ryan was walking down Broxton in the fading light and smiled when he saw me standing beneath the marquee.

"Hey," he said at the ticket booth, reaching for his wallet and quickly making the *What's up?* face at me.

"Hey," I said, nodding, smiling, hands in my pockets.

He had showered and his hair was brushed back and he was wearing jeans, and a blue Lacoste to match his eyes and a Members Only jacket, and he smiled at me once again as we walked to the lobby, handed our tickets to an usher and then headed to the concession stand.

"You getting anything?" he asked.

"I'm okay," I said and watched as he bought a small carton of Milk Duds.

The soundtrack from *Chariots of Fire* was playing throughout the semi-deserted auditorium, and I let Ryan choose the seats, which were in the middle of the theater and farther back than I would have sat, and he preferred the center of the row, though I liked the aisle. The lights dimmed and the curtain lifted and the already famous Vangelis score began and I was vaguely paying attention to young runners sprinting along the water's edge of a cloudy beach in slow motion—the music was supposed to stir us but I immediately located a sadness in the score that was quickly killing me and I started tearing up but clenched myself so tightly that the moment passed.

I thought Ryan might have snickered at this opening sequence, lean in and say something dirty, comment on the runners, but he didn't. He was quiet and kept concentrating on the screen as the story unfolded, every so often lifting a Milk Dud to his mouth and chewing contemplatively. I knew who the cinematographer David Watkin was and I thought the movie looked good but I didn't find any of the British guys attractive even though they were young college athletes because, I suppose, I was distracted by sitting so closely to Ryan, and I became self-conscious about any movement I might make. I wanted to touch him, rub my fingers along the edge of his zipper, pull his cock out and jack him off, just so I could watch his face during orgasm and smell his semen, and I grew instantly hard thinking about this. *Chariots of Fire* wasn't my kind of movie (there was no action or violence or sex or nudity—it was resolutely PG) and I deflated a little when I realized it was going to include a lecture about anti-Semitism. My increasing boredom and the closeness to Ryan was maddening: the movie was so well intentioned and noble that by a certain point I didn't even know what was going on. I wanted to touch Ryan's cock. I wanted to kiss his mouth. I wanted to run my finger between the crevice of his ass. I had to refrain from glancing over at him and when I finally did he was staring intently up at the screen, occasionally chewing on a Milk Dud, his jaw clenching and unclenching, seemingly lost in the movie. At one point he noticed me looking at him and offered the yellow carton, thinking that's what I wanted, and I shook my head no. I began to assume that Ryan was more immersed in the movie than me because it was about athletes—it was basically a simple sports movie, I realized, and it was about the camaraderie of men: men watching each other, men sizing each other up, men admiring each other because of their physical accomplishments—and it also had a religious element. One of the runners was racing for God, which Ryan either responded to or rejected—I didn't know. "Run in God's name," someone said, and I wondered if this stirred something in him.

Suddenly Ryan got up without saying anything and walked away from me down the row to the aisle on the other side of the theater. I turned my head and watched as he exited the auditorium. He was gone for only a few minutes and then he came back and took his seat. "What did I miss?" he asked, leaning in. I could smell the soap that he had washed his hands with—he had used the restroom, I realized. "Um, he can't run on the Sabbath," I explained. Ryan nodded and looked back at the screen. The movie ended with an anticlimactic race in slow motion

I wasn't prepared for, and then it was over. Ryan stood up as the credits played and stretched exaggeratedly to loosen up and then I followed him into the lobby. I had to use the restroom and Ryan told me he'd be outside. I walked up the stairs to the men's room and stood at the urinal thinking about how to approach the rest of the night. If everything was lost, then why not throw in a grenade: tell Ryan that you loved him and just let everything blow up. What difference did it make if nothing was going to happen? I zipped my jeans and washed my hands and proceeded back to the lobby, where I noticed Ryan was standing on the terrazzo floor beneath the marquee, staring at the poster for *Venom*—the word in bright-yellow letters and shaped like fangs next to a drawing of a snake slithering out of a vent. "You liked the movie?" he asked. We started walking next door to Hamburger Hamlet. "Yeah, it was okay," I said. He nodded, a simple affirmation.

We were on Weyburn when he casually said, "Do you care if Robert joins us?" I had no idea what he was talking about at first, and even though I'd been thinking about the two of them together for the past twenty-four hours it still didn't register who he was referencing. "What?" I asked, turning to him as we moved along the sidewalk.

"Do you care if Robert comes to dinner?" Ryan asked. "He's joining us."

I stopped walking. He turned and looked at me, quizzically, his brow furrowed, wondering why I'd stopped.

"What are you doing?" I asked.

"What do you mean?" he asked back blankly.

"Why are you inviting Robert to join us?" I asked.

"I thought you wouldn't mind," he said, confused. "Is something wrong?"

"I thought it was just going to be us," I said.

"What's the difference?" he asked, still confused, and then, "Did you want to hold hands?"

I was stifled with embarrassment when Ryan said this.

"Do you have a problem?" Ryan asked. "With Robert?"

"He's crazy," I said quietly. "And you've got to be crazy hanging out with him."

"What are you talking about?" he asked. "How is he crazy?"

"He had a breakdown at Susan's party—" I started.

"A breakdown?" Ryan interrupted. "What does that mean?"

"He went fucking nuts. He had this meltdown. He's on a bunch of different drugs. He's on fucking Thorazine—" I was saying this all in a low rush.

"I don't know what that is—" Ryan interrupted again, confused.

"He was in a mental institution," I said quietly. "A fucking mental institution. In Illinois. Just this past year. He's sick. There's something wrong with him, there's—"

"I think you need to take it easy—" Ryan said, speaking over me.

"You shouldn't be hanging out with him, Ryan—"

"Wait a minute, wait a minute," he said, holding up a hand. "Who said I'm hanging out with him?"

I stared straight at his face. "You're not hanging out with him? Is that what you're saying? You're saying you're not hanging out with Robert Mallory?" This was leveled at Ryan as an accusation.

Ryan looked back at me, annoyed and impatient. "Why would you care if I was hanging out with Robert?" he asked. "I'm not saying I have but even if I was what's the big deal?"

"Are you?" I asked, accusingly. "Have you been?"

Ryan just stared, unsure as to where he should steer the conversation.

"Maybe," he said. The evasive way he uttered this infuriated me, especially when I knew that Ryan desired Robert.

"You know, he's not gay," I said. "He's not going to have sex with you, if that's what you're hoping. He's in love with Susan Reynolds. He's not going to have sex with you."

Ryan stared at me for a beat as if he was trying to figure every- thing out, and then he looked away and down Weyburn, his eyes fixed on the streets curving up toward UCLA beyond the sign for the West- world arcade. "Why do you say shit like that?" he quietly asked. A young couple was passing by. We just stood there, not moving out of their way. They walked around us.

"I don't think you know the truth," I said.

"I think that you are losing it," he countered, carefully. "I mean, I just want to have a good time." He paused. "And you're causing all of this drama—"

"Ryan, he had something to do with Matt Kellner," I said, my voice low and controlled. "He had something to do with Matt's death. He was with Matt when he died. He contributed. He was a factor in Matt's death—"

Ryan recoiled from me, his eyes wide, his mouth shaped into a grimace.

"What are you talking about?" he asked.

"Ryan, you've got to believe me," I said. "He's connected to the missing girls. The Trawler. There's something going on with him. And I know he had something to do with Matt. There's a tape. His voice is on it—"

Ryan was walking away from me and toward the entrance of the restaurant. I hadn't realized how frantic I'd become.

"Stop it, just fucking stop it," I heard Ryan mutter.

"Ryan—" I reached out and grabbed his shoulder.

He whirled around. "What are you doing? What are you talking about? Do you know how fucking crazy you sound?" He calmly checked his watch. "He should be here any minute. Maybe you should go home. I don't know."

"When did you invite him?" I asked. "Did you invite him when we were watching the movie—"

"I invited him at lunch," Ryan said patiently. "I was going to tell you at school but I didn't see you the rest of the day."

He was about to push open the door. I was staring at the Halloween decorations adorning the windows of the Postermat and I was about to tell Ryan to fuck it, that I'd be heading home and that I'd see him tomorrow at Buckley, when I suddenly noticed a vehicle slowly approaching in the distance, crossing Westwood Boulevard and gliding along Weyburn. It was a beige-colored van. And I was struck mute as the van drove past us, my eyes trailing it. I turned and watched as the van cruised past Hamburger Hamlet and then Broxton and toward Gayley, where it waited until the light turned green and made a left. I couldn't tell if it was the same van I'd seen in Palm Springs on Saturday night or the one I glimpsed in Century City yesterday afternoon, flashing its lights at me before making that wide U-turn on Avenue of the Stars. All I knew was that it rendered me helpless and I shut down. I turned to Ryan, who stood at the entrance of the restaurant, his hand on the door, waiting. I must have suddenly looked different—scared, pale, dumbstruck—because Ryan's expression became concerned. "Are you okay?" he asked. "What just happened?" I touched my forehead—I could feel my fingers trembling. "I just . . . I just need to sit down . . ." In a daze I moved past Ryan and walked into the restaurant. "Bret?" I heard him say as he followed me in. "Bret? Are you okay?"

I MUTTERED that I had to go to the restroom and jogged up the staircase adjacent to the entrance and fell against the men's-room door, clutching and unclutching my fists while taking in a number of deep and steady breaths: I had never experienced this level of fear and panic before and nothing prepared me for how deep and over-whelming it was. I splashed cold water on my face and wiped it off with a paper towel. I stared at myself in the mirror. I regained some kind of composure and made my way back downstairs—I'd be telling Ryan that I wasn't feeling well and needed to get home. But Ryan and Robert were already sitting across from each other in one of the red booths in the front room, at a window table overlooking Weyburn, and they both glanced up from their oversized menus as I neared them. I had no idea what Ryan had told Robert, but I suspected nothing about what I'd said earlier on the sidewalk, because Robert raised his eyes and smiled innocently at me as I decided to slide into the booth. I realized I wasn't going to let Ryan sit alone with Robert for any amount of time if I could help it and so I erased the fake excuse and sat down next to Ryan and across from Robert.

Ryan was giving a rundown of what he thought about *Chariots of Fire* and I was supposing Ryan was under Robert's spell and trying to sound more sophisticated than he actually was, but Robert wasn't gay, so why was Ryan trying to impress him? Then I realized Ryan wasn't gay either, so none of this mattered in the manufactured dream we existed in. But I decided to be real and started interrupting Ryan and criticized the movie and the things I didn't like about it—it was bor-ing, it was anticlimactic, there was no excitement, I made fun of the religious element. This was a performance and it took a physical com-mitment that was exhausting, but I maintained it. Robert responded to my harsh assessment with occasional laughter while Ryan kept jok-ingly trying to defend the movie and I was okay for a while—we briefly talked about Terry Schaffer's party on Saturday, Ryan wasn't going, Robert and I were—but after we ordered, things quickly fell apart. Robert mentioned it was his eighteenth birthday in two weeks and invited both of us to the dinner he was planning. It was going to be at a restaurant called Le Dome, he said, and it would be just Thom and Susan, Debbie and myself, Jeff and Tracy and Ryan. When Robert said that Susan Reynolds had suggested the restaurant, my rage returned and I immediately allowed the paranoid anger to envelop me.

"Is Susan throwing the birthday dinner for you?" I asked, pretending to be curious.

"No," Robert said. "I'm taking everyone out—actually my aunt is paying. Susan just suggested the restaurant."

"When did she suggest this?" I asked.

"I think, um, last week," Robert said.

He sat back as the waitress placed our drink orders down—everyone had a Coke.

"Not while you guys were in Palm Springs?" I asked.

"No," Robert said without missing a beat. "We didn't see each other in Palm Springs." This was said so effortlessly I had to nod, impressed.

"Okay, okay," I said.

"I was just asking her what some cool places were," Robert said. "And she mentioned Le Dome."

"It's pretty fancy," I said. "Are you sure you don't want to go somewhere more casual?"

"I don't know what Le Dome is," Ryan admitted.

"It's a place on Sunset, a block from Tower Records," I said not looking at him, just staring at Robert.

"My aunt took me the other night," Robert said. "It's cool. It's pretty good. I don't think it's too fancy. My aunt's paying."

There wasn't any trace of animosity in the conversation and to someone overhearing us it probably sounded innocuous, despite my growing rage, because I was trying to keep it together by treating this as a game—it wasn't real, it could never be real, because everyone was hiding something, everyone was a liar. Ryan was trying not to eye me warily because of what I had admitted outside (Robert was in love with Susan Reynolds, Robert was involved with Matt Kellner's death, Robert was connected to the Trawler) and kept steering the conversation back to *Chariots of Fire* and then asked what movies Robert had seen recently—an attempt to steer the conversation into legitimately innocuous territory, because I knew Ryan Vaughn didn't care and wasn't particularly invested in movies. Robert admitted he hadn't seen any films lately.

"Why not?" I asked suddenly.

"Because, I guess, I've been busy," he said, his eyes darting from me to Ryan.

"Busy with what?" I asked.

"School, homework, studying," Robert said.

"And going to Palm Springs," I reminded him.

"I've been out a couple times." He shrugged, sipped his Coke.

"Who do you stay with out there?" I asked.

"A friend of the family's," he said, unfazed. "In Rancho Mirage."

"So you never saw any movies with Matt?" I asked softly.

"What?" Robert asked.

"Did you and Matt ever go to the movies?"

"Matt?" he asked. "No." Pause. "I didn't really know Matt."

"Don't bring Matt up," Ryan said quietly. "Come on, Bret."

"Why not?" I asked. "Matt and Robert were friends. They hung out."

"Not really," Robert said. "I mean I tried to get to know him but—"

"What happened?" I asked too quickly. "You tried? How?"

"Well, you knew him," Robert said, hesitantly. "You know how hard it could be to reach him."

"Reach him?" I murmured, nodding. "Yeah, I guess." I paused. "How hard did you try?" I paused again. "I mean, to reach him."

"Well, we'd eat lunch together sometimes," he said. "We talked at school—"

"Did you ever go over to his house?" I asked. "On Haskell Avenue?"

"No," Robert said.

"Did he ever come over to yours?" I asked.

"No."

"So you didn't really try *that* hard to reach him."

Robert stared at me. I'd finally activated the whirring behind the eyes, even though a smile was frozen on his face.

"Are you accusing me of something?" he asked lightly, containing himself. "What's going on?"

"No, no," I said, acting completely complacent. "I'm sorry if it came off like that. I'm just, I guess, interested, considering, you know, what happened . . ."

"Right, right," Robert said, nodding. "I understand."

"So you didn't really hang out with him?" I asked.

"Bret," Robert said, sighing. "I talked to Ronald Kellner. If you want to know what I said to him, you can just call him yourself."

"It's funny, because Ronald said Matt was going to see you before he disappeared," I said. "I've already talked to Ronald, by the way."

Ryan glanced at me, and then over to Robert, utterly confused.

"Yeah, supposedly Matt said this . . ." Robert confirmed. "And we had vague plans. I'd given Matt my number and he was supposed to call me—"

"Which number?" I interrupted.

"My number," Robert said. "Not the one in the roster." A beat. "It's private."

"So—you never saw Matt Kellner the week he disappeared?" I asked.

"Bret," Ryan said. I ignored him.

"What do you mean?" Robert squinted at me, confused. "See him?"

"I mean did he ever stop by your place?" I asked. "Did you guys talk? Did he ever call you the week he was missing? Or make any kind of contact?"

"No, we hadn't talked, and no, he didn't make any kind of contact with me." Robert sat very still in the booth, his eyes whirring, trying to figure out how to play this game and combat me.

"You guys didn't drive out to Crystal Cove together?" I asked gently. "You guys didn't record some tapes together?"

"Bret," Ryan warned again.

"What are you talking about?" Robert asked back. "Tapes? I've never been to Crystal Cove."

"I'm just asking," I said soothingly.

Robert's gaze hardened. "Whatever was going on between you and Matt is none of my business." He paused. "I understand," he said, "that it was hard for you." He paused again. "Considering, y'know, the nature of your friendship." He realized how this sounded and then clarified: "Whatever that was."

I was too shocked to say anything but since Ryan already knew about Matt and me it didn't really explode.

"But I didn't know Matt," Robert said. "So I don't know what you're asking me."

"How do you know what was going on between Matt and me?" I asked in defensive mode. "Did Matt tell you? Did he actually tell you?"

"No," Robert said. "He just told me you had a falling out and that the two of you weren't hanging anymore." He paused. "I asked what the falling out was about but he was kind of vague." He paused again, offered a little shrug. "I assumed it was something that was none of my business."

"Why would you assume that?" I asked. "Why would it be none of your business?"

"Susan mentioned something," Robert said. "That you guys were . . . close."

I wanted to scream. I wanted to leap out of the booth. Instead, I just stared at Robert, paralyzed. But I was also on the verge of collapsing and crawling away from the table to find a corner to cover my face with my hands and cower in.

"And you thought what?" I asked. "You believed her?"

"Yeah, sure," Robert said. "Why shouldn't I believe her?"

And then I couldn't stop myself: it rushed out of me.

"Well, Susan mentioned to me that you'd been institutionalized part of your junior year before you came to Buckley." I paused. "Should I believe that?"

Robert flinched, then turned away. Ryan was looking back and forth between the two of us, again utterly confused at where we had taken the conversation. Robert didn't prolong the moment and turned back to me with a wary expression.

"Yeah, um, I was dealing . . . with some stuff," Robert admitted, sighing. "Yeah, I, um, was in a place outside of Jacksonville for a couple months." He paused. "And I was figuring things out." He stopped. "My father placed me there. I didn't think I needed to go."

"But you told us you were in Roycemore," I said quietly. "When you first came to Buckley you said you were in Roycemore. You never mentioned anything about a mental institution—"

"It wasn't a mental institution," Robert said. "It was a . . . facility." He made a gesture with his hand. "And what? Come on. I'm just supposed to blurt that out? My first day of school? When I just met you guys?"

"I don't know," I said, shaking my head. "I just don't know . . ."

"You don't know what?" he asked.

"I don't know if you're fucking crazy or not," I said.

Silence. The three of us just stared at each other.

And then I started laughing, trying to pass the whole thing off as a joke. And it worked, because Ryan took my cue and started to laugh as well, whether he wanted to or not, which caused Robert to uneasily smile and nod. "Hey, I'm sorry, I'm just fucking around," I said, reaching across the table and grabbing his wrist. "You cool?"

Ryan and Robert realized that we had been unwittingly playing some kind of game I'd created that teetered on the edge of cruelty and that this had all been an elaborate joke. Dinner arrived and within the returning pantomime everything was smooth and easygoing. Part of the tension had broken and everyone was relieved that the conversation about Matt was over, but, if I look back, only part of the tension had cracked, because Robert never told us why he was in the facility in Jacksonville and I didn't press it and I also didn't tell Robert I knew about Susan Reynolds, that Robert had lied about being in Palm Springs with her, and that I had followed him to an abandoned house on Benedict Canyon on a number of afternoons that fall and that I didn't believe him about Matt Kellner because I had in my possession a tape that was made the last night Matt was alive and the pretend voice taunting Matt had come from the mouth of the boy sitting across from me in the red leather booth at Hamburger Hamlet and the tape was left in my mailbox by him sometime before he'd headed off to Palm Springs that weekend and that I found Sunday morning.

But I didn't have to wait long to find out exactly why Robert Mallory was placed in that developmental center outside of Jacksonville during the second half of his junior year in the spring of 1981. I found out the next day.

23

ON WEDNESDAY MORNING ROSA MENTIONED that a message on my mother's answering machine had been left for me. It was eight-forty and I'd just walked into the kitchen in my school uniform and tossed the Gucci backpack onto the island while I opened the refrigerator and swigged from a carton of orange juice. I avoided the copy of the *Los Angeles Times* waiting for me next to a bowl of berries Rosa had laid out, afraid of what might be in it, and walked through the house to my mom's room, where I sat on the bed and pressed PLAY on the answering machine. I waited. And then I heard a woman's voice I didn't recognize. "Bret, I hope this is the right number, though I suppose you might have your own . . . number, but this is the only one in the roster." I leaned toward the machine. I was apprehensive. I automatically thought I was in some kind of trouble. But then the hesitant voice said, "This is Abby Mallory, I'm Robert's aunt, we talked on the phone I think on Friday, when you called and I told you Robert was in Palm Springs. I think you went out with him and Ryan last night?" She asked this as a question even though it wasn't—she knew and also apparently knew Ryan Vaughn well enough to refer to him by his first name.

"Anyway, Robert already left for school this morning and . . ." She stopped. I wasn't breathing. "He told me some things that you, um, said to him last night and I think that maybe you . . . and I should talk." She paused again as if weighted down by what she wanted to tell me. "I don't want him to know that I called you and I don't want to do this over the phone, so if you could meet me somewhere I would appreciate it." She paused. "I think there are things you need to know." My stomach dropped and I found myself gripping the comforter on my mother's bed. She paused again. "There is . . . something . . . that I think needs to be clarified for you . . . about Robert." There was another pause. "I hope you get this message and you call me back." I thought she was about to hang up but then she left a number, which I scrawled down on the pad by the phone on my mother's nightstand. Abigail Mallory ended the message with "Sooner is better. I could meet this afternoon. I'll be in Beverly Hills at my lawyer's office and I could meet afterward, around five, when you're out of school. I hope you get this before you head to Buckley. If you call back don't leave a message. If I don't hear from you I'll try again." She paused. "And please, please, don't tell Robert I called." There was an abrupt click.

I sat still on my mother's bed only a moment before I reached for the phone. Abigail answered immediately and after a brief conversation she asked me to meet her at La Scala Boutique at five o'clock.

I PULLED the 450SL into the half-filled parking lot adjacent to La Scala Boutique and easily found a space. I walked the short distance to the entrance still wearing my school uniform and took off my Way-farers as I opened the door. The restaurant, which sat on the corner of Beverly Drive and Little Santa Monica Boulevard, was ringed with booths and there were a number of tables tightly packed together in the middle of the space and a small bar that sat six was in the corner, decorated with hanging Chianti bottles. At the booth before the entrance to the kitchen sat a woman dressed in a cream-colored blouse and a black blazer, wearing sunglasses and smoking a cigarette, which she stubbed out in an ashtray next to a glass of white wine— she was the only person in the entire restaurant. "I didn't know if you were coming or not," Abigail said as she took off her sunglasses and I neared the table. She was younger than I expected, probably early thirties, and then I remembered she wasn't Robert's mother—she was the younger sister of his father, and she was striking in ways similar to Robert and I was suddenly curious as to what his father looked like, if he was as handsome and sexually alluring as his son. I sat down across from her and realized I didn't need to say my name. "Do you want a drink?" she asked quietly. I shook my head.

"I'm sorry if I'm a little off," she started. "I just came from a meet-ing with my attorney," she explained. "My husband and I are in the middle of a rather protracted divorce. And he is being fairly difficult. Though I know he says the same thing about me." She paused and added a sad little smile. "And these appointments have become very unpleasant." She lifted the glass and finished the wine. "I should have probably rescheduled this. I'm sorry." She was so reserved it was like sitting with an actress straining to play a part in a scene she hadn't remembered the lines to.

I didn't know what I was supposed to say as a seventeen-year-old costumed in a private-school uniform, so I just stared at her and qui-etly nodded as if I understood. I didn't have anything to say, because I didn't know where to begin, and I also realized, sitting in the booth at La Scala, that I didn't want to know anything and that maybe I should just leave and let everything play out without knowing why Robert's aunt thought it was so important to meet, especially with the added caveat that I'd been warned Robert should never know about this meeting or the phone call that set it up. She was studying me without expression as if trying to neutrally figure out who this boy was she had summoned to meet her and if she could trust him. I finally looked away and down at the table and waited until she said some-thing. The maître d', who I recognized from my frequent visits to the restaurant with my parents, walked out of the kitchen wearing slacks and a Polo shirt, and asked her if she'd like another glass of wine, and Abby nodded without saying anything. I watched as he went to the bar and came back with a half-empty bottle of chilled Pinot Grigio and poured it until her glass was filled to the brim. Abby nodded thanks and the maître d' asked me if I'd like a drink. I just shook my head and murmured no.

"Robert told me he saw you last night," she finally said.

"Yeah, Ryan invited him to dinner after we went to the movies," I said. "In Westwood," I uselessly added.

"Robert told me you were . . . upset, it seemed." She paused and waited for me to say something.

"No, not really," I lied. "I wasn't upset. We were—I mean, I was kind of joking around," I said. "I was joking around. Whatever I said wasn't meant to be taken so seriously."

"Robert said that you said that but that's not what Robert thought . . ." She took a sip of wine. "He didn't believe you when you said you were just joking."

I didn't say anything at first. A vague annoyance was rising within me that I tried to tamp down. "Well, I can't help it if he couldn't take a joke."

She considered this and took another sip of wine. "He said that you, well, went after him last night. He said that you seemed to be accusing him of something that he said he has nothing to do with and knows nothing about." I felt a chill when I heard this but Abigail said it in a calm voice—she wasn't accosting me. She was just relating the facts that Robert had supplied her with. The Valium, as usual, was steadying me and I was able to stare at her without breaking down over Matt Kellner and the terrible things I imagined Robert had done to him.

"But I said I was joking. I said it was a game. It was a guy thing, y'know, just screwing around, testing limits, being a dick. I mean everything seemed fine afterward." I paused. I was lying and I didn't care and I flashed on how I had sobbed on the drive back from West-wood to the empty house on Mulholland, and now in La Scala I became emboldened. "What did Robert take so seriously that he had to tell you about it?" This was a dare on my part and the first moment in the conversation when I felt like an adult—that I had risen to the occasion and was defending myself from whatever her fucked-up nephew had accused me of. Abigail was still studying me and didn't answer my question. Instead, she went in a different direction. She wasn't evasive but genuinely curious.

"Robert has mentioned you a lot," she said. "In fact since the first day of school." She was staring at me but there was no anger, she wasn't admonishing, she was just telling me things. "He said you saw him somewhere, at a movie, over a year ago." She paused. "A movie that he told you he wasn't at. And you didn't believe him." She sipped the wine. "And later that day you followed him." She paused again. "After school."

"No, I didn't follow him," I said calmly. "I was driving to the Galleria and he started following me. And he followed me *into* the Galleria. I wasn't following anybody."

She just stared at me as if she was deciding whether she could believe me or not.

"He doesn't know you're here, right?" Her expression and her voice became concerned. "You didn't mention anything about meeting me here, right?"

"No, no, he doesn't," I said quietly. "You told me not to." I paused and then said, "I don't really talk to Robert." I paused again. "I don't really trust him."

"He became very interested in you," she said. "From the first day." She paused. "He talks about you a lot." She sipped her wine. "He said that you . . . unsettled him . . . when you told him you were positive you saw him at that movie theater over a year ago."

I felt another chill, a wave of apprehension. "Why . . . did that unsettle him?" I asked. "I know he was there. I don't know why he was lying about it."

"Don't you know?" she asked. "Or are you pretending you don't know why?" She leaned in. "Look, we can sit here all day and evade whatever your situation is, Bret—"

"What's *my* situation?" I asked, and realized my voice sounded helpless and reedy like a child. "Why does everyone need to be so careful around Robert? And why do I need to believe what Robert says? I think he's a fucking liar—"

"I didn't say that," she said, surprised. "That's not what I meant."

"You're implying that I've done something wrong," I said. "That I've said something wrong. When Robert is, I believe, a pretty screwed-up guy. What's *my* situation?"

She didn't say anything. She kept studying me as if she couldn't figure out if I was trustworthy or not, someone who could act with her in this scene she was creating as a confidant, a co-conspirator, another performer who would get on her level. "Well, you told Robert last night that you thought he was crazy."

"Is he?" I asked. "Is he messed up? Is he dangerous? Why do I need to be so careful around him?" I asked. "Why is he on Thorazine?" I asked.

"He's not on Thorazine," Abigail said, confused. "Robert's not on Thorazine," she said again. "Who told you that?"

I stopped and retraced the days back to Susan's party, where I heard her utter this by the edge of the pool. "I think he . . . told some-one this," I said quietly. "I think he told Susan Reynolds this."

"No, he's not on Thorazine," she said, sipping the wine again. "He takes a benzodiazepine but nothing heavier than that." She furrowed her brow. "Thorazine?"

"Look, I'm not sure what Robert is exactly capable of," I said, trying to carefully formulate how I wanted to relay this. "I think he is . . . or I've come to believe that he is . . . a somewhat troubled . . . individual who is responsible for . . . a number of things." I said this without emotion, and it sounded hollow, devoid of reason or fact, something bland and bureaucratic. Abigail was silent. I looked around the empty room. The restaurant had a panoramic view of Santa Monica Boulevard and Beverly Drive as well as Little Santa Monica Boulevard, the streets backed up with rush-hour traffic. The sky was darkening and it would soon be night. Suddenly I was scan-ning the streets for a glimpse of the beige-colored van. In the ensuing silence I asked: "Why was Robert in that . . . facility? The one outside of Jacksonville?" I paused. "What happened?"

"How did you find out about that?" she asked, unsurprised but curious.

"Susan Reynolds told me," I said.

"Susan," she said, smiling to herself. "Do you know that I've never met her?"

"Why . . . would you have met her?" I asked.

"Because Robert is quite taken with her," Abigail said. "That's why."

"She has a boyfriend," I automatically said. "And Thom's my best friend."

"I know. I understand that," she said. "It's a delicate situation for everyone, isn't it?"

I didn't want to talk about that. It was already playing out between Robert and Susan. I knew what was going on and what would eventu-ally happen and I wanted to postpone the reality for as long as I pos-sibly could. Thom would be back in four days. "Why was Robert in that facility?" I asked again.

"His father put him there," she said simply.

"What did he do?" I asked. "What did Robert do so he had to be put in whatever the fuck it is? A mental institution?"

"I wasn't . . . there," Abigail said vaguely. "I only . . . heard things." She paused. "Robert disputed them but a few things happened that alarmed his father, supposedly." She paused again. "As well as his stepmother." She sipped her wine. "And there was an incident with his stepsister that was, I am supposing, the final straw. Though Robert denied it ever happened."

"So he was only there once?" I asked. "He hadn't been institution-alized any times before that?"

"No," she said and then carefully explained, "His mother's death seemed to be the catalyst for Robert going off the rails a bit, which is to be expected, but I think he was hit exceptionally hard and it just exacerbated whatever else was going on with Robert before her death." She didn't know how much more she should offer and abruptly stopped. It was all tinged with vagueness and in that moment I thought I preferred it that way, but I realized I didn't: I needed specifics.

"So his father put him in there," I said, coaxing her. "And it was only once."

"It was about four and a half months," Abigail said. "January until May."

"Can you tell me what happened?" I asked gently.

"Well, I don't know what exactly happened," she said, and then, "What did Robert tell you?"

"He told us his mother died, and that he didn't get along with his father or his stepmother and that he wanted to move to Los Angeles and live with you, and that his dad ultimately agreed." I paused and then asked as delicately as possible: "What happened to his mother?"

"We don't really know," Abigail said matter-of-factly. "I didn't know my sister-in-law very well, but supposedly this was an accident. She had fallen from the upstairs landing in her home, tripped over the banister, and landed in such a way that she was killed instantly." Abigail paused, sipped the wine—the glass was now almost empty. She was completely unemotional when she said this, though the wine had caused her face to flush. She looked around for the maître d' and then at the boy sitting across from her. "But there were always questions—"

"Questions?" I interrupted her.

"Discrepancies," she clarified, momentarily distracted. "There were always questions on William's part. It didn't quite add up for him. She'd have to be in a certain position by the banister, the railing, on the second floor, William said . . ." She paused, debating if she should go on. "But, look, it had been a contentious divorce and William, that's Robert's father, hated Carol, he really hated her by then, and the case, which was never not referred to as an accident despite the suggestive nature of William's inquiries, was simply closed and that was it. And then Robert moved in with William and Diane, his stepmother, and Ashley, his younger stepsister from Diane's previous marriage, even though William wanted to send Robert away to a boarding school, but it was already May—Carol died in April—and the plan was to enroll Robert somewhere in September." Abigail paused and then decided to take another path. "Look, I wasn't entirely correct about Carol's death being the only thing impacting Robert. Something was happening before. There were things happening to Robert that were affecting him in strange ways before her death. This was according to both Carol and William. And I have to reiterate, Bret, I wasn't there. I was living out here. And I really only know what either William or Robert or Carol told me." She suddenly waved a hand through the air as if it signified something. "The specifics aren't important, it's just differing versions of events, but there was definitely a part of Robert that I became worried about, that concerned me—there were drugs, there was acting out, he had threatened a classmate." She paused again and then realized something. "I guess I'm telling you this so you *would* be more careful around him, because he's very . . . sensitive." I realized that Abigail was buzzed and this was causing her to ramble. "And that I'm not quite sure what you think he *is* capable of. I'm saying he's not the dangerous individual you seem to say he is—"

"Yes, you are," I interrupted. "You're afraid of him."

She paused. "Well, I think you need to define what you mean by dangerous—"

"Jesus Christ, what are you saying? Why am I fucking here? I don't want to know any of this shit. I don't want you to tell me anything. You're basically telling me that Robert's dad thinks Robert might have had something to do with his mother's death? Is that what I was supposed to take away from that—"

"But you need to know these things," she said quietly. "Because you need to stop this feeling you have about Robert—"

"I changed my mind," I said. "I'm afraid of this. I don't want to know anything else about this."

"Maybe that's a good thing," she said, grasping. "Being afraid. Keeping alert—"

"I'm sick of being afraid," I said. "And you're afraid, too. That's why you're here. That's why you called me. You're scared."

She shrugged. "You get used to it."

"Oh, fuck this," I muttered, and then, staring at her, I couldn't help but ask, "What do other people think happened to his mother? Do they think Robert had something to do with it?"

"Of course not, Bret," she said, looking around the restaurant for the maître d', her fingers lightly clenched around the stem of the empty wineglass. "Of course they don't, because Robert had nothing to do with it—"

"I don't believe it," I said. "I believe people thought he had something to do with it, whether he did or not. There must have been rumors."

"Well, there were always rumors about Robert but William started those . . ." Abigail stopped and just stared at me. "According to my brother . . ." Abigail looked past me, almost as if she was making sure there was no one around to hear her. "Carol had to have been standing in a certain position, somewhere mid-railing, above the floor, in order to fall from the landing—"

"And had she been?" I cut in.

Abigail looked at me. "No one knows," she answered quietly.

"Had she been pushed? Had she been thrown off? Is that what people thought? What are you trying to say? Did Robert do it?"

She released her grip on the wineglass and folded her hands on the table.

"It was an accident," she repeated. "There were irregularities, but the cause of death was listed as an accident. No one knew why she was in a position to fall the way she did but it was an accident." Abby suddenly became impatient. "This isn't what I wanted to talk to you about. I don't have anything to say about what happened to Carol."

"What did Robert say?" I asked. "About what happened to his mother?"

"He wasn't home," she said. "But he was the one who found her."

"Did he have an alibi?" I couldn't help but ask.

"An alibi?" she said, stunned. She asked it again, as if in disbelief. "Alibi?" Her expression shifted, as if she was suddenly seeing me in a new light and it confirmed something about the boy sitting across from her and the word he used. *Alibi.*

I was just staring at Abigail, breathing deeply, trying to control myself—the Valium wasn't working and small threads of anxiety were unspooling all around me in the air, tendrils creeping across the table-cloth in La Scala, wrapping themselves around my arms, my chest, my neck. Abigail started talking again and I tried to pay attention to what she was saying but I didn't want to. The noise of her voice entered in and out of my consciousness as my eyes scanned the streets for the sight of a beige-colored van.

"Robert did have . . . anger issues, and, yes, he acted out, and, yes, there were drugs—and, yes, he threatened people, classmates, and he wasn't focused anymore—and, yes, the marijuana and what-ever else he was taking, peyote, mushrooms, LSD, whatever, con-tributed to this, of course—but he wasn't dangerous, Bret. Except maybe to himself." Abigail stared at me for emphasis when she said this. "I don't believe he was necessarily violent. In fact there was one occasion when Robert was found in, what Carol described, a cata-tonic state in his bedroom and that was when the benzodiazepine was finally prescribed." She paused. "As for rumors about Robert, well, William mentioned that before Carol died she had told him there were a number of neighborhood pets that had either disappeared or were found dead and that she was very worried that people thought Robert had something to do with it, and William told her he probably did." She paused. "Yes, that is the type of father my brother is."

I felt sick when I heard this and I wanted her to stop talking, but I couldn't say anything. I suddenly remembered glimpsing Robert standing in front of Vince's Pets on the first floor of the Galleria in

Sherman Oaks on that September day after school, and a wave of revulsion swept through me. Abigail kept talking.

"Nothing was ever pinned on Robert but William assumed things about him, which just exacerbated the paranoia, his paranoia, Robert's paranoia." She looked at the empty glass and then scanned the room again for the maître d'. She sighed. "Anyway, Carol died in April, and after about a month living with his father, when Robert was finishing his sophomore year at Roycemore, William didn't want Robert living with them, he said there was something going on with Ashley, who was only twelve, something inappropriate, and so Robert came to L.A. and stayed with me during the summer of 1980." She stopped talking and reached for a cigarette and lit it. She blew the smoke away from me as I just stared at her. The maître d' suddenly appeared and without asking poured Abigail a third glass of white wine and then walked over to the bar to answer the phone. The cigarette and the refilled glass relaxed her into asking me: "And that's when you said you saw him. Right? At that movie theater in May."

I DIDN'T SAY ANYTHING because she knew Robert had been at the Village Theater on that Saturday at the early matinee of *The Shining.* He had wandered down one aisle and then up another, looking for someone. Robert had told Abigail on September 8 that someone at school had seen him that day—stunned that someone could have remembered him from only one sighting. And the way Abigail looked at me in La Scala, I realized that she knew why Robert had made such an impression and why he had stayed with me for so long—why I still remembered this boy fifteen months after I'd first seen him. She knew I thought he was beautiful, desirable, someone I wanted, and this answered a number of questions about me that she didn't need to ask. She had figured me out. I'd been attracted to her nephew in such an impactful way that she knew what my secret was. In some ways I barely cared, because the fear was erasing everything, but I suddenly felt naked and lightly ashamed in front of her. She was very relaxed now. Her trepidation about me had disappeared—she no longer seemed to care. I was just a boy. She thought she knew so much more than I did as she quietly got drunk. She started talking again.

"At first, Robert seemed better when he visited me here in 1980; this was in mid-May, after his sophomore year at Roycemore ended, though I hadn't experienced him in Chicago so I couldn't really compare—in fact I had rarely seen my nephew before," she said. "I don't think he was on drugs out here, because I told Robert he couldn't have a car if he took drugs. My husband and I had recently separated and he had moved to Brentwood and I had moved to Century City and he had bought a new car and left his Porsche and I let Robert drive that. And it was just me and Robert that summer and I really didn't see him much at all—he was gone a lot and I didn't ask where he was or what he was doing. He was out most nights, and I noticed that he had spent a lot of money on gas because of the credit card I'd given him—and in strange places, up and down the coast, sometimes as far away as Monterey or beyond San Diego, just driving—but he was also very social and he met girls easily, so I just assumed he was with them."

I'd love to put my tongue up that tight little pussy, all pink and wet . . . Little honey pot . . . really fuck that ass hard . . . make her scream . . .

"He seemed, at first, I don't know, to really thrive in Los Angeles," Abigail continued. "I don't think there was any way he had processed his mother's death yet—it had only been a couple of months, it was too soon—but he seemed okay. I assumed the impact of it would hit him later." She paused and then drank half the glass of wine. She had loosened up considerably and was no longer intently focusing on me. She was just talking freely, uninhibited. "But something had happened at the beginning of the summer, just a month or so after Robert arrived, that was the catalyst for Robert to vanish for days, even a week, at a time." She inhaled on the cigarette, exhaling a stream of smoke away from me. "This was the beginning of the paranoia. This was when he said someone had started following him. And this started happening after a girl Robert had been seeing on and off . . . disappeared."

She paused. I waited.

"You were right," Abigail said. "Robert was at that theater in

Westwood on that Saturday in May." She paused. "You did see him. He was there with a girl."

"With who?" I managed to ask through the dread.

"With a girl named Kathy Latchford," she said. "Katherine Latchford."

She paused again and studied me, curious as to what my reaction would be to that name.

"I know who that is," I said quietly. But my voice trembled because my heart was beating too quickly and I found it difficult to speak.

"SO YOU CAN UNDERSTAND why Robert didn't want anyone to know he had been with her, after she disappeared." She looked at me and slightly cocked her head. "And why he denied being there to you." She inhaled on the cigarette. "It was never a serious thing with Kathy. They went to the movies, they went to a concert, Kathy was seeing a lot of different people, Robert was going back to Chicago in September, it was casual." Abigail paused. "There were other boys Kathy was involved with that the police talked to after she disappeared . . ."

"But not Robert," I said.

"No, not Robert," she confirmed.

"He didn't come forward or . . . say anything?"

"No." Abigail crushed the cigarette out in the ashtray. "He wouldn't. Because he said he didn't know anything." She paused and looked around the room. "And I believed him." She looked back at me. "And both his father and myself agreed that, considering Robert's recent problems, well, he should just leave himself out of it."

I didn't say anything. I was just looking at Abigail dead-eyed. I couldn't believe how fast the nausea overwhelmed me—it was caused by pure panic that the anxiety had exploded into. I just sat very still to let the sickness pass, and then it slowly started dimming after the second wave crested. I wanted to get out of La Scala and go home and smoke weed and take another Quaalude, until I was stoned enough to annihilate myself and crawl under the blankets on my bed and fall into a deep and dreamless sleep.

"So you know about Katherine Latchford and what happened to her," Abigail was saying.

I nodded slowly. "Yes." I swallowed. "The Trawler."

"Yes." She nodded. "The first girl."

My jaw was clenched so tightly I thought my teeth were going to crack. I managed to unclench the jaw and murmur, "So that's why he said he hadn't been at the movie." I paused. "He didn't want someone to make the connection . . ."

Abigail continued. "There was one thing that Robert told me about Kathy that bothered me, but there was this person who was calling her and hanging up and she thought someone had gotten into her bedroom and rearranged a shelf of her books and gone through a drawer of her T-shirts and panties." She paused. "And she told Robert a few pairs of panties were missing." And then Abigail was trying to focus intently on me as she spoke so she could keep gauging my reaction to the information she was relaying instead of just being lost in the buzz of three glasses of wine. "She thought Robert had left her that poster, that gift, that the police became interested in much later . . ." She stopped. "But he hadn't."

"The Madness poster," I confirmed quietly. "For *One Step Beyond.*"

"Robert hadn't left her any poster," Abigail said. "I don't know what the poster was but he hadn't left anything for her." She paused. "Someone else had."

One Step Beyond. Second Edition. Three Imaginary Boys. Gang of Four.

I knew that the Foreigner 4 poster was part of this narrative.

I knew that Matt Kellner was somehow connected. But I had no idea how.

"On that day you saw him in Westwood, Robert told me that after the movie Kathy thought she saw someone suspicious in the parking lot, a guy, in the distance, wearing sunglasses, someone staring at her, and so when she disappeared from that party a few weeks later Robert assumed she was just hiding out for a couple of days—doing drugs, probably with another boy she'd been seeing, dealing with her paranoia." She sipped the wine. It was almost gone.

"Yeah?" I said, just gazing at Abigail.

"And then, when it became apparent that something was seriously wrong and that Kathy was in fact missing, Robert said someone had begun to follow . . . him." She paused dramatically to let this land. I said nothing, remembering what Thom told me in the car on the way to the airport: Robert had told him he was being followed, *stalked*, some freak.

"And there were phone calls on his private line where no one said anything, a number of hang-ups," Abigail said, breathing in. "And he sensed that when he was out in public he was being . . . watched. According to Robert this never let up during that summer here in L.A., the summer Katherine was missing and before her body was found, and on one level he just got used to it. Sometimes he even made jokes about it, but I knew he was going through something." She paused. "He still thinks someone is following him. He said it stopped in Chicago but when he returned to Los Angeles that December, to spend the holidays with me, he felt it again—this invisible presence, he called it. He had started receiving anonymous letters with no return address that he never showed me—I don't know what was in them. And then the phone calls started up again around Christmas. It was a replay of the summer. And Robert started breaking down." She paused. "And of course Kathy's body had been found in August."

And Sarah Johnson would disappear that first week in January, the writer reminded me.

"Who did he think it was?" I heard myself ask and then flashed on Robert in the Galleria when he told me: *I don't like being followed.*

"He doesn't know," Abby said. "He never did."

"Abby." I breathed in. "Do you really believe him? Do you really believe he had nothing to do with Katherine's disappearance? And what happened to her? You don't think he's capable of that?"

Her expression hardened for the first time since I'd sat down. "That response is exactly why Robert didn't go to the police." She shook her head slightly. "That response is part of the problem, Bret. The first thing he told me when he got home from that first day of school in September was that someone from Buckley had seen him at that movie he had gone to with Kathy Latchford. He was panicked about it." She paused. "He hadn't seen you. He doesn't remember seeing you. He was walking around looking for Katherine—she had been dropped off by her mother." She paused again. "But when you ask me something like that—is Robert capable of this, if he has an *alibi,* if he was responsible for his mother's death—it makes me realize that you obviously think he's sick and—"

"There's a time line," I said, leaning in. "Abby. There's a time line. Katherine disappeared when Robert was here and then her body was found before he left. Sarah Johnson disappeared when he was here and—"

"Bret." Abigail had raised her voice. "I don't want to hear this."

"Was he here in L.A. during the past summer?" I asked. "In June? Was Robert here in June?"

"Well, um, on and off . . ." Abigail started. "Yes, he was here in June. Yes."

"So he was here when Julie Selwyn disappeared," I said. "In June. He was here in June."

"Who's Julie Selwyn?" Abigail Mallory asked, confused.

"WHAT HAPPENED IN CHICAGO?" I asked. "Why was Robert placed in that facility?" I paused. "You don't want to tell me. You can't tell me, can you? You don't want me to know, because it'll confirm something about Robert," I said. "You don't want me to know."

"I don't know what happened, Bret," Abigail said. "I only know what I heard and there were two differing versions—"

"What happened?" I interrupted. "Jesus, just tell me so I can get out of here."

She stared at me—she was drunk and alive to the possibilities of whatever she was going to tell me and yet she wanted to make me understand something by defending Robert against whatever he had been accused of in Illinois. If she had been sober I don't think she would have been capable. But, buzzed on three glasses of wine, she decided to be honest and give it a shot.

"It seemed that Ashley—" she began quietly.

"Who's Ashley?" I asked, not remembering.

"His stepsister," she said.

"Okay, Ashley." I nodded.

"Ashley said . . . something happened between her and Robert."

I stared at Abigail. "What?"

"I suspect she always had a crush on Robert, or that's what Carol had mentioned once or twice when I talked to her," Abigail said. "Even though Robert lived with his mother he occasionally stayed with his father when Carol was away on business. And I think Ashley accused Robert of certain things, certain sexual things that he didn't do. But William and Diane wanted to believe . . ."

"Like what?" I asked. "Like what sexual things?"

"Robert was back at Roycemore in January and wasn't doing well—I heard about peyote and LSD, which Robert admitted to—and he was having problems with his father and with Diane—they hadn't been able to find a boarding school that Robert would agree to—and it just kept escalating until . . . Ashley said something happened to her. That Robert did something to her."

I waited.

Abigail sighed. "She had developed a . . . rash and she blamed it on Robert," Abigail said, after taking a long pause. "She said that Robert had done . . . something to her. That he had told her to . . . shave . . ." Abigail stopped. "There was the insinuation that he had done something to her. That he had . . . done something sexual to her. Robert said it wasn't true, that she was lying, and then . . ."

I waited. "And then?"

"And then Robert overdosed and I don't think it was a serious attempt but maybe a way to make William feel guilty about believing Ashley and then William wanted to place Robert in that facility—he said it was to get him clean as well as to get a complete psychiatric evaluation—and it all happened fairly quickly. Robert was placed in Jacksonville a week after he returned to Chicago and by the time he was released it was decided that he should move out here with me," she said. "Look, I just want you to understand that he has been through a lot and I think unfairly treated. And I think that whatever you want to hang on him is also unfair and dangerous and I want you to—"

I leaned in again. I could feel my skin reddening. I was suddenly furious.

"He was with Matt Kellner, okay, Abby?" I said quietly. "The week Matt disappeared he knew where Matt was, and I have a tape that was made the night Matt died and I believe the other voice on it is Robert's and that he helped fucking kill him—"

"Stop it—"

"I believe that on that weekend Matt came over to the house on Benedict Canyon and that Robert drugged him and that he drove him down the coast to Crystal Cove and that he beat the shit out of him and then drove him back and this is just a fucked-up game Robert likes to play—"

"Stop it, Bret, please—"

"And he staged it to look like Matt drowned after a psychotic break—"

"You have to stop this, Bret—"

Abigail had reached for the pack of cigarettes and then dropped her hand.

"Robert cut his fucking cat's head off, Abby. Your fucking nephew nailed it to a column. He gutted it—"

"Robert already talked to Ronald Kellner, Bret." She looked up at me and there were tears in her eyes.

"You don't believe he was involved with the home invasions that began when he was here in the summer of 1980? Along with the assaults and Katherine Latchford disappearing?" I said. "The time line fits. The time line completely fits. He was here when Sarah Johnson disappeared and he was here when Julie Selwyn disappeared and he wasn't on the goddamn field at school the night Audrey Barbour disappeared." I stopped, exhausted. "He was in fucking Woodland Hills, stalking her at the Promenade—"

"I don't really know who those other girls are. I guess I haven't been following this as closely as you, Bret," Abigail said softly. "I'm not sure I know who those girls are exactly."

"So it's just bad luck that Robert dated the girl who was the first victim of the Trawler," I said. "And bad luck that his twelve-year-old stepsister said he raped her—"

"You have to stop accusing him of things," she said. "He has no one. He has no one but me—"

"Stop it," I said. "Just stop it—"

But a sudden pang expanded in my chest when she said this because I felt the same way about myself: *You have no one either.*

—

SHE LEANED ACROSS the table—the desperation was palpable. "You should get to know him, Bret," she said quietly. "I think if you knew him you'd realize it wouldn't be possible for him to do what you're suggesting." She stopped and then sat back. She reached for the pack of cigarettes, picked one out but refrained from lighting it. And then she suddenly looked slightly confused. "How . . . did you know about the house on Benedict Canyon?"

"I don't remember," I automatically lied. "I think Robert mentioned it to a group of us at lunch or something," I muttered. "There was some house on Benedict he mentioned . . ." I didn't tell her I'd followed Robert there and that I roamed the backyard.

"It's where my husband and I first lived. He's now in Scottsdale. He hasn't put the house on the market because he has to give me half of it. He's being a prick." She was having trouble focusing on me. I realized she was trying to light the cigarette and for some reason couldn't. "Robert keeps some things there. Upstairs. He has a key."

I was overwhelmed. I finally stood up. I looked at her blankly. In that moment I saw Abigail Mallory as a clueless drunk and I wondered how many times she had censored herself during our conversation. Even though she seemed afraid and vulnerable she made me feel pitiless, as if I was capable of wiping her out. "You want me to be friends with him?" I asked quietly. "You want me to hang out with Robert?"

She looked up at me but didn't nod.

"I'll hang out with him. Whatever." I realized my back was completely damp with sweat and fused with my Polo shirt. "You want me to be nice to him? Fine. Whatever." I said this numbly, with no emotion.

Her face relaxed and she seemed surprised. "That easily?" she asked softly. "You've changed your mind that easily?"

"I haven't changed my mind about anything," I said.

She stared at me, confused.

"I'm worried about what's going to happen to Susan Reynolds," I said. "I'm worried about what he's going to do to Susan."

24

I DIDN'T GO TO SCHOOL on Thursday—I couldn't handle the notion of it after what was revealed to me at La Scala Boutique and so I stayed in bed with the comforter swathed around my body. I over-slept, even with Rosa trying to wake me up and walking into my room to assist a whimpering Shingy, who was scratching at the door that led onto the deck, as I fell in and out of sleep. I spent the day going over the conversation I'd had with Abigail Mallory while ignoring phone calls from Debbie and trying to concentrate on homework with the help of the dwindling supply of weed I'd bought from Jeff on Sun-day. What happened in La Scala Boutique could become, if I let it, my only point of reference, and I needed to be distracted from it, and the bowls I kept smoking from the glass pipe helped me focus on other things. That night I took a Quaalude to zone out and easily fell asleep, and on Friday I dutifully got out of bed when the alarm I'd set the night before began quietly beeping on my nightstand and went through the morning ritual, though I didn't jerk off that day—I had no desire. I swam, took a shower, got dressed in the Buckley uniform, glanced over the homework I had completed the night before and then stared at myself in the mirror and realized I looked good, I looked normal, I looked friendly, I looked calm, I was the tangible participant and I was going to get along with everybody that day. And I was going to become Robert Mallory's friend—because there wasn't any choice.

As I walked toward the bell tower with the Gucci backpack slung over my shoulder I took notice of everyone's cars in the parking lot: there were Susan's and Debbie's respective BMWs, there was Ryan's black Trans Am and Robert's Porsche—everyone was there but me.

(Then I remembered: Thom Wright's Corvette wasn't there either.) It was almost nine o'clock and American Fiction was about to begin. *Slaughterhouse Five* had been assigned and I'd quickly read the first half of the novel the day before, stoned, out by the pool, after I called Buckley and told one of the secretaries that I wasn't feeling well and wouldn't be coming to school that day—there was no suspicion in her voice, only concern and understanding; this was how Buckley worked, this was what being a senior meant, this was the privilege we'd inherited. Susan smiled at me as I took the seat next to hers and I smiled back reassuringly and then I nodded over at Ryan, who hesitantly nodded at me, as if surprised I'd acknowledged him, and then class began. The day really became effortless once you faked it and it actually became *more real* because of your changed demeanor; the *act* became the reality and it affected everything in what seemed like a positive way. In fact, it was preferable to reality.

BY THE TIME lunch was playing itself out, with just Debbie and Susan and Robert and myself occupying the center table beneath the shadow of the Pavilion, I had metamorphosed into so many people I actually wasn't: I was now Debbie Schaffer's amiably amorous boyfriend, telling her I'd spent Thursday at home thinking about us and how I wanted—and *needed*—to be more committed to *us,* and I promised her I had vanquished the zombie who had overtaken me earlier that semester. I was now constantly touching and caressing her and kissing her on the lips every time we ran into each other between classes on that Friday, and though I begged off on her coming over to the house on Mulholland for a quick fuck after school she didn't argue, because she was not only so touched by my newfound allegiance but too preoccupied with the equestrian charity event, which was far more glamorous and extravagant than I'd supposed—it would be televised, there were sponsors, there were movie and TV stars attending, it was tied into something bigger I couldn't comprehend. Spirit had been acting nervous and skittish and needed to refocus on his performance, Debbie would mention to me, something had spooked him—and she was training the horse daily in order to calm him because it was a complicated routine, and she was almost constantly in Malibu when she wasn't at Buckley. I acted concerned and asked the appropriate questions even though I was completely bored and didn't care—and she, in turn, was giddy and relieved that I was so attentive and at one point suspiciously asked me if I was high on something and I assured her I wasn't—"only you," I added. What was happening was *real*, I insisted. And then, because of my admission, Debbie told me she was disappointed with *herself* and that it was *her* fault that we hadn't been able to spend more time together and I reassured her that we'd completely reconnect when the charity event was over and that I was looking forward to being in the stands to support her. When I said this she was so surprised on that last Friday in October she looked happier than I'd ever seen her, and I wondered why I hadn't accepted this way of *being* in June, when we fell on that chaise longue by the lit pool at Anthony Matthews's house and I let the relationship start to take us to the unsteady place where we were now at. I hoped it wasn't too late.

I WAS ALSO THE BEST FRIEND to Susan Reynolds—I stopped her in the pathway under the eaves after our first class and held her hand as I sincerely told her how sorry I was about Palm Springs and that it was her life and I loved her no matter what she decided and I'd never tell Thom and please forgive me. Susan was too exquisitely numb to break down with relief but her eyes teared up and she hugged me tightly as Ryan Vaughn passed by with a blank expression, heading to his next class, ignoring me, but even that was okay, because I now understood that it was never going to happen with us anyway—that had always been the painful reality.

"Thank you," Susan said.

"I'm really going to try, I'm really there for you," I said. "And I'm going to try and be friends with Robert," I said. "Matt's death messed me up—I've gotten everything so wrong," I told her.

I tried not to zone out during assembly when I suffered a brief and painful moment that unexpectedly broke the tangible participant: I noticed Thom's absence—it was suddenly undeniable and everywhere. A huge part of Buckley was missing without him. I couldn't believe how much I craved his presence and in a panic immediately willed the tangible participant back and turned this desire about Thom onto Robert, and while the sea of blue blazers intoned the Pledge of Allegiance and the Buckley Prayer I leaned in to Robert and apologized for what had happened at Hamburger Hamlet on Tuesday night in Westwood: it was all a joke, it was all a misunderstanding, and I was really, really sorry. Robert acted totally unfazed and shrugged it off. He leaned in and said in a low voice, "It's cool, dude."

THIS KINDNESS CONTINUED at lunch, when I—along with Debbie and Susan—tried explaining to Robert my "weird" sense of humor and how perverse I could get, pushing things into uncomfortable realms or just embellishing stuff, and warned him not to take it too personally and again apologized for any discomfort I might have caused. I was just a writer, we had issues, we had problems, we were all a little nuts. The girls had apparently been filled in about what happened at Hamburger Hamlet in Westwood the other night, and though Debbie accepted it as just another facet of myself as a writer, Susan seemed more hesitant, because she had actually heard first-hand *from me* what I'd been thinking about Robert and his connection to Matt Kellner, but on that Friday she seemed grateful I was making an effort and appreciated the fact that I was preparing myself for whatever was going to happen between her and Robert Mallory.

I made a point at lunch to remind Robert that I was still up for seeing a movie with him and hanging out this weekend if he'd like to. "Maybe we could all do something together," I innocently suggested.

And then the girls reminded me that it was Terry's party Saturday night and somehow it was suddenly decided that the tangible participant should go with Robert to Stone Canyon, just the two of us, together. Susan was already going to be there with Debbie, getting their hair done by José Éber and their makeup by Rick Gillette, something arranged by Liz Schaffer, who was always professionally made up before any kind of public appearance. "Yeah," Debbie said brightly. "Why don't the two of you come together?" I was shocked by this request but I smiled and looked over at Robert, who shrugged and said, "Sure, I guess."

This was the last thing I wanted to do but it was also, I realized, part of a plan I began constructing, a new story I wanted to write.

The SHARDS

—

ON SATURDAY NIGHT I headed over to Century City in the 450SL with the top up—it had taken me longer than I expected to get my hair exactly how I liked it. *Evita* was still playing at the Shubert Theater in the ABC Entertainment Center and the valet in front was lined with waiting cars and behind the valet a large crowd had gathered and was entering the lobby, the Century Towers looming closer in the darkness as I drove toward them on Avenue of the Stars. I pulled past the white brick wall announcing the Century Towers in gold cursive lettering and told the security guard I was there to pick up Robert Mallory and he instructed me to check in at the front desk in the lobby of the building that was situated closest to Pico Boulevard and then directed me to a parking spot. The circular fountain was lit blue and dancing with water as I walked toward the entrance of the tower and into a spare and modern lobby with a crystal chandelier hanging over a waiting area consisting of a floral-patterned couch and a pair of armchairs that bracketed a glass coffee table where a lone orchid sat. The space exuded sleekness: stone floors, a vaulted ceiling. There was a man in a uniform at the front desk, which was set off to the right side as you entered the vast lobby, who barely noticed me as I walked up to him announcing my arrival. The elevator bank was directly parallel to the glass doors of the entrance and I could have walked straight to them unnoticed and bypassed the front desk altogether, but I followed protocol and checked in, even though Robert was expecting me.

The doorman lifted a phone, waited, and then told whoever had picked up that "Bret" was here; after a beat, the doorman said "Certainly" and then told me I could go up, gesturing toward the elevator banks.

ABIGAIL MALLORY'S condo was a penthouse at the top of the twenty-eight-story building, and as I stood in the quickly rising elevator I felt a strange calm lightly reverberating with a faint erotic charge— there was something I found so intimate about walking into the condo where Robert resided and where he combated his insanity with the routine of a normal seventeen-year-old boy: maybe he slept naked, or maybe he wore pajamas, maybe he jerked off when he showered, I imagined him eating meals, a bowl of cereal, and getting dressed and undressed, using the bathroom, doing his homework, and yet I also imagined him dreaming about planning another abduction, creating another *assemblage* depending on the current lunar cycle, using Susan Reynolds's body as the source of the *alterations* and what the Trawler called the *remakings*. I was entering into Robert's world that night and I hadn't fully realized until I was shooting up to the twenty-eighth floor how badly I'd desired this—there was a sexual tinge attached to it.

The elevator door opened and I walked into a hallway and looked around—and when I saw a door slightly ajar I realized it was the entrance to Abigail's penthouse. I knocked and loudly said, "Hello?" I heard Robert call back from somewhere in the condo, "Hey, I'll be out in a sec," and then the sound of a blow-dryer.

I entered into a massive living room with a marble floor and dimmed recessed lighting, which accentuated the stunning views spread out behind a window wall overlooking West Hollywood and the hills of Sunset in the far distance. There was an opened sliding glass door that led onto a balcony where a chaise longue and a small table sat, and past the edge of the balcony was the Hillcrest Country Club and Rancho Park. And far below a series of lit tennis courts bordered a darkened golf course next to where traffic flowed on Pico Boulevard. It was completely silent on the balcony—the world below the penthouse seemed very far away.

Everything about the condo was minimalist: the sleek sectional that took up most of the space in the living room was light gray and modern, and suggested nothing comfortable. A large print of the Hockney painting *Portrait of an Artist* hung on a wall next to the white granite fireplace and it was the blue of the pool, the green of the hills, and the pink blazer of the boy that seemed to be the only real color in the otherwise stark monochromatic room. There was a dining area beneath a chandelier where, at a rectangular glass table, eight anonymous high-backed gray-cushioned chairs sat; I assumed it was never used, judging how barren the condo was. This room flowed into a surprisingly narrow kitchen that was completely uncluttered with objects. I noticed a knife rack next to a blender, and a few tangerines piled in a ceramic bowl on a wooden cutting board. The blow-dryer had stopped and Robert called out, "I'm in here," expecting me to locate him from the vague direction of his voice. I walked slowly down a hallway—the marble became hardwood floors and there were no paintings or photographs on the walls—until I came to a room whose door was open.

THE FIRST THING I noticed was a bulky TV that sat on a stand in the corner, and because it was Halloween, *Night of the Living Dead* was playing—it had just started—and the spare black-and-white images complemented the décor of the gray bedroom, which had the same sweeping view of L.A. as the rest of the condo and was just as chic and minimal, and also looked as if no one lived there. It wasn't decorated for permanence—it was a transitory space, barely furnished, with a queen-sized bed tightly fitted with a light-gray comforter that melded in with the gray headboard and the flat gray carpet that surrounded it. A desk, a set of drawers, a nightstand with a lamp, all minimal and nondescript—and I also noticed there wasn't a phone in Robert's room and wondered where the phone with the number I found in Matt Kellner's drawer was located. (My mind immediately flashed: it was at Benedict Canyon.) There were no posters, there weren't any books except for the mass-market paperback of *Slaughterhouse Five* we were reading in American Fiction that lay folded open-faced down on the desk. There wasn't a stereo, just a boom box with a couple of cassettes scattered around it.

Robert was standing in a walk-in closet, knotting a crimson tie in front of a full-length mirror. I stopped, stunned at how handsome Robert looked that night, tall and sleek in a simple fitted black suit with a white dress shirt. I was also wearing a suit but it was assembled from a variety of pieces: a Polo button-down and slacks from I. Magnin along with the tweed jacket I favored that year, a Gucci belt, an Armani tie and black penny loafers. Robert's simplicity was classic and timeless and I imagined I looked like a preppie oaf by comparison. He had styled and combed back his hair, which accentuated the angles of his face, and I almost didn't recognize him even though I'd seen him only the day before. I realized he was taking Terry's party seriously in a way that I no longer could—he badly wanted to make an impression and

I didn't care anymore; this had been zapped out of me in the bunga-low at the Beverly Hills Hotel weeks ago. He smiled genuinely as he walked out of the closet and then checked himself in a mirror in the bathroom adjacent to the stark bedroom. I noticed a bottle of cologne and various toiletries and an array of seashells carefully arranged next to the sink, which I zoned out on while Robert inspected himself before he switched off a light and the bathroom went dark.

I thought I had come up for a drink but I heard him say, "Let's go," as I stared at the boom box and wondered if it was what Robert used to record Matt as he was breaking him down in Crystal Cove the last night of Matt's life, and how many ski masks did Robert keep in the chest of drawers by the television playing *Night of the Living Dead*?

But I forced a smile and said, "Let's do it," and then added, "We're running a little late."

He nodded okay and smiled at me again and it was hard to believe that this was the smile of a boy who had tried to kill himself, accord-ing to Abigail Mallory, less than a year ago in his bedroom in Chicago.

ELTON JOHN'S "FUNERAL for a Friend" started playing on KLOS as we drove from Century City toward Bel Air.

I took Avenue of the Stars and would make a left onto Santa Monica and then drive South Beverly Glen until it hit Bel Air Road where I'd swing right onto Bellagio, which would take us to Stone Canyon—it was a simple route, maybe ten minutes; the Schaffers lived up the street from the Bel Air Hotel and there'd be a valet, so we wouldn't have to worry about finding a parking space. Nothing much was said as I drove: the drama of the music was what he seemed to concentrate on, though I was so acutely aware of Robert's pres-ence that I barely heard the song; his scent lightly filled the cabin of the Mercedes: clean, the ocean, the drift of sandalwood, it suggested purity, something fresh and erotic. I wanted to tell him how good he smelled but refrained, just concentrating on the rising intensity of the song. It could have been any night in L.A.: we didn't pass anyone trick-or-treating and traffic was sparse on that Saturday.

Whatever conversation we had on the drive to Bel Air was so tentative and perfunctory—we didn't mention the girls, neither of us mentioned Thom Wright, Robert never said anything about his aunt meeting me on Wednesday in Beverly Hills, and not a whisper about last weekend in Palm Springs. But there wasn't anything awkward about the situation either—he seemed silenced by the anticipation of the party and he was into the song, with him at one point air-drumming, and soon I was more relaxed, focusing on the upcoming traffic signal at Beverly Glen and Sunset when "Funeral for a Friend" gave way to "Love Lies Bleeding" and in that moment I thought I saw the beige-colored van pull up behind us, just before I drove through the light on Beverly Glen and toward Bel Air's East Gate, but when I glanced again at the rearview mirror I watched as the headlights veered left onto Sunset and sped away, toward Westwood.

This happened so fast that I almost didn't have time to process the van or connect any meaning to it and yet felt a sharp panic, even though I couldn't be sure if it was the van. But why did I feel any fear? It was just a van. I was attaching something to it that hadn't even announced itself yet. It was just a beige-colored van whose license plates I'd never bothered to notice. It was just a flash, it was just an image, maybe it was nothing, maybe I was imagining it, and the force of Robert's presence and the expectation of Terry's party overrode any ominous thoughts that might have lingered. "Love Lies Bleeding" kept playing as we climbed the streets to Stone Canyon toward the Schaffers' mansion, and I didn't say anything to Robert about the van but I'd begun wondering: Was the van following me? Or, I thought, was the van following Robert?

I PULLED up to the valet stand in the circular driveway, where a surfer in white jeans and a white Polo shirt jogged around the hood of the car to open the driver's-side door as another surfer opened the passenger side, and when I got out the surfer handed me a ticket. There was a small army of surfer valets that night, opening doors and escorting women and men from a series of Mercedes and Porsches and Jaguars and Rolls, quickly moving the line of cars out of the driveway. The surfers were a Terry Schaffer touch: his parties always had an all-male staff consisting of young good-looking dudes who acted as valets, bartenders, servers, waiters, because supposedly the women who attended the parties didn't want their spouses and boy-friends distracted by hot young chicks offering them canapés and pouring champagne: just another piece of etiquette in the social world of Terry Schaffer that seemed practical and I admired.

I joined Robert and as we walked up the steps toward the open door of the house, where the butler, Paul, in uniform, warmly greeted the guests, ushering them in, Robert leaned in to me and asked, "Is that Jacqueline Bisset?"

I hadn't noticed and turned to see the actress heading toward us with a brooding platinum-blond hulk who I realized was Alexander Godunov, the Russian ballet dancer who had defected to the United States a couple of years previous, and they were now a couple.

"Yeah," I said in a low voice.

"God, she's so hot," Robert said, hushed, as Paul recognized me and nodded and then I introduced him to Robert. "He goes to Buck-ley with us," I said, expecting Paul would care and, of course, he pre-tended to—that was part of his job as the Schaffers' butler.

"Nice to meet you, Robert," Paul said graciously. "Please come in."

And then Paul leaned in to me and said, "Deborah and Susan are out by the pool, and supper will be served at nine."

Stepping into the foyer, I noticed that this party was darker than others, with candles flickering everywhere as the main source of light, and couples were casually sitting on the steps of the grand curving staircase and there were guests upstairs on the landing as well, every-one holding drinks and flatteringly lit by the burning candles.

AS WE STEPPED into the packed living room I realized why every-thing was darker than usual: this was one of Terry's starrier parties, and I noticed that Steven Reinhardt wasn't around to photograph the celebrities who had stopped by that night because this was a private event and it wasn't promoting anything. Terry's parties weren't par-ticularly lavish—they were cool, understated affairs, and there was a low-key, tossed-off attitude about them that made the movie stars in attendance seem all the more startling. Sometimes there were no reasons for the party—it was just Terry Schaffer hosting on a Satur-day night and everyone simply came. The living room was flickering with candlelight and loud with voices that drowned out the music—mostly seventies rock and recent disco hits, "You Make Loving Fun" by Fleetwood Mac was playing—as I led Robert to the bar set up in the corner, manned by two surfer bartenders. Robert wasn't drinking but I asked for a beer and was handed an ice-cold Corona with a wedge of lime that I pushed through the bottle's neck. I'd been attending Terry's parties since I'd turned sixteen, and invited by Debbie because we were friends, and for some reason that was the age at which Terry started allowing us in, and I was surprised how quickly jaded I'd become: I liked movies and movie stars but I also liked secrets, and seeing them in the flesh diminished their power for me.

But this was Robert's first Terry Schaffer party and he slowly looked around the living room as if stunned: Paul Newman was talking to Dudley Moore with Susan Anton towering over him. Jane Fonda was explaining something to Terry—it had been announced in the trades she was going to star in a movie Terry was producing but it never happened. I hadn't seen Terry since that afternoon at the Beverly Hills Hotel and I suddenly felt both emboldened and ashamed and looked away after he first noticed Robert and then me and lifted his drink. A director whose work I was enamored with—Walter Hill—was holding a tumbler and leaning in to Mel Gibson, whom I'd excitedly seen at the last party Terry threw, but on that Halloween night he just didn't have the same sexual impact. I was, however, still intrigued by the filmmakers I noticed in the crowd and knew that Robert wouldn't recognize: Tony Richardson, Franco Zeffirelli, Herbert Ross, John Schlesinger, and James Bridges, who was talking to John Travolta. I looked back at Terry, who kept listening to something Jane Fonda was telling him but was staring at Robert too intently, and I became completely unnerved.

I told Robert we should go outside and find the girls.

A LARGE GROUP had gathered by the glowing rectangle of the pool, next to another bar manned by surfers, and Robert stood for a moment to take in the vast yard dotted with Tiki torches, music coming from speakers hidden in the trees—"Brandy" by Looking Glass—a white tent set up and filled with thirty circular candlelit dining tables with ten folding chairs at each and a buffet being laid out by a group of uniformed servers.

Robert breathed in and then actually looked at me as he took in the grounds and said, "Amazing."

The smokers were usually outside even though cigarettes were allowed in the house, and Robert nudged me as we walked down the flagstone path to the pool: he had already spotted Jack Nicholson puffing on a Marlboro and standing with Angelica Huston and Diane Keaton and Warren Beatty, who had taken a break from busily editing *Reds* in New York, and Barry Diller, who was running Paramount at the time—the studio would be releasing Beatty's film in December. "This is crazy," Robert muttered as we moved closer to the crowd by the pool, where Liz Schaffer was smoking a cigarette in one hand and holding a near-empty glass in the other, stunningly put together in Halston, looking far younger than thirty-eight, and she was talking to Steve Martin and Carrie Fisher. Liz noticed me but only smiled tightly and turned away without any other acknowledgment, which I found oddly startling, and then she laughed at something Carrie said. I assumed her reticence was due to the embarrassment she felt because of the last time I'd seen her, drunk and naked beneath an opened Bijan robe in the living room on the Sunday before Labor Day.

I finished the first Corona and ordered another one when we arrived at the pool bar. Billie, the golden retriever, wandered out from wherever he'd been placed for the night and was padding around searching for affection and I petted him but Robert didn't—he just stared at the animal without interest, then looked away. Robert followed me as we walked around the crowd gathered by the pool and onto the lawn, the candlelit house looming above us, the windows flickering, though the fully staffed kitchen remained brightly lit. The two of us headed toward the stairs that led up to Debbie's room, because I assumed that's where the girls were, and then we stopped: Susan and Debbie were already carefully stepping down the stairs as we stood on the lawn rising up to the house; we waited silently as they neared us. They were both wearing vintage strapless taffeta dresses—Debbie's was pink, Susan's was black—and the first things I noticed were how the dresses accentuated their cleavage and I was shocked that Debbie had colored her hair—it was no longer platinum but an ashier blond, more natural-looking—and it was a different cut, less harsh and more girlish. And their makeup, from where we stood, seemed simple, just mascara and pink lipstick, and I couldn't understand what the makeup artist had accomplished, though as they got closer it became apparent: there was a flawless, understated radiance to their complexions. Susan was wearing a strand of pearls and Debbie wore a pair of black jade earrings and a matching black bangle on her wrist, a cool New Wave contrast with the elegant pink dress. They were holding empty champagne flutes as they moved toward us across the lawn, and I wondered if they'd been sharing coke in Debbie's bedroom. I also wondered if Thom's name ever came up anymore when they talked.

"I'm not going to drink too much, so I can drive you home whenever you'd like," I told Robert before the girls walked over to us.

He looked at me. "You're not staying with Debbie tonight?"

I took a swig from the Corona bottle and looked back at him. "No," I said. "I hadn't planned on it. Why?" I realized my voice had a slightly confused tone.

"Oh, well, don't worry about it," Robert said. "I'm good. I'll be fine."

"Okay," I said tentatively, and then, "How are you getting back?"

"Susan's driving me," he said, as the girls got closer.

I immediately asked, "Where?"

Robert calmly said, "Century City."

"Oh. Okay." I nodded quickly. And then backed up. "Wait, I don't understand," I said like a fool.

"There was a reason I asked my aunt if she'd like to head up to Santa Barbara for the weekend," Robert said in a low voice.

"Oh, so you could have the condo to yourself," I said, nodding. I thought I was going to be sick. Something cracked open within me that could never be sealed again.

"Okay, I get it," I said. Why don't you just take her to Benedict Canyon? the writer wanted me to ask. Because Robert didn't know that I knew about the house on Benedict Canyon, I replied to the writer.

"And Susan might be staying over," Robert confirmed. "I don't know. It's an option."

467

"Oh, okay," I said. "I didn't know that. Cool."

"But that's just between you and me," Robert said. "Right?"

"Oh yeah, yeah, of course, right," I said, having no idea what that meant exactly. "I won't say anything."

MINDLESS FORMALITIES about our arrival time (we were late) and how well "you boys" cleaned up and what movie stars Robert had seen became the jumbled dialogue I couldn't follow because I was having trouble breathing. I gripped the Corona bottle to steady myself. I realized an anxiety attack was imminent and I wanted to be alone—I didn't want anyone to see me as I broke down. Debbie took my hand as Robert and I helped lead the girls, balancing in their high heels, on the sloping lawn back to the pool so they could refill their flutes with champagne. I could only imagine how messed up the expression on my face was: a crumpling grimace. I tried to keep it together but Debbie was saying something to me that I couldn't hear because I was watching Susan's hand clenching Robert's—this particular intimacy was allowable now. I was blindly moving toward the pool, which had become blurry, when I suddenly told Debbie I needed to go back into the house and use the restroom. "Use mine," she said, gesturing to the stairs leading up to her room.

"No, it's okay," I said. "I'll be right back."

A series of jump cuts and I was barely aware that I'd floated through the open French doors and into the candlelit living room, which seemed even more packed and louder than before—"One of These Nights" by the Eagles was playing, I wrote down in my journal later that night—and was now asking the bartender for another beer and then changed my mind and ordered a vodka on the rocks. I needed something stronger, or maybe I would cool down if I simply drank nothing, maybe just a Perrier or a Coke. And then I felt a hand clasp mine as I took the tumbler of vodka. It was Terry's.

"I was looking for you," he said, grinning, buzzed. "Come with me. I want to show you something."

"Terry," I said. "I've gotta go back outside. Debbie's waiting for me."

He had already turned away and started pulling me through the crowd by my wrist until we walked up the steps out of the living room and across the foyer, where Terry passed by the guests hanging on the stairs, and I followed him down the hallway toward his office and a bathroom no one was using and I let him drag me in and shut the door behind us and lock it.

He immediately pushed me against the counter and roughly kissed my mouth. Both of us were holding drinks, and I had to be careful finding a place near the sink I could set the glass down while Terry continued devouring my lips and tongue until I started pushing him away. I realized he was on the cusp of totally wasted and this enforced his horniness and when he dropped to his knees and began unzipping my slacks I just leaned against the counter and was almost grateful that something else had eradicated the anxiety and bad mood and dread I was experiencing—this was comical by comparison. "Terry, come on," I finally said, when it became apparent I wasn't getting hard and I leaned over and lifted him up by his armpits. He was wearing a black suit and a dress shirt and it was unbuttoned to the middle of his chest—it was supposed to be sexy, masculine, and maybe at another time it might have worked for me but not on that night. Terry smiled drunkenly and pressed against me. "I want to suck your cock," he said matter-of-factly. "Is there anything wrong with that?" he asked, weaving. "You liked it the last time," he said in a singsong voice. I didn't know what to say—I just wanted to get out of the bathroom and away from Terry. "Yeah, maybe, but later," I said, trying to placate him. "I can't, just not here." He kissed me again, his mouth tasting like vodka and weed, and I was calm about it; in fact I was kissing him back, but I hoped this was enough, because I felt no excitement even as he continued massaging my crotch.

Finally Terry realized it wasn't happening and backed off and checked himself in the mirror. He reached into the pocket of his blazer and pulled out a small vial of cocaine and held it up to me. "Maybe this will get you in the mood," he said, again in that singsong voice, and I realized I had never seen Terry quite this high—he was on the verge of seriously trashed. He unscrewed the top and dipped the tiny spoon into the vial and quickly snorted two bumps before offering it to me. I shook my head, declined. "You're no fun tonight," he said mock-sadly. There wasn't any point in bringing up the screenplay and I realized that dream was over—I'd have to wait for him to mention it again, if he ever would. He checked his nostrils in the mirror and then patted his hair into place.

"Who's that stunner you're with?" He sniffed and looked away from the mirror at me, waiting for an answer.

"His name is Robert," I said quietly. "He's a new kid at Buckley."

Terry whistled and then said "Woof" and the way he said this made me reach for the tumbler of vodka and down it in one gulp.

"He's straight," I said wearily.

Terry smiled at me and said, "We'll see about that." It was supposed to be a joke but the way Terry said it, drunk and high, made it sound like something menacing, a threat. "Ready to roll?" Terry asked, opening the bathroom door. "I actually need to use the . . ." I gestured at the toilet.

"Go for it," Terry said, exiting the bathroom; he headed back into the din of his party, almost tripping over the edge of the carpet lining the hallway, and then regained his balance by placing a hand against the wall.

I turned and looked at myself in the mirror without closing the door—there was no one in this part of the house. I used a hand towel to wipe Terry's saliva off my penis and then tossed it in the hamper and zipped up my slacks. I washed my hands and then lowered my head toward the faucet and drank from it, cleansing my mouth. I left the bathroom and wandered toward the foyer: I was going to head up the staircase to Debbie's room, where I'd decompress before I went back outside to rejoin the party, but I got interrupted and briefly found myself in a conversation with the director John Schlesinger, who remembered me because at the last party I'd told him I liked *The Day of the Locust*, his 1975 adaptation of the Nathanael West novel, and this had intrigued him and he ended up mildly flirting with me, especially when I started asking him questions about the movie he made that helped me fall in love with Richard Gere, the World War II drama *Yanks*—though I never told him about my crush on the actor. On that Saturday night in October we briefly talked about how maybe I could stay with him and Michael in Palm Springs now that the season was beginning and the weather was cooler, and then Anthony Perkins joined us and I said I had to excuse myself and get something for Debbie and then climbed over the couples lounging on the staircase and walked the darkened hallway to Debbie's room, where I pushed open the door, closed it and then headed for the bed, and lay down on the coral-pink comforter, shutting my eyes.

THE VODKA along with the two beers stabilized me but I needed something else if I wanted to go back to the party. I sat up and looked around the room: at the wall of shelves lined with ribbons and trophies and a bookcase where two hardcover Judith Krantz novels were prominently displayed, at the rows of cassette tapes and the expensive stereo, at the posters overlapping each other on one wall of the room—they were always being replaced, depending on Debbie's whim. I opened the drawer of the nightstand by the bed and rummaged through it: the Buckley roster, a tin of Djarum clove cigarettes, bracelets and rings, ticket stubs, Polaroids of Debbie and me at the Seven Seas over the summer, various photos of Debbie and Susan goofing off, another Polaroid of Thom Wright in just a swimsuit standing at the edge of the Schaffers' pool (why?) and then, in the second drawer, there were a few small packets of coke I wasn't interested in, a large square hand mirror dusted with it, a white phallic-shaped vibrator, a small pad with phone numbers next to the names "D. Henley" and "B. Squire" and "Shore Lanes," a name I didn't recognize, as well as a paperback copy of Sydney Omarr's 1981 Leo forecast, and then I found what I was looking for: a canister of pills and multicolored capsules. I opened the canister and poured the contents into my palm and sorted through them to find the Valium, which I located easily; I swallowed one and then placed three in the pocket of the tweed blazer, along with, just in case, a Quaalude. I wouldn't drink anything else, so I'd be able to drive home—it would all work out, I thought morosely.

On the edge of the bed I waited for the Valium to take effect. I stared at the pink rotary phone and the copy of The Beverly Hills Diet that had sat next to it all summer and then thought about leaving the party without telling anyone. I badly wanted to make the escape but I also knew that it would cause too much drama: I was essentially trapped by the party, and what I had let myself so passively drift into with Debbie Schaffer. I had tricked her and was paying the price, I thought, as I stared over at the wall of posters, deflated: the burning "X" of the *Los Angeles* poster, Pink Floyd's *The Wall*, the Go-Go's wearing only towels and face cream, the Talking Heads' *Remain in Light*, Prince, a poster of the Police, Oingo Boingo, and a poster I hadn't remembered seeing before—it was retro and plain, something from what looked like the early 1970s and not as up-to-date as Debbie liked to consider herself: a quintet of black faces floating in space and smiling, the three men lightly bearded, the two women with smooth, flat hair. It reminded me of something my parents owned, a relic from another time, and brought a memory back from childhood that I was about to locate and define when I was startled by the sudden ringing of the pink rotary phone on the nightstand. I actually gasped because it had been so silent in the room—the sounds of the party outside just a distant ambient hum. Debbie's answering machine picked up. The person who called didn't say anything—it was silent for about five seconds and then they hung up. I left the room through the doorway that took me to the stairs outside.

THE FIRST THING I noticed was Terry Schaffer talking to Robert Mallory, standing away from the group by the pool, alone on the lawn, only the two of them, both in their black suits, Terry drunk, Robert sober. Robert smiled bashfully as Terry leaned in to him, Gerry Rafferty's "Baker Street" blaring from the trees. It looked as if Terry was confiding something to Robert, who just kept nodding and laughing nervously. Terry had a particular stance that unambiguously suggested he was interested in Robert sexually: he was obviously hitting on him, as any gay man would have, I realized, in the right setting, and Robert was trying to react as any polite and amiable straight dude in a similar circumstance: I'm tolerating this with good humor but it's not going to happen. I realized that I was awkwardly frozen in place and that I had to continue down the staircase until I hit the lawn, but then I would have nowhere I wanted to go.

As I began nearing Terry and Robert, Liz Schaffer walked up to her husband and said something and I noticed that the guests by the pool had started heading toward the white tent. Terry bowed charmingly to his wife and excused himself from Robert, then bounded up to the house, probably to tell the guests inside that dinner was being served. Liz said something to Robert and he nodded and as she walked away she noticed me and just smiled tightly without saying anything—again, this distant stance from Liz was startling but not entirely unexpected, I reassured myself. Robert walked up the lawn to where I was standing and wasn't smiling anymore. In fact he seemed mildly shaken by the conversation he'd just had with Terry. I experienced a brief flash of satisfaction—and maybe it was the initial flowering of the Valium as well—when I asked Robert, "What were you and Terry talking about?"

Robert looked around, as if he was nervous about something. He suddenly seemed vulnerable, for maybe the first time since I'd met him.

"Oh, he just wanted to know if I ever modeled," Robert said, tossing it off, casually, unsure of what he should admit to me. "Or if I wanted to, um, act."

"And what did you tell him?" I asked.

"Bret, come on," Robert said, as if we had an understanding about something secret.

"What?" I shrugged, pretending to be innocent.

"I didn't know he was Debbie's dad. I'd never met him. I thought he was just some random dude." Robert said this conspiratorially and leaned in. "He wanted to meet me for a drink at the Beverly Hills Hotel tomorrow."

"And are you going to?" I asked casually, but the light flicker of dread threatened to return.

"No, I had to pass on that," Robert said, looking at me strangely. "I'm . . . not really interested."

"Not interested in what?" I pressed.

"I'm not interested in having a drink at the Polo Lounge with Terry Schaffer," Robert said, amused. "For many reasons, Bret."

"Well, it wouldn't be in the Polo Lounge anyway," I murmured.

"Whatever," he said, looking around for Susan. "It doesn't matter. I'm not interested."

"Why not?" I asked, curiously. "He's an important guy. He can make you a *stah*."

"Are you fucking with me?" Robert asked, his almond eyes tinged with alertness and worry. "What are you asking me?"

"I'm just curious why you won't meet Terry Schaffer for a drink at the Beverly Hills Hotel." The Valium was beginning to create a barrier—and once behind it I didn't care anymore.

Robert looked at me, pissed, and then said, "How about because he's scary."

"Ooh, scary Terry," I said, pretending to shiver. And then: "Why is he so scary?" I asked. "Because he hit on you?"

Robert seemed surprised I said this out loud. He blushed. He whispered, confused, leaning toward me again, "Debbie's dad is gay, right?"

"I guess you didn't know this," I said. "Yeah, Terry's into guys."

"So he thought I was going to have sex with him just because he's gay," Robert said flatly. "Is he out of his mind?" And then, looking at me as if trying to figure something out, said, "You're fucking with me."

"He's just high," I said, realizing how relaxed the Valium was making me. "He attacked me in the bathroom tonight." I shrugged. Robert looked at me horrified.

"And you let him?" Robert asked, appalled. "You didn't do anything?"

"I think *you're* overreacting," I said. "I think you can take care of yourself."

"He's Debbie's dad, Bret," Robert said.

"Yes, he is," I said. "And I'm not telling Debbie it happened."

"He touched me," Robert said, staring. "He touched me right here on the lawn."

"Yeah, Terry does things like that," I said coolly.

"You seem okay with it," Robert said, still semi-stunned.

"You get used to it," I said.

"He's a freak," Robert said quietly. "It's not acceptable. You don't just grope your daughter's friends at a fucking party."

The Valium momentarily vanished and I wanted to scream at him about all the unacceptable things Robert had done since he'd come into our lives and the accusations made against him in Chicago. His reaction about Terry was disgusting, especially compared with the horror I imagined he had created and was still causing, but the Valium ultimately wouldn't let me—I became placid. I also found what I saw as Robert's overreaction to Terry's advances faintly homophobic, but, then, I thought, I wasn't a straight guy, and I suddenly remembered how offended I'd been by the idea of Liz Schaffer hitting on me drunkenly last year and momentarily connected to Robert's supposed outrage. I saw Susan and Debbie walking up the lawn to where we were standing. "Welcome to L.A.," was all I said.

"You really think it's okay?" Robert said, again quietly. "Or are you playing your little game now? Let's see how many buttons I can push until someone reacts."

"I think you'll survive," I said in a low voice. "I think you're a big boy."

Robert said, "That's really fucked up."

"Fucked up is relative," I said, turning to him.

"WHAT'S FUCKED UP?" Susan asked as she leaned in to Robert suggestively, buzzed enough not to care how it looked in front of me. He had been staring at me hard as if he was being challenged and didn't like it. But Susan's presence had a calming effect, and when Debbie wrapped her arm around my waist, he smiled at Susan and said, "This party is so crazy it's fucked up," as if this was what Robert and I had been talking about and not Terry Schaffer hitting on him and groping his dick. Behind us guests were slowly walking down from the house and toward the white tent, which lightly billowed in the warm wind. The girls admitted they weren't hungry and suggested we go inside. I shrugged why not and Robert seemed confused at first as to why we were climbing the stairs up to Debbie's room instead of joining the guests for dinner, and then realized why as Debbie locked the door behind us and sat on the bed and opened the second drawer of the nightstand. Susan sat next to Debbie as she started pouring one of the packets filled with cocaine onto the hand mirror. I slumped in a pink armchair across the room and studied Robert as he watched Debbie cutting the pile into lines. Robert shifted uncomfortably, his hands in his pockets, as if he was waiting impatiently for the girls to quickly complete this task so we could get to the tent for dinner. But it also seemed that the appearance of the cocaine was activating something in him that he didn't want to confront. A sudden scratching at the door overly startled him. Billie barked from behind it.

"Babe, can you let him in?" Susan asked.

I just smiled at the way Susan called him babe—the Valium had fully kicked in, everything was really so ridiculous behind the barrier: the party, Matt's death, the cocaine, Terry groping Robert, Terry on his knees in the bathroom downstairs, the Trawler's madness, the disappearing girls—all of it. The casual use of "babe" was another confirmation of what was happening, a beam of light in a darkened cave where other beams of light were suddenly appearing, illuminating the truth. Robert turned and opened the door and the golden retriever immediately padded over to Debbie, who ignored the dog as she kept cutting lines. Susan absently petted Billie and then noted Robert's shifting stance—he seemed uncomfortable around the dog and he made no move to interact with it or pet the perpetually grinning head. In fact it seemed as if he was looking at the animal with a vague disdain—the dog seemed to distract and even repel him. Debbie had to remind Robert to reclose the door and then lock it, which he did. I noticed there was an expression on his face as he watched Debbie cutting the lines that indicated he was making a decision about something: he didn't want to be in the room anymore.

"Are you okay?" Susan noticed this as well. "I'm just doing a line, nothing major," she reassured him.

"Yeah, I know," Robert said. "But . . ." He made a gesture toward the door he had just closed and locked. "I'm going to get something to eat, I guess."

"Okay," Susan said. "We'll be down soon."

Robert nodded and then Susan said, "You're not mad, are you?"

"No, babe, no," he said. "Being around it just makes me a little uncomfortable, that's all," he admitted and then paused. "I'm just hungry. I want you to have a good time."

"Could you go out the other way?" Debbie asked, pointing to the door that led to the second-story landing and the staircase that would take Robert to the foyer. If he had left through the door that led to the outside staircase Debbie and Susan could have been clearly visible to any of the guests walking along the lawn toward the tent.

"Oh, yeah, sure," Robert said crossing the room, and I watched as he carefully opened the door and then entered the darkened hallway, giving me a quick smile before closing it behind him, and I wondered what the smile meant—so many things, I imagined, floating. He won, Thom lost, I was nowhere. It was silent in the room as Debbie leaned over and sniffed the first line off the mirror, and moved aside so Susan could do the next. Debbie looked over at me, the cocaine hitting, and I just offered a Valium grin and shook my head at nothing. She gestured at the mirror lined with coke. "I'm okay," I said. Susan did another line and then so did Debbie, and I hadn't noticed there was an opened bottle of Dom Pérignon until Debbie was pouring it into the flutes they'd carried with them back to the room, and then Debbie lit a cigarette and opened the window above her bed, blowing the smoke outside. Susan wanted a drag and inhaled deeply on the clove Debbie handed her. I looked over at the posters again as Susan walked over to the stereo and lifted the needle and placed it on the record that was already on the turntable. And it was something I remembered from my childhood, something my parents used to play, an up-tempo ballad on an eight-track: "Last Night I Didn't Get to Sleep at All" and then I shifted in the armchair and looked at Susan, who had stood up and was swaying to the song.

"Thom gets back tomorrow," I said. "What are you going to do?"

"Actually Thom gets back Monday night," Susan said dreamily. "He's staying an extra day." She paused, swayed. "Lionel got tickets to a football game." She paused again and kept swaying to the music. "At *Giants Stadium*," she enunciated. "The *Giants* are playing the *Jets*," she said in a lightly sardonic tone as if the sport was a joke and the names of the teams were punch lines. She was making fun of something Thom took seriously enough to stay an extra day so he could go to the game, and this was a tone and an angle I had never heard from her before and it was another step away from Thom and their past. But I was remarkably relaxed as I watched Susan take the cigarette from Debbie, who walked past me to look through her records as the song continued playing. *"The sleeping pill I took was just a waste of time,"* the woman sang. Susan moved back to the window and exhaled smoke through it.

"So Thom gets back to school on *Tuesday*," I said. "What are you going to do?"

"What are *you* going to do?" she asked back lightly.

"You told him," I said. "You told Robert."

"Told him what?" Susan asked, waving another stream of smoke into the night air. She looked over at me as if locating my presence in a haze.

"You're staying with him in Century City," I said quietly. "He let me know that."

"I might," Susan said, unfazed. "But I might not."

"But it's an option," I said. "Or that's what Robert told me."

"Oh, did he?" she asked, now mildly amused. The numbness activated by the cocaine was Susan at her most distant. None of what I said seemed to bother her at all, and this suggested that she had a plan for dealing with Thom she wasn't telling anyone—it would have been awful to be in her presence if I hadn't been lightly stoned on the vodka and Valium, but since I was numb none of this particularly bothered me in that moment.

"He told me this was just between him and me," I said. "You going to Century City tonight." I paused. "So you told him. And I asked you not to."

"I didn't tell him anything," she said. "I don't know what you're talking about."

"You didn't keep your promise," I said. "The promise I asked you to make in Palm Springs."

"That's not true," she sighed. "I don't know what you're talking about," she said again.

I didn't say anything. I was just listening to the music. *I couldn't close my eyes 'cause you were on my mind* . . . and I realized, embarrassingly, the song was in that moment about my feelings for Thom and that Susan didn't hear it that way at all: in fact she wasn't even thinking about Thom Wright anymore. She said something in the break between when the song ended and a new one began. I hadn't heard her and asked Susan to repeat what she'd just said.

"Do you really care?" she asked.

"Susan," I said, and then I said her name again.

Susan traced her finger over the mirror and rubbed the residue of coke along her gums, and then took another drag off the cigarette, lost in the drug and champagne and the promise of romance, a night with Robert Mallory at the penthouse in Century City. One song ended and another one began: it was the same group, another single from my childhood, "Up, Up and Away," and I was wondering why Debbie was playing this retro music and why she hadn't entered into our conversation, and helped steer it from the druggy evasions of Susan, and just allowed it to play out between us instead. My eyes glanced at the poster of the black faces again and I sat up a little, suddenly interested in the name of the band in yellow at the top of the poster's edge—it was hard to see from where I was sitting. I couldn't remember the name of the group, and when I peered closely at it they were whom I thought—the 5th Dimension—and the poster was for *Their Greatest Hits* and I wondered why this poster was pinned up in Debbie's room now and why she was listening to them.

I was on the verge of asking her about the poster when we were jolted by the screaming that was suddenly coming from outside Debbie's bedroom door.

THE SCREAMS weren't celebratory or joyous but shocked and anguished and loud enough to burst through the walls of Debbie's room and over the music we were listening to. Billie started barking furiously and dashed to the door and pawed at it, whimpering, desperately looking over at Debbie, who was kneeling by her record collection and then stood up, frozen, confused, looking at the door behind which the screams were coming from, and Susan's coy numbness was immediately replaced with a newfound concern and she crushed the cigarette out and was the first of us to walk over and open the door, with Billie scrambling past her and down the darkened hallway. There existed only one person screaming now—the chorus of screams had subsided and there was just a soundtrack of worried voices—and the one scream had become a kind of bellowing, and it was guttural and male and I remember Jigsaw singing "Sky High" suddenly being turned off mid-verse as Susan, Debbie and I quickly walked to the landing on the second floor, which was flickering with candlelight and where guests were gathered around the railing looking down onto the foyer—a frantic murmuring was rising toward us from below, where the screaming was coming from, and then the crystal chandelier blasted light across the landing, revealing the grand curving staircase and the white-tiled foyer and that's when Debbie pushed between where Susan and me were standing and looked down at Terry Schaffer lying in the middle of the foyer, on his back, red-faced and screaming, the veins bulging in his neck.

Terry's right leg was bent up beside him so that his foot touched his torso—it was such an unnatural angle that it looked almost cartoonish, unreal, and then I noticed the blood quickly pooling beside the bent leg and realized that Steven Reinhardt was kneeling next to Terry below the bright light, and there were two surfer valets trying to calm Terry down, an array of horrified guests standing in the background. Steven had carefully pulled up the right leg of Terry's slacks, which revealed a large bone—it was the snapped mid-tibia—piercing through the skin of his right shin, and this was where the blood was both spraying and then simply gushing out across the floor of the foyer, and Debbie started crying and put her hands over her ears and fell to her knees. Susan just stood at the railing stunned and I kept staring at the bone. And then Terry stopped screaming, his face crimson and the veins in his neck still bulging absurdly, and suddenly he looked surprised as he vomited onto the foyer—it just shot out of his mouth—and then he vomited again and fainted. I was realizing that Terry had fallen from the second story landing and crashed onto the tiled floor at an angle that rendered this injury possible. Billie was frantically sniffing around Terry and then started nervously lapping up the vomit until the two surfers pushed the dog away and someone led it into the kitchen. I looked up across to the other side of the landing and there wasn't anyone standing at the railing looking down from where Terry had fallen. The landing was empty.

LIZ SCHAFFER had pushed through the crowd and it took a moment for her to realize what had happened: her husband was lying unconscious, a widening pool of blood spreading from his leg, the glass tumbler Terry was holding when he fell shattered next to him. Liz was drunk and, instead of instinctively kneeling down with Steven and the surfers to aid her husband, just started yelling at Terry's prone body on the floor, his head next to a spray of vomit. "What did you do?" she yelled. "This is just great! What in the fuck did you do, you stupid fucking bastard! Why do you ruin everything, you fucking stupid bastard? You fucking stupid fag bastard!" And then she gasped and started weeping when she saw the extent of the wound and the bone sticking half out of the shin and the calf and dramatically collapsed as guests cried out surprised. Two men carried Liz into the living room, where we heard her quickly regain consciousness and start yelling angrily again while weeping about why Terry was such a mess. *"He thinks I have a problem! He's a fucking cokehead! He's a cocksucker!"* she screamed.

Debbie had started walking slowly down the curving staircase and for some reason she kept her ears covered with her hands as she wept and made it a few feet before getting to where Steven and two of the surfers were now trying to tie a tourniquet made from Terry's belt around the bleeding wound, and then Steven searched Terry's pockets and found the vial of coke and slipped it into his own jeans. Steven had already made a number of fast emergency phone calls and suddenly so many sirens pierced the night air coming up Stone Canyon. Bel Air Security and the Los Angeles Police Department and an ambulance dispatched from the UCLA Medical Center arrived almost simultaneously, all within minutes after Terry had fallen, and their vehicles crowded the circular driveway. The sirens abruptly stopped and the red and blue lights of the police cars swirled through the diamond-patterned windows on the second-story landing where Susan and I still stood. Terry was lifted onto a stretcher and quickly loaded into the ambulance and then Steven drove Liz and Debbie to the Medical Center in Westwood. No one really knew what to do in the minutes after they left: the music had stopped, the lights had been turned on all over the house, there was a stunned and confused silence hanging everywhere. People started leaving and the valets began pulling their cars forward after the ambulance and the LAPD and the host and the hostess had all left—there was no one to get any instructions from about where to go or what to do. Paul was mopping up the blood and the vomit and Maria, the Schaffers' housekeeper, was helping him.

SUSAN AND I realized there were still people down by the tent and that's where Robert probably was but in fact he was already walking up the lawn to the house when we met him, looking anxious and asking what happened, and Susan told him that Terry had fallen from the upstairs landing and broken his leg and was just taken to the hospital and Robert seemed confused and didn't understand what we were talking about—"Terry fell? He broke his *leg*? It was an accident? Is he okay?"—and then Susan, who had been so calm, suddenly burst into tears and hugged Robert and he hugged her back, his face over her shoulder, averting his eyes from mine. I stared for a moment at Susan convulsing against Robert and then looked away: the guests who had heard the sirens were murmuring worriedly to each other as they wandered out of the tent. Susan quickly composed herself and pulled back from Robert, wiping her face with the back of her hand, and muttered that she just wanted to get out of there, the party was over, it was time to leave. "Bret?" she said, as if I needed to confirm this. "Yeah, you're right," I said. "Let's just go home."

And then the three of us were walking back to the house and through the foyer, which had now been completely cleaned, and a few stunned guests were still standing around sobering up. Susan and Robert waited until the valet brought my car—Susan had parked her BMW in one of the spaces in the garage when she arrived earlier that afternoon and the keys were in it. When the 450SL pulled up I hugged Susan and then, surprisingly, Robert and I hugged—but it was loose, two dudes, nothing tight—and I was thankful that they'd waited with me, because there was no way I could bear to watch Robert get into Susan's BMW, which he would probably be driving—he was sober and she was upset and coked up—back to the condo in Century City, where he'd spend the night comforting her with his tongue, his fingers, his cock. I drove back to the empty house on Mulholland and took another one of Debbie's Valiums and watched *Saturday Night Live* alone in my bedroom. Donald Pleasence, who played Dr. Loomis in *Halloween*, was hosting and the musical guest was Fear but I couldn't concentrate on any of the skits because I was behind the barrier, calmly thinking about not only a woman falling to her death from the second-story landing in a townhouse in Chicago but also the meaning of a poster in Debbie Schaffer's bedroom pinned to a wall in the mansion on Stone Canyon.

25

I NEEDED TO ask Debbie where she found the 5th Dimension poster.

This was one of three things that preoccupied me on that Sunday, along with the image of Terry's shattered leg and Carol Mallory falling off a similar landing when she crashed to her death in a Chicago townhouse in the spring of 1980. In my narrative Robert also pushed Terry off the landing in Stone Canyon after he left Debbie's bedroom and I imagined Terry had been in the house telling everyone dinner was being served and ran into Robert on the landing and hit on him again, groped his dick, tried to kiss him, the two of them just silhouettes in the darkness on the landing, so no one saw what happened. Robert escaped through the hallway on the other side of the landing, parallel to the one that led to Debbie's bedroom, which took Robert to the back of the house and down a stairwell that led to the maid's room and then through the kitchen and outside to the tent—perhaps completely unnoticed. There was no way to prove this on that Sunday afternoon and I realized we'd have to hear from Terry Schaffer as to whether some version of this happened or not, though I also realized Terry might never admit it: coming on to an underage kid, who pushed away from his advances, resulting in the injury he sustained when he fell over the railing. Because Abigail Mallory mentioned to me that this was exactly how Robert's mother, her sister-in-law, died, I made this connection and though it was tenuous I was haunted by it. And since I felt so alone that day it became a friend.

—

I WAS IN THE kitchen when I heard the phone from my bedroom ringing and I walked down the hallway and reached for the receiver before the answering machine clicked on. It was Debbie. She seemed surprised that I picked up. "I knew it was going to be you," I said softly, and then asked if she had slept. "Yeah, a little," she said, and then proceeded to tell me what happened at the hospital after she and Liz and Steven Reinhardt arrived at UCLA Medical Center, where her father had already disappeared into the ER's operating room, and how Debbie and Liz became entangled in a screaming match in the fluorescent-lit waiting area, each blaming the other for Terry's fuck-ups. Liz was drunk and flailing angrily as Debbie screamed back in tears and began coming down from the cocaine while Liz kept referring to me as "that boyfriend of yours" until Steven—talking to the emergency physician and Terry's own personal doctor, who had driven over from Brentwood—interrupted the two women because he was told by members of the staff it would be a good idea to take Liz and Debbie back to Bel Air, but not before Liz demanded a tranquilizer and after one was administered wept in the car as Steven drove them to Stone Canyon, where he basically carried Liz to her bedroom and Debbie cried herself in and out of sleep, exhausted, until she finally took something and was knocked out until two in the afternoon.

"I thought my mother liked you," Debbie said. "I had no idea what she was referring to." I calmly explained what I'd seen on the Sunday before Labor Day in the living room, her mom drunk and naked, and Debbie said, "Maybe that's it. She's so erratic." She asked me why I hadn't waited for her at the house last night and I told her I had no idea if she was coming back or not, and what could I have done anyway? Debbie only sighed and murmured, "I guess." I asked about Terry and what actually happened. Did he say anything? Does anyone know? No, she said. Steven told her that Terry was under sedation and that he'd be at UCLA for a few days and then transferred to Cedars, where he'd have to undergo a number of operations—the damage was so bad that Terry wouldn't be able to get around on crutches for a week and Debbie and Liz couldn't see or talk to him until tomorrow. There was so much blood, Debbie finally murmured.

"I need to see you. I need to be with you." She paused, and then asked, "Why didn't you leave any messages when you called?"

The SHARDS

I asked her what she meant. And she explained that there were six empty messages on her answering machine when she woke—just silence and then a hang up. "Wasn't that you?"

I didn't know what to say. I hadn't called. I didn't want to scare her and explain over the phone who I thought the calls were coming from. I would tell her when I saw her. "Oh yeah," I said. "I wanted to see how you were." I found myself blushing at the lie. "But you never picked up so I just . . ." I trailed off.

"I need to see you," she said again.

"Yes, yeah, of course," I said. "Do you want to come over?"

"Yeah," she said. "I've got to get out of here. I don't want to be around when Liz wakes up."

"I'll see you soon" was all I said.

SHE ARRIVED AROUND FOUR and we tried to have sex but I couldn't get hard and Debbie seemed aroused in only a desultory way and so I went down on her—I had, by the time I started having sex with Debbie, watched enough straight porn to kind of know what to do and I always managed to make Debbie have an orgasm. After its release she cried and I held her and then we walked to the kitchen, where she found a bottle of white wine in the back of the refrigerator and opened it. She poured herself a glass of the Chardonnay and I made sure Shingy had enough food and then we moved silently back to my room and lay on the bed while I used the remote to try and find something to watch on TV. It was night by now and through the large bay window I could see the ground lamps in the yard lit up by the automatic timer. The sound on the television was low and I finally asked, very quietly, "How long have you known about Susan and Robert?"

"I don't know," she murmured, resting against me, in one of the Camp Beverly Hills T-shirts she favored that year and a simple pair of pink underwear. "I guess Susan mentioned him the first day," she said. "After school. When we were in Fiorucci's. That she liked him. That he was cute." She paused and just stared at the TV screen. *Electrifying,* I remembered Susan saying. "And then it happened." She paused again. "It just happened. Somewhere along the line it happened. She was moving away from Thom." She took a sip of wine and I suddenly flashed on Debbie becoming a drunken Liz in five years. I didn't say anything—I just kept my eyes fixed on the screen, concentrating on surfing the channels, finding something we could watch. I didn't know what to say—I wanted to tell her who the phone calls were coming from but I wasn't ready yet.

"I knew you were in Palm Springs," Debbie said softly.

I swallowed and finally felt that wave of dread I had known was out there to sweep away the numbness and it did, my relentless companion during that fall.

"Susan told me," Debbie said, and then, "It doesn't matter."

"No," I finally said. "I guess it doesn't."

"I was going to confront you at school, on that Monday," she said. "But it doesn't matter."

And what more did I need to know about Susan Reynolds and Robert Mallory? It was happening and it had nothing to do with me—I wasn't connected to the relationship that had formed itself among us during that first semester of our senior year. Debbie didn't say anything else, didn't offer any details or snatches of conversations between the two girls about the new boy, nothing. And though I might have thought I had questions, in the end I really didn't: there was nothing else I wanted to know. It would play itself out and we'd have to deal with it. Something else was more compelling to me in that moment.

"Can I ask you a question?" I said.

She nodded once, curled against me, staring at the TV screen.

"Where did you get that poster?" I asked. "The one for the 5th Dimension?"

"It was on the table in the foyer where all the mail was," Debbie said.

I paused and felt suddenly nauseous. The hand holding the remote had begun to tremble and I almost lowered it onto my lap.

"I think it was from my dad," she said vacantly. "I know that Susan likes them." She paused and sipped the wine. "It's kind of a cool poster."

"When did you find it?" I managed to ask.

"Sometime last week," she said in the same vague way. "I get free posters all the time. My dad gets stuff. Liz." She kept staring at the screen but she wasn't looking at anything specifically. She was too far away from me. She wasn't paying close enough attention. She didn't know anything. She hadn't been following the narrative. She knew nothing about the clues. This applied to who Debbie thought I was as well.

"You're playing a game, right?" I asked. I was trembling as if the temperature in the room had suddenly plummeted.

"What kind of game?" she asked tonelessly.

"Debbie," I started but then didn't know what to say. Debbie and Susan knew nothing about the Trawler, they hadn't been following his story, they didn't know the warning signs. I was stalled. "It's just . . ."

"It's just what?" she asked in a completely uninterested way.

"The Trawler," I managed in a weak voice.

"The Trawler—what is that?" she asked.

"The girls that have been getting killed . . ." I started.

"I don't really follow the news," she said. "What does that have to do with anything?"

"It leaves posters," I said as evenly as possible. "It leaves . . . posters for people. There's a . . . sequence."

I felt Debbie shift beside me as she turned her head to look at my face.

"Sometimes a poster is just a poster, Bret," she said. "You're scaring me."

"Maybe you should be scared," I said quietly.

"No, not that. *You* are scaring me," she clarified. "Talking like this. And you've been scaring Susan as well. She told me that you thought Robert was somehow connected to what happened to Matt."

My eyes had dropped from the TV to the drawer with the Maxell cassette in it. And for a moment I thought I was going to stand up and play the tape for her at the highest volume possible so she could hear every terrible moan and shriek, but then decided not to—I couldn't listen to it again. It was too horrible. And why did I have it? And why was Matt being questioned about having sex with a man? What man? Who was the ghoul talking about? I had already realized: it was me.

"And you've been . . . receiving phone calls," I said quietly as if I hadn't heard her. "That's part of the pattern as well . . ." Silence.

"I'm getting more wine," she finally muttered, pushing up off the bed.

I waited a beat and then opened the nightstand drawer and took one of the Valiums: it would work, I would be able to relax again, I would drift off into the nowhere zone, become numb and erase the anxiety. Debbie came back and stood at the edge of the bed. I looked up at her innocently but I also wanted to convey my fear. "I'm concerned . . ." she started and let the words hang there.

"About what?"

"About you," she said. She had refilled the wine glass and took a swallow.

"I'm concerned about . . . you," I said, trying to keep my voice from quaking.

"Well, we're a couple," she said. "We should be concerned about each other."

In any other scene this would have deeply irritated me—a reminder that we actually weren't a couple and that Debbie only thought we were and that this was ultimately my fault: I had helped create the illusion that she was buying into.

"I know things that you don't," I said. I felt I was spacing out and that no matter what I managed to explain it wouldn't matter—it would, in fact, become part of a larger concern she'd have about me.

"You know things about a serial killer," Debbie said. "And you know things that connect Robert to Matt Kellner's death. Is this what you know?"

"Yes, I think so," I said in a faraway voice.

"Have you ever thought about talking to someone?" she asked. She sat down on the edge of the bed.

"I'm talking to . . . you," I said, confused. "Do you mean the police?"

"No, I meant a professional," she said gently.

Something got activated. "What do you mean?" I asked.

"I mean someone to talk to about these . . . concerns." She let the sentence hang there. "Someone you could talk to about . . . these fears."

"You mean a shrink," I said hollowly.

"Yes," Debbie said. "A psychiatrist or a psychologist—"

"You don't know anything," I said. "And I do."

"I think . . . you twist things," she said. "I think you don't like Robert."

"Debbie, if you only knew you wouldn't—"

"And I understand that," she said. "You're close to Thom—"

"We're all close to Thom!" I said loudly. The fear was ratcheted up.

She wasn't listening. "But that doesn't mean Robert's out there abducting girls and that he had anything to do with Matt—"

"There's a time line," I stressed quietly, closing my eyes. "There's a time line, Deborah. And he's dangerous. He's a liar and he's dangerous." I paused. "I'm worried he's going to do something to Susan."

She didn't say anything. She looked at the wineglass she was holding. And I realized: she was reconsidering my sanity, and suddenly it all felt hopeless as I became spacier—I was almost behind the barrier. I slid down until I was prone on the bed, my eyes shut tightly; a maddening helplessness I couldn't control was washing over everything. I wanted to explain *the time line* to her but something was holding me back. "Okay, okay," I finally said. "I understand."

"What do you understand?" she asked. She was staring, expecting me to relinquish my narrative and conform to hers. I was already performing this to a degree and so it ultimately wasn't difficult to keep moving through the pantomime I'd built for us. I told myself, vaguely, that I would figure it out, whatever that meant, I had no idea, everything was formless, just air. "I'm sorry" is all I said. "I'm tired." I paused. "I'm sorry," I said again.

"You're crying," she said. "Why are you crying?"

I touched my face. I hadn't realized my cheeks were wet. And then I burst into a massive sob. I covered my face with my hands as I started convulsing on the bed, completely overwhelmed.

"Baby, baby," Debbie said. I heard her put the wineglass down on the nightstand and then the weight of the bed shifted as she leaned in to me and tried to gently take one of the hands off my face. The sobbing was so intense I sounded like an animal. And then I forced it to stop and I turned away from her, folding into myself, reaching for a Kleenex and wiping my face and then blowing my nose. I was lightly panting from the force of the tears—they had come from fear, from the stress of being afraid all the time, along with the relief that the Valium was bringing me. She had wrapped her legs around mine and was running her hand through my hair, softly telling me everything was going to be all right, and I fell asleep in my tennis shorts and T-shirt and the Valium kept me unconscious until Debbie woke me at seven-thirty the next morning by gently kissing my lips, reminding me I was going to be late for school. She was dressed—she'd been up since seven and fed Shingy and let him out and took a dip in the pool—and Rosa had just arrived, earlier than usual, and Debbie said that she had to get back home to change into her Buckley uniform and that if she didn't see me beneath the bell tower before nine then we'd meet by the lockers after first period. I nodded and watched her walk out of the room and down the hall. I could hear her speaking quiet Spanish to Rosa and then the clattering of Shingy's paws as he followed Debbie to the front door, and then she was gone.

26

I ARRIVED AT BUCKLEY LATE on that Monday in November, after first period began, and pulled the 450SL into a space in the senior parking lot and then made my way under the bell tower and headed to the administration building, fingering the Maxell cassette that was in the pocket of my blazer. The hush in the office was occasionally interrupted by a phone ringing and the sporadic clicking of an electric typewriter as I waited until one of the secretaries, Mrs. Davies, hung up the phone and I told her I needed to talk to Dr. Croft. Concerned, she asked me if I had an appointment and I told her no, I didn't. She made a questioning face and then looked across a piece of paper on a clipboard and asked, "What is this about, Bret?" and I said, "It's just very important that I speak to him." She stared at me. "It's private," I said brusquely. "It's personal." Mrs. Davies lifted the phone, even though I could see the entrance to Croft's office from where I stood and the door was open—I could have just bypassed her and walked in, but the formalities at Buckley never would have allowed me to do that even as a senior and despite all the perks that came with being a member of the twelfth grade. I heard the phone ring and then Croft picking up but I didn't hear what she quietly said as I paced away from her desk, my eyes scanning past a giant vase of stargazer lilies, the LeRoy Neiman painting, the grandfather clock that announced it was nine-fifteen, all the while fingering the cassette tape in the pocket of my jacket. Croft actually came out of his office—he was dressed in a suit and tie and looking at me curiously. "Why aren't you in class, Bret?" he asked. I muttered, "I need to talk to you. It's very important." Croft must have noticed how upset I looked even though I'd been careful putting myself together that morning so there could be less of an excuse to not believe what I was about to tell him: the tie wasn't loosened, I was wearing a regulation white shirt, not something Polo or Armani, I shaved, my hair was neatly brushed, I was wearing the traditional penny loafers and not Topsiders. I wanted to look like a model student. Croft said, "Well, come in."

I FOLLOWED HIM into the office. It was Buckley-elegant: the sleek and uncluttered mahogany desk, two chairs across from it, a rolled-arm sofa, with identical floral pattern upholstery, behind the chairs and flanked by floor lamps, a coffee table with a black-and-white chess set laid out, lush ferns bordering the sides of a wide window offering a view of two walkways leading to the first rows of stucco bungalows that led into the rest of the school, in one of which was being taught a class I should have been in—Mr. Robbins, American Fiction—and where I should have been sitting next to Susan Reynolds and talking about the symbolism in *Slaughterhouse Five* while I tried not to look at Ryan Vaughn. The only institutional touch in Croft's office was the panels of fluorescent lights above us, which I glanced at nervously as Croft waved me in, positioning himself in the leather swivel chair behind his desk. I asked him if I could close the door and he paused before he nodded, as if realizing he didn't want to agitate any further an already nervous student.

I had known Croft for three years by that point—he first arrived in the fall of 1978—but I had no idea where he was from, where he had worked before, what his interests were, why we referred to him as *Dr.* He was good-looking, no older than forty, and there was something masculine about him that I vaguely responded to: brown wavy hair and a beard that accentuated a pair of thick lips, and his eyes were almond shaped and there was something youthful about his overall demeanor. He was the opposite of the bureaucratic disciplinarian that the much older Headmaster Walters embodied—someone more invested in the original idea of the Buckley tradition and its principles. Croft was casual with the students, and certainly looser then the last principal, a chain-smoking elfin Frenchman who wore silvery YSL suits and seemed to have an amusing disdain for the job as well as the students he'd been hired to preside over—there was something about Mr. Renaud that suggested he was better than Buckley and the job was somehow beneath him. Croft was younger and the students liked him, he had a friendly vibe—there were no nasally impressions or gross rumors connected to him, unlike with Renaud; he was approachable, and I'm sure there were female students who found him attractive. I suppose I knew he was married but I didn't know if he had any children, and I realized, as I sat in his office on that first Monday of November, that Dr. Croft was a blank, because he was an adult, and therefore was someone I didn't quite know yet—I was just beginning to enter that world. He actually knew far more about me than I knew about him. For myself, in that moment, he was just the most easily accessible authority figure available, and I needed to talk to someone.

CROFT REACHED INTO a drawer and pulled out a folder—I didn't know it was mine at first—and opened it, scanned a few pages he lifted before saying anything. Croft looked up at me and asked quizzically, as if he also already knew the answer, "Did you retake the SATs last week?" I looked at him, surprised that this was what he thought I wanted to talk about or that he even knew this. "No, I . . . rescheduled them," I said, haltingly. He sighed, a little disappointed, and then said, looking through the file, "Mrs. Zimmerman says you made and then canceled a number of appointments with her—"

"It was only two," I interrupted Croft. In that moment I thought I was going to explode with frustration. I tried not writhing in the chair. "I'll make another appointment with her but I'm not here to talk about that." I made a nervous gesture with my hand. "About colleges and SATs." I glanced over at the wide window and even though no one would be able to clearly make us out, because it was tinted green, I still felt exposed sitting there. The other hand was in my pocket, the fingertips pressing against the cassette tape.

"Okay," Croft said, leaning back in his chair. "So what's up?"

I immediately started talking. "I think there's something wrong with one of the students here," I said calmly but with emphasis. "Robert Mallory. I know all about the developmental center he was in before he came here and the suicide attempt, the overdose, and I talked to his aunt and she's concerned about him as well and I think he had something to do with Matt Kellner's death." I was looking at Croft directly when I said this to underscore the seriousness of the situation—my eyes didn't dart nervously around the room, I wasn't fidgeting or crossing and recrossing my legs, I was completely still. Croft was just staring at me, his expression unchanged even though I sensed he was disturbed that this was what I wanted to talk about. But I knew that our parents paid far too much tuition for Croft to dismiss me or any other student immediately and that his job involved listening to the students no matter how outlandish or lost or entitled they sounded.

Croft continued to stare at me blankly; there was a long pause in which he wondered which direction to go. This gave me hope but it also disturbed me. I breathed in.

"Are you okay, Bret?" he finally asked.

"Yes, yes," I said. "I am." I realized something. "No, I'm not on drugs. I'm not high. If that's what you're thinking."

"No, no." He held up his hands, surprised. "I wasn't thinking that—"

"Then why did you ask that?" I interrupted him.

"You just seem very agitated," Dr. Croft said. "I'm a little concerned."

"I'm fine, I'm fine," I said. "I just need you to hear me out—"

"Hear you out about—" He was talking over me.

"I think Robert Mallory was involved with Matt's death."

"Yes, I heard you, um . . ." Croft considered this before saying, "But you know that Matt Kellner's death was ruled accidental—"

"But his parents don't think that." I cut him off. "Ronald Kellner doesn't think it was accidental at all. He thinks—"

"Well, Ronald Kellner is very upset, as he should be," Croft interrupted gently. "The pain of losing a child must be enormous and I'm not sure his judgment is fully intact."

It was silent in the office as Croft just stared back at me after he said this. He had no interest in my file anymore. He closed the folder. He understood now that the meeting I requested had nothing to do with any of the information in the file: this wasn't about academics or my SAT scores or getting into the right college or whatever my GPA was.

"Did you see the autopsy report?" I asked quietly. "Did you know about the bruises? Did you know there were bruises all over Matt's body? And that someone hit him with something? And that someone hit his forehead with a hammer or something?"

"I did not see the autopsy report," Croft said, then realized and asked, surprised, "Did you?"

"Yes," I nodded. "Yes, I saw it. Mr. Kellner showed it to me." I stopped, unsure if I should offer the following. "And I also saw photos. Of Matt. Of what Mr. Kellner called the crime scene." Silence. "It wasn't accidental. It didn't look accidental."

"Why would Ron Kellner do that?" Croft asked, more curious now than surprised. "Why would he show you these things?"

"I went over to Matt's house," I explained as evenly as I could. "After he died. I talked to Ronald. I wanted to know what happened to Matt. No one knew anything. No one still knows anything. It's like everyone just doesn't want to know that he was *attacked*." I breathed in. My fingers kept pressing down on the cassette tape in the pocket of the blazer.

Croft studied me and it seemed that he made a decision to treat me like an adult: there was a moment when I felt the mood in the room change and I rose to it, but it didn't happen. "A student with a drug problem had a psychotic break by abusing hallucinogens and then overdosing on Quaaludes and then mutilated himself and drowned," Croft said, very softly. "This is not, as far as I know, a *criminal* investigation, even if Ronald Kellner wants to make it one." Croft paused and stared at me. "And besides, Buckley has nothing to do with the death of Matt Kellner." He paused again. "Matt didn't expire on school grounds. We have no connection to whatever happened, so we are left out of the loop."

I remember that word forty years later: *loop*. It sounded so casual, so offhand. I immediately thought of a Froot Loop. The use of the word seemed to diminish the seriousness of what I wanted to impart. Walking into the administration building, I had felt in such command of the information that I was going to lay out for Dr. Croft that I would end up controlling the conversation. But that wasn't happening, I realized, confused, trying to get my narrative back on the track I wanted it to run on. In this respect it was reminding me of the movie pitch I tried to sell Terry Schaffer in the bungalow at the Beverly Hills Hotel and that he ultimately rejected as well.

"Okay, okay, that doesn't matter . . ." I started. I blinked a couple of times, breathed in and shook my head to let Croft register my frustration. "Matt wasn't a drug addict," I said. "He smoked a ton of weed but he wasn't a drug addict and he never tripped on acid and he never took 'ludes and—"

Croft gently interrupted me again. "And we know that Matt told his father he was going to see Robert Mallory before he disappeared and that Ronald Kellner, in fact, talked to Robert, who denied that he ever saw Matt that week." Croft was staring at me. He said this to make sure I was aware of the information as well, so that it should limit what I wanted to tell him next. Croft even relayed this as a warning: that I needed to calm down and be careful with whatever I wanted to reveal or else there would be no point to having the meeting last any longer and he'd have to excuse me and suggest I get back to class.

"Yes, I know that, too, Dr. Croft," I said quickly. "But what if Robert lied? What if Robert wasn't telling the truth? I think he's a liar. He lies all the time. Why should we believe him about this? He was institutionalized. He tried to commit suicide. He's sick."

For one brief moment I thought Croft became invested in what I was saying when he asked me, "How do you think Robert was involved?"

The following came out in a rush: "I think, I think, that Matt went over to Robert's that weekend, and not the condo in Century City but a house on Benedict Canyon, and I think Robert drugged him and I think he was the one who drove him out to Crystal Cove in his Porsche and then proceeded to beat the shit out of him and I think he was the one who drove Matt's car back to Haskell Avenue from Benedict, was the one who'd kept Matt high and strung out for seven days—he gave him the hallucinogens, he fed him the Quaaludes, it was torture, something he got off on—and then back in Encino he slashed Matt's arm open on that Friday night or early Saturday morning after Crystal Cove and then hit him with something, I don't know, a hammer or something, and then dumped the body in the pool and staged it. I don't know why—I think it was Robert who was having a psychotic break. And then he fucking killed the cat and . . ." I caught a breath, I sat back, I thought I was going to start crying.

Croft looked at me utterly confused. "What . . . *cat*?" he asked. "A cat was killed? I don't understand." I realized that Croft only knew the clean and official narrative and nothing else. My hand kept fingering the Maxell cassette and my eyes scanned the room for something to play it on but I didn't see anything. "He recorded torturing Matt. I don't know why but he left me a tape. It's like a game he's playing with me. Like a dare." I stared at Croft hoping I hadn't sounded desperate but I knew that I'd become overtly emotional and there was nothing I could do about it: an involuntary adolescent reaction.

"Is Matt's voice on the tape?" Croft asked lightly.

"Yes," I said, and then, "Well, I . . . think so, it's hard to tell. But I think it's him . . ."

"Is Robert's voice," Croft asked, "on this tape?"

"No, it's, um, it's a disguised voice," I said. "It's like a fake voice. Like someone pretending to be like a monster or something."

I realized as I said this that I wasn't quite ready to show Croft the tape—there was something off about his attitude. He wasn't a believer. He was already suspicious of me, and then he confirmed it.

"A monster?" he asked with an incredulity that bordered on amusement. "A *monster*? Oh, Bret, please—"

"Look, Dr. Croft—"

"Why would Robert go to such lengths to do this to Matt Kellner?" Croft asked, looking away from me and then back at the folder, which he reopened. A gesture that relayed he wasn't taking any of this seriously anymore. "Why would he do this?"

"I don't know," I said. "Because he's insane. Because he was in a mental institution and I think he's a deeply disturbed individual. I think he has a mental disorder and he's taking pills and he had this breakdown at Susan Reynolds's party, like a psychotic breakdown, and . . ." I was trying to sound professional, and using terms that I thought made me seem like an adult: *deeply disturbed individual, mental disorder, psychotic breakdown.* But I stopped talking because I was losing Croft and I wanted to clarify myself before he completely dismissed me. And then I couldn't help it—my need to push the story expanded and started crossing the line into an even darker narrative than the one about Matt Kellner and the beating at Crystal Cove and the staging of a suicide in Encino. "I think that . . ." I started and then stopped.

"You think what?" Dr. Croft asked blankly, looking up from my file.

"Do you know what . . . the Trawler is?" I asked.

"The Trawler?" Croft asked back. "You mean the serial killer?"

"Yes, yes," I said, nodding. "The serial killer. Four girls—well, three. They haven't found the fourth one yet. And, um, maybe there have been more and we just don't know, maybe boys too—"

"I've been reading about the case," Croft said hesitantly, wondering where I was going with this. "It's very disturbing."

"Robert Mallory went out with the first girl who died," I said. "Katherine Latchford. He dated her. In the weeks before she disappeared. In 1980. When he first came out here and was staying with his aunt."

Croft studied me, and I thought from the expression on his face that he had become increasingly concerned about what I was telling him, or so I hoped, and that he wanted to hear more. I continued, unable to stop myself.

"And there's a time line that fits whenever Robert was in L.A. The home invasions and the assaults that began in the summer of 1980 started when Robert was first out here from Chicago. And then they stopped once he left. They began again when he returned for the holidays and then in January, while he was still here, um, Sarah . . ." I'd forgotten her last name for a moment. "Sarah Johnson disappeared and the same with Julie Selwyn—he was here, just after Roycemore, in June, his aunt told me. And now Audrey Barbour." I was so keyed up I had to stop myself and look down. I was clutching my knees and trying to steady my breathing. My fingers had left the cassette what seemed like a long time ago.

Finally, I heard Croft say softly, "That's an awfully big leap."

This caused me to look up and stare directly at him. "Did you know what happened to his mother? How she died?"

"She had a terrible accident," Croft said, nodding. "Something about a fall."

"Just like Terry Schaffer fell on Saturday night," I said. "It was exactly like what happened to Terry Schaffer. And Robert was at that party. And I believe he was responsible."

A silence lasted longer than it should have as Croft studied me, deciding what to say next. "I heard about Terry," Croft finally murmured. "Does anyone know what happened? You're close to Debbie, aren't you?"

"I believe Robert was responsible for that accident," I was saying. "I think he pushed Terry off the landing just like I think he pushed his mother . . ."

Croft looked at me helplessly, as if he was getting increasingly impatient with my presence. "Again, why would he possibly do this, Bret?"

"Because he's insane, he's sick," I said. "He raped his stepsister. Did you know that? That he told her to shave her pussy and that he raped her?" Someone walked past the window and startled me and I jumped in my chair: but it was only Miguel, the head of maintenance, with one of the gardeners.

"Bret," Croft said, his face a strained grimace, "I really want you to calm down."

"I am calm," I said, trying to sound as cool as possible. "I'm calm but you don't seem to be taking any of this seriously."

"You don't seem like you're calm," Croft said. "In fact you're saying some fairly incendiary things and you're accusing a classmate of some pretty serious stuff—"

Stuff. The word *stuff* minimized what I was conveying to Dr. Croft and it caused me to stumble, because I realized I'd lost whatever control I thought I had in the conversation when he used that word.

"Look, I'm fine, I'm fine—"

"I don't think you are," Croft said over me, his eyes wide with concern. "You seem to be freaking out."

"I'm not freaking out," I said. "I'm the only one putting the pieces together."

"I think this all sounds kind of speculative," Croft said in a sympathetic way, suggesting I needed not only to relax but to rethink everything I was telling him.

"You don't know what I know," I said.

"I guess I don't." He closed the file again and leaned back, studying me. With the door shut Croft's office was completely silent: you couldn't hear the phones ringing or the electric typewriters or the sounds of faculty leaving the lounge and heading toward their second-period classes, the soft murmurs of the secretaries. I stared back at Croft. It seemed he was hesitant about telling me something. He cocked his head and continued taking me in. He sighed. "Liz Schaffer called me last week," Croft finally said.

I just stared at him. "Yeah? So?" I asked.

"I don't know what prompted this but she was under the assumption that you and her husband are, um, somehow . . ." Croft didn't know how to say this without being indirect. ". . . involved with each other somehow. That you've become close to Terry . . ."

I continued to stare at him, paralyzed, even though it felt like my entire body was dropping through the air with no landing in sight: just one continuous free-fall that would last forever. It was mild outside and the office was air-conditioned but I was sweating beneath the Buckley uniform: my armpits were wet and sticky and my back was damp. Croft kept talking.

"Now, she seemed a bit out of it when she called and I assume this is a delusion of hers—"

"She's an alcoholic," I managed to say.

Croft closed his eyes and held his hands up in a diplomatic manner. "Yes, I'm aware of Mrs. Schaffer's problem and I know that she can be rather high-strung, but she seems to think that she has . . . proof."

I kept staring at Croft. The world was receding. Robert Mallory was receding. My whole reason for being in Dr. Croft's office was becoming dismantled. This was no longer the conversation I wanted to have. I had mentioned the Trawler and somehow Liz Schaffer was taking precedence over a serial killer. "About what?" I asked. "Proof of what?"

"That you and Terry are having . . . some kind of relationship." Croft shrugged, widened his eyes.

"She's a sick drunk," I said.

Croft ignored that and instead conceded, seeming to side with no one, "You're not legally an adult but you're almost eighteen. However, Bret—"

"It's not true," I said. "It's a lie."

"Well, I hope it is," Croft said. "It sounded unlikely." But he didn't seem entirely convinced when he said this. The expression on his face suggested that the student sitting across from him was capable of doing anything and saying anything and making horrendous shit up and that whatever acquaintance I had with Croft was now irreparably damaged. He would never look at me in the same way again. He would always be distrustful of me. He would always think I was crazy. But I suddenly didn't care: I'd be out of Buckley in eight months.

"This isn't about Terry or Liz—" I started.

"But *you* brought Terry up—"

"Because of Robert Mallory," I said. "This was always about Robert Mallory." I paused. "I didn't come here to talk about Liz or Terry Schaffer. I came here to talk about Robert Mallory and what I think he's capable of."

Croft paused again, pondering something—a thought, an idea—that maybe he shouldn't relay to me but that I had somehow forced him into admitting because the nature of the conversation I'd initiated demanded it. This was somehow my fault.

"I have to say, Bret, that this is all very strange, very odd," Croft murmured. "You coming in here and telling me that you think Robert is connected to Matt Kellner."

"What is?" I asked. "I don't understand. Why?"

"Well, because I spoke to Robert almost three weeks ago," Croft said. "I actually wanted to talk to him about Matt and find out what he knew, considering what Ronald Kellner told us: that Robert was the last person Matt had mentioned to him."

"Robert was in here?" I asked. "I don't understand," I said, squinting at him. I had shifted to the edge of the chair.

"Well, he seemed to think"—Croft placed his hands together and clasped them—"well, that *you* had something to do with Matt's, um, predicament, is what he, um, called it—"

"Predicament?" I asked.

"Well, about whatever led up to what happened," Croft said. "Not what ultimately happened, of course—he didn't accuse you of that or anything like that. But Robert said you and Matt were, again, involved in . . ." Croft trailed off and then found his voice. ". . . a fairly intense friendship and that . . ."

My hands were clenched into one fist on my lap.

"Wait," I said, my eyes closed. "Robert came in here and told you that I was involved in a . . ." I said softly and then stopped.

"Not with his death," Dr. Croft clarified. "But that Matt and you had a falling out over something." He paused. "Something intimate."

I felt any hope quickly drain out of me. I was suddenly light-headed and exhausted, even though I had slept for almost fourteen hours last night. It was over. *Did you like inserting the cock in your anus? Did you like sucking the cock? Did you like the cock in your asshole?* Why was the person asking Matt that? Who was the person that had inserted his cock into Matt? Who was the person whose dick Matt sucked? It was mine. I had done all of these things to Matt and people knew: Susan, Ryan, Robert, probably Debbie. This was the moment when I realized why I hadn't played the tape for anyone and that I probably was never going to play the tape for anyone: I'd be the only one implicated.

"I mean, who are we to believe?" Croft asked. "Two boys with rather active imaginations?" He paused. "Do you have something against Robert Mallory?" he asked. "Did he do something to you?"

"He's a liar," I muttered. "Don't compare me to him." And then in a helpless voice asked, "He actually said I had something to do with Matt?" I looked down and muttered, "He's a liar. He lies all the time."

"You do know that Ronald Kellner doesn't think Robert Mallory had anything to do with Matt's death," Croft said. "Ron certainly told you that, correct?"

I would become a suspect if I wanted to pursue this, I realized.

"You want to be a writer, I heard," Croft was saying, placing the folder about me back into the drawer he had lifted it from. "Mrs. Zimmerman told me that you were looking for a college with a good writing program. Mr. Robbins said he read a couple of pieces you wrote and that you have talent." He paused. "They were rather provocative, Mr. Robbins said—'really wild' were his exact words. Very imaginative." He paused. I had shown Mr. Robbins two sections from an early draft of *Less Than Zero*—a chapter where Julian was the narrator and describing a sexual tryst he had with an older businessman in a motel room. And there was another chapter that involved a missing girl who turned up dead in a backyard in Bel Air, mauled to death by what turned out to be a werewolf—the details were gory, lurid, sexualized, her vagina had been torn open. This fact seemed to sum up and prove something for Dr. Croft.

Croft was already standing and this announced the meeting had ended and soon we could hear the chiming of the bells indicating first period was over and in five minutes second period would begin and the day would move along in its contained and regulated way. This meant I was supposed to stand up too, and I grabbed the arm of the chair to steady myself as I stood. I suddenly wanted to lunge toward him, grab him by his jacket and plead that he had to believe me, that if he didn't believe me I wouldn't know where else to go, what else to do, everything would be lost, Robert Mallory would get away with everything, who knew if Audrey Barbour was dead or still alive, something could get saved if Croft believed me, Susan Reynolds was in danger and so was Deborah Schaffer, my girlfriend—and then I remembered: Thom Wright would be back tomorrow.

"How long have your parents been away?" I heard Croft ask.

"They left . . . um, the week before Labor Day," I said quietly.

"And when are they coming back?" he asked.

"They are coming back . . ." I had to think about it, do the math. "In two or three weeks," I suddenly said, surprised how soon they were returning and how long they'd been traveling. "Before Thanksgiving."

"So they've been gone about two months now," Croft said, confirming this.

"Yes."

Croft had stepped around the desk and was guiding me toward the door he was opening. The sounds of the office returned but were louder now, with faculty walking in and out during the break between first and second periods and a few students inquiring about schedules and requests with a number of secretaries.

"My guess is that you've been alone and isolated," Croft said. "And that maybe this has affected you in ways that might have ignited your imagination." He said this as if it was supposed to make me feel better.

I still had enough strength and self-respect to say, "No, no, that's not it."

"Okay, well, I want you to take it easy," Croft said. "And let the authorities figure this out. Let them handle it." He paused and then he felt the need to add, "I want you to realize this conversation was confidential. It wasn't on the record. Cone of Silence, and all that."

He suddenly called out to his secretary, "Sherry, are the Wilsons still coming in at ten?" Sherry nodded yes and Croft turned back to me. "Look, if you need to talk to someone the school has references for a number of doctors that we could recommend." I smiled shakily at him and muttered that I was fine, everything was fine, I was sorry I bothered him, maybe I've been isolated, maybe I've been fitting the pieces together in the wrong way and I'd take a break from all this and just focus on my homework and reschedule retaking the SATs and make an appointment with Mrs. Zimmerman. Croft clasped my shoulder before I walked away and left the administration building. He looked at me. I looked at him. We didn't know what else to say—that was it. I took the walkway that would lead me back to the senior parking lot, away from the rest of Buckley. I noted where Robert's Porsche was parked as I slid into the 450SL and headed to the house on Benedict Canyon.

AT TEN O'CLOCK on that first Monday in November there was very little traffic heading up Beverly Glen. At its peak I made a left onto a deserted Mulholland, and then turned right onto Benedict Canyon, which was also empty. When I arrived at the house I noticed only a pool-cleaning van parked up the street and about three houses down was a gardener's flatbed truck—there were no other cars around. I turned into the driveway and put the Mercedes in PARK and got out to push open the wrought-iron gate with the mud-streaked WARNING: NO TRESPASSING sign hanging crookedly on it and then, back in the car, I steered it up the gravel road that smoothed out into the stone driveway curving in front of the house. There was nothing menacing or decrepit about the condition of the house—its exterior was clean and well kept. It might have been abandoned during the protracted divorce between Abigail Mallory and her husband but it was maintained in such good condition—or so it seemed from the outside—that the white paint coating the house looked fresh, as did the gleaming pine-green shutters (nonfunctional and purely a decorative touch), and the gray shingles that adorned the sloping roof looked new. The house itself was anonymous, not fancy, almost featureless—it could have existed in any town or city—but because of its location in the canyons of Los Angeles there was something exotic about it and it was probably worth a lot of money. I had no fear anymore, or at least not in that moment—it had blown up in Dr. Croft's office—and what carried me toward the house was anger.

I knew the front door, white and lined with green trim, was going to be locked when I walked through the arched entry, though I tried it anyway, and the large bay window was concealed with thin venetian blinds so you couldn't see into the living room. I walked around to the right side of the house, but there wasn't a door until I entered the backyard, where the towering oaks and sycamores looming over the property shaded the house from the mid-morning sun. If the front of the house seemed well taken care of the backyard was a shambles by comparison: the old tennis court with a sagging net was still strewn with leaves and the pool was mostly empty, except there was about a foot of blackish water in the deep end, also blanketed with leaves, and the patio furniture scattered around the deck was rusted. A pair of French doors I expected led into the kitchen and a den were both curtained and locked. I then walked around to the other side of the house and noted how eerily quiet it was at the bottom of the canyon as I glanced up at the steeply rising hillside behind the backyard. There were three aluminum trash cans lining this side of the house, along with a number of wooden boards leaning against the gray stucco wall, and there was a single windowed door, also shaded, and I was suddenly electrified when I gripped the knob and it turned. This door was, for some reason, unlocked. I opened the door and entered the house.

I WALKED into a small and musty room that contained a washer and dryer. There was a shelf above them where a bottle of detergent, a can of Lysol, a folded towel and a red toolbox sat. I opened the toolbox: it contained nothing but a hammer, a few nails, a screwdriver, a pair of pliers and oversized scissors. It didn't mean anything, it didn't prove anything, the tools were clean, they were just objects in a toolbox, they weren't weapons—my mind raced calmly. I pocketed the pair of pliers and left the laundry room and moved down a short hallway and past a guest bathroom and then I was standing in the foyer, where the living room and what was probably the den or a dining room and a kitchen were all within my line of vision, huge rooms spread out in a vast space. And the house was almost completely devoid of furniture, though there was a couch in the empty living room and a table with no chairs in the kitchen, and I suddenly realized I didn't know how Abigail Mallory or her ex-husband made a living—he had done business, I vaguely remembered, with Ronald Kellner—and that the furniture in the Century City condo would have been too modern, almost awkward, in this particular and more conventional house, which had a homier feel, something a family could live in, and maybe someday would if the place was ever sold. The house was immaculate—it had recently been cleaned. There didn't seem to be dust anywhere and it smelled as if the kitchen was mopped. There was a door I thought was a closet but when I found it locked I realized it probably led to the garage.

But I wasn't as interested in the first floor of the house as I was the second story. I wanted to go upstairs and find the room Robert occupied. As I made my way up the staircase, set off by the foyer and across from the kitchen, the house was so silent that I involuntarily jumped when the heel of the penny loafer I was wearing slipped and knocked against one of the polished oak steps that led to the second floor. Again, this wasn't necessarily fear—just a pulsing, heightened sense of anger: Robert had reduced me to this. No one was trying to put the pieces together but me.

And then I remembered Thom Wright was returning to L.A. that night and the anger enlarged itself.

THE SECOND FLOOR of the house was much larger than it seemed from outside—the sloping roof had suggested something cozier, more compact. There was one big empty space directly across from the top of the stairs, its windows concealed with venetian blinds, that I assumed was the master bedroom, and then I walked down a wide carpeted hallway and passed another large empty room, again darkened. There was a long stretch of hallway without any doorways or rooms but suddenly I stopped at a bathroom when I noticed items in it: a can of shaving cream, a bar of soap, towels hung from a rack, and when I looked in the shower stall there was a brown bottle of Vidal Sassoon shampoo, a jar of Noxzema, and a razor. And then, just past the bathroom, was the space that Robert occupied, which was the room at the very end of the long hallway: a futon mattress with a large bunched-up gray blanket and a couple of pillows with gray cases, and a Tensor lamp sat on the bare wooden floor next to the mattress—this was beneath a window that looked over the driveway; an empty bottle of 7Up sat on its ledge. The room smelled like weed and I automatically located a small bag next to the futon: there were rolling papers and a glass pipe and an ashtray, and large white candles surrounded the futon on paper plates, some melted down further than others. An electric typewriter sat on a small makeshift desk made from the same kind of boards that were leaning against the left side of the house, and as did a boom box similar to the one in Robert's bedroom in Century City, cassette tapes scattered around it—the English Beat's *Wha'ppen*, Was (Not Was), Tom Verlaine's *Dreamtime*—along with a small stack of mass-market paperbacks we'd be reading that term: *The Catcher in the Rye, On the Road, The Grapes of Wrath.* There wasn't a chest of drawers but I noticed a closet door that was slightly ajar and walked over and opened it: a pile of mostly black T-shirts, a couple pairs of tennis shorts, sandals, two pairs of black jeans. I didn't see any underwear and suddenly wondered if Robert even wore them when not at school and became faintly aroused. I wanted to smell a shirt I lifted off the floor, and that's when I uncovered an issue of *Penthouse* from July, and a *Hustler* from June, and the first thing that shocked me in the house on Benedict Canyon was the jar of Vaseline that I reached for and opened—the image of the gel traced by his fingers was abstractly erotic.

I THEN went back to the makeshift desk, where there were two spiral-bound notebooks that had nothing written in them. I froze anyway, but since it had already been revealed to me what I discovered in one of them wasn't a complete surprise, just quietly ominous: a number of articles about Katherine Latchford that had been clipped from the *Los Angeles Times*, beginning during the summer of 1980 and laying out a long narrative of what happened to the girl: articles about her disappearance from the party, about her social life, her academic life, articles detailing the weeks she was missing, interviews with family members and friends, the first details of the mysterious phone calls, and the rearrangements in her bedroom, and then the discovery of the body, and countless follow-up articles about the murder. There was a copy of *Los Angeles Magazine* from November of 1980 with Ann-Margaret on the cover that also had an article about what happened to Katherine Latchford. But there were no clipped articles about the other girls: nothing about Sarah Johnson or Julie Selwyn or Audrey Barbour. I closed the notebook and noticed that a number of keys were on the desk and one was marked "CC 2802"—this was a key to the door of Abigail Mallory's penthouse on the twenty-eighth floor of the Century Towers, which I pocketed. And then I realized I wanted to see if any of the other keys would open the locked door downstairs. But none of them opened it—none of them even fit into the keyhole. I went back upstairs and replaced the keys on Robert's desk. I reopened the notebook with the articles about Katherine Latchford, because some of them were paper-clipped together, and I pulled the clip from a two-page article and unfolded it as I walked back downstairs and to the locked door I figured led to the garage. This was all done in a calm and purposeful manner—my anger had dissipated and there wasn't anything else replacing it. I was alone in an abandoned house off a canyon road where a murderer sometimes resided, but whatever fear and dread I should have experienced there was now simply a numbness that blanketed everything. The paper clip slid into the keyhole on the handle and I quickly unlocked the door, revealing a darkened stairwell that led not to the garage but to what looked like a basement, a rarity in L.A. It was completely silent.

THERE WAS ONLY a moment of trepidation before I started moving toward the stairway and then my hand wandered the wall in the darkness and landed on a switch and a lone lightbulb in the ceiling at the bottom of the stairs suddenly lit up.

I noticed nothing unusual about the space as I slowly made my way down the stairs—in fact it seemed totally unused. It was just an empty room that smelled damp and faintly of rot. And then I realized that the stairway led to another door, deeper into the basement. But the paper clip would not open that door—there were two keyholes and it was seemingly bolted tightly from within. When I turned away from the door I was surprised to see that a small corner of the basement was actually being used as storage space: there were deflated rafts and a number of blue kickboards for the pool, a broom, a mop. I neared a large wall of floor-to-ceiling cupboards. I opened one and didn't understand what I was looking at. It took a moment to adjust. There was a large bag half filled with dry dog food, maybe twenty tins of Purina Cat Chow, a bag of birdseed, and then I saw on the bottom shelf a row of empty glass bowls that might seem innocent enough but were, I realized, for fish—empty fishbowls lined in a row. In the adjoining cupboard were a number of small steel cages that were used to transport animals—a pet, a small dog, a cat, a guinea pig, hamsters. And then I became genuinely startled when I noticed something staring at me from a glass box—it was completely still and I didn't know what it was at first, only that it was alive.

It was, I realized finally, an iguana in a sad facsimile of whatever its natural habitat would have been. The glass cage was lined with sand dotted with rocks and there was a small bottle of water affixed to the side of the cage with a spigot. The reptilian face just stared at me until it didn't, and I finally found my breath. I suddenly felt sick and I quickly closed the cupboard doors and shambled up the staircase, forgetting to close and relock the door I'd jimmied open. I rushed down the hallway to the laundry room and burst out of the house, slamming the door shut behind me. I walked quickly to my car and got in and started it. I drove the car across the stone driveway and then down the gravel path that led to Benedict Canyon. I drove the car past the opened gate, put it into PARK and got out to close the gate. I pulled the gate closed and then, just as I was about to get back into the car, I saw a vehicle parked about four houses down on the other side of the canyon road, just idling as if it was waiting for someone, or paused before heading to Hutton and the stoplight there. It was the beige-colored van.

I DON'T KNOW why exactly but I started walking toward it, and slowly at first, because a horrible curiosity overwhelmed whatever fear had previously enveloped me, and there was the need for an answer, and then I started running at the van as it pulled away from the curb. I yelled out "Hey!" and ran faster along the canyon road and then tripped over a fallen tree branch and skidded hard onto the asphalt as the van sped down Benedict. My palms were scratched and I'd torn the knee on the gray slacks and scraped the skin. As I pushed myself up I saw that the van had stopped again and without thinking I scrambled toward it, but then the van lurched away from me. And then it braked suddenly, the red taillights flashing on, sunlight reflected in the windows of its back doors, which were tinted black. I realized I'd hurt my leg more than I initially thought and I was limping toward the van; there were no other cars coming either up or down the canyon road and it was so quiet. It was almost as if whoever was driving the van was taunting me, or being instructed by someone else inside the van, I thought, to tease this meddler, this little pussy, the *maricón*. I moved closer to the van as it idled on the canyon road, and then it decided to drive away, but slowly, until it disappeared around a curve. I waited a beat and then hurriedly headed back to the car, my palms and knee stinging from the fall, as a crushing sense of disappointment dropped onto me: I had failed to see the license-plate number. A few cars eventually passed on my way back to the Mercedes, where I got into the driver's seat and gripped the steering wheel hard in order to calm myself. And then I mindlessly decided to turn left onto the canyon road and press down on the accelerator, trying to catch up with the van. But I didn't find it—I drove all the way to Sunset Boulevard above the speed limit and realized the van must have made a turn onto one of the many roads that streamed and twisted across the canyons.

—

The SHARDS

I NEVER WENT back to Buckley that day. Instead I just drove aimlessly.

I made it as far out as Bakersfield and then to Barstow and then I don't know how I found myself in Lancaster—I was just driving without any sense of destination or purpose. I filled the car up at a 76 station in Littlerock, where I washed my scratched palms in the men's-room sink and wetted a towel and wiped the gravel still stuck to my scraped knee and then ended up in Pasadena and drove all the way down to Anaheim, and when I hit Huntington I realized I could find the beach at Crystal Cove and park on the bluff where Matt Kellner's bloodstained backpack had been found and where he was tortured in front of a bonfire, but decided I couldn't—what would the point be, why would I hurt myself like that? I wasn't listening to music; it was completely silent within the cabin of the Mercedes as I just kept processing what I'd seen in the house on Benedict Canyon and then just as quickly trying to forget what was in it. I drove up the coast and got all the way to Malibu by the time night was falling and thought about stopping at Jeff Taylor's in the Colony to buy Quaaludes and weed but realized I couldn't talk to anybody. I wouldn't be capable of speech; a conversation, let alone a transaction, would have been impossible. Thousand Oaks, Simi Valley, and then I hit traffic on the 405 heading back to the empty house on Mulholland. By the time I returned home it was almost nine o'clock and the gas tank was near empty—I had filled it up again at a gas station on Pacific Coast Highway at dusk. I was starving and exhausted as I let myself into the house. Shingy danced around me while I opened the refrigerator and just stared into it until I began to weep. I moved to the bedroom and took off my uniform and ignored the red light blinking on the answering machine and opened the drawer of my nightstand and took the two Valiums I had left and then spent forty minutes in the shower, until I was tired enough to dry myself off and fall into bed, where my only point of reference was the blank, wide face of an iguana staring at me from a glass cage in the locked basement of a house on Benedict Canyon. That night I slept through the six phone calls that landed hourly, a silent message recorded each time; I could barely hear the shallow breaths on the other end of the line when I listened to them the next morning.

27

TUESDAY. I took half of a Quaalude before I left for Buckley. I drove into the parking lot and could feel the drug lightly pressing down on me, slowly erasing any fear or sadness, worry or doubt—it was going to transform Bret into the tangible participant and promised to ease me through the day, which would be watery, with everything shimmering in the glow of the Quaalude. I drove by Ryan Vaughn talking to Thom Wright, the two of them standing by the white Corvette no one had seen for a week, and I offered a surprised face at Thom, who smiled tightly at me and then turned back to Ryan. I parked in my space and sat still, controlling my breathing, murmuring to myself that it was going to be okay, until I felt relaxed enough to confront the morning—it wasn't as if the Quaalude had already hit (this usually took about thirty minutes—I was almost there) but it was the *idea* it would be hitting me soon that offered comfort and peace.

As I got out of the car and slung the Gucci backpack over my shoulder I noticed, one row over, Debbie talking to Rita Lee and Tracy Goldman by her BMW. Debbie automatically noticed me and offered a casual wave, unsmiling as she kept talking, and I nodded at her as I headed to Thom. I didn't see Susan's car and I didn't even bother looking for Robert's Porsche. In my tracking shot I watched as Ryan clapped Thom on the back and began walking out of the moving frame—this would ordinarily have wounded me but the thought of the Quaalude overtaking my consciousness was making everything bearable and I smiled as I approached Thom. His hair was wavier than usual and there was light stubble on his face, which meant he probably hadn't shaved all week. He offered a wan smile as I neared him. He seemed tired up close and thinner. "Welcome back. How was the trip?" I asked. "Change your mind and going to UMass?" He offered a forced grin and shook his head. "No," he said quietly. "Don't think so." He checked his watch and looked out over the parking lot, distracted. And then he turned back to me. I knew that he was looking for Susan's car and that he'd been waiting for her. It was nearing nine o'clock and we watched as the girls started heading toward us, moving across the parking lot, a reminder that class was starting soon. "You stayed for a football game," I said. "So it must've been fun."

"I didn't want to stay," Thom said. "But my dad already had the tickets."

"Why didn't you want to stay?" I asked.

He became briefly annoyed. "I was already gone a week."

"How's Lionel?" I asked, wanting to engage him and erase this distance that was separating us.

"He's good, I guess," Thom said, unenthusiastic. He started telling me about the trip but he was going through the motions—he didn't care and really had nothing to say. And then he stopped as if he remembered something. "I talked to Susan last night," he said as we neared the bell tower. "When I got back." I dreaded the mention of her name but knew it was inevitable.

"Yeah?" was all I asked.

"She told me what happened to Terry," Thom said. "Jeez, how did *that* happen?"

I stopped walking. "Thom."

He turned. "Yeah?"

I just stared at him, not knowing what to say. He quickly became concerned.

"What is it, dude?" he asked quietly.

"I think, um, that . . ." I began. I felt I could say anything. I was about to start melting and I was feeling so loose that I could have simply blurted out the truth: Susan and Robert are together. And I almost did, before we were interrupted. Thom looked up and I felt a hand on my neck and then Debbie kissed me on the lips and smiled at Thom as Rita and Tracy passed us.

"Welcome back," she said.

"Hey, Debbie." Thom cocked his head. "There's something different about you . . ."

Debbie cocked her head as well, waiting.

"It's the hair," he said, smiling, as if pleased with himself for figuring it out, momentarily taking him away from whatever was troubling him. "Looks great."

"Thanks."

Debbie walked with us beneath the bell tower, heading toward our first class.

"We were just talking about what happened to your dad," Thom said.

"You talk to him?" I asked her. "Did you find out what happened?"

"No," she said. "He doesn't remember. He had been, in his own words, inebriated and wasted. *Blitzed.* He remembers nothing. He doesn't even remember what he was doing upstairs." Liz and Debbie had visited him, separately, at UCLA Medical Center on Monday afternoon. "Where were you yesterday?" she softly asked me.

This was how Terry was going to play it, I dully realized in that moment. He wasn't going to blame anyone, no one was pushed, he wasn't going to bring Robert Mallory into the narrative, which would now fade away because it was an accident Terry couldn't remember.

I ignored Debbie's question. "So he doesn't remember if it was an accident?"

"What would it be otherwise?" she asked. "Why wouldn't it be an accident?"

"Maybe he was pushed," I suggested, remarkably calm.

"Pushed by who, Bret?" Debbie sighed heavily.

"I mean, I just wondered if he actually fell or if he was pushed," I said. "I guess Terry doesn't remember."

"No, my father doesn't remember," she said with a quiet finality that I translated into: Don't ever ask me this again.

We arrived at the bungalows just past the administration building and Thom paused at the classroom I was about to enter and then checked his watch and without saying anything headed off to his first period, and Debbie waited until he was out of earshot to ask me if I was all right. This was becoming her mantra to me, and if I hadn't been on the verge of getting stoned I might've said something allusive and bitchy, but the Quaalude let me kiss her forehead and assure her I was fine. She wasn't convinced and stared at me hard. "What?" I asked, feeling completely relaxed. "What's wrong?"

"Are you high?" she said. "You're high, aren't you?"

"A little," I confessed. "I took half a 'lude before school."

"Why?" she asked. "Are you still upset?"

"No," I lied. "I'm better. Everything is fine."

"What were you talking to Thom about?"

"Nothing," I said. Debbie's presence was suddenly straining against the oncoming blurry warmth of the drug.

And then she said in a low voice, "You're not going to do something stupid and tell Thom anything, right?" I waved a hand in front of her face to indicate she had nothing to worry about and kissed her again and then floated into American Fiction and sat at my desk, glancing over at where Susan should have been. I was able to acknowledge Ryan and pulled out my copy of *Slaughterhouse Five* and smiled woozily at Mr. Robbins. The bells were chiming and I noticed a figure dashing along the walkway beyond the tinted windows and it was Susan, who made it to class just before the bells faded. She nodded at Mr. Robbins and then slid into the seat next to mine. I realized that she had purposefully arrived late, not wanting to see Thom—or anyone else—in person. I don't remember saying anything to her and I can't remember the next class, but at assembly the dream threatened to unravel when Robert Mallory appeared, standing in the courtyard beneath the Pavilion, where I watched as Thom gave him a very quick dude-hug. I had thought that Thom was figuring something out, that he had spent the week putting the pieces together, that somehow he knew Robert Mallory wasn't gay, and that Susan's new blankness was tied into moving away from Thom, preparing herself for a future without him—but apparently not.

After assembly Thom and Susan were standing beneath the flagpole before Phys Ed and I could finally feel the faint new spike in the narrative that would be altering everything soon. They were softly talking to each other; this was a seemingly normal conversation—placid, even. Thom seemed to be asking soft questions and Susan seemed to be softly answering him and there was nothing angry or defiant in either of their stances. But only if you didn't know the secret history that was playing itself out. You would have thought this was a couple in love, a dream, the sensitive jock and the numb beauty, the high school cliché, reunited after a week apart.

BUT ON GILLEY FIELD Thom walked up to where I was lying on the bleachers, his body blocking everything out except the crisp neon-blue autumn sky edged around him. I was enjoying my high, stoning out on the small green world below, prone at the top of the stands, forgetting everything I'd seen in the abandoned house on Benedict Canyon, and the beige-colored van, and the 5th Dimension poster hanging in Debbie's bedroom, and the phone calls both she and I had been receiving. Thom stood over me, backlit, just a shadow, and I took off my sunglasses and stared up at him. "Did you know that Susan went to Palm Springs last weekend?" was the first thing he asked. I didn't know how to answer that.

"Yeah." I shrugged. "To see her grandparents. Right?"

Thom was silent. I struggled to sit up. He just stood over me.

"She didn't pick up any of my calls," he said tonelessly. "She was never home to pick up any of my calls. She only called back once. The entire week."

"But weren't . . . you traveling around?" I managed to ask.

He ignored me. "She never told me she was going to Palm Springs and she goes the day I left? She never told me that." He turned and looked at the field as if he was searching for her. She was standing by the tennis courts with Debbie—they were both holding rackets and wearing sunglasses. Robert wasn't on the field. Thom's outline turned back to me. "Did she go with anybody? Did she go with Debbie?"

"I don't think she—"

"Had she mentioned anything to you?" He cut me off.

"No, she hadn't," I said. "Didn't she tell you?"

"That she was going to Palm Springs to see her grandparents? No." He paused. "She said that she had and that I'd forgotten."

Anger was about to obliterate the high I was coasting on.

"Robert was out in Palm Springs, too," I said, controlling myself to not go any further than that. Thom had to piece this together on his own. He would never forgive me if I told him the truth—I would always be connected to his pain.

"Robert?" Thom asked. "Mallory?"

"Yeah," I said. "He was out there, too, that weekend . . ."

"So what?" he said, confused, and then, "Were they together?"

"I don't know," I said. "Robert was staying in Rancho Mirage."

"What are you trying to say, Bret?" Thom asked in the coldest voice I'd ever heard from him.

"I don't think Robert is gay," I said quietly.

Thom didn't say anything. He just stood there, immobile.

"How do you know that," Thom finally said. He did not inflect this as a question.

"Thom . . ." I started, again yearning to tell him what I knew.

He just stood above me, looking down, trying to process whatever I was attempting to tell him—processing not the precise information exactly but why I seemed so tentative and lost when I was trying to talk to him about his girlfriend and Robert Mallory. The shape standing above me seemed gripped in a small but rising panic. He knew I wanted to tell him something he really didn't want to hear, and I ultimately didn't. I was both surprised and not surprised that it had taken Thom Wright as long as it did to figure out that something was very wrong.

HE MADE the connection at lunch that day and I remember I had never seen anything as magical as Thom silently staring at Susan and Robert beneath the shadow of the Pavilion and realizing something— his silent realization was more thrilling than any elaborate special effect. I didn't want to sit with anyone, so I arrived at the row of senior tables early and sat two over from the center table—I didn't want my high interrupted. But when Debbie saw where I was sitting she just slid in across from me, followed by Susan and Thom, who also sat across from each other—and I noted that Thom hadn't brought a lunch, which suggested something had been misplaced or broken, a lack of order had surfaced in Thom's world; he didn't care anymore. The talk between Debbie and Susan was chatty and perfunctory, with Thom and me often not saying anything. And then Robert showed up and sat next to Susan and it was that one moment when Susan and Robert casually ignored each other that gave Thom the meaning he needed to help him see more of what was going on and expand the narrative. I watched Thom while Susan and Debbie kept talking, and though they tried, once or twice, to engage me or Thom, they completely ignored Robert. This was the wrong move, the bad tactic, the thing that made Thom suspect, the strain was so obvious. I stared as Thom noticed this and his face subtly shifted expressions: it was so light there was barely a signal, but I was the one watching Thom pretending to listen to the girls' conversation. I was the one who saw his eyes moving from Susan to Robert as the conversation continued. I was the one who felt his frustration and the betrayal. He actually pushed away from the bench and scowled lightly to himself at one point, as if he suddenly remembered something he had to do after school and had forgotten about. It was a very small motion and I was the only one who saw it, I thought, closing my eyes for a moment.

"So you were out in Palm Springs, too," Thom finally said, staring at Robert, with something like wonder.

He had interrupted the conversation between the girls and it suddenly stopped.

"Two weekends ago," Thom said quietly. "When Susan was out there. Visiting her grandparents."

Robert said, "We didn't even know we were both out there until I got back to school on Monday."

"How did you know this?" Susan asked Thom, curious. "I mean that Robert was out there."

"Bret told me," Thom said flatly.

I could tell Susan looked over at me but I was staring at Thom.

"Oh," she said. I heard her ask me, "You did?" I ignored her.

"What were you doing there?" Thom asked.

"Visiting some friends," Robert said.

"What friends?" Thom asked. "I didn't think you had any friends. Friends from L.A.? Who else do you know in L.A. but us?"

"Friends of my family," Robert said. "Friends from Chicago."

"Really?" Thom asked. "They're out in the desert? In Rancho Mirage? Your friends from Chicago."

"Yeah," Robert said. "Why?"

"I don't know," Thom said, looking between Susan and Robert, his eyes darting from one blank face to the other. "It just sounds weird."

"No, it doesn't," Susan said. "You sound weird."

"Yeah, babe, it does," Thom countered. "You're both out there the same weekend and you never told me you were going out there in the first place?"

The way Susan said, "What are you trying to say?" was both an awful tease and a rehearsed denial. What was maddening about witnessing this was that if you knew the truth—as everyone at that table did except Thom, who was just now realizing it—this was a kind of torture for Thom, and I didn't understand what their plan was, how they were going to let him down easy, if they were even going to tell Thom at all. Maybe they just hoped he'd figure it out for himself without any confirmation and then move away from Susan and on to someone else.

"I'm not trying to say anything," Thom said casually. He shrugged.

"Hey, dude," Robert said, leaning forward.

"Stop it," Thom snapped. "Just stop it."

"I think you're tired," Susan said, reaching over the table and grabbing Thom's hand. "I think you had a long week and we haven't talked and we need to hang out after school. Okay? Can we do that? Is that okay?"

Thom stopped pulling away from her and relented. He wasn't saying anything.

"Thom?" Susan asked, trying to refocus him. "Can we please hang out after school today?"

"I have practice," Thom muttered.

"After practice." Susan sighed.

"Sure, babe," he said tightly. He then glanced over at Robert and changed his mind and softened. "It's been a long week. Susan's right. I'm sorry." When Thom admitted this the mood at the table lightened up, even though he sounded just as rehearsed as Susan had. It was happening, I thought to myself. It was really happening.

THE school day ended with me sitting in the passenger seat of Jeff Taylor's Porsche 924 as he separated a number of white pills out of a plastic baggie and dropped them into my open palm, which was lightly scratched with scabs from when I fell on Benedict Canyon the day before, and which I pocketed before handing him fifty dollars. The car reeked of weed—it had settled into the upholstery and the dashboard—and Jeff was tan from surfing and his hair was bleached by the sun and I was still high from the half-Quaalude I'd taken—150 milligrams could usually carry me over eight to ten hours but I wanted to make sure I had a supply in case of another anxiety attack—and the BusBoys were singing "Did You See Me?" and I felt I had to tell Jeff that I wasn't taking the 'ludes recreationally. For some reason on that afternoon it was necessary to impart this to Jeff—I needed them to get through my days, that was it, did he understand, was he truly my friend. "I don't care, brother," Jeff said good-naturedly. "Do whatever you want." I watched through the windshield as Robert walked by himself, a load of books under his arm, to the black Porsche and simply got in without looking around.

"I heard you and Tracy were invited to Robert's birthday dinner," I said, feeling a coldness, a dark chill, drifting over the sunny warmth created by the drug.

"Yeah," Jeff said tentatively, sealing the bag and reaching over my lap, placing it back into the glove compartment. "I'm not sure we're going." He clarified. "At least I'm not going."

"Why not?"

"I'm getting some weird vibes from whatever the situation is," Jeff said vaguely.

"What's the situation?"

"You haven't noticed?" he asked.

"Noticed what?"

"What's going on between Robert and Susan?" He looked at me.

"Oh, that," I said, quietly stunned that Jeff had paid enough attention and knew about this.

"Until they all figure it out, or at least tell Thom about whatever they're doing, I'm staying out of it," he said, and then he asked, "Don't you know what's happening?"

"No, I don't. I mean yeah, of course, yeah, of course I do," I said, watching Robert's Porsche glide out of the parking lot. I wondered if he was heading to Century City or the abandoned house on Benedict

Canyon as I got out of Jeff's car and floated to the Mercedes and drove home. It was around three-thirty when I pulled into the garage.

THE PHONE RINGING IS WHAT WOKE ME UP. When I squinted over at the clock I saw it was nine and the room was completely dark. I vaguely remember driving home from Buckley and dropping into the pool after taking my uniform off. I swam through the cool water and it heightened the sensation of the drug and then I remember actually trying to work out in the makeshift gym— something I had been doing regularly because it helped manage the fear—push-ups, biceps curls, and I had muscles now, there was definition. But a wave of exhaustion had washed over me and I remember lying down to rest—something I never did during the day—and falling into what turned out to be a long sleep. I didn't recognize the voice that was coming from the answering machine. "Bret. Pick up. Bret. Pick up." It was a man, and I thought at first it was my father calling from some distant country overseas and I reached for the phone and fumbled with the cord, untangling it as I sat up in bed. "Hello?" I said.

"Bret. It's Terry."

"Hey, Terry," I said, squinting around the darkness of the room. The Santa Anas had started up again and the wind was softly wailing across the backyard. I turned on the Tensor lamp by the bed, which made the rest of the room seem suddenly darker.

"I need you to do me a favor," he said.

"Where are you?" I asked, confused.

"I'm at Cedars," he said. "I was transferred today. Look, I need you to do something for me. It's important."

"Okay," I said tentatively. "What . . . is it?"

"I need you to drive out to Malibu," he said. I noticed that his voice sounded strained, slightly desperate.

"What time is it?" I knew what time it was but needed to reorient myself after the drug-induced nap.

"I don't know. Nine, I think," Terry said.

"What's wrong, Terry?" I was suddenly scared for myself. I initially thought this had something to do with me, or whatever happened between us weeks ago in the bungalow at the Beverly Hills Hotel—why else would Terry Schaffer call me at nine o'clock on a Tuesday night? He said, "Something happened to the goddamn horse at the stables."

It took me a moment. I said the horse's name. "Spirit."

"Yeah," Terry sighed. "Look, Steve left for New York this morning or else I'd send him out there," Terry was saying, referring to Steven Reinhardt. "But he's gone—"

"I can't go, Terry," I said. "It's nine o'clock." I paused. "It's a school night," I lamely added.

"Connie Myerson is heading over there now. She's the owner of the stables," Terry said. "She's expecting you in—"

"What happened?" I asked, interrupting him.

He sighed. "A security guard was making the rounds earlier and there was something wrong with the horse. I don't know. They won't tell me what. It was injured, it was involved in an accident, I don't know—they just said there had been an accident of some kind and that someone needs to come out there to verify something for the insurance policy." Terry paused. "Look, I need you to drive out and tell me what happened. Just be my witness. I already told Connie Myerson I'm sending you."

"Terry—" I started.

"I need to know what happened to the horse, Bret," Terry insisted. "It's now considered a crime scene but they will not tell me what happened over the phone."

I got out of bed and stood there naked, my legs wobbling. Terry's fear had made me clearheaded and ready to obey him and I automatically started getting dressed, reaching for the jockey shorts and then the uniform lying on the floor next to the bed that I'd been wearing earlier that day. "What am I supposed to do?" I asked.

"This shouldn't take more than a couple of hours and I'll owe you big-time," Terry said. "Drive out there, see what happened to the horse, call me, and then you can go home." He paused. "I'll owe you big-time," he said again. "We can talk about that script you want to write. I've been thinking about it."

The SHARDS

I was cradling the phone in my neck as I pulled the gray slacks on and reached down to pick up the white shirt. "Yeah?" I asked. "Really?"

"Yeah, yeah," he said hurriedly.

"Cool," I said. "Okay."

"Debbie doesn't need to know anything yet and I want it kept that way until I find out what happened," Terry said. "I want you to call me directly from the stables and inform me on what happened. It's simple. I'll owe you."

I sighed and then slipped my feet into the loafers I'd worn to school.

"You know where it is?" he asked. "Windover Stables?"

"Yeah," I muttered. "I remember."

"And call me as soon as you find out," he said. "They have the number to reach me here. Connie has it."

I TOOK MULHOLLAND to the 405 and drove the brightly lit freeway through the darkened Sepulveda Pass until I reached the 10 and curved right and moved across the empty lanes until it merged onto the Pacific Coast Highway. This would be faster than taking Sunset all the way to the beach, which was usually my preferred route to Malibu, and the one I'd probably take home after checking out Spirit and leaving the stables. I passed the Jonathan Club and sped along the coast, flying through every light until I reached Malibu, and the Santa Anas were gusting and the ocean off to my left was alive with waves below a huge orange moon. As I neared the turn for the Windover Stables whatever sparse traffic had lightened up to the point where it seemed there was no one around, just faraway headlights slowly cruising toward me down the coast, only darkness in the distance mirrored in the rearview. The road leading up to the stables wasn't lit and so I relied on my high-beams to guide the Mercedes up the winding hillside until I arrived at the parking lot, where two Malibu sheriff's cars and a Windover Stables van and a Volvo station wagon were parked outside the front office. I pulled the Mercedes next to one of the sheriff's cars. The wind thrashed the bending trees lining the trail behind the front office, leading to the stables, and then died down just as quickly as it rose up toward the sky again. I opened the door to the offices.

A WOMAN IN her early fifties, elegant yet also vaguely haggard, was smoking a cigarette while talking quietly on the phone, dressed in a long wool coat, wearing a flowered headscarf. Behind her were two Malibu sheriff's officers conferring with each other next to a table where a security guard sat with his arms on his knees, ashen, shell-shocked, and the officers were subdued as well, talking in low murmurs. The atmosphere surrounding the narrative about what had happened to Spirit suddenly changed for me as I stood in the office. It was more serious than I thought. There didn't seem to be any sudden rush to repair the horse, to heal it or take care of it. It seemed that something had already concluded itself. There was no accident, no injuries, no life to save. The four people noticed me but no one said anything. Connie talked to whoever was on the other line about "the problems" with the cult in Venice and then in Santa Monica, the incidents that had been occurring along the coast—she didn't say the name but I knew she was talking about the Riders of the Afterlife. Connie Myerson hung up the phone and stared at me wearily. "I'm Bret Ellis," I said. "Terry Schaffer sent me." Connie nodded and motioned for the sheriff's officers. "They'll take you to the stables and then you can come back and call Terry from here," she said softly.

I followed the two officers in the darkness, their flashlights guiding us along the tree-lined trail, the wind gusting up and dying down in rhythmic patterns, until we reached the stairs that led to the darkened arena and past that, the lit stables, and beyond the stables stood a forest of trees blocking the Pacific, and only the orange moon could be seen through the black branches surrounding the stables. There was another sheriff's officer standing by a large green-and-white-striped structure, a barn, who held a walkie-talkie to his mouth, which he lowered as he saw the other officers approaching with me hanging behind them. A jolt of fear struck me as I saw how grim-faced he looked. None of the men said anything—just nodded at each other. "What happened?" I asked. No one answered. One of the officers gestured for me to follow him into the barn—I noticed how eerily quiet everything was once we entered. The floor of the barn was packed with dirt and lit with fluorescent lights and the officer stopped at a door, its top half open; I could now hear a whirring sound inside. The officer stepped into the space and made a gesture with his hand. Again, it meant I should follow him. We walked into a darkened area. He flicked on the lights.

THE FLOOR WAS LINED with hay and there were bales of it stacked against the wall. The space we walked into was where they were housing Spirit and it led toward a shoulder-high fence and past that the open center of the barn ringed with other private stables, all closed—we had come in through a side door. There were two large rotating fans moving back and forth across the stall where something huge was covered with what looked like a beige canvas tarpaulin. It was bloodstained.

"Why are the fans on?" I asked, swallowing, confused.

"To keep away the insects and the bats," the officer said, reaching out to pull the tarpaulin off the shape.

At first I didn't know what I was looking at. But it was the horse. It was Spirit. It was somehow sitting up, propped against the wall, its hind legs splayed out in front of the animal, its front hooves hung over its chest, and its hide was wet with fresh blood everywhere though only two or three places seemed opened up; the most glaring was a large bright-pink wound where the animal had been gutted, its stomach carved open, purple and blue entrails bulging out. I looked down and finally noticed the pool of blood that reached out to where I was standing—I hadn't seen it when I walked in. I looked back at the horse. The ears were sliced off and its tongue had been pulled all the way out of its throat and was draped over its chest—just like Alex the cat. The horse's eyes were kept widened with what looked like giant silver nails, so that the animal seemed surprised at what had happened to it. When I looked back down at the floor there was a massive glistening pink snake between the horse's hind legs that I realized was the animal's penis, which had been pulled completely out of its body. I noticed that small silvery bats had appeared from nowhere and were fluttering against the fans and toward the horse and a few had landed and were crawling along the carcass, fighting the manufactured wind. The officer waved them away with a broom and quickly asked, "You good?" I nodded dumbly. And then he threw the tarpaulin over the animal's corpse, grunting with the effort. I looked up and saw that a number of bats had lined the ceiling, waiting.

Back in the front office I called Terry in his private suite at Cedars and tried to describe what I'd seen, until he told me to stop and that he didn't need to hear anything else. He asked me to hand the phone to Connie, who took it from me and turned away. After hanging up, she handed me something to sign attached to a clipboard. I numbly did, not knowing what it was, and then realized I wasn't needed any longer and simply drifted out to where the cars were parked. It was only in the Mercedes, when the immediate shock started fading, that I realized with a horrifying force that someone had actually done this. Whether it was the Trawler or the Riders of the Afterlife didn't matter—*someone* had felt the need to move through the grounds of the Windover Stables on that Tuesday night in November and target Debbie Schaffer's horse and then kill and mutilate it. I drove across Sunset through the darkened hills and canyons, the orange moon always visible through the branches of the trees, and I was shaking and moaning out loud. Fear was the only sensation. I knew everything was ending and the paranoia that had been humming around us was now flowering everywhere. It was back in the house on Mulholland where I became positive that someone had broken in and rearranged the towels in my bathroom, though I had no proof and couldn't remember. I made sure all the doors were locked, like I always did. I made sure the butcher knife was in the drawer by my bed. I made sure Shingy slept next to me, so he could bark out a warning when the intruder wearing the ski mask broke into my room, his eyes wide with madness.

Debbie didn't make it to school on Wednesday, and no one but me, not even Susan, knew why yet.

28

WEDNESDAY MORNING Terry contacted his daughter before she left Stone Canyon for school and asked her to visit him at Cedars-Sinai—he said it was very important. Terry was going into a second operation later that day and wanted to talk to her beforehand. Debbie arrived at the private suite and Terry told her that something had happened to Spirit—the horse hadn't been mutilated; instead it had an unchecked "heart abnormality" that led to a severe seizure the previous night and had to be put down by Mike Stevens, the veterinarian overseeing Spirit. There was no mention about the Riders of the Afterlife cult, who the Malibu sheriff's office had convinced themselves were responsible for the death of the horse but about whom they kept quiet at Terry's insistence, and there was no mention, or warning, about whether this was the work of the Trawler. Debbie, according to Terry later that week, was in a state of shock, as if she didn't believe her father (she had thought he was going to tell her that he and Liz were separating), and she left Cedars in a rage. Instead of heading to Buckley she drove out to Malibu, and at the stables she confronted Connie Myerson, who tried to calm Debbie with a series of evasions and lies. Debbie ran down the trail and across the arena to the barn, but Spirit, of course, had already been disposed of—Terry made sure that happened quickly when he heard about what had been done to the animal. Mike Stevens made arrangements, and at midnight on Tuesday a truck rolled into the back of the stables and the three Malibu sheriff's officers and two assistants from the veterinary clinic hauled the horse onto a forklift and had it driven to a crematorium to be disposed of, and the stable was hosed down with bleach. There were photographs taken for insurance reasons but nobody saw what had happened to the horse except for that small group of witnesses on Tuesday night. Including myself. In order to get through Wednesday, I pretended it wasn't real, I *concealed* it. I didn't go to school that day.

After listening to the anguished, nonsensical messages Debbie left on her answering machine when Susan got back from school, she drove to Bel Air, where Debbie was sitting in her bedroom in the dark, wasted in a bikini; she sobbed to Susan that no one would tell her what had happened, and that she kept calling Mike Stevens, Spirit's veterinarian, and he hadn't been taking her calls and then he suddenly did and confirmed what Terry had told her in Cedars-Sinai earlier that day, but "They're all lying to me!" she wailed even though she had no proof, and Susan kept trying to calm her down and asked why anyone would be lying to her—what would the point be? Debbie finally passed out, exhausted with grief, and it was six when Susan drove back to North Canon Drive. The mistake that Susan made after Debbie Schaffer talked to her Wednesday night: Susan drove over to Robert Mallory's in Century City and not to Thom Wright's on North Hillcrest. This was the decision that caused the movement in Thom's narrative to leap forward. This simple decision helped speed everything up. Thom found out when he got home from football practice and immediately called Susan at seven and instead spoke to Gayle Reynolds, who had no idea what was going on between Robert and her daughter and simply told him—innocently—that Susan had gone to see Robert. Thom kept calm and then slammed down the phone and called me, but by then, I had turned off the answering machine and lowered the sound of the phone so that you could barely hear it ringing. I did this because of the phone calls where no one said anything. And because I couldn't talk to Thom.

Debbie didn't come to school Thursday either. But I did.

EVERYTHING SEEMED DREAMLIKE on that Thursday—a silent movie played out in slow motion, and it was about evasion, encroaching despair, secrets, everything leading up to a vague trap, and we were aware that we were all in the same film even though we all wanted different endings. Susan arrived late so she wouldn't have to deal with Thom, who was waiting for either Susan or Robert to arrive in the parking lot, and I waited silently with him on that Thursday morning—he was too upset and distracted to have a conversation, pacing by the bench beneath the bell tower, scowling at the parking lot as it kept filling up. I didn't know what was wrong until Thom eventually told me he'd called Susan's number a dozen times last night without her answering and almost drove over to the house on Canon before he regained his cool and tried to concentrate on homework, but he barely slept—he was a wreck. When it seemed apparent that neither Susan nor Robert was going to arrive before nine we both walked toward our first-period classes and said we'd see each other at assembly. He looked exhausted. I had slept with the help from half a Quaalude and was just trying to keep it together. Susan arrived at five after nine to Mr. Robbins's class and took her seat without saying anything to me. And then I saw Robert walking by the green-tinted windows of the classroom moments later and realized they had arrived together.

THERE WAS A TENSE conversation between Thom and Susan after first period ended—Thom was already waiting outside American Fiction and I walked quickly away from them and busied myself at my locker while Ryan Vaughn ignored me. During assembly Dr. Croft scanned the crowd from where he stood behind the microphone next to Susan and his eyes briefly landed on mine as he spoke and briefly stopped before he continued the scan while he kept talking—a reminder of the demented meeting I instigated in his office on Monday. Robert was standing away from the crowd, in the distance, on the steps leading up to the courtyard, where he could barely be seen. I didn't go to Gilley Field but PE wasn't coed that day and so Thom and Susan were separated until lunch, and that was when Thom and I and Robert and Susan sat at the center table—it seemed like everyone else was avoiding us, the bad vibes that Jeff Taylor had noticed were spreading out everywhere. We were pretending that everything was okay when it obviously wasn't and I knew something was about to crack and I wanted it to—we needed to free ourselves from the airlessness of the situation, we needed to get real, the pantomime had finally become an obstacle. Susan was talking about Debbie's horse but, considering what was going on between Robert and Thom, it barely registered with them. I didn't tell anyone that I'd seen what happened to Spirit because I was at the Windover Stables on Tuesday night and that whoever murdered the horse had positioned long steel nails through the animal's face in order to widen its eyes, which popped out of its head, mimicking an exaggerated expression of surprise. I nodded at Susan and went along with the narrative about the heart abnormality and the seizure.

And then Robert let us know that he had canceled his birthday dinner at Le Dome—Ryan had bailed, Tracy and Jeff had bailed, Debbie wasn't coming. However, Robert suggested that maybe the four of us could have dinner that night instead. "Get together and talk," he added.

"TALK ABOUT WHAT?" Thom asked, suddenly animated by the suggestion. I noticed he wasn't eating his lunch. He had it spread out in front of him—but he wasn't touching it. He just stared curiously at Robert. And it became impossible not to realize that the four of us sitting together at the center table beneath the Pavilion was a bad idea the minute we all took our places.

"I think we need to clear the air about stuff," Robert said, tentative.

"Clear the air about what?" Thom asked patiently. "Stuff?"

"I think there are things we need to talk about," Robert said.

Thom mulled this over, or pretended to, while Susan dully stared at him.

"Maybe he's right," I said, more to Thom than anyone else. "Maybe we should."

"Why don't we just talk here," Thom said quietly. He stared back at Susan. "I don't want to go out to dinner." And then, "Why wait?"

"Thom, come on," Susan said.

"No, really, why don't we just talk here," Thom said. "What do you want to say?"

Susan located the hostility in Thom's tone and shifted on the bench apprehensively. It was happening, I thought. It was really happening.

"Okay, well . . ." Robert started. "I think there has been some, um, misapprehension about me that isn't totally valid . . ." Robert stopped and glanced over at where I was sitting and then his gaze calmly landed back on Thom, who was very still and staring at Robert. "And I think you should tell me what's on your mind and just be honest instead of—"

"My girlfriend has been trying to convince me ever since I got back that we should take a break," Thom said as if Susan wasn't there. "But she wouldn't say why. She just gave me these vague reasons—she needed to find her own space, she wanted to spend her last year not as a couple but on her own. And I kept asking her why—why is she so unhappy and distant?—and she insisted that she wasn't unhappy but that we should just be friends and I had to ask her—though it just didn't seem possible—if there was someone else." Thom paused. "She said no, but I didn't believe her. That there wasn't someone else."

Robert nodded. "What do you mean by someone else?"

"You," I suddenly said—it had become unbearable enduring this evasion. "You," I said again simply and with no rancor. "Why don't you two just admit it and get everything over with."

Susan looked at me with a coldness I'd never experienced from her before. I was furious but contained it.

"What?" I asked. "Is there something wrong, Susan?"

Thom was sitting very still.

"Well, nothing has happened," Robert said.

"That's bullshit," I said.

"Bret," Susan warned.

"That's bullshit."

"So you're admitting it," Thom suddenly asked them.

We were all talking softly in low, hushed voices so no one around us could hear what we were saying but we were giving off bad vibes, and I quickly glanced around to see if anyone had noticed the tension rising off the center table. I was startled to see Ryan staring at us while the rest of his table was either pretending nothing was happening or just legitimately ignoring the situation.

"You want me to do this here so I won't make a scene in front of everyone?" Thom was staring at Susan. "You don't want to do this in private?" His tone carried a faint hint of disgust.

"Why would you make a scene?" she asked. "We're just talking. Jesus, Thom."

I looked over at Thom, who was in profile next to me. He was grinning but it was frozen and fake—it was scary. He didn't want to express embarrassment or weakness and he kept very still. "I'm not going to make a scene," he said in a mild voice. "But I thought you were a friend." He directed this at Robert. And then looked at Susan: "Both of you."

"He was never your friend, Thom," I said. "He was never anybody's friend."

"What is wrong with you?" Robert said to me.

"There's nothing wrong with me," I said. "You're a liar and a freak," I said, unable to control myself.

"If you say so, Bret." He sighed exaggeratedly. "But that's the pot calling the kettle black."

"Going to Croft and telling him that I was somehow involved with Matt's death is pretty fucked up—" I started.

"I didn't go to anybody," Robert interrupted, talking over me. "I was called in—"

"And you wanted to implicate me in—"

"You implicated yourself," Robert said. "Stop it, Bret." And then I activated something. "Just shut the fuck up."

Susan laid a hand on Robert's wrist to calm him down. Thom noticed.

"You want me to tell Thom?" Robert asked. "About you and Matt?"

Without turning to him, I could see that Thom was now looking at me.

"Well, do you want to tell them what you did to him?" I asked. "And the tape you made at Crystal Cove? And that you dated Katherine Latchford?" I turned to Thom and then back at Susan. "She was the first victim of the Trawler and this fucking freak dated her. And who the fuck knows what else he did." I was sickened by his presence but my voice remained low and calm.

No one said anything until Robert asked, "What do you think

you're piecing together? You're making up some kind of story about me?" His face was a confused grimace. "Is that what you're doing? Making up a story about me?"

"I know all about you," I said. "You're a sick creep."

"Bret, stop it," Susan said harshly, but only lightly raising her voice.

Thom suddenly interrupted, leaning across the table, toward Robert.

"You came here, we took you in, I thought you were my friend, we included you, we save your ass from some stupid freak-out where you could've drowned, and we all knew about your past and I listened and was sympathetic about your little stalker, this person following you around, and this is what you do?" Thom swallowed and sat back. "You fucked my girlfriend."

Robert and Susan immediately leaned in to Thom and started quietly talking over each other: "That's not true, we haven't done anything, stop it, that's not true."

"You didn't spend the night with him on Saturday?" I asked accusingly.

"No," Susan said. "I didn't."

"I just don't believe you, man," Thom was saying to Robert.

Robert stood up and gathered his lunch into a brown paper bag and simply walked to another table, where he forced a smile and sat next to Ryan Vaughn, who slid over on the bench to accommodate him. Robert tried to make this seem natural, as if he had just decided to change tables and nothing else, but there had to be a reason and everyone at that table knew something had happened at ours—a confirmation of the quiet drama that had taken place. I saw Jeff looking over at me and mouthing *What happened?* and I turned away.

"I'm done," Susan said. "I don't want to be with you anymore," she said. "We're breaking up." She spoke in a low voice but she was furious—I had never seen her this enraged.

"I know that," Thom said stoically. "You can fuck off now."

"Good," she said, pushing away from the table. "Just leave me alone for a while and don't call me." She walked down the steps and through the courtyard and out of the plaza, leaving Thom and me sitting there alone at the center table. I was so embarrassed for Thom that I was locked in place and didn't know what to say. When he tried to put his uneaten lunch back into the bag his hands were shaking. He was breathing evenly but when he suddenly looked over at me there were tears in his eyes that he managed to control until he couldn't and then he got up, leaving his bag on the table, and jogged quickly to the men's restroom located in the lobby of the Pavilion; he didn't come out for the rest of lunch. I sat alone at the table and realized this was the final act. It would all be over soon. No one from any of the other senior tables came over to ask what had happened.

I didn't see Thom the rest of the day, until school ended, when I noticed that he was sitting in the Corvette in the senior parking lot sobbing and I cautiously walked over until he noticed and looked up. I knelt next to the driver's side and Thom composed himself and then unrolled the window. He wiped his wet and reddened face with the back of his hand and then reached for a Kleenex to blow his nose. "I have practice in fifteen minutes," he said in a strained voice that was on the verge of breaking down again. "I don't know if I can do it." I just nodded and had an overwhelming need to comfort Thom, to stroke his jaw and run my fingers through his hair and tell him it would be okay and then we'd kiss, our lips brushing against each other, I'd be there, he could be with me, I'd never leave Thom for someone else.

Instead, I finally said, "We have to do something about him."

I DIDN'T drive back to the house on Mulholland. I drove through the canyons and cruised Century City and then headed to Westwood, where I aimlessly walked around until dusk and bought a ticket to *Shock Treatment*. I was the only person in the theater and couldn't concentrate on the movie because of everything collapsing around us—the shrill, satiric musical numbers activated my fear: the movie's manufactured absurdity made everything so unbearable I could barely watch it. After it was over I walked across Wilshire Boulevard to a sushi bar and sat at the counter and ordered sake with my fake ID and a California roll but I wasn't hungry. Buzzed from the sake, I just drove around—I made it all the way out to the beach in Venice and then I was driving through Culver City and soon the skyscrapers of downtown were in the distance and in seconds it seemed I was on South Figueroa, cruising past the Bonaventure Hotel, "Nowhere Girl" playing continually in the tape deck. I was on the freeway and realized in a daze that I was flying through the Cahuenga Pass when I saw the Hollywood Cross lit above the Ford Amphitheatre and I found myself racing across the 101 passing through Burbank and Studio City and then Sherman Oaks and Encino and Tarzana, until I was out in Woodland Hills, where I drove through the now empty parking lot of the Promenade, the place where Audrey Barbour had disappeared, and I tried to imagine that night: a girl getting into a handsome boy's Porsche, or was the beige-colored van idling up next to her instead? The parking lot was ghostly and dotted with sodium lights illuminating empty spaces and I was running low on gas and filled up at a 76 station on Ventura Boulevard. I thought about driving past the Kellners' house on Haskell Avenue but it was nearing ten o'clock and I realized that the night was passing by in a blur.

On Mulholland I parked the car in the garage and made sure it was completely closed. I stepped into the hallway and was relieved that Rosa had left the lights on—I wasn't capable of walking into a darkened house. Everything was quiet as I stepped into the kitchen. I was craving the sedation of a Quaalude and knew I would have to take one—and smoke weed—to get any sleep. I needed to move through Friday and then escape into the weekend. I walked down the hallway toward my bedroom, unnerved at how quiet it was.

I stopped after I opened the door and stood there, confused as to what I was seeing.

Spread out on the neatly made bed were the jockey shorts I took from Matt Kellner's house and the Maxell cassette resting on top of them.

I realized in that moment that I hadn't seen Shingy and I looked around the room and called his name.

And I had just thought *Why would Rosa have left the lights on?* when the phone suddenly rang and I cried out.

I picked it up and heard Debbie Schaffer screaming.

—

ON THAT THURSDAY NIGHT Debbie stayed in her bedroom in the house on Stone Canyon, finishing the packets of cocaine she had stashed in her nightstand drawer while drinking champagne. By eight o'clock: Liz Schaffer had passed out in her bedroom, Steven Reinhardt would be flying in from New York the following morning to guide Terry Schaffer out of Cedars-Sinai and back to Bel Air, Maria was asleep in the maid's quarters and Paul had left for the day and driven to Baldwin Hills, where he lived with his wife and young son. Earlier that evening Susan Reynolds had called Debbie, distraught about the scene that played out at lunch between her and Thom and convincing herself that the pain was equal to the loss of Spirit—Susan reminded us later—who had only been with Debbie for about five months, compared to the more than two years she and Thom Wright were together. Susan told us that Debbie had sounded high and slightly drunk and said that she didn't want to talk and hung up on her. It was nine-fifteen when Bel Air Security received a call from the Schaffer residence: it was Debbie who told the security guard that their dog, Billie, was missing, and a patrol car arrived at the house on Stone Canyon. Debbie gave a description of the absent pet to the patrolman, who took down the information regarding the dog and noted that "Miss Schaffer" seemed, in his estimation, "inebriated" and after he told her they'd start looking for the dog that night, suggested that she go to bed and get some sleep. Miss Schaffer became offended and told the patrolman to go "fuck yourself" and then closed the front door. And then another call came into Bel Air Security twenty minutes later, again from Debbie Schaffer.

DEBBIE HAD DECIDED to go swimming that night but the pool lights weren't working—later it was found out the wires had been cut—and after diving in and during a lap "someone" grabbed her foot in the pool and tried to pull her under, according to Miss Schaffer. This seemed highly unlikely to the guard in the Bel Air Security office but the patrolman who had taken down the information about Billie drove back to the house on Stone Canyon, where a "hysterical" Miss Schaffer, who was wet and shivering and waiting in the driveway wearing only a bikini with a beach towel draped over her shoulders, said that she had been "attacked" by "someone" in the darkened pool. "Someone grabbed my fucking foot in the fucking pool" were her exact words and she said that she had screamed and then "kicked at it"—and then "a hand" grabbed her ankle again—and Debbie desperately splashed out of the pool and ran up the lawn to the house. She was positive that someone had slipped into the pool while she was swimming and was going to "drown" her. She also mentioned the calls: the phone in her room kept ringing and someone kept hanging up. Debbie had contacted the Beverly Hills Police Department as well and while she was talking to the Bel Air Security patrolman two cops pulled into the driveway on what was a slow Thursday night and decided to search the property. Maria slept through this. Liz slept through this as well. Neither had any recollection of hearing anything when asked in the following days about the disappearance.

It was at this point that Debbie called Susan and told her that she was coming over and spending the night and Susan said that was fine and waited for her arrival. Debbie never made it to North Canon Drive.

Out by the pool one of the policemen discovered a blood drag—as if an animal had been attacked and wounded and then dragged away. The blood drag continued across the concrete surrounding the pool and all the way to the lawn and the two cops followed the blood-splattered grass with their flashlights until the blood drag died out. It was decided by the policemen that a coyote had probably attacked the Schaffers' pet and dragged it off somewhere in the canyons, where the dog was presumably eaten. They would let Miss Schaffer know at a later date—she was too keyed up and wasted at this point.

DEBBIE WAS walking down the staircase to the foyer, dressed and carrying an overnight bag, when she stopped and finally noticed the manila envelope Liz had left earlier that evening on the table that sat next to the front door. It had Debbie's name written on it in Liz's handwriting. The photos of Terry and me were explicit—I saw them later—and there was no denying who was in the photos or what we were doing on that Sunday afternoon in October in a bungalow at the

Beverly Hills Hotel. And this was when Debbie called me, at ten-fifteen, and started screaming hysterically in front of the two police officers and the Bel Air Security patrolman: *How could you have done this with my father, I knew about Matt Kellner, I didn't care, I thought you'd been experimenting, Susan told me, but Terry is my father,* she screamed, and then she started screaming about Liz, who stayed passed out during Debbie's breakdown, for marrying Terry, for having a child, for being a fucking alcoholic. And then she hung up and, according to the three witnesses, collapsed on the floor and sat there sobbing, the pornographic photos scattered around her. She composed herself minutes later and told the Beverly Hills Police Department and Bel Air patrolman they could leave, not to worry, she wasn't getting behind the wheel of a car, they could just go, she was going to bed, and after checking the first floor of the house the three men reluctantly agreed.

But the next morning Debbie's BMW was gone and there were blood droplets spattered across the driveway and she never arrived at Susan's, or the empty house on Mulholland or at Buckley the following day.

29

AFTER DEBBIE hung up I was trembling so hard from the shock of what she screamed that I could barely make my way to the nightstand where the Quaaludes were waiting—I was involuntarily shaking so hard I was vibrating. I sat on the edge of the bed after swallowing one, not knowing how I was going to survive without losing my mind until the pill hit me twenty minutes later. The world was collapsing, wreckage was strewn everywhere, I had no control over anything. *But you never had,* I realized when I could finally stand up and look down at Matt's jockey shorts and the Maxell tape that had been laid out on the bed. My first thought was that Rosa had straightened the drawers and simply laid these items out, wondering if I wanted to keep them—this had happened once or twice before, especially if I told her I was looking for something that I'd lost. But other thoughts blocked that very real possibility and though I tried ignoring any other ominous scenarios I couldn't help but think: *Why were all the lights in the house on?*

And then I remembered: "Shingy."

I called the name uselessly as I floated through the house but he didn't appear. I was quickly going under as I stumbled to my mom's room, where I locked the door behind me and then dragged the comforter off her bed and shut myself in the walk-in closet and let myself be knocked out. I actually fell to my knees as blackness crashed over me. I woke up when I thought I heard Shingy barking from somewhere within the house but it was only loudly in my dream, because when I unlocked the bedroom door and walked through the empty living room in the early dawn light the dog was nowhere to be seen:

not on his pillow in the kitchen, not outside on the lawn, or under the desk in my bedroom—his food and water bowls were empty. But the Quaalude I'd taken last night was calming enough to help me pretend everything was normal: The Quaalude would help me go to school and accept whatever my fate was going to be that day. The Quaalude would help me deal with the humiliation of Debbie confronting me. And then I thought calmly, with the Quaalude's help: let everyone know the truth, you'll be free, you can vanquish the tangible participant and be yourself, you're too young to play a role, you're too young to become an adult yet.

In my bedroom I placed Matt's jockey shorts and the cassette back in the bottom drawer. And though I was still moving underwater because of the drug I took the night before, I could also accept *anything* while it kept flowing through my system—nothing would faze me, nothing could hurt me. I had finally achieved a level of numbness that I didn't think was possible. I was floating over the same empty desert plains Susan was floating over and toward which ultimately we were all heading: some of us just arrived there sooner than others. *It means nothing to me. This means nothing to me. Oh, Vienna.*

BEFORE I LEFT FOR BUCKLEY that morning the phone in my bedroom rang and it was Steven Reinhardt calling from the American Airlines terminal at LAX after landing from a 5:00 a.m. flight out of JFK, to ask if Debbie was with me. I didn't pick up and he ended up leaving a message about how Debbie had disappeared from Stone Canyon and Terry and Liz were having him reach out to anyone who was close to her and see if she'd driven over to their house to spend the night—there was blood by the pool, there was blood on the driveway, everyone was worried. I carefully drove to school and parked in the senior lot and saw Susan waiting for someone beneath the bell tower. "She didn't come to your house?" was the first thing Susan asked me as I approached her. "No," I said. "I had no idea she left Bel Air." I was genuinely shocked at first that Susan had told Debbie about Matt Kellner at some point during the past few weeks and anger briefly flared below the constant warmth created by the drug but in the end it didn't really matter—Debbie was gone, Matt was gone—and I wasn't going to confront Susan about this on that morning when everything else mattered so much more. Things were speeding up: an added urgency seemed to touch everyone.

"Something happened last night, she sounded crazy," Susan said in a whispered voice. "She was freaking out. I talked to Liz this morning," she said, and then added, "They say they're going to file a missing-person report." Susan was trying to remain calm but light traces of panic permeated the numbness she had perfected.

"Maybe she's just, um, hanging with, um, someone we don't know," I mumbled, completely numb from the Quaalude. "I don't think they're going to file anything yet."

"This isn't like Debbie," Susan said. "You know that, Bret."

I nodded. "Yeah, yeah, I know."

"Did she call you?" Susan asked. "Last night?"

I nodded again.

"What did she say?" Susan asked.

"She was . . . fucked up," I said, shrugging. Looking back, I realized in that moment that neither Susan Reynolds nor Steven Reinhardt knew about the photos of me and Terry yet. "She wasn't making any sense," I said. "I couldn't understand what she was saying." I paused. "I thought she might come over but she never did." I paused again. "I thought about going to Bel Air but it was late . . ." I trailed off.

"She was supposed to come to my place," Susan said. "I don't know what happened. Her car was gone. There was blood on the driveway. Billie was gone." Susan suddenly held a hand to her mouth and choked back a sob. Her eyes were tearing. The fear had finally eradicated the numbness.

"What do you mean . . . Billie is gone?" I asked hollowly.

Susan was watching something behind me. I turned. Robert's Porsche was pulling into the parking lot. I remained calm as I watched him get out of the car, but desire and disgust messed everything up and I had to turn away. As I left her Susan felt she had to say, "I'm with him now. You know that, right, Bret? That I'm with Robert now."

"I know," I said, walking away from her. "Yeah, I know."

"And are you okay?" she asked. "About that?"

"I'll see you in class," I murmured and floated beneath the bell tower on the walkways below the eaves.

Thom Wright never showed up to school that day.

AFTER ASSEMBLY the senior class was told by Coach Holtz that PE had been canceled. Instead, we sat around the courtyard beneath the Pavilion, and by then everyone had heard not only about Debbie's horse but that Debbie was actually missing, and a number of the girls—Michelle Stevenson, Tracy Goldman, Karen Landis, Nancy Dalloway, Katie Harris, Rita Lee, Danielle Peters—were being brought into the administration offices one by one, and seated across from Dr. Croft as Liz Schaffer asked them questions over the speaker phone from the house on Stone Canyon. But no one knew where Debbie was—she had legitimately vanished. And then the whispered conversations began, when each girl came back to the courtyard and joined the group assembled there and another one was called in. There were coded lines of dialogue that if you translated them carefully revealed perhaps that Debbie was unstable, perhaps she used heavy drugs, maybe Debbie fucked guys in bands, maybe Debbie was a slut, maybe Debbie had gotten mixed up with the "wrong people," and there was a rumor that she had found "something" out about her dad, and wasn't Terry gay and did this have anything to do with the accident that happened on Saturday night at the Schaffers' party? I was sitting among these girls and Tony Matthews and Jeff Taylor and Dominic Thompson and Kyle Colson, and the conversation about Debbie proceeded anyway—it continued as if the presence of her boyfriend didn't matter. Most of the senior class left during lunch, and a group met up at the McDonald's in Sherman Oaks but I was so unnerved by my invisibility I couldn't join them. Robert and Susan sat on the periphery of the courtyard, only talking to each other. No one spoke to me—without Debbie I just quietly disappeared. Thom Wright's not showing up to school that day was the catalyst for me to go home—it was an indication that we had reached the end of the pantomime.

—

The SHARDS

AT THE HOUSE ON MULHOLLAND Rosa was concerned about Shingy and I told her she should leave for the day and that the dog would come back or I assured her I'd find him. I assured her it had only been a day. I assured her that he'd run away before even though he hadn't. Rosa wanted to contact my mother but I told her not to—"They'll be back soon," I said. "Don't worry my mom," I said. "Wait until Shingy comes home," I said. Rosa was apprehensive but she usually left early on Fridays and I told her to relax and have a nice weekend and that I'd see her Monday and that Shingy would probably be back by then as I guided her to the front door and watched as she hesitantly walked down the steps to the orange Nova she drove from East Los Angeles. But before she left I had to ask her if she went through the drawers of my desk yesterday and placed a pair of underwear and a cassette tape on the bed and Rosa turned and said no—she didn't know what I was talking about.

"Did you leave the lights on?" I asked. "Last night?" I clarified. "Before you left?"

She looked up at me confused and said, "No, I didn't leave the lights on. I never leave the lights on."

I stood on the steps leading out to the driveway and watched her get into the car, feeling nothing, though I should have been afraid. I heard my phone ringing past the open door and turned around slowly, listening until it stopped. Whoever it was didn't leave a message. But for some reason I knew they would call back. I stepped into the foyer, closed the front door and then locked it and had started moving down the hallway toward my room when the phone began ringing again. I stood in the doorway listening as the answering machine picked up. "Bret." Pause. "Bret. Are you there?" Pause. "Bret. Pick up. It's Terry." I moved slowly to the phone and though I didn't want to pick it up I had to find out how Debbie knew about what happened at the Beverly Hills Hotel. I reached for the phone and lifted the receiver.

"Hello?" I said hollowly.

"Hey," Terry said. "It's me." He sounded sedated and faraway, groggy from whatever medication he was taking.

"Where are you?" I asked.

"I'm still at Cedars." He sighed. "They wouldn't discharge me.

Doctors all ganged up." He paused. "Look, I can't really talk right now but you need to know something."

I knew what he was going to say but I didn't tell him what Debbie had screamed at me over the phone the night before.

"What?" I said, standing in the bedroom as the afternoon light began fading away.

"Liz had me followed for a couple weeks in October," Terry said quietly. And then he stopped, as if this information was enough.

I didn't say anything.

"I don't know how the fuck it happened," he said. "I'm usually discreet. But someone ended up photographing us at the hotel."

"Photographing us?" Hearing this from Terry *himself* made me nauseous and I had to sit down on the bed. I was dizzy. I thought it was just a rumor Debbie had convinced herself was real. And then I remembered the *proof* that Dr. Croft had mentioned—the *proof* that Liz Schaffer told him existed.

"And Debbie found out," Terry said. "I think that's maybe why she disappeared. Liz told her."

I couldn't say anything.

"I'm sorry about this, Bret," Terry said. "But I'm taking the blame. It's my fault."

"What should I do?" I finally asked.

"Nothing," Terry said. "I just wanted to, um, warn you." He paused. "I'll try to smooth this out on my own. But . . ." He trailed off, suddenly distracted. Something was happening in the suite at Cedars. And then Terry said, "I can't talk now."

"Terry?" I said.

Suddenly there was an agitated voice in the background. I heard it ask, "Who are you on the phone with? You shouldn't be on the phone." It was Liz.

Terry lied, made up a name, someone named Sam.

There was a rustling sound and I heard Liz speaking directly into the phone. "Who is this? Is this Sam?" She paused, and then I could hear her look over at Terry. "Who is on the phone, Terry?" Terry was now talking to Steve Reinhardt, who had entered the room, and he ignored his wife. I should have hung up but I didn't. I wanted to explain to Liz that none of this was my fault. "Hello?" she was saying. I said nothing. "You're such an asshole," I heard her say to Terry. I continued to say nothing. "Hello, who is this?" And then she abruptly stopped and realized something. I heard an intake of breath; a kind of borderline gasp, and then Liz said in a low voice, "How dare you call here. How *dare* you. You are *not* welcome anywhere near me or my husband or my daughter. You are not welcome anywhere near us. You are a very sick young man. You should be ashamed of yourself." I could barely hear both Terry and Steven telling Liz to hang up and then I heard the phone being wrested away from her—what sounded like a brief struggle occurred before someone else was holding the phone. It was Steven Reinhardt calmly saying something while Liz screamed incoherently at Terry. "Hey, Bret," he said coolly. "We're having some problems here. You shouldn't call anymore, okay? You should have known better." He paused. "You've been warned." There was another pause. "Remember that. I warned you." He said this over Liz screaming in the background. "Okay? Got it?" And there was a click and then silence.

I ENDED UP in the makeshift gym, where I tried to work out. The exertion eradicated the pain and replaced it with something else. It was momentarily calming and moved me away from myself. I took a shower and threw on a bathing suit and a Polo shirt and walked outside, where I called Shingy's name again. It was around four o'clock and there was nothing—just the ambient sound coming from the canyons below and cars racing along Mulholland behind the boxwood hedge. I spent the next ten minutes barricading the house for the night by making sure everything was securely locked: the garage, the front door, the side doors, the kitchen doors, all the windows latched tight. I debated unplugging the phone, because it kept ringing and someone always hung up and I wasn't going to be the victim that would answer it, playing along with the game the caller was instigating, I wasn't going to be the target unknowingly drawn to their fate. Instead I turned the volume on the ringer down and at five o'clock fell onto the bed and drifted in and out of a Quaalude sleep, willing it to come so it would annihilate me into an endless unconsciousness:

silence, slow-motion waves, a night sky scattered with faraway stars, a healing peace. In one of the sleepless moments I thought I heard the doorbell ringing and then, after a moment of confusion, realized the doorbell actually was ringing and I clutched myself, adrenaline coursing through me. I waited. It was night now and the yard was lit. And through the bay window of my bedroom I saw someone walking across the lawn. It was Robert Mallory and he was calling my name. "Bret, I know you're here. Bret, open the door. Let me in."

I THOUGHT THAT IT WAS A DREAM at first, and that I was still sleeping, but realized that this was real. And I wasn't as frightened as I thought I'd be if he ever showed up, because I was now used to him, he was *known* and he was still wearing the Buckley slacks and the shirt from earlier in the day and he wasn't the wide-eyed madman in the ski mask with the butcher knife assaulting me in a planned home invasion. He was just the ultimate version of the prep-pie fantasy boy I jerked off to—in this incarnation he seemed safe. I got off the bed and turned the lights on in my room—it was seven o'clock—and then moved down the hallway and watched as he came to the kitchen doors, which he leaned toward and peered through. "I know you're in there," he said loudly. "Open up." He paused. "We need to talk." I hesitated before I touched the panel on the wall and the kitchen bloomed with light. I walked toward the locked door he was standing behind.

"What are you doing here?" I asked. "I don't want you here. I'm going to call the police."

"And tell them what?" he called out, confused.

"That you're trespassing," I said loudly. And then realized how weak I sounded. *Don't be a pussy,* I heard Ryan Vaughn admonish me, and blushed at the memory, ashamed that I could sound like this.

"You're crazy," Robert said. "Just open up. Or come out here. We can talk by the pool."

I slowly moved toward the kitchen door and unlocked it. I pushed it open.

"I know what happened in Chicago," I said. "What do you want?"

"This whole thing has got to stop." He ignored the remark about

Chicago and didn't make any move to enter the house. "I mean you've got to get a grip, dude."

"What whole thing?" I asked. "What whole thing has to stop?"

"This thing you have about me," he said. "Your version of who you think I am." He paused, and then for emphasis added, "It's going to get both of us in a lot of trouble."

"What's the *version*, Robert?" I asked. "Oh, fuck it," I said turning away. "I don't care anymore. You're going to do what you're going to do. I can't stop you. You got Susan, whatever."

I walked over to the hallway leading to my room. I turned and waited to see what he was going to do.

Robert hesitantly entered the kitchen and then stood next to the island in the middle of the space. He was concerned, on the verge of worry but, like me, capable of calmness, and acting as if nothing bothered him, except you could see the whirring behind the eyes and intuit from this that Robert was locked into a kind of madness he'd never escape.

"Yeah, Susan and I are together," he said. "I'm sorry if that bothers you."

"No, you're not," I said. "You're not sorry about anything."

And then he suddenly asked, "Did you break into my house? The house on Benedict?" He paused, staring at me—I was shocked by the way he referred to it as *my house.* "Did you go through my things?" He was asking this sincerely with traces of confusion. "Were you there? How did you find out about it?"

"No," I said. "I don't know what you're talking about."

Robert just stared, trying to figure out whether he believed me or not.

He sighed and started walking toward me.

"You're all alone here?" he asked softly. "Tonight? There's no one else here?"

I nodded and didn't realize I was backing down the hallway until I passed the door to the garage, where I thought about simply bolting, but the keys to the Mercedes were in my bedroom.

"What do you want?" I asked.

"Who do you think I am?" he asked back.

I couldn't help myself. It came automatically. "I think . . . you're connected to the Trawler," I said quietly. "I think you're responsible for . . . those girls . . ."

"Stop it, Bret," he said in a soft voice.

I kept backing down the hallway. He kept slowly heading toward me.

"You're the Trawler," I whispered. "And I think you did something to Debbie."

"Your girlfriend," he said. "Why would I do something to your girlfriend?"

"I don't know," I whispered. "But I think you did something to her."

"Your girlfriend?" Robert asked.

"Yeah, my girlfriend."

"The one you're so serious about."

"Yeah," I whispered. "I think you did something to her."

"Stop it," he said tiredly. "You don't know what you're talking about."

"Where are you keeping her?" I asked. "Are you keeping her at Benedict Canyon?"

"Are you one of the freaks that keep following me?" he countered. "Is that you, Bret? Are you with them? Did they contact you?"

"I don't know . . . who you're talking about," I barely managed to say.

"Did they contact you?" he asked. "Are you with them now?"

"You were at the Village Theater," I said. "You were with Katherine Latchford the week she disappeared . . . You lied . . ."

"So what?" he asked with a confidence that I found chilling. "What does that prove?" He paused. "Maybe you were the creep who started following us. Maybe you were the creep she said was staring at her in the parking lot."

"I have that tape you left," I said, ignoring him. "The one with you and Matt on it—"

"I didn't leave you a tape, Bret."

I realized I didn't want to play the tape for Robert and have to reach into the drawer where Matt's underwear was—and it didn't matter, since it implicated me far more than anyone else. We were in my room now and he was standing in front of me. I didn't know what to say anymore, because there was nothing else to say—nothing registered with him, it was like talking into a mirror. He studied me for a moment and then cocked his head. He looked around the room, taking it in; his eyes landed on the Elvis Costello poster. The room was silent. He suddenly grinned and looked away and then back at me, almost shyly. He slowly reached out a hand and I slapped at it, shocked that he was going to touch me.

"Shhh," he said. "Just calm down. Just relax."

I backed away but my legs hit the bed and I lost my balance and sat there.

And then he was standing over me and I was staring at the bulge of his crotch encased in the tight gray slacks. He reached out and lightly ruffled my hair and a bolt of lust ignited within me. He lowered his hand and then he was tracing my jaw and then lightly the side of my neck and then the hand was back on my cheek, stroking it. I was trembling. He looked at me with a distant expression, almost lost, as if he couldn't figure out why he was doing this but was compelled to anyway. "Relax," he said again and his thumb stopped on my lips and then he lightly tried pushing it into my mouth. He finally pushed the thumb in and out of my mouth and I let him—it tasted salty and felt rough and I sucked on it like a cock and I wanted to suck his other fingers. He stopped and leaned down into my face and his lips lightly touched mine and then he pressed harder. I was instantly stiff as he lowered himself onto the bed and lay on top of me, his mouth on mine, and then he started grinding his hips against me, and I was grinding back, remembering him naked by the pool of Susan's house—his big dick, the taut ass. "Yeah, you like that?" he whispered huskily, his breath milky and wet, and then he started kissing me harder, his tongue pushing into my mouth, and I became overwhelmed and started fiercely kissing him back and my cock had gotten so hard I thought I was on the verge of orgasm and my face was so red it was burning and Robert noticed how hard I was and stopped pumping his crotch and grinned, his face inches from mine and whispered, "You like that, don't you?" I nodded and could smell his breath, his scent. I had my hands clasped on the cheeks of his small tight ass, kneading them, spreading them apart beneath the gray slacks and the jockey shorts. I couldn't control my breathing. My penis was so hard now it actually hurt. I had opened my legs and spread them wide and I reached down to unbutton my bathing suit and pulled my cock out. He looked down at the pulsing erection and then back at me and whispered, "Yeah, stroke it." I had barely started touching myself when I realized I was going to ejaculate and stopped and reached for his cock instead but I couldn't find it and then realized Robert wasn't hard.

I looked up at his face and the sexy grin was gone and he pushed back and sat on the edge of the bed and then looked down at me and with a faint trace of disgust wiped his mouth with the back of his hand and muttered, "Fucking faggot." And then, "I knew it."

I LAY there immobile as he stood up and then he just stared out the bay window at the darkened yard, the trees lit by ground lamps, the glowing blue rectangle of the pool and the black canyons below winding all the way down to where the lights of the Valley began. I don't know how long he stood there—time didn't exist for me in that moment. He squinted at something and then whispered to himself—I couldn't hear what it was—and then without looking at me he simply turned and left the bedroom. I heard his shoes walking along the hallway and then the front door opened and then it closed and he was gone. I couldn't help myself and within seconds I came so hard the force of it blinded me, and then I slid off the bed and crumpled to the floor and started sobbing.

30

THE FOLLOWING was culled together from various police reports, eyewitness accounts and testimonials concerning what happened on Saturday night, November 7, 1981.

Susan Reynolds made plans with Robert Mallory for him to arrive at the house on North Canon Drive at eight o'clock. Donald and Gayle Reynolds would be out to dinner with friends, actually at Le Dome, where Susan had suggested Robert celebrate his eighteenth birthday—it was that night, and Robert and Susan were going to spend it together in her bedroom watching TV, maybe *The Love Boat*, and then maybe *Fantasy Island*, maybe *Saturday Night Live;* Lauren Hutton was hosting. Maybe Robert would stay the night, maybe he wouldn't; nothing was decided. Regardless, Susan and Robert would have the house to themselves until about eleven, when Donald and Gayle returned home—they were meeting another couple for cocktails at a house on Maple Drive before heading to the restaurant for a seven-thirty reservation.

At around seven-fifteen Susan took a shower and put on a white terry-cloth robe and began getting ready for Robert's arrival. She was listening to music—"Private Eyes" by Hall and Oates, she remembered—in front of the mirror at her dressing table while blowing her hair dry when she thought she heard something: a "slamming" noise downstairs in the empty house. But she couldn't be sure. She turned off the blow-dryer and sat still, listening. She leaned over and lowered the volume on the stereo. She was still anxious about Debbie's disappearance—no one had heard from her since she was last seen on Thursday night, no phone calls, her car wasn't found—and the Valium she'd taken earlier wasn't sufficiently calming. She sat in her chair and waited, staring at her face in the lit mirror, willing herself to calm down. She reached for the phone and called Robert, but he didn't pick up, which meant he was either taking a shower or maybe had already left Century City and was heading over earlier than planned. She resumed drying her hair and didn't turn the volume back on. Five minutes later Susan heard what she thought was another "slamming" noise coming from downstairs and she turned off the blow-dryer and automatically called out, "Mom? Dad?"—she realized it was too early for Robert and she would have had to let him in since he didn't have a key, so who else could it have been? Susan convinced herself in that moment that nothing was downstairs when she didn't hear anything else. But she became distracted and decided to see what it was she'd actually heard.

SUSAN couldn't shake it off: she had an "uneasy feeling," as if there was "a presence" inside the house while she made her way downstairs. She didn't think about calling the police at first: Robert would be there soon and what could possibly happen to her in a mansion on North Canon Drive on a Saturday night in Beverly Hills, is what she was thinking. She'd always been safe, protected, taken care of, nothing could happen to her, she wasn't reckless like Debbie, she was in control. Susan convinced herself that she was being silly and at that point she was sufficiently unafraid. In the living room the phone rang, startling her, and it kept ringing until she picked it up and said "Hello?" and then someone hung up. That's when she saw that the sliding glass door leading from the backyard into the dining room was wide open. Susan walked over to the door, curious, and stared out into the darkened yard. She thought the pool lights had been turned on earlier but the pool was just a long black rectangle and the Christmas lights from her party, lacing the massive bougainvillea, were darkened as well. Again she couldn't be sure if the backyard had been lit before she'd taken the shower. And that was when Susan imagined she saw a figure standing next to the tree—though after a few seconds she realized that maybe no one was there. Maybe she had imagined it, she thought—it was so dark. But at this point Susan made the decision to wait outside the house for Robert, in her car, even though she really had no idea if the sliding glass door had been open earlier, before her parents left for dinner, or not. She slid the glass door closed and a wave of apprehension swept over her even though she told herself she was just keyed up, anxious because of Debbie; maybe she needed another Valium, maybe she just needed to see Robert, she was sad about Thom.

She remembered to lock the door before she walked away from it.

SUSAN DIDN'T get dressed—she was just going to pull the BMW out of the garage and park on the curb and wait for Robert to arrive. This was all so silly, she thought, but she didn't want to stay in the house any longer. Still wearing her robe, she walked out to the garage and got into the car, but it wouldn't start. She turned the key in the ignition: the BMW revved up and then made a sputtering sound and died out. This happened three times before the car wouldn't start at all. (Later it would be discovered that the motor oil had been drained and replaced with a mixture of salt and Pepsi; a crushed can was discarded in one of the trash bins in the garage.) Her parents had taken Gayle's Mercedes to dinner; Donald's Cadillac was in the garage, but back inside the house Susan couldn't find the keys. She told herself to calm down and had just walked upstairs to her room to quickly get dressed so she could stand on the bluestone pathway lined with the Mexican fan palms and wait for Robert when she heard something downstairs—it was the sliding glass door being slammed open again. She was positive about this—she wasn't imagining it. And then she realized: she had locked it.

Someone had opened it from within the house.

And that's when Susan called Thom Wright. Thom was in his bedroom on North Hillcrest and he picked up when he heard Susan's voice on the answering machine. She told him that she was frightened and that there was something wrong and could Thom please forget everything and please come over please. Thom listened silently and was about to hang up on her—he was furious that she had called and asked him this. "Where's Robert? Why don't you call him?" And

Susan whispered back: "There's someone in the house." And then the line went dead.

SUSAN THOUGHT that Thom had hung up on her but when she tried to call him back she realized that someone had cut the phone lines. Susan now knew that something was very wrong and moved quickly down the upstairs hallway, still in her robe and barefoot, and arrived at the top of the stairs and was looking into the stark white-lit living room, at least the half she could see. She carefully stepped down until she was midway between the upstairs and the first floor, and then she saw something. It was a person standing very still in the middle of the vast white space, wearing black jeans and a long-sleeved black T-shirt and a black ski mask. It seemed to be waiting for her. A black-gloved hand was clutching a butcher knife. There was a moment of confusion where Susan and the intruder just stared at each other. His eyes were unusually wide and his mouth was open and baring his teeth. The weird pause continued until the figure lunged toward her.

Susan turned, screaming, and fell against the stairs as the intruder leapt on her and then dragged her by a leg to the bottom of the stair-case. She kicked at him and her robe opened—she was only wearing panties beneath it—and then the "thing" straddled her, pressing her down on the floor and staring at her breasts. The eyes remained wide and the mouth was a grimace—and then it was opening and closing as if the intruder couldn't help it, as if he was trying to form sentences but couldn't make any sounds, and then Susan registered the butcher knife again and it was almost as if the intruder remembered he was holding it as well and he lowered it until the tip of the knife ran across the upper band of her panties and Susan involuntarily grabbed at the blade to stop it, slicing her hand open while the intruder kept the knife pressed hard against her vagina; blood from Susan's palm started seeping out and immediately stained the panties and then the intruder lifted the knife and swiped it hard across her chest, slicing into Susan's right breast, slitting it wide open. The knife was so sharp that she didn't realize what had happened at first and when she looked down she was confused: there was a hot red sheet coating her torso. And then she realized: it was blood. The breast had collapsed, it sagged open, and a flap of flesh hung against her chest, and then the pain caused her to start screaming again.

ON HILLCREST, THOM ran to his Corvette in only a bathing suit and a T-shirt and he was barefoot. He raced the car along Elevado, speeding through every stop sign until he hit Canon and then swerved left, braking the car into a skid on the driveway, and ran to the front door, which was locked; he could hear Susan screaming from inside the house. He ran around to the back of the residence, where the sliding glass door was open, and found Susan in the living room, sitting on the floor, hunched over, her robe drenched with blood. Thom was suddenly paralyzed; he couldn't register what was happening.

When Susan looked up and saw Thom she screamed, "He's in here!" She screamed it again, "He's in here!" Thom didn't know what he was looking for or what she meant. "He's in here!" she screamed. "He's in here!" And then he saw it.

The figure wearing a ski mask, holding a butcher knife, smeared with blood, rushing toward Thom while Susan kept screaming as the intruder and Thom fell to the floor. The intruder quickly sat up, repositioned himself, raised the knife and automatically plunged it into Thom's left buttock as Thom lay on his side and then immediately slashed downward, sawing the flesh open as it sliced down the leg, blood spraying out, all the way to the knee, the entire meat of it folded open, peeling away from the rest of the leg. The knife had missed the femoral artery but blood was pouring onto the white marble floor in a quickly widening pool. Thom started screaming.

And then the intruder turned to Susan; she tried to scramble up but the figure grabbed her from behind and held her in place with his arm crooked around her neck. For some reason Susan left the following detail out of the initial police reports: she instinctively grabbed the arm with both hands and moved her chin down and forced her mouth onto the sleeve of the intruder and bit hard onto his forearm and wouldn't let go. She tasted blood as the intruder tried to pull his arm away from her grip—the intruder was shouting out in pain—until he stabbed her in the arm and she finally let go. He reeled away and hesitated before striking her across the face with a gloved fist and she fell backward onto the floor. Susan's mouth was filled with blood—she had bitten so deeply into the forearm that she could feel hard flecks of flesh in her mouth that she started spitting out—this detail was told to someone five days later. The intruder fled through the open sliding glass door and disappeared into the darkness of the backyard.

SUSAN CRAWLED through the massive pool of blood in the living room to where Thom was sheet-white and bleeding out, shaking uncontrollably, and then she lifted herself and shambled toward the phone and picked it up but she had forgotten that the lines had been cut and the phone was dead and she lunged out the front door of the house screaming for help. She crossed over the yard and out onto Canon, her robe drenched in blood, the deflated breast flapping against her chest; her entire torso was painted red and streaked with tissue, and her panties were sopping with blood as well, her face smeared with it. And then she whirled around when the headlights of Robert's Porsche suddenly blinded her and he braked the car and ran to where Susan had collapsed in the street and she shouted at him, weeping, that Thom was inside: he was bleeding, he was dying, you have to save him. Robert ran into the house as horrified neighbors began emerging from their homes on North Canon. Someone had called the police but Robert came out of the house carrying Thom, who was losing consciousness, his mangled leg looking "unreal" according to one witness—cleaved open, part of it "hanging off" the side—and he didn't wait for the police or an ambulance. Robert placed Thom in the front seat of the Porsche and then Susan got in, squeezing next to Thom. Robert drove to the closest hospital, which was Cedars, racing along Santa Monica Boulevard, swerving recklessly in and out of traffic, and then down to Beverly, where the Porsche lurched into the emergency parking area and where Robert ran in shouting for help. A group of attendants immediately wheeled gurneys out and placed Thom, now unconscious, on one and a hysterical Susan on the other, and then she grabbed Robert's arm before she was taken into the emergency OR and told him to call Le Dome and page her parents, which Robert did from a phone at the nurses' station, and Donald and Gayle arrived at Cedars twenty minutes later.

I HAD PACKED a bag and was moving to a motel on Sepulveda Boulevard not far from the Sherman Oaks Galleria—I wasn't going to risk it and spend another night in the house on Mulholland—when the phone in my bedroom rang at nine and it was Donald Reynolds. In a stunned voice he explained that Susan and Thom had been attacked by an intruder at the house on Canon Drive and said, "Susan told me to call you on this number and she wanted me to tell you that she's worried about you. She wants you to know that someone's out there. That maybe you guys, I don't know, have all been targeted . . . by someone . . . That's what she said . . ." I automatically asked where Robert Mallory was and Donald quickly filled me in on what Robert had told him when he found Thom and Susan and that Robert was the one who had driven them to Cedars. Thom was in surgery and he was barely going to make it and Laurie Wright had just arrived and was in shock. All I could ask, standing numb in my bedroom, was "Is Robert still there?" I waited. "Um, no, he left. He went back to Century City," Donald said. "There was no reason for him to stay. He already talked to the police. He said that—" I thanked Donald and hung up on him in mid-sentence.

LATER, ACCORDING TO the valet and the front desk at the Century Towers, Robert was last seen walking into the lobby at eight-fifty, his clothes and face covered with dried blood and a black duffel bag slung over his shoulder, and he was trying not to weep but also assured the doorman that he was okay and that there had been a "terrible accident" he witnessed and that he was going to clean up before going back to the hospital. I drove the Jaguar to Century City and stopped at the valet beyond the gates of the Century Towers and said that Robert Mallory had called and that he needed to see me. "I rushed straight over," I said. "I go to school with him. I'm a friend. I have no idea what he wants. He sounded . . . desperate." The valet gravely nodded—he had seen the condition Robert was in when he had arrived thirty minutes ago—and motioned me to a parking space directly by the fountains in front of the entrance but didn't tell me to check in with the doorman. I guessed he assumed I just would. I got out of the car and walked quickly to the lobby and paused, glancing over for a moment at the faraway front desk, behind which the lone doorman was situated. I just decided to risk it and walked directly to the other side of the lobby and stepped into an elevator and pressed "28."

I USED THE KEY I had found in the room Robert occupied in the abandoned house on Benedict Canyon and quietly opened the front door of Abigail's condo.

The recessed lighting in the living room was dimmed, accentuating the massive views of West Hollywood and the hills above Sunset braided with lights, and Pico Boulevard was sparse with traffic on that Saturday night. Everything seemed so far away that the world in that moment felt unreal and I acted accordingly. I bolted the door shut and then quickly dismantled the doorknob with the pair of pliers I was carrying, wrenching the handle off the door, rendering the door useless, it couldn't be opened—the process was louder than I intended, making a screeching sound that echoed throughout the apartment when I finally pulled the knob off and it clattered to the floor. I expected Robert to run out from wherever he was to see what had caused the noise coming from the entrance hall but he didn't. And then I proceeded into the kitchen, where I pulled a knife out of the countertop block. I unplugged the phone and yanked out the cord from the wall and then made my way past Robert's bedroom, where I heard the shower running, and went into Abigail's bedroom and unplugged the line to that phone as well, removed the cord and placed it in the nightstand, and then I moved down the darkened hallway toward Robert's bedroom.

The shower in the bathroom adjacent to the bedroom was running and I made my way toward the sound of the water as if solely guided by it. I stood in the doorway of the bedroom and saw the black duffel bag sitting on the gray comforter of the bed and it was in the process of being packed—T-shirts, underwear, a pair of jeans, a toiletries kit. And then I saw the tennis shorts and yellow Polo shirt stained with blood that Robert had been wearing earlier now lying in a pile by the bed, along with a pair of underwear and white blood-spattered Topsiders. There was no other sound in the apartment except for the water streaming from the shower Robert was taking. I moved slowly into the bathroom, which was shrouded in steam, and simply neared the shower stall and slowly reached toward the chrome handle with the fist holding the knife. When I opened the door the stall was empty. I stared at the hot water blasting out of the showerhead, confused.

And then I heard someone shout my name behind me and I screamed and whirled around.

ROBERT'S HAIR WAS WET and he was only wearing jockey shorts and a white T-shirt and I realized he'd been crouching behind the bed when I walked in and was now standing on the other side of it, directly across from me. We stared at each other in what seemed like a mutually surprised state of shock. I looked down and saw that he was clenching a butcher knife in his fist. And then he saw the knife I was holding. I remembered what my motives were: I wanted to talk to him. I wanted him to confess.

"What were those noises?" he asked. "What did you do?"

"I didn't do anything, Robert," I said softly.

"How did you get in, Bret?" he asked in a calm steely voice. But I could tell he was unnerved and trying not to show it. "What are you doing here? How did you get up? What were those noises?"

It took me a moment to find my voice again. I hadn't expected this to be part of the narrative: the shower, the knife, Robert hiding behind the bed. "I . . . just wanted to talk to you . . ." I said softly. "I just wanted to make sure I could talk to you . . ."

"Why are you holding a knife, Bret?" he asked calmly.

"Susan and Thom were . . . attacked tonight," I said.

"Why are you holding a knife, Bret?" he asked again.

"It was . . . you, right?" I said. "You . . . tried to . . . hurt . . ." I couldn't finish the sentence.

"I found them," Robert said. "I took them to the hospital. You didn't answer me. Why are you holding a knife, Bret?"

I ignored him and breathed in and carefully said, "I want to know what you did with Debbie—"

"Get the fuck out of here," he said softly.

"Where is she?" I asked.

He hadn't moved. He just stood behind the bed, very still. "I don't know where she is, Bret."

"I . . . don't think that's true," I said softly.

"I don't care what you think is true," he said. "But I'm going to take you downstairs to the lobby and I'm going to have the doorman escort you out of here—"

"No, you're not," I said.

He paused and tried not to appear shocked by my tone.

"What do you mean—no, I'm not?" he asked.

"You're going to tell me where Debbie Schaffer is," I said. "And then we're going to call the police." I paused. "You need help, Robert. You're sick. And you need help." I stared at him.

Robert didn't say anything. He just stood frozen, clutching the butcher knife. He had put the jockey shorts and T-shirt on when he was still wet and there were oval outlines where the dampness had touched the fabric. The almond eyes squinted slightly and he realized something. "You're with them, aren't you?" he said softly.

"With who, Robert?" I asked, as if speaking to a child.

"You're one of them," he said, softly convincing himself.

"I just want you to tell me where Debbie is," I said. "And I just want you to get help."

"You're one of the freaks who've been following me," Robert murmured, staring at my face, and then his eyes were roaming my body. "Ever since that summer . . . after the movie . . . when it started . . ." He trailed off as if lost in a reverie. "You were there . . ."

"I don't know who you're talking about, Robert," I said.

"You're with them, aren't you?" he said in a trance. He slowly took a step back. "The freak who follows me."

"Robert, tell me where Debbie is," I said, straining.

"You're one of them," he said. "You're one of the freaks who've been following me. Just fucking admit it, Bret."

"I'm not one of them, Robert," I said. "I just want to talk to you about where Debbie is."

"Get the fuck out of here," he said. "Get the fuck away from me."

Something was rising in the room. This couldn't stay sustained—it was looking for a release. The building up toward it was becoming intolerable. Everything felt pressurized.

"I just want to help you," I said again. And then I started slowly moving around the bed to where he stood. "Where's Debbie? Where did you take her?"

"Get away from me." He made a sudden movement: he swiped the butcher knife through the air. And then he leapt onto the bed, where he towered over me as he carefully balanced on the mattress. I turned direction and stared up at him from where I stood.

"Where's Debbie, Robert?" I said, my voice rising.

"Get out of here," he shouted. "You're with them! Get the fuck out!"

"Where's Debbie?" I shouted back.

In that moment Robert leapt forward and slashed the knife at me and I felt the tip of it across my face, opening up my forehead and cheekbone. Before I could react he slashed again and I could feel it slice across my nose and lips. Blood started dripping down my face and I had to blink it out of my eyes. I blindly stumbled forward with my knife raised but Robert had run out of the room and I collapsed against the sink in the bathroom but couldn't see my reflection because there was too much steam—the water was still pouring out of the shower. I wiped my face off with a hand towel I grabbed by the sink and looked at it as I walked back into the bedroom. It had immediately been stained red. I turned it over and pressed it against my face again and the other side came back just as red. I held the towel up against my forehead to stop the blood from dripping into my eyes as I moved into the hallway.

I COULD HEAR the grunting noises of panic coming from Robert as he tried to open the front door of the apartment. "What did you do?!?" he screamed. "What in the fuck did you do?" I kept the towel held against my forehead as I moved toward the living room. I heard him run into the kitchen and fumble with the disconnected phone, which he threw against the floor. There were animal noises of fear coming from him as he started to pound on the front door again, his arms slamming against it. "Help!" he shouted. "Help!"

"Robert," I said, moving toward the darkness of the living room. "I just want to talk."

Suddenly there was silence. I pulled the towel from my forehead and scanned the space but couldn't locate Robert. He wasn't by the front door and he wasn't in the kitchen. I walked carefully by the dining table and the granite fireplace and the Hockney print. The bleeding had slowed down—blood wasn't dripping into my eyes anymore—but I could taste it on my lips and my face was wet with it. I was about to call his name again when he suddenly emerged from the darkness at an angle I hadn't expected and pushed me back against a wall and then lifted his arm and stabbed me in the chest, but the knife hit the breast bone, which only caused the blade to drag down, slicing across the pectoral, and I could feel blood draping across my abdomen. I automatically pushed Robert away and then slashed wildly at him with the knife: a large red line was suddenly swiped across his chest and his rib cage and down to his torso—the white T-shirt flowered red. It wasn't deep but blood started spattering across the marble floor. He lunged forward and tried to stab me again in the chest and again it didn't go deeper than the breastbone—this all happened in a matter of seconds. I pushed him away and fell against the wall and turned toward it, sliding, shocked not only at how much blood was smearing across the white expanse but also that it was my blood.

ROBERT WAS opening the sliding glass door that led out to the balcony and I rushed toward him and slashed the knife across his back. He turned and lifted a leg to kick me away—and I fell backward onto the floor. When he returned to the door and opened it I could see that his back was now red with blood. He fully opened the sliding glass door and stepped onto the balcony and then slammed the door shut, holding on to it, while shouting for help. He kept holding on, because he couldn't lock it from outside, and he kept shouting for help while I started to pry the glass door open. He pushed against it, holding the door in place. I immediately stepped away from the door and kicked at it hard. And then I kicked it again. Robert kept holding it in place, shouting for help, red-faced. His ripped T-shirt was now covered completely with blood and blood was spattering all over the smooth white-tiled floor of the balcony. I brushed from my eyes drops of blood that were dripping down my forehead again. Robert kept shouting for help, now in a crouch, still holding on to the door handle—but he was so far above the world, who could have possibly heard him? I kicked the door again and the glass finally cracked. I kept kicking and the crack splintered upward. Robert kept shouting for help while holding on to the door, his muscles straining, blood running down his legs. I kicked again and the entire door burst open in a cascading sheet of glass that littered the balcony.

Robert backed away and looked over the railing. I thought he was going to jump and rushed toward him with the knife and knocked him onto the balcony floor and held him there, straddling his waist. He was writhing against the shattered glass and it was cutting into my knees as I tried to grab the wrist with the hand holding the knife but he managed to stab my thigh, digging the blade in and then pulling it out and pushing it in again, and I screamed and rolled off him onto the carpet of broken glass and I could feel it cutting into my back and neck. I clutched Robert's forearm and slammed it down onto the glass and forced it up, then slammed it down, trying to knock the knife out of his grasp. He managed to pull away and grabbed the railing with a hand encrusted with broken glass and then I watched in horror as he climbed onto it.

"Robert," I shouted. "Don't."

He crouched on the railing and threw the knife over it and then lifted one leg and then another while gripping the railing and then he dropped out of sight.

I screamed and crawled to the railing, momentarily forgetting the broken glass that was cutting into my knees and palms, and looked down.

—

ROBERT HAD DROPPED onto the lit balcony below, which jutted out four feet past the railing on the top floor of the Century Towers. I heard Robert pounding on the sliding glass door of the unit and calling out for help but no one was answering, it was locked, the lights inside were off, nobody was home. Waves of adrenaline were shooting through me as I climbed onto the railing, slippery with blood, and pretended that I wasn't twenty-eight stories up and that it was a miniature world below me and that none of this was real and, still clutching the knife, I easily landed on the lit balcony, maybe a drop of eight feet. I rushed toward Robert, who was slick and shiny with blood, and pulled him away from pounding on the sliding glass door now streaked red as he shouted desperately into the darkened apartment beyond it, and I started shaking him, screaming into his face, *"WHERE IS SHE WHERE IS DEBBIE?"* I didn't feel it when he stabbed me in the arm—the blade didn't go deep enough to register at first. He was screaming back at me, *What did you want what do you want from me why were you following me?* He was delirious with fear and anger and there was shattered glass stuck along his legs and arms and after holding me back he lunged at me, swinging the knife, and I could feel the blade tear through my shirt and slash my chest again. I clumsily ran the blade of my knife across his bare arm and blood started pouring out. With the same arm he clenched his fist and punched the side of my head with such force that I fell to my knees stunned. I saw white for a moment and I could feel my eyes roll back into my sockets as I staggered to my knees. I felt wet with blood everywhere.

I looked down at the blood-splattered patio and then lifted my head—I thought I was going to be sick when I saw Robert climb over the railing on the twenty-seventh floor but I lurched forward and grabbed his leg and pulled him toward me. He fell back onto the patio and started kicking at my face and I held on to his calf to steady him but he managed to land the heel of his foot against my cheek. His T-shirt and underwear completely stained red with blood, he heaved himself up and straddled me while I lay there, everything blurry and echoing around me, and I felt his hands on my throat, and they were slowly crushing it. But the hands were too wet with blood and slippery and he couldn't get the proper traction, apply the correct pressure, and I was able to reach up with the hand holding the knife and blindly stab him. One hand let go of my throat and he knocked the knife out of my fist and it clattered against the bloodied balcony. The moment the knife flew away I grabbed his throat with both my hands and pulled him closer to me until we were face to face. He strained upward, pulling away, and then scrambled off me and turned to grip the railing.

I HEAVED myself up, choking, and stopped him from climbing onto it. We were now leaning, half over the railing, in an embrace and I realized he was trying to throw me off the balcony. I could smell the coppery aroma of blood everywhere and it was so quiet and what happened between us had only been going on for barely two minutes—it all happened so fast—but I was fading. We stayed locked in a frozen grip—neither one could move the other. I was suddenly so exhausted that Robert was able to finally push away from me and grabbed the railing again: I just stared and realized he was going to jump onto the balcony below this one. And in a matter of seconds he swung over and hung from the railing and was trying to swing onto the twenty-sixth-story balcony. But it was the same size as this one—only the twenty-eighth floor had the smaller balcony. I crawled over to the railing, where just Robert's hands were visible, the knuckles not covered with blood white from the strain. The floor of the balcony was wet, as if it had rained or been hosed down with water, but it was our blood and I slipped in it while I staggered to the railing and then, on my knees, looked down and watched as Robert tried to swing his body onto the twenty-sixth floor.

"Robert, please, I want to help," I shouted. "Robert, don't!"

And then I raised a bloodied fist and brought it down on the back of his hand.

He was making desperate panting sounds. He kept swinging his body forward, trying to aim for the balcony.

I raised my fist again and brought it down on the back of his other hand, hard.

"Robert, don't!" I cried.

And then he fell silently into the darkness.

—

THERE WAS ONLY SILENCE—no screaming—and then an awful cracking sound when the body hit the roof of the garage that you could hear twenty-seven stories up. I looked down but I couldn't see anything. I started weeping and collapsed into a corner of the patio and soon I could hear the sirens in the distance. I stayed crouched on the blood-smeared tiles, clutching myself. At one point I heard the front door being rammed open in the unit above. There were voices. I started crying out for help. And then the lights in the darkened unit on the twenty-seventh floor illuminated the empty apartment and the voices neared me. I was crying nonsensically—the smell of rust was everywhere but that was the congealing blood. The sliding glass doors opened but I was blinded with blood and couldn't really see anything and I was hysterical. *"I tried to help him he killed himself he was my friend I loved him I loved him I tried to save him he attacked two of my friends earlier he jumped he jumped."* I was being lifted up. *"He trapped me in the apartment I thought he was going to kill me."* Paramedics placed me on a stretcher, my face was wiped clean, and an oxygen mask covered my nose and mouth. I was wheeled through the apartment and then was carried down in the elevator. I saw the vaulted ceiling of the lobby as I kept ranting even though no one could hear me through the oxygen mask. *"He killed those girls he killed Debbie he attacked Susan he told me to come he needed me he attacked me he tried to kill me before he jumped I loved him I loved him."* I was pleading to anyone who was listening. I was wheeled into the courtyard, whirling with blue and red lights, sirens piercing the air, and the last thing I saw before losing consciousness was another stretcher being slowly wheeled toward an ambulance, two paramedics by its side, and on it was something completely misshapen, a mound, something that had rearranged itself when it hit the roof of the Century Towers garage and become something else and the sheet covering it was stained with red and purple and yellow—it was some kind of sculpture, sections of it sticking upward beneath the sheet: it was something that couldn't have fit into a body bag. And when I realized that under the sheet were the remains of Robert I started screaming until I blacked out.

31

I WAS IN A DARKENED room in Cedars-Sinai and Laurie Wright was standing over me when I woke up in the middle of the night.

There were actually no serious injuries, though I received 115 stitches. The stab wounds Robert Mallory inflicted upon me weren't deep or "invasive" enough for serious medical attention, I was told by a physician. Besides the light slashing across my face—which didn't require stitches—I was stabbed in the breastbone, in the left thigh, in the arm and slashed across my chest numerous times. I learned it was difficult to get stabbed deeply in a knife fight. I learned it's hard to inflict a lethal injury. I learned it is hard to "get by" the rib cage. I learned you have to stab in a very specific way and at a very specific angle for the wound to be fatal. None of my organs were touched and none of my major blood vessels were punctured. I might have arrived in the emergency room at Cedars-Sinai a bloodied mess, but there was nothing remotely lethal about my injuries. In retrospect everything felt vaguely routine, as if I'd been rehearsing this for a long time: I told the police what had happened to me in Unit 2802 of the Century Towers and there was no one to refute it. I said that Robert had called me *after* he left the hospital from a pay phone "somewhere" and that he was "extremely upset" and that he needed to see me. I told the police that I knew he had mental issues and had spent time in an institution in Illinois after a suicide attempt in January and that I believed he was somehow connected to the crimes of the Trawler, and that Robert had dated Katherine Latchford in the summer of 1980 before she vanished, and I explained the time line I had figured out that tied Robert to the other girls; I also told them I believed

Robert was responsible for the disappearance of Debbie Schaffer—the officers knew nothing about this—and that it was Robert Mallory, in fact, who had attacked Susan Reynolds and Thom Wright in the house on North Canon Drive, and after he fled pretended to rescue them—he was a sick individual, I explained; he was a maniac, I told them; he wanted to hurt Susan, he had *seduced* her, this was part of the game; and he had something to do with the death of Matt Kellner, but no one I talked to had any idea who that was.

I repeated this story to anyone who would listen: the Reynolds, Laurie Wright, the police officers who took down my statement, the doctors who attended to me. I had gone, I told them over and over, to help a "distraught" friend, someone who had told me on the phone that he was going to kill himself, and so I "raced" to Century City to try and stop the friend from committing suicide because I knew he had tried to once before. I was in a panic, I told them. When I arrived in the apartment I couldn't find Robert. I was looking for him in the master bedroom when I heard a noise. And then I saw that Robert had dismantled the front door—he had bolted it shut and removed the handle so that I couldn't open it—to "entrap me" and that I had defended myself with a knife I found in the kitchen. I kept shouting for help but apparently no one heard, I said. Even after Robert managed to stab me several times I tried to pull him off the railings on both the twenty-eighth- and twenty-seventh-story balconies while attempting to defend myself. I reiterated: Robert was mentally unstable. Robert had been in an institution. He had raped his stepsister. He had attempted suicide once before. He had killed my friend. I reiterated: I tried to help him. And then he jumped.

All this was taken down with very few questions—when one was asked I answered it wearily, often tearing up and bursting into sobs—and then I signed my statements with a bandaged hand that had earlier been encrusted with shattered glass.

LAURIE WRIGHT told me that my parents had been contacted but they wouldn't be back in Los Angeles for two nights due to their complicated and circuitous route out of Europe. It would take a day for the ship they were sailing to dock and then they would be driven to the closest airport and fly into London, where they'd take the Concorde to New York and then barely make a nonstop American Airlines flight to LAX.

I discharged myself from the hospital late Sunday afternoon—I demanded it—and Laurie Wright brought me to the house on North Hillcrest, where I'd be staying until my parents arrived. I was going to sleep in Thom's room and Laurie guided me to the bed with the plaid comforter crumpled across it because I was shuffling stiffly even though the pain pills made me feel as if I was floating in slow motion, and as I eased myself onto the mattress I inhaled Thom's scent—it enveloped me—and I pulled a pillow to my side and pretended it was him, wincing at the soreness in my chest and arms and thigh penetrating through the painkillers, and zoned out instead at the Griffin pennant that hung on the wall over Thom's desk and its innocence comforted me. I didn't really know then the extent—the severity—of Thom's injury, only that his leg had been "damaged," and yet I worried for him and his future. The pain pills helped me sleep and I didn't get out of bed until late Sunday night. There were bandages across my chest and on my right thigh, but my face, despite the awful red-and-purple swelling where Robert's kick had landed, only looked like someone had scratched it when I stared at myself in the mirror of Thom's bathroom—there was a very thin scab that ran down my forehead and there was another one bisecting my nose and lips. Laurie went back to the hospital and spent the rest of Sunday there as Thom went through another surgery to put his leg back together, and though he was briefly conscious and talked to his mother for a moment before he went into the operating room there was nothing for Laurie Wright to do but wait. Lionel was flying in from New York on Tuesday and I idly wondered what had happened to the handsome young man I'd seen Laurie with at Homecoming, which now seemed like it took place in another world an eternity ago.

I ASKED Laurie how Susan was doing when she came back to the house on Hillcrest late that evening with some prepared food she had picked up at a nearby deli before it closed. Laurie shrugged as she opened a bottle of white wine. "I don't know, I guess she's going to be okay," she said and then mentioned something about reconstructive surgery and how advanced it had become. "Reconstructive . . . surgery?" I asked, confused. Laurie glanced at me and wouldn't clarify. "I didn't see her. She goes home Wednesday." Laurie drank the first glass of wine as I sat at the table in the kitchen with her, high, almost dreaming: I didn't feel anything, I could barely eat the turkey sandwich Laurie had brought me, I could barely lift my bandaged hand, and yet I felt oddly free.

"But it's hard," Laurie was saying after pouring herself a second glass of wine. She paused while contemplating something. "She broke my son's heart. I have sympathy for her but I don't really like her much anymore."

We watched the ABC local news that night at eleven and the lead story was about the prep-school boy who leapt to his death from a Century City high-rise after assaulting a classmate and of course this story was tied to the attack on Susan and Thom since Robert was connected to both, and briefly, after my statement was made, there were hints about the Trawler and that if Robert *wasn't* the Trawler there were connections Robert had to the serial killer that were becoming more apparent after Robert's suicide. But none of us knew what these connections were yet.

ON MONDAY MORNING before Laurie went to the hospital at nine we watched the ABC local news during *Good Morning America;* a dozen squad cars had descended upon the house on Benedict Canyon late Sunday night, while we were sleeping. The swirling red and blue lights bathed the house in a psychedelic wave of color, and the body of Audrey Barbour, the fourth known victim of the Trawler, was found in a soundproofed room in the makeshift basement of the house—the room that I had tried to get into but couldn't. I sat on the couch in the den on Hillcrest Drive wearing one of Thom's robes—dark green with a Polo horse on it, smelling lightly of Aramis and Old Spice—and stared dully at the TV screen in a Vicodin haze. I was thinking: this was the house that ate people. I was thinking this was the house where Matt Kellner had been holed up in for several days while Robert Mallory tortured him after gaining his trust. This was the house where Robert Mallory made his awful plans. There was footage of a body bag being carried out from the side of the house—I recognized the unlocked door I had entered only days ago. Laurie Wright started crying. It was months later when we found out what the Trawler meant by the things he referred to in his letters as "the alterations" and "the assemblages" and "the remakings." Audrey Barbour's sacrificed body was found stapled together with the limbs from a succession of missing animals by the Trawler and "his friends" who had been "following the moon"—this was "the project" that the Trawler created, all of it meticulously sewn together like a patchwork quilt. This was an elaborate variation on what had also been done to the other three girls, who had also perhaps spent time in that house.

Inside the space that had been soundproofed by someone in the abandoned house on Benedict Canyon a sheet of Audrey Barbour's rotting flesh that had been removed from her back and shoulders hung in the doorway like a curtain you had to push aside before you entered the room where she was being presented: her body had been "decorated"—her mouth was stuffed with fish, the head and neck of a cat had been splayed across her forehead and stapled to it, the rest of its body was hanging out of her vagina, her legs bent and spread as if she was giving birth to it. Audrey's head was adorned with the limp bodies of dead snakes, their heads cut off, and a wig of them crowned her skull. Her breasts were missing—they had been removed and two cats' heads had been placed in the empty, mangled wounds. Her anus was forced open with the snout of a decapitated dog and another dog's raggedly mutilated neck was stapled to that. As I've said we didn't learn about these details until months later, and only a few of them: it took a year for the awfulness of what the Trawler "accomplished" to be fully revealed. Even though the body of the fourth victim of the Trawler had been found in the house on Benedict Canyon, Robert Mallory never appeared as the key suspect in the days that followed—I later learned that it had been a "tempting" theory but that certain elements about it simply didn't add up.

DEBBIE SCHAFFER ARRIVED back at Stone Canyon that Monday morning, November 9.

She had left Bel Air on Thursday night and driven to the Hollywood Hills home of a thirty-year-old musician she had been seeing on and off for the past year, before anything had happened between us, and during our relationship as well, whose stage name was Shore Lanes; he was the guitarist in a little-known local band called Line One who were never going to make it—Susan Reynolds knew about Shore and his was the first place she had called on Friday morning but Debbie had told anyone who answered the phone to say that she wasn't there. Debbie spent the weekend at Shore's trying to obliterate from her mind the photos she had seen of her father and myself on that bed in the Beverly Hills Hotel and she was in a house high above the city on Appian Way along with various band members and their groupies in a three-day-long cocaine binge and joined by two girls and a boy, Riders of the Afterlife kids, all of them seventeen, who the band had befriended. Debbie hadn't heard anything about what happened to Susan and Thom until Monday morning because no one knew where she was or could contact her and Debbie had wanted it that way. Dealers kept dropping by and time disappeared, the band rehearsed tracks off a new album that was never going to be released even though they had received a large advance from the record company, there was no news from the world outside the rented house, just a constant supply of cocaine and vodka and tequila, and bowls filled with Valium and Quaalude, deliveries from the neighborhood liquor store, crates of beer, cartons of cigarettes, huge bottles of margarita mix—all aiding in Debbie's obliteration.

And when Debbie, exhausted, retreated to Shore's bedroom, the small TV in the corner was flickering and as she lay on the mattress and stared in a stupor at its screen, unable to sleep, she realized at one point that she was staring at Susan Reynolds's house on North Canon Drive and then a photo of Robert Mallory from the Roycemore yearbook appeared and Debbie said she thought she'd been dreaming but then she sat up and in a panic couldn't find the remote to turn up the volume. There was footage of the house on Benedict Canyon swirling with red and blue lights. There was the body bag being carried out through the side door. There was a shot of TV vans lined up and down the canyon road. There was a shot of the Century Towers. Yearbook photos of Thom Wright, Susan Reynolds and Bret

Ellis flashed across the screen. Debbie got dressed and wandered out of the house into the cold light of morning and, walking the street, it took her thirty minutes to locate her car, until she remembered it had been hidden in the garage since she didn't want anyone to find her, and then she drove across Sunset back to Bel Air. Maria wailed when she saw Debbie and fell to her knees, and Steven Reinhardt called Terry at Cedars; he wanted to talk to his daughter but she refused to speak to him. She also refused to speak to Liz. Debbie instead stoically listened as Steven told her what had happened—the attack on Susan and Thom, and later myself and then Robert's suicide that only I had witnessed. The first thing Debbie Schaffer asked after a moment of silence while she just stared impassively at Steven's face: "A suicide? Is that what Bret said it was?"

I GRABBED MY mother and fell into her arms weeping when she appeared at Laurie Wright's house early Tuesday morning to take me back to Mulholland in a black limousine that was waiting curbside in front of the residence on North Hillcrest.

ON FRIDAY I called Susan and asked if I could see her and she agreed.

I hadn't been to school that week and I hadn't talked to anyone except my mother and someone from the LAPD who wanted to question me again about what happened in the condo on the twenty-eighth floor of the Century Towers—Abigail Mallory supposedly had her doubts about my narrative—but I gave the detective the same story, though embellishing details about Robert to make it more dramatic and frightening. Again, who was going to refute it? And I was disappointed that the detective didn't ask about Katherine Latchford or Matt Kellner or anything else except the events that led to the attack in the apartment. I was just sitting outside at a patio table spacing out on the remainder of the Vicodin next to Marty Reed, my parents' lawyer, but there really was no physical pain any longer. I spent a lot of time naked in the bathroom inspecting the wounds Robert Mallory had inflicted upon me and I'd peel back the bandages and stare at the stitched-up spaces, fascinated mostly by the long line that began at my breastbone and traveled down my rib cage: a dark-purple centipede is what I thought it looked like.

I mostly avoided the news about what happened that night, but the discovery of Audrey Barbour supplanted the attack on Canon Drive and the suicide in Century City, with the media only nominally connecting Robert with the Trawler and his crimes—and I couldn't understand why. There had been no news at all about Deborah Schaffer: no mention of her disappearance appeared anywhere and I'm fairly sure Terry and Liz made this happen or simply hadn't filed the missing person report. Debbie was simply gone for the weekend and then she was back at the house on Stone Canyon the following Monday morning. And she had been the only one Susan allowed in her bedroom on Canon Drive, where she was recuperating while awaiting another reconstructive surgery.

GAYLE LET ME IN on that Friday afternoon and I walked through the living room behind her and up the stairs and down the hall to where Susan was in her bedroom—it had been six days since the attack.

Susan was propped up in bed and Gayle asked her if she needed anything and Susan shook her head no. Susan was sedated on pain-killers, semi-lost in a medicated daze, and she was listening to Icehouse. She was wearing a robe but I could see part of the bandage that was wrapped around her chest—it was impossible not to notice that one side of her was simply flattened out and I held in a gasp. When we tried hugging each other we both laughed as we winced with pain and then started crying. I sat down on the bed next to Susan, and her bandaged hand, where she had grabbed the intruder's knife, covered her mouth as tears spilled quickly out of her eyes, and then I bowed my head and started convulsing with sobs—we didn't need to acknowledge what we were both crying over: we knew it was everything, what happened to Thom, what happened to Robert, the attacks we separately suffered, the song that was playing, everything. We talked quietly and made promises to each other. Susan had seen Thom on Wednesday, before she was discharged, and told me he was going to be okay. I nodded and then started crying again and she asked if I'd seen anyone and I told her no—I hadn't been back to Buckley, I barely left my room, I was high on Vicodin all the time, I probably shouldn't have driven over to Beverly Hills. She smiled.

Icehouse kept filtering softly through the room and I realized at one point there had been a manila envelope resting in Susan's lap along with a series of eight-by-ten photos she'd been looking at. I craned my neck as she turned the photos to me. They were in black and white and seemingly taken with a telephoto lens: Susan and Robert in Palm Springs at Las Casuelas—this was from across the street on North Palm Canyon Drive as they sat at a table in the cantina. Susan and Robert in the backyard of her grandparents'—Robert in a bathing suit, Susan in a bikini, lounging on a chaise. Susan and Robert wading in the pool. Susan and Robert standing next to each other by the white BMW in the senior parking lot—this was taken from somewhere within the hillsides surrounding Buckley. Everything was taken from far away, as if the photographer was hiding. Susan: getting out of her BMW and walking into the Century Towers. Susan: standing alone on Gilley Field holding a tennis racket. I looked up at her.

"Do you know who took these?" I asked.

She shook her head no. "They were left in the mailbox," she said dreamily. I was distracted by the photos and suddenly felt lightly fearful. Susan was too high to really care. She was just looking at the ones with Robert in them. "Did you?" she asked slyly. "Did you take them?"

"No." I shook my head.

"I know you loved me," she was saying. "And I know you loved Thom."

I didn't say anything.

"I hope we never hurt you," she said.

"No," I said. "No, you never hurt me." This wasn't true but we were past that place now—it didn't matter any longer.

"It could have been you," Susan said. "If things were different."

Again, I didn't say anything.

"How did you . . ." She stopped. "How did you manage to play it so well all these years?"

"Play what?" I asked, pretending not to know what she meant.

She didn't say anything until she smiled sadly and looked away. "The role, Bret."

"I don't think I played it so well," I finally said, my voice cracking.

"I remember the first time I talked to you," she said, high. "It was the first week of seventh grade." She paused. "And it was at lunch and do you know what I thought?"

I shook my head. The painkillers were talking through her.

"I thought: I'm going to marry him one day," she said. She grinned, stoned, studying me for a reaction, curious as to what I might say.

"You're high," I said.

"Maybe . . ."

"What happened?" I asked, playing along. "Why didn't you?"

"I figured you out," she said. "I kept you free."

"Why Robert?" I asked. "I understand Thom, but why Robert?"

"I don't know," she said. "I can't explain it."

I said nothing.

"I fell in love with him," she said. "I thought I had met . . ." She trailed off, almost ashamed of what she was going to say next. Her mouth was slightly open, as if she had just received a blow. And then she recovered.

"You thought you met who?" I asked.

There was barely a pause before she said, "A dream."

I looked down and tried to compose myself.

Susan asked me, "What happened on Saturday night, Bret? In Robert's apartment?" She paused. "Tell me what really happened."

I reached up and placed a finger to her lips and she smiled understandingly and closed her eyes—the gesture we often made to each other indicating we didn't need to hear what the other person was going to say because we already knew and it wouldn't make a difference anyway.

When Susan opened her eyes they were automatically drawn to something. I was wearing a blue Polo dress shirt, long-sleeved, buttoned up, but one of the sleeves had draped down when I lifted my arm to press the finger to her lips and I realized she was looking at something there. The stoned smile was gone and then her eyes looked up at mine and then she looked back at the arm. The mellow, exhausted mood in the room reversed itself and something got activated—everything was humming. Susan began shaking as she looked up at me again. Before I could stop her she reached over and pulled the sleeve farther down. She didn't say anything at first but I realized that Susan was looking at a deep wound on my forearm surrounded by purple-and-yellow bruising.

Susan thought she was looking at a bite mark. She said this out loud.

Susan thought this bite mark was in exactly the same place where Susan had bitten the intruder on Saturday night.

Susan thought the indentations of her teeth were plainly visible.

She just stared at me. She didn't say anything else. She started crying. And then she threw up on the front of her robe.

"What's wrong?" I asked softly.

She was pulling away but I was clutching her bandaged hand.

"Susan, what's wrong?" I asked again.

She turned away from me, trembling. She was slowly shaking her head back and forth like a little girl, her chin coated with drool and vomit.

"Please, Susan," I said softly. "Don't worry. He's gone. Robert's gone. He can't hurt you anymore."

Susan turned back to me, trembling violently now. I was gripping her hand so tightly she couldn't pull away.

"Is my secret safe with you?" I asked softly. "Is my secret safe with you?" I whispered again.

I was squeezing her hand with such force that I could feel it begin to snap apart—I kept crushing it while telling her in a soothing voice, "He's gone, Robert's gone, it's all going to be okay, you're safe," until I heard something in her hand breaking. She fainted and slid off the bed. I sat very still, composing myself, and then slowly stood up, paused, and ran out of the bedroom and called out to Gayle that Susan said she felt weird and that she had told me she'd taken too many painkillers and then she threw up and passed out and fell and I think maybe she broke something in her hand. Gayle hurried up the stairs and I followed her into Susan's room, where we both helped lift her onto the bed. But the bed was wet with urine and so I lifted Susan back up and placed her in another room as Gayle stripped the sheets and then called a doctor.

I ASSUMED SUSAN NEVER told anybody about what she thought she saw and I never talked to her again. Susan Reynolds didn't return to Buckley—she finished out her senior year at Marymount, where she graduated in June. I never saw her after that scene in her bedroom until she was standing under an umbrella at the valet in front of the Palihouse Hotel on that December afternoon almost forty years later. And it was almost twenty years later when I found out that Susan actually had told someone about what she thought she'd seen in her bedroom on Friday the 13th of November, 1981.

IT WAS MONDAY of the following week when I went back to school and became the object of fascination, briefly kind of a hero, because there was no one else to talk with about what had happened: Susan Reynolds and Thom Wright weren't coming back to Buckley their senior year and I had vanquished Robert Mallory—there were rumors still swirling around him—and I was the boy who fought off a supposed serial killer and I seemed dangerous and tough and people wanted to talk to me: I was seen in a new light, I had an aura of celebrity. I was the center of attention in a way I'd never been before, now that Thom and Robert and Susan were gone and Debbie Schaffer wasn't returning until December. So I told my audience, whoever it was in those first days back, about what I heard had happened on Canon Drive on that Saturday night and what had *physically* happened to both Susan and Thom, how they'd both been attacked and mangled by a butcher knife Robert Mallory was wielding—Susan across the chest, and Thom's leg sawed open—and that once Robert fled the house Susan stumbled out onto Canon Drive "covered in blood" and "screaming for help," and Robert's Porsche suddenly and suspiciously appeared and he rushed them to Cedars-Sinai, pretending that he hadn't been in the house when he was in fact the intruder who stabbed them.

And then I told the version of what happened in the Century

Towers I'd already told everyone else. My classmates listened, rapt with horror at my description of the attack, and they would gasp and dramatically turn when I unbuttoned my shirt midway and showed off the stitches that crisscrossed my chest and went down to my rib cage. *We had all been attacked by the Trawler*, I told them. The Trawler was Robert Mallory, I told them. And when he had been found out, he leapt to his death but not before he tried to kill me. Ryan Vaughn was the only person who had no interest in my story—he listened once, at lunch, and during it, he stood up, collected his things and walked to another table, as if he was too unnerved. But this didn't deter me. Emboldened by the reaction I was receiving, I continued with the story—the stabbings, the jump to the balcony below, the struggle, the blood that was splattered everywhere—and I prolonged it, teasing the incident out, stopping myself in order to supposedly regain my composure. And afterward people were so grateful that I was okay. They were so relieved that I had "survived" the experience. I was congratulated. I was thanked. Everywhere I walked students from all grades would stare at me and they'd whisper that I was the boy who had killed the Trawler—everyone knew who he was now and what he had been capable of. He had actually gone to school with them and Robert wasn't there anymore. We were saved because of me.

But something happened that stopped this narrative from continuing.

ANOTHER GIRL WAS ABDUCTED, who turned out to be the Trawler's final victim in Los Angeles County: a seventeen-year-old named Leslie Slavin vanished on a crowded Saturday night in Westwood—November 21—after leaving a group of friends at Yesterdays and walking to her car, which had been parked in a garage on Glendon Avenue, and then a few random home invasions started again, but less violent than the one the Trawler had supposedly committed at the Reynolds residence on North Canon Drive, it was noted, and he ended up denying that was him—he tacitly acknowledged the other home invasions but not the one in Beverly Hills. A letter from the Trawler sent to the *Los Angeles Times* and verified by the LAPD confirmed this and referenced Robert Mallory not by name but just as "the God" who another gift was left to in the house that "the God" occasionally inhabited on Benedict Canyon. The gift was a sacrifice and the sacrifice was Audrey Barbour, as all the other girls had been, starting with Katherine Latchford, and the letter absolved "the God" of any "wrongdoing" or "suspicion." In fact the Trawler seemed offended that people briefly thought "the God" had anything to do with *his* crimes, his *projects*, this new girl being the last of them, the Trawler promised—the one that would be offered to the deceased boy that the Trawler called "the God." The Trawler wanted the credit for Audrey Barbour and the others and resented the fact that people may have thought Robert was somehow responsible. The letter confirmed that the Trawler and "his friends" had themselves soundproofed the basement of the abandoned house on Benedict Canyon, which "the God" sometimes visited, and that "the sacrifice" had been there for days before being killed and then discovered on that Sunday night. I realized sickeningly while reading the article that Audrey Barbour's body may have been there the day I wandered through the house and into the basement.

The Trawler also wrote that he had become "intimate" with many of "the acquaintances" of "the God," and his friends had too, and "enjoyed" their "time with them," though he didn't name anyone. He mentioned "gifts" he had left for "the God's classmates"—mementos, photos, the posters.

AND THEN ABIGAIL Mallory released the letters—the fan notes— that had been sent to Robert beginning in the summer of 1980, after Katherine Latchford had disappeared, and through the early fall of 1981 and he was suddenly exonerated—they were obviously from the same voice. It was the Trawler.

The letters had no specific references to any of the victims—they were just love letters to "the God" reminding him that the Trawler and his friends were always watching "the God" and that they were leaving "gifts" and "sacrifices" for him all over the city and he would find out about them very soon—"treasures," the Trawler called them. There was never enough in the letters for Robert to piece anything together by the time Audrey Barbour had disappeared. No names of victims, no references to home invasions—just a constant stalking, telling Robert he'd been "spotted" various places, and that "the God" was being "watched over." Robert had not been paying attention to the narrative beyond the letters as closely as I'd assumed—he didn't make the connection between the crimes and the letters. In fact he thought at one point, according to Abigail, that the letters were coming from a group of "psycho chicks" or maybe from a girl he'd dated and then abandoned those first months in California. The realization, swift and brutal, was that there had been people stalking Robert for almost a year and a half, as well as the students closest to him once he arrived at Buckley: these followers were the Trawler and his supposed friends.

Abigail Mallory once again publicly disputed what she believed had happened between her nephew and Bret Ellis in her condo on the night of November 7. But she hadn't been there. And my account was forceful and dramatic enough so that it became the core truth on which the rest of the remaining narrative was carried: Robert may not have been the Trawler but he was a dangerous and suicidal figure who wanted to harm a student that had been suspicious of him. But this narrative wasn't enough to save me.

I QUICKLY BECAME A PARIAH in ways that I didn't notice at first after the Trawler abducted Leslie Slavin and took credit for the death of Audrey Barbour and it was clearly apparent that Robert Mallory hadn't killed anyone, as I had so insisted, but was in fact a *victim* of the Trawler's mind games and his overall obsession with Robert.

I realized the mood about me had shifted fast but it was subtle when it started—it came in what I thought were only imagined evasions, people forgetting to say hi or acknowledge me as I walked the pathways under the eaves, teachers glancing away as I passed them, pretending to be in conversation with one another, and certain students avoiding me as I pulled books out of my locker between classes. I found myself standing alone in the courtyard during assembly. No one was waiting for me in the senior parking lot or under the bell tower when I arrived there before school started—not anymore. I noticed I wasn't being invited out to lunch on the days when the people I'd thought were my friends headed to Teru Sushi or Du-par's in Studio City, or the McDonald's or Hamburger Hamlet in Sherman Oaks, and I often found myself eating alone at one of the far tables below the shadow of the Pavilion, away from the center table, where I used to sit, now occupied by Ryan Vaughn and Jeff Taylor and Tracy Goldman and Michelle Stevenson, who Ryan had started dating.

When Debbie Schaffer failed to invite me to Jeff Taylor's eighteenth-birthday party she was throwing at the house on Stone Canyon I understood why—we rarely talked the rest of our senior year and I never spoke to Terry or Liz again. But the exclusion was more painfully clear when a group of guys including Jeff, Kyle Colson, Anthony Matthews and Dominic Thompson made plans to see a movie in Westwood and I hadn't been invited; this was when I realized I was going to exist on a solitary plane the rest of my senior year— a loner, an outsider, the person I always knew I was. The tangible participant simply walked away and muttered *adios, hasta luego, maricón*. Whatever status I had once enjoyed completely disappeared. And maybe if I hadn't been so close with Thom and Susan for all those years this was how it would have always been anyway and I was just realizing that without their presence in close proximity to mine I might have been as invisible then as I was becoming now. Everything faded from me.

Thom Wright attended the Harvard School for Boys during the remainder of twelfth grade and I didn't see him again for almost twenty years.

IN DECEMBER I received a manila envelope addressed to me only by my name scrawled across it, BRETT misspelled with two "t"s.

It was sealed and lying on top of the island in the kitchen along with the rest of the mail and various magazines when I returned home from school on an overcast Thursday afternoon before Christmas break began. I slowly walked the hallway to my bedroom, where I closed and locked the door and sat on the bed before opening the envelope. I pulled out a series of photos, there were maybe forty of them, eight-by-tens in black and white and many of them taken with a telephoto lens: the first five were of me at the top of the bleachers on Gilley Field, alone, and then with Robert Mallory—whoever was taking the photos must have been somewhere in the forested hills below Beverly Glen on that day in October when Robert revealed his suspicions about me and Matt Kellner.

And then there were a series of photos taken across the street from the house on Benedict Canyon. I was wearing my school uniform and standing next to my mother's Jaguar parked on the curving stone driveway and I was looking up at the house. In another photo I tried turning the handle on the front door. In another I walked around the side of the house. There were another series of photos: me pushing open the wrought-iron gate. There was a photo of me stepping out of the 450SL this time. There was a shot of me opening the side door of the house and slipping in. There was also a photo I didn't recognize at first because it seemed as if it was taken in another era so far away that I couldn't place where I was. But then I realized: it was Haskell Avenue and I was leaving Matt in the pool house, the last time I ever talked to him, my face was a grimace and clenched with tears, or maybe it could have been construed as anger. I realized—it had been taken from the back of a van parked down the street.

And there were five photos that had nobody in them: an empty living room, a large bedroom, a kitchen, a bathroom, the view from behind a sliding glass door of a swimming pool and a backyard: a tiled fountain, a ficus tree. I didn't understand where this location was until I realized they were taken within my aunt's house in Palm Springs on South Toledo Avenue.

And then there were five more photos, all taken from inside the house on Mulholland: the garage without the 450SL in it, an empty living room, my bathroom, my bedroom, the comforter where the Maxell tape and Matt's jockey shorts were laid out.

When I arrived at the last series of photos I saw that they were clear, in medium and close-up shots—they weren't taken with a telephoto lens—and they were of Matt Kellner in a windbreaker standing on a bluff above the Pacific as the sky darkened behind him and he was staring into the lens blankly, his mouth partly open, a backpack slung over his shoulder, and someone had drawn a pentagram in black marker onto the glossy mat of the photo. There was another photo of Matt standing in a deserted parking lot, looking lost, staring into the lens of the camera, and he wasn't frightened. Another one of him:

looking away and half-smiling at someone out of the photo's reach. This was, I realized, at Crystal Cove before night fell and the bonfire was built. I was numb, gazing at his beautiful face, how innocent he seemed, his full lips and the tousled sun-streaked hair. And then I noticed it: behind Matt, over his right shoulder, plainly visible, was the beige-colored van, parked off to the side, almost blending into the whiteness of the sand and sky, its door opened all the way, positioned so that you couldn't see a license plate in the photo.

Scrawled above Matt was the word *shhhhh*.

I realized there was one more photo at the bottom of the stack and I placed it over the photo of Matt in the parking lot at Crystal Cove. It was a photo of Shingy, a medium shot, staring at whoever was taking the picture, in an empty room somewhere adorned with nothing, bare white walls, only a cardboard box behind the dog. He wasn't wearing his collar and he had been completely shorn of all his hair beneath the neck, as if he was being prepared for something. A pentagram hovered above his cocked head drawn in red felt marker. There was something wrong in the photo and then I realized what it was when I looked more closely at it: one of his eyes was missing and someone had cut off his tail.

BESIDES MATT AND ROBERT, the other casualty took place in January. It was simple and there was no mystery involved—it was an accident, bad luck, fate, nothing to do with Robert Mallory or the Trawler.

Anthony Matthews and Doug Furth were convoying on Pacific Coast Highway, heading to Jeff Taylor's father's place in Malibu. It was the last weekend of Christmas vacation and they'd met in Westwood to see *Taps* at the Avco Center and afterward drive to the Colony to spend the night—it was a Saturday and the movie started at four o'clock. They took separate cars and by the time they were on the I-10 it was almost seven—and because it was raining there was very little traffic as they neared Point Dume. Anthony was driving his Camaro and Doug was trailing him in his BMW. Anthony was speeding, according to Doug, but it didn't appear dangerously so, and neither one of them was high. It happened simply, in a matter of seconds—Doug said what happened seemed so far away he couldn't understand why the Camaro's taillights had only "pulled over" to the side of the road in the rainy darkness.

Doug drove closer until the BMW's headlights illuminated the wreckage of the Camaro. The car had skidded off the highway and slammed into the cliff side—simple, a human error, miscalculation, free of meaning or mystery. Doug pulled his car over and walked carefully toward the Camaro, shouting Anthony's name: steam was billowing out from under the crushed hood and the engine kept making an awful rapid clunking sound that abruptly stopped and Doug didn't understand at first what had been flung through the windshield: but it was Anthony. And he was already dying, stretched across the crumpled hood, completely jeweled with glass that was slowly turning purple in the glare of the headlights, and Doug could actually hear the glass crackling from the warm blood that was quickly streaming out of the spaces on Anthony's broken body.

I WAS LUCKY. I was a Pisces. I was the sign of two fish swimming in opposite directions—a dreamer, moving ceaselessly upstream, not entirely rational, prone to notions, but blindly pursuing whatever I wanted, a romantic, an individualist who needed no part of the crowd. My trajectory was simple: Bennington, reinventing myself, the publication of *Less Than Zero* when I was twenty-one, its success and the celebrity that followed, moving to Manhattan, where other novels were written by this young and infamous fish in the deep span of empire, a role I played until I didn't want to any longer but found myself trapped in regardless. There were the usual soap operas: various failed relationships, cocaine and Klonopin, I threw so many parties, the doomed boyfriend who died at thirty of an aortic aneurism, which was the catalyst for me to finally move back to Los Angeles after being gone for almost twenty-five years. One scene that still haunts me from those decades when I lived away from Los Angeles and was trying to forget that awful fall of 1981 happened in Boston in January of 1999, at the beginnings of what turned out to be a fifteen-month world book tour for my fifth work of fiction, *Glamorama.* I was in college when *Less Than Zero* was published so I didn't have to do one—I had an excuse—and by the time my second book was released I had amassed enough of a say to dissuade my publisher from a book tour; no one wanted me to tour for my third novel, the notorious *American Psycho,* and I only hit a few cities for a collection of stories in 1994 called *The Informers*—a couple of boutique bookstores, nothing more. I had never wanted to participate in a book tour because I'd feel too exposed. The Trawler had never been captured.

However, too much money had been invested in the new novel for me not to participate in an endless publicity tour and I wasn't happy about what the next year was shaping into. In Boston, on the first leg of the North American tour, I read for about twenty minutes to a packed audience at Boston College and then answered questions and afterward was led to a book signing that would last about two to three hours—this was determined by the size of the line that snaked through the lobby of the auditorium.

At one point a surprisingly handsome man who was probably around thirty-five, my age, handed me a hardcover copy of *Less Than Zero* in pristine condition, a novel that was almost fifteen years old, a novel that had nothing and yet everything to do with what happened to me in the fall of 1981. I was signing books, flanked by two PR girls from my publishing house, and we were working as a team to get all the books signed. They were there to help move the line along quickly—one would open the books and slide them to me, I'd sign them, then slide the books to the girl on my other side, and we'd keep the line moving. I briefly glanced up at the handsome man and smiled, because I wanted to make eye contact with whoever was in line to get a book signed, and I did a double take because he seemed so familiar. He was wearing a suit, Brooks Brothers, and a tie and a long camel-hair coat and he was holding an umbrella, his hair short and lightly graying at the sides, and his face was smooth-shaven and classically boyish. He just stared at me and I felt frightened, and then lustful, and then confused. He had the body of an athlete: trim, with slightly broad shoulders, but also compact, a runner, muscular and lithe. I didn't say anything. And the man didn't say anything either. When I glanced up at him again he just stared at me with a slightly wary smile. He seemed reticent, conservative, probably a business-man, a professional, a banker. He was so familiar—someone from my faraway past, a person I hadn't seen in years. I looked up at him helplessly. Everything froze.

"It's for Thom," he said. "Spelled with an 'h.' "

I pretended at first not to know who this was but it was Thom Wright, who I had not seen or spoken to since 1981. It immediately became awkward. He was waiting for my recognition.

And after I signed his full name without his asking me to he looked up from the title page and smiled.

"If you wait," I said, staring up at his face, "we can talk." I paused. "After this."

He checked his Rolex. He briefly thought about something. And then he nodded.

IT WAS SNOWING that day in Boston and I found Thom standing outside, in front of the lobby of the auditorium where the book sign-ing had taken place. A black sedan was waiting for me at the curb—I was being driven to a TV station for a live interview promoting tomor-row's in-store signing, wherever that was. I told Sloane and Karen that I needed to talk to an old friend. One of them reminded me we had to be at the station in thirty minutes and there was traffic. The snow was lightly drifting toward us as we stood in the overhang and made small talk about how Thom had been following my career since 1985, our breath steaming in the ice-cold air, and it was getting dark out.

"I don't know what to say," I finally said. "I can't believe you're here."

"I wasn't going to come," Thom said. "But I couldn't help it."

"Why haven't we seen each other in twenty years?" I asked. "What happened, Thom?" I just stared at him. "I thought of you so many times . . ."

Thom stared back at me, deciding something. His face flickered with a thought, and then became darkly animated. I noticed he sud-denly seemed troubled. There was doubt.

"She called me in the hospital after she saw you," he said. "Susan."

I nodded and kept staring at him.

"She sounded high, desperate." Thom stopped. "She said she saw something on your arm."

"I know," I said.

"She wanted us to call the police," Thom said. "She thought . . ." He didn't know how to say this without being ashamed, and then he did: ". . . that you had done it."

Thom breathed in, exhaled. I needed a cigarette but for some reason didn't want to smoke in front of Thom and refrained from reaching for the pack of Marlboros in the pocket of my Armani overcoat. All my boyish desires about him had returned with a feeling that was tidal. He resumed talking but hesitantly, unsure of himself. "I told her she was . . . crazy and that I would deny it. That this sounded insane. Totally insane . . ." He stopped, distracted by the two women waiting by the black sedan—their stances suggested I needed to hurry. Thom sighed, breath steaming from his mouth. "But it also . . . scared me. She seemed . . . so positive . . . it was you. And I told her she was crazy and that I wasn't going along with this crazy shit and that she should just stop it." He paused. "I told her she'd hurt me enough, leave me alone, I don't want any part of it. I don't know." Thom paused again. "I didn't really want to see you or really anybody after what happened to me . . ." The slightly quizzical expression flattened out into blankness. "But . . . it wasn't you, right?" It had been years he'd been waiting to ask me this. I breathed in, and shook my head no.

"Thom," I said. "It wasn't me." I looked away from him and at the snow drifting over the sedan and the two women standing next to it as the sky got darker—the sky was turning black—and then I was looking at Thom. "She was so high that day on painkillers when I saw her . . ." I stopped. "When she thought she saw . . . the thing on my arm . . ."

Thom just stared at me. "Who was it, then?" he asked quietly.

Again, there was doubt—it was slight but it hovered everywhere. The wind kept the snow drifting toward us beneath the overhang. I noticed how it dusted Thom's shoes.

I shrugged. I paused. "Maybe it was the Trawler . . . I don't know . . ."

Thom stared at me until he nodded. He remained blank-faced.

"They never found out who that was," Thom said. "Did they." It wasn't a question. He knew the answer. "The Trawler."

I slowly shook my head. "No, they didn't." I glanced over at the two girls. One of them tapped her wrist with a finger, indicating it was time to finish up.

"I guess she was traumatized and saw . . . things everywhere for a while, signs and signals, and she became paranoid . . . Everything was an . . . omen, a reminder," Thom said. He had glanced over at the sedan as well and realized time was running out. "But we never got back together. So. It didn't really matter to me what her state of mind was."

"Thom," I said. "I'm . . . sorry."

He seemed surprised. "For what?" he asked. "What do you have to be sorry for?"

"For not reaching out to you," I said. "For all those years of not reaching out to you." I paused, and then said it, "Explaining how I felt about you."

He considered this, looked away, and squinted at the snow blanketing the sidewalk. I had confirmed something that he didn't want to hear. "Well, for a long time I wasn't reachable," is all Thom said, offering a tight smile.

I asked Thom if he wanted to meet for dinner later that night, back at my hotel, I was staying at the Ritz-Carlton. Thom politely backed off and said that he had plans but that it was good to see me, however briefly, and thanked me for signing his book. I gave him my number in New York but he didn't call and I never saw him again.

I BEGAN THIS version of the book last spring: something cracked and it came easily in ways it never had before. The *facts* from that fall were receding from memory but *being* seventeen actually became clearer to me emotionally, more focused and pressing than it ever had at fifty-six, and I realized I had needed this distance of forty years to finally begin writing the book. And it was no longer a story about its most dramatic and eerie element—the mystery of the Trawler and his victims and our interaction with him—but it was about Matt Kellner, who began haunting my dreams, his presence trailing me throughout my days, holding on to my hand as I walked through the aisle of a supermarket or sitting in the passenger seat of my car as I drove aimlessly through the empty city or lying next to me in bed as I streamed a movie late at night. There were weeks that spring when he was the only person I ever thought about and I remembered the way he smelled, chlorine and suntan lotion and semen, and the salted way he tasted, how beautiful he was—and my days would get altered. The book was no longer, as it had been when I tried writing it in 1983 and 1999 and 2006 and 2013, only about the lead-up to the awful attacks we survived on November 7, but about the complicated reserves of desire I had for Susan Reynolds and her numbness—which became the guiding aesthetic in my work, which I adopted from her: she was, in many ways, my inspiration. It also surprised me that I found myself writing about my love for Thom Wright, which had been ignited at that moment when I glimpsed his naked body in the locker room after a summer away, lust igniting the flow of memory, when I came to the crushing conclusion I've yet to meet a man I wanted to live with for the rest of my life as much as I did with Thom Wright. Forty years passed and I never found one because, at a certain point, I realized such men simply didn't exist or at least not in the ways I wanted—in so many aspects I'd remained a child. Another reason I started writing the book had to do with Debbie Schaffer, who I realized was more complex as I laid the story out—I thought she would end up simply entitled, a princess, but when I remembered the specifics of the narrative this didn't turn out to be true. I had almost reached out to Debbie when I heard Terry had killed himself in the summer of 1992—my father had died a month earlier—but I knew she wouldn't have wanted to talk to me. I've always had a hard time finding peace with that. Nothing was resolved.

THE BOOK DETAILED more than I thought it would about Ryan Vaughn and I comforted myself with the notion that we were simply too young and born in the wrong time and though we should have been allowed to be ourselves there was no way this was going to happen in 1981. And since then I had often wondered if we could have made it work together after we left Buckley: in New York, in Vermont, in San Francisco, which is where Ryan Vaughn eventually moved. He barely spoke to me the rest of our senior year, and once, at graduation in June of 1982, we bumped into each other accidentally in the boys' bathroom in the Pavilion after the ceremony, both of us draped in red robes and still wearing the mortarboard caps: there was a surprised silence that I broke by saying "Ryan—" and then he interrupted with "See ya!," making the *What's up?* face we used to share. Ryan had no social-media presence—I realized this when I tried to find him in 2013, as I dreamt about another version of this book—and I had no idea what actually happened to him until I was at a cocktail party at the Sunset Tower in 2018, where I ran into Tracy Goldman, who I hadn't seen since graduation, and we started talking about our long-ago classmates, since we had nothing else in common, and when I asked her if she knew anything about Ryan Vaughn she told me that she heard, though she couldn't exactly remember where, he was an architect in San Francisco and living with his *partner*—it was obvious what she meant with that word and the way she lightly pressed down on it, expecting me to be as surprised as she was where Ryan Vaughn had ended up. I don't know why this wounded me to the extent that it did—it had been almost forty years since we'd kissed—but I left the party immediately after that conversation and drove the streets of the city as I used to on nights when I was sad and seventeen in the fall of 1981.

DESPITE MY FAMILIARITY with the events, the book frightened me, as love does, as dreams do, and almost drove my partner mad when he read the things I was revealing to this new friend who had moved into our house and who I now spent time with daily in my office. Todd and I would have fights in which he disputed the "veracity" of certain events that I adamantly confirmed, and as the writing of the book carried me to the ending, it filled him with such palpable fear that being near me became almost unbearable. And he would leave the condo on Doheny for days at a time while I wrote in my office, and scanned old journals filled with lists, the school yearbook *Images* opened to a certain page, notes littered with song titles everywhere. Some nights Todd slept in motels he could afford on the darker side of Hollywood and I drank more than usual—after I moved through a particular chapter or sequence of events I found myself wiped out and immediately reached for the bottle of Tanqueray in the kitchen cabinet and simply drank the gin quickly in a glass with some ice. If that failed to move me away from the chill I'd take a Xanax or an Ativan that our dealer supplied us with and then, lightly stoned, I would end up back in my office, listening to the music from that period on YouTube, almost every night while I was writing the book, sometimes three or four hours in a row, the songs that summed up that period, anthems about hope for the future, the new metamorphosis, leaving childhood behind: *Vienna, Nowhere Girl, Icehouse, Time For Me To Fly.* But many of the songs now sounded like desperate desire and rejection and running away. If the songs were about, as I once thought, a child who became a man, they were also, for me at fifty-six, about a man who stayed a child.

—

The SHARDS

A WEEK AGO I saw a beige-colored van parked at the 7-Eleven on Holloway and La Cienega, next door to the Palihouse Hotel, where I first glimpsed Susan Reynolds after not seeing her for thirty-eight years, and whenever I see a similar van I connect it with the Trawler and his obsession over Robert Mallory and the fact that he was never captured—he had drifted to other states perhaps, beginning new narratives, staking out a different story, and sometimes I dream about Robert and in the dreams he's a different person that I meet up with in a vast hotel or an empty airplane, sometimes disguised as someone else, sometimes older, but mostly young, and staring at me fixed in that moment of his teenage beauty, a place where he would always reside—he would never age. And sometimes when I wake up from one of my dreams about Robert, or Matt, or Ryan Vaughn, or Thom, or Susan, I'm reminded that the fall of 1981 wasn't the dream that I sometimes pretended it was in the decades that followed. But I always slipped whenever I heard those faraway voices calling out to me, and I would find that record with the platinum-blonde girl on the cover, and turn the volume up, and play it loud, close my eyes and lie back and listen to a song about dreaming.

A Note About the Author

BRET EASTON ELLIS is the author of six novels, a collection of essays, and a collection of stories, which have been translated into thirty-two languages. He lives in Los Angeles and is the host of the *Bret Easton Ellis Podcast,* available on Patreon.

A Note on the Type

This book was set in Caledonia, a typeface designed by W. A. Dwiggins (1880–1956). It belongs to the family of printing types called "modern face" by printers—a term used to mark the change in style of the type letters that occurred around 1800. Caledonia borders on the general design of Scotch Roman but it is more freely drawn than that letter. This version of Caledonia was adapted by David Berlow in 1979.

Typeset by Scribe
Philadelphia, Pennsylvania

Printed and bound by Berryville Graphics
Berryville, Virginia

Designed by Michael Collica